P9-BYY-433

in the
presence
of the
enemy

also by elizabeth george

A Great Deliverance
Payment in Blood
Well-Schooled in Murder
A Suitable Vengeance
For the Sake of Elena
Missing Joseph
Playing for the Ashes

in the presence of the enemy

elizabeth george

BANTAM BOOKS
New York   Toronto   London
Sydney   Auckland

IN THE PRESENCE OF THE ENEMY
A Bantam Book / April 1996

All rights reserved.
Copyright © 1996 by Susan Elizabeth George.

Book design by Maria Carella.
Map designed by Laura Hartman Maestro.

No part of this book may be reproduced or transmitted in any form or by any means,
electronic or mechanical, including photocopying, recording, or by any information storage
and retrieval system, without permission in writing from the publisher.
For information address: Bantam Books.

Library of Congress Cataloging-in-Publication Data
George, Elizabeth.
In the presence of the enemy / Elizabeth George.
p.   cm.
ISBN 0-553-09265-0
I. Title.
PS3557.E478I5   1996
813'.54—dc20   95-37670
CIP

Published simultaneously in the United States and Canada

Bantam Books are published by Bantam Books, a division of Bantam Doubleday Dell Publishing
Group, Inc. Its trademark, consisting of the words "Bantam Books" and the portrayal of a rooster,
is Registered in U.S. Patent and Trademark Office and in other countries. Marca Registrada.
Bantam Books, 1540 Broadway, New York, New York 10036.

PRINTED IN THE UNITED STATES OF AMERICA

BVG   0 9 8 7 6 5 4

In loving memory of Freddie LaChapelle
1948–1994

I grant you immortality in the one small
way I can.

Go with God, dearest Freddie.

For neither man nor angel can discern
Hypocrisy, the only evil that walks
Invisible, except to God alone.

JOHN MILTON, *Paradise Lost*

part
one

1

CHARLOTTE BOWEN THOUGHT she was dead. She opened her
eyes into cold and darkness. The cold was beneath her, feeling just
like the ground in her mother's garden planter, where the never-stop
drips from the outdoor tap made a patch of damp that was green and
smelly. The darkness was everywhere. Black pushed against her like a
heavy blanket, and she strained her eyes against it, trying to force out of
the endless nothing a shape that might tell her she wasn't in a grave.
She didn't move at first. She didn't reach out either fingers or toes
because she didn't want to feel the sides of the coffin because she didn't
want to know that death was like this when she'd thought there'd be
saints and sunlight and angels, with the angels sitting on swings playing
harps.

Charlotte listened hard, but there was nothing to hear. She sniffed,
but there was nothing to smell except the mustiness all round her, the
way old stones smell after mould's grown on them. She swallowed and
tasted the vague memory of apple juice. And the flavour was enough to
make her recall.

He'd given her apple juice, hadn't he? He'd handed over a bottle
with a cap that he'd loosened and shiny beads of moisture speckling its
sides. He'd smiled and squeezed her shoulder once. He'd said, "Not to
worry, Lottie. Your mum doesn't want that."

Mummy. That was what this was all about. Where was Mummy?
What had happened to her? And to Lottie? What had happened to
Lottie?

"There's been an accident," he'd said. "I'm to take you to your
mum."

"Where?" she'd said. "Where's Mummy?" And then louder, because her stomach felt liquidy all of a sudden and she didn't like the way he was looking at her, "Tell me where's my mum! Tell me! Right now!"

"It's all right," he'd said quickly with a glance about. Just like Mummy, he was embarrassed because of her noise. "Quiet down, Lottie. She's in a Government safe house. Do you know what that means?"

Charlotte had shaken her head. She was, after all, only ten years old and most of the workings of the Government were a mystery to her. All she knew for sure was that being in the Government meant that Mummy left home before seven in the morning and usually didn't come back till after she was asleep. Mummy went to her office in Parliament Square. She went to her meetings in the Home Office. She went to the House of Commons. On Friday afternoons she held surgery for her constituents in Marylebone, while Lottie did her school prep, tucked out of sight in a yellow-walled room where the constituency's executive committee met.

"Behave yourself," her mother would say when Charlotte arrived after school each Friday afternoon. She'd give a meaningful tilt of her head in the direction of that yellow-walled room. "I don't want to hear a peep out of you till we leave. Is that clear?"

"Yes, Mummy."

And then Mummy would smile. "So give us a kiss," she would say. "And a hug. I want a hug as well." And she would stop her discussion with the parish priest or the Pakistani grocer from the Edgware Road or the local schoolteacher or whoever else wanted ten precious minutes of their MP's time. And she'd catch Lottie up in a stiff-armed hug that hurt. Then she'd swat her bottom and say, "Off with you now," and turn back to her visitor, saying, "Kids," with a chuckle.

Fridays were best. After Mummy's surgery, she and Lottie would ride home together and Lottie would tell her all about her week. Her mother would listen. She would nod, and sometimes pat Lottie's knee, but all the time she kept her eyes fixed to the road, just beyond their driver's head.

"Mummy," Lottie would say with a martyred sigh in a useless attempt to wrest her mother's attention from Marylebone High Street to herself. Mummy didn't *have* to look at the high street after all. It's not as if *she* was driving the car. "I'm *talking* to you. What're you *looking* for?"

"Trouble, Charlotte. I'm looking for trouble. You'd be wise to do the same."

Trouble had come, it seemed. But a Government safe house? What was that exactly? Was it a place to hide if someone dropped a bomb?

"Are we going to the safe house?" Lottie had gulped down the apple juice in a rush. It was a little peculiar—not nearly sweet enough—but she drank it down properly because she knew it was naughty to seem ungrateful to an adult.

"That we are," he'd said. "We're going to the safe house. Your mum's waiting there."

Which was all that she could remember distinctly. Things had got quite blurry after that. Her eyelids had grown heavy as they drove through London, and within minutes it seemed that she hadn't been able to hold up her head. At the back of her mind, she seemed to recall a kind voice saying, "That's the girl, Lottie. Have a nice kip, won't you," and a hand gently removing her specs.

At this final thought, Lottie inched her hands up to her face in the darkness, keeping them as near as possible to her body so that she wouldn't have to feel the sides of the coffin she was lying in. Her fingers touched her chin. They climbed slowly up her cheeks in a spider walk. They felt their way across the bridge of her nose. Her specs were gone.

That made no difference in the darkness, of course. But if the lights went on . . . Only how were lights to go on in a coffin?

Lottie took a shallow breath. Then another. And another. How much air? she wondered. How much time before . . . And why? Why?

She felt her throat getting tight and her chest getting hot. She felt her eyes burn. She thought, Mustn't cry, mustn't ever ever cry. Mustn't ever let anyone *see* . . . Except there was nothing to see, was there? There was nothing but endless black upon black. Which made her throat tight, which made her chest hot, which made her eyes burn all over again. *Mustn't*, Lottie thought. Mustn't cry. No, no.

—⁂—

Rodney Aronson leaned his kettle-drum bum against the window-sill in the editor's office and felt the ancient venetian blinds scrape against the back of his safari jacket. He fished in one of the jacket's pockets for the rest of his Cadbury whole nut bar, and he unwrapped its foil with the dedication of a paleontologist scrupulously removing soil from the buried remains of prehistoric man.

Across the room at the conference table, Dennis Luxford looked completely relaxed in what Rodney called the Chair of Authority. With a triangular grin on his elfin face, the editor was listening to the day's final report on what Fleet Street had the previous week dubbed the Rent Boy Rumba. The report was being given, with considerable animation, by the best investigative reporter on staff at *The Source*. Mitchell Corsico was twenty-three years old—a young man rather idiotically given to cowboy attire—with the instincts of a bloodhound and the tremulous sensitivity of a barracuda. He was just what they needed in the current rich climate of parliamentary peccadilloes, public outrage, and sexual shenanigans.

"According to this afternoon's statement," Corsico was saying, "our esteemed MP from East Norfolk declared that his constituency is solidly behind him. He's innocent until proven and all the et ceteras. The loyal party chairman asserts the entire brouhaha is the fault of the gutter press, who, he claims, are attempting yet again to undermine the Government." Corsico flipped through his notes in an apparent search for the appropriate quote. Finding it, he shoved his treasured Stetson back on his head, struck a heroic pose, and recited, " 'It's no secret that the media are set on a path to bring down the Government. This rent boy business is merely another attempt by Fleet Street to determine the direction of parliamentary debate. But if the media wish to destroy the Government, the media shall find more than one worthy opponent waiting to do battle from Downing Street to Whitehall to the Palace of Westminster.' " Corsico flipped the notebook closed and shoved it into the back pocket of his well-worn jeans. "Lofty sentiment, that, wouldn't you say?"

Luxford tilted his chair back and folded his hands across his exceedingly flat stomach. Forty-six years old with the body of a teenager *and* a full head of dusty blond hair to boot. He needed to be euthanised, Rodney thought blackly. It would be a mercy for his colleagues in general and Rodney in particular not to have to lumber along in his elegant wake. "We don't need to bring down the Government," Luxford said. "We can sit back and watch while they bring down themselves." Idly, he fingered his silk paisley braces. "Is Mr. Larnsey still holding to his original story?"

"Like a barnacle," Corsico said. "Our esteemed MP from East Norfolk has reiterated his earlier statement about, as he called it, 'this unfortunate misunderstanding arising from my presence in an automobile behind Paddington Station last Thursday night.' He was gathering data for the Select Committee on Drug Abuse and Prostitution, he maintains."

"Is there a Select Committee on Drug Abuse and Prostitution?" Luxford asked.

"If there isn't, you may depend upon the Government's establishing one straightaway."

Luxford cushioned the back of his neck with his hands and tilted his chair another degree backwards. He couldn't have looked more pleased with the developing events. In the present stretch of Conservative control over the reins of the Government, the nation's tabloids had uncovered MPs with mistresses, MPs with illegitimate children, MPs with call girls, MPs engaged in auto-eroticism, MPs with shaky real estate deals, and MPs with questionable ties to industry, but this was a first: a Conservative MP caught in as *flagrante* a *delicto* as there ever was, in the embrace of a sixteen-year-old male prostitute behind Paddington Station. This was such stuff as circulation dreams were made of, and Rodney could see Luxford mentally assessing the next pay rise he would likely be given once the books were balanced and the profits were in. Current events were allowing him to make good on his promise to elevate *The Source*'s circulation to number one. He was a lucky bastard, blast his rotten little heart. But to Rodney's way of thinking, he wasn't the only journalist in London who could sink his incisors into an unexpected opportunity and rip a story from it like a hound with a hare. He wasn't the only warrior in Fleet Street. "Another three days before the Prime Minister jettisons him," Luxford predicted. He glanced in Rodney's direction. "What's your bet?"

"I'd say three days might be stretching it, Den." Rodney smiled inwardly at Luxford's expression. The editor hated diminutive forms of his name.

Luxford evaluated Rodney's reply through narrowed eyes. No fool, our Luxford, Rodney thought. He hadn't got to where he was by ignoring the daggers waiting at his back. Luxford gave his attention again to the reporter. "What do you have on next?"

Corsico ticked items off with his fingers. "MP Larnsey's wife swore yesterday she'd stick by her man, but I've a source who's told me she's moving out tonight. I'll need a photographer on that."

"Rod'll see to it," Luxford said without another glance in Rodney's direction. "What else?"

"The East Norfolk Conservative Association is meeting tonight to discuss their MP's 'political viability.' I've had a call from someone inside the association who says Larnsey's going to be asked to stand down."

"Anything else?"

"We're waiting for the Prime Minister to comment. Oh yes. One thing more. An anonymous phone call claiming Larnsey always fancied boys, even at school. The wife was a front from the day of the wedding."

"What about the rent boy?"

"He's in hiding at the moment. At his parents' home in South Lambeth."

"Will he talk? Will the parents?"

"I'm still working on that."

Luxford lowered his chair. "Right then," he said and added wickedly with that triangular grin, "Keep up the good work, Mitch."

Corsico gave a mock tip of his Stetson and headed out of the office. He reached the door as it opened to Luxford's secretary, sixty years old and bearing two stacks of letters, which she carried to the conference table and placed in front of *The Source* editor. Stack one was opened, and these went on Luxford's left. Stack two was unopened, marked *Personal* or *Confidential* or *Editor's Eyes Only*, and these went on Luxford's right, after which the secretary fetched the letter opener from the editor's desk and placed it on the conference table a precise two inches from the unopened envelopes. She fetched the wastepaper basket as well and situated this next to Luxford's chair. "Anything else, Mr. Luxford?" she asked, which is what she asked deferentially every evening before she left for the day. "A blow job, Miss Wallace," Rodney silently replied. "On your knees, woman. And moan while you do it." He chuckled in spite of himself at the thought of Miss Wallace—decked out as always in her twin set, her tweeds, and her pearls—on her knees between Luxford's thighs. To hide his amusement, he quickly lowered his head to examine the rest of his Cadbury bar.

Luxford had begun flipping through the unopened letters. "Phone my wife before you leave," he said to his secretary. "I shouldn't be later than eight this evening."

Miss Wallace nodded and vanished in silence, trodding across the grey carpet towards the door in her sensibly crepe-soled shoes. Alone with *The Source* editor for the first time that day, Rodney slid his bum from the windowsill as Luxford reached for the letter opener and began on the envelopes at his right. Rodney had never been able to understand Luxford's predilection for opening personal letters himself. Considering the political bent of the newspaper—as far left of centre as one could get without being called Red, Commie, Pinko, or any other less-than-salutary sobriquet—a letter marked *Personal* might well be a bomb. And far better to risk Miss Wallace's losing fingers, hands, or an eye than for the newspaper's chief editor to make himself the potential bull's-eye in a crackpot's target. Luxford, of course, wouldn't see it that way. Not that he would worry over Miss Wallace's exposure to risk. Rather, he would point out that it was an editor's job to take the measure of the public's response to his newspaper. *The Source*, he would declare, was not going to achieve the coveted top position in the circulation wars by having its chief editor directing its troops from behind the battle lines. No editor worth his salt lost touch with the public.

Rodney watched as Luxford perused the first letter. He snorted, balled it up, and flicked it into the wastepaper basket. He opened the second and scanned it quickly. He chuckled and sent it to join the first. He'd read the third, fourth, and fifth and was opening the sixth when he said in an absent tone that Rodney knew was deliberate, "Yes, Rod? Is there something on your mind?"

What was on Rodney's mind was being done out of the very position Luxford was occupying: Lord of the Mighty, imprimatur, head boy, senior prefect, and otherwise venerable editor of *The Source*. He'd been elbowed aside for the promotion he bloody well deserved just six months back in favour of Luxford, told by the swine-faced chairman in his plummy voice that he "lacked the necessary instincts" to make the sort of changes in *The Source* that would turn the tabloid around. What sort of instincts? he'd enquired politely when the paper's chairman broke the news to him. "The instincts of a killer," the chairman had replied. "Luxford has them in spades. Just look at what he did for the *Globe*."

What he'd done for the *Globe* was to take a languishing tabloid largely dedicated to film star gossip and unctuous stories on the Royal Family and transform it into the highest-selling newspaper in the country. But he hadn't done it through raising standards. He was too attuned to the times for that. Rather, he'd done it by appealing to the baser instincts of the tabloid's readers. He'd offered them a daily diet of scandals, of sexual escapades of politicians, of Tartuffery within the Church of England, and of the ostensible and highly occasional chivalry of the common man. The result was a veritable feast of titillation for Luxford's readers, who by the millions slapped down their thirty-five pence each morning as if *The Source*'s editor alone—and not its staff and not Rodney, who had *just* as many brains and five years' more experience than Luxford—held the keys to their contentment. And while the little rat gloried in his increasing success, the rest of the London tabloids fought to keep pace. All of them together thumbed their noses and said, "Kiss my arse, then" each time the Government threatened to force some basic controls upon them. But *vox populi* held no water in Westminster, not when the press were lambasting the Prime Minister each time a fellow Tory MP did his part to underscore what was appearing more and more to be the essential hypocrisy of the Conservative Party.

Not that seeing the Tory ship-of-state sinking was a painful spectacle for Rodney Aronson. He'd voted Labour—or at worst Liberal Democrat—ever since casting his first ballot. To think that Labour might benefit from the current climate of political unrest was extremely gratifying to him. So under other circumstances, Rodney would have enjoyed the daily spectacle of press conferences, outraged telephone calls, demands for a special election, and dire predictions of the outcome of local elections due to be held within weeks. But under these circumstances, with Luxford at the helm where he would probably remain indefinitely, occluding Rodney's own rise to the top, Rodney chafed. He told himself his discomfort grew from the fact that he was the superior newsman. But the real truth was that he was jealous.

He'd been at *The Source* since he was sixteen years old, he'd worked his way from a factotum to his present position of Deputy Editor—second in command, mind you—on sheer strength of will, strength of character, and strength of talent. He was *owed* the top job, and everyone knew it. Including Luxford, which was why the editor was watching him now, reading his mind like the fox he was, and waiting for him to reply. You don't have the instincts of a killer, he'd been told. Yes. Right. Well, everyone would see the truth soon enough.

"Something on your mind, Rod?" Luxford repeated before dropping his gaze again to his correspondence.

Your job, Rodney thought. But what he said was, "This rent boy business. I think it's time to back off."

"Why?"

"It's getting old. We've been leading with the story since Friday. Yesterday and today were nothing more than a rehash of Sunday and Monday's developments. I know Mitch Corsico is on the trail of something more, but until he's got it, I think we need to take a break."

Luxford set letter number six to one side and pulled at his overlong—and trademark—sideburns in what Rodney knew was a spurious demonstration of editor-considers-subordinate's-opinion. He picked up envelope number seven and inserted the letter opener beneath its flap. He held that pose while he replied.

"The Government has placed itself in this position. The Prime Minister gave us his Recommitment to Basic British Values as part of the party manifesto, didn't he? Just two years ago, wasn't it? We're merely exploring what the Recommitment to Basic British Values apparently means to the Tories. Mum and Dad Greengrocer along with Uncle Shoemaker and Granddad Pensioner all thought it meant a return to decency and 'God Save the Queen' in the cinema after films. Our Tory MPs seem to think otherwise."

"Right," Rodney said. "But do we want to look like we're trying to bring down the Government with an endless exposé of what one half-witted MP does with his dick on his own free time? Hell, we've plenty of other grist to use against the Tories. So why don't we—"

"Developing a moral conscience at the eleventh hour?" Luxford raised a sardonic eyebrow and went back to his letter, slitting open the envelope and slipping out the folded paper inside. "I wouldn't have thought it of you, Rod."

Rodney felt his face grow hot. "I'm only saying that if we're going to aim the heavy artillery at the Government, we might want to start thinking about directing fire at something more substantial than the off-hours bonking of Members of Parliament. Papers have been doing that for years, and where has it got us? The berks are still in power."

"I dare say our readers feel their interests are being served. What did you tell me the most recent circulation figures were?" It was Luxford's usual ploy. He never asked that sort of question without knowing the answer. As if to emphasise this, he gave his attention back to the letter in his hand.

"I'm not saying we ought to ignore the extra-marital bonking that's going on. I know it's our bread and butter. But if we just spin the story so it looks like the Government . . ." Rodney realised that Luxford wasn't listening. Instead, he was frowning at the letter he held. He pulled at his sideburns, but this time the act and the consideration accompanying the act were both genuine. Rodney was certain of it. He said with rising hope that he was careful to expunge from his voice, "Something wrong, Den?"

The hand that held the letter screwed it into his palm. "Balls," Luxford said. He threw the letter into the rubbish with the others. He reached for the next one and slit it open. "What utter bullshit," he said. "The great unthinking populace speaks." He read the next letter and then said to Rodney, "That's where we differ. You apparently view our readers as educable, Rod. While I view them as they are. Our nation's great unwashed and greater unread. To be spoon-fed their opinions like lukewarm porridge." Luxford pushed his chair away from the conference table. "Is there anything else this evening? Because if there isn't, I've a dozen phone calls to return and a family to get home to."

There's your job, Rodney thought once again. There's what I'm owed for twenty-two years of loyalty to this miserable rag. But what he said was, "No, Den. There's nothing else. At the moment, that is."

He dropped his Cadbury wrapper among the editor's discarded

letters and headed for the door. Luxford said, "Rod," as Rodney pulled the door open. And when he'd turned to Luxford, "You've got choco-late in your beard."

Luxford was smiling as Rodney left him.

—𝔪—

But the smile faded instantly once the other man was gone. Dennis Luxford swung his chair to the wastepaper basket. He pulled out the letter. He uncrinkled it against the surface of the conference table and read it again. It was composed of a one-word salutation and a single sentence, and it had nothing to do with rent boys, automobiles, or Sinclair Larnsey, MP:

> Luxford—
> Use page one to acknowledge your firstborn child, and
> Charlotte will be freed.

Luxford stared at the message with a heartbeat thumping light and fast in his ears. He swiftly assessed a handful of possible senders, but they were so unlikely that the only conclusion he could reach was a simple one: The letter had to be a bluff. Still, he was careful to sort through the remaining rubbish in such a way so as not to disturb the order in which he'd thrown away the day's post. He rescued the letter's accompanying envelope and studied it. A partial postmark made a three-quarter moon next to the first class stamp. It was faded, but legible enough for Luxford to see that the letter had been posted in London.

Luxford leaned back in his chair. He read the first eight words again. *Use page one to acknowledge your firstborn child.* Charlotte, he thought.

For the past ten years, he had allowed himself to reflect upon Charlotte only once a month, a quarter of an hour's admission of pater-nity that he'd managed to keep secret from everyone in his world, Charlotte's mother included. The rest of the time he forced the girl's existence to diminish in his memory. He'd never spoken to a soul about her. Some days he managed to forget altogether that he was the father of more than one child.

He scooped up both the letter and its envelope and carried them to the window where he looked down at Farrington Street and listened to the muted noise of traffic.

Someone, he knew, someone quite close by, someone in Fleet Street or perhaps in Wapping or as far away as that soaring glass tower on the Isle of Dogs, was waiting for him to make a wrong move. Someone out there—well-versed in how a story completely unrelated to current events gained momentum in the press and whetted the public's appetite for a very conspicuous fall from grace—anticipated his inadvertently laying a trail in reaction to this letter and, through laying that trail, forging a link between himself and Charlotte's mother. When he'd done that, the press would pounce. One paper would uncover the story. The rest would follow. And both he and Charlotte's mother would pay for their mistake. Her punishment would be a pillory followed by a quick descent from political power. His would be a more personal loss.

He was sardonically amused to note how he was being hoist with his own petard. If the Government had not been facing even more certain damage should the truth about Charlotte be known, Luxford would have assumed the letter had been sent from Number Ten Downing Street in a gesture of how-does-it-feel-to-be-on-the-receiving-end-for-once. But the Government had as much interest in keeping the truth about Charlotte buried as had Luxford himself. And if the Government was not involved in the letter and its obliquely minatory message, then it stood to reason that another sort of enemy was.

And there were scores of them. From every walk of life. Eager. Waiting. Hoping that he would betray himself.

Dennis Luxford had been playing the game of investigative one-upmanship too long to make a false move. He hadn't turned the tide of *The Source*'s declining circulation by being oblivious of the methods used by journalists to reach the truth. So he decided that he would toss out the letter and forget about it and thus give his enemies sod all to work with. If he received another, he'd toss out that one as well.

He balled up the letter a second time and turned from the window to throw it with the others. But in doing so, he caught sight of the correspondence his secretary had already opened and stacked. He considered the possibility of yet another letter, not marked this time for his eyes only, but sent unmarked so that anyone could open it, or sent to Mitch Corsico, or to one of the other reporters who were currently on the scent of sexual corruption. This letter wouldn't be phrased so obscurely. Names would be mentioned, dates and places would be manufactured, and what had started as a thirteen-word bluff would become a full-blown hue and cry for the truth.

He could prevent that. All it would take was a single phone call and an answer to the only questions possible at this point: Have you told someone, Eve? Anyone? At any time? In the last ten years? About us? Have you told?

If she hadn't, the letter was nothing but an attempt to rattle him, and easily dismissable at that. If she had, she needed to know that both of them were about to come under a full-blown siege.

2

_____

HAVING PREPARED HER AUDIENCE, Deborah St. James lined up three large black-and-white photographs on one of the worktables in her husband's laboratory. She adjusted the fluorescent lights and stood back to wait the judgement of her husband and of his workmate, Lady Helen Clyde. She'd been experimenting with this new series of photographs for four months now, and while she was fairly pleased with the results, she was also feeling more and more these days the pressure to make a real financial contribution to their household. She wanted this contribution to be a regular one, not one restricted to the sporadic assignments she had so far been able to glean from beating on the doors of advertising agencies, talent agencies, magazines, wire services, and publishers. In the last few years since completing her training, Deborah had begun to feel as if she were spending most of her waking hours lugging her portfolio from one end of London to the other, when all along what she wanted was to be successful shooting her photographs as pure art. From Stieglitz to Mapplethorpe, other people had done it. Why not she?

Deborah pressed her palms together and waited for either her husband or Helen Clyde to speak. They'd been in the midst of evaluating the transcript of a forensic deposition Simon had given a fortnight ago on water-gel explosives, and they had intended to go on from there to an analysis of tool marks made on the metal surround of a doorknob in an attempt to establish a case for the defence in an upcoming murder trial. But they'd been willing enough to take a break. They'd been going at it since nine that morning with only a pause for lunch and a second for dinner, and from what Deborah could see now at half past nine in the evening, Helen, at least, was ready to call it a day.

Simon was bent over the photograph of a National Front skinhead. Helen was studying a West Indian girl who stood with an enormous Union Jack curled through her hands. Both the skinhead and the girl were positioned in front of a portable backdrop that Deborah had devised from large triangles of solidly painted canvas.

When neither Simon nor Helen spoke, she said, "You see, I want the pictures to be personality specific. I don't want to objectify the subject in my old way. I control the background—that's the canvas I was working on in the garden last February, do you remember, Simon?—but the personality is specific to the individual picture. The subject can't hide. He—or she, of course—can't falsify himself because the film speed's too slow and the subject can't sustain artifice for as long as it takes to get the proper exposure. So. What d'you think?"

She told herself that it didn't matter what either of them thought. She was on to something with this new approach, and she meant to keep with it. But it would help to have someone's independent verification that the work was as good as she believed it was. Even if that someone was her own husband, the person least likely to find fault with her efforts.

He moved away from the skinhead, skirted Helen who was still studying the West Indian flag holder, and went to the third picture, a Rastafarian in an impressively beaded shawl that covered his hole-dotted T-shirt. He said, "Where did you take these, Deborah?"

She said, "Covent Garden. Near the theatre museum. I'd like to do St. Botolph's Church next. The homeless. You know." She watched Helen move to another picture. She kept herself from gnawing at her thumbnail as she waited.

Helen finally looked up. "I think they're wonderful."

"*Do* you? Do you really? I mean, do you think . . . You see, they're rather different, aren't they? What I wanted . . . I mean . . . I'm using a twenty-by-twenty-four-inch Polaroid, and I've left in the sprocket marks as well as the marks from the chemicals on the prints because I want them to sort of *announce* that they're pictures. They're the artificial reality while the subjects themselves are the truth. At least . . . Well, that's what I'd like to think . . ." Deborah reached for her hair and shoved its copper-coloured mass away from her face. Words left her in a muddle. They always had. She sighed. "That's what I'm trying . . ."

Her husband put his arm round her shoulders and soundly kissed the side of her head. "A fine job," he said. "How many have you taken?"

"Oh dozens. Hundreds. Well, perhaps not hundreds, but a great many. I've only just started making these oversize prints. What I'm really hoping is that they'll be good enough to show . . . in a gallery, I mean. Like art. Because, well, they *are* art after all and . . ." Her voice drifted off as her eyes caught movement at the edge of her vision. She turned to the door of the lab to see that her father—a long-time member of one or another of the St. James family's households—had come quietly to the top of the Cheyne Row house.

"Mr. St. James," Joseph Cotter said, adhering to his history of never once using Simon's Christian name. The length of their marriage aside, he had never been able to adjust fully to the fact that his daughter had married her father's youthful employer. "You've visitors. I've put them in the study."

"Visitors?" Deborah asked. "I didn't hear . . . did the doorbell ring, Dad?"

"Don't need the doorbell, these visitors, do they?" Cotter replied. He entered the lab and frowned down at Deborah's photographs. "Nasty bloke, this," he said in reference to the National Front ruffian. And to Deborah's husband, "It's David. Along with some mate of 'is, done up in fancy braces and flashy shoes."

"David?" Deborah asked. "David St. James? Here? In London?"

"Here in the 'ouse," Cotter pointed out. "And looking 'is usual worse for wear. Where that bloke buys 'is clothes is a mystery to me. Oxfam, I think. You want coffee all round? They both look like they could do with a cup."

Deborah was already heading down the stairs calling, "David? David?" as her husband said, "Coffee, yes. And knowing my brother, you'd better bring along the rest of that chocolate cake." He said to Helen, "Let's put the rest of this on hold till tomorrow. Will you be off, then?"

"Let me say hello to David first." Helen switched off the fluorescent lights and trailed St. James to the stairs, which he took with a slow care necessitated by his braced left leg. Cotter followed them.

The door to the study was open. Within the room, Deborah was saying, "What are you *doing* here, David? Why didn't you phone? Nothing's wrong with Sylvie or the children, I hope?"

David was brushing his sister-in-law's cheek with a kiss, saying, "Fine. They're fine, Deb. Everyone's fine. I'm in town for a conference on Euro-trade. Dennis tracked me down there. Ah. Here's Simon. Dennis Luxford, my brother Simon. My sister-in-law. And Helen Clyde. Helen, how are you? It's been years, hasn't it?"

"Last Boxing Day," Helen replied. "At your parents' house. But there was such a crush that you're forgiven for not remembering."

"No doubt I spent most of the afternoon grazing at the buffet table anyway." David slapped both hands against his paunch, the one feature he possessed that distinguished him from his younger brother. Otherwise he and St. James were, like all the St. James siblings, remarkably similar in appearance, sharing the same curling black hair, the same height, the same sharp angularity of features, and the same eye colour that could never decide between grey or blue. He was indeed dressed as Cotter had described him: oddly. From his Birkenstock sandals and argyll socks to his tweed jacket and his polo shirt, David was eclecticism personified, the sartorial despair of his family. He was a genius in business, having increased the profits of the family's shipping company fourfold since their father's retirement. But one would never guess it to behold him.

"I need your help." David chose one of the two leather armchairs near the fireplace. With the assurance of a man who commands a legion of employees, he directed everyone else to sit. "Rather more to the point, Dennis needs your help. That's why we've come."

"What sort of help?" St. James observed the man who had come with his brother. He was standing more or less out of the direct light, near the wall on which Deborah regularly hung a changing display of her photographs. Luxford, St. James saw, was extremely fit-looking, a middle-aged man of relatively modest stature whose natty blue blazer, silk tie, and fawn trousers suggested a beau but whose face wore an expression of mild distrust that at the moment appeared to be mixing with a fair amount of incredulity. St. James knew the source of the latter, although he never saw it without a momentary sinking of his spirits. Dennis Luxford wanted help in some matter or another, but he didn't expect he'd be able to receive it from someone who was obviously crippled. St. James wanted to say, "It's just the leg, Mr. Luxford. My intellect continues to function as always." Instead, he waited for the other man to speak while Helen and Deborah made places for themselves on the sofa and the ottoman.

Luxford didn't seem pleased that the women had apparently settled in for the duration of the interview. He said, "This is a personal matter. It's extremely confidential. I'm not willing—"

David St. James interposed. "These are the three people in the country least likely to sell your story to the media, Dennis. I dare say they don't even know who you are." And then to the others, "Do you, in fact? Never mind. I can see by your faces that you don't."

He went on to explain. He and Luxford, he said, had been together at Lancaster University, adversaries in the debating society and boozing mates after exams. They'd stayed in touch through the years since leaving the University, keeping tabs on each other's successful career. "Dennis is a writer," David said. "Damned finest writer I've ever known, truth to tell." He'd come to London to make his mark in literature, David told them, but he'd got sidetracked into journalism and decided to stay there. He started out as a political correspondent for the *Guardian*. Now he was an editor.

"Of the *Guardian?*" St. James asked.

"*The Source.*" Luxford said it with a look that directed a challenge towards any of them who might choose to comment. To begin at the *Guardian* and end up at *The Source* might not exactly be considered a celestial ascent in one's fortunes, but Luxford, it seemed, was not about to be judged.

David appeared oblivious of the look. He said with a nod in Luxford's direction, "He took over *The Source* six months ago, Simon, after making the *Globe* number one. He was the youngest editor in Fleet Street history when he ran the *Globe*, not to mention the most successful. Which he still is. Even the *Sunday Times* admitted that. They did quite a spread on him in the magazine. When was that, Dennis?"

Luxford ignored the question and seemed to chafe under David's encomium. He appeared to ruminate for a moment. "No," he finally said to David. "This isn't going to work. There's too much at risk. I shouldn't have come."

Deborah stirred. "We'll leave," she said. "Helen. Shall we?"

But St. James was studying the newspaper editor, and something about him—was it a smooth ability to manipulate the situation?—made him say, "Helen works with me, Mr. Luxford. If you need my help, you're going to end up with hers as well, even if that doesn't appear to be the case at the moment. And I do share most of my work with my wife."

"That's it, then," Luxford said and made a movement to depart.

David St. James waved him back. "You're going to have to trust someone," he said and went on to his brother. "The problem is, we've got a Tory career on the line."

"I should think that would please you," St. James said to Luxford. "*The Source* has never made a secret of its political leaning."

"This is a rather special Tory career," David said. "Tell him, Dennis. He can help you. It's either him or a stranger who might not have Simon's ethics. Or you can choose the police. And you know where that leads."

As Dennis Luxford was considering his options, Cotter brought in the coffee and chocolate cake. He set the large tray on the coffee table in front of Helen and looked back to the door where a small long-haired dachshund hopefully watched the activity. "You," Cotter said. "Peach. Didn't I tell you to stop in the kitchen?" The dog wagged her tail and barked. "Likes chocolate, she does," Cotter said in explanation.

"Likes everything," Deborah amended. She moved to take cups from Helen as she poured the coffee. Cotter scooped the dog up and headed again towards the back of the house. In a moment they heard him climbing the stairs. "Milk and sugar, Mr. Luxford?" Deborah asked amiably, as if Luxford hadn't been questioning her integrity a moment earlier. "Will you have some cake as well? My father made it. He's an extraordinary cook."

Luxford looked as if he knew the decision to break bread with them—or in this case cake—would be crossing a line he would prefer not to cross. Still, he accepted. He moved to the sofa, where he sat on the edge and brooded while Deborah and Helen continued passing round the cake and the coffee. He finally spoke. "All right. I can see that I have little choice." He reached into his blazer's inner pocket, revealing the paisley braces that had impressed Cotter. He brought out an envelope, which he passed to St. James with the explanation that it had come to him in the afternoon's post.

St. James studied the envelope before removing its contents. He read the brief message. He went at once to his desk and rooted in the side drawer for a moment, bringing forth a plastic jacket into which he slipped the single piece of paper. He said, "Has anyone else handled this?"

"Only you and I."

"Good." St. James passed the plastic jacket to Helen. He said to Luxford, "Charlotte. Who is she? And who's your firstborn child?"

"She is. Charlotte. She's been kidnapped."

"You've not phoned the authorities?"

"We can't have the police, if that's who you mean. We can't run the risk of any publicity."

"There won't be publicity," St. James pointed out. "Procedure calls for keeping kidnappings under wraps. You know that well enough, don't you? I'd assume a newspaperman—"

"I know well enough that the police keep the newspapers up-to-date with daily briefings when they're dealing with abduction," Luxford said sharply. "With all parties understanding that nothing goes into print until the victim's returned to the family."

"So why's that a problem, Mr. Luxford?"

"Because of who the victim is."

"Your daughter."

"Yes. And the daughter of Eve Bowen."

Helen met St. James's eyes as she passed the kidnapper's letter back to him. He saw her eyebrows rise. Deborah was saying, "Eve Bowen? I'm not entirely familiar. . . . Simon? Do you know . . . ?"

Eve Bowen, David told her, was the Undersecretary of State for the Home Office, one of the Conservative Government's most high-profile Junior Ministers. She was an up-and-comer who, with astonishing rapidity, was climbing the ladder to become the country's next Margaret Thatcher. She was the Member of Parliament for Marylebone, and it was from Marylebone that her daughter had apparently disappeared.

"When I got this in the post"—Luxford gestured to the letter—"I phoned Eve at once. Frankly, I thought it was a bluff. I thought someone had somehow linked our names. I thought someone was trying to get me to react in a way that would betray the past relationship between us. I thought someone was in need of some sort of proof that Eve and I are connected through Charlotte, and the pretence that Charlotte had been abducted—plus my reaction to that pretence—would be the proof required."

"Why would anyone want proof of your connection to Eve Bowen?" Helen asked.

"In order to sell the story to the media. I don't need to tell you how it would play out in the press if it became known that I—of all people—am the father of Eve Bowen's only child. Especially after the way she's . . ." He seemed to search for a euphemism that eluded him.

St. James concluded the thought without resorting to a more pleasant way of expressing it. "The way she's used the child's illegitimacy to benefit her own ends in the past?"

"She's made it her standard," Luxford admitted. "You can imagine the field day the press would have with her once it was known that Eve Bowen's great crime of passion involved someone like me."

St. James could well imagine. The Marylebone MP had long portrayed herself as a fallen woman who'd made restitution, who'd eschewed an abortion as a solution reflecting the erosion of values in society, who was doing the right thing by her bastard child. The fact of her daughter's illegitimacy—as well as the fact that Eve Bowen had nobly never named the father—was at least part of the reason she'd been elected to Parliament in the first place. She publicly espoused morality, religion, basic values, family solidarity, devotion to Monarch and country. She stood for everything that *The Source* derided among Conservative politicians.

"The story's served her well," St. James said. "A politician who's admitted publicly to her imperfections. That's hard for a voter to resist. Not to mention a Prime Minister seeking to bolster his Government with female appointees. Does he know the child's been kidnapped, by the way?"

"No one in the Government's been told."

"And you're certain she's been kidnapped?" St. James indicated the letter that was lying on his knee. "This uses a form of block printing. It could well have been done by a child. Is there any chance that Charlotte herself could be behind this? Does she know about you? Could this be an effort to force her mother's hand in some way?"

"Of course not. Good God. She's only ten years old. Eve's never told her."

"Can you be sure of that?"

"Of course I can't be sure. I can only go by what Eve's told me."

"And you've told no one? Are you married? Have you told your wife?"

"I've told no one," he said firmly, without acknowledging the other two questions. "Eve says she hasn't either, but she must have let something drop at one time or another—some reference, some chance remark. She must have said something to someone who bears a grudge against her."

"And does no one bear a grudge against you?" Helen's dark eyes were guileless and her expression bland, both implying that she had no idea that The Source's primary philosophy was to dig up the dirt fast and publish it first.

"Half the country, I dare say," Luxford admitted. "But it's hardly going to ruin me professionally if word gets out that I'm the father of Eve Bowen's illegitimate child. I'll be a laughingstock briefly, considering my politics, but that'll be the end of it. Eve, not I, is in the vulnerable position."

"Then why send you the letter?" St. James asked.

"We both received one. Mine came in the post. Hers was waiting at home, hand delivered sometime during the day, according to her housekeeper."

St. James re-examined the envelope in which Luxford's letter had been mailed. It was postmarked two days previously.

"When did Charlotte disappear?" he asked.

"This afternoon. Somewhere between Blandford Street and Devonshire Place Mews."

"Has there been a demand for money?"

"Just the demand for public acknowledgement of Charlotte's paternity."

"Which you're unwilling to make."

"I'm willing to make it. I'd rather not, it would cause me difficulties, but I'm willing. It's Eve who won't hear of it."

"You've seen her?"

"Talked to her. After that I phoned David. I remembered his having a brother . . . I knew you were involved in criminal investigations somehow, or at least that you had been. I thought you might help."

St. James shook his head and returned letter and envelope to Luxford. "This isn't a matter for me to handle. It can be dealt with discreetly by—"

"Listen to me." Luxford hadn't touched either his cake or his coffee, but he reached for the coffee now. He gulped down a mouthful and replaced the cup in its saucer. Some of the coffee sloshed out, wetting his fingers. He didn't make a move to dry them. "You don't know how newspapers actually work. The cops will go to Eve's house first and no one will hear of it, true. But they'll need to speak to her more than once, and they won't be willing to wait for an hour when she's in seclusion in Marylebone. So they'll go to see her at the Home Office because that's near enough Scotland Yard, and God knows this particular kidnapping is going to be a Scotland Yard case unless we do something to head that off now."

"Scotland Yard and the Home Office live in each other's pocket," St. James pointed out. "You know that. Even if that weren't the case, the investigators wouldn't go to see her in uniform."

"Do you actually think they need to be in uniform?" Luxford demanded. "There isn't a journalist alive who can't tell when he's looking at a cop. So a cop shows up at the Home Office and asks for the Undersecretary of State. A correspondent for one of the papers sees him. Someone in the Home Office is willing to snout—a secretary, a filing clerk, a caretaker, a fifth-rank civil servant with too many debts and too much interest in money. However it happens, it happens. Someone talks to the correspondent. And his newspaper's attention is now zeroed in on Eve Bowen. Who *is* this woman, the paper starts asking. What's going on that the police have come to call? Who *is* the father of her child, by the way? It's only a matter of time before they trace Charlotte to me."

"If you haven't told anyone, that's unlikely," St. James said.

"It doesn't matter what I've told or not told," Luxford said. "The point is that Eve's told. She claims she hasn't, but she must have done. Someone knows. Someone's waiting. Bringing in the police—which is what the kidnapper expects us to do—is just the ticket to get the story into the press. If that happens, Eve's finished. She'll have to stand down as Junior Minister and I dare say she'll lose her seat as well. If not now, because of this, then in the next election."

"Unless she becomes a figure of public sympathy, in which case this entire affair serves her interests quite well."

"That," Luxford said, "is a particularly vile comment. What are you suggesting? She's Charlotte's mother, for God's sake."

Deborah turned to her husband. She'd been sitting on the ottoman in front of his chair, and she touched his good leg lightly and got to her feet. "Could I have a word, Simon?" she asked him.

St. James saw that she was flushed. He regretted at once allowing her to be part of the interview. The moment he'd heard it was about a child, he should have sent her from the room on some pretext. Children—and her inability to bear them—were her greatest vulnerability.

He followed her into the dining room. She stood by the table with her hands behind her, resting them against the polished wood. She said, "I know what you're thinking, but it isn't that. You've no need to protect me."

"I don't want to get involved in this, Deborah. There's too much risk. I don't want it on my conscience if something happens to the girl."

"This doesn't appear to be a typical abduction though, does it? No demand for money, just a demand for publicity. And no threat of death. If you don't help them, you know they'll just go to someone else."

"Or they'll go to the police, which is where they should have gone in the first place."

"But you've done this sort of work before. So has Helen. Not recently, of course. But you've done it in the past. And you've done it well."

St. James made no reply. He knew what he ought to do: what he'd already done. Tell Luxford that he wanted no part of the situation. But Deborah was watching him, her face a mirror of the absolute faith she'd always had in him. To do the right thing, to be wise when necessary.

"You can put a time limit on it," she said reasonably. "You can . . . What if you say that you'll give it . . . what, one day? Two? To establish a trail. To talk to people who know her. To . . . I don't know. To do something. Because if you do that much, at least you'll know that the investigation is being handled properly. And that's what you want, isn't it? To be sure that everything's handled properly?"

St. James touched her cheek. Her skin was hot. Her eyes seemed too large. She looked little more than a child herself despite her twenty-five years. He shouldn't have let her listen to Luxford's story in the first place, he thought again. He should have sent her off to work on her photographs. He should have insisted. He should have . . . St. James brought himself round abruptly. Deborah was right. He always wanted to protect her. He had a passion to protect her. It was the bane of their marriage, the largest disadvantage of being eleven years her senior and having known her since her birth.

"They need you," she said. "I think you ought to help. At least talk to the mother. Hear what she has to say. You could do that much tonight. You and Helen can go to her. Right away." She reached for his hand that still grazed her cheek.

"I can't promise two days," he said.

"That won't matter, so long as you're involved. Will you do it, then? I know you won't regret it."

I already do, St. James thought. But he nodded his assent.

—m—

Dennis Luxford had plenty of time to put his psychological house in order before returning home. He lived in Highgate, a considerable drive north from the St. James home near the river in Chelsea, and while he was guiding his Porsche through the traffic, he assembled his thoughts and constructed a facade that his wife, he hoped, would not be able to pierce.

He'd phoned her after talking to Eve. Estimated time of arrival had changed, he explained. Sorry, darling. Something's come up. I've a photographer in South Lambeth waiting for Larnsey's rent boy to come out of his parents' house; I've a reporter ready when the boy makes his statement; we're holding up the presses as long as possible to get it in the morning's edition. I need to stand by here. Am I ballsing up your evening plans?

Fiona said no. She'd just been reading to Leo when the phone rang, or rather reading *with* Leo because no one read *to* Leo when Leo wanted to do the reading himself. He'd chosen Giotto, Fiona confided with a sigh. Again. I do wish his interest might be caught by another period of art. Reading about religious paintings quite puts me to sleep.

It's good for your soul, Luxford had said in a tone that tried to achieve wry amusement although what he had thought was, Shouldn't he be reading about dinosaurs at his age? About constellations? About big-game hunters? About snakes and frogs? Why in hell was an eight-year-old reading about a fourteenth-century painter? And why was his mother encouraging him to do so?

They were too close to each other, Luxford thought not for the first time. Leo and his mother shared too much of the same soul. It would do the boy a world of good when he was finally packed off to the

Baverstock School for the autumn term. Leo didn't like the idea, Fiona liked it less, but Luxford knew it would serve them both well. Hadn't Baverstock done as much for him? Made him a man? Given him direction? Wasn't being sent off to public school the reason he was where he was today?

He quashed the thought of where he was today, tonight, this minute. He had to obliterate the memory of the letter and everything that had followed from the letter. It was the only way to maintain the facade.

Still, thoughts lapped like small waves against the barriers he had built to contain them, and central to the thoughts was his conversation with Eve.

He hadn't spoken to her since she'd told him she was pregnant all those years ago, five months to the day after the Tory conference where they'd met. Or not met exactly, because he'd known her from the University, known her only in passing on the staff of the newspaper and found her attractive even as he found her politics repellent. When he'd seen her in Blackpool among the grey-suited, grey-haired, and generally grey-faced power brokers of the Conservative Party, the attraction had been the same, as had the repulsion. But they were fellow journalists at that time—he two years into his command of the *Globe*, she a political correspondent for the *Daily Telegraph*—and they had occasion, dining and drinking among their colleagues, to lock horns and intellects over the Conservatives' apparent stranglehold on the reins of power. Locking horns and intellects led to locking bodies. Not once, because at least there might be an excuse for once: Ascribe it to excessive drink and more excessive randiness and forget about it please. But instead, the affair had gone on feverishly throughout the length of the conference. The result was Charlotte.

What had he been thinking of? Luxford wondered. He'd known Fiona for a year at the time of that conference, he'd known he intended to marry her, he'd set upon a course to win her trust and her heart, not to mention her voluptuous body, and at the first opportunity, he'd cocked things up. But not entirely, because Eve not only hadn't wanted to marry him, she wouldn't hear of marrying him when he made the perfunctory offer upon learning she was pregnant. She had her sights set on a career in politics. Marriage to Dennis Luxford was not part of her plan to achieve that career. "My God," she'd said. "Do you actually believe I'd hook myself up with the King of Sleaze just to have a man's name for my baby's birth certificate? You must be more demented than your politics suggest." So they'd parted. And in the intervening years, as she climbed the ladder of power, he sometimes told himself that Eve had successfully done what he himself could not manage: She'd made a surgical cut into her memory and amputated the dangling appendage of her past.

That hadn't been the case, as he discovered when he'd phoned her. Charlotte's existence wouldn't allow it.

"What do you want?" she'd asked him when he had finally managed to track her down in the Chief Whip's office at the House of Commons. "Why are you phoning me?" Her voice had been low and terse. There were other voices in the background.

He'd said, "I need to talk to you."

"Frankly, I don't feel likewise."

"It's about Charlotte."

He heard her breath hiss in. Her voice didn't change. "She's nothing to do with you and you know it."

"Evelyn," he said urgently. "I know I'm phoning out of the blue."

"With remarkable timing."

"I'm sorry. I can hear you're not alone. Can you get to a private phone?"

"I've *no* intention—"

"I've had a letter. Accusing me."

"That's hardly a surprise. I should think that a letter accusing you of something would be a regular event for you."

"Someone knows."

"What?"

"About us. About Charlotte."

That seemed to rattle her, if only for a moment. She was quiet at first. He thought he could hear her tapping a finger against the mouthpiece of the phone. Then she said abruptly, "Nonsense."

"Listen. Just listen." He read the brief message. Having heard it, she said nothing. Somewhere in the office with her, a man's voice gave a bark of laughter. "Firstborn child, it says," Luxford said. "Someone knows. Have you confided in anyone?"

"Freed?" she said. " 'Charlotte will be *freed*'?" There was another silence in which Luxford could almost hear her mind working as she assessed the potential for damage to her credibility and measured the extent of the political fall-out. "Give me your number," she finally said. "I'll phone you back."

She had done so, but when she had, it was a different Eve on the phone. She'd said, "Dennis. God *damn* you. What have you *done*?"

No weeping, no terror, no mother's hysteria, no breast-beating, no rage. Just those eight words. And an end to his hopes that someone was bluffing. No one was bluffing about anything, it seemed. Charlotte was

missing. Someone had her, someone—or someone employed by someone—who knew the truth.

He had to keep that truth from Fiona. She had made a sacred
mission of keeping no secrets from him during their ten-year marriage.
It didn't bear thinking what would happen to the trust between them
should she discover the one secret he'd kept from her. It was bad
enough that he'd fathered a child he never saw. Fiona might learn to
absolve him for that. But to have fathered this child in the midst of his
pursuit of Fiona herself, in the midst of forging a bond with her . . .
She would see everything that had passed between them from that
moment on as one variation or another of falsehood. And falsehood was
what she would never forgive.

Luxford made the turn from Highgate Road. He followed the
curve of Millfield Lane along Hampstead Heath where small bobbing
lights moving along the path by the ponds told him that bicyclers were
still enjoying the late May weather, despite the hour and the darkness.
He slowed as the brick wall edging his property emerged from a hedge
of privet and holly. He turned in between the pillars and cruised up the
slope of the drive towards the villa that had been their home for the
past eight years.

Fiona was in the garden. From a distance, Luxford saw the movement of her white muslin dressing gown against the emerald-black
backdrop of ferns, and he went to join her. He followed the haphazard
arrangement of paving stones, his shoe soles brushing against baby's
tears that were already dotted with the night's dew. If his wife had
heard the car arrive, she gave no notice. She was heading for the largest
tree in the garden, an umbrella-shaped hornbeam under which a
wooden bench sat at the edge of the garden pool.

She was curled on this bench when he reached her, her endless
mannequin's legs and shapely feet hidden beneath the folds of her
dressing gown. She'd pinned her hair away from her face, and the first
thing he did when he joined her on the bench, after kissing her fondly,
was to unpin it so that it fell to her breasts. He felt the same stirring for
her that he always felt, a mixture of awe, desire, and amazement at the
fact that this glorious creature was actually his wife.

He was grateful for the darkness, which made the task of this first
meeting between them an easier one. He was grateful that she'd chosen
to come outdoors as well, because her garden—the crowning achievement in her domestic life, as she liked to call it—provided him with the
means of distracting her.

"Aren't you cold?" he asked. "Would you like my jacket?"

"The night's lovely," she replied. "I couldn't bear to be indoors.

Do you expect we'll have a horrible summer if it's this gorgeous in May?''

"That's the general rule."

A fish broke the surface of the pool before them, its tail fin slapping on a lily pad. "It's an unfair rule," Fiona said. "Spring should make a promise that summer fulfills." She gestured towards a stand of young birches in a hollow some twenty yards from where they sat. "The nightingales have come again this year. And there's a family of whinchats that Leo and I watched this afternoon. We were feeding the squirrels. Darling, Leo must be taught not to feed the squirrels from his hand. I've spoken to him about it time and again. He argues that there's no such things as rabies in England, and he refuses to consider the danger he's putting the animal in when he allows it to become too accustomed to human contact. Won't you speak to him again?''

If he was going to speak to Leo about anything, Luxford thought, it wouldn't be about squirrels. Curiosity about animals was typical to a growing boy, thank God.

Fiona continued. Luxford could tell she was speaking with care, which gave him an uneasy moment until her choice of subject became clear to him. "He talked again about Baverstock, darling. He does seem so reluctant to go. Haven't you noticed? I've explained and explained about its being your school and wouldn't he truly like to be an old Bavernian like his father? He says no, he doesn't much care for the idea, and what does it matter because Grandpa isn't an old Bavernian nor is Uncle Jack and they've done quite well for themselves, haven't they?''

"We've been through this, Fiona."

"Of course we have, darling. Time and again. I only want to tell you what Leo said so that you're prepared for him in the morning. He's declared that he is going to speak to you about it over breakfast—man to man, he said—providing you're up before he sets off to school. I did tell him you'd be coming in late tonight. Listen, darling. There's the nightingale. How lovely. Did you get the story, by the way?''

Luxford almost stumbled. Her voice had been so quiet. He'd been enjoying the softness of her hair against the palm of his hand. He'd been trying to identify the scent she was wearing. He'd been thinking of the last time they'd made love out of doors. So he very nearly missed the delicate transition, that gentle feminine shifting of conversational gears.

"No," he said and continued with the truth, glad that there was a truth he could tell her. "The rent boy continues in hiding at the moment. We went to press without him."

"Dreadful to have to waste an evening waiting for nothing, I imagine.''

"A third of my job is waiting for nothing. Another third is deciding what will go in nothing's place on tomorrow's front page. Rodney's suggesting we back off on the story. We had a go-round about it this afternoon."

"He phoned here for you this evening. Perhaps that's what his call was about. I told him you were still at the office. He'd phoned there but couldn't get you, he said. No answer on your private line. Around half past eight. I expect you'd popped out for something to eat, hadn't you?"

"I expect. Half past eight?"

"That's what he said."

"I had my sandwich round then, I think." Luxford stirred on the bench, feeling sticky and uncomfortable. He'd never lied to his wife, at least not after a single lie about the endless tedium of that fateful Tory conference in Blackpool. And Fiona hadn't been his wife then, so it didn't much count in the truth and faithfulness department, did it? He sighed and picked up a flake of stone from beneath them. He used his thumb to flick it into the pool. He watched the flurry of interest at the surface of the water as the fish zipped to the spot in hopes of catching a bug. "We should have a holiday," he said. "The South of France. Hire a car and drive through Provence. Take a house there for a month. What about it? This summer?"

She laughed quietly. He felt her cool hand on the back of his neck. Her fingers sought their way into his hair. "When would you ever take a month away from the paper? You'd be mad with boredom within a week. Not to mention tormented by the thought of Rodney Aronson busily ingratiating himself with everyone from the chairman to the office cleaners. He means to have your job, you know."

Yes, Luxford thought, that's exactly what Rodney Aronson meant. He'd been monitoring Luxford's every movement and decision since his arrival at *The Source*, just waiting for the single mistake that he could carry to the chairman and secure his own future. If Charlotte Bowen's existence could possibly be designated that single mistake . . . But there was no possibility that Rodney knew about Charlotte. There was *no* possibility. None. At. All.

"You're so quiet," Fiona remarked. "Are you exhausted?"

"Just thinking."

"About?"

"The last time we made love in the garden. I can't remember when it was. I just remember that it rained."

"Last September," she said.

He looked over his shoulder at her. "You remember."

"Over there by the birches where the grass is longer. We had wine and cheese. We had music on in the house. We had that old blanket from the boot of your car."

"We had?"

"We had."

She looked wonderful in moonlight. She looked like the work of art that she was. Her full lips were inviting, her throat an arch that asked for his kiss, her statuesque body a wordless temptation. "That blanket," Luxford noted. "It's still in the boot."

The full lips curved. "Go get it," she said.

3

*E*VE BOWEN, UNDERSECRETARY OF STATE for the Home Office
and six-year Member of Parliament for Marylebone, lived in Devonshire Place Mews, a hook-shaped length of London cobblestones lined
with erstwhile stables and garages long ago converted to housing. Her
house stood at the northeast end of the mews, an impressive double-
width affair that was three storeys of slate, white woodwork, and brick,
with a roof terrace from which draped swags of ivy.

St. James had spoken to the Junior Minister before leaving Chelsea.
Luxford had made the call, said merely, "I've found someone, Evelyn.
You need to talk to him," and handed the phone to St. James without
waiting for her response. St. James's conversation with the MP had
been brief: He would be coming to see her immediately; he would be
bringing an associate with him; did the Junior Minister wish him to
know anything prior to their arrival?

Her initial response had been a brusque question. "How do you
know Luxford?"

"Through my brother."

"Who is he?"

"A businessman in town for a conference. From Southampton."

"Has he an axe to grind?"

"With the Government? The Home Office? I seriously doubt it."

"All right." She recited her address, concluding cryptically with,
"Keep Luxford out of this. If anyone appears to be watching the house
when you arrive, drive on and we'll meet later. Is that clear?"

It was. A conscientious quarter of an hour after Dennis Luxford
had departed, St. James and Helen Clyde began to wind their way up to
Marylebone. It was just after eleven when they swung off the high

street into Devonshire Place Mews, and after driving the mews' entire length to assure themselves that no one was loitering in the vicinity, St. James pulled his old MG to a halt in front of Eve Bowen's house and quietly released its manual clutch.

A porch light burned above the front door. Inside, another light brushed uneven strips of illumination against the closed curtains of the ground floor front windows. When they rang the bell, brisk footsteps immediately sounded against an entry of either marble or tiles. A well-oiled bolt was drawn. The door swung open.

Eve Bowen said, "Mr. St. James?" She stepped back from the light almost as soon as it fell upon her, and once St. James and Helen were in the house, she shot the door closed and bolted them in. She said, "In here," and led them to the right, across terra-cotta tiles, into a sitting room where a briefcase stood open upon a side table next to a chair, spilling out manila folders, pages of typing, news cuttings, telephone messages, documents, and pamphlets. Eve Bowen snapped its lid down without stopping to shove its bulging contents into place. She picked up a thick green wineglass, drained it, and poured more white wine from a bottle that rested in a bucket on the floor. She said, "I'd be interested in knowing how much he's paying you for this charade."

St. James was nonplussed. "I beg your pardon?"

"Luxford's behind this, of course. But I can see by your expression that he hasn't yet made you aware of that fact. How wise of him." She took the seat she had apparently been sitting in prior to their arrival and directed them to a sofa and chairs that resembled enormous umber pillows sewn together. She rested her wineglass in her lap, using both hands to hold it against the trim, matchstick skirt of her suit. This was black, pin-striped. Seeing it, St. James recalled reading an interview with the Junior Minister shortly after she'd been tapped by the Government to serve in her current position as Undersecretary of State for the Home Office. No one would find her drawing attention to herself in the manner of her female colleagues in the Commons, she had asserted. She saw no need to plume herself in scarlet in the hope of distinguishing herself from the men. She'd let her brain do that for her.

"Dennis Luxford is a man without conscience," she said abruptly. Her words were brittle, her tone cut from glass. "He's the maestro conducting this particular orchestra. Oh, not directly, of course. I dare say snatching ten-year-olds off the street is probably beyond even his willingness to stoop to skulduggery. But make no mistake, he's playing you for a fool, and he's trying to do the same to me. I won't have it."

"What gives you the impression he's involved?" St. James lowered himself to the sofa, finding it surprisingly comfortable despite its amorphous nature. He adjusted his bad leg to an easier position. Helen stayed where she was, standing at the fireplace near a collection of trophies displayed in a niche, the better to observe Ms. Bowen from a spot in the room where she wouldn't be conspicuously doing so.

"Because there are only two people on earth who know the identity of my daughter's father. I'm one of them. Dennis Luxford is the other."

"Your daughter herself doesn't know?"

"Of course not. Never. And it's impossible that she could have found out on her own."

"Your parents? Your family?"

"No one, Mr. St. James, save Dennis and me." She took a measured sip of her wine. "It's his tabloid's objective to bring down the Government. At the moment, he finds himself with the right set of circumstances to crush the Conservative Party once and for all. He's attempting to do so."

"I don't follow your logic."

"It's all rather convenient, wouldn't you say? My daughter's disappearance. A putative kidnapping note in Luxford's possession. A demand for publicity in that note. And all of it falling directly on the heels of Sinclair Larnsey's shenanigans with an underage boy in Paddington."

"Mr. Luxford wasn't acting like a man in the midst of orchestrating a kidnapping for the tabloids to exploit," St. James noted.

"Not for the tabloids in the plural," she replied. "For the tabloid in the excessively singular. He's hardly going to let the competition scoop his own best story."

"He seemed as intent as you are upon keeping this quiet."

"Are you a student of human behaviour, Mr. St. James? Along with your other talents?"

"I think it's wise to make an assessment of the people who ask me for help. Before I agree to help them."

"How perspicacious. When we have more time, perhaps I'll ask for your assessment of me." She set her wineglass beside her briefcase. She removed her circular tortoiseshell spectacles and rubbed their lenses against the arm of the chair as if to polish them and to study St. James simultaneously. The tortoiseshell frames were largely the same shade as Eve Bowen's unruffled pageboy hair, and when she replaced the spectacles on her nose, they touched the tips of the fringe she wore overlong to cover her eyebrows. "Let me ask you this. Don't you find anything out of order in the fact that Mr. Luxford received this kidnapping note by post?"

"Obviously," St. James said. "It was postmarked yesterday. And possibly posted the day before that."

"While my daughter was quite safe at home. So if we examine the facts, we can agree that we have a kidnapper fairly sure of a successful outcome to his kidnapping when he posts his letter."

"Or," St. James said, "we have a kidnapper who knows it won't matter if he fails because if he fails, the letter will have no effect upon its recipient. If the kidnapper and the recipient of the letter are one and the same person. Or if the kidnapper has been hired by the letter's recipient."

"So you see."

"I hadn't overlooked the postmark, Ms. Bowen. And I don't take what's said to me only on face value. I'm willing to agree that Dennis Luxford may be behind this in some way. I'm equally willing to suspect that you are."

Her mouth curved briefly. She gave a sharp nod. "Well, well," she said. "You're not as much Luxford's lackey as he supposes, are you? I think you'll do."

She got up from her chair and went to a trapezoidal bronze sculpture that stood on a pedestal between the two front windows. She tilted the sculpture and from beneath it she took an envelope which she carried to St. James before returning to her chair. "This was delivered sometime during the day. Possibly between one and three o'clock this afternoon. My housekeeper—Mrs. Maguire, she's left for the day— found it when she returned from her weekly visit to her turf accountant. She put it with the rest of the post—you can see it has my name on it—and didn't think about it until I phoned her at seven o'clock, asking about Charlotte, after Dennis Luxford phoned me."

St. James examined the envelope Eve Bowen had given him. It was white, inexpensive, the sort of envelope one could buy almost anywhere, from Boots to the local newsagent's. He donned latex gloves and slid the envelope's contents out. He unfolded the single sheet of paper and placed it within another plastic jacket that he'd brought from his home. He removed the gloves and read the brief message.

> *Eve Bowen—*
> *If you want to know what's happened to Lottie, phone her father.*

"Lottie," St. James noted.

"That's what she calls herself."

"What does Luxford call her?"

Eve Bowen didn't falter in her belief in Luxford's involvement. She said, "The name wouldn't be impossible to discover, Mr. St. James. Someone's obviously discovered it."

"Or has already known it." St. James showed the letter to Helen. She read it before speaking.

"You said you phoned Mrs. Maguire at seven this evening, Ms. Bowen. Surely your daughter had been missing a number of hours by then. Mrs. Maguire didn't notice?"

"She noticed."

"But she didn't alert you?"

The Junior Minister made a minute alteration in her position in the chair. Her breath eased out in what could have passed for a sigh. "Several times in the past year—since I've been at the Home Office—Charlotte has misbehaved. Mrs. Maguire knows I expect her to handle Charlotte's mischief on her own without disturbing me at work. She thought this was an instance of misbehaviour."

"Why?"

"Because Wednesday afternoon is her music lesson, an event Charlotte doesn't particularly like. She drags herself to it each week and most Wednesday afternoons she threatens to throw herself or her flute down a street drain. When she didn't turn up here immediately after her lesson today, Mrs. Maguire assumed she was up to her usual tricks. It wasn't until six that she began phoning round to see if Charlotte had gone home with one of her schoolmates instead of going to her lesson."

"She goes to the lesson alone, then?" Helen clarified.

The MP apparently heard the unspoken but inevitable secondary question behind Helen's words: Was a ten-year-old girl running about unsupervised on the streets of London? She said, "Children travel in packs these days, in case you haven't noticed. Charlotte would hardly have been alone. And when she is, Mrs. Maguire attempts to accompany her."

"Attempts." The word wasn't lost on Helen.

"Charlotte doesn't much like being trailed by an overweight Irishwoman given to wearing baggy leggings and a moth-eaten pullover. And are we here to discuss my child-minding practices or the whereabouts of my child?"

St. James felt rather than saw Helen's reaction to the words. The air seemed to thicken with a mixture of one woman's aggravation and the other's disbelief. Neither emotion would bring them any closer to locating the child, however. He shifted gears.

"Once she found that Charlotte hadn't gone home with a schoolmate, Mrs. Maguire still didn't phone you?"

"I'd made rather a point about her responsibility to my daughter after an incident last month."

"What sort of incident?"

"A typical display of pigheadedness." The MP took another sip of her wine. "Charlotte had been hiding in the boiler room at St. Bernadette's—that's her school, on Blandford Street—because she didn't want to keep an appointment with her psychotherapist. It's a weekly appointment, she knows she has to go, but every month or so she makes up her mind not to cooperate. This was one of those times. Mrs. Maguire phoned me in a panic when Charlotte failed to appear in time to be taken to her appointment. I had to leave my office to hunt her down. It was after that that Mrs. Maguire and I sat down and became quite clear on what her responsibilities towards my daughter were going to be. And through what hours those responsibilities would extend."

Helen looked increasingly perplexed by the Junior Minister's approach to child-minding. She seemed to be ready to question the other woman further. St. James headed her off. There was no point to putting the Junior Minister any more on the defensive, at least not at the moment.

"Where exactly was the music lesson?"

She told him the lesson took place not far from St. Bernadette's School, in a mews area called Cross Keys Close near Marylebone High Street. Charlotte walked there every Wednesday directly after school. Her teacher was a man called Damien Chambers.

"Did your daughter show up for her lesson today?"

She had shown up. Mrs. Maguire had phoned Mr. Chambers first when she started her search for Charlotte at six o'clock. According to him, the girl had been there and gone at her regular time.

"We'll have to speak to this man," St. James pointed out. "And he'll probably want to know why we're asking him questions. Have you considered that and where it could lead?"

Eve Bowen had apparently already accepted the fact that even a private investigation into her daughter's disappearance could not be made without questioning those who had seen her last. And those who had last seen her would no doubt wonder why a crippled man and his female companion were nosing about, dogging the child's movements. It couldn't be helped. The curiosity of those questioned might lead them to drop an intriguing suggestion to one of the tabloids, but that was a risk Charlotte's mother was apparently willing to take.

"The way we're going about it, the story is nothing but speculation," she said. "It's only with the police involved that things become definite."

"Speculation can fan itself into a firestorm," St. James said. "You need to bring in the police, Ms. Bowen. If not the local authorities, then Scotland Yard. You've the pull for that, I assume, because of the Home Office."

"I have the pull. And I want no police. It's out of the question."

The expression on her face was adamantine. He and Helen could argue the point with her for another quarter of an hour, but St. James could tell that their efforts would be futile. Finding the child—finding her quickly—was the real point. He asked for a description of the little girl as she'd appeared that morning, for a photograph as well. Eve Bowen told them that she hadn't seen her daughter that morning, she never saw Charlotte in the morning because she was always gone from the house before Charlotte awakened. But she'd been wearing her school uniform, naturally. Upstairs somewhere there was a picture of her wearing it. She left the room to fetch the photograph. They heard her climbing the stairs.

"This is more than odd, Simon," Helen said in a low voice once they were alone. "From the way she's acting, one could almost think—" She hesitated. She tucked her arms round herself. "Don't you find her reaction to what's happened to Charlotte rather unnatural?"

St. James got to his feet and went to examine the trophies. They bore Eve Bowen's name and had been awarded for dressage. It seemed fitting that she would have won her dozen or more first places for such an activity. He wondered if her political staff responded to her signals as well as her horse had apparently done.

He said, "She thinks Luxford's behind this, Helen. It wouldn't be his intention to harm the child, just to rattle the mother. She apparently doesn't intend to be rattled."

"Still, one would expect to encounter a fissure or two here in private."

"She's a politician. She's going to play her cards close to the chest."

"But this is her daughter we're talking about. Why is she out on the streets alone? And what's her mother been doing from seven o'clock till now?" Helen gestured at the table, the briefcase, the documents that the briefcase disgorged. "I'd hardly expect the parent of a kidnapped child—no matter who kidnapped her—to be able to keep her mind on her work. It isn't natural, is it? None of this is natural."

"I agree entirely. But she knows quite well how things are going to appear to us. She hasn't got where she is in the brief time it's taken her to get there without knowing in advance how things will look." St. James examined a gallery of photographs that stood in haphazard ranks among three houseplants on a narrow chrome and glass table. He noted a picture of Eve Bowen and the Prime Minister, another of Eve Bowen and the Home Secretary, a third of Eve Bowen in a receiving line along which the Princess Royal appeared to be offering greetings to a rather scant gathering of minority police constables.

"Things," Helen said with delicate irony on the word St. James had chosen, "are looking rather remarkably detached, if you ask me."

A key turned the dead bolt of the front door as Helen was speaking. The door opened and shut. The bolt sounded again. Footsteps barked on the tiles and a man stood at the doorway to the sitting room, nearly six feet tall, narrow-shouldered, and spare. He moved his tea-coloured eyes from St. James to Helen, but he didn't speak at first. He looked tired and his hair the colour of old oak was disarranged boyishly, as if he'd ruffled it with his fingers in order to drive more blood to his head.

He finally spoke. "Hullo. Where's Eve?"

"Upstairs," St. James replied. "Fetching a photograph."

"A photograph?" He looked at Helen, then back to St. James. He appeared to read something in their expressions because his tone altered from friendly indifference to instant wariness. "What's going on?" He asked the question with an edge of aggression in his voice, which suggested that he was a man used to being answered at once and with deference. Even Government ministers, it seemed, did not entertain guests at nearly midnight without grave cause. He called sharply towards the stairs, "Eve?" And then to St. James, "Has something happened to someone? Is Eve all right? Has the Prime Minister—"

"Alex." Eve Bowen spoke, beyond St. James's line of vision. He heard her come quickly down the stairs.

Alex said to her, "What's going on?"

She avoided the question by introducing Helen and St. James, saying, "My husband. Alexander Stone."

St. James couldn't remember ever reading that the Junior Minister was married, but when Eve Bowen introduced her husband, he realised that he must have done and filed the information somewhere in the dustier part of his memory since it was unlikely he would have entirely forgotten that Alexander Stone was the Junior Minister's husband. Stone was one of the country's leading entrepreneurs. His particular interest was in restaurants, and he owned at least a half dozen upscale establishments from Hammersmith to Holburn. He was a master chef, a Newcastle boy who'd managed to shed his Geordie accent sometime during the admirable journey he'd made from pastry maker at Brown's Hotel to flourishing restaurateur. Indeed, Stone was the personification of the Conservative Party's ideal: With no social or educational advantages—and certainly no drawing upon government assistance—he'd made a success of himself. He was possibility incarnate and private ownership nonpareil. He was, in short, the perfect husband for a Tory MP.

"Something's happened," Eve Bowen explained to him. She put a gentling hand on his arm. "Alex, I'm afraid it's not very pleasant."

Again, Stone looked from St. James to Helen. St. James was trying to digest the information that Eve Bowen had not yet made her husband aware of her daughter's abduction. Helen, he could see, was doing the same. Both of their faces gave great scope for study, and Alexander Stone took a moment to study them while his own face blanched. "Dad," he said. "Is he gone? His heart?"

"It's not your father. Alex, Charlotte's gone missing."

He fixed his eyes on his wife. "Charlotte," he repeated blankly. "Charlotte. Charlie. *What?*"

"She's been kidnapped."

He looked dazed. "What? When? What's going—"

"This afternoon. After her music lesson."

His right hand went to the disheveled hair, dishevelling it further. "Fuck, Eve. What the *hell?* Why didn't you phone? I've been at Couscous since two. You know that. Why haven't you phoned me?"

"I didn't know till seven. And things happened too quickly."

He said to St. James, "You're the police."

"No police," his wife said.

He swung round to her. "Are you out of your mind? What the *hell*—"

"Alex." The MP's voice was low and insistent. "Will you wait in the kitchen? Will you make us some dinner? I'll be in in a moment to explain."

"Explain what?" he demanded. "What the fuck is going on? Who are these people? I want some answers, Eve."

"And you'll get them." She touched his arm again. "Please. Let me finish here. Please."

"Don't you bloody dismiss me like one of your underlings."

"Alex, believe me. I'm not. Let me finish here."

Stone pulled away from her. "Bloody *hell*," he snarled. He stalked through the sitting room, through the dining room beyond it, through a swinging door that apparently led to the kitchen.

Eve Bowen contemplated the path he'd taken. Behind the swinging door, cupboards opened and slammed shut. Pots cracked against work tops. Water ran. She handed the photograph to St. James. "This is Charlotte."

"I'll need her weekly schedule. A list of her friends. Addresses of the places she goes."

She nodded, although it was clear that her mind was in the kitchen with her husband. "Of course," she said. She returned to her chair where she took up a pen and a notebook, her hair falling forward to hide her face.

Helen was the one who asked the question. "Why didn't you phone your husband, Ms. Bowen? When you knew Charlotte was missing, why didn't you phone?"

Eve Bowen raised her head. She looked quite composed, as if she'd taken the time of crossing the room to wrest control over any emotions that might have betrayed her. "I didn't want him to be one of Dennis Luxford's victims," she said. "It seemed to me there are enough of them already."

—⁂—

Alexander Stone worked in a fury. He whisked red wine into the mixture of olive oil, chopped tomatoes, onions, parsley, and garlic. He lowered the heat beneath the pan and strode from his prized state-of-the-culinary-art cooker to the chopping board where he sent his knife flashing through the caps of a dozen mushrooms. He swept them into a bowl and took them to the cooker. There, a large pot of water was beginning to boil. It was sending steam towards the ceiling in translucent plumes, which made him suddenly think of Charlie, with no defence. Ghostbird feathers, she would have called them, dragging her footstool to the cooker and chattering while he worked.

Sweet Jesus, he thought.

He clenched a fist and pounded it hard against his thigh. He felt his eyes burning and he told himself that his contact lenses were reacting to the heat from the cooker and the pungency of the simmering onions and garlic. Then he called himself a spineless liar and stopped what he was doing and lowered his head. He was breathing like a distance runner, and he tried to be calm. He brought himself face-to-face with the truth: He didn't yet have the facts, and until he had them, he was pouring precious energy into rage. Which would serve him ill. Which would serve Charlie ill.

Right, he thought. Yes. Good. Let's be about our business. Let's wait. Let's see.

He pushed himself away from the cooker. He pulled from the freezer a packet of fettuccine. He had it completely unwrapped and ready to drop into the boiling water before he realised that he couldn't feel its cold on his palm. The realisation made him release the pasta so quickly into the pot that a geyser shot up and spat against his skin. That he could feel, and he took an instinctive leap away from the cooker like a novice in the kitchen.

"God damn," he whispered. "Fuck it. God damn."

He walked to the calendar that hung on the wall next to the telephone. He wanted to make sure. There was always a chance that he hadn't written down his week's schedule for once, that he hadn't left the name of the restaurant whose chefs and waiters he'd be overseeing that day, that he hadn't made sure his whereabouts were available to Mrs. Maguire, to Charlie, to his wife, that he had failed to allow for the odd emergency when his presence would be a desperate necessity. . . . But there it was in the square marked for Wednesday. *Couscous.* Just as the day before had *Sceptre* written across it. Just as tomorrow had *Demoiselle.* Which meant that there was no excuse at all. Which meant that he had the facts. Which meant that his rage could rage at will, fists crashing through cupboards, glasses and dishes smashing to the floor, cutlery hurled against walls, refrigerator dumped and its contents mashed beneath his feet. . . .

"They've left."

He swung around. Eve had come to the doorway. She removed her glasses and polished them wearily on the black silk lining of her jacket. "You didn't have to make anything fresh," she said with a nod at the cooker. "Mrs. Maguire probably left us something. She would have done. She always does for—" She stopped herself by returning her glasses to her nose.

For Charlotte. She wouldn't say the two words because she wouldn't say her daughter's name. Saying her daughter's name would give him an opening before she was ready. And she was a bloody politician who bloody well knew how to keep the upper hand.

As if a meal were not in the midst of cooking in that very room, she went to the refrigerator. Alex watched her bring out the two covered plates that he'd already inspected, carrying them to the work top and unwrapping Mrs. Maguire's Wednesday night offering of macaroni cheese, mixed veg, and boiled new potatoes dressed with a daring dash of paprika.

"God," she said, staring down at the lumps of cheddar that pockmarked the agglutinant gobbet of macaroni.

He said, "I leave her something for Charlie every day. All she has to do is warm it, but she won't. 'Fancy names for muck' is what she calls it."

"And this isn't muck?" Eve dumped the contents of both plates into the sink. She flipped the switch and let the disposer eat its fill. The water ran and ran and Alex watched her watching it, knowing that she was using the time to prepare herself for the coming conversation. Her head was bowed and her shoulders drooped. Her neck was exposed. It was white and vulnerable and it begged for his pity. But he wasn't moved.

He crossed to her, switched off the disposer, and turned off the tap. He took her arm to swing her to him. She was rigid to the touch. He dropped his hand.

"What happened?" he demanded.

"Just what I told you. She disappeared on the way home from her music lesson."

"Maguire wasn't with her?"

"Apparently not."

"God *damn* it, Eve. We've been through this before. If she can't be relied on to—"

"She thought Charlotte was with friends."

"She thought. She bloody fucking *thought*." Again he felt the need to strike. Had the housekeeper been there, he would have gone for her throat. "Why?" he asked sharply. "Just tell me why."

She didn't pretend to misunderstand. She turned. She cupped each elbow with her hands. It was a choice of position that cut her off from him more effectively than had she moved to the other side of the room. "Alex, I had to think what to do."

He felt gratitude for the fact that she at least didn't try to expound on her previous lie of things happening too quickly, of there being no time. But it was a meagre gratitude, like a seed that fell onto barren soil. "What exactly is there to think about?" he asked with a deliberate, polite calm. "It seems a simple four-step problem to me." He used his thumb and three fingers to tick off each step. "Charlie's been snatched. You phone me at the restaurant. I fetch you from your office. We go to the police."

"It's not as simple as that."

"You seem to be quagmired somewhere on step one. Is that right?" Her face didn't change. It still wore its expression of complete sang-froid, so essential in her line of work, a tranquillity that was quickly obliterating his own. "God damn it. Is that *right*, Eve?"

"Do you want me to explain?"

"I want you to tell me who the fuck those people were in the sitting room. I want you to tell me why the fuck you haven't called the police. I want you to explain—and let's go for ten words or less, Eve—why you didn't seem to think it important to let me know my own daughter—''

"Stepdaughter, Alex."

"Jesus Christ. So if I was her father—obviously defined by you as provider of a sodding sperm—I'd have merited a call to let me know that my child had gone missing. Am I getting it right?''

"Not quite. Charlotte's father already knows. He's the one who phoned me to tell me she'd been taken. I believe he's arranged to have her taken himself.''

The pasta water chose this moment to boil over, gushing in a frothing wave down the sides of the pot and onto the burner beneath it. Feeling as if he were slogging hip-deep through porridge, Alex went to the cooker and carried through the motions of stirring, lowering the heat, lifting the pot, setting a diffuser into position, while all the time he heard *Charlotte's father, Charlotte's father, Charlotte's father* roaring round the room. He set his stirring fork on its holder carefully before he turned back to his wife. She was naturally fair-skinned, but in the light of the kitchen she looked deadly pale.

"Charlie's father," he said.

"He claims to have received a kidnapping note. I received one as well." Alex saw her fingers tighten on her elbows. The gesture looked to him like a girding of mental or emotional loins. The worst, he realised, was yet to come.

"Keep going," he said evenly.

"Don't you want to see to your pasta?''

"I haven't much of an appetite. Have you?''

She shook her head. But she left him for a moment and returned to the sitting room, during which time he numbly stood stirring his sauce and his pasta and wondering when he'd feel like eating again. She returned with an opened bottle of wine and two glasses. She poured at the bar that extended from the cooker. She slid one of the glasses in his direction.

He realised that she wasn't going to say it unless he forced her. She would tell him everything else—what had apparently happened to Charlie, at what time of day, and exactly how and with what words she had come to learn about it. But she wouldn't speak the name unless he insisted. In the seven years he'd known her, in the six years of their marriage, the identity of Charlotte's father was the one secret she hadn't revealed. And it hadn't seemed fair to Alex to press her. Charlie's father, whoever he was, was part of Eve's past. Alex had wanted only to be part of her present and her future.

"Why's he taken her?"

She answered emotionlessly, a recital of conclusions she'd already reached. "Because he wants the public to know who her father is. Because he wants to embarrass the Tories further. Because if the Government continues to be faced with sexual scandals that erode the public's faith in their elected officials, the Prime Minister is going to be forced to call a general election and the Tories are going to lose it. Which is what he wants."

Alex homed in on the words that chilled him most and told him most about what she'd kept hidden for so many years. "Sexual scandals?"

Her lips curved mirthlessly. "Sexual scandals."

"Who is it, Eve?"

"Dennis Luxford."

The name meant nothing to him. Years of dreading, years of wondering, years of speculating, years of calculating, and the name meant absolutely sod bloody all. He could tell that she saw he was making no connection. She gave a sardonic and self-directed chuckle and walked to the small kitchen table that sat in a bay window overlooking the back garden. There was a rattan magazine holder next to one of the chairs. It was where Mrs. Maguire kept her lowbrow reading material that entertained her through her daily elevenses. From this rattan holder Eve took a tabloid. She carried it to the bar and laid it before Alex.

Its masthead was a blaze of red into which garish yellow letters spelled out *The Source!* Beneath this masthead three inches of headline screamed *Love-Cheat MP.* The headline was accompanied by two colour photographs, one of Sinclair Larnsey, MP for East Norfolk, looking grim-faced as he emerged from a building in the company of a cane-wielding elderly gentleman who had *Constituency Association Chairman* incised all over him, the other of a magenta Citroën, under which ran the caption: "Sinclair Larnsey's mobile love nest." The rest of the front page was devoted to Win A Dream Holiday (page 11), Breakfast With Your Favourite Star (page 8), and Cricket Murder Trial Coming (page 29).

He frowned at the tabloid. It was tawdry and noisome, as it no doubt intended to be. It howled for attention, and he could imagine it being scooped up by the thousands as commuters sought something diverting to read on their way to work. But surely its very shoddiness declared the level of impact it might have on public opinion. Who read this sort of shit, anyway, aside from people like Mrs. Maguire who could not exactly be described as a major intellectual force in the country.

Eve was walking back to the rattan holder. She rooted out three more copies of the tabloid and laid them carefully on the bar before him. *PM's Latest Skeleton: Top Aide on the Take!* took up one entire front page. *Tory MP Mistress X4!* decorated another. *Royal Flush: Who's Keeping the Princess Warm at Night?* leapt from the third.

"I don't get it," Alex said. "Your case is different to these. What are the newspapers going to crucify you about? You made a mistake. You got pregnant. You had a baby. You've raised her, cared for her, and gone on with your life. It's a non-story."

"You don't understand."

"What's there to understand?"

"Dennis Luxford. This is his newspaper, Alex. Charlotte's father edits this newspaper and he was editing another one just about this disgusting when we had our little—" She blinked rapidly and for a moment he thought she would actually lose her composure. "That's what he was doing—editing a tabloid, digging up the most salacious gossip he could find, smearing whomever he wished to humiliate—when we had our little fling in Blackpool."

He tore his eyes from her and looked back at the papers. He told himself that if he hadn't heard her correctly, he wouldn't have to believe. She made a movement, and he looked to see that she had taken up her wineglass and held it in a toast, which she did not make. Instead, she said, "There was Eve Bowen, future Tory MP, future Junior Minister, future Premier, the ultra-conservative, God-is-my-bedrock, morally righteous little reporter making the two-backed beast with the King of Sleaze. My God, what a field day the papers will have with that story. And this one will lead the pack."

Alex searched for something to say, which was difficult because all he was able to feel at the moment was the coating of ice that seemed to be growing rapidly round his heart. Even his words felt deadened. "You weren't a Member of Parliament then."

"A fine point that the public will be more than willing to overlook, I assure you. The public will take great tickling pleasure imagining the two of us slinking round the hotel in Blackpool, hotly setting up our assignations, I spread-legged on a hotel room bed, panting for Luxford to plumb my depths with his mighty organ. And then the next morning rearranging myself to look like Miss Butter-Wouldn't-Melt for my colleagues. And living with the secret for all these years. Acting as if I found morally reprehensible everything the man stands for."

Alex stared at her. He looked at the features he'd been looking at for the past seven years: that unruffled hair, those clear hazel eyes, the chin too sharp, the upper lip too thin. He thought, This is my wife. This is the woman I love. Who I am with her is not who I am with anyone else. Do I even know her? He said numbly, "And don't you? Didn't you?"

Her eyes seemed to darken. When she responded, her voice sounded oddly removed. "How can you even ask me that, Alex?"

"Because I want to know. I have a right to know."

"To know what?"

"Who the hell you are."

She didn't answer. Instead, she met his gaze for the longest time before she took the pot from the cooker and carried it to the sink, where she dumped the fettuccine into a colander. She used a fork to lift a strand of it. She said quietly, "You've overcooked your pasta, Alex. Not the kind of mistake I'd expect you to make."

"Answer me," he said.

"I believe I just did."

"The mistake was the pregnancy," he persisted, "not the choice of partners. You knew what he was when you slept with him. You had to have known."

"Yes. I knew. Do you want me to tell you that it didn't matter?"

"I want you to tell me the truth."

"All right. It didn't matter. I wanted sex with him."

"Why?"

"He engaged my mind. Which is the one thing most men don't bother to try when it comes to seducing women."

Alex grasped onto the word because he needed to grasp it. "He seduced you."

"The first time. After that, no. It was mutual after that."

"So you fucked him more than once."

She didn't flinch from the word as he would have liked her to do. "I fucked him for the length of the conference. Every night. And most of the mornings as well."

"Brilliant." He gathered the tabloids together. He replaced them in the rattan holder. He went to the cooker and grabbed the pan of sauce. He dumped it into the sink and watched it burble into the disposer. She was still standing next to the draining board. He could feel her proximity, but he couldn't face her. He felt as if his mind had received some sort of death blow. All he could manage was, "So he's taken Charlie. Luxford."

"He's arranged it. And if he publicly acknowledges the fact that he's her father—on the front page of his paper—then she'll be re-turned.''

"Why not phone the police?''

"Because I intend to call his bluff.''

"Using Charlie to do it?''

"Using Charlotte? What do you mean?''

This he could feel at last, and he revelled in the sensation. "Where's he got her, Eve? Does she know what's going on? Is she hungry? Is she cold? Is she mad with terror? She was snatched off the street by a total stranger. So are you concerned with anything besides saving your reputation and winning the game and calling this bastard Luxford's bluff?''

"Don't make this a referendum on motherhood,'' she said quietly. "I made a mistake in my life. I've paid for that. I'm still paying for it. I'll pay till I die.''

"This is a child we're talking about, not an error in judgement. A ten-year-old child.''

"And I intend to find her. But I'll do it my way. I'll rot in hell before I do it his. Just look at his newspaper if you can't decipher what he wants from me, Alex. And before you condemn me for my gross self-interest, try asking yourself what allowing a fine sex scandal into the papers would do to Charlotte.''

He knew, of course. One of the greatest nightmares in political life was the sudden appearance of a skeleton that one had believed long and safely buried. Once that skeleton dusted off its creaking bones and made its debut in the public eye, it turned suspect every action, remark, and intention of its owner. Its presence—even if it did no more than hug the periphery of the owner's current life—begged that motivations be examined, comments be placed beneath a microscope, footsteps be dogged, letters be analysed, speeches be dissected, and everything else be nosed as intimately as possible to try to detect the scent of hypocrisy. And this scrutiny didn't end with the skeleton's owner. It tainted every member of the family whose names and whose lives were also dragged through the mud of the public's God-given right to be kept informed. Parnell had known this. Profumo likewise. Yeo and Ashby had both felt the scalpel of scrutiny incise the flesh of what they had considered their private lives. Since neither her predecessors in Parliament nor the Mon-archy itself was exempt from public exposure and ridicule, Eve knew that she would not be an exception, and certainly not in the eyes of a man like Luxford who was driven by the mutual demons of his circula-tion figures and his personal loathing of the Conservative Party.

Alex felt weighted by burdens. His body demanded action. His mind demanded understanding. His heart demanded flight. He was caught between aversion and compassion, and he felt tattered by the battle of their antagonism within him. He fought his way to compassion, if only for the moment.

He said with a tilt of his chin in the direction of the sitting room, "So who were they? That man and woman."

He could tell by her face that she believed she had prevailed. She said, "He once worked for Scotland Yard. She's . . . I don't know. She assists him in some way."

"You're confident they can handle this?"

"Yes. I am."

"Why?"

"Because when he asked me to make a schedule of Charlotte's activities, he had me do it twice. Once in writing. Once in printing."

"I don't get it."

"He has both kidnapping notes, Alex. The one I received. The one Dennis received. He wants to look at my writing. He wants to compare it to the writing in the notes. He thinks I may be involved. He doesn't trust anyone. Which means, I believe, that we can trust him."

4

"*AROUND FIVE PAST FIVE*," Damien Chambers said. He spoke with the unmistakable broad vowels of the Belfast native. "She sometimes stays longer. She knows I don't give another lesson till seven, so she sometimes hangs about for a while. She likes me to play the whistle for her while she plays the spoons. But today she wanted to be off at once. So she was. Round five past five." With three long fingers he shoved wispy filaments of his apricot hair back into the long ponytail that he'd banded into place at the base of his neck. He waited for St. James's next question.

They'd got Charlotte's music teacher out of bed, but he hadn't complained at the intrusion. He'd merely said, "Missing? Lottie Bowen's gone missing? Hell!" and excused himself for a moment to dash up the stairs. Water began to roar energetically into a bathtub. A door opened then closed. A minute passed. The door opened and closed again. The water shut off. He'd clattered back to join them. He wore a long dressing gown of red plaid and nothing beneath it. His ankles were exposed. These, like the rest of him, were as white as bleached bones. He had tattered leather slippers on his feet.

Damien Chambers lived in one of the mole-sized houses of Cross Keys Close, a rabbit warren of cobbled passageways with antique street-lamps and a dubious atmosphere that encouraged looking over one's shoulder and hurrying along. St. James and Helen hadn't been able to drive into the area—the MG wouldn't fit, and even if it had done, there would have been no way to turn it around—so they'd left it in Bulstrode Place, just off the high street, and they'd worked their way through the maze of passages to find Number 12, where Charlotte Bowen's music teacher lived.

They now sat with him in his sitting room, which was not much larger than a compartment on an old-fashioned railway carriage. A spinet piano shared the limited floor space with an electric keyboard, a cello, two violins, a harp, a trombone, a mandolin, a dulcimer, two lopsided music stands, and a half dozen dustballs the approximate size of sewer rats. St. James and Helen used the piano bench for their sitting. Damien Chambers perched on the edge of a metal chair. He tucked his hands deeply into his armpits, a posture that made him look more diminutive than his five feet and five inches.

"She wanted to learn the tuba," he said. "She liked its shape. She said tubas look like gold elephant ears. Of course, they would have been brass, not gold, but Lottie isn't much of a one for details. I could have taught her the tuba—I can teach almost anything—but her mother wouldn't have it. She said violin at first, which we tried for six weeks, till Lottie drove her parents round the bend with the screeching. She said piano after that, but she didn't have space in the house for a piano and Lottie refused to practise on the piano at her school. So we've moved to the flute. Small, portable, and without much noise. We've been going at it for nearly a year now. She's not much good because she won't practise. And her best mate—a little girl called Breta—hates to listen and always wants her to play. Play with her, I mean. Not play the flute."

St. James reached into his jacket pocket for the list Eve Bowen had assembled for him. He ran his gaze down it. "Breta," he said. The name wasn't listed. Nor, he noted with some surprise, was any name other than those adults Charlotte met with who were listed by profession: dancing teacher, psychotherapist, choir director, music teacher. He frowned at this.

"That's right. Breta. I don't know her surname. But she's quite the rapscallion, according to Lottie, so she shouldn't be hard to track down if you want to talk to her. She and Lottie are always up to one trick or another. Pinching sweets together. Giving pensioners a hard time. Sneaking into the betting shop where they oughtn't be. Slipping into the cinema without a ticket. You don't know about Breta? Ms. Bowen didn't tell you?"

His hands burrowed farther into his armpits. His shoulders caved in as a result. Damien Chambers must have been at least thirty years old, but in that position, he looked more like one of Charlotte's contemporaries than a man who was technically old enough to be her father.

"What was she wearing when she left you this afternoon?" St. James asked.

"Wearing? Her clothes. What else would she have been wearing?

She took nothing off here. Not so much as her cardigan. I mean, why would she?"

St. James felt Helen's uneasy glance upon him. He showed Chambers the photograph that Eve Bowen had given them. The music teacher said, "Yes. This is what she always wore. It's her school uniform. Ugly colour, that green, isn't it? Looks like mould. She didn't much like it. Her hair's shorter now than in this picture though. She'd just got it cut last Saturday. Sort of an early Beatles cut, if you know what I mean, that Dutch-boy thing? She was grousing about it this afternoon. She said it made her look like a boy. She said she wanted to wear lipstick and earrings now that her hair was chopped off, so people would know she was a girl. She said Cito—that's what she called her stepfather, but I expect you know that already, don't you? It's from *Papacito*. She's studying Spanish. She said Cito told her that lipstick and earrings were no longer prime indicators of the wearer's sexuality, but I don't think she really knew what he meant. She pinched one of her mother's lipsticks last week. She was wearing it when she came for her lesson. Looked like a little clown because she hadn't a mirror with her when she smeared it on, so it was a bit crooked. I had her go upstairs to the loo and look in the mirror to see what a mess she'd made of herself." He coughed into his fist, returned the fist to his armpit, and began to tap his foot. "That was the only time she was upstairs, of course."

As Helen tensed on the piano bench next to him, St. James observed the music teacher and considered the potential sources of his agitation—including whatever or whoever had taken him on his rush up the stairs when they'd first arrived. He said, "Did this other child— Breta—ever come with Charlotte to her lesson?"

"Nearly always."

"Today?"

"Yes. At least Lottie said that Breta was with her."

"You didn't see her yourself?"

"I won't allow her inside. Too much of a distraction. I make her wait at the Prince Albert pub. She hangs about those tables outside on the pavement. You probably saw them yourselves. In Bulstrode Place, on the corner."

"That's where she was today?"

"Lottie said she was waiting, which is why she wanted to be off so quick. And that's the only place to wait." He looked thoughtful and pulled his lip inward with his teeth. "You know, I wouldn't be surprised if Breta's behind this in some way. I mean behind Lottie's running off. Because she *has* run off, hasn't she? You said she's missing, but you

don't expect that there's—what d'you call it—some kind of foul play?"
He grimaced at the last two words. His foot tapped more energetically.

Helen leaned forward. The room was so tiny that they'd all been sitting with their knees nearly touching. She used this proximity to place her fingers gently on Chambers' right knee. He stopped tapping the foot.

"Sorry," he said. "I'm nervous. Obviously."

"Yes," Helen said. "I can see that. Why?"

"It puts me in a bad light, doesn't it? All this about Lottie. I could have been the last one to see her. That doesn't look good."

"We don't yet know who was last to see her," St. James said.

"And if it gets into the papers . . ." Chambers hugged himself closer. "I give music lessons to children. It's hardly going to be good for business if it gets known that one of my pupils disappeared after her lesson with me. I'd rather that didn't happen. I live a quiet life here and I'd like very much to keep it that way."

There was sense in that, St. James had to admit. Chambers' livelihood was at stake, and no doubt their presence and their questions about Charlotte were illustrating how delicate his grip was upon it. Nonetheless, his reaction to their visit seemed extreme.

St. James pointed out to Chambers that whoever had abducted Charlotte—assuming she had been abducted and was not hiding somewhere with a friend—had to be familiar with the route she took from the school to her music lesson and from there to her home.

Chambers agreed. But her school was a brief walk from his house and there was only one way in and out of the immediate vicinity—the way St. James and Helen had come—so learning Lottie's route would not have been a time-consuming task for anyone, he said.

"Have you noticed anyone hanging about in the last few days?" St. James asked.

Chambers looked as if he would have liked to say yes, if only to take the spotlight away from himself. But he said no, no one at all. Of course, he went on more hopefully, there were foot police in the area—one could hardly avoid noticing them—and the occasional odd tourist taking a wrong turn and ending up in Marylebone instead of Regent's Park. But other than them and the usual people one expected to see like the postman, the dustmen, and the working people who hung about the Prince Albert pub at lunchtime, there had been no one who had seemed out of place. On the other hand, he didn't get out much, so Mr. St. James would do well to ask at the other houses in the close. Someone had to have seen something, right? How could a child simply disappear without anyone noticing something out of sorts? If she's disappeared. Because she *could* be with Breta. This could be another of Breta's tricks.

Helen said, "But there's something more, isn't there, Mr. Chambers?" in a voice that was soft with sympathy. "Isn't there something more you'd like to tell us?"

He looked from her to St. James. St. James said, "There's someone in the house with you, isn't there? Someone you rushed up the stairs to talk to when we first arrived?"

Damien Chambers blushed to the colour of plum pith. He said, "It's nothing to do with this. Honestly."

Her name was Rachel, he told them in a low voice. Rachel Mountbatten. No relation, of course. She was a violinist with the Philharmonic. They'd known each other for months and months. They'd gone out to a late dinner tonight. He'd asked her back for a drink and she'd seemed happy to oblige and when he'd invited her upstairs to his room . . . It was their first time together in that way. He wanted it perfect. Then there'd come their knock at his door. And now this.

"Rachel's . . . well, she's not exactly free," he explained. "She thought it was her husband at the door when you knocked. Shall I call her down? I'd rather not. I expect it'll cook things between us. But I'll fetch her if you like. Although," he added, "it's not like I'd use her for an alibi or anything if it came down to it. I mean, if an alibi is going to be necessary. That's not exactly the done thing, is it?"

But because of Rachel, he went on, he'd prefer to be kept in the background of whatever it was that had happened to Lottie. He knew it sounded heartless and it wasn't as if he wasn't concerned about the little girl's whereabouts, but this thing with Rachel was awfully important to him. . . . He hoped they understood.

On their way back to St. James's car, Helen said, "Curiouser and curiouser, Simon. Something's off with the mother. Something's off with Mr. Chambers. Are we being used?"

"For what?"

"I don't know." She slid into the MG and waited until he had joined her and switched on the ignition before she continued. "No one's behaving as I would expect. Eve Bowen, whose daughter has vanished off the street, wants no police involved despite the fact that in her position at the Home Office she could well have the cream of Scotland Yard at her fingertips with no one the wiser. Dennis Luxford, who by all rights should be wild to pursue the story, wants nothing to do with it. Damien Chambers, with a lover upstairs—and I'm willing to bet he had no intention of producing her for us—is afraid of being connected with the disappearance of a ten-year-old girl. If it *is* a legitimate disappearance. Because perhaps it isn't. Perhaps every one of them knows where Charlotte is. Perhaps that's why Eve Bowen seemed so calm and why Damien Chambers seemed so anxious, when one would expect the opposite of them."

St. James guided the car in the direction of Wigmore Street. He turned towards Hyde Park without replying.

Helen went on. "It wasn't your inclination to take this on, was it?"

"I've no expertise in this area, Helen. I'm a forensic scientist, not a private eye. Give me bloodstains or fingerprints and I'll produce a half dozen answers to your questions. But with something like this, I'm out of my depth."

"So why . . . ?" She gazed at him. He could feel her reading his face with her usual acumen. "Deborah," she said.

"I told her I'd speak to Eve Bowen, that's all. I told her I'd urge her to bring in the police."

"You did do that," Helen pointed out. They negotiated the traffic congestion at Marble Arch and made the turn into Park Lane with its curve of brightly lit hotels. "What's next, then?"

"We can go two ways. Either handle it ourselves until Eve Bowen breaks or bring in Scotland Yard without her approval." He glanced away from the road at her. "I don't have to tell you how easy the latter would be."

She met his gaze. "Let me consider it."

—⁂—

Helen kicked off her shoes inside the front door of the building in which she lived. She whispered, "Mercy," at the sweet sensation of feet being released from agonising servitude to the god of fashion, and scooping them up, she padded wearily across the marble entry and up the stairs to her flat, six rooms on the first floor of a late Victorian building, with a drawing room overlooking a rectangle of green that was South Kensington's Onslow Square. A light, as she had seen from the street, was on in the drawing room. Since it wasn't on a timer and since she hadn't turned it on before leaving for Simon's lab that morning, its beacon glowing through the sheer curtains on the balcony door told her she had a visitor. It could be only one person.

She hesitated outside the door, her key in her hand. She reflected on Simon's words. How easy it would be indeed to bring in Scotland Yard without Eve Bowen's knowledge or approval, especially since a detective inspector from the Yard's CID was at this moment waiting for her somewhere beyond this heavy oak door.

A word to Tommy was all that would be required. He would take it from there. He would see to it that all the appropriate measures were taken: listening devices placed on telephones where the Yard deemed it necessary; background checks on everyone remotely involved with the Junior Minister, *The Source* editor, and their daughter; a minute analysis of the two letters received; an army of detective constables to walk the streets of Marylebone in the morning, interviewing potential witnesses to the girl's disappearance and scouring every inch of the borough for a clue that would explain what had happened to Charlotte Bowen this day. Prints would be taken and handed over to the National Fingerprint Office. Descriptions of Charlotte would be inputted into the PNC. The case would be given top priority, and the best officers available would be assigned to it. Tommy, in fact, would probably not be involved at all. Undoubtedly the case would be handled by people more powerful than he in Scotland Yard. Once he let it be known that the daughter of Eve Bowen had been kidnapped, the search for the child would be taken out of his hands.

Which meant, of course, that the Yard would follow established procedures. Which meant, of course, that the media would be informed.

Helen frowned at the key ring in her palm. If she could depend upon Tommy and Tommy alone as the police officer involved . . . But she couldn't, could she?

She called his name as she swung the door open. He answered, "In here, Helen," and she followed the sound of his voice to the kitchen, where he stood watch over the toaster, with his shirtsleeves rolled to the elbows, his collar unbuttoned and tie removed, and a jar of Marmite open and ready on the work top. He held a batch of papers. He was reading from these with the kitchen light glinting off his rumpled blond hair, and he looked over the top of his spectacles at her as she dropped her shoes to the floor.

"Late night," he said, setting his papers on the work top and his spectacles on top of them. "I'd almost given you up."

"That's not your dinner, is it?" She lumped her shoulder bag onto the table, gave a look through the day's post, pulled out a letter from her sister Iris, and carried it over to Tommy. He put his hand beneath her hair in his usual fashion—his palm warm against the back of her neck—and kissed her. First her mouth, then her forehead, then her mouth again. He held her against his side as he waited for his toast. She crackled open her letter, saying, "It's not, is it?" And when he didn't reply immediately, "Tommy, tell me that's not all you've had for dinner. You are the most exasperating man. Why don't you eat?"

He pressed his mouth to the side of her head. "Time gets away from me." He sounded tired. "I spent most of the day and on into the evening with the crown prosecutors on the Fleming case. Statements being taken from all parties. Charges being brought. Lawyers making demands. Reports being requested. Press conferences being organised. I forgot."

"To eat? How on earth is that possible? Don't you notice that you're hungry?"

"One does forget, Helen."

"Hmph. Not I."

"How well I know." His toast popped up. He speared it with a fork and lathered it with Marmite. Leaning against the work top, he munched for a moment, after which he said with some apparent surprise, "Good Lord, this is awful. I can't believe I ate so much of it at Oxford."

"The taste buds are different when you're twenty years old. If you had a cheap enough bottle of plonk to drink, you'd find yourself transported back to your youth." She unfolded her letter.

"What's up?" he asked.

She read a few lines and recited the facts for him. "How many calves have been born on the ranch so far this year. Great joy at having survived another Montana winter. Jonathon's school marks are not what they should be and do I think he ought to be sent to England to boarding school? (*Definitely* not.) Mummy's visit was a great success only because Daphne was there to keep them from leaping at each other's throats. When am I coming for a visit? I may invite you as well, it seems, now that things—as she puts it—are official. And when is the wedding because she needs to diet for at least three months in order to be fit to be seen in public." Helen folded the letter and crammed it back into its envelope. She edited out her sister's extended rhapsody on Helen's engagement to Thomas Lynley, eighth Earl of Asherton, with its heavily underlined *at last at last at last*, its dozen exclamation points, and its ribald speculations on what life was going to be like in the future with, as Iris put it, a Lynley on the lead. "That's it."

"I meant," Tommy said past the toast, "tonight. What's up?"

"Tonight?" Helen aimed for insouciance, but only managed something that sounded to her like an uneasy truce between inanity and guilt. Tommy's face altered marginally. She tried to assure herself that he looked more confused than suspicious.

"Rather late hours at work," he pointed out. But his brown eyes were watchful.

To escape their scrutiny, Helen went for the kettle and spent a moment filling it and plugging in its flex. She plopped it down and rubbed her hand against the water that sloshed from the spout. She fetched the tea tin from the cupboard and spooned tea into a porcelain pot.

"Ghastly day," she said as she spooned. "Tool marks on metal. I was gazing through microscopes till I thought I'd go blind. But you know Simon. Why stop at eight in the evening when there are four more hours to be worked through before one collapses from exhaustion? At least I managed to squeeze two meals out of him, but that's only because Deborah was at home. He's as bad as you are when it comes to eating. What's wrong with the men in my life? Why do they have such an aversion to food?"

She could feel Tommy studying her as she tapped the lid onto the tea tin and returned it to its cupboard. She hooked two cups onto two fingers, placed them on saucers, and pulled two spoons from a drawer.

"Deborah's taken some wonderful portraits," she told him. "I meant to bring one along to show you, but I forgot. No matter. I'll get one from her tomorrow."

"Working again tomorrow?"

"We've hours and hours left, I'm afraid. Days, probably. Why? Had you something planned?"

"Cornwall, I thought, when this Fleming business is taken care of."

Her heart lightened at the prospect of Cornwall, the sun, the wind off the sea, and Tommy's company when his mind wasn't taken up with his work. "That sounds lovely, darling."

"Can you get away?"

"When?"

"Tomorrow evening. Perhaps the day after."

Helen didn't see how. At the same time, she didn't see how she could tell Tommy that she didn't see how. Her work for Simon was sporadic at best, and even when he had deadlines fast approaching or testimony coming up in court or a lecture to be given in the immediate future or a course to prepare for the university, Simon was the most tractable of employers—if he even could be called her employer—when it came to Helen's presence in his lab. They had fallen into the casual habit of working together over the past few years. It had never been a formal arrangement. So she could hardly claim to Tommy that Simon might protest if she wanted to go to Cornwall for a few days. He wouldn't protest at all under normal circumstances, and Tommy knew that quite well.

Of course, these weren't normal circumstances. Because under normal circumstances she wouldn't be standing in her kitchen wishing the water in the kettle would boil so that she would have another distraction that would keep her from having to manufacture a variation on the truth that was not an outright lie. Because she hated the thought of lying to Tommy. Because she knew that he would know she was lying and he would wonder why. Because she had a past that was nearly as colourful as his own, and when lovers begin prevaricating—lovers possessed of tangled pasts that unfortunately happen to exclude each other—there is usually a reason from one of their pasts that has slithered unexpectedly into both of their presents. Wasn't that the case? And isn't that just what Tommy would think?

Lord, Helen thought. Her head was spinning. Would the water *never* boil?

"I'd need half a day to go over the estate books once we got there," Tommy was saying, "but after that the time would be ours. And you could use that half day with Mother, couldn't you?"

She could. Of course she could. She hadn't yet seen Lady Asherton since—as Iris would have put it—"things" had finally become official with Tommy. They'd spoken on the phone. They had both agreed that there was much to discuss about the future. Here was an opportunity to do so. Except that she couldn't get away. Certainly not tomorrow, and with all probability, not the day after that either.

Now was the moment to tell Tommy the truth: There's just a little something we're investigating, darling, Simon and I. What, you ask? Nothing really. So inconsequential. Nothing to trouble yourself over. Truly.

Another lie. A lie on a lie. A terrible muddle.

Helen looked hopefully at the kettle. As if in answer to her prayers, it began to steam. It switched itself off, and she dashed to attend to it.

Tommy was saying, ". . . and they're apparently set to descend on Cornwall as soon as possible to celebrate. I think that's Aunt Augusta's idea. Anything for a party."

Helen said, "Aunt Augusta? What are you talking about, Tommy?" before she realised he'd been chatting away about their engagement while she'd been ruminating over how best to lie to him. She said, "I'm sorry, darling. I drifted off for a moment. I was thinking about your mother." She poured water into the teapot, stirred it vigorously, and went to the refrigerator where she rooted round for the milk.

Tommy said nothing as she assembled the teapot and everything else on a wooden tray. She picked up the tray, saying, "Let's collapse in the drawing room, darling. I'm afraid I've run out of Lapsang Souchong. You'll have to settle for Earl Grey instead," to which he replied, "What's going on, Helen?"

She thought, Damn. She said, "Going on?"

"Don't," he said. "I'm not a fool. Is there something on your mind?"

She sighed and reached for a variation on the truth. "It's nerves," she said. "I'm sorry." And thought, Don't let him ask anything more. And to keep him from asking, "It's the change between us. Finally having everything definite. Wondering if life is going to work out."

"Are you getting cold feet about marrying me?"

"Cold, no." She smiled at him. "I'm not getting cold feet at all. Although the poor things are miserably sore. I don't know what I was thinking when I bought those shoes, Tommy. Forest green, the perfect match for this suit, and absolute agony. By two o'clock I had a fairly good idea what the bottom half of a crucifixion would feel like. Come along and rub them for me, will you? And tell me about your day."

He wasn't buying. She could tell that by the way he was observing her. He was favouring her with his detective inspector's inspection, and she wouldn't emerge unscathed from the scrutiny. She turned from it quickly and went to the drawing room. She poured the tea, saying, "Have you brought the Fleming case to a conclusion, then?" in reference to the investigation that had taken up so much of his time for the past several weeks.

He was slow to join her, and when he did, he walked not to the sofa where she had his tea ready, but rather to a floor lamp, which he switched on, then to a table lamp next to the sofa, then to another next to a chair. He didn't stop until every shadow had been eliminated.

He came to join her, but he didn't sit next to her. Rather, he chose a chair from which he could face her, from which—she knew—he could easily study her. This he did as she picked up her cup and took a sip of her tea.

She knew he was going to insist upon the truth. He was going to say, What's really going on, Helen, and please don't lie to me any further because I can always tell when someone's lying to me since I've years of exposure to liars of the highest calibre and I'd like to think that the woman I'm marrying isn't one of them so if you don't mind shall we clear the air right now because I'm having second thoughts about you and about us and until those second thoughts are banished I can't see how we can move onwards together.

But he said something quite different, hands clasped loosely between his knees, tea untouched, face grave, and voice . . . Did he really sound hesitant? "I know that I press in too close sometimes, Helen. My only excuse is that I always feel in a hurry about us. It's as if I believe we don't have nearly enough time and we need to get on with things now. Today. Tonight. Immediately. I've always felt that way when it comes to you."

She set her teacup on the table. "Press in . . . I don't understand."

"I should have phoned to tell you I'd be here when you got home. I didn't think to do it." He shifted his gaze off hers and onto his hands. He seemed to aim for a lighter tone, saying, "Listen, darling, it's quite all right if tonight you'd rather . . ." He raised his head. He drew in, then blew out a chestful of air. He said, "Hell," then plunged on with, "Helen. Would you prefer to be alone tonight?"

From her place on the sofa, she observed him, feeling herself going soft in a hundred different ways. The sensation was not unlike sinking into quicksand, and while her nature insisted that she do something to extricate herself, her heart informed her that she could not do so. She had long resisted the qualities in Tommy that had encouraged others to label him such an outstanding catch in the marriage game. She was generally impervious to his good looks. His wealth did not interest her. His passionate nature was sometimes trying. His ardour was flattering, but she had seen it directed at enough women in the past to have doubts about its reliability. While it was true that his intelligence was appealing, she had access to other men who were equally as quick, as clever, and as able as Tommy. But this . . . Helen did not possess the armour to combat it. Surrounded by a world of stiff upper lips, she was putty in the hands of a man's vulnerability.

She rose from the sofa. She went to him and knelt by his chair. She looked up into his face. "Alone," she said quietly, "is the very last place that I want to be."

—⚬⚬⚬—

Light awakened her this time. It dazzled her eyes so much that Charlotte thought it was the Holy Trinity bestowing Grace upon her. She remembered the way that Sister Agnetis explained the Trinity during religious studies at St. Bernadette's, drawing a triangle, labelling each corner The Father, The Son, and The Holy Spirit, and then using her special yellow-gold chalk to create giant sunbeams spurting out from the triangle's sides. Only they weren't supposed to be sunbeams, Sister Agnetis explained. They were supposed to be Grace. Grace was what you had to be in a perfect state of in order to get into heaven.

Lottie blinked against the white incandescence. It had to be the

Holy Trinity, she decided, because it floated and swung in the air just like God. And coming from it in the darkness, a voice spoke, just like God to Moses from the burning bush. "Here's something. Eat."

The shining lowered. A hand extended. A tin bowl clattered next to Lottie's head. Then the light itself sank down to her level and hissed like air spouting out of a tyre. The light made a clank against the floor. She shrank from its burning. She got far enough from it to make out that its fire wore a hat and was mounted on a stand. Lantern, she realised. Not the Trinity at all. Which must mean that she still wasn't dead.

A figure moved into the pool of radiance, black-garbed and distorted in her vision, like a carnival mirror. Lottie said through a very dry mouth, "Where's my specs? I don't have my specs. I must have my specs. I can't see prop'ly without them."

He said, "You don't need them in the dark."

"I'm not in the dark. You've brought a light. So you give me my specs. I want my specs. If you don't give me my specs, I'll tell. I will."

"You'll get your specs back in due time." A clink as he set something on the floor. Tall and tubular. Red. Thermos, Lottie thought. He uncapped it and poured liquid into the bowl. Fragrant. Hot. Lottie's stomach growled.

"Where's my mum?" she demanded. "You said she was in a safe house. You said you were taking me to her. You *said*. But this isn't a safe house. So where is she? Where *is* she?"

"Quiet down," he said.

"I'll yell if I want. Mummy! Mummy! Mum!" She began to get to her feet.

A hand shot forward and clamped over her mouth, fingers digging like tiger claws into her cheeks. The hand yanked her across the floor. She fell to her knees and the rough edge of something that felt like a stone cut into her.

"Mummy!" she shouted when the hand released her. "Mu—" The hand shut off her voice, doused her head in the soup. The soup was hot. It burned. She squeezed her eyes closed. She coughed. Her legs kicked. Her hands scrabbled against his arms.

He said into her ear, "Are you quiet now, Lottie?"

She nodded. He raised her up. Soup dripped from her face down the front of her school uniform. She coughed. She wiped her face against the arm of her cardigan.

It was cold where he'd brought her, wherever it was. The wind was coming inside from somewhere, but when she peered about she found she couldn't see beyond the circle of radiance provided by the lantern.

Even of him she could see only a boot, a bent knee, and his hands. She shrank from these. They reached for the Thermos and poured more soup into the bowl.

"No one'll hear you if you shout."

"Then why'd you stop me?"

"Because I don't like little-girl noises." He used his toe to push the bowl in her direction.

"Got to go to the loo."

"After. Eat that."

"Is it poison?"

"Right. I need you dead like I need a bullet in my foot. Eat."

She looked about. "I haven't got a spoon."

"You didn't need a spoon a moment ago, did you? Now eat it."

He moved farther out of the light. Lottie heard a *svit* and saw the flaring of a match. He was hunched over it and when he turned back to her, she saw the firefly tip of his cigarette.

"Where's my mum?" She lifted the bowl as she asked the question. The soup was vegetable, like Mrs. Maguire made. She was hungrier than she'd ever remembered being, and she drank it down and used her fingers to help the vegetables into her mouth. "Where's my mum?" she asked again.

"Eat."

She watched him as she raised the bowl. He was just a shadow and without her specs he was a very blurry shadow as well.

"What're you gawping at, then? Can't you look somewhere else?"

She lowered her eyes. It was no use, really, trying to see him. All she could manage was his outline. A head, two shoulders, two arms, two legs. He was careful to keep out of the light.

It came to her then that she had been kidnapped. A shiver went over her, so strong a shiver that she slopped vegetable soup out of the bowl. It dribbled across her hand and onto the skirt of her uniform's pinafore dress. What happened when people were kidnapped? she wondered. She tried to remember. It was all about money, wasn't it? And being hidden somewhere until someone paid money. Except Mummy didn't have very much money. But Cito did.

"D'you want money from my dad?" she asked.

He snorted. "What I want from your dad's got nothing to do with money."

"But you've kidnapped me, haven't you? Because I don't think this is a safe house at all and I don't think my mummy's anywhere in it. And if this isn't a safe house and Mummy isn't here, then you've snatched me cause you want money. Haven't you? Why else . . ." She remembered. Sister Agnetis was hobbling back and forth across the front of the classroom, telling the story of St. Maria Goretti who died because she wanted to stay pure. Had St. Maria Goretti been snatched as well? Isn't that how the dreadful story had begun? With someone taking her, someone eager to defile her Precious Temple of the Holy Spirit? Carefully, Lottie set her bowl on the floor. Her hands felt sticky where she'd spilled soup on them and she rubbed them against the skirt of her pinafore dress. She wasn't exactly sure how one's Precious Temple of the Holy Spirit was defiled, but if it had to do with drinking vegetable soup given to one by a stranger, then she knew she had to refuse to drink it. "I've had enough," she said and remembered to add, "Thank you very much indeed."

"Eat it all."

"I don't want any more."

"I said eat it. Every scrap. You hear?" He came forward and poured the rest of the Thermos into the bowl. Little beads of yellow dotted the broth. They moved towards each other and formed a circle like a fairy's necklace. "You need me to help you do the job?"

Lottie didn't much like his voice. She knew what he meant. He'd shove her face into the soup again. He'd keep her face there till she drowned or she ate. She didn't think she would much like to drown, so she picked up the bowl. God would forgive her if she ate the soup, wouldn't He?

When she was finished, she placed the bowl on the floor. She said, "I got to use the loo."

He clanked something into the circle of light. Yet another bowl, but this one deep and thick, with a ring of daisies painted on it and a curving lip round its rim like an octopus mouth. She stared at it, confused. She said, "I don't want more soup. I ate what you gave me. I got to go to the loo."

"Go," he said. "Don't you know what that is?"

She saw that he meant her to go in the bowl, that he also meant her to do it in front of him. He meant her to lower her knickers and squat and pee and he'd be watching and listening all the time. Just like Mrs. Maguire did at home, standing on the other side of the door, calling, "Are you having a movement this morning, dearie?"

She said, "I can't. Not in front of you."

He said, "Then don't," and took the bowl away. Quick as a gnat's blink he snatched up the Thermos, the soup bowl, and the lantern. The light went out. Lottie felt a *whoosh* as something plopped onto the floor right next to her. She gave a cry and shrank away. A stream of cold air passed over her like the flight of ghosts coming out of a graveyard. Then a *clunk* sounded, followed by a *swetch*, and she knew she was alone.

She patted her hand on the floor where the *whoosh* had sounded. He'd thrown down a blanket. It was smelly and rough to the touch, but she picked it up and hugged it to her stomach and tried not to think what being given a blanket meant about her stay in this dark place.

She whimpered, "But I got to go to the loo." And she felt the lump in her throat and the tightness in her chest all over again. No, no, she thought. Mustn't mustn't. "I got to go to the loo."

She sank to the floor. Her lips were trembling and her eyes were welling. She pressed one hand to her mouth and squeezed her eyes closed. She swallowed and tried to make the lump in her throat go back to her stomach.

"Think happy thoughts," her mother would say.

So she thought about Breta. She even said her name. She whispered it. "Breta. Best best friend, Breta."

Because Breta was the happiest thought to think. Being with Breta. Telling tales. Playing pranks.

She made herself consider what Breta would do if she found herself here. Here in the dark, what would Breta do?

Pee first, Lottie thought. Breta would pee. She'd say, You have me stowed in this dark hole, mister, but you can't make me do what you say. So I'm going to pee. Right here and right now. Not into some bowl but right on the floor.

The floor. She should have known it wasn't a coffin, Lottie thought, because it had a floor. A hard floor like rocks. Only . . .

Lottie felt the same floor he'd dragged her across, the very same floor she'd cut her knee on. This, of course, would have been the first thing that Breta would have done had she awakened in the dark. Breta'd have tried to suss out where she was. She'd never have just lain there and whimpered like a baby.

Lottie snuffled and let her fingers feel round the floor. It was slightly ridged, which is how she must have cut her knee. She traced the ridging in the shape of a rectangle. Then another rectangle next to the first. Then another.

"Bricks," she whispered. Breta would be proud.

Lottie thought about a floor made of bricks and what a floor made of bricks might tell her about where she was. She realised that if she moved about much, she was liable to get hurt. She might stumble. She might fall. She might plunge headlong into a well. She might—

A well in the dark? Breta would have asked. I don't think so, Lottie.

So on hands and knees Lottie continued to feel along the floor until her fingers finally nudged into wood. It was rough-surfaced and splintery, with tiny cool heads of nails driven into it. She felt edges and corners. She felt up the sides. A crate, she decided. More than one. A group of them that she inched along.

She hit a different kind of surface rising up from the floor. It was smooth and curved, and when she gave it an enquiring prod with her knuckles, it moved with an uneven and spluttery sound. A familiar sound, reminding her of saltwater and sand, of playing happily at the edge of the sea.

"Plastic bucket," she said, proud of herself. Breta couldn't have named it as fast as that.

She heard a slosh from inside and lowered her face to sniff. There was no scent. She dipped her fingers into the liquid and put them to her tongue. "Water," she said. "A bucket of water."

She knew at once what Breta would do. She'd say, Well, I got to pee, Lot, and she'd use the bucket.

Which is what Lottie did. She tipped the water out of the bucket, lowered her knickers, and squatted over it. The hot gush of pee surged out of her. She balanced on the bucket's edge and rested her head against her knees. One knee was throbbing where the brick had cut into it. She licked at the throb and tasted blood. She felt suddenly weary. She felt very alone. All thoughts of Breta vanished just like popped bubbles.

"I want Mummy," Lottie whispered.

And even to that, she knew exactly what Breta would say.

Did you ever think Mummy might not want you?

5

ST. JAMES LEFT both Helen and Deborah on Marylebone High Street, in front of a shop called Pumpkin's Grocery, where an elderly woman with an impatient fox terrier on a lead was picking through punnets of strawberries. Supplied with the photograph of Charlotte Bowen, Helen and Deborah would walk the areas surrounding St. Bernadette's Convent School on Blandford Street, Damien Chambers' tiny house in Cross Keys Close, and Devonshire Place Mews near the top of the high street. Their purpose was twofold. They would look for anyone who might have seen Charlotte on the previous afternoon. They would map out every possible route the girl could have taken from the school to Chambers' house and from Chambers' house to her own. Their assignment was Charlotte. St. James's assignment was Charlotte's friend, Breta.

Long after he had dropped Helen at her flat, long after Deborah had gone to bed, St. James had roamed restlessly round the house. He started in the study, where he drew books from the shelves in haphazard fashion while he drank two brandies and pretended to read. He went from there to the kitchen, where he brewed himself a cup of Ovaltine—which he didn't drink—and spent ten minutes tossing a tennis ball from the stairway to the back door for Peach's canine entertainment. He climbed the stairs to his bedroom and watched his wife sleep. He finally took himself up to his lab. Deborah's photographs were still spread on the worktable where she had laid them out earlier in the evening, and in the overhead light he studied the picture of the West Indian girl with the Union Jack in her hands. She couldn't, he decided, be much more than ten years old. Charlotte Bowen's age.

St. James returned the photographs to Deborah's darkroom and fetched the plastic jackets into which he had placed the notes that Eve Bowen and Dennis Luxford had received. Next to these notes he laid the printed list that Eve Bowen had assembled. He switched on three high-intensity lamps and took up a magnifying glass. He studied the two notes and the list.

He concentrated on the commonalities. Since they shared no common words, he had to depend upon common letters. *F*, double *t*, the lone *w* beginning *will* in one note and *want* in the other, and the most reliable letter for analysis and code-breaking, the letter *e*.

The crosspiece of the *f* in Luxford's note matched exactly the crosspiece of the *f* in Bowen's: In both cases the crosspiece was used to form part of the letter that followed the *f*. The same style of crossing had been used in the double *t* in *Charlotte* and the double *t* in *Lottie*. The *w* in both letters stood entirely alone, rounded at the bottom with no point of connection to the letters that followed it. On the other hand, the downsweep of the *e* always connected to the letter following it while the initial curve of the letter stood alone and was never joined to what preceded it. The overall style of both notes was something between printing and cursive, resembling an intermediate step between the two. Even to the unschooled eye engaged in a cursory examination, it was clear that both notes had been composed by the same hand.

He picked up Eve Bowen's list and looked for the kind of subtle similarities that even one attempting to disguise his writing generally failed to obscure. How a letter is formed is so unconscious an activity that without giving purposeful attention to each stroke of the pen or the pencil, someone attempting to disguise his handwriting is bound to make an unintentional mistake. Such a mistake was what he was looking for: the distinct loop of an *l*, the starting point of an *a* or an *o*, the curve of an *r* and where that curve began, a similarity in spacing between words, a uniformity in the manner in which the pen or the pencil was lifted at the end of a word before beginning another.

St. James went over individual letters with the magnifying glass. He examined each word. He measured the space between words and the width and the height of the letters. He did this to both of the kidnapping notes and to Eve Bowen's list. The result was the same. The notes had been composed by the same hand, but that hand did not belong to Eve Bowen.

St. James sat back on his stool and considered in what logical direction this sort of analysis of writing samples would inevitably lead him. If Eve Bowen had been telling the truth—that Dennis Luxford was the only other person who knew the identity of Charlotte's natural father—then the most reasonable next step would be to gather a sample of

Luxford's printing to study. Yet carrying this journey through the labyrinth of chirography to that end seemed a profligate expenditure of his time. Because if Dennis Luxford was indeed behind Charlotte's disappearance—with his background in journalism and his attendant knowledge of the workings of the police—he would hardly have been foolish enough to pen the notes announcing her kidnapping.

And that was what St. James found so unusual. That was what was causing his disquiet: that someone had penned the notes in the first place. They hadn't been typed, they hadn't been composed of letters cut from magazines or newspapers. This fact suggested one of two possibilities: The kidnapper was someone who didn't expect to be caught. Or the kidnapper was someone who didn't expect to be punished once the complete truth of the kidnapping was brought to light.

Whatever the case, whoever had taken Charlotte Bowen off the street had to be someone who either knew the child's movements intimately or had spent some time studying them before her abduction. If the former was the case, a family member had to be involved, however remotely. If the latter was the case, it was a good possibility that Charlotte's kidnapper had stalked her first. And a stalker attracts notice eventually. The likeliest person to have noticed a stalker was Charlotte herself. Or her companion, Breta. It was with Breta in mind that St. James drove north to Devonshire Place Mews after leaving his wife and Helen Clyde in Marylebone High Street.

A cappella singing was going on behind the closed door of Eve Bowen's house. When he rang the bell, St. James could hear the kind of steady male chant one expects to encounter in a monastery or a cathedral. In response to his thumb on the bell, the singing stopped abruptly. A moment later, the bolts were drawn on the other side of the door and it opened.

He'd expected to see either Eve Bowen or her husband. But standing before him was a red-faced woman shaped much like a pear. She wore a bulky orange sweater over crimson leggings, which bagged at the knees.

She said briskly, "I want no subscriptions, no witnessings of Jehovah, and no readings from the Book of Mormon, thank you," in a brogue that sounded as if she'd arrived from the Irish countryside only last week.

St. James decided that based upon the MP's description of her, this would have to be Mrs. Maguire the housekeeper. Before she could close the door, he identified himself and asked for Eve Bowen.

Mrs. Maguire's tone immediately altered from dismissiveness to quiet intensity. "You're the gentleman who's seeing about Charlie?"

St. James said yes. The housekeeper quickly stepped back from the door. She led him into the sitting room, where a sombre *Sanctus* was issuing from a tape player at a much subdued volume. The player stood next to a coffee table on which a make-shift altar had been assembled. Two lit candles flickered on either side of a crucifix, themselves flanked by a slender statue of the Virgin with her chipped hands extended and another of a bearded saint with a green shawl thrown over saffron robes. At the sight of this altar, St. James turned back to Mrs. Maguire and noticed that her right hand was closed round a string of rosary beads.

"I'm doing all the mysteries this morning," Mrs. Maguire said obscurely with a nod of her head in the direction of the altar. "Joyful, sorrowful, and glorious, all three of them. And I won't be getting up off my knees till I've done my part to bring Charlie home, small part though it be. I'm praying to St. Jude and the Blessed Mother. One of them will take care of this business."

She seemed oblivious of the fact that she was off the same knees which she had just declared she would remain on. She moved to the tape player and punched a button. The chanting ceased. "If I can't be in a church, I can make my own. The Lord understands." She kissed the crucifix at the end of the rosary and laid the beads lovingly at the sandal-shod feet of St. Jude. She took a moment to arrange them so that no bead touched another and the crucifix lay carefully corpus-side up.

"She's not here," she said to St. James.

"Ms. Bowen's not at home?"

"Nor Mr. Alex."

"Are they out looking for Charlotte?"

Mrs. Maguire touched her blunt fingers to the rosary's crucifix again. She looked like a woman who was sifting through a dozen possible responses for the most favourable one. She apparently gave up the search because she finally said, "No."

"Then where—"

"He's gone in to one of his restaurants. She's at the Commons. He would have stayed home, but she's wanting to have things appear as normal as possible. Which is why I'm here and not kneeling in St. Luke's as I'd like to be, saying my rosaries in front of the Blessed Sacrament." She seemed to sense and expect St. James's surprise at this business-as-usual reaction to Charlotte's disappearance because she continued quickly. " 'Tisn't near as harsh as it seems, young man. Miss Eve phoned me at quarter past one this morning. Not that I was asleep—not that she had even *tried* to sleep, God protect her—as I didn't as much as close an eyelid from dark to dawn. She told me you'd be looking into this terrible business with Charlie and while you were doing that, the rest of us—Mr. Alex, herself, and me—would need to keep ourselves calm and busy and as close to normal as ever we could. For Charlie's sake. So here I am. And there she is, God love her, going off to work and trying to pretend that the only concern she has in the world is passing another piece of legislation on the IRA."

St. James's interest quickened at this bit of news. "Ms. Bowen's been involved in IRA legislation?"

"Has been from the first. No sooner was she at the Home Office two years back but she was up to her knickers in anti-terrorism this, anti-possession of Semtex that, and this bill and that bill on increasing prison terms for the IRA. Not that there wasn't a simpler solution to the problem all along than nattering about it in the House of Commons."

Here was something to gnaw upon mentally, St. James realised: IRA legislation. A high-profile MP would not be able to keep her political position on the troubles a secret, nor, probably, would she be interested in doing so. This—in addition to the Irish involved however peripherally in her daily life and in the life of her child—was something to consider should Breta not be able to give them the assistance they needed in finding Charlotte.

Mrs. Maguire gestured in the direction Alex Stone had taken upon leaving the sitting room on the previous night. "If you want to talk, then it's best I go about my business while we do it. Perhaps acting normal will help me feel it," and she led him through the dining room and into a high-tech kitchen. On one of the work tops a mahogany case containing silver cutlery gaped open. Next to it stood a squat jar of polish and a handful of blackened rags.

"Normal Thursday," Mrs. Maguire said. "I can't think how Miss Eve holds herself together, but if she can do it, then so can I." She uncapped the jar of polish and set its lid on the granite work top. Her lips curved downward. She scooped up a green wedge of polish on a rag. She said in a lower voice, "Just a babe. Dear Lord, help us. She's only a babe."

St. James took a seat at the bar that extended from the cooktop. He watched Mrs. Maguire fiercely apply the silver polish to a large serving spoon. He said, "When did you last see Charlotte?"

"Yesterday morning. I walked her to St. Bernadette's like I always do."

"Every morning?"

"Such mornings as Mr. Alex doesn't take her. But it isn't exactly walking *with* the girl that I do in the morning. It's walking *after* her. Just to make sure she gets to school proper and doesn't end up where she oughtn't be."

"Has she played truant in the past?"

"Early on. She doesn't like St. Bernadette's. She'd prefer a state school, but Miss Eve's not having any of that."

"Ms. Bowen's Catholic?"

"Miss Eve's always done her proper service to the Lord, but she's not Catholic. She does a Sunday regular at St. Marylebone's."

"Odd that she would choose a convent school for her daughter, then."

"She thinks Charlie needs discipline. And if a child needs discipline, a Catholic school is where to find it."

"What do you think?"

Mrs. Maguire squinted at the spoon. She applied her thumb to the bowl of it. "Think?"

"Does Charlotte need discipline?"

"A child brought up with a firm hand doesn't need discipline, Mr. St. James. Wasn't that the case with my own five? Wasn't that the case with my brothers and sisters? Eighteen of us there were, sleeping in three rooms in County Kerry, and never a slap on the bum was needed to keep us walking the straight and narrow. But times have changed, and I'm not one to cast stones at the mothering done by an upstanding fine woman who gave in to a moment of human weakness. The Lord forgives our sins, and He's long since forgiven hers. Besides, some things come natural to a woman. Other things don't."

"Which things?"

Mrs. Maguire gave her attention to the polishing of the spoon. She ran a clipped thumbnail along its handle. "Miss Eve does her best," she said. "She does the best she knows and always has done."

"You've been with her long?"

"Since Charlie was six weeks old, I've been with her. And such a squaller that baby was, like God sent her to earth to try her mother's patience. She never did settle into life proper until she learned to talk."

"And your patience?"

"Raising five children on my own taught me patience. Charlie's fussing was nothing new to me."

"What about Charlotte's father?" St. James slid the question in easily. "How did he deal with her?"

"Mr. Alex?"

"I'm talking about Charlotte's natural father."

"I don't know the black heart. Has there ever been a word or a card or a phone call or a sign from him that he fathered this child? No. Not once. Which, Miss Eve says, is how she would have it. Even now. Even *now*. Just think of it. Blessed Jesus, how that monster hurt her." Mrs. Maguire raised a bulky sleeve to her face. She pressed it first beneath one eye and then beneath the other, saying, "Sorry. I'm feeling that helpless, I am. Sitting here in this house and acting at everyday Thursday business. I know it's for the best. I know it had to be done for Charlie's sake. But it's mad. *Mad*."

St. James watched her lift a fork, doing her duty as Eve Bowen had instructed. But her heart appeared to be elsewhere, and her lips trembled as she rubbed the polish into the silver. The woman's emotion seemed genuine enough, but St. James knew that his expertise lay in the study of evidence and not in the evaluation of witnesses and potential suspects. He directed her back to the morning walks to the school, asking her to recall anyone on the street, anyone who might have been watching Charlotte, anyone who appeared to be out of place.

She stared at the case of silver for a moment before replying. She hadn't noticed anyone in particular, she finally told him. But they walked along the high street, didn't they, and there were always people out and about there. Delivery men, professionals on their way to work, shopkeepers opening up for the day, joggers and cyclists, people hurrying to catch the bus or the tube. She didn't notice. She didn't think to notice. She kept her eyes on Charlie and she made certain the child took herself to school. She thought about the day's work ahead and she planned Charlie's dinner and . . . Dear God forgive her for not being aware, for not keeping an eye open for the devil's work, for not watching over her Charlie like she was meant to watch, like she was paid to watch, like she was trusted to watch, like she was . . .

Mrs. Maguire dropped the silver and polish. She fished a handkerchief out of her sleeve. She blew her nose mightily on it and said, "Dear Lord, don't let a hair of her head come to harm. We will try to see Your hand at work in this business. We will come to understand Your meaning in it all."

St. James wondered how the child's disappearance could have a greater meaning beyond the simple horror of her disappearance. Religion, he found, did not explain the mysteries, the gross cruelties, or the inconsistencies of life in any way. He said, "Prior to her disappearance, Charlotte was apparently in the company of another child. What can you tell me about a girl called Breta?"

"Little enough and not much of it good. She's a wild one from a broken family. From Charlie's chatter, I've taken the impression that her mum's more interested in disco dancing than in putting her thumb on Breta's comings and goings. She's done Charlie no service, that child."

"She's wild in what way?"

"Up to mischief. Always wanting Charlie to be part of it." Breta was an imp, Mrs. Maguire explained. She pinched sweets from the vendors on Baker Street. She sneaked past the ticket takers at Madame Tussaud's. She wrote her initials in marking pen in the tube.

"Is she a schoolmate of Charlotte's?"

She was indeed. Charlie's days and nights were scripted so tightly by Miss Eve and Mr. Alex that the only opportunity she even had for making friends was at St. Bernadette's. "When else would the child have time to be with her?" Mrs. Maguire asked. She herself, she went on in further answer to his questions, didn't know the girl's surname, and she had not yet met her, but she was willing to bet that the family were foreigners. "*And* on the dole," she added. "Dancing all night, sleeping all day, and taking government assistance without a blush of shame."

St. James considered the disturbing oddity of this new fact about Charlotte Bowen's young life. His own family had known the names, the addresses, the telephone numbers, and probably the blood types of all his childhood companions and their parents. When he had chafed under their scrutiny of his acquaintances, his mother had informed him that such inspection and approval was part and parcel of their job as his guardians. So how did Eve Bowen and Alexander Stone do their jobs in Charlotte's life? he wondered.

Mrs. Maguire seemed to read his mind, for she said, "Charlie's kept busy, Mr. St. James. Miss Eve sees to that. The child's got her dancing lessons after school on Monday, her psychologist on Tuesday, her music lesson on Wednesday, after-school games on Thursday. Friday she goes directly to Miss Eve at the constituency office for the afternoon. There isn't time for friends anywhere but at school and that's under the supervision of the good Sisters, so it's safe. Or it ought to be."

"So when does Charlotte play with this girl?"

"When she can snatch a moment. Game days at school. Before her appointments. Children can always make time for a friendship."

"At the weekends?"

Charlie was with her parents at the weekends, Mrs. Maguire explained. Either with them both, or with Mr. Alex in one of his restaurants, or with Miss Eve at the office in Parliament Square. "Weekends are for the family," she said, and her tone suggested the rigidity of this rule. She went on as if concluding what St. James was thinking. "They're busy. They should know Charlie's friends. They should know what she's up to when she's not with them. They don't always and that's the way of it. God forgive them, because I don't see how they'll forgive themselves."

—m—

St. Bernadette's Primary School stood on Blandford Street, a short distance to the west of the high street and perhaps a quarter of a mile from Devonshire Place Mews. Four storeys of brick with crosses acting as finials on its gables and a statue of the eponymous saint in a niche above the wide front porch, the school was run by the Sisters of the Holy Martyrs. The Sisters were a group of women whose mean age appeared to be seventy. They wore heavy black robes, large wooden rosary beads round their waists, white bibs, and wimples that somewhat resembled decapitated swans. They kept their school as spotless as a polished chalice. The windows sparkled, the immaculate walls looked like the interior of a good Christian's soul, the grey linoleum floors glittered, and the air smelled of polish and disinfectant. If the atmosphere of cleanliness was anything to go by, the devil could not hope to have truck with this school's inhabitants.

After a brief conversation with the head of the school, a nun called Sister Mary of the Passion who listened with hands folded piously beneath her bib and sharp black eyes riveted on St. James's face, he was ushered up the stairs to the second floor where he followed Sister Mary of the Passion down a silent corridor behind whose closed doors the cause of serious scholarship was being furthered. At the second door from the end, Sister Mary of the Passion rapped once sharply before entering. The class—perhaps twenty-five young girls seated in orderly rows—leapt to their feet with a scraping of chairs. They held fountain pens and rulers in their hands. They chorused, "Good morning, Sister!" to which the nun nodded curtly. The girls dropped silently back into their chairs and went about their business. This seemed to be the meticulous diagramming of sentences, and their fingers and thumbs were crosshatched with ink from wielding pens and rulers as they drew the appropriate grammatical lines.

Sister Mary of the Passion had a brief, low-voiced conversation with a nun who walked to meet her at the front of the classroom with the hitched gait of a recipient of a recent hip replacement. She had a dried-apricot face and thick, rimless spectacles. After a terse exchange, the second nun nodded and came towards St. James. She joined him in the corridor and shut the door behind her while Sister Mary of the Passion did duty as substitute teacher.

"I'm Sister Agnetis," she told him. "Sister Mary of the Passion has explained that you've come about Charlotte Bowen."

"She's gone missing."

The nun pursed her lips. Her fingers reached for the beads that circled her waist and hung to her knees. "Little spit," she said. "This doesn't surprise me."

"Why is that, Sister?"

"She's after attention. In the classroom, in the dinner hall, at games, at prayers. This will doubtless be another one of her ploys to make herself the focus of everyone's concern. It won't be the first time."

"Are you saying that Charlotte's run off before?"

"She's acted up before. Last week it was with her mother's cosmetics, which she brought to school and painted herself up with in the lavatory during lunch. She looked like a clown when she came into the classroom, but that's what she intended. Everyone who goes to a circus tends to watch the clowns. Am I correct?" Sister Agnetis paused to go spelunking into the cavernous depths of her pocket. She brought out a crumpled tissue which she pressed to either side of her mouth, daubing up spittle that had gathered as she spoke. "She won't stay at her desk for twenty minutes at a time. She's browsing through the books or poking at the hamster's cage or shaking the collecting tins—"

"Collecting tins?"

"Money for the missions," Sister Agnetis said, and reembarked the train of her thoughts. "She wanted to be form president, and when the girls cast their votes for another, she got quite hysterical and had to be removed for the remainder of the afternoon. She doesn't see the need for neatness in her person or her work, she won't follow rules that she doesn't like, and when it comes to religious studies, she announces that as she isn't Catholic, she shouldn't be made to attend. Which is what comes, I dare say, of taking non-Catholics into the school. Not my decision, of course. We *are* here to serve the community." She returned the tissue to her pocket and, like Sister Mary of the Passion, adopted a posture with hands folded beneath her bib. When St. James took a moment to assimilate her information and assess what it added to his knowledge of Charlotte, she added, "You no doubt think I'm being harsh in my judgement of the girl. But I feel quite confident that her mother would be happy to confirm the child's difficult nature. She's been here more than once for a conference."

"Ms. Bowen?"

"I spoke to her only last Wednesday night about the affair of the cosmetics, and I can tell you that she punished the child severely—as she needed to be punished—for making off with her mother's belongings without permission."

"Punished her in what way?"

Sister Agnetis's hands slid out from beneath her bib and made a gesture indicating they were empty of information. "However she punished her, it was sufficient to subdue the child for the remainder of the week. On Monday, of course, she was back to normal."

"Difficult?"

"As I said, back to normal."

"Perhaps Charlotte's difficult periods are encouraged by her classmates," St. James said.

Sister Agnetis received this as an affront. She said, "I am noted for my discipline, sir."

St. James made noises of reassurance. "I was referring to a friend of Charlotte's here at the school. There's a very good chance that she knows where Charlotte is. Or, failing that, that she might have seen something on their way home from school that could give us an idea where she is. It's this girl I've come to talk to. She's called Breta."

"Breta." Sister Agnetis drew the snaggled remains of her eyebrows together. She stepped to the small window in the door of her classroom and gazed inside as if in search of the girl. She said, "There's no one called Breta in my class."

"I dare say it's a nickname," St. James suggested.

Back to the window. She gave the class another scrutiny and said, "Sanpaolo, perhaps. Brittany Sanpaolo."

"May I speak with her?"

Sister Agnetis fetched the girl, a sullen-faced ten-year-old whose uniform stretched uneasily over a tubby frame. She wore her hair cut too short for her moonlike face, and when she spoke, her mouth glittered with a grillwork of braces.

She made her feelings quite clear. "Lottie Bowen?" she said in an incredulous voice. She went on with a hissing of sibilant s's. "She's not *my* friend. No *way* she's my friend. She makes me want to puke." She cast a hasty glance at Sister Agnetis and added, "Sorry, Sister."

"As well you ought to be," Sister Agnetis said. "You answer the man's questions."

What Brittany could tell St. James was little enough. And she told it as if she'd been waiting since the first term at school for just such an opportunity to unload about Charlotte. Lottie Bowen made fun of other students, Brittany confided. She made fun of their hair, she made fun of their faces, she made fun of the answers they gave in class, she made fun of their weight, she made fun of their voices. Particularly, it seemed to St. James, she made fun of Brittany Sanpaolo herself. He gave caustic mental thanks to Sister Agnetis for foisting the disagreeable child upon him and he was about to break into her litany of Charlotte Bowen's sins—Lottie brags about her mother all the time, she brags about the holidays she goes on with her parents, she brags about the gifts her parents give her—when she commenced what was clearly the peroration of her remarks with the fact that no one liked Lottie, no one wanted to eat lunch with her, no one wanted her to be in the school, no one wanted to be her friend . . . except that thick Brigitta Walters and everyone knew why *she* hung about Lottie.

"Brigitta?" St. James said. Here was progress. If nothing else, *Brigitta* sounded closer to *Breta*, the way a child might mispronounce an older sibling's name.

Brigitta was in Sister Vincent de Paul's class, Brittany informed them. She and Charlotte sang in the school choir together.

Five minutes were all that were required to discover from Sister Vincent de Paul—easily eighty years old with indifferent hearing—that Brigitta Walters was not in school this day. No message from her parents as to the nature of her illness, but isn't that what one came more and more to expect from parents these days? Too busy to phone, too busy to be involved in the lives of their children, too busy for courtesy, too busy for—

St. James thanked Sister Vincent de Paul hastily. With Brigitta Walters' address and phone number in his possession, he made his escape.

It seemed as if they were getting somewhere.

6

"SO WHAT HAVE WE GOT on for tomorrow?" Dennis Luxford pointed a finger at Sarah Happleshort, his news editor. She tongued her chewing gum to the side of her mouth and picked up her notes.

Round the table in Luxford's office, the rest of the news meeting waited for the conclusion to their daily conference. This was the gathering to determine the contents of tomorrow's *Source*, to decide how stories would be spun, and to hear Luxford's decision on what would run on the front page. Sports had been arguing for heightened coverage of the selection of the England cricket team, a suggestion that had been greeted with hoots of derision despite the recent death of England's best batsman. In comparison to the Rent Boy Rumba, the asphyxiation of an eminent cricketer was minuscule potatoes no matter who had been arrested and charged with orchestrating said asphyxiation. Besides, that was old news and it didn't carry the amusement value of the Tories' attempts at damage control faced with Sinclair Larnsey, the rent boy he was caught with, and the steamy-windowed Citroën—"The slime-ball doesn't even buy British," Sarah Happleshort said, her dudgeon high—in which the pair were purportedly "discussing the dangers of solicitation" when abruptly interrupted by the local police.

Sarah used a pencil to point to items on her list. "Larnsey's met with his constituency committee. No precise word yet, but we've got a reliable source telling us he's going to be asked to stand down. East Norfolk is willing to put up with the occasional dalliance, it seems. All pardonable in the light of let's-practice-Christian-forgiveness and let-him-without-sin-proceed-with-the-stone-toss. But they appear to draw the line at human weaknesses involving married men, teenaged boys, closed automobiles, and an exchange of body fluids and cash. The crucial question among the committee appears to be whether they want to force a by-election while the PM's popularity is on the wane. If they don't, they look like they don't care about the Recommitment to Basic British Values. If they do, they're going to lose the seat to Labour and they know it."

"Politics as usual," the sports editor complained.

Rodney Aronson added, "The story's getting tired."

Luxford ignored them. The sports editor was going to go to the gallows for his cricket story, no matter the current change of events, and Rodney had his own axe to grind, one having nothing to do with dust settling on a story. He had been watching Luxford all day, like a scientist studying a dividing amoeba, and Luxford was becoming certain that the scrutiny had little to do with the contents of *The Source*'s next edition and much to do with speculation about why Luxford hadn't eaten all day, why he had started more than once at the ringing of the telephone, why he had grabbed the first delivery of the day's post and flipped through the letters with too much concentration.

"The rent boy has made his bow to the public," Sarah Happleshort was continuing, "through the vehicle of his dad. The statement: 'Daffy is dead sorry for what Mr. Larnsey's going through. Seems to Daffy he's a nice enough bloke.' "

"Daffy?" the picture editor asked incredulously. "Larnsey's actually bonking a rent boy called *Daffy*?"

"Perhaps he quacks when he comes," the business editor said.

Appreciative guffaws all round. Sarah went on. "We do have, however, a quote from the boy that I think we may want to use as our lead." And to Sports, who was drawing breath to argue for his asphyxiated cricketer once more, "Come on, Will. Be realistic. We spent six days running Fleming's death on page one. The story's stale bread. But this . . . Think of it with a photo. Daffy speaks to the press. He's asked about his lifestyle. How does it feel to be doing it in cars with middle-aged men? He says, 'It's a living, i'n't it?' That's our headline. With a suitable commentary on page six about what the Tories, through gross mismanagement of the Government and the economy, have brought teenagers to. Rodney can write it."

"Glad to under any other circumstances," Rodney said genially. "But this should go out under Dennis's name. His pen's mightier than mine by a long shot, and the Tories deserve a thrashing from the master. What say, Den? Are you up for it?" He was popping a piece of an Aero bar into his mouth as he spoke. He arranged his features into an expression of concern when he added, "You look peakish today. Coming down with something?"

Luxford favoured Rodney with a five-second scrutiny. What Rodney wanted to say was "Losing the edge, Den? Your balls on the shrivel?" but he lacked the courage to be so open. Luxford wondered if he had enough dirt filed away to sack the worm as he deserved. He doubted it. Rodney was too slick by half.

Luxford said, "Larnsey takes page one. Run the rent boy photo. Mock me up a copy of the headline with the photo before you run it. Put cricket back in sports." And he went through the rest of the stories without referring to his notes. Business, politics, world news, crime. He could have looked at his notebook without any loss of respect on the part of the editors, but he wanted Rodney to see and remember who had his fingers on the pulse of what at *The Source*.

The general shuffle of a meeting's end ensued, with Sports grumbling about "basic human decency," and Photo calling into the newsroom, "Where's Dixon? I need a blow-up of Daffy" to catcalls and quacking. Sarah Happleshort gathered up her papers, joking with Crime and Politics. The three of them headed for the door where they broke ranks for Luxford's secretary.

Miss Wallace said, "Phone call, Mr. Luxford. I told him earlier that you were in a meeting and tried to take a number from him, but he wouldn't give it. He's phoned back twice. I've got him on hold."

"Who?" Luxford asked.

"He won't say. Just that he wants to talk to you about . . . the kid." She removed the flustered look from her face by waving at the air in front of her as if it were filled with gnats. "That's the expression he used, Mr. Luxford. I assume he means the young man who . . . the other night . . . at the train station . . ." She coloured. Not for the first time Dennis Luxford wondered how Miss Wallace had survived at *The Source* for so long. He'd inherited her from his predecessor who'd had many good laughs at the expense of her delicate sensibilities. "I did tell him that Mitch Corsico was the reporter working on the story, but he says he's sure you don't want him talking to Mr. Corsico."

"Want me to take it, Den?" Rodney asked. "We don't want every Tom, Dick, and Harry off the street phoning in whenever they want to have a chat with the editor."

But Luxford was feeling his stomach muscles tightening at the possibility implied behind the words *wants to talk about the kid*. He said, "I'll take it. Put the call through," and Miss Wallace walked back to her desk to do so.

Rodney said, "Den, you're setting precedent here. Reading their letters is one thing, but taking their calls . . . ?"

The phone was ringing. Luxford said, "I appreciate the sentiment, Rod," as he walked to his desk for the phone. There was always, he admitted, the possibility that Miss Wallace was correct in her assumption, that the caller had information about the rent boy, that the call itself was no more than another intrusion into a busy day. He picked up the receiver and said, "Luxford."

A man said, "Where was the story, Luxford? I'm going to kill her if you don't run that story."

—⚬—

By cancelling one meeting and postponing another, Eve Bowen managed to get to Harrods by five. She'd left her political assistant juggling her schedule, phoning round with apologies and suitable excuses, and casting evaluative looks in her direction as she ordered her car brought round at once. She could have walked from Parliament Square to the Home Office, and Joel Woodward knew it. So he also knew that her terse "Something's come up. Cancel the four-thirty meeting," had nothing to do with governmental matters.

Joel would wonder, of course. Her political assistant was nothing if not disturbingly curious when it came to her private affairs. But he wouldn't ask questions for which she would have to construct elaborate lies in response. Nor would he share with others whatever suspicions he might be harbouring about the nature of the actual phone call that she had indeed received. He might casually ask upon her return, "The meeting went well?" and attempt to read her response for its level of veracity. He might also phone round and check up on her movements, looking for inconsistencies between them and what she said about them. But whatever conclusions Joel reached, he would keep them to himself. He was the embodiment of For Queen and Country, not to mention For Employer, and he liked the questionable importance of his job too much to risk it by garnering her displeasure. To Joel Woodward, it was better to be in the partial know—in a situation in which silence and a significant, meaningful nod to lesser mortals would telegraph his intimacy with the affairs of the Home Office Undersecretary—than to be relegated to a position in which he knew nothing at all and would therefore have to rely upon intellect and performance alone as a means of establishing his position in the office hierarchy.

As far as her driver went, his job was to drive. And he was quite used to transporting her in a single day to places as diverse as Bethnal

Green, Mayfair, and Holloway Prison. He would hardly give a thought to an order to take her to Harrods.

He dropped her at the entrance on Hans Crescent. To her "Twenty minutes, Fred," he responded with a simian grunt. She ducked in the bronze doors where security guards kept watch for terrorists determined to upset the flow of business, and she made for the escalators. Despite the late hour of the afternoon, these were crowded with shoppers, and she found herself sandwiched between three women chador-shrouded from head to foot and a gaggle of Germans loaded down with shopping bags.

On the fourth floor, she weaved through bodywear, swimsuits, girls in straw hats, and Rastafarians to make her way to the trendy pacesetters' department where—behind a display of black jeans, black tank tops, black bolero jackets, black waistcoats, and black berets—the Way In coffee shop catered to the department's trend-setting clientele.

Dennis Luxford, she saw, was already there. He'd managed to procure a grey-topped table that was situated in a corner and partially screened by an enormous yellow pillar. He was drinking something tall and fizzy and making a pretence of studying the menu.

Eve hadn't seen him since the afternoon he had learned she was pregnant. Their paths might have crossed in the intervening ten years—especially once she ventured into public life—but she had seen to it that that did not happen. He had seemed just as happy to keep his distance from her, and since his position as editor first of the *Globe* and then of *The Source* didn't actually require him to rub elbows with politicians if he did not wish to do so, he had never again been present at a Tory conference or at any other occasion where the two of them might meet.

He had changed very little, she saw. The same thick, sandy hair, the same dapper clothes, the same trim figure, the same overlong sideburns. Even—and this as he stood when she reached his table—the same serrulated scar across part of his chin, souvenir of a dormitory fight during his first month at Baverstock School for Boys. They'd compared their facial scars in between bouts of sex in her hotel room in Blackpool more than ten years before. She had wanted to know why he didn't grow a beard to cover his. He had wanted to know why she wore her fringe overgrown to camouflage hers, a starburst cicatrix that bisected her right eyebrow.

"Dennis," she said now in greeting and ignored the hand he held out to her. She moved his glass to the opposite side of the table so that he and not she would be facing the interior of the department store. She deposited her briefcase on the floor and sat where he had been sitting. "I can give you ten minutes." She shoved the menu to one side and said when the waiter appeared, "Coffee, black. Nothing else." And then to Dennis when the waiter departed, "If you've a photographer waiting out there to capture this tender moment between us for tomorrow's edition, I sincerely doubt you'll be able to make much of the back of my head. And as I have no intention of leaving the premises in your company, there will be no other opportunity for your reading public to know there might be a connection between us."

Always a credit to his extraordinary talent at dissimulation, Dennis managed to look disconcerted by her words, she noted. He said, "For God's sake, Evelyn, I didn't phone you for that."

"Please give me some credit for intelligence. We both know where your political loyalties lie. You'd love to bring down the Government. But don't you think you're taking a risk that has the potential to destroy your career if your connection to Charlotte is made known?"

"I've said from the first that I'd admit to the world I'm her father if that's what it takes to—"

"I'm not talking about that connection, Dennis. Ancient history is not nearly so interesting as are current events. Surely you know that better than anyone. No, what I'm talking about is a more recent connection than your fathering my daughter." She gave gentle emphasis to the procreative word and sat back in her chair as the coffee was delivered. The waiter forced the metal plunger down through the granules in the cafetière. He asked Dennis if he'd like another Perrier, and when Dennis nodded his assent, he disappeared to fetch it. While he did so, Dennis studied Eve. His look was one of perplexity, but he made no comment until they were alone again with their drinks some two minutes later.

"There is no more recent connection between Charlotte and me," he said.

She stirred her coffee thoughtfully and returned his observation of her with her own of him. There appeared to be a beading of perspiration at the edge of his hairline. She wondered what was causing it: the effort at dissembling or the apprehension attendant to successfully carrying this scene off prior to the presses' beginning their run with tomorrow's edition of his scurrilous newspaper.

"I'm afraid there is a more recent connection," she said. "And I'd like you to know that your plan isn't going to work the way you'd imagined. You may hold Charlotte hostage for as long as you like in an attempt to manipulate me, Dennis, but it's going to make no difference to the eventual outcome of this situation: You'll have to return her, and I shall see to it that you're charged with kidnapping. Which, I dare say, will not do much to enhance your career or your reputation. Although it will, admittedly, make extremely good copy for the newspaper which you will no longer be editing."

He was keeping his eyes fastened on hers, so she was able to see the quick dilation of his pupils. He, no doubt, was attempting to evaluate her words for their degree of bluff. He said, "Are you mad? I don't have Charlotte. I'm not keeping Charlotte. I haven't taken Charlotte. I don't even bloody *know*—"

Laughter from the next table interrupted him. Three shoppers had just plopped into the seats. They were vociferously debating the merits of fruit tarts over lemon cake as a suitable energy booster after the exertions of an afternoon at Harrods.

Dennis leaned forward and said tersely, "Evelyn, God damn it, you'd better listen to me. This is real. *Real.* I don't have Charlotte. I have no idea where Charlotte is. But someone does and he was on the phone to me ninety minutes ago."

"So you said," she said.

"So it *was*," he declared. "For God's sake, why would I make this up?" He picked up his napkin and crushed it in his fingers. He went on once again in a lower voice. "Just listen. All right?" He glanced at the nearby table where the shoppers were opting loudly for the lemon cake all round. He turned back to Eve. He shielded both his words and his face from the restaurant and its occupants, giving her the momentary impression—and nicely done, she thought with a mental salute in his direction—that he felt it as crucial as she that no one know they were meeting. He recounted his supposed conversation with the kidnapper.

"He said that he wants the story in tomorrow's newspaper," Dennis said. "He said, 'I want the facts of your first kid in the paper, Luxford. I want them on page one. I want you to tell the whole story yourself and tell it straight and leave nothing out. Especially her name. I want to read her name. I want the whole bloody story.' I told him that might be impossible. I told him that I had to talk to you first. I said that I wasn't the only person involved, that there were the feelings of the mother to be considered as well."

"How good of you. You always did go in big for the feelings of others." Eve poured herself additional coffee and added sugar.

"He didn't buy it," Dennis said, ignoring her jibe. "He asked when I had ever cared about the feelings of the mother."

"How prescient of him."

"Just listen, God damn it. He said, 'When did you ever care for Mum, Luxford? When you did the deed? When you said "Let's have a talk." Talk. Right. What a laugh, you little prick.' Which is what made me think . . . Evelyn, it has to be someone who was at the conference in Blackpool. We talked there, you and I. That's how it began."

"I know how it began," she said icily.

"We thought we were being discreet, but we must have put a foot wrong somewhere. And someone out there has been biding his time ever since, waiting for the moment."

"To?"

"To bring you down. Look." Dennis shifted his chair towards her. She successfully vanquished the inclination to shift her own chair away. "Despite what you may be thinking about my intentions, this snatching of Charlotte isn't about bringing down the entire Government."

"How can you possibly argue that, considering how your newspaper's been frothing at the mouth over Sinclair Larnsey?"

"Because this isn't remotely a Profumo-type situation. Yes, the Larnsey case makes the Government look idiotic what with the Recommitment to Basic British Values business, but the Government stands little chance of actually falling. Not because of Larnsey and not because of you. These are sexual peccadilloes we're talking about. This isn't an MP lying to Parliament. There are no Russian spies involved. So this isn't a plot. This is personal. And it's personal about you and about your career. You've got to see that."

He'd reached across the table impulsively as he was speaking. He'd closed his fingers round her arm. She could feel the heat of his fingers, and it quickly rode up through her veins to burn in her throat. She said, looking past him, "Take your hand off me, please." And then when he did not move his hand at once, she looked back at him. "Dennis, I said—"

"I heard you." Still he did not move. "Why do you hate me so much?"

"Don't be ridiculous. To hate you I'd have to take time to think about you. And I don't."

"You're lying."

"And you're self-deluding. Remove your hand from my arm before I douse it with coffee."

"I offered to marry you, Evelyn. You refused."

"Don't recount my history. I know it well enough."

"So it can't be that we didn't marry. So it must be because you knew I didn't love you in the first place. Did that offend your puritan principles? Does it still? Knowing you were my sexual peccadillo? Having slept with a man who wanted, at heart, only to fuck you? Or was the act itself not as grave an offence as the enjoyment that went with it?

Your enjoyment, by the way. Mine is implicit through Charlotte's existence.''

She felt the impulse to strike him whip through her arm. Had they not been in so public a place, she would have done so. Her palm longed for a stinging contact with his face.

"You're despicable," she said.

He removed his hand. "For which offence? Touching you then? Or touching you now?"

"You don't touch me," she said. "You never could."

"Self-deluding, Eve. Wasn't that your term of choice?"

"How dare you—"

"What? Speak the truth? What we did, we did, and we both enjoyed it. Don't rewrite history because you'd rather not face it. And don't blame me for showing you the only good time you've probably had in your life."

She pushed her coffee cup into the centre of the table. He anticipated her intention by getting to his feet. He dropped a ten-pound note next to his Perrier glass. He said, "This bloke wants the story in tomorrow's paper. He wants it on the front page. He wants the whole story, start to finish. I'm willing to write it. I can hold up the presses till nine o'clock. If you decide to take this seriously, you know where to find me."

"The size of your ego was always the least appealing of your personal attributes, Dennis."

"And yours was a desperate need to have the last word. But you can't come out on top in this situation. You'd do well to realise that before it's too late. There is, after all, another life at stake. Beyond your own."

He turned on his heel and left her.

She found that the muscles of her neck and shoulders had locked on themselves. She kneaded her fingers against them for relief. Everything—*everything*—she despised in men had its embodiment in Dennis Luxford, and this encounter had done nothing more than reinforce that belief. But she hadn't clawed her way into her present position by submitting to any male's attempt at domination. She wasn't about to capitulate now. He could try to manipulate her with apocryphal kidnapping notes, with fictive telephone calls, with utterly specious displays of even more specious paternal concern. He could try to pluck at the cord of maternal instinct, which he so obviously believed was intrinsic to the female constitution. He could act the part of outrage, sincerity, or political perspicacity. But none of that could obviate the simple fact that *The Source*, under six months of Dennis Luxford's aegis, had done everything within its filthy power to humiliate the Government and advance the cause of the Opposition. She knew this as well as anyone with the ability to read. And for Luxford to think—simply because he had managed to involve her daughter—that now Eve Bowen would stand up in public, confess her past sins, destroy her career, and thereby allow another faggot to be placed round the stake upon which the press was intending to incinerate the Government . . . Nothing on earth could possibly be more ridiculous.

And this was about his newspaper, at the bottom of it all. This was about circulation wars and political positioning and advertising revenues and editorial reputation. She had merely become a pawn in whatever rise to or maintenance of power Dennis Luxford was orchestrating. His only mistake was in assuming she would allow herself to be moved on the chessboard to a position of his liking.

He was a swine. He had always been a swine.

Eve stood and gathered up her briefcase. She headed for the restaurant exit. Dennis was long since gone, so she had no fear that anyone might connect her presence in Harrods to his. A pity for him, she thought. Not everything in his life was going to work out as he had it planned.

—៣—

Rodney Aronson saw but did not quite believe. He'd been skulking round the racks of clothes and the displays of black headgear ever since Luxford had gone into the restaurant. He'd missed the arrival of the woman—jockeyed from his viewing position for thirty seconds by a sweating stock boy wheeling in a rack of double-breasted black blazers with silver buttons the size of Frisbees. And while he'd tried to get a decent glimpse of her once Mr. Sweat had fussily rearranged two racks of trousers to his liking, all he'd managed to see was a slim back in a well-tailored jacket and a smooth fall of autumn-beech-leaf hair. He'd tried to see more, but he failed. He couldn't risk attracting Luxford's attention.

It had been one thing to watch Luxford's body tighten at the telephone call, to watch his chair swivel round to hide his face, to be dismissed with a summary "See to the editorial on the rent boy, Rodney," to play the waiting cat and see Luxford the mouse slip out and snag a taxi in Ludgate Circus, to follow him in a taxi of one's own just like the detective in a low-budget film noir. That was all excusable activity, conveniently falling under the heading Keeping the Newspaper's Interests at Heart. But this . . . This was dicey. The intensity of the conversation between *The Source* editor and Beech-Leaf Hair suggested more than a professional meeting which might be interpreted to *The Source* chairman as a betrayal of the newspaper's concerns. That was what Rodney was looking for, of course. A chance to bring down Luxford and assume his own rightful place at the head of the news meeting each day. But this encounter that he was witnessing—and damn the excruciating distance he had to maintain—had all the earmarks of an amorous assignation: the heads bending towards each other, the shoulders hunching to guard breathless conversation, Luxford twisting his chair towards hers, that tender little moment of physical contact—hand-on-arm in place of hand-up-skirt. And the most indisputable earmark of them all: arriving separately and leaving the same way. There was no doubt about it. Old Den was doing some knicker-trolling on the side.

The dipshit must be out of his mind, Rodney thought. He followed the woman at a distance and evaluated her. She had good legs and a terrific little arse and the rest of her was probably decent as well if the severe tailoring of her suit was anything to go by. But let's not forget that unlike Rodney, who had Butterball Betsy waiting at home for his nightly ministrations, Dennis Luxford had Fiona decorating his hearth. Fabulous Fiona. Fiona of the gods. She who had been simply dubbed the Cheeks in reference to the most famous facial bones ever to grace the cover of a fashion magazine. With Fiona to come home to—and Rodney could only hotly imagine the state of dress, state of mind, and state of anticipation in which an ethereal enchantress like Fiona would greet her lord and master upon his return from Fleet Street each night—what in God's name was Luxford doing playing bury the banger with anyone else?

It made no sense to Rodney why any man would cheat on a woman like Fiona, why any man would *want* to cheat on a woman like Fiona. But having a torrid little poke-and-dash on the side while married to the Cheeks *did* explain Luxford's recent preoccupation, the questionable state of his nerves, and his mysterious disappearance last night. Not at home, according to the spectacular spouse. Not at work, according to the newsroom nosies. Not in the car, according to his cellular service. At the time Rodney had accepted the suggestion that Luxford had probably slipped out for dinner. But now he knew that if any slipping had been done, Luxford had been doing it with Beech-Leaf Hair.

She looked damned familiar too, although Rodney couldn't quite put a name to her face. She was someone though. A high-powered lawyer or a corporate somebody.

He edged closer to her as they approached the escalators. He'd had only one look at her face as she came out of the restaurant; everything else had been the back of her head. If he could manage somehow to have a good fifteen-second study of her, he was certain he'd be able to name her.

It was impossible, he found. Short of throwing himself in front of her on the escalator and then riding it backwards so as to face her, there was really no way. He had to make do with trailing her in the hope that something would give her away.

She rode directly to the ground floor in a mass of shoppers, most of whom, like her, were heading for the exits. They were a roiling lava flow of green shopping bags. They yammered in a dozen languages and gesticulated wildly to punctuate their words. He was reminded for the second time that day—the first time had been on the ride upwards in Luxford's wake—why he never darkened the doorway of Harrods.

The hour caused the ground floor to be jammed, a jostling mass of shoppers making for the doors. As Beech-Leaf Hair headed out with them, Rodney prayed that her chosen direction on the street would be towards the Knightsbridge tube station. It was true that her manner of dress suggested limos, taxis, or a car of her own. But one could still hope. Because if she took the tube, he was on her tail. All he had to do was follow her home and her identity would be a matter of formality.

Hope was defeated, however, as he gained the street doors some ten seconds behind her. He searched the pavement for the familiar colour of her hair, looking hopefully through the throngs heading round the corner of Basil Street towards Knightsbridge Station. He saw her among them, and at first he thought she was going to cooperatively ride the tube. But as he trotted along behind her and made the turn into Hans Crescent, he watched her stride towards a black Rover, out of which a dark-suited chauffeur was climbing. She turned in Rodney's direction as she slid into the back seat, and again for an instant he saw her face.

He memorised that face: the straight hair framing it, the tortoise-shell specs, the full lower lip, the pointed chin. She wore power cloth-ing, she carried a power briefcase, she had power posture, she walked with a determined, powerful gait. She wasn't at all what he figured a bastard like Dennis Luxford would go for in a vigorous round of cheat-ing-on-the-wife. But on the other hand, there was no doubt a primitive caveman satisfaction to be found in wrestling a woman like that to the mattress. Rodney himself didn't go in for the dominant types. But Luxford—a dominant type himself—would probably find the challenge of thawing her first, seducing her second, and vanquishing her third a veritable aphrodisiac. So who *was* she?

He watched her car slide into the slipstream of late afternoon traffic. It rolled in his direction. As it passed him, Rodney shifted his attention from the passenger to the driver to the car itself. Which is when he saw the number plate and, more important, the plate's last three letters. His eyes widened at the sight of them. They were part of a series, making the Rover part of a fleet of cars. And he'd hung round Westminster long enough in his past to know exactly where that fleet of cars came from. He felt his mouth curve upward happily. He heard himself crow.

As the car swept round the corner, the vision of it remained in Rodney's mind. As well as the interpretation of that vision.

The number plates belonged to the Government. Which meant the Rover belonged to the Government's fleet. Which meant Beech-Leaf Hair was a member of the Government. Which meant—and at the thought Rodney could not and did not bother to contain his shout of joy—that Dennis Luxford, putative supporter of the Labour Party, editor of a Labour newspaper, was bonking the Enemy.

7

WHEN ST. JAMES told Eve Bowen's political assistant that he would wait for the MP's return, he was favoured with a pinched-nose look of disapproval. The man said, "Whatever you like. Sit over there, then," but his expression implied that St. James's presence was something akin to a noxious gas emanating from the office's central heating. He went about his business with the air of a man intending to demonstrate how much of a burden this unscheduled visit was going to put on everyone. There was much dashing about: from phone calls to fax machines, from filing cabinets to an oversize calendar that hung on the wall. Watching him, St. James was reminded of the White Rabbit in *Alice*, although his physical appearance was more suggestive of a flag-pole from which was waving a bulbous banner of Guinness-coloured hair.

The young man was on his feet in an instant when Eve Bowen entered the office some twenty minutes after St. James's arrival. He crossed to the door, saying, "I was about to send out the bloodhounds on you," and reaching for her briefcase. He scooped up a handful of telephone messages as he went on. "The committee meeting's been put off till tomorrow. The Commons debate begins at eight tonight. The delegation from Customs wants to schedule a lunch, not a dinner. Lancaster University would like you to speak before the Conservative Feminist Association in June. *And* Mr. Harvie is asking if you intend to give him an answer on the Salisbury question within the next decade: *Do we really need another prison and must it be in his constituency?*"

Eve Bowen snatched the messages from him. "I don't think I've lost my ability to read in the last two hours, Joel. Isn't there something more productive you could be doing?"

At the rebuke, an eyeblink of anger flashed on the assistant's face. He said formally, "Virginia's left for the day, Ms. Bowen. I thought it best, as this gentleman wished to wait for your return, not to leave the office unoccupied."

At this, Eve Bowen looked up from her messages and saw St. James. Without looking at Joel, she said, "Take a break for dinner. I won't be wanting you again before eight." To St. James she said, "In here, please," and led him into her office.

A wooden desk faced the door, and Eve Bowen went to the credenza behind it, where she poured herself a plastic cup of water from a Thermos. She fished in her desk drawer, brought out a bottle of aspirin, shook four into her hand. Once she had taken them, she sank into the green leather chair behind the desk, removed her spectacles, and said, "Well?"

St. James told her first what Helen and Deborah had managed to unearth after their day in Marylebone. He had met with them at the Rising Sun pub at five o'clock. And they, like him, had been satisfied that the information they were gathering was beginning to form a pattern that might prove to be the trail which would lead them to Charlotte Bowen.

From her photograph, the little girl had been recognised in more than one shop. "Chatty little thing," or "Quite the talker, that missy," was the general assessment of her. While no one had been able actually to name her, those who had recognised her were able to say with at least a fair degree of certainty when they had seen her last. And California Pizza on Blandford Street, along with Chimes Music Shop on the high street and Golden Hind Fish and Chips on Marylebone Lane, had been able to pinpoint exactly their last sighting of the girl. In the case of the pizza place and the music shop, Charlotte had been in the company of another girl from St. Bernadette's, a girl with a happy willingness to allow Charlotte Bowen to spend a fistful of five-pound notes on her: on pizza and Cokes in the former location, on CDs at the latter. This had been on the Monday and the Tuesday, respectively, prior to Charlotte's disappearance. At the Golden Hind—the shop closest to the music teacher's home and hence the shop closest to the possible location of Charlotte's abduction—they discovered that the little girl was a regular visitor on Wednesdays. On Wednesdays she fingered a handful of sticky coins across the glass counter and always made the same purchase of a bag of chips and a Coke. She doused the chips with enough vinegar to cross the eyes of a creature with more sensitive taste buds, and she took them along with her to eat. When asked, the shop owner chewed over the possibility of Charlotte's being in the company of another girl at the time of her purchases. He said at first no, then yes, then perhaps, then he declared he couldn't really say for a certainty because the fish and chips shop was a regular hang-out for the local "little buggers" after school, and he couldn't tell the girls from the boys these days, let alone who was with who.

However, from the pizza place and the music shop, Helen and Deborah had obtained a description of the girl who had been in Charlotte's company on the afternoons preceding her disappearance. She was frizzy-haired, she favoured fuchsia berets or, alternately, neon headbands, she was heavily freckled, she bit her fingernails down to the quick. And, like Charlotte, she wore the school uniform of St. Bernadette's.

"Who is this?" Eve Bowen asked. "And why is she with Charlotte when Charlotte is supposed to be at a dancing lesson or with her psychologist?"

Chances were, St. James told her, that Charlotte was in her company prior to her afternoon's assigned activity. Both shops confirmed that the girls had been there in the half hour immediately after school. The girl in question was called Brigitta Walters. Did Eve Bowen know her?

The MP said she didn't. She'd never met the girl. She said she herself had little enough opportunity to be with Charlotte, so when the time allowed, she chose to spend it with her daughter alone or with her daughter and her husband, but not in the company of her daughter's friends.

"So chances are you don't know Breta either," St. James said.

"Breta?"

He recounted what he knew about Charlotte's friend. He said, "I thought at first that Breta and Brigitta were one and the same since Mr. Chambers told us that Breta generally accompanies Charlotte to her music lesson on Wednesdays."

"But they aren't one and the same?"

In answer, St. James told her about his meeting with Brigitta, who was tucked up in bed with a furious headcold in Wimpole Street. He'd met with the girl under the watchful eye of her crimp-haired grandmother, who sat in the corner of her bedroom in a rocking chair like a suspicious duenna. As soon as he had walked into the child's room, he had known this was Charlotte's unnamed companion at California Pizza and Chimes Music Shop. Even if her hair hadn't been as frizzy as freshly gathered fleece, even if her neon-green headband hadn't given her away, she was chewing on her fingernails with the singular passion of a performance artist, and she ceased only when a reply to one of his questions was necessary.

He'd thought at first that he was at the end of the trail, with Breta at last. But she wasn't Breta and Breta wasn't a nickname for hers. *She* had no nicknames, she informed him. She was, in fact, named for her great-aunt who was Swedish and who lived in Stockholm with her fourth husband, with seven greyhounds, and with gobs of money. More money than Lottie Bowen ever had, she said. Brigitta visited her great-aunt every summer hols, along with Gran. And here was Auntie's picture, if he wanted to see it.

St. James had asked the child if she knew Breta. Indeed she did. Lottie's mate from one of Marylebone's *state* schools, she confided with a meaningful look in her grandmother's direction, where they had *normal* teachers who dressed like *humans*, not ancient old *ladies* who *slobbered* when they talked.

"Have you any idea what school this might be?" St. James asked Eve Bowen.

She considered the question. "It might be the Geoffrey Shenkling School," she told him. It was in Crawford Place, not far from the Edgware Road. The MP named it as a likely location where St. James might find Breta because the Shenkling school was where Charlotte had wished to be enrolled. "She wanted to go there rather than to St. Bernadette's. She still wants to, in fact. I've no doubt that some of the scrapes she gets into are designed to get her expelled from St. Bernadette's so that I'll have to send her to Shenkling."

"Sister Agnetis did tell me that Charlotte caused a small scene when she took your cosmetics to school."

"She's always into my make-up. If not that, then my clothes."

"It's something you row about?"

The minister rubbed the skin above her eyes with thumb and forefinger, as if urging her headache to be on its way. She returned her glasses to her nose. "She isn't the easiest child to discipline. She's never seemed to have any particular need either to please or be good."

"Sister Agnetis told me that Charlotte was punished for taking your make-up. She used the term 'punished severely,' in fact."

Eve Bowen regarded him evenly before replying. "I don't ignore it when my daughter disobeys me, Mr. St. James."

"How does she generally react to punishment?"

"She generally sulks. After which she even more generally works herself up to disobedience again."

"Has she ever run off? Or threatened to run off?"

"I note your wedding band. Have you children of your own? No? Well, if you did, you would know that the most common threat a child makes to a parent when being corrected for an act of defiance is 'I'm going to run away and then you'll be sorry. See if you won't.' "

"How might Charlotte have met this other girl: Breta?"

The MP got to her feet. She walked restlessly to the window, hands cradling elbows. "I see the direction you're heading in, naturally. Charlotte reveals to Breta that her mother beats her—which would no doubt be the manner in which my daughter would portray five hard smacks on the bum administered, by the way, only upon the third occasion of her pinching my lipstick. Breta suggests that the two of them give Mum a proper little shake-up. So they scarper off and wait for Mum to learn her lesson."

"It's something to consider. Children often act without full comprehension of how their behaviour is going to affect their parents."

"Children don't act like that often. They act like that all the time." She studied Parliament Square below them. She raised her eyes and appeared to reflect upon the Gothic architecture of the Palace of Westminster. She said without turning from the view, "If the other girl goes to the Shenkling school, Charlotte probably met her in my constituency office. She's there each Friday afternoon. Breta most likely came to my surgery with one of her parents and wandered off while we were talking. If she'd poked her head into the conference room, she would have seen Charlotte doing her schoolwork." She turned back from the window. "But this isn't about Breta, whoever she is. Charlotte isn't with Breta."

"Nonetheless, I need to talk with her. She's the best possible chance we have of getting a description of whoever it is holding Charlotte. She may have seen him yesterday afternoon. Or earlier, if he was stalking your daughter."

"You don't need to find Breta to get a description of whoever snatched Charlotte. You already have the description since you've met him yourself. Dennis Luxford."

At the window, framed by an early evening sky, she told him of her meeting with Luxford. She related Luxford's tale about the telephone call from the kidnapper. She told him about the threat to Charlotte's life and the demand that the story of her birth—with names, dates, and places included—be run on the front page of tomorrow's *Source* and written by Dennis Luxford himself.

Every mental alarm went off in his head when St. James heard that a threat had been made against the child's life. He said firmly, "This changes everything. She's in danger. We must—"

"Rubbish. Dennis Luxford wants me to *think* she's in danger."

"Ms. Bowen, you're wrong. And we're phoning the police. Now."

She walked back to the credenza. She poured herself another cupful of water from the Thermos. She drank it down, looked at him steadily, and said with utter calm, "Mr. St. James, have another think. I'd like to point out how easily I could obstruct an unnecessary police investigation into this matter. It's as easy as making a single phone call. And if you think I can't—or won't—do that from my position at the Home Office, then you don't understand much about who wields what power and where."

St. James felt astonishment coursing through him. He would not have believed that such an obdurate lack of reason was possible in any man or woman caught up in such circumstances. But when she continued with her previous line of conversation, he not only recognised the situation for what it was, but he also realised that there was only one course left open to him. He cursed himself for having become involved in this wretched mess.

As if she were a party to his mental processes and to the conclusion he'd reached, she went on. "You can imagine what publication of the story would do for Mr. Luxford's circulation and his advertising revenue. The fact that he himself is intimately involved in the story will hardly adversely affect the sale of newspapers. On the contrary, his involvement will probably stimulate sales and he knows it. Oh, he'll be a little embarrassed to have been caught out, but Charlotte is, after all, living evidence of Mr. Luxford's virility, and I think you'll agree that men tend to be boyishly sheepish—and only momentarily sheepish— over public revelations of their sexual prowess. In our society, it's the woman who pays the bigger price for being publicly unveiled as a sinner."

"But Charlotte's illegitimacy isn't a secret."

"No. Indeed. Her paternity is. And it's her paternity—and what will be seen as my unfortunate and inarguably hypocritical choice of lovers—that will go down as my sin. Because despite what you think, this is about politics, Mr. St. James. This isn't about life or death. This isn't even about morality. And while I'm not as high profile a politician as the Prime Minister or the Home Secretary or the Chancellor of the Exchequer, publication of this story—following hard on the heels of Sinclair Larnsey and his rent boy—will cost me my career. Oh, I shall be able to remain Marylebone's MP for the present. In a constituency where I began with a mere eight hundred vote majority, I'm unlikely to be asked to stand down and thus force a by-election. But odds are very good that I'll be de-selected by my committee at the next general election. And even if that isn't the case, and even if the Government manages to survive this latest blow, to what level of political power do you expect I'll be able to rise after my romp with Dennis Luxford is made public? This isn't a situation in which I had a long-term love affair, in which my foolish little female heart ached for a man I adored but could not have, in which I was seduced like Tess of the bloody D'Urbervilles. This is about sex, hard and sweaty sex. With, of all people, the Conservative Party's public enemy number one. Now, Mr. St. James, do you honestly expect the Prime Minister to reward me for that? But what a story it will make across the front page, I'm sure you'll agree."

St. James could see that she was finally shaking. When she uncradled her elbows long enough to adjust her spectacles on her nose, her hands were trembling. She looked round the office and seemed to see in its collection of notebooks, binders, reports, letters, photographs, and framed commendations the newly defined limits of her political life. She said, "He's a monster. The only reason he's never run the story before is that the occasion wasn't right. With Larnsey and the rent boy, now it is."

"There have been other exposés of sexual misconduct in the last ten years," St. James pointed out. "It's difficult to believe that Luxford would wait until now."

"Look at the polls, Mr. St. James. The PM's approval rating has never been this low. A Labour newspaper couldn't have a better moment to whack away at the Tories and hope against hope that their whacking is enough to fell the entire Government. For which whacking, I assure you, I shall be held responsible."

"But if Luxford's behind this," St. James said, "he's risking everything himself. He stands to go to prison for kidnapping if we can construct a chain of evidence that leads to him."

"He's a newspaperman," she pointed out. "They risk everything as a matter of course, if it means a story."

—ᴍ—

A flash of yellow dressing gown at the laboratory doorway caught his attention and St. James looked up. Backed by the darkness of the corridor, Deborah stood watching him.

"Coming to bed?" she asked. "You were up awfully late last night. Are you staying up late again?"

He set the magnifying glass on top of the plastic jacket in which lay the kidnapping note sent to Dennis Luxford. He straightened on the stool and winced at the cramping of muscles held too long in one position. Deborah frowned as he reached to massage his neck. She came to him and gently shooed his hands away. She brushed aside his overlong hair, dropped a loving kiss on the back of his neck, and took over the massaging herself. He leaned back and let her minister to him.

"Lilies," he murmured as the muscles she was working on began to warm.

"What about them?"

"Your scent. I like it."

"That's good, especially if it can manage to lure you to bed at a decent hour."

He kissed her palm. "It can manage that, and at any hour."

"We could do this more easily in the bedroom anyway."

"We could do many things more easily in the bedroom," he replied. "Shall I suggest a few?"

She laughed. She moved closer to him and slipped her arms round his waist, holding him snugly against her, back to front. She said, "What are you working on? You were so quiet all through dinner. Dad asked afterwards if you'd taken a sudden dislike to his duck *à l'orange*. I told him that so long as he continues to make duck *à l'orange* with chicken, it should never present a problem. Ducks and rabbits, you know, I told him. Simon will never put his teeth to a duck or a rabbit. Or a deer. Dad doesn't quite understand that. But then he's never had your partiality for Donald, Thumper, and Bambi."

"Too much Walt Disney as a child."

"Hmm. Yes. I'm still trying to recover from the death of Bambi's mother myself."

He chuckled. "Don't remind me. I had to carry you sobbing from the cinema. Even an ice cream did no good. Had you stayed until the conclusion of the film, you would have seen that it does have a happy ending."

"But it did strike rather close to home, my love. At the time."

"Of course, I realised that later. Less than a year after your mother died . . . What had happened to my brains? But at the time I thought, 'I shall take little Deborah to see this nice film for her birthday. I saw it myself when I was her age and I enjoyed it thoroughly.' I thought your father would have my head in a basket when I explained to him why you were so upset."

"He's quite forgiven you. As have I. But you always did have the strangest ideas of what we ought to do to celebrate my birthday. Looking at mummies. The Chamber of Horrors at Madame Tussaud's. Watching Bambi's mother get shot."

"So much for my capacity to deal with children," he said. "Perhaps it's just as well that we haven't—" He stopped himself. He dropped his hands to hers and held her where she was before she could withdraw. "Sorry," he said. When she didn't respond at once, he turned on the stool so that he faced her. She looked as if she was mentally chewing over his words, testing them for their flavour as well as for their gist. "I'm sorry," he repeated.

"Did you mean it?"

"No. I was just talking aimlessly. I was talking without thinking. I let my guard down."

"I don't *want* you to be on guard with me." She took a step away from him. Her hands—so recently warming his body—twisted the ties of her dressing gown's belt. "I want you to be who you are. I want you to say what you think. Why won't you stop trying to protect me from that?"

He thought about her question. Why did people guard their thoughts from others? Why did they veil their language? What did they fear? Loss, of course. Which was what everyone feared, although everyone tended to survive loss when it occurred in their lives. Deborah knew that better than anyone.

He reached for her. He felt her resistance. He said, "Deborah. Please," and she came to him. "I want what you want. But unlike you, I don't want it more than anything in the world. What I want more than anything in the world is you. Each time you lost a baby, I lost part of you. I didn't want to go on in that way because I knew where it would end. And while I could cope with losing part of you, I knew I couldn't cope with losing you altogether. And that, my love, is the unguarded truth. You want children at any price. I don't. For me, some prices are far too high."

Her eyes filled with tears, and he thought with despair of descending the quick downward spiral of yet another painful discussion with his wife, a discussion that might well last till dawn, reach no resolution, bring neither of them peace, and trigger another lengthy depression in her. But she surprised him, as she frequently did.

"Thank you," she whispered. She used the sleeve of her dressing gown to wipe at her eyes. "You really are the most remarkable man."

"I'm not feeling particularly remarkable tonight."

"No, I can see that. You've had something on your mind ever since you got home, haven't you? What is it?"

"A growing sense of unease."

"Charlotte Bowen?"

He told her of his conversation with the little girl's mother. He told her of the threat to Charlotte's life. He saw concern growing upon her as one of her hands rose to her lips.

"I'm caught," he explained. "If the child's to be found, it's up to me."

"Should we phone Tommy?"

"Useless. From her level at the Home Office, Eve Bowen can stonewall a police investigation into eternity. And she gave me little doubt that she'd do it."

"Then what can we do?"

"Hope Bowen's right and soldier on."

"But you don't think that she's right?"

"I don't know what to think."

Her shoulders drooped. "Oh, Simon," she said. "Oh, God. I've done this to you, haven't I?"

St. James could not deny that he'd become involved because of her request, but he knew there was little to be gained and much to be lost by pointing the finger of blame either at Deborah or at himself. So he said, "Rationally, I should see that we've made some progress. We know the route Charlotte took to get home from school or from her music lesson. We know the shops she stopped in. We've tracked down one of her companions and we have a good lead on the other. But I'm uneasy about where we're heading."

"Is that why you're studying the notes again?"

"I'm studying the notes again because I can't think what else to do at this point. And I like that fact even less than I like feeling uneasy about what I've been doing all day in the first place." He leaned past her and switched off the two high-intensity lamps that were blazing brightly on the laboratory table, leaving the ceiling lights to shine with a softer glow.

"That must be how Tommy feels all the time when he's in the midst of an enquiry," Deborah noted.

"Well and good for him because he's a police detective. He has the patience required to gather the facts, to piece them together, and to allow the evidence to fall into place. I haven't that patience. And I doubt I'm going to be able to develop it at this late date." St. James gathered up the plastic jackets and the other handwriting sample. He returned them to the top of a filing cabinet next to the door. "And if this is a bonafide kidnapping and not what Eve Bowen's determined to believe it is—a hoax perpetrated by Dennis Luxford to hurt the Government and to benefit his newspaper—then there's a real urgency to get to the bottom of everything that no one seems to feel but me."

"Dennis Luxford seemed to feel it."

"But he's as adamant as she about how the case is handled." He returned to the laboratory table, to her. "That's what bothers me about this whole mess. And I don't like to be bothered. I don't like the distraction. It keeps muddying the waters for me. Which I don't like in the least because my waters are generally as clear as Swiss air."

"Because bullets and hairs and fingerprints can't argue with you," she pointed out. "They have no point of view that they need to express."

"I'm used to dealing with things, not with people. Things cooperate by lying inertly beneath the microscope or inside the chromatograph. People won't do that."

"But the way seems obvious at this point, doesn't it?"

"The way?"

"To proceed. We've got the Shenkling school to look into. And those squats on George Street."

"Squats? What squats?"

"Helen and I told you about them this afternoon, Simon. At the pub. Don't you remember?"

He did, then. A row of abandoned buildings not far from either St. Bernadette's School or Damien Chambers' house. Helen and Deborah had both waxed enthusiastic about them over tea. They were close to the possible point of abduction, convenient in location to the child's home, and at the same time they were too decayed and forbidding in appearance for the casual passerby to want to explore them. But for someone looking for a hiding place, they were perfect as a potential element in the puzzle of Charlotte's disappearance. They hadn't been part of this day's agenda, so Helen and Deborah had left them for tomorrow when blue jeans, plimsolls, sweatshirts, and torches would make their exploration easier. St. James sighed with disgust at the realisation that he'd forgotten about the buildings. "Another reason I couldn't possibly hope to have success as a private detective," he said.

"So we have a direction to head in."

"I don't feel any better for the knowledge."

She reached for his hand. "I have confidence in you."

But her voice betrayed the anxiety she felt with another day coming and a child's life on the line.

Charlotte swam up from sleep, the way she swam up to the boat in Fermain Bay when they went on holiday to Guernsey. But unlike a summer's holiday on Guernsey, she swam into darkness.

Her mouth felt like cat's fur. Her eyes felt like glue had been thumb-printed into their corners. Her head felt heavier than the bag of flour Mrs. Maguire dug into when she started her scones. And her hands were so weary that they could barely pluck at the smelly wool of the blanket in order to pull it closer to her shivering body. Feel crumpy, she thought, and she could almost hear her granny saying to her grand-dad, "Peter, come have a look at the child. I think she's ailing."

She'd got dizzy first. Then her legs had begun to quiver. She hadn't wanted to sit on the brick floor, and she'd tried to find her way back to the crates so she could sit on them. But she'd got turned about some-how and she'd tripped over the blanket he'd left on the floor. She'd forgotten all about the blanket. Its edges were soaked with the water she'd sloshed from the bucket when she'd decided to use the bucket as a loo.

At the thought of that water, Lottie tried to swallow. If she hadn't dumped it out, she'd have something to drink. Now there was no telling when she would be given some water, some apple juice, or even some soup to make the cat's fur in her mouth go away.

It was Breta's fault. Lottie's mind struggled to hold on to the thought rather than sink into the blackness again. It was all Breta's fault. Dumping out the water was just the sort of thing that Breta would do. It was something naughty; it was something unplanned.

She always thought she knew everything, Breta did. She always said, "You want me for your best friend, don't you?" So when Breta said, "Do this, Lottie Bowen," or "Do that right now," Lottie obeyed. Because it was special to be someone's best friend. Best friend meant an invitation to a birthday party, someone to play let's pretend with, gig-gles in the night on a special sleep-over, postcards on holidays, and secrets shared. Lottie wanted a best friend more than anything in the world. So she always did what it might take to gain one.

But perhaps Breta wouldn't have dumped out the bucket of water at all. Perhaps she would have peed in front of him, peed into the octopus mouth that he'd set on the floor, peed and laughed in his face while she did it. Or perhaps she'd have taken the time to search for something to use once he'd gone away. Or perhaps she wouldn't have worried about using anything at all. Perhaps she'd just have squatted by those wooden boxes and made a mess. If Lottie had done any of that, she'd have water to drink now. It might be dirty water. It might be brackish. But at least it would make the cat's fur in her mouth go away.

"Cold," she murmured. "Thirsty."

Breta would demand why she was staying on the floor if she was cold and thirsty. Breta would say, This isn't exactly a camping trip, Lottie. So why're you acting like it is? Why're you being so goody good *good*?

Lottie knew what Breta would do. She would hop to her feet and explore the room. She would find the door that he had entered by and left from. She would shout. She would scream. She would bang on that door. She would force someone to notice her.

Lottie felt her eyes close. They were too weary to fight against the black all round her. There was nothing to see anyway. She'd heard the sounds that told her he'd locked her in. There was no way out.

Which was, of course, something that Breta would never believe. She'd say, No way out? What a twit! He came in. He went out. Find the door and break it down. Don't just lie there whinging, Lottie.

Not whinging, Lottie thought.

To which Breta would say, You are. You are. What a baby you are.

Lottie pulled the blanket closer to her. The damp spots from the spilled water made clammy patches against her legs. She pulled her legs up, pulled herself into a ball. She tucked her hands into fists and buried the fists beneath her chin. She pressed the fists against her throat so she wouldn't have to feel how thirsty she was.

Baby, she could hear Breta mock her.

"Not a baby."

No? Then prove it. Prove it, Lottie Bowen.

Prove it. That was how Breta always got what she wanted. Prove you're not a baby, prove you want to be my friend, prove you like me better than anyone else, prove you can keep a secret. Prove, prove, prove, prove. Pour all of the bubble bath into the tub and let it run over so it looks like snow. Nick your mother's best lipstick and wear it at school. Flush your knickers down the loo and run about the rest of the day without them. Pinch that Twix for me . . . no, pinch two. Because best friends do stuff like that for each other. That's what being a best friend is. Don't you want to be someone's very best friend?

Lottie did. How she did. And Breta had friends. Breta had dozens and dozens of friends. So if Lottie was going to collect friends as well, she was going to have to be more like Breta. Which is what Breta had been telling her from the very first.

Lottie pressed her hands against the bricks and raised herself. Dizziness came at her like a swell on the sea. She brought her knees up so that only her feet and her bottom were still touching the floor. When the dizziness passed, she got to her feet. She swayed, but she didn't fall.

On her feet, she didn't know what to do. She took a hesitant step forward in the black, her fingers flipping like a bug's antennae. She shivered with the cold. She counted her steps. They inched her forward across the floor.

What was this place? she wondered. It wasn't a cave. It was dark like a cave but a cave didn't have a floor of bricks and it didn't have a door. So what was it? Where was she?

Hands stretched before her, she came to a wall. The shapes upon it and the texture of those shapes were familiar to her, something she'd felt already. Bricks, she realised. She shuffled along the wall like a blind mole. Her hands moved against its surface, first up, then down. She was looking for a window—walls generally had windows in them, didn't they?—a boarded window that offered a crack through which she would peer.

Isn't going to be a window, Lottie, Breta would have said as Lottie patted and searched. You'd see cracks of light through the boards and there're no cracks of light so there isn't a window and you're being a twit.

Breta was right. But Lottie found the door. The wood of it was scratchy and musty-smelling, and she felt up it and down it, seeking the knob. She twisted this to no avail. Then she pounded. And she shouted. "Let me out! Mummy! Mummy!"

There was no response. She pressed her ear against the wood but heard nothing at all. She pounded upon the door another time. She could tell by the dull thudding her fists made against the wood that the door was very thick, like a door of a church.

A church? Was she in the crypt of a church?

Where they stuff dead bodies? Breta would have laughed. And she would have made ghost noises and flittered round the room with a sheet on her head.

Lottie cringed at the thought of bodies and ghosts. She picked up the pace of her exploration. She thought, Out, out, out. Got to get out. And she crept along the wall till she bumped her sore knee.

She winced but didn't moan or cry out. Instead, her fingers reached out to find what she had bumped. More wood, but not rough like the crates. Her fingers raced over it. It felt like a board. It was two hands wide. Above it was another board the exact same width. Below was a third. A fourth seemed to run diagonally up the wall, the width of it fixed against the bricks. . . .

Stairs, she thought.

She pulled herself up them. They were awfully steep, more like a stepladder than stairs. She had to use her hands as well as her feet. As she climbed, she remembered a day trip to Greenwich and the *Cutty Sark* and climbing into the ship on stairs just like these. But this couldn't be the inside of a ship that she was in, could it? A ship made of bricks? It would sink like a stone. It wouldn't float for a second. Besides, if this was a ship that she was in, wouldn't she feel the sea beneath her? Wouldn't the floor rock? Wouldn't she hear the creak of wooden masts and smell the salt air? Wouldn't she—

Her head bumped the ceiling. She gave a yowl of surprise. She crouched. She thought about stairways that led up to ceilings—instead of to landings, where a door could be pounded on—and she knew that stairs didn't go up to ceilings without a purpose. There had to be a door, didn't there, a trapdoor perhaps, like in the barn at Granddad's, where you climbed a ladder to get into the loft.

Her palm reached blindly for the ceiling above her. She finished her climb with greater care. She traced her fingers on the ceiling, moving outward from the wall. She found what felt like a trapdoor's corner, cut into the wood. Then another corner. She moved her hands away from these, trying to centre them. Then she gave a push. Not a fierce one because her arms were feeling all tingly and peculiar. But it was a push all the same.

She felt the trapdoor give. She rested and then tried another push. The door was heavy, like a weight sat on top of it so she couldn't get out, so she would stay in her place, so she wouldn't be a bother to anyone. Like always. That made her lose her temper. "Mummy!" she called. "Mummy, are you there? Mummy! Mummy!"

No answer. She gave another push. Then she crawled up and used her back and her shoulders. She heaved once as hard as she could and then twice more, grunting the way she heard Mrs. Maguire grunt when she moved the fridge to clean behind it. With a creak, the trapdoor opened.

Dizziness and weakness fled in an instant. She'd done it, she'd done it, she'd done it herself. Even without Breta here to tell her how.

She climbed into the chamber above her. It was dark like the one below it, but unlike the other it was not pitch black. Some three feet away, what looked like a blurry ebony rectangle was edged with a shimmery kind of soot grey. She picked her way to this rectangle and found that it was a recessed window, thickly boarded over but not so completely that no light filtered in along the edges. That was the shimmery grey she saw: the nighttime darkness outside, broken up by the moon and the stars, in contrast to the solid wall of gloom inside.

In the shadows and aided by the shimmery grey light, Lottie could make out shapes, even without her specs. A pole stood in the centre of the room. It was like a maypole she'd seen once on the green in the village near her granddad's farm, only ever so much fatter. Above it a thick beam stretched across the room and above that beam, barely visible in the murk, what appeared to be a huge wheel hung on its side, like a flying saucer. The maypole shot up to meet this wheel and extended beyond it, disappearing into the darkness above.

Lottie edged to the pole and touched it. It was cold. It felt like metal, not wood. And knobby metal, like it was old and rusty. It had sticky goopy stuff round its base. She squinted above, trying her best to make out the wheel. It seemed to have huge teeth cut into it, like a giant gear. A pole and a gear wheel, she thought. She curved her arm round the pole and considered what she'd found.

She'd seen the insides of a clock once, a clock from the mantelpiece in Granny's sitting room, curved like the shape of a wave. Uncle Jonathon had given it to Granny for her birthday, but it hadn't worked properly because it was an antique. So Granddad had taken it apart on the kitchen table. It was made of wheels that fit into other wheels which together with the first wheels made the ticking work. All those little wheels were shaped like this one, with teeth.

Clock, she decided. A gigantic clock. She listened for the ticking. She heard nothing at all. No ticking, no tocking, no movement of gears. Broken, she thought. Just like the mantelpiece clock at Granny's. But unlike the mantelpiece clock at Granny's, this was a huge clock. A church clock, perhaps. A tower clock standing proudly in the centre of a square. Or a clock in a castle.

The thought of castles took her in another direction. To dungeons with cells. To firelit rooms that were filled with sprockets and gears, toothed wheels and spikes. To prisoners shrieking and leather-masked gaolers demanding they confess.

Torture, Lottie thought. And the fat pole she clung to and the giant wheel above it took on a new meaning. She dropped her arm and backed away from the pole. Her legs felt rubbery. Perhaps it would have been better not to know.

Suddenly, cold gushed up from the floor and swirled round her knees. Then a loud *whump* seemed to bounce from the walls in the room below her. Silence rushed in to replace the cold, followed by a metallic scrape.

Lottie saw that the square in the floor through which she had climbed now shone with a bobbing light. Rustling sounded next, someone moving below her in heavy clothes. Then a man said, ''Where the . . ." and the wooden crates on the floor below began to bump and creak together.

He thought she'd escaped, Lottie realised. Which meant that there was a *way* to escape. And if she could keep him from knowing she'd found the stairs and climbed them, if she could keep him from knowing she'd located the trapdoor, then once he went in search of her, she could find that escape route and escape for real.

She slipped across the room and lowered the door quietly. She sat on it and hoped her weight would hold it closed if he tried it.

Through the cracks in the floor, she could see the light get brighter. She could hear his heavy tread on the stairs. She held her breath. The trapdoor rose a quarter of an inch. It lowered, then lifted a quarter of an inch again. "Shit," he said. *"Shit."* The door lowered once more. Lottie heard him descend the stairs.

The light went out with a scrape. The outer door opened and then thunked closed. Then it was quiet.

Lottie wanted to clap her hands. She wanted to shout. She forgot all about the cat's fur in her throat and instead she swung the trapdoor up. Breta could not have done any better. Breta could not have fooled him so well. In fact, Breta would probably have hit him in the face with that bucket and run for her life, but Breta would never have thought to outsmart him, to make him think she'd run for her life already.

It was dark below, but the dark didn't frighten Lottie this time because she knew it was so close to being over. She felt her way down the stairs and scooted towards the wooden crates. *That's* where her exit route was, of course. The crates hid an opening that was just Lottie's size.

Lottie set her shoulder against the first of them. Wouldn't Breta be surprised to hear of this adventure? Wouldn't Cito be amazed that Lottie had prevailed? Wouldn't Mummy be proud to know her very own daughter had—

A sudden clank of metal.

Light arced in her direction like a swinging fist.

Lottie spun around, hands balled at her mouth.

"Daddy's the one who's getting you out of here, Lottie," he said. "You're not doing it yourself."

She squinted. He was all in black. She couldn't see him, just the shape of him behind the light. She lowered her fists to her sides.

"I can get out," she said. "You just see if I can't. And when I do, my mummy's going to get you good. She's in the Government. She puts people in gaol. She locks them in the Scrubs and she throws away the key and that's what's going to happen to you. You just wait, you."

"Is that what's going to happen, Lottie? No, I don't think so. Not if Dad tells the truth like he should. He's a prize, is Dad. He's a class-A bloke. But no one's ever known that, and now he has the chance to show his stuff to the world. He can tell the real story and save his little sprog."

"What story?" Lottie asked. "Cito doesn't tell stories. Mrs. Maguire tells stories. She makes them up."

"Well, you're going to help Dad make one up. Come here, Lottie."

"I won't," Lottie said. "I'm thirsty and I won't. You give me a drink."

He placed something on the floor with a *snick*. His toe moved it into the light as well. The tall red Thermos. Lottie took an eager step towards it. "That's right," he said. "But after. After you give Dad some help with his story."

"I'll never help you."

"No?" He rattled a paper bag that was somewhere out of the light. "Shepherd's pie," he said. "Cold apple juice and hot shepherd's pie."

The cat's fur was back, thick as ever on the roof of her mouth and clear down her throat. And her stomach was empty, which she hadn't really noticed before now. But when he'd mentioned shepherd's pie, her insides went all hollow like a bell.

Lottie knew she should turn her back on him and tell him to go, and if she hadn't been so thirsty, if her throat had been able to manage a swallow, if her stomach hadn't started to rumble, if she hadn't smelled the pie, she surely would have done so. She would have laughed in his face. She would have stomped her feet. She would have screamed and yowled. But the apple juice. Cool and sweet and after that the food . . .

She marched into the light, in his direction. All right. She would show him. She wasn't afraid. "What am I s'posed to do?" she asked.

He chuckled. "How very nice," he said.

8

IT WAS AFTER TEN in the morning when Alexander Stone rolled to the edge of the king-size bed and peered at his digital alarm clock. He gazed at the red numbers in disbelief and said, "Hell," when their significance finally soaked into his brain. He hadn't awakened when Eve's own alarm sounded on her bedside table at the usual hour of five. Nearly two-thirds of a bottle of vodka—downed between nine and half past eleven last night—had seen to that.

He'd sat in the kitchen to do his drinking, at the small square table in the inglenook overlooking the garden. He'd mixed the first tumblerful of vodka with orange juice, but after that he'd taken it straight. He'd been twenty-four hours into what he'd started calling the Truth at Last, and among knowing the truth, wondering if the truth had anything to do with Charlie's whereabouts as Eve so fervently believed, and trying to avoid a consideration of what his wife's actions and reactions implied about that truth, he felt pretty much paralysed. He wanted action but he had no idea what kind of action was called for. There were too many questions pounding inside his skull. There was no one in the house to answer them. Eve would be at the Commons embroiled in debate until after midnight. He'd decided to drink. To drink to get drunk. It seemed at the time the single best means of obliterating the knowledge he could have gone the rest of his life without possessing.

Luxford, he thought. Dennis Fucking Luxford. He hadn't even known who the bastard was before Wednesday night, but since that time Luxford and Luxford's intrusion into their lives had been dominating his thoughts.

He sat up warily. His guts churned in uneasy response to a change in position. The furniture in the bedroom seemed to undulate queasily, partly as a result of the vodka still unabsorbed in his body, partly as a result of having yet to put his lenses into his eyes.

He reached for his dressing gown and eased himself to his feet. He swallowed a throatful of sickness down and made his way to the bathroom, where he turned on the taps. He looked at his image in the bathroom mirror. The image was blurry without his lenses in, but its most outstanding details were clear enough: the bloodshot eyes, the haggard face, the skin that seemed to be surrendering to a gravitational pull that had been encouraged by ten hours of drink-induced unconsciousness. I look like dried shit, he thought.

He splashed handful after handful of cold water onto his skin. He dried his face. He put his lenses in his eyes and reached for his shaving gear. He tried to ignore both his nausea and his headache by concentrating on lathering his face.

Vague noise came from somewhere downstairs—a sound not unlike monastic singing—but it was deeply muffled. Eve would have told Mrs. Maguire to keep her daily din to a minimum. "Mr. Stone wasn't well last night," she would have said before leaving the house at her usual pre-dawn time. "He needs his sleep. I don't want him disturbed." And Mrs. Maguire would have obeyed, which was what everyone did when Eve Bowen gave one of her implicit orders.

"There's no point in your confronting Dennis," she'd said to him. "This is something I have to handle alone."

"As Charlie's father for the last six years, I think I have something to say to this bastard."

"Resurrecting the past isn't going to help, Alex."

It was another implicit order. Stay away from Luxford. Keep your distance from that part of my life.

Alex wasn't the sort of man who kept his distance from anything. He hadn't got to where he was as a businessman from hanging back and letting others plan the strategies and fight the battles. After spending the night of Charlie's disappearance lying in bed with his eyes on the ceiling and his mind leaping from one plan to another that he knew would result in her safe return, he'd gone cooperatively to work yesterday for Eve's peace of mind, in order to keep up the pretence of normalcy that she seemed so intent upon maintaining. But at nine in the evening he'd finally had enough. He decided he wasn't going to spend another useless day without putting at least one of his plans into action. He phoned Eve's office and insisted that her unctuous assistant get a message to her at the House of Commons. "Do it now," he'd told Woodward when the assistant had begun with a string of excuses all designed to put him off. "Pronto. Emergency. Got it?" She'd finally phoned back at half past ten, and he could tell from her voice that she believed Luxford had relented and Charlie was returned.

"Nothing new," he'd said in answer to her low, intense, "Alex. What's happened?"

She'd said with an alteration in tone, "Then why are you phoning?" which, along with the drink, set him off.

"Because our daughter's missing," he said with deliberate courtesy. "Because I've just spent the entire day in a bloody charade of business as usual. Because I haven't talked to you since this morning and I'd like to know what the hell is going on. Is that all right with you, Eve?"

He could picture her casting a glance over her shoulder, because her low voice lowered another degree. "Alex, I'm returning your call from the Commons. Do you understand what that means?"

"Patronise your colleagues. Don't try it with me."

"Believe me, this isn't the time or the place—"

"You might have phoned me yourself, by the way. At any time during this goddamned day. Which would have taken care of the delicate problem of having to return my call from the House of Fucking Commons. Where, of course, anyone might listen in. That's what you're worried about, isn't it, Eve?"

"Have you been drinking?"

"Where's my daughter?"

"I can't go into it right now."

"Shall I come there, then? You can always give me an update about Charlie's disappearance with a lobby journalist listening in. That would make for good press, wouldn't it? But, hell, I forgot. Press is just what you don't want. Right?"

"Don't do this to me, Alex. I know you're upset, and you have good reason—"

"Thank you very much."

"—but you've got to see that the only way to handle this is—"

"Eve Bowen's way. So tell me, how far do you intend to let Luxford push you?"

"I met with him. He knows my position."

Alex's fingers closed round the telephone cord. Would it were Luxford's neck. "You met with him when?"

"This afternoon."

"And?"

"He doesn't intend to return her. At the moment. But he's going to have to return her eventually because I've made it clear that I won't play his game. All right, Alex? Have I told you enough?"

She wanted to get off the phone. It was obvious she wanted to return to the Commons. To a debate, a vote, or another opportunity to prove how superbly she could crush an opponent's cobblers between her teeth.

"I want to talk to this bastard."

"That'll do no good. Stay out of this, Alex. Promise me you'll stay out of it. Please."

"I'm not going through another day like today. All this business-as-usual bullshit. With Charlie out there somewhere . . . I'm not doing it."

"Fine. Don't. But don't go near Luxford."

"Why?" He couldn't keep himself from asking the question. It was, after all, at the root of everything. "You want him alone? All for yourself? Like Blackpool, Eve?"

"That's a disgusting remark. I'm ending this conversation. We can talk again when you're sober. In the morning."

And she'd hung up the phone. And he'd drunk the vodka. He'd drunk it until the kitchen floor had begun to tilt. Then he'd staggered up the stairs and fallen crosswise and fully clothed upon the bed. Sometime during the night she must have removed his trousers, shirt, and shoes because he was wearing only his boxer shorts and his socks when he crawled out of the bed.

He downed six aspirin and made his way back to the bedroom. He dressed slowly, waiting for the aspirin to have some effect against the thunder within his skull. He'd forfeited his morning's conversation with Eve, but it was just as well. In his present condition he would have been no match for her. He had to admit that she'd shown an uncharacteristic mercy in leaving him to sleep the binge off instead of awakening him and forcing him to engage in the conversation he'd been so insistent upon having with her. She would have ground him to powder in three or four sentences without employing a quarter of her brain power. He wondered what it indicated about Eve—and about the state of their marriage—that she'd chosen to leave without a demonstration of suzerainty. Then he wondered why he was wondering about the state of their marriage at all, when he'd never wondered about it before. But he knew the answer to that piece of speculation and, despite his attempt to remove the answer from his mind, when he went downstairs to the kitchen, he saw it lying on the table.

Mrs. Maguire was not in sight, but her copy of *The Source* lay where she had left it.

Bloody odd, Alex thought. Mrs. Maguire had been bringing that piece of shit to their house every day for as long as he could remember. But until Wednesday night, when Eve had deliberately brought the papers to his attention, he hadn't once looked at any of them. Oh, he'd glanced at a story here and there when he had occasion to wrap coffee grounds in the paper. He'd wondered derisively about how many brain cells Mrs. Maguire numbed out when she read it each day. But that was the extent of it.

Now the tabloid seemed to have a magnetic power over him. Ignoring his body's demand for hot coffee, he went instead to the table and stared down at the paper.

It's a Living, I'n't It? emblazoned the front page, running parallel to a photograph of a teenage boy in purple leather. The boy was in the act of strolling down a brick path from a terraced house, and he smirked at the camera as if he'd known in advance the headline that would accompany his picture. He was identified as Daffy Dukane, and the tabloid was labelling him the rent boy who had been caught in an automobile with Sinclair Larnsey, East Norfolk's MP. The caption to the photograph suggested that Daffy Dukane's circumstances—educationally disadvantaged, chronically unemployed, and statistically one of the unemployable—had forced him into sharing his favours on a regular basis as a means of survival. The reader willing to turn to page four would find an editorial excoriating the Government that had brought scores of sixteen-year-old boys to this pass. *It's Come to This* was the editorial's headline. But when Alex saw that it had been written by someone called Rodney Aronson and not Dennis Luxford, he passed it by. Because it was Dennis Luxford he wanted to know about. For reasons that went deeper than Luxford's politics.

How had she put it: They'd fucked every night, every morning as well. And not because the sod had seduced her but because she'd wanted it, she'd wanted him. They'd gone at it like monkeys, and who Luxford was and what he stood for hadn't meant a thing to her in light of what she wanted from him.

Alex flipped through the pages of the tabloid, looking. He didn't admit to himself what he was looking for, but he looked all the same. He went through the paper from front to back, and when he'd seen it all, he riffled through the rattan holder and pulled out every other copy of *The Source* that Mrs. Maguire had brought into the house.

He could see the hotel room. He could see its orange curtains and its bland, pseudo-oak institutional furniture. He could see the maddening clutter Eve always generated wherever she went: briefcase, paperwork, magazines, cosmetics, shoes on the floor, hair dryer on the chest of drawers, damp towels left in sodden heaps. He could see a room service trolley with the remains of a meal spread across it. In a stream of light left burning in the bathroom, he could see the bed and its crumpled sheets. He could even see her because he knew—had years and years of knowing—that her knees would be lifted, her legs would be locked round his torso, her hands would be in his hair or on his back, and she would take her pleasure so amazingly quick with a cry of delight saying darling, no, stop, it's too much . . . and that was all he could see.

In disgust, he swept the stack of tabloids to the floor. This is about Charlie, he told himself, and he tried to drive that information into his head. This is not about Eve. This is not about ten years ago when I did not know her, when I was ignorant of her entire existence, when her actions and her relationships were no concern of mine, when who and what she was . . . But that *was* the issue, wasn't it? Who and what his wife had once been, who and what she now was.

Alex went for coffee. He stood at the sink and drank it black and bitter. It was a suitable, if only momentary, distraction from his torturous thoughts. But once he'd downed it, scalding the roof of his mouth and his throat, he was brought back to her.

Did he know her? he wondered. Was it even possible to know her? She was, after all, a politician. She was used to the chameleon requirements of her career.

He considered that career and its implications. She had joined the Marylebone Conservative Association, which is where they had met. She had worked for the party at his own side. She had proved herself so thoroughly and so often that in a break with tradition the constituency committee had asked *her* to put her name on the candidates' list, she had not volunteered to do so herself. And he'd sat in on her interview before her selection as Marylebone's Conservative candidate. He'd heard her passionate advocacy of the party ideals. He himself had shared her strong views about the value of family, about the incalculable importance of small businesses, about the deleterious aspects of government assistance, but he could never have expressed his views as she did. She seemed to know what the constituency committee would ask her before they even decided themselves. She spoke of the need to take their nighttime streets back and make them safe. She outlined her plans for increasing the party's majority in Marylebone. She delineated all the ways in which she had determined she could support the Prime Minister. She had something provocative to say about the care of battered wives, about sex education in the schools, about abortion, about prison terms, about the care of the elderly and the infirm, about taxing and spending and innovative campaigning. She was quick and clever and she impressed the committee with her command of facts. Alex knew this had been no difficulty for her, which is why he wondered: Did she mean what she said? Was she real, as well?

And he wondered which fact bothered him more: the fact that Eve might not be who she claimed to be or the fact that she might have brushed aside who she was in order to have a fuck with someone who stood for everything she opposed.

Because that was the truth about Luxford. He wouldn't have been editing the paper he was editing if he stood for anything else. His politics were a given. What remained to be discovered was the physical nature of the man himself. Because surely to discover his physical nature was to understand. And to understand was essential if they were ever to get to the bottom of—

Right. Alex grinned sardonically. He congratulated himself for his complete decomposition. In less than thirty-six hours he'd managed to metamorphose from rational human being to pissing twit. What had started out as soul-scoring desperation to find his daughter and to spare her in any way had disintegrated to a Neanderthal need to find and obliterate his sexual partner's previous mate. No lies now about seeing Luxford in order to understand. Alex wanted to see him in order to make bruising contact with his flesh. And not for Charlie. Not because of what he was doing to Charlie. But because of Eve.

Alex realized that he had never asked his wife to identify Charlie's father because he had never really wanted to know. Knowledge demanded reaction to knowledge. And reaction to that particular knowledge was what he had wished to avoid.

"Shit," he whispered. He leaned into the sink, his hands on the draining boards on either side of it. Perhaps, like his wife, he should have gone to work today. At least there were motions to be gone through at work. Here there was nothing except his thoughts. And they were maddening.

He had to get out. He had to do something.

He poured another mug of coffee and drank it down. He found that his head had stopped pounding and the nausea was beginning to fade. He became aware of the monastic chanting that he'd heard upon waking, and he moved towards its location, which seemed to be the sitting room.

Mrs. Maguire was on her plump knees in front of the coffee table, where she'd set up a cross and some statues and candles. Her eyes were closed. Her lips moved silently. Every ten seconds precisely, she slid another bead of her rosary through her fingers, and as she did so, tears leaked from beneath her sooty lashes. They dripped off her round cheeks and onto her pullover, where two splodges of damp on her ample breasts told him how long she had been weeping.

The chanting came from a tape recorder, from which solemn male voices were intoning the words *miserere nobis* again and again. Alex knew no Latin, so he couldn't translate. But the words sounded appropriate. They brought him back to himself.

He couldn't do nothing. He could act and he would. This wasn't about Eve. This wasn't about Luxford. This wasn't about what had happened between them or why. This was about Charlie, who couldn't hope to understand the battle going on between her parents. And Charlie was someone he could do something about.

—⁂—

Dennis Luxford waited for a moment before honking the horn when Leo came out of the dentist's surgery. His son stood in a blaze of late morning sunlight, his white-blond hair ruffling in the breeze. He looked left and right, perplexity creasing his forehead. He expected to see Fiona's Mercedes, parked three buildings down from Mr. Wilcot's surgery where she had dropped him an hour earlier. What he did not expect was to find that his father had decided upon a man-to-man lunch before returning Leo to his Highgate school.

"I'll fetch him," Luxford had told Fiona when she was about to leave the house to pick up their son and ferry him back to school. And when she'd looked doubtful, he'd gone on with, "You said he wanted to talk to me, darling. About Baverstock. Remember?"

"That was yesterday morning," she replied. There was no reproach in her words. She wasn't angry that he'd failed to rise in time to have that breakfast conversation with their son. Nor was she angry that he hadn't returned till long past midnight last night. She had no idea he'd waited fruitlessly until after eleven for a message from Eve Bowen telling him to run the truth about Charlotte on the front page of the paper. As far as she was concerned, last night was all about his job's making another necessary intrusion into their lives. She knew the odd hours his career frequently demanded of him, and she was merely offering him the facts, as she always did: Leo had spoken about talking to his father two days ago; he'd planned the conversation for yesterday morning; she couldn't be certain that he still wanted to talk to his father today. She had good reason for this line of thought. Leo was as changeable as the English weather.

Luxford honked the horn. Leo spun in his direction. His hair swept outward—sun lighting its ends like a halo—and his face brightened with a smile. It was an enchanting smile, very like his mother's, and whenever he saw it Luxford's heart tightened at the exact same moment that his mind enjoined Leo to toughen up, smarten up, walk with his fists cocked, and think like a yob. Naturally, Luxford didn't want his son actually to be a yob, but if he could just get him to think like one—even like one-tenth of one—his general manner of confronting life wouldn't be so troubling.

Leo waved. He swung his rucksack up to his shoulder, gave a little skip, and headed happily in his father's direction. His white shirt, Luxford noticed, was hanging outside his trousers and below his navy uniform pullover on one side. Luxford liked the look of this dishevelment. Lack of interest in neatness was completely out of character in Leo but definitely in character for the average boy.

Leo climbed into the Porsche. He said, "Daddy!" and quickly corrected himself to, "Dad. 'Lo. I was looking for Mummy. She said she'd be at the bakery. Over there." He crooked a finger in that direction.

Luxford took the opportunity to sneak a look at Leo's hands. They were perfectly clean, their nails clipped, no dirt beneath them. Luxford catalogued this information along with everything else that concerned him about his son. He felt impatient with it. Where was the dirt? the scabs? Where were the hangnails? the plasters? Damn it all, these were Fiona's hands he was looking at, with long, tapering fingers and oval nails with perfect half moons at the cuticles. Had any of his own genetic material gone into the making of his son? Luxford wondered. Why should similarity of appearance translate to similarity of everything else as well? Leo was even going to inherit Fiona's willowy height, not Luxford's own more compact frame, and Luxford had spent many thoughtful hours considering what use Leo might make of his body. He wanted to think of his son as a distance runner, a hurdler, a high jumper, a long jumper, a pole vaulter. He did not want to think of his son as Leo thought of himself: a dancer.

"Tommy Tune is quite tall," Fiona had pointed out when Luxford said no, no, definitely not to a pair of tap shoes Leo had wanted for his birthday. "And Fred Astaire. Wasn't he tall as well, darling?"

"That's hardly the point," Luxford had replied from behind clenched teeth. "For God's sake, Leo isn't going to be a dancer, and he's not getting any tap shoes."

So Leo had taken matters into his own hands. He superglued pennies to the toes and the heels of his best pair of shoes and tapped energetically on the tiles in the kitchen. Fiona had labelled this behaviour inventive. Luxford called it destructive and disobedient, and he gated Leo for two weeks as punishment. Not that being gated mattered to Leo. He sat contentedly in his room, reading his art books, caring for his finches, and rearranging his photographs of the dancers he admired.

"At least it's modern dance," Fiona pointed out. "It's not as if he wants to study ballet."

"Out of the question, and that's my final word on it," Luxford said, and he made certain that Baverstock School for Boys hadn't added dancing—tap or otherwise—to its curriculum since he had been a pupil.

"We were going to have toasted teacakes," Leo was saying. "Mummy and I. After the dentist. My mouth's all numb, though, so I don't expect I would have much enjoyed eating them. Does it look peculiar, Dad? My mouth? It feels quite odd."

"It looks fine," Luxford said. "I thought we'd have lunch. If you can miss another hour of school and if your mouth isn't bothered."

Leo grinned. "Wicked!" He squirmed round in his seat and reached for his seat belt. He said, "Mr. Potter wants me to sing a solo on Parents' Day. He told me yesterday. Did Mummy tell you? It's to be an alleluia." He squirmed back into position. "It's not an actual solo, I suppose, since the rest of the choir will sing as well, but there's a part where I get to sing all alone for something like a whole minute. That counts as a solo, I expect. Doesn't it?"

Luxford wanted to ask if there wasn't something else his son could do for Parents' Day, like build a science project or give a speech exhorting his fellow pupils into a political uprising. But he bit off the words and started the car, guiding it into the late morning traffic. He said, "I'll look forward to hearing you," and added mendaciously, "I always wanted to be in the choir at Baverstock. They have a fine one, but I couldn't carry a tune. Whatever I sang always sounded like stones clattering round in a bucket."

"Did you really?" Leo homed in on the lie with a disconcerting perspicacity also inherited from his mother. "That's funny. I wouldn't ever expect you to want to be in a choir, Dad."

"Why not?" Luxford glanced at his son. Leo was delicately pressing his fingertips into his upper lip, curiously testing his mouth for its degree of numbness.

"I expect you could get your lip mashed up after the dentist and you wouldn't even know it," the boy said thoughtfully. "I expect you could chew it off and not know it either. Brilliant, that, isn't it?" And then, again like his mother, that unexpected shifting of conversational gears so as to take the listener by surprise. "I expect you'd think it was rather sissy, being in a choir. Wouldn't you, Dad?"

Luxford wasn't to be sidetracked off the topic of his choice. He also wasn't going to allow his son to turn the conversation into an analysis of the father. Fiona did enough of that. "Have I mentioned that Baverstock has a school canoe club? That's something new since I was a pupil. They practise on the swimming pool—these are one-man canoes, by the way—and they make a yearly expedition to the Loire." Was that a flicker of interest on Leo's face? Luxford decided it was and went on. "It's part of the C.C.F., the canoeing. They make their own canoes. And during the Easter holiday they have a week's camp for adventure training. Climbing, parascending, shooting, camping, first aid. You know the sort of thing."

Leo's head lowered. His pullover had got rucked up by the seat belt. The buckle of his trouser belt was exposed, and he fingered this.

"You're going to like it even more than you expect," Luxford said, aiming for a tone that indicated his blithe assumption of Leo's complete cooperation. He made the turn up Highgate Hill, heading for the high street. "Where shall we have lunch?"

Leo shrugged. Luxford could see his teeth chewing at his lip. He said, "Don't do that, Leo. Not while it's numb," and Leo seemed to sink farther into his seat.

Since no suggestion was forthcoming from his son, Luxford chose randomly, sliding the Porsche into an available parking space near a trendy-looking cafe in Pond Square. He ushered Leo inside, ignoring the fact that his son's usually light-hearted gait had altered to a heavy-hearted trudge. He squired him to a table, handed him a laminated ivory menu, and read the illuminated chalkboard aloud for the daily specials.

He said, "What'll it be?"

Leo shrugged again. He set down the menu, rested his cheek in his palm, and kicked the heel of his shoe against the iron chair leg. He sighed and with his other hand he rotated the vase at the table's centre and repositioned the sprig of white flowers and their accompanying greenery so that they could be viewed from every angle. He did this with apparent unconsciousness, a second-nature activity that raised his father's hackles and destroyed his patience.

"Leo!" Luxford's voice had completely lost its air of paternal bonhomie.

Leo hastily withdrew his fingers from the vase. He picked up the menu and made a show of studying it. "I was just wondering," he said in a low voice, his chin drawn in to illustrate the fact that his wondering was a wondering wondered to himself.

"What?" Luxford demanded.

"Nothing." The foot kicked at the chair leg again.

"I'm interested. What?"

Leo lifted his nose towards the flowers. "Why Mummy's lunaria has smaller flowers than those."

Luxford set his own menu down with painstaking diligence. He looked from the flowers—whose name he could not have uttered even under threat of death—to his maddening son. Baverstock School for Boys was called for, all right. And the sooner the better. Without it, in another year Leo's eccentricities would be beyond remedy. How did he *know* the damn things he knew anyway? Fiona talked about them, true, but Luxford knew his wife didn't sit Leo down and lecture to him on the marvels of botany any more than she encouraged him to devour art books or admire Fred Astaire. "Dennis, he's beyond me," she said more than once late at night long after Leo had gone to bed. "He's his own person, and it's a lovely person, so why are you trying to make him you?"

But Luxford wasn't trying to make Leo into a miniature version of himself. He was just trying to make Leo into a miniature version of Leo the future adult. He didn't want to think that this current Leo was a larval form of the Leo to come. The boy merely needed guidance, a firm hand, and a few years away at school.

When the waitress came for their order, Luxford chose the veal special. Leo gave a shudder, said, "That's a baby cow, Dad," and selected a cottage cheese and pineapple sandwich. "With chips," he added, and told his father in a typical display of honesty, "They're extra."

"Fine," Luxford said. They both ordered their drinks and when the waitress left them, they both stared at the lunaria that Leo had rearranged.

It was early for lunch, just before noon, so they had most of the restaurant to themselves. There were only two other occupied tables, and these were at the far end of the restaurant and sheltered by potted trees, so they had no means of true distraction. Which was just as well, Luxford decided, because they needed to have their talk.

He made the first foray. "Leo, I know you aren't particularly happy about going to Baverstock. Your mother's told me. But you must know I wouldn't make a decision like this if I didn't think it was for the best. It's my own school. You know that. And it did wonders for me. It shaped me, gave me backbone, made me feel confident. It'll do the same for you."

Leo went the direction Fiona had predicted. His foot kicked rhythmically at the chair leg as he spoke. "Granddad didn't go there. Uncle Jack didn't go there."

"Right. Quite. But I want more for you than either of them has."

"What's wrong with the shop? What's wrong with the airport?"

It was an innocent enquiry made in a calm and innocent voice. But Luxford wasn't about to engage in a discussion of his father's appliance shop or his brother's position in security at Heathrow. Leo would have liked that, since it would have directed the spotlight onto someone else and possibly caused a complete shift in the conversation if he played his cards right. But Leo wasn't in charge at the moment.

"It's a privilege to go to a school like Baverstock."

"You always say privilege is bosh," Leo pointed out.

"I don't mean privilege that way. I mean that to be able to go to a school like Baverstock is something not to be turned from lightly, since any boy in his right mind would be happy to take your place." Luxford watched his son toy with his knife and fork, balance the blade of the one between the tines of the other. He couldn't have looked less impressed with the privilege his father was attempting to explain to him. Luxford went on. "The teaching's top notch. And it's up-to-date. You'll work with computers. You'll learn advanced science. They have a technical activities centre where you can build anything you'd like . . . a hovercraft, even, if you've a mind for it."

"I don't want to go."

"You'll make dozens of friends, and within the year you'll be enjoying it so much that you won't even want to come home for half terms."

"I'm too little," Leo said.

"Don't be absurd. You're nearly twice the size of other boys your age, and by the time you get there in the autumn, you'll be six inches taller than anyone else in your year. What is it you're afraid of? Being bullied? Is that it?"

"I'm too little," Leo insisted. He slumped in his chair and stared at the knife-and-fork sculpture he'd made.

"Leo, I've already pointed out that your size—"

"I'm only eight years old," he said flatly. And he looked at his father with those highland-sky eyes of his—damn if he didn't have Fiona's eyes as well—brimming with tears.

"For God's sake, don't cry about it," Luxford said. Which, of course, caused the floodgates to open. "Leo!" Luxford said his name in a tightened-jaw command. "For God's sake. Leo!"

The boy lowered his head to the table. His shoulders shook.

"Stop it," Luxford hissed. "Sit up. Right now."

Leo tried to control himself but only ended up sobbing, "C . . . c . . . can't. Daddy, c . . . can't."

The waitress chose this moment to arrive with their food. She said, "Should I . . . would you . . . is he . . ." and stood a hesitant three steps from the table with a plate in each hand and her face dissolving into an expression of sympathy. "Oh, the poor dear little one," she said in a voice one would use to coo to a bird. "Can I get him something special?"

Some backbone, Luxford thought, which I doubt is on the menu. He said, "He's all right. Leo, your lunch is here. Sit up."

Leo raised his head. His face looked mottled like strawberry skin. His nose had begun to dribble. He heaved a breath. Luxford fished out his handkerchief and handed it to him. "Wipe," he said. "And then eat."

"Perhaps he'd like a nice sweet," the waitress said. "Would you like that, luv?" And to Luxford in a lower voice, "What a beautiful face on him! He looks like one of them painted angels."

"Thank you," Luxford said, "but he has all he needs at the moment."

But beyond the moment? Luxford didn't know. He picked up his knife and fork and cut into the veal. Leo drew disconsolate squiggles of brown sauce across his network of chips. He set the bottle down and looked at his plate, his lips quivering. More tears were forecast.

Luxford said past the veal, which to his surprise was succulently cooked and absolutely delicious, innocent baby cow or not, "Eat your lunch, Leo."

"Not hungry. My mouth feels peculiar."

"Leo, I said eat."

Leo snuffled and picked up a single chip from which he took a chipmunk-size bite that he proceeded to chew between his front teeth. Luxford forked up more veal, and he eyed his son. Leo took a second tiny bite from the chip and then a third that was even smaller. He had always been an artist at telegraphing defiance through an act of ostensible obedience. Luxford knew he could bully him into eating properly, but he didn't want another round of public tears.

He said, "Leo."

"I'm eating." Leo picked up half of the sandwich and held it in such a way that a third of its cottage cheese and pineapple slid from between the slices of bread onto the tabletop. "Yuck," he said.

"You're behaving like a . . ." Luxford sought another word as he heard his wife's reasonable voice say, "He's behaving like a child because he is a child, Dennis. Why do you expect him to be what he can't possibly be when he's only eight years old? He certainly has no unreasonable expectations of you."

With his fingers, Leo scooped up the cottage cheese and pineapple and let it plop onto the top of his chips. He took more brown sauce and poured it onto the mess. He stirred it with his index finger. He was trying to push his father, and Luxford knew it. He didn't need a session with one of Fiona's psychology books to tell him that. He also didn't intend to be pushed.

He said, "I know you're frightened about going away." And when the lips began to quiver again, he went hastily on. "That's normal, Leo. But it's not as if Baverstock is that far away. You'll be only eighty miles from home." But he could see from the boy's face that *only eighty miles* translated into the distance from the earth to Mars, with his mother on one planet and himself on another. Luxford knew that nothing he could possibly say was going to change the fact that when Leo went to Baverstock, Fiona wouldn't be going with him. So he said in finality, "You're going to have to trust me, son. Some things are for the best, and believe me this is one of them. Now eat your lunch."

He gave his attention fully to his own lunch, his actions implying that their discussion was over. But it hadn't gone as he'd intended and the single tear trailing down Leo's cheek told him he'd made a botch of their encounter. He'd be hearing as much from Fiona tonight.

He sighed. His shoulders ached, a physical manifestation of everything he seemed to be carrying round at the moment. He had too much on his mind. He couldn't deal simultaneously with Leo, with Fiona, with Sinclair Larnsey's peripatetic roguery, with Eve, with whatever Rod Aronson was up to at work, with anonymous letters, with threatening phone calls, and most of all with what had happened to Charlotte.

He'd tried to dismiss the little girl from his mind and he'd succeeded in doing so for most of the morning, telling himself that it was upon Evelyn's head that the sin of inaction would lie should anything happen to Charlotte. He was no part of her life—at the wish of her mother—and nothing he could do would make himself part of her life now. He was not responsible for what happened to the child. Except that he was. In the single but most profound manner, he was utterly responsible for Charlotte, and he knew it.

Last night he'd sat at his desk with his gaze on the telephone, saying, "Come on, Evelyn. Phone me. Come *on*," until he could hold up the presses no longer. He had the story written. The names, the dates, and the places were there. All he needed was a phone call from her and the story would run on page one where her abductor wanted it and Charlotte would be released and returned to her home. But the phone call hadn't come. The paper had run with the rent boy story on the front page. And now Luxford waited for the sky to fall in whatever way it might.

He tried to tell himself that the kidnapper would merely take the story to another paper, the *Globe* being the most logical choice. But the moment he had himself nearly convinced that it was only publicity the kidnapper wanted, publicity that could come from any source, he heard the voice at the other end of the telephone again. "I'll kill her if you don't run that story." And he did not know which part of the message took precedence in the kidnapper's mind: the threat to kill, the demand for the story itself, or the requirement that the story run in Luxford's own paper.

In not running the story, he was calling a bluff that he had no right to call in the first place. The fact that Evelyn was doing the same did nothing to alleviate his anxiety. She'd made it clear at Harrods that she believed he was behind Charlotte's disappearance and thinking that, she would call what she thought was his bluff indefinitely, secure in the knowledge that he'd never lift a hand to harm his own child.

There was only one solution that he could see. He had to alter Evelyn's belief. He had to do battle with her entire pattern of thinking. He had to make her understand that he wasn't the man she thought he was.

He hadn't the vaguest idea how to go about it.

9

HELEN CLYDE COULDN'T RECALL where she had first heard the expression "pay dirt." It had probably been part of the dialogue in one of the American detective programmes that she used to watch with her father during her formative years. Her father was nothing if not a devotee of the hardest of hard-boiled gumshoes. When he wasn't engaged in one sort of financial wizardry or another, he was reading Raymond Chandler and Dashiell Hammett to tide him over until the next Humphrey Bogart film was shown for the thousandth time on television. He preferred Humphrey Bogart to everyone else if he could get him. And on the desperate occasions when Sam Spade and Philip Marlowe were on assignment elsewhere from the BBC, Helen's father made do with the pale counterfeits of more recent years. This is where "pay dirt" must have come from, a seed from the dialogue, planted in her mind during hours in front of those shifting images from the cathode-ray tube. The seed sprang to full flower during her morning's efforts in the environs of Cross Keys Close in Marylebone. And pay dirt was what she triumphantly hit when she interviewed the inhabitant of Number 4.

They'd made a three-way division of labour at the St. James house at half past nine that morning. St. James would continue on the path to Breta, taking on the Geoffrey Shenkling School. Deborah would collect a sample of Dennis Luxford's printing in order to eliminate him as a potential author of the kidnapping notes. Helen would question the denizens of Cross Keys Close to find out if anyone had been lurking in the area in the days preceding Charlotte's disappearance.

"The Luxford business is probably unnecessary," St. James had told them. "I can't believe he'd write the note himself if he took the girl. But we need to eliminate him as a matter of course. So, my love, if you don't mind taking on *The Source* . . ."

Deborah flushed. She said, "Simon. Good grief. I'm terrible at this sort of thing. You know that. What on earth shall I *say* to him?"

"The truth will do," St. James had told her. Deborah looked unconvinced. Her entire experience in this line of work had so far been limited to a single episode of quasi-breaking-and-entering in Helen's company nearly four years in the past, and even then Helen had sallied forth in the lead, requiring Deborah only to footsoldier along behind her.

"Darling," Helen told her, "just think of Miss Marple. Or Tuppence. Think of Tuppence. Or Harriet Vane."

Deborah had finally settled upon taking her cameras with her as a security blanket to shelter her from the inclement weather of the vast unknown. "It's a newspaper office after all," she explained anxiously, lest St. James and Helen rush her out of the Chelsea house unarmed. "I won't feel quite so odd if I have them with me. I won't look out of place. They have photographers there, don't they? Lots of photographers? At the newspaper office? Yes. Of course. Well, of course they do."

"Incognito," Helen cried. "Darling, that's it. The very absolute thing. No one who sees you will know why you're there and Mr. Luxford will be so appreciative of your thoughtfulness in sparing him that he'll cooperate forthwith. Deborah, you were made for this line of work."

Deborah had chuckled, her most reliable trait an ability to be joked out of her natural reticence. She'd gathered her cameras and gone on her way. St. James and Helen had done likewise.

From the time he had dropped her at the corner of Marylebone High Street and Marylebone Lane, heading himself west towards the Edgware Road, Helen had been asking questions. She'd started in the shops along Marylebone Lane, and she'd framed her questions round the disappearance of a child whose photograph she flashed once again but whose name she was careful not to give. Helen pinned the highest of her hopes upon the owner of the Golden Hind Fish and Chips Shop. Since Charlotte stopped there as a matter of course on Wednesdays prior to her music lesson, what better place was there for someone to wait for her and to watch for her than at one of the Golden Hind's five wobble-legged tables? There was one specifically where a watcher could have waited, tucked into a corner behind a fruit machine but with a clear view of anyone who might have come strolling along Marylebone Lane.

But the shop owner, despite Helen's encouraging mantra-like murmuring of "It could have been a man, it could have been a woman, it might well have been someone you've never seen here before," shook his head and continued pouring vegetable oil into one of his capacious cooking vats. There might have been someone new hanging about, he said, but how was he to know? His shop was busy—and thank the Lord for that in these sorts of times—and if someone new was to come in for a nice bit of cod, chances are he'd think it was someone from one of the businesses that backed onto Bulstrode Place. *That's* where she should be asking round, anyway. The buildings that them businesses were in had picture windows looking down on the street. More'n once he'd seen a secretary or a clerk-type gawping out the windows instead of seeing to their work. Which is why, tell you, Miss, the whole flipping country is going to hell. No work ethic. Too many bloody bank holidays. Everybody with a hand out, looking for the government to lay something in their palms. When he took a breath to expatiate further upon his chosen theme, Helen thanked him hastily and left him St. James's card. If he did happen to remember anything . . .

The businesses backing onto Bulstrode Place took up several hours of her time. She had to bring to bear all of her skills at artfully blending persuasion and prevarication in order to manoeuvre past receptionists and security personnel so as to gain access to anyone having a work station, office, or desk near the windows that overlooked Bulstrode Place and Marylebone Lane. But here, again, she gained nothing but a questionable job offer for a more questionable job from a leering executive.

She did little better at the Prince Albert pub, where the publican greeted her question with an incredulous laugh. "Someone hanging about? Someone looking out of place?" he guffawed. "Luv, this's London, this is. Hangers about're my business. And what's looking out of place these days? 'Less someone came in dripping blood like a vampire, I wouldn't even take notice. Even then I might not, times being what they are. My only question's can they pay for their drinks."

After that she began the painstaking sojourn through Cross Keys Close. She'd never actually been in a section of London so reminiscent of Jack the Ripper's haunts. Even in broad daylight the area made her nerves jangle. Tall buildings stood on each side of narrow alleyways, so the only sunlight that broke into the gloom was the occasional blade of it, which slashed at a roofline, and the even more occasional pool of it that managed to gather on a front step possessing a fortuitous exposure. There was virtually no one about in the area—which certainly suggested the distinct possibility of a stranger's presence having been noted—but there was also virtually no one at home in most of the mousehole dwellings either.

She avoided Damien Chambers' house, although she did take note of the electric keyboard music issuing from behind the closed door. She concentrated on the music teacher's neighbours and worked both sides of the thread's-width cobbled street. Her only companions were two cats—one ginger, one tabby, and both with hip bones jutting out at starvation angles—and a small furry creature with a pointed snout. This last skittered on tiny legs along the front of one building. His presence suggested that as brief an exposure to the area as possible was what was called for.

Helen showed Charlotte's photograph. She explained her disappearance. She sidestepped natural questions like Who is she? and Are you suggesting foul play? She went to the heart of the matter once the preliminaries were completed: Chances were very good that the girl had been abducted. Had anyone been seen in the immediate vicinity? Anyone suspicious? Anyone lingering around too long?

From Number 3 and Number 7, two women whose televisions were coincidentally roaring with the same chat show, she received the same information as she and Simon had received from Damien Chambers on Wednesday night. Milkman, postman, the odd delivery man. Those were the only people who'd been seen in the mews. From Number 6 and Number 9 she received dull-faced blank stares. From half a dozen more she received nothing at all since no one was at home. And then she scored at Number 5.

She thought she might be in good hands when she first knocked on the door. Happening to glance above—just as she had kept glancing round uneasily as she made her way through the network of alleys—she saw a wizened face watching her surreptitiously through a crack in the curtains at the single first floor window. She raised a hand in greeting and tried to look as pleasantly non-threatening as possible. She called out, "May I speak to you for a moment, please?" and she saw the eyes narrow. She smiled encouragingly. The face disappeared. She knocked again. Nearly a minute went by, then the door cracked open on a chain.

Helen said, "Thank you so much. This won't take a moment," and rustled in her shoulder bag for Charlotte's photo.

The eyes in the wizened face watched her warily. Helen couldn't yet tell if they belonged to a woman or to a man, since their owner was dressed asexually in a green tracksuit and trainers.

"Whatchawan?" Wizened-Face asked.

Helen produced the picture. She explained Charlotte's disappearance. Wizened-Face took the picture in an age-spotted hand and held it between fingers with bright red nails. That, at least, settled the question of sex, unless the poor dear was an elderly transvestite.

"This little girl has disappeared," Helen said. "Possibly from Cross Keys Close. We're trying to establish if anyone has been lurking round the area in the past week or so."

"Pewman rang the police," the woman said, and thrust the photograph back at Helen. She wiped her nose on the back of her hand and jerked her head at Number 4 across the alley. "Pewman," she said again. "Wasn't me."

"The police? When?"

She shrugged. "Was a tramp hanging about early week. Know the sorts, doanchew? Go through them rubbish bins looking for food. Pewman don't like that. Well, none of's do. But Pewman, he'd be the one rang the police."

Helen worked on putting this information together. She spoke quickly lest the woman decide she'd said enough and slam the door. "You're saying there was a vagrant in the neighbourhood, Mrs. . . ." She waited hopefully for an appellation to hang upon the woman, an indication of growing warmth and trust between them. Wizened wasn't having any. She sucked on her teeth and favoured Helen with a look that spoke volumes, none of which had anything to do with amity. Helen continued. "This vagrant was here for several days? And Pewman . . . Mr. Pewman? . . . He phoned the police?"

"Constable run him off." She grinned. Seeing her teeth, Helen made a mental vow to visit her dentist more regularly. "I saw that much, I did. Tramp fell into the rubbish bin howling 'bout police brutality. Pewman did it though. Phoned the police. Jus' ask him."

"Can you describe . . ."

"Hmmm. Can do. Good-looking, he were. No-nonsense type. Dark hair like a cap. Real nice. Real clean. Li'l bit of caterpillar on his lip. Look of authority 'bout him, there was."

"Oh dear, I'm sorry," Helen said, and forced her voice to remain patient and pleasant, "I meant the vagrant, not the policeman."

"Ah. Him." The woman made another wipe at her nose. "Was dressed in brown, like army stuff."

"Khaki?"

"Thassit. All crumpled up like he slept in it. Heavy boots. No laces. Rucksack . . . one o' them big things."

"A duffel bag?"

"Thassit. Right."

The description would probably fit ten thousand men currently wandering round London. Helen pressed further. "Did you notice any-thing else about him? A physical characteristic. His hair, for instance. His face. His body."

Wrong question to ask. The woman grinned and Helen was regaled by yet another display of her teeth. "Was looking at the copper more'n him. Nice little arse on the copper, there was. I like a man with a tight little arse, doanchew?"

"Quite. I'm an absolute martyr to the male posterior," Helen said. "As to the other man . . ."

She was able to add only his hair. "Mostly grey, it were. Hanging out in straggles from beneath a knitted cap. Cap itself . . ." She used one of her fingernails to rub along her gumline and down between two teeth as she thought. "Navy in colour. Pewman phoned the coppers on him when he's going through his dustbin. Pewman'd know what he looked like better'n me."

Pewman, blessedly, did know. And even more blessedly, he was at home. A screenplay writer, he explained, and Helen had caught him mid-sentence, so if she didn't mind . . .

Helen went directly to the vagrant without explanation.

Pewman said, "Oh yes, I remember him," and supplied Helen with a description that made her marvel at his powers of observation. The man was fifty to sixty-five, he stood perhaps five feet ten inches tall, his face was dark and deeply lined as if from too much sun, his lips were so badly chapped that they were white with dead skin, his hands were roughed up—barely healing cuts on the backs of them, his trousers were held up by a maroon tie that was worked through the belt loops. "And," Pewman concluded, "one of his shoes was built up."

"Built up?"

"You know. One sole was about an inch thicker than the other. Polio in childhood, perhaps?" He gave a boyish laugh at Helen's look of astonishment at his powers of observation. "Writer," he said in appar-ent explanation.

"Sorry?"

"He looked like a good character, so I wrote a description of him when I saw him going through the rubbish. One never knows when something's going to be useful."

"You phoned the police as well, according to your neighbour, Mrs. . . ." Helen waved vaguely across the alley, where, she saw, her conversation with Mr. Pewman was being observed from a crack in the curtains.

"I?" He shook his head. "Nope. Poor bugger. I wouldn't have

phoned the cops on him. There wasn't much in my rubbish, but he was welcome to it. It was probably one of the others. Probably Miss Schickel from Number 10." He rolled his eyes and tilted his head in the direction of Number 10, farther down the alley. "She's one of those up-by-their-bootstraps types. I lived through the Blitz, etc., etc. You know the sort I mean? They've got zero tolerance for the down-at-heel. She probably warned the bloke off and when he didn't disappear, she'd have phoned the cops. And kept phoning till they came round and rousted him."

"Did you see him get rousted?"

He hadn't, he said. He'd just seen him going through the rubbish. He couldn't have said for certain exactly how long the man had been hanging about the area, but he knew it was more than one day. Despite her lack of tolerance for her less fortunate fellow man, Miss Schickel was unlikely to phone the cops after only one incursion into her rubbish bin.

Did he know the exact day when the vagrant had been rousted?

He thought about this, playing a pencil through his fingers. He finally said that it must have been a couple of days ago. Perhaps Wednesday. Yes, Wednesday for sure, because his mum always phoned on Wednesday and when he'd been talking to her, he'd looked out the window and seen the poor bloke. He hadn't seen the man since, come to think of it.

Which was the moment when Helen thought of the gumshoe expression. She'd finally hit pay dirt. It was a solid lead.

—◊—

The existence of a lead ameliorated the frustration St. James was suffering. With the blessing of the headmistress of the Geoffrey Shenkling School, he'd spoken to every female child possessing a name even remotely close to the nickname Breta. He'd interviewed eight- to twelve-year-old Albertas, Bridgets, Elizabeths, Berthes, Babettes, Ritas, and Brittanys of every race, every creed, and every possible disposition. Some were shy. Some were frightened. Some were outspoken. Some were delighted to be out of their lessons. But none of them knew Charlotte Bowen, either as Charlotte, as Lottie, or as Charlie. And none of them had ever been to Eve Bowen's Friday afternoon surgery with a parent, a guardian, or a friend. He'd come away from the school with a list of the day's absentees and their phone numbers. But he had a feeling that the Shenkling school was going to be a complete dead end.

"And if that's the case, we're left with having to check every other school in Marylebone," St. James said, "while time continues to pass. Which is, of course, to the kidnapper's advantage. You know, Helen, if we hadn't had confirmation from two other sources that Breta's indeed a friend of Charlotte's, I'd be willing to lay money on Damien Chambers' having cooked her up on Wednesday night on the spot to get us off his back."

"His bringing up Breta did give us an instant direction to head in, didn't it?" Helen noted thoughtfully. They'd joined forces in the Rising Sun pub on the high street, where St. James was brooding into a Guinness and Helen was fortifying herself with a glass of white wine. They'd arrived during that quiet period between lunch and dinner, so aside from the publican who was polishing and shelving glasses, they had the bar to themselves.

"But you'd be hard pressed to make me believe he managed to get both Mrs. Maguire and Brigitta Walters to corroborate his story about Breta. Why would they?"

"Mrs. Maguire's Irish, isn't she? And Damien Chambers? That was an Irish accent, surely."

"Belfast," St. James said.

"So perhaps they share a common interest."

St. James again considered Eve Bowen's position at the Home Office and what Mrs. Maguire had alluded to about the MP's special interest: putting the screws to the IRA. But he shook his head. "That doesn't explain Brigitta Walters. How does she fit in? Why would she tell the same tale about Breta if it wasn't the truth?"

"Perhaps our concentration's too limited in looking for Breta," Helen said. "We've thought of her as a school friend or a neighbourhood friend. But Charlotte could know the girl from somewhere else. What about from a church group? Sunday school? Choir?"

"There's been no mention of that."

"Girl guides?"

"We'd have been told."

"What about her dancing class? We've not looked into her dancing class, and it's been mentioned more than once."

They hadn't looked into it. And it was a possibility. There was her psychologist as well. Both leads needed following up; both leads might hold the key they were looking for, so why did he feel so reluctant to deal with them? St. James wondered. But he knew the answer. He curled his fingers and felt the tips of his nails dig into his palm. He said, "I want to get out of this, Helen."

"It isn't making either of our lives any easier, is it?"

He glanced her way quickly. "You've told him?"

"Tommy? No." Helen sighed. "He questioned me, naturally. He knows I'm preoccupied with something. But so far I've managed to convince him it's nothing but premarital nerves."

"He won't like being lied to."

"I haven't actually lied. I do have premarital nerves. I'm still not sure."

"About Tommy?"

"About marriage to Tommy. About marriage to anyone. About marriage full stop. All this till-death-do-us business makes me uneasy. How can I vow eternal love for one man when I can't even maintain a month's devotion to a single pair of earrings?" She dismissed the subject by pushing her wineglass away. "But I *have* come up with something to cheer us."

She went on to explain. Her explanation was the leaven that finally acted upon St. James's frustration. The presence of the vagrant in Cross Keys Close was the first piece of information that actually fitted in with another piece of information already in their possession.

"The squats on George Street," St. James said meditatively after considering Helen's information for several moments. "Deborah reminded me of them last night."

"Of course," Helen said. "They'd be the perfect doss-house for a vagrant, wouldn't they?"

"They'd certainly be perfect for something," St. James said. He drained his glass. "Let's get on with things, then."

—⚋—

Deborah was getting restless. She'd started out her day with a two-hour wait for Dennis Luxford in the reception area of *The Source*, occupying herself by watching the journalists come and go.

She checked with the reception desk every half hour during this time. But the answer to her question was always the same. Mr. Luxford had not yet come in. And no, he would be *highly* unlikely to come in a rear entrance. When she insisted that the receptionist phone Dennis Luxford's office to make certain the editor had still not arrived, the young woman had done so with post-adolescent ill grace. "*Is* he in yet?" the receptionist demanded into the mouthpiece of her phone. Her nameplate said that she was called Charity, a gross misnomer to Deborah's way of thinking.

An hour after lunchtime, Deborah left the building and went in search of sustenance. This she found in a winebar near St. Bride Street, where a plate of *penne all'arrabbiata*, an entire basket of garlic bread, and a glass of red wine did nothing for her breath but much for her spirits. She hauled herself and her cameras back to Farrington Street.

This time, someone else was waiting for Dennis Luxford, as Charity informed her with a "You're *back*? Don't give up easy, do you? Well, join the crowd."

Deborah discovered that among Charity's many gifts was hyperbole. The crowd consisted of a single man. He was sitting on the edge of one of the sofas in the reception area. Every time someone came through the revolving doors, he looked as if he intended to jump to his feet.

Deborah nodded at him pleasantly. He frowned and snapped the cuff of his shirt off his wrist to examine his watch, after which he strode to the reception desk and had a few sharp words with Charity. She was saying rather hotly, "Hey. Chill out. I don't exactly have a reason to lie to you, do I?" when at last Dennis Luxford came through the front door.

Deborah got to her feet. Charity said, "*See*," and called out, "Mr. Luxford?" The man who'd been waiting for the editor swung round from Charity's desk.

He said, "Luxford?"

Luxford looked immediately wary at the tone, which suggested that this was no friendly visit. He shot a glance at the security guard who stood near the door. The guard began to approach.

The man said, "I'm Alexander Stone. Eve's husband."

Luxford examined him, then gave a minute shake of his head to the guard, telling him to retreat. He said, "This way," and turned to the lifts, which is when he saw Deborah.

Deborah knew at once that she was wildly out of her depth. Good grief, this was Eve Bowen's husband who'd been waiting for Luxford, Eve Bowen's husband who—according to what they'd been told—didn't even know that Dennis Luxford was the father of Eve Bowen's child. And here he was, wearing an expression of such steely control that Deborah knew in an instant he'd been told the truth and was still in the process of reeling from that truth. Which meant he could do anything, say anything, cause a scene, resort to violence. He was what they called a loose cannon. And the miserable fates—not to mention her husband's directions—had placed *her* in a position where she might have to deal with him.

She wanted to sink not only through the floor but directly through the earth as well. Where would she come out if she sank through the earth? China? The Himalayas? Bangladesh?

Luxford gave a curious glance to her camera bag. He said, "What's this? Have you news?"

Stone said, "Luxford, I want a word with you."

Luxford said over his shoulder, "You'll get it," and to Deborah, "Come to my office."

Stone wasn't about to be left in the lobby. When the lift doors slid open, he followed Deborah and Luxford inside. The security guard again made a movement indicating he'd intervene. Luxford held up a hand, said, "It's fine, Jerry," and punched a button for the eleventh floor.

They were alone in the lift. Luxford said to Deborah, "Well?"

She wondered how it would play: I need a sample of your printing so that my husband can assure himself you're not the kidnapper. That should be sufficient to make Alexander Stone go for the other man's throat. He was emanating enough antipathy to suggest discretion was in order.

She said, "Simon asked me to stop by. There's just a small detail that he wants to rule out."

Stone seemed to realise that her presence had a connection to his stepdaughter's disappearance. He said brusquely, "What do you know? What have you uncovered? Why the hell haven't we heard from you about what's going on?"

Deborah, flustered, said, "Simon spoke to your wife yesterday afternoon. She hasn't told . . . ?" Well, *obviously* she hasn't told him, you twit, Deborah lectured herself. She said, hoping she sounded like the voice of confidence, "Actually, he made a complete report to her of how things stand at her office. I mean, he went to her office. The report wasn't about her office." Wonderful, she thought. Perfectly professional. She used her teeth to pull in on her upper lip. Anything to keep it from flapping.

At the fifth floor, the lift doors opened and two men and a woman climbed aboard, so Deborah was saved from sinking deeper into verbal quicksand. They were having a conversation about politics, the woman saying quietly, "According to a reliable source," at which the men chuckled knowingly, which prompted her to say, "No. Listen. He was at a dinner in Downing Street. And the PM actually *told* someone during drinks that the public doesn't care who's stuffing whom where, just so long as taxes don't rise. Now, it was all *sotto voce*, but if Mitch can just get confirmation, we can—"

"Pam," Luxford said. The woman looked his way. "Later." She glanced from Luxford to his companions. She gave a small grimace of apology for her indiscretion. When the lift doors opened on the eleventh floor, she vanished into the newsroom.

Luxford led Deborah and Alexander Stone to his office, at the far side of the newsroom to the left of the lifts. A group with notebooks and papers in their hands were milling about near his secretary's desk, and as Luxford approached, a dumpy-looking man in a safari jacket came forward and said, "Den? What's—" He shot a glance at Deborah and Stone, but particularly at Deborah's camera bag, which he seemed to take as an omen of something. "I was about to run the news meeting without you."

"Push it back an hour," Luxford said.

"Den, is that wise? Can we afford another delay? Last night's was bad enough, but—"

Luxford directed Deborah and Stone into his office. He spun on his heel. "I've something to deal with, Rodney," he said. "We'll have the meeting in an hour. If the print run's delayed, the world will not end. Clear?"

"That's another day of paying overtime," Rodney noted.

"Yes. Another day." Luxford shut the door. "Now," he said to Deborah.

Stone intervened. "Listen to me, you bastard," he said quietly, and planted himself in Luxford's path to his desk. He was, Deborah saw, about four inches taller than *The Source* editor, but both men appeared equally fit. And Luxford didn't look like the type to quail when faced with an attempt at intimidation.

"Mr. Luxford," she said bravely. "Actually, it's only a formality, but what I need is—"

"What have you done with her?" Stone demanded. "What have you done with Charlie?"

Luxford didn't so much as flinch. "Evelyn's conclusion is wrong. Obviously, I wasn't able to convince her of that. But perhaps I can convince you. Sit down."

"Don't you bloody tell me—"

"Fine. Then stand. But get out of my way, because I'm not accustomed to speaking into someone's nostrils and I don't intend to become accustomed to that now."

Stone didn't back off. The two men were virtually eyeball to eyeball. A muscle worked in Stone's jaw. Luxford tensed in response. But his voice remained calm.

"Mr. Stone, hear me. I don't have Charlotte."

"Don't try to tell me that someone like you would bother to draw the line at abducting a ten-year-old."

"Then I won't," he said. "But I will say this. You don't know the first thing about what 'someone like me' is like, and unfortunately I've no time to shed any light on the subject for you."

Stone made a rough gesture at the wall next to the conference table. A line of framed front pages hung there. They represented some of *The Source*'s more lurid stories, spanning everything from a *ménage à trois* enjoyed by three putatively wholesome stars of a postwar television drama called—much to the newspaper's amusement—*No Home But This* to a delighted exposé of cellular phone calls placed by the Princess of Wales.

Stone said, "I don't need any more light shed. Your pathetic excuse for journalism is light enough."

"Fine." Luxford looked at his watch. "That should add to the brevity of our conversation. Why are you here? Can we get to the point, because I've work to do and Mrs. St. James to talk to."

Deborah, who had placed her camera case on a beige sofa that stood against the wall, seized the opportunity Luxford passed her way. She said, "Yes. Right. What I'm going to need is—"

"Types like you hide." Stone took an aggressive step closer to Luxford. "Behind their jobs, their secretaries, their public school voices. But I want you out in the open. Understand?"

"I've already told Evelyn that I'm willing to come out in the open. If she hasn't seen fit to make that clear to you, I don't know what I can do about the fact."

"You keep Eve out of this."

One of Luxford's eyebrows rose, barely a fraction's movement. He said, "Excuse me, Mr. Stone," and sidestepped the other man to go to his desk.

Deborah said hopefully, "Mr. Luxford, if I can—"

Stone caught Luxford's arm. "Where's Charlie?" he demanded.

Luxford's eyes fixed on Stone's rigid face. He said quietly, "Stand away from me. I recommend you don't do something you'll regret. I haven't taken Charlotte, and I have no idea where Charlotte is. As I explained to Evelyn yesterday afternoon, I have no reason to want our mutual past played out in the press. I have a wife and son who know nothing about Charlotte's existence, and believe me, I'd like to keep it that way despite what you and your wife might think. If you and Evelyn communicated on a more regular basis, perhaps you'd know—"

Stone increased his grip on Luxford's arm and jerked it roughly.

Deborah saw the editor's eyes narrow in response. "This isn't about Eve. Don't bring Eve into this."

"She's already into this, isn't she? It's her child we're talking about."

"And yours." Stone said the two words like an execration. He dropped his grip on Luxford's arm. The editor stepped past him and went to his desk. "What sort of man fathers a child and walks away from the fact, Luxford? What sort of man won't take responsibility for his past?"

Luxford punched a button on the monitor of a computer and scooped up a handful of messages. He riffled through these, set them aside, and did the same to a stack of unopened letters. He picked up a padded mailing envelope that lay beneath the letters and looked up to speak. "And it's the past you're more concerned about, isn't it?" he asked. "This isn't about the present at all."

"Why, you fucking—"

"Yes. Fucking. That's it. Tell me, Mr. Stone, what is it you're truly concerned about this afternoon? Is it Charlotte's disappearance or the fact I fucked her mother?"

Stone lunged. Deborah did likewise, astonishing herself with the speed of her decision to act. Stone made it to the desk. His hands shot out to grip Luxford. Deborah caught his left arm and yanked him away.

Stone spun to her, clearly having forgotten she was there. His fist was clenched. His arm was cocked. He swung, and Deborah tried to leap out of the way, but she wasn't quick enough. He caught her sharply on the side of the head. With one hard blow he sent her to the floor.

Above the ringing in her ears, Deborah heard cursing. Then Luxford's voice barked, "Get a security guard up here. Now. *Now.*"

She saw feet, the bottom of trouser legs. She heard Stone saying, "Oh Jesus. Fuck. Fuck."

She felt a hand on her back and another on her arm. She said, "No. It's all right. Really. I'm quite . . . It's nothing . . ."

The office door opened. Another male voice said, "Den? Den? Gosh, is there anything—"

"Get the hell out!"

The door closed.

Deborah lifted herself to a sitting position. She saw that Stone was the one assisting her. His face had gone to the colour of bread dough. He said, "I'm sorry. I didn't mean . . . Jesus. What's happening?"

"Move aside," Luxford said. "God damn it. I said move aside." He raised Deborah to her feet, led her to the sofa, and squatted before her to have a look at her face. He answered Stone's question. "What's happening is assault."

Deborah raised a hand to fend off the words. "No. No. Please. I was . . . I got in the way. He clearly didn't know . . ."

"He doesn't know sod all," Luxford snapped. "Here. Let me look at you. Have you hit your head?" His fingers went into her hair and moved with gentle, quick confidence across her skull. "Hurt anywhere?"

She shook her head. She was more shaken than hurt, although she assumed she would probably ache later. She was also embarrassed. She hated to be a cynosure—fading happily into the woodwork was more in her line—and her unthinking response to Stone's sudden leap had landed her directly where she didn't want to be. She used the moment to say what she had to say, feeling that Alexander Stone wouldn't be likely to fly off the handle a second time in five minutes. "Actually, I've come for a sample of your printing," she told *The Source* editor. "It's just a formality, but Simon wants to . . . You see, if he can just have a look at it."

Luxford nodded sharply. He didn't seem the least offended. He said, "Of course. I should have thought to give him a sample the other night. You're sure you're all right?"

She nodded and offered what she hoped was a convincing smile. Luxford got to his feet. Stone, she saw, had retreated to a conference table at the far side of the office. He'd pulled out a chair and sunk into it. His head was in his hands.

Luxford took a sheet of paper and began to write. The office door opened. The uniformed guard said, "Mr. Luxford? A problem?"

Luxford looked up. He took a moment to evaluate Stone before he said, "Stay close by, Jerry. I'll let you know if I need you." The guard disappeared. Luxford said to Stone, "I ought to have you ejected from the building. And I will—believe me—if you aren't prepared to listen."

Stone didn't raise his head. "I'll listen."

"Then hear me. Someone has Charlotte. Someone's threatened her life. Someone wants the truth about Evelyn, about me. I don't know who that someone is and I don't know why he's waited till now to use the thumbscrews. But the fact is he's doing it. We can either cooperate, bring in the police, or call his bluff. Which, I may tell you, I don't believe is a bluff in the first place. So you have two options as I see it, Stone. Either go home and convince your wife that this situation is deadly serious, or play the game her way and live with the consequences. I've done what I can."

Stone said dully, "Into your hands." He gave a muted, sardonic laugh.

"What?"

"I've played right into your hands." He raised his head. "Haven't I?"

Luxford's expression was incredulous.

Deborah said, "Mr. Stone, surely you see that—"

"Don't bother," Luxford interposed. "He's found his villain. They both have. Save your breath."

He turned his attention to the padded envelope he'd been holding. It was stapled shut, and he ripped it open. He said, "We have nothing more to say, Mr. Stone. Can you see yourself out or do you need assistance?" He upended the envelope without waiting for a response. He stared at its contents. Deborah saw him swallow.

She got to her feet, rather unsteadily, and said, "Mr. Luxford?" and then, "No. Don't touch it," when she saw what lay among the rest of his mail.

It was a small tape recorder.

10

RODNEY ARONSON KEPT ONE EYE on his computer screen and the other on Luxford's office door, no mean feat since his own office was on the other side of the newsroom from Luxford's and the intervening space was taken up by a score of desks, filing cabinets, computer terminals, and the constantly moving bodies of *The Source* journalists. The rest of the news meeting members had drifted off to other responsibilities once Luxford had postponed the conference for an hour. If they found the editor's order for a delay a curiosity, none of them had mentioned it. But Rodney had lingered. He'd got a good look at the face of the man who'd been accompanying Luxford, and there was something about his expression of barely controlled hostility that suggested to Rodney that he hang about Miss Wallace's compulsively neat cubby-hole on the off chance something of interest occurred.

Something *had* occurred, but when Rodney responded to the sound of raised voices and crashing bodies by throwing open the editor's office door in a display of his deep and abiding concern for Luxford's safety, the last thing he expected to see was the red-haired woman sprawled out on the floor. Mr. Hostility had been lurching over her, which suggested that he was the one who'd put her there. What in hell was going on?

Once Luxford—always the personification of gratitude—summarily ordered him out of the office, Rodney considered the possibilities. Red-Hair was a photojournalist to be sure. There was no other explanation for the camera bag she had with her. She'd probably come to sell some photographs to the paper. *The Source* bought pictures from free-lancers on a regular basis, so it wasn't unusual for a photographer to show up with a clutch of dandy and potentially embarrassing snaps of one notable figure or another, from a member of the Royal Family looking downright unroyal, to a political figure making undignified whoopie. But free-lancers with pictures to sell didn't generally peddle them to the chief editor of the paper. They didn't even meet with him. They met with the photo editor or one of his assistants.

So what did it mean, Luxford squiring Red-Hair into his office? No, that wasn't quite it, was it? It was Luxford *hustling* Red-Hair into his office. And Luxford making damn sure that no one had a chance to talk to her. Or to Mr. Hostility, for that matter. And who the hell was *he?*

Since Hostility'd scored a neat TKO against the redhead, Rodney could only assume that the man was determined to keep her photos out of the paper. Which suggested he was somebody. But who? He didn't look like somebody. He didn't look like anybody. Which itself suggested that he was featured in the photos with a somebody whose honour he was there to protect.

Quite a charming thought, that. Perhaps the days of chivalry weren't dead. Which did make one wonder what Mr. Hostility was doing decking a woman. By all rights, he should have simply decked Luxford.

Rodney had been keeping his eye on dear Den since the Harrods rendezvous. He'd spent last evening at *The Source*, where he'd seen to it that Luxford's nerves were kept on edge by dropping by his office every hour or so and making anxious noises about when the presses were going to run the morning's edition. Luxford told him twice to go home, but Rodney hung about, sniffing round for an indication of why Luxford was pushing the print delay to the danger point. It was his duty to keep an eye on things, wasn't it? If Luxford was cracking as it seemed he was cracking, then someone had to be there to sweep up the pieces when he broke apart.

Rodney decided that the delay had to do with the meeting at Harrods. He decided that he had misunderstood that meeting altogether. While he'd first assumed that Luxford was bonking the woman he'd met, he'd had to shift his thinking round when the printing delay fell immediately upon the assignation's heels.

It had to do with a story, of course. Which—setting aside that tender moment of physical contact in the restaurant—did make a hell of a lot more sense than an affair. After all, Luxford had nightly—not to mention morningly and afternoonly—access to the statuesque charms of the Fabulous Fiona. The woman in Harrods had been something of a moderate looker, but she was nothing in comparison to the Wondrous Wife.

Besides, she was in the Government, which made it even more likely that she had a story to tell. And if that was the case, then it had to be one hell of a page-turner involving the biggest of bigwigs: the Chancellor of the Exchequer, the Home Secretary, maybe even the PM himself. The most stupendous stories usually involved the high-level bonking of low-level bonkees, especially if secrets pertaining to national security were part of the pre- or post-coital encounter. And it did rather make sense that a female member of the Government, her feminist nature boiling with outrage at the callous use of her sisters, had decided to play the whistle-blower. If she was going to blow the gaff about someone important, if she wanted to ensure her safety and her anonymity, and most important if she was able to make a connection with a newspaper's editor, why not take the story directly to him?

Of course, of course. Hadn't Luxford been pounding away at the keyboard of his computer when Rodney returned from Harrods yesterday? And what else could he have been holding up the presses for if not for confirmation of a story? Luxford was no fool. He wouldn't run an exposé of anyone's experiences in the seamier side of pinch-and-plunge without at least two independent confirmations. Since the source was female, she was also potentially a woman scorned. Luxford was too wily a newsman to get caught in the middle of someone's thirst for vengeance. So he'd waited, he'd held up the printing of the paper, and when she hadn't been able to produce anyone to verify her accusations, he'd killed his own story.

Which still didn't answer the question of who the devil she was.

Since he'd returned from Harrods, Rodney had been using his free time to scroll religiously through back issues of *The Source*, looking for a clue to the woman's identity. If she was a member of the Government, surely they'd done a story involving her at one time or another. He'd given up the project at half past eleven last night, but he'd gone back to it this morning whenever time allowed. Shortly before noon, while in the midst of Mitch Corsico's report on the latest developments in the Rent Boy Rumba (Larnsey had met at length with the PM; he would make no comment upon exiting Number Ten; Daffy Dukane had taken on an agent who was willing to negotiate terms for an exclusive interview but it was going to be costly), Rodney had latched on to a Corsico remark about "doing some browsing in the library" and mentally smacked himself on the forehead. What the hell was he doing sifting through back issues of the newspaper for a clue when all he had to do to uncover the identity of the woman in Harrods was to stroll down three floors to the tabloid's library and flip through *The Times Guide to the House of Commons* to see if Luxford's source was indeed an MP and not some civil servant with access to a government car?

And there she was, smiling up from page 357 with her overlarge spectacles and her overlong fringe. Eve Bowen, the MP from Marylebone and Undersecretary of State at the Home Office. Rodney whistled appreciatively at the information. She was indeed a moderate looker but, the Fab Fi aside, it was even more obvious now that Luxford hadn't been meeting with her because of those looks.

If she was a Junior Minister, Bowen was ranked somewhere round third to fifth in importance at the Home Office. That put her into the regular company of movers and shakers of the highest importance. What she was offering Luxford must be pure gold, Rodney decided. So how the hell was he going to find out what it was so that he could pass the information on to the chairman in an aside that would enhance Rodney's persona as a ruthless newshound, a sagacious editor, and a beloved confidant of the mighty? Aside from reading Luxford's mind for the code word that would give him access to Luxford's computer terminal, where with any luck he could find the story the editor had been writing the previous night, Rodney didn't have a clue. But he'd made progress with the discovery of Eve Bowen's identity, and there was cause for celebration in that.

Her identity was a sure first step. With that as a starting point, Rodney knew he could call in a few debts that were owed him from several of the lobby correspondents at Parliament. He could get on the phone with one or more of them and see what he could dig up. He'd have to be careful how he did it. The last thing he wanted was to set another paper on the trail of a story that *The Source* was about to break. But handled with finesse . . . somehow connecting his curiosity to current events . . . perhaps revealing the paper's intention to examine the role of women in Parliament . . . even going so far as to claim he was seeking the female reaction to the male MPs' recent rash of trouser dropping . . . Surely he could uncover a detail that might mean nothing to a lobby journalist but everything to Rodney who knew about Bowen's private meeting with Luxford and therefore who would also know how to interpret an aberration in her behaviour that might otherwise go disregarded by others.

Yes, yes. This was the answer. He reached for his Filofax. Sarah Happleshort popped into his doorway, unwrapping a stick of Wrigley's spearmint.

"You're on," she said. "A star is born."

He looked at her blankly, his thoughts taken up with which one of the lobby correspondents would most likely be taken in by his call.

"The understudy's dream has come true." Sarah's elbow jutted out in the general direction of Luxford's office. "Dennis had an emergency. He's left for the day. You're in charge. Do you want the crew in here for the news meeting? Or shall we use his office?"

Rodney blinked. Sarah's meaning became clear. The mantle of power settled over his shoulders, and he took a moment to savour its warmth. Then he did his best to look appropriately concerned and said, "An emergency? Not something wrong with the family? His wife? His son?"

"Couldn't say. He left with the man and woman he came in with. D'you know who they are? No? Hmmm." She looked over her shoulder and across the newsroom. Her next words were thoughtful. "Something's up, I expect. What d'you say?"

The last thing Rodney wanted was Happleshort's quivering nose on the scent. "I say we have a paper to get out. We'll meet in Den's office. Gather the others. Give me ten minutes."

When she left to do his bidding—how he liked to think of it in those lofty terms—Rodney went back to his Filofax. He leafed through it quickly. Ten minutes, he thought, was more than enough time to place the phone call that would secure his future.

—⁂—

What Helen and Deborah had described to him as squats were really more like squats in the making, St. James discovered. They sat in a derelict row on George Street, a short distance away from a chi-chi–looking Japanese restaurant possessing the rare luxury of a car park behind it. St. James and Helen left the MG there.

George Street was typical of modern London, a street offering everything from the dignified presence of the United Bank of Kuwait to abandoned tenements waiting for someone to invest in their future. The particular tenements that he and Helen walked to had once been shops with three floors of flats above them. Their ground floor display windows and their glass doors had been replaced with sheets of metal over which had been nailed a diagonal striping of boards. But the windows above street level were not boarded, nor were they broken, which made the flats above the shops desirable as squats.

As St. James looked the buildings over, Helen said, "There's no way someone could get in from the front."

"Not with the way they've been boarded up. But no one would chance going in through the front anyway. The street's too busy. There's too much risk of someone seeing, remembering, and later phoning the authorities."

"Phoning . . . ?" Helen looked from the tenements to St. James. Her voice quickened with excitement. "Simon, you don't think Charlotte's here, do you? In one of these buildings?"

He was frowning at the buildings. He didn't respond until she said his name and repeated the questions. Then it was only to say, "We need to talk to him, Helen. If he exists."

"The vagrant? Two different people in Cross Keys Close mentioned having seen him. How on earth could he not exist?"

"I agree they saw someone," St. James said. "But didn't anything about Mr. Pewman's description of the man strike you as odd?"

"Just the fact that he could describe him so accurately."

"There's that. But didn't the description seem remarkably generic, exactly what one would expect a dosser to look like? The duffel bag, the old khaki clothes, the knitted cap, the hair, the weathered face. Particularly the face. The memorable face."

Helen's own face brightened. "Are you saying the man was in a disguise?"

"What better way to recce the area for a few days?"

"But of course. Of *course*. He could rustle through rubbish bins and keep his eye peeled for Charlotte's movements. But he wouldn't be able to snatch Charlotte dressed like that, would he? She'd have been terrified. She'd have caused a scene which someone would have remembered. So when he knew her comings and goings well enough, he'd drop the disguise altogether and snatch her then, wouldn't he?"

"But he would have needed a place to change. To change without being seen. To become the tramp and then unbecome him when it was time to take Charlotte."

"The squats," she said.

"It's a possibility. Shall we have a look around?"

Although squatters were protected by law in the country, there was a procedure one had to go through in order to avoid being charged with breaking and entering private property. A squatter was required to change the locks on the doors and to put up a sign declaring his intention of occupying an abandoned residence. He was also required to do this prior to police intervention. But someone who didn't wish to draw attention to himself, someone who especially didn't want to be an object of interest to the local police, would not seize the rights to a building or a flat in the typical manner. Rather, he would make his takeover as surreptitious as possible, gaining access to a building through a less conventional means.

"Let's try round the back," St. James said.

The row of buildings was offset at either end by an alley. St. James and Helen chose the closest one and followed it to a small square. One side of the square was taken up by a multi-storey car park, two sides by the backs of buildings on other streets, one side by the back gardens of the tenements on George Street. These back gardens were walled in, enclosed by at least twelve feet of sooty bricks with their tops overgrown by whatever straggling plantlife was able to flourish without a gardener's care. Unless a squatter had come prepared with rock-climbing equipment in order to clamber over the wall, the only way in appeared to be at the near end of the alley.

Here, two unlocked wooden gates opened into a small brick-walled courtyard, one side of which comprised the looming wall of one of the back gardens. This courtyard was filled with the detritus of previous inhabitants of the building: mattresses, box springs, dustbins, a hosepipe, an old perambulator, a broken ladder.

The ladder looked promising. St. James dragged it out from behind one of the mattresses. But its wood was rotten and its rungs—where they existed at all—didn't look as if they'd support a child's weight, let alone the weight of a fully grown man. So St. James discarded it and considered instead a large abandoned and empty dumpster. It sat behind one of the courtyard's wooden gates.

"It's on wheels," Helen noted. "Shall we?"

"I think so," St. James said.

The dumpster was rusty. It didn't look as if its wheels would turn. But when St. James and Helen positioned themselves on either side of it and began to heave it towards the garden wall, they found it rolled quite easily, as if it had been oiled for the purpose.

Once it was in position, St. James could see that the dumpster would easily provide a means of scrambling over the wall. He tested the strength of the metal sides and the lid. They appeared sound. Then he saw Helen watching him uneasily, a frown drawing a line between her eyebrows. He knew what she was thinking: Not exactly an activity for a man in your condition, Simon. She wouldn't say it, though. She wouldn't want to run the risk of wounding him with a reminder of his disability.

"It's the only way in," he responded to her unspoken concern. "I can manage it, Helen."

"But how are you going to get back over the wall from the other side?"

"There'll be something in the building I can use. If there isn't, you'll have to go for help." She looked doubtful about this plan. He said again, "It's the only way."

She thought about it, apparently accepted the idea, and yielded, saying, "Let me at least help you get over. All right?"

He gauged the height of the wall and the height of the dumpster. He nodded his agreement to her modification of his plan. He heaved himself awkwardly to the top of the dumpster, assisted by an upper-body strength which had increased over the years since his lower body had been disabled. Once standing on the lid, he turned back to Helen and pulled her up to join him. From where they stood, they could reach the top of the brick wall, but they could not see over it. Helen was right, St. James realised. He was going to need her assistance.

He cupped his hands for one of her feet. "You first," he said. "I'll need your help to get to the top." He gave her a boost. She gripped the mound of mortar that fashioned the wall's cap. With a grunt and a heave, she straddled it. Once in a secure position, she took a moment to examine the back of the building and its garden.

"This is it," she said.

"What?"

"Someone's been here." Her voice was tinged with the thrill of the chase. "There's an old sideboard that's been upended next to the wall inside. So someone could get in and out easily. Here." She extended her hand to him. "Come have a look. There's a chair as well, for getting down off the sideboard. And there's even a path that's been tramped through the weeds. It looks fairly fresh to me."

With his right hand on the wall and his left gripped in hers, St. James strained his way up to join her. It was no easy feat, despite his words of assurance to her a moment earlier. One dead leg encased in a brace however lightweight did nothing to make his life easy. His forehead was damp with perspiration when he'd finally completed the activity.

He saw what she was talking about, however. The sideboard—weathered enough to look as if it had spent years in the back garden even while the building was still occupied—appeared to have been dragged from beneath one of the windows, in part creating the path through the weeds that Helen had mentioned. And the path did indeed look fresh. Where it cut through shrubbery, the broken ends of the branches of overgrown bushes had not yet browned with exposure to the weather.

"Pay dirt," Helen murmured.

"What?"

She smiled. "Nothing. There's a clear way out of here if we use the sideboard. Shall I join you, then?"

He nodded, glad of her company. She lowered herself to the up-ended sideboard and from there to the chair that stood next to it. St. James followed her.

The garden was little more than a square measuring twenty feet on all sides, and it was densely overgrown with weeds, with ivy, and with broom. This shrub had apparently flourished under a regime of neglect: A blaze of yellow blooms burned like sunlight along three sides of the garden's perimeter and next to the building's back door.

This, they found, was a security door, a single piece of steel cut to fit the frame and bolted straight into the wood. There was neither doorknob to turn nor hinges to remove. The only way to get through it and into the building beyond it was to unbolt the entire affair.

The back windows on the ground floor, however, had not been made so secure. While they were boarded on the inside, their glass was broken on the outside and, upon inspection, St. James found that one of the boards had been loosened enough so that without too much trouble someone could easily climb in and out. Helen fetched the chair as he worked the board out of their way.

She said, "With the door closed up like that, one wonders why the owners didn't do more with the windows."

St. James used the chair to lift himself to the sill, saying, "Perhaps they thought the door would be discouragement enough. I can't think that someone would want to continually use this as a means of entrance and exit."

"But as a temporary measure . . ." Helen spoke thoughtfully. "It *is* perfect, isn't it?"

"It's that," St. James said.

The window, he found, gave into what seemed to be a storage room for whatever business would occupy the ground floor of the building. It contained cupboards, shelves, and a dusty linoleum floor across which—even in the dim light—he could see footprints.

St. James eased from the window to the floor, waited for Helen to join him, and slipped a torch from his pocket. He directed it along the path of the footprints, which went towards the front of the building.

The air in the storeroom was tinctured with the odours of mildew and wood rot. As they carefully picked their way along a corridor that led to the front of the building, they became aware of additional smells: the throat-closing foetid scent of excrement and urine seeping out of a lavatory where a long-unflushed toilet stood, the sharp smell of plaster emanating from holes that had been kicked into the corridor's walls, the sickly sweet odour of a dead body's decay. This last appeared to be rising from a partially eaten rat that lay at the foot of the stairs, where the storeroom behind joined the shop in front.

The footprints, they saw, did not go into the shop, which was as dark as nighttime because of its metal-covered windows and door. Rather, they climbed the stairs. Before climbing them in turn, St. James flashed his torchlight round the room that would have served as the shop. There was nothing to be seen, aside from a toppled magazine rack, an ancient refrigerated storage bin missing its lid, a collection of yellowed newspapers, and perhaps half a dozen crushed cardboard boxes.

St. James and Helen turned back to the stairs. They followed the footprints, Helen sidestepping the dead rat with a shudder and compulsively gripping St. James's arm.

"Lord, are those *mice* moving in the walls?" she whispered.

"Rats, more likely."

"It's hard to imagine someone actually staying here."

"It's not the Savoy," St. James admitted. He climbed to the first floor, where the unboarded windows allowed the late afternoon sunlight to illuminate the rooms.

There appeared to be one flat on each of the upper floors. The footprints they were following, which seemed to come and go and constantly overlap on the stairs, led them past the first floor flat, where a glance inside its partially unhinged door showed them little more than a room with graffiti spray-painted onto the walls—featuring "Kop Killers Deuce Two" in large blue letters surrounded by hieroglyphs ostensibly translatable only by fellow graffiti artists—and orange carpeting ripped up in great patches. There was little else helpful in this flat, aside from an astounding array of cigarette ends, crumpled cigarette packets, empty bottles, beer cans, and fast-food paper cups and bags, as well as a gaping hole in the ceiling which told them that the lighting fixture had been nicked.

The second floor flat was much the same, with the variation being the graffiti artists' choice of spray paint. Here the colour was red, which had apparently inspired the painters to use more blood-thirsty imagery along with their hieroglyphs. "Kop Killers Deuce Two" was accompanied by drawings of disembowelled policemen. Here also the carpeting was in tatters and littered with rubbish. A sofa and armchair that stood on either side of the kitchen door sported burn holes in them, one large enough to qualify as evidence of a bonafide fire.

The footprints continued to the top of the building. They went into the final flat where they were absorbed by what carpeting was left there. This, like the other two flats', was orange and while it had been pulled away from the walls at one time, more recently it had been rolled back into place. It wasn't ripped, but it bore ancient stains in a variety of hues suggesting everything from red wine to dog urine.

Like the other two flats', the door was standing open, but it was still on its hinges. Additionally, a hasp was fixed onto its exterior, its hinge on the door frame and its staple on the door itself. St. James fingered the hinge reflectively as Helen moved past him into the room. The hasp looked new: It was scratchless and clean.

He joined Helen inside the flat. The hasp suggested an accompanying padlock nearby, and he glanced about for it. He saw that unlike the two flats they had already seen, this one was free of rubbish although its walls bore graffiti not much different to the other flats'. There was no lock lying on the floor or on any of the shelves of the metal bookcase fixed to one wall, so he went into the kitchen to see if he could locate a lock there.

He looked through drawers and cupboards, finding a tin cup, a tine-bent fork, some loose nails, and two dirty jars. Water dripped from the tap in the kitchen sink, and he turned it on to note that the water ran perfectly clear, not cloudy or brownish as if it had lain in rusting pipes for a year or two.

He returned to the sitting room as Helen emerged from the bedroom. Her face was bright with discovery.

She said, "Simon, have you noticed—"

"Yes. Someone's been here. And not just to prowl about but to stay."

"So you were right. About the vagrant."

"It could be a coincidence."

"I don't think so." She gestured back the way she had come, saying, "The mirror in the bathroom's been cleaned. Not all of it, but a section. Big enough to see one's reflection in." She seemed to be waiting for a reaction because when St. James didn't give her one, she continued impatiently. "He'd need a mirror, wouldn't he, if he was making himself up to look like a tramp?"

It was a possibility, but St. James was reluctant to conclude upon so little evidence that they had tracked down the vagrant's hideaway upon their first try. He went to the window in the sitting room. It was generally filthy, save for a quarter of one of its four panes. This had been wiped clear.

St. James peered through the glass. He considered the contrast between this flat and the others, considered the footprints, considered the hasp and the suggestion it made of a lock being used recently on the flat door. It was clear that no one was squatting here permanently—the absence of furniture, of cooking utensils, of clothing, and of food gave testimony to that. But that someone had dossed here briefly and recently. . . . The replacement of the carpeting, the water in the pipes, the complete absence of rubbish, all urged him to that conclusion.

"I agree that someone's been here," he said to Helen as he gazed through the cleared spot in the window. He saw that the window faced George Street. He also saw that on an angle, the window lined up with the entrance to the car park of the Japanese restaurant where he'd left his MG. He shifted his position to look in that direction. "But as to whether it's actually your vagrant, Helen, I couldn't—" He stopped. He squinted at what he beheld just beyond the car park, one street to the north. It couldn't be, he thought. It was hardly possible. And yet there it was.

"What is it?" Helen asked.

He reached for her blindly and pulled her to the window. He stood her in front of him, positioned her head towards the Japanese restaurant, and rested his hands on her shoulders. "Do you see the restaurant? The car park beyond it?"

"Yes. Why?"

"Look beyond the car park. Do you see the other street?"

"Of course I see it. My vision's quite as good as yours."

"And across that street, the building? Do you see it?"

"Which . . . oh, the brick building? With the steps going up? I see the front doors and a few of the windows." She turned back to him. "Why? What is it?"

"Blandford Street, Helen. And that—through this window, the only cleaned window in the entire flat, mind you—is a very clear view of St. Bernadette's School."

Her eyes widened. She whirled back to the window. "Simon!" she said.

—⁂—

After leaving Helen in Onslow Square, St. James found a spot for the MG on Lordship Place and used his shoulder against the weather-worn gate that led into the back garden of his house on Cheyne Row. Cotter, he discovered, was busy in the kitchen, scrubbing new potatoes at the sink with Peach sitting at his feet ever hopeful of a handout. The dog looked in St. James's direction and wagged her tail in greeting, but she clearly believed that her current position at Cotter's feet was the one more likely to meet with edible success. The household cat—a large grey called Alaska who was approximately twice the size of the miniature dachshund—lolled on the windowsill above the sink and acknowledged St. James's arrival with typical feline ennui: The tip of his tail lifted and fell, whereupon he returned to the state of semi-somnolence that was his principal characteristic.

"About time, if you ask me," Cotter said to St. James, attacking a bad spot on one of the potatoes.

St. James glanced at the rusty-faced clock above the cooker. It was not yet time for dinner. He said, "A problem?"

Cotter harrumphed. He used his potato peeler to indicate the stairs. "Deb's brought two blokes 'ome with her. Been 'ere more'n an hour, they 'ave. More like two. They've done tea. They've done sherry. They've done more tea. They've done more sherry. One of them's wanted to leave, but Deb's not having any of that. They've been waiting for you."

"Who are they?" St. James joined him at the sink where he took a handful of chopped carrots and munched on them.

"That's for dinner," Cotter warned him. He plopped the new potato into the water and reached for another. "One of them's that bloke from the other night. The one'oo came with David."

"Dennis Luxford."

"The other, I don't know. Some bloke looking like a stick of dynamite getting ready to blast. They been at each other—both those blokes—since they got 'ere. You know the sort o' thing. Talking through their teeth like they mean to be civil but only because Deb won't leave the room and let them go at it like they want."

St. James popped the rest of the carrots into his mouth and climbed the stairs, wondering what he'd let his wife in for when he'd asked her to get a sample of Luxford's printing. It had seemed an uncomplicated enough task. So what had happened?

He discovered soon enough when he found them in the study, along with the remains of afternoon tea and sherry. Luxford was speaking to someone on the phone at St. James's desk, Deborah was nervously kneading the knuckles of her right hand with the fingers of her left, and the third man—who turned out to be Alexander Stone—was watching Luxford from his position at the bookshelves with such undisguised loathing on his face that St. James wondered how Deborah had managed to keep him under control.

She jumped to her feet, saying, "Simon. Thank goodness, my love," with a fervency that told him how rattled she was.

Luxford was saying tersely, "No, I'm not giving approval. Hold it up till you hear from me. . . . This is not a moot decision, Rod. Is that clear, or do I need to spell out the consequences if you go your own way?"

Alexander Stone said, apparently to Deborah, "Finally. Now play that thing for him so we can blow Luxford's game."

Deborah hastily brought St. James into the picture. As Luxford concluded his conversation by abruptly slamming down the phone on whoever it was on the other end of the line, Deborah went to the desk for a padded mailing envelope. She said to her husband, "Mr. Luxford received this this afternoon."

"Be accurate with the facts, if you don't mind," Stone said. "That was on Luxford's desk this afternoon. It could have been placed there anytime. By anyone."

"Don't let's go through this again," Luxford said. "My secretary gave you the information, Mr. Stone. It was delivered by messenger at one o'clock."

"A messenger you could have hired yourself."

"For God's sake." Luxford sounded monumentally tired.

"We didn't actually touch it." Deborah handed the envelope to her husband and watched him glance inside at the tape recorder. "But we did play it when we saw what it was. I used an unsharpened pencil to press the start button. The wood part, not the rubber." She added this latter explanation with a flush, saying in a lower voice, "Was that the best way? I wasn't entirely certain, but I did think we ought to at least know if the recording related in some way."

St. James said, "Well done," and fished in his pocket for his latex gloves. He donned them, pulled the recorder from the envelope, and played its message.

A reedy child's voice spoke. "*Cito—*"

"Jesus." Stone turned to the bookshelves and reached for a volume at random.

"*This man here says you c'n get me out. He says you're s'posed to tell everyone a story. He says you're to tell the truth. He says you're a real fine bloke and no one knows and you're s'posed to tell the truth so everyone will know. If you tell the proper story, he says you'll save me, Cito.*"

At the bookshelves, Stone raised a fist to his eyes. He lowered his head.

On the tape, there was a barely audible click and the voice continued. "*Cito, I had to make this tape in order that he would give me some juice 'cause I was so thirsty.*" Another small click. "*D'you know what story you're s'posed to tell? I said to him that you don't tell stories. I said to*" *him that Mrs. Maguire tells stories. But he says you know what story to tell.''* An additional click. *''I've only got a blanket, and I haven't got a loo. But there's bricks.''* Click. *''A maypole.''* Click. The tape ended abruptly.

"This is Charlotte's voice?" St. James asked.

Stone said in answer, speaking to the shelves, "You fucker, Luxford. I'm going to kill you before we're through."

St. James held up his hand to prevent Luxford from responding. He played the tape a second time. He said, "You can hear it's been edited, but inexpertly."

"So what?" Stone demanded. "We know who made it."

St. James went on. "We can assume one of two possibilities: Either the kidnapper doesn't have access to the right equipment or he doesn't care that we know it's been edited."

"The bricks and the maypole?" Deborah asked.

"Left in to confuse us, I dare say. Charlotte thinks she's giving her stepfather a clue to her whereabouts. But the kidnapper knows the clue won't help. Because she isn't where she thinks she is." He said to Stone, "Damien Chambers told me she calls you Cito."

Stone nodded, still facing the shelves.

"Since she's speaking to you on it, the kidnapper obviously hasn't yet told her who her father really is. We can assume he provided her with the basic contents of the message she was to relay: Her father must openly tell the truth to gain her release. She thinks he means you're to tell the truth, not Mr. Luxford."

Stone shoved the volume he'd taken from the bookshelves back into place. "Don't tell me you're going to fall for this shit?" he demanded of St. James incredulously.

"What I'm going to do is assume, for the moment, that the tape is genuine," St. James explained. "You agree it's Charlotte's voice."

"Of course it's her voice. He's got her somewhere. He's had her make the tape. And now we're to crumble and dance to his tune. Jesus Christ. Just look at the envelope if you don't believe me. His name. The newspaper's name. The street. Nothing else. No stamps. No postmarks. Nothing."

"There wouldn't necessarily be either if it was delivered by messenger."

"Or if he 'delivered' it himself. Or had it delivered by whoever's in this with him." Stone left the bookshelves and came to the sofa where he stood at its back, gripping it. He said, "Look at him. Just bloody God damn *look* at him. You know who he is. You know what he is. You know what he wants."

"I want Charlotte's safety," Luxford said.

"You want your fucking story. Your story. Eve's."

St. James intervened, saying, "Upstairs please. To the lab," and then quietly to his wife, "You've managed heroically, my love. Thank you." She gave him a tremulous smile and slipped from the room, obviously grateful to be out of the mess.

St. James took the tape recorder, the envelope, and the sample of Luxford's writing to the top floor of the house. The other men followed him. The tension between them was palpable. Feeling it like a throbbing fog, St. James marvelled at the fact that Deborah had successfully coped as long as she had done with the two men's obvious need to beat each other to a pulp.

"What's this all about?" Stone demanded.

"Eliminating a few of my concerns," St. James responded. He flipped on the overhead lights of the lab and went to one of the grey steel cupboards, where he pulled out an ink pad and half a dozen heavy white cards. He set these on one of the worktables, adding to them a jar of powder, a large fluffy brush, and the small torch he'd carried in his pocket that day.

"You first, please," he said to Dennis Luxford, who was leaning against the jamb of the laboratory door as Alexander Stone prowled among the worktables, scowling at the mass of St. James's equipment. "Then Mr. Stone."

"What?" Stone asked.

"Fingerprints. Merely a formality, but one I'd like to get out of the way. Mr. Luxford . . . ?"

Dennis Luxford shot Stone a long look before he walked to the worktable and allowed St. James to take his fingerprints. It was a look that communicated his continued and complete cooperation in addition to his having nothing to hide.

St. James said, "Mr. Stone . . . ?"

"Why the hell—"

"As he said," Luxford commented while he wiped the ink from his fingers, "we're eliminating his concerns."

Stone hissed, "Shit," under his breath, but he came forward and allowed himself to be fingerprinted as well.

Having taken their prints, St. James turned to the tape recorder. He examined it first with the torch's light, looking for patent prints that would show themselves when the recorder was held at the appropriate angle. He popped the tape from inside the cassette and did the same. Nothing showed in the light.

While the other two men watched from opposite ends of the worktable, he dipped his brush into the powder—he'd chosen red as the most workable contrast to the black recorder itself—and dusted it lightly, one side at a time.

"It's been wiped clean," he commented when no prints became visible under the powder.

He went through the same process with the tiny cassette. Again, nothing emerged.

"So what bloody concerns are we eliminating?" Stone demanded. "He's not a fool. He's not going to leave his prints on anything."

St. James made a noise of agreement in his throat. "The first concern's been addressed, then, hasn't it? He isn't a fool." He flipped the recorder so that its back was exposed. He slid open the cover of the battery compartment, removed it, and laid it on the table. Gently, using a scalpel that he took from a drawer, he removed the batteries as well. These he set on a sheet of white paper. He took the torch and directed it both upon the back side of the battery compartment's cover and upon the two batteries themselves. He smiled at what he saw. "At least not a complete fool," he said. "But then, no one actually thinks of everything."

"Prints?" Luxford asked.

"One very nice patent on the back of the cover. Some partials on the batteries." He used the powder again. The other men stood silently as he dusted, brushing carefully in the direction of the flow of the print, removing excess powder with a puff of breath. He kept his eyes on the prints—admiring them, studying them—as he reached for the pressure-wound tape. The back of the cover, he knew, would be easy to work with. The batteries would prove more difficult.

He carefully pressed the tape onto the prints, making certain he was leaving no pockets of air. Then he pressed harder, using his thumb on the cover of the battery compartment, using a pencil's rubber on the batteries themselves. He lifted the tape in one motion and then pressed the prints onto the extra cards he'd taken from the cupboard. He quickly labelled them.

He indicated the print that had come from the back of the battery cover. He pointed out the ridges and the fact that they flowed up and inward. He said, "Thumbprint, right hand. The others—from the batteries—it's harder to say because they're partials. I'd guess index finger and thumb."

St. James compared them to Stone's first. He used a magnifying glass, more for effect than for anything else because he could see they were not his prints. He went on to Luxford's with much the same results. The whorls on all three of the thumbprints—Stone's, Luxford's, and the print from the recorder—were completely different, one plain, one accidental, and the other double looped.

Stone seemed to read St. James's conclusion from his face. He said, "You can't be surprised. He's not in this alone. He can't be."

St. James made no immediate reply. Instead, he took the sample of Luxford's printing and compared it to the notes he and Eve Bowen had received. He took his time about studying the letters, the spaces between words, the small peculiarities. Again, he could see no point of comparison.

He raised his head. He said, "Mr. Stone, I want you to see reason because you're the only one who's going to be able to convince your wife. If the tape recording hasn't convinced you of the urgency of—"

"Jesus Christ." Stone's voice was filled more with wonder than with outrage. "He's got you as well. But that's no surprise. He's the one who hired you in the first place. So what else could we expect but that you'd support his claim to be uninvolved?"

"For God's sake, Stone, see reason," Luxford said.

"I see reason just fine," Stone replied. "You're out to ruin my wife and you've found the means to do it. As well as the personnel to help you carry it out. This"—a jerk of his thumb to encompass the room— "is all part of the pretence."

"If you believe that, go to the police," St. James said.

"Of course." Stone smiled without humour. "You've set us up so that's our only recourse. And all of us know where bringing in the police will take us. Right to the newspapers. Right where Luxford wants us. All of this—the notes, the tape recording, the fingerprints—is nothing more than part of a trail we're meant to follow, one that's intended to lead us to play Luxford's game. Eve and I won't do it."

"With Charlotte's life hanging in the balance?" Luxford said. "God in heaven, man, you must see at this point that you can't take the risk that some maniac will kill her."

Stone spun in his direction. Luxford's stance changed swiftly, in preparation.

St. James said, "Mr. Stone, hear me. If Mr. Luxford wanted to throw us off the track, he wouldn't have arranged for someone to leave a single fine thumbprint on the inside of the tape recorder. He would have arranged to leave prints all over it. That print on the recorder—as well as the ones on the batteries—tells us that the kidnapper made a simple mistake. He didn't buy fresh batteries when he wanted Charlotte to record her message. He merely tested the ones that were in there already and forgot that when he first put them in—however long ago that was—he would have left his prints on them and on the back of the compartment's cover. That's what happened. He used gloves for the rest. He wiped the cassette and the recorder clean. And I'd be willing to bet that if we test the kidnapping notes for fingerprints as well—which we can do, although it'll take more time than I believe we have—we'll find only Mr. Luxford's and mine on his and only your wife's on hers. Which will take us nowhere. Which will cause delay. Which, whether you want to hear it or not, will put your stepdaughter's life at greater risk. I'm not suggesting that you urge your wife to allow Mr. Luxford to run his story in the paper. I am suggesting that you urge your wife to phone the authorities.''

"It's one and the same," Stone said.

Luxford seemed to snap. His fist hit the worktable. "I've had ten years to ruin your wife," he said. "Ten God damn years when I could have slapped her face on the front page of two different papers and humiliated the hell out of her. But I haven't done it. Have you ever wondered why?''

"The time wasn't right.''

"Listen to me! You've said you know what I am. All right. You know what I am. I'm a man of absolutely no compunction. I don't need the God damn time to be right. If I'd wanted to run the story of my relationship with Evelyn, I would have run it without a second thought. I've no respect for her. Her politics revolt me. I know what she is, and believe me I'd love to expose her to the world. But I haven't. I've wanted to time and again, but I haven't. So *think*, man. Ask yourself why.''

"Why would you smear yourself if you could avoid it?''

"This goes beyond me.''

"Really? To whom?''

"For God's sake. To my daughter. *Because* she's my daughter.'' Luxford paused, as if waiting for the information to sink into Stone's brain. In the moment that passed before Luxford spoke again, St. James saw the subtle change in Stone: the marginal slumping of the shoulders, the curve of the fingers as if he wished to grasp something that wasn't there. Luxford said more quietly, "If I'd aimed for Evelyn, I'd have ended up hitting Charlotte. Why would I put my own child through that? Knowing she's my child. I live in the world I've created, Mr. Stone. Believe me, I know how the publicity would ricochet off Evelyn and strike the girl.''

Stone said, his voice dull, "Those were Eve's words as well. She won't make a move because she wants to protect Charlie.''

Luxford looked as if he'd have liked to argue this point. But instead he said, "Then you must convince her to make a move. Whatever the move may be. It's the only way."

Stone rested his knuckles on the top of the worktable. He ran them back and forth and watched their movement. "I wish to God that there was a God to tell me what to do," he said quietly to himself, his eyes on his hand.

The others said nothing. Outside, somewhere down in the street a child's voice called, "You liar! You dirt-face! You said you would and you didn't and I'm going to tell! I am!"

Stone drew a deep breath. He swallowed, raised his head. "Let me use your telephone," he said to St. James.

11

WHEN MR. CZVANEK left Eve Bowen's office, he was apparently satisfied that his local MP had heard, sympathised with, and vowed to do something about his complaint: the recent opening of a video arcade directly beneath his flat in Praed Street. It was a location already made noisy by the presence of traffic, by its proximity to Paddington Station, and by the nightly business manoeuvring of rent boys and streetwalkers that the police were doing nothing about despite his regular phone calls to them. Mr. Czvanek—who lived with his ageing mother, his wife, and their six children in three rooms from which they hoped to build a better life—was fast losing his dreams, not to mention his patience.

He'd said in his broken English, "I come to you as last hope of my family, Mrs. Parliament. My neighbours, they say I talk to MP for getting help. My family, we not mind the street, the cars. But my little ones, is for them no good to grow up with looking at sin everywhere. These people who sell themselves on the street. These young ones with their smokes and their drugs in the video arcade. This is for my children no good. My neighbours, they say you can make difference. You can make . . ." He struggled for a word and as he did so, he twisted the trouser turn-up on his left ankle where it was balanced against his right knee. He'd been doing so for most of their interview. It was fairly well mangled as he reached the conclusion of his remarks. "You can make the bad ones shove away. So my children grow up to be proper. Is a father's dream, how the children grow up. You have children of your own, Mrs. Parliament?" He'd picked up the politically correct family photograph of Eve, Alex, and Charlotte all looking simultaneously winsome and devoted to one another. He left a shovel-sized thumbprint on the silver frame. "This your family? Your child? So you understand?"

Eve had made the correct noises and the correct notes. She'd explained the nature of the committee that was currently studying the problem of enhancing policing in the area. She expounded upon the fact that Praed Street was a centre for business as well as for vice and while she could guarantee that more crackdowns would be made upon the fleshpeddlers of the area, she couldn't, unfortunately, control the businesses that lined the street since the street was zoned for such establishments. So the video arcade was probably going to remain his close neighbour unless lack of interest forced it out of business. She could promise, however, that the local police would make periodic inspections of the arcade itself, checking for drugs, alleviating illegal drinking, and sending young ones on their way after hours. She said that there were always compromises one had to make in living in big cities. In Mr. Czvanek's life, the video arcade was going to be one of them, at least for the present.

He'd seemed satisfied. He'd stood. He'd smiled. He'd said expansively, "What a great country, this. A man like me to see Mrs. Parliament. Just to walk in and sit down and see Mrs. Parliament myself. A great thing, this."

Eve had shaken the man's hand as she always shook her constituents' hands upon their visits to her surgery: one of theirs sandwiched between both of hers. When the door shut behind him, she buzzed her secretary. She said, "Give me a few minutes, Nuala. How many more?" to which Nuala replied in a low voice from the outer office, "Six. And Mr. Woodward's phoned again. He said it's quite urgent. He's said you're to phone him as soon as you have a break."

"What's it about?"

"I did ask, Ms. Bowen." Nuala's voice indicated how little she liked Joel Woodward's propensity for playing at spymaster, guarding information as if the national security were involved every time he had a message to pass on. "Shall I phone him for you? Get him on the line?"

"I'll see the other constituents first. Presently."

Eve removed her spectacles and laid them on the desk. She'd been at the constituency association office since three o'clock. It was her regular Friday afternoon surgery, but nothing except the flow of constituents and the meeting scheduled with her association chairman had been regular about it. Instead of being in command of every interview, with a ready response for each question and request, she'd found her attention drifting. More than once under the guise of taking notes, she'd had to have points repeated and elucidations made. While this was normal operating procedure for an MP meeting with constituents at a weekend surgery, it was not normal operating procedure for Eve Bowen. She prided herself on a capacious memory and a prodigiously facile mind. That she was having difficulty now, meeting with constituents whose troubles she should have been able to field, to catalogue, and to solve with barely an expenditure of brain power, told her how easily she could be interpreted as experiencing the fissure she had been determined no one would see.

Going through the motions was what Charlotte's disappearance had called for. So far she'd managed it, but the strain was starting to shake her. And the fact that she *was* feeling shaken rattled her more than did Charlotte's disappearance itself. It had been only forty-eight hours since her daughter had been taken, and Eve knew that in order to win this battle with Dennis Luxford she had to hold on for a lengthy siege. The only way to do this was to focus completely on the task at hand.

For this reason, she had not returned Joel Woodward's phone calls. She could not risk allowing her political assistant to throw her off her stride any more than she was already thrown off it.

She slipped out the side door of her office, the one that led down the corridor to the rear of the building. There, she shut herself into the loo where she washed her palms of Mr. Czvanek's oily handshake. She patted a thin layer of cover-up beneath her eyes, and she used rose pencil on her upper lip. She brushed a hair off her jacket. She straightened the collar of her blouse. She stepped back from the mirror and evaluated her appearance. Normal, she decided. Save for her nerves, which were jangled and had been jangled since she'd left her office in Parliament Square.

The encounter with the journalist had been nothing. More, it had meant less than nothing. MPs were accosted by journalists—lobby journalists and others—every day of the week. They wanted quick answers to questions, they wanted interviews, they wanted background information, they wanted confirmation of a story. They promised anonymity, they guaranteed accuracy, they swore another source would be the one named for purposes of attribution. But they were always around, either in the members' lobby at the Commons, or coming and going at the Home Office and Whitehall, or lounging with an eye to possible activity in One Parliament Square. So it was nothing unusual for a journalist to approach her as she crossed the lobby on her way to her car, already an hour late for her Friday afternoon's surgery at the office in Marylebone. What *had* been unusual was everything that followed that initial approach.

Her name had been Tarp. Diana Tarp, she said, although Eve could read that well enough on the press pass she wore on a chain round her neck. She represented the *Globe* and she wanted to arrange an interview with the Undersecretary of State. As soon as possible, if Ms. Bowen didn't mind.

Eve had been so surprised by this frontal approach that she stopped in her progress to the door where she could see her Rover and its driver waiting at the kerb. She'd said, "I beg your pardon?" And before Diana Tarp could respond, she continued with, "If you want an interview, Ms. Tarp, may I suggest you phone my office and not accost me like a streetwalker with a proposition? Excuse me, please."

As she moved past the journalist, Diana Tarp said quietly, "Actually, I'd thought you'd be grateful for a more intimate approach, rather than have me go through your office personnel."

Eve had turned towards the door, but she slowed, then stopped. "What?"

The journalist gave her a level look. "You know how offices work, Ms. Bowen. A journalist phones in but won't leave a precise message. Five minutes later half the staff knows. Five more minutes later and the rest of the staff is speculating why. I thought you might like to avoid that. The knowledge and the speculation, that is."

Eve had felt a chill with her words. But it was followed by an anger so wild that for a moment she didn't trust herself to speak. So she shifted her briefcase from one hand to the other and looked at her watch as she instructed her blood not to wash across her face.

At last she said, "I'm afraid I haven't the time to accommodate you at the moment, Ms.—" and she gazed at the other woman's identification.

"Tarp," she said, "Diana Tarp," in a voice that told Eve she was unconvinced by and unimpressed with her performance.

"Yes. Well. If you have no wish to arrange an interview through my office, Ms. Tarp, then give me one of your cards and I'll phone you when I can. That's the best I can do. At the moment, I'm already overdue at my surgery."

After a pause in which they examined each other as potential opponents, Diana Tarp handed over a card. But she'd never moved her eyes from Eve's face as she pulled that card from her jacket pocket.

"I do hope to hear from you," she said.

In the back of the Rover, as she rolled towards Marylebone, Eve inspected the card. It bore the woman's name, her home address, her work phone, her office phone, her pager, and her fax. Clearly, if there was a story to be got from any source about any subject, Diana Tarp had made herself available to get it.

Slowly Eve tore the card in half, then in quarters, then in eighths. When she had reduced it to the size of confetti, she spread the pieces across the palm of her hand and, when the Rover drew up in front of the constituency association office, she dropped them into the gutter, where a rivulet of bronze-coloured water was trickling in the direction of a drain. So much for Diana Tarp, Eve thought.

It had been nothing, she concluded now. The journalist's approach was unusual but that, perhaps, was merely her style. She could be working on a story about the growing numbers of women in Parliament, about the need for more women in the Cabinet. She could be investigating any one of a dozen areas that were the responsibility of the Home Office. She might want to know about changes in immigration policies, about centralised policing, about prison reform. She might wish to discuss the Government's position on refugee resettlement, on the movement towards a permanent cease-fire with the IRA. She might be digging into something potentially nasty regarding MI5. It could have been anything. It could have been nothing. It was merely the timing that had unnerved her.

Eve returned her spectacles to her nose and adjusted her hair so that its fringe did the job to cover her scar. She said to her image in the mirror, "Member of Parliament. Undersecretary of State," and when she had those elements of her persona in place, she returned to her office and buzzed in her next constituent.

That meeting—a convoluted conversation with an unmarried mother of three who had a fourth on the way and who had come to protest about her current position on the list for council housing—was interrupted by Nuala. She didn't buzz this time. Rather, she tapped discreetly on the door and opened it as Miss Peggy Hornfisher was demanding, "So, zit s'posed to be *my* fault they've all got the same dad? Why's that disqualify me? If I slept round and popped out kids without a blink as to who their dads were, I'd be at the top of that list and don't we both know it. And don't tell *me* to talk to the councillors. I been talking to the councillors till I'm blue in the face. *You* talk to them. That's why we voted for you, isn't it?"

Nuala's "Excuse me, Ms. Bowen," saved Eve from having to explain the finer points of qualification for and distribution of council housing to Miss Hornfisher. And the fact that Nuala had interrupted in person suggested a matter that required immediate attention.

Eve went to the door and joined Nuala outside her office. The secretary said, "Your husband's just phoned."

"Why didn't you put him through?"

"He didn't want to be put through. He said you're to come home at once. He's on his way and you're to meet him there. That's all." Nuala shifted uncomfortably from foot to foot. She'd spoken to Alex in the past. She would know how unusual it was for him to give his wife a directive without talking to her personally. "He didn't say anything else."

Eve felt the touch of panic, but she reached for what Alex had reached for on Wednesday night. She said with perfect sangfroid, "His father's not well," and returned to her office. She made her excuses to Miss Hornfisher, followed them with promises, and began to stuff her belongings into her briefcase as Miss Hornfisher lumbered from the room. She tried to remain composed even as her mind careened from one thought to the next. It was Charlotte. Alex was phoning about Charlotte. He wouldn't have told her to come home otherwise. So there was word. There was news. Luxford had relented. Eve had held firm, she had refused to cave in, she had been unmoved by Luxford's performance, she had stood her ground, she had shown him who had balls, she had—

The phone rang. She snatched it. "What?" she snapped.

"It's Joel Woodward again," Nuala said.

"I can't talk to him now."

"Ms. Bowen, he says it's urgent."

"Oh damn it, put him through," she said and in a moment heard Joel's voice saying with uncharacteristic insubordination, "Shit! Why haven't you answered my calls?"

"Exactly who do you think you're talking to, Joel?"

"I know who I'm talking to. And I know something else. Something dodgy's going on over here, and I rather thought you'd be interested in knowing what it is."

—m—

The Friday night traffic was bad. The month of May, the beginning of the season's largest influx of tourists, the rush to get to the theatre: All these elements combined to clog the streets.

St. James rode with Luxford, following Stone. Luxford used his car phone to speak to his wife, delaying his arrival home. He did not tell her why. He said to St. James, "Fiona doesn't know about any of this. I can't think how to tell her. God. What a cock-up." He kept his eyes on the car in front of them, his hands low on the steering wheel. He said, "Do you think I'm involved in this? In what's happened to Charlotte?"

"What I think isn't important, Mr. Luxford."

"You regret your own involvement."

"Yes. I do."

"Why did you take this on?"

St. James looked out the side window. They were passing Hyde Park. Through gaps in the great plane trees, he could see that people still walked along the pathway in the fading evening light. With dogs on leads. With arms about each other. With small children in push-chairs. He caught sight of one young woman lifting a child high into the air, the sort of play that a baby loves. He said, "It's rather too complicated to explain, I'm afraid," and he was grateful when Luxford said nothing more.

When they reached Marylebone, Mrs. Maguire was just leaving, with a yellow poncho slung over one shoulder and a plastic bag dangling from her arm. She spoke to Alexander Stone while Luxford pulled into a vacant spot farther down the mews. By the time they walked back to the house, she was gone.

"Eve's home," Stone said. "Let me go in first."

They waited outside. The occasional car passed on Marylebone High Street. The muffled babble of conversation drifted in their direction from the Devonshire Arms on the corner. Other than that, the mews was silent.

Several minutes passed before the door opened. Stone said, "Come in."

Eve Bowen was waiting for them in the sitting room. She stood next to the sculpture from under which she had taken the kidnapper's note two nights earlier. She looked poised the way a warrior is poised before hand-to-hand combat. She was a picture of the sort of equanimity that is intended to intimidate.

"Play the tape," she said.

St. James did so. Eve's face didn't alter as Charlotte's voice piped among them, although St. James thought he saw her swallow when the little girl said, "Cito, *I had to make this tape in order that he would give me some juice 'cause I was so thirsty.*"

When the tape finished playing, Eve said to Luxford, "Thank you for the information. Now you may leave."

Luxford's hand shot out as if he would touch her, but they stood at opposite sides of the room. "Evelyn—"

"Leave."

"Eve," Stone said, "we'll phone the police. We don't need to play the game his way. He doesn't need to run the story."

"No," she said. Her face was as stony as her voice. St. James realised that she hadn't taken her eyes off Luxford since they'd all walked into the room. They stood about like actors upon a stage, each having taken a position from which none of them moved: Luxford by the fireplace, Eve across from him, Stone by the entry to the dining room, St. James by the sofa. He was nearest to her and he tried to read her, but she was as guarded as a wary cat.

"Ms. Bowen," he said and he kept his voice low, the way one would speak to maintain calm at all costs, "we've made progress to-day."

"Such as?" Still, she looked at Luxford. As if her look were a challenge, he did not avoid it.

St. James told her about the vagrant, about the sightings of him that had been confirmed by the two residents of Cross Keys Close. He told her about the policeman who had run the vagrant off, saying, "One of the constables at the Marylebone station is going to remember that man and that description. If you phone them, the detectives won't be starting from nothing in an investigation. They'll have a good lead."

"No," she said. "Try your best, Dennis. You can't have it your way." She was communicating something to Luxford with the words, something beyond merely her refusal to act. St. James couldn't guess what it was, but it seemed to him that Luxford could. He saw the editor's lips part fractionally, but he didn't reply.

Stone said, "I don't see that we have a choice, Eve. God knows I don't want you to go through this, but Luxford thinks—"

He was silenced by her look, so swift it might have been shot from a gun. Treason, it said to him, treachery, betrayal. "You as well," she said.

"No. Never. I'm on your side, Eve."

She smiled thinly. "Then know this." Her gaze went back to Luxford. "One of the lobby journalists requested an immediate inter-view with me this afternoon. Convenient to the circumstances, wouldn't you say?"

"That means nothing," Luxford said. "For the love of God, Eve-lyn, you're a bloody Junior Minister. You must get requests for inter-views all the time."

"As soon as possible, she said." Eve continued as if Luxford hadn't spoken. "Without mentioning the fact to any of my staff because, she told me, I might not want my staff to know she was talking to me."

"From my paper?" Luxford asked.

"You wouldn't be that foolish. But from your former paper. And I find that fascinating."

"It's just coincidence. You must see that."

"I would have done had it not been for the rest."

"What?" Stone asked. "Eve, what's going on?"

"Five journalists have phoned since half past three this afternoon. Joel took the calls. They have the scent that something's up, he told me, they all want a word, so do I know what it is they're after and how would I like him to handle the sudden influx of interest in . . . What *is* it they're suddenly interested in, Ms. Bowen?"

Luxford said urgently, "No. Evelyn. I haven't told a soul. That has nothing to do—"

"Get out of my house, you bastard," she said quietly. "I'll die before I cave in to you."

St. James spoke to Luxford outside, standing next to his car. The last person in the world he would ever have expected to feel a stirring of pity for was the editor of *The Source*, but he felt pity now. The man looked haggard. Patches of damp the size of dinner plates soddened his natty blue shirt. His body was rank with the scent of perspiration.

He said in a shell-shocked voice, "What next?"

"I'll talk to her again."

"We've no time."

"I'll talk to her now."

"She won't give." His gaze went to the house, which told neither of them anything other than the fact that more lights had been switched on in the sitting room and another in a room upstairs. "She should have aborted," he said. "All those years ago. I don't know why she didn't. I used to think it was because she needed a concrete reason to hate me."

"For?"

"Seducing her. Or making her want to be seduced. The latter, I suspect. It's terrifying to some people when they learn to want."

"It is." St. James touched the roof of Luxford's car. "Go home. Let me see what I can do."

"Nothing," Luxford predicted.

"Nonetheless, let me see."

He waited until Luxford had driven off before he went back to the house. Stone answered the door.

"I think it's high time you buggered off," he said. "She's been through enough. Jesus. When I think I almost bought into his performance myself, it makes me want to punch holes in the walls."

"I'm not on anyone's side, Mr. Stone," St. James said. "Let me talk to your wife. I haven't finished telling her what she needs to know about today's investigation. She has a right to that information. You'll agree with that."

Stone evaluated St. James's words through eyes that narrowed. Like Luxford, he looked worn to nearly nothing. But Eve Bowen, St. James realised, had not looked like that at all. She had looked ready to go another fifteen rounds and ready to come out the victor.

Stone nodded and stepped back from the door. He climbed the stairs heavily as St. James returned to the sitting room and tried to think what to say, what to do, and how to move the woman into action before it was too late. He saw that in place of the altar that Mrs. Maguire had set up, on the coffee table a chess set was now spread out. The pieces were untraditional, however. St. James picked up the opposing kings. Harold Wilson was one. Margaret Thatcher was the other. He replaced them carefully.

"He's made you think he cares about Charlotte, hasn't he?"

St. James looked up to see Eve Bowen in the doorway. Her husband stood behind her, a hand on her elbow.

"He doesn't, you know. He's never even seen her. One would think, in the ten years of her life, that he might have tried. I wouldn't have allowed it, of course."

"Perhaps he knew that."

"Perhaps." She came into the room. She sat in the same chair she had chosen on Wednesday night, and the light from the table lamp showed her face as composed. "He's a master dissembler, Mr. St. James. I know that better than anyone. He'll want you to think that I'm bitter about our affair and how things turned out. He'll want you to see my behaviour as a reaction to the weakness in myself that caused me to fall victim to his plethora of charms all those years ago. And while your attention is focused on me and on my refusal to recognise Dennis Luxford's essential decency, he'll move nimbly behind the scenes, orchestrating our anxiety from one level to the next." She rested her head against the back of the chair. She closed her eyes. "The tape was a nice touch. I might have believed it all myself had I not known he would stoop to anything."

"It was your daughter's voice."

"Oh yes. It was Charlotte."

St. James went to the sofa. His bad leg burdened him like a hundredweight; his back ached from the strain of heaving his body over brick walls. All he would need to make affliction complete was one of his migraines. There was a decision to be taken, and the very reluctance he felt pulling at his body with every movement told him how necessary it was that he take it.

He said, "I'll tell you what I know at this point."

She said, "And then you'll leave us to fend for ourselves."

"Yes. I can't in good conscience carry on with this."

"You believe him, then."

"Ms. Bowen, I do. I don't particularly like him. I don't much like what he stands for. I think his newspaper ought to be blasted from the earth. But I do believe him."

"Why?"

"Because, as he's said, he could have told his story ten years ago. He could have told his story when you first stood for Parliament. He has no reason to tell his story now. Except to save your daughter. His daughter."

"His offspring, Mr. St. James. Not his daughter. Charlotte is Alex's daughter." She opened her eyes and turned her head to him without lifting it from the back of the chair. "You don't understand politics, do you?"

"At your level? No. I suppose I don't."

"Well, this is politics, Mr. St. James. As I've said from the first, this is all about politics."

"I don't believe that."

"I know. That's why we're at an impasse." She made a weary gesture in his direction. "All right. Give us the rest of the facts. Then go. We'll decide what to do and your hands will be utterly clean of the decision."

Alexander Stone sat in the pillowlike chair that matched the sofa, next to the fireplace and across from his wife. He sat on the edge of it, elbows on his knees, head bent, eyes on his feet.

Released from a responsibility he hadn't wanted to assume in the first place, St. James didn't find himself freed at all. Rather, the weight he was carrying felt heavier and more dreadful. He tried to work past it. This was not his obligation, he told himself. But still he felt the tremendous effort attendant to shrugging it off.

He said, "I went to the Shenkling school, as we discussed." He saw Alexander Stone raise his head. "I spoke to girls from eight to twelve years old. The girl we're looking for wasn't there. I have a list of the absentees from today if you'd like to phone them."

"What's this about?" Stone asked.

"A friend of Charlotte's," his wife explained as St. James passed her the list.

St. James said, "Charlotte's music teacher—"

"Chambers," Stone said.

"Damien Chambers. Yes. He told us Charlotte was generally in the company of another girl on the Wednesdays of her music lessons. This girl was apparently with Charlotte this past Wednesday as well. We've been looking for her in the hope she'd be able to tell us something about what happened that afternoon. So far, we haven't been able to find her."

"But the description of the vagrant," Eve Bowen said. "That gives us something."

"Yes. And if you can find the girl and get her to confirm that description—perhaps to confirm that the vagrant was back in the area at the time Charlotte went in to her music lesson—you'd have something more solid to give the authorities."

"Where else could she be?" Eve Bowen asked. "If not at St. Bernadette's and not at the Shenkling school?"

"One of the other schools in Marylebone. Or there are other possibilities. Her dancing class, for instance. Someone from the neighbourhood. A child who sees the same psychotherapist. She has to be somewhere."

Eve Bowen nodded. She raised her fingers to her temple in a thoughtful gesture. "I hadn't thought before this, but the name . . . Are you certain it's a girl we're looking for?"

"The name's unusual, but everyone I've spoken to says it's a girl."

Alexander Stone spoke. "Unusual name? Who is it? Why isn't it someone we know?"

"Mrs. Maguire knows her. Or at least knows of her. As do Mr. Chambers and at least one of Charlotte's mates from St. Bernadette's. She's apparently a girl Charlotte sees on a catch-as-catch-can basis."

"Who is it?"

"It's a girl called Breta," Eve Bowen said to her husband. "Do you know her, Alex?"

"Breta?" Alexander Stone rose. He went to the fireplace, where he picked up a photograph of a toddler on a swing, himself behind the swing laughing into the camera. "God," he said. "Jesus."

"What?" Eve asked.

"Have you spent the last two days looking for Breta?" Stone asked St. James wearily.

"In large part, yes. Until we had the information about the vagrant, it was the only thing we had to go on."

"Well, let's hope your information about the vagrant is more viable than your information about Breta." Stone gave a desperate-sounding laugh. He set the photograph facedown on the mantel. "Brilliant." He looked at his wife and then away. "Where have you been, Eve? Where the bloody fuck have you been? Do you live in this house or just make visits?"

"What are you talking about?"

"I'm talking about Charlie. I'm talking about Breta. I'm talking about the fact that your daughter—my daughter, our daughter, Eve—doesn't have a single friend in the world and you don't even know it."

St. James felt the ice washing through his veins as what Stone said and what he might mean began to coalesce ineluctably. Eve Bowen, he saw, had finally for a moment lost a vestige of her mien of cool tranquillity.

"What is this?" she demanded.

"The truth," Stone said. And he laughed again, but this time the laugh rose the scale and teetered on the verge of hysteria. "Breta is no one, Eve. She's no one. *No one.* Breta isn't real. You've had your hired gun spend the last two days combing Marylebone for Charlie's imaginary friend."

12

CHARLOTTE WHISPERED, "BRETA. Best friend Breta," but her lips felt caked and her mouth felt like it was filled with crumbs of old dried bread. So she knew that Breta couldn't hear her and, more important, that she wouldn't respond.

Her body was achy. Every place it was supposed to bend, it hurt. She couldn't tell at all how long it had been since she'd made the tape for Cito, but it seemed like days and months and years. It seemed like forever.

She was hungry and thirsty. Her eyes felt like there was a cloud behind them that pressed against her eyelids and filled the rest of her head. She didn't know when she had ever been so tired, and if she hadn't felt so draggy in the body and heavy in the arms and legs, she might have been more than a little cut up about the fact that her tummy had started to hurt because it had been so long since the shepherd's pie and the apple juice. But she could still taste them—couldn't she?—if she rubbed her tongue against the roof of her mouth.

A pang shot through her stomach. Lying where she was on the damp blanket, she dragged her knees up and clutched herself round the middle, which dislodged the blanket a degree or two and exposed her to the dank air of her lightless prison. She said, "Cold," through those same caked lips, and she released her stomach to tighten her cardigan round her body. She put one hand between her legs to keep it warm. The other she stuffed into her cardigan's pocket.

She felt him, then, inside that pocket, and her eyes opened to the darkness all round her as she wondered how she'd forgotten little Widgie. Poor friend *she* was, thinking about herself, wishing she could talk to Breta when all the time Widgie was no doubt cold and anxious and hungry and thirsty, just like Lottie.

She murmured, "Sorry, Widge," and closed her fingers over the hump of clay, which had—as Cito had carefully explained—been fired and glazed and long ago put into a Christmas cracker for a child who had lived decades and decades before Charlotte's own birth. She felt the ridges on Widgie's back and the point at one end that served as his snout. She and Cito had seen him one day among a display of other similarly tiny figurines in a shop in Camden Passage, where they'd gone to scout out something special for Mummy for Mothering Sunday. "Hedgehog, hedgehog!" Lottie had squealed and pointed at the tiny creature. "Cito, he's just like Mrs. Tiggy-Winkle."

"Not exactly like, Charlie," Cito had said.

Which was true, because, unlike Mrs. Tiggy-Winkle, the hedgehog in question wasn't wearing a striped petticoat, a cap, or a gown. He wasn't wearing anything at all except his hedgehog prickles and his especially precious hedgehog face. But despite his lack of attire, he was still a hedgehog and hedgehogs were Lottie's favourite extra-special live things. So Cito had bought him for her and presented him to her on the palm of his hand, and he had ridden in her pocket ever since, like a lucky charm, no matter where she went. How had she managed to forget about Widgie when he'd been with her all along?

Lottie took him from her pocket and held him against her cheek. At the touch of him, she felt a blueness settle inside her. He was cold, like ice. She should have kept him warmer. She should have kept him safer. He depended upon her and she had failed him.

She patted in the darkness for a corner of the blanket on which she was lying, and she rolled the hedgehog into it. She said through the lips she could hardly move, so caked they were, "Snug like that, Widge. Don't you worry. We'll be going home soon."

Because they *would* be going home. She knew that Cito would tell the story that the kidnapper wanted, and that would be the end of all this. No more dark. No more cold. No more bricks for a bed and bucket for a loo. She only hoped that Cito asked Mrs. Maguire for help with his story before he told it. He wasn't very good at telling stories, and they always started out the same. "Once upon a time, there was an evil, ugly, twisted magician and a very *very* beautiful little princess with short brown hair and spectacles . . ." If the kidnapper wanted something different for his story, Cito was going to need Mrs. Maguire's help.

Lottie tried to gauge how long it had been since she'd made that tape for Cito. She tried to gauge how long it would take Cito to create his story once he heard the tape. She tried to decide what kind of story would please the kidnapper best and she wondered how Cito would get the story to him. Would he say it into the tape recorder like she had? Would he tell it on the phone?

She was too tired to think up answers to her questions. She was too tired to even suppose what the answers might be. With one hand scrunched deep into her cardigan pocket and her other hand tucked tightly between her legs and her knees drawn up so that her stomach didn't hurt, she closed her eyes and thought about sleep. Because she was so tired. She was so awfully and terribly tired . . .

Light and sound crashed upon her simultaneously. They came like lightning, only in reverse. First a furious crank and a desperate *smash-boom*, then the backs of her eyelids suddenly were red and glowing, and Lottie opened her eyes.

She gave a gasp because it hurt so much to have light falling on her. Not the regulated incandescence from a lantern this time, but real light that came from the sun. It blazed through a doorway in the wall and for a second nothing else was there. Just the light, so bright, so difficult to look at. She felt like a mole, cringing back and squinting and giving a cry that sounded like, "Ahtch," and curling farther into a ball.

Then through the slit in her eyelids, she saw him. He moved into the doorway and stood there framed with the light at his back. In the triangle of his legs, she could see the colours blue and green and she thought about daytime and the sky and trees, but she couldn't tell what was what because she hadn't her specs.

She mumbled, "Need my specs."

"No," he said. "That's what you don't need. You don't need your specs."

"But I—"

"Shut your gob!"

Lottie cowered into her blanket. She could see the shape of him, but with the light behind him—so bright, so furious, like it wanted more than anything just to eat her up—she couldn't see anything else. Except his hands. On them he wore gloves. In one of his hands he carried the red Thermos. In the other he held something that looked like a tube. Lottie's eyes fixed on the Thermos thirstily. Juice, she thought. Cold, sweet, and wet. But instead of uncapping the Thermos and pouring her a drink, he threw the tube onto the bricks by her head. She squinted hard and saw it was a newspaper.

"Dad didn't tell the truth," he said. "Dad didn't say a word. Isn't that too bad, Lottie?"

There was something in his voice. . . . Lottie felt her eyes prickle and her insides seemed to be trying to shove something hard into her throat. She murmured, "I tried to tell you. I tried to say. Cito can't tell proper stories."

"And that's a problem, isn't it? But no matter, because all he needs is a little encouragement. We're going to give it to him, you and I. Are you ready for that?"

"I tried to tell him . . ." Lottie attempted to swallow. She reached an arm out towards the Thermos. "Thirsty," she said. She wanted to lift her head from the bricks, she wanted to run into the light behind him, but she couldn't manage it. She couldn't manage a thing. She felt tears leaking from the corners of her eyes.

What a baby, Breta would have said.

He used his foot to kick the door closed. It swung to, but it did not latch. A strip of light remained, telling Lottie where it was. A strip of light that told her what direction to run in.

But too much of her ached. Too much of her couldn't move. Too much of her was hungry and thirsty and tired. Besides, he was three steps away, and in less than a second he'd taken those steps and she was looking at his shoes and the bottom of his trousers.

He knelt and she cowered away from him. She felt a lump beneath her head and knew she'd accidentally rolled onto Widgie. Poor Widgie, she thought. I've not been much of a friend to Widgie. She moved herself off him.

"That's better," he said to her. "When you don't fight, it's better."

Through a blur, she saw him uncap the Thermos. She said, "My specs. Could I have my specs?"

He said, "For this, you don't need your specs." He slipped his left hand beneath her neck and drew her head upwards.

"Dad should have run the story," he said. His fingers tightened. They pulled on her hair. "Dad should have followed the rules."

"Please . . ." Lottie felt her insides quiver. Her feet began to scrabble. Her hands clawed at the floor. "Hurts," she said. "Don't . . . My mummy . . ."

"No," he said. "This isn't going to hurt. Not the least little bit. Are you ready for your drink?"

He was holding her firmly yet her spirits lifted. He didn't mean to hurt her after all.

But instead of pouring juice from the Thermos into its cuplike top, instead of lifting that cuplike top to her mouth, he gripped her neck harder and tipped her head backwards and brought the Thermos itself up to her mouth. He began to pour.

"Swallow," he murmured. "You're thirsty. Swallow. It will be all right."

She coughed. She sputtered. She gulped the liquid. It was cold and wet, but it wasn't juice. She said, "It isn't—"

"Juice?" he said. "Not this time. But it's wet, isn't it? Fast as well. Come on. Drink it up."

She struggled against him, but when she squirmed, he only held her tighter. So she knew the way to freedom was to do as he said. She drank and she gulped. He poured and he poured.

And before she knew it, she was drifting and floating. She saw Sister Agnetis. She saw Mrs. Maguire. She saw Mummy and Cito and Fermain Bay. And then the darkness returned.

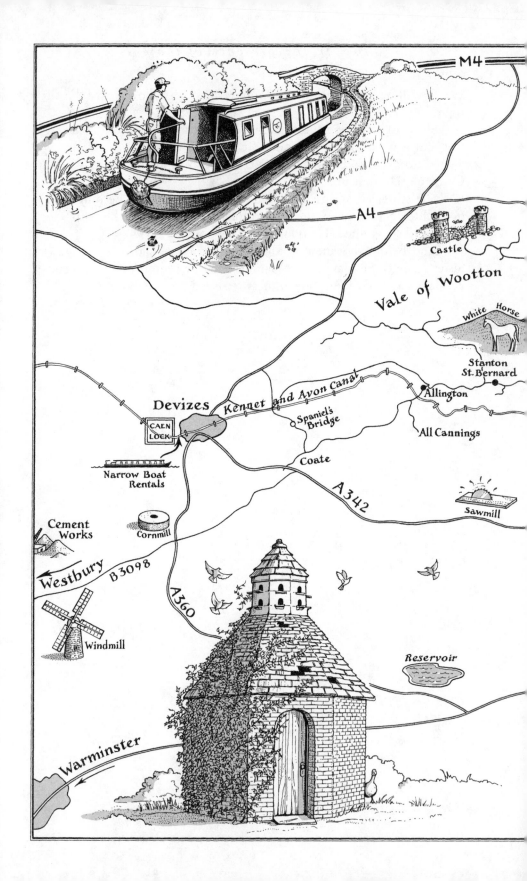

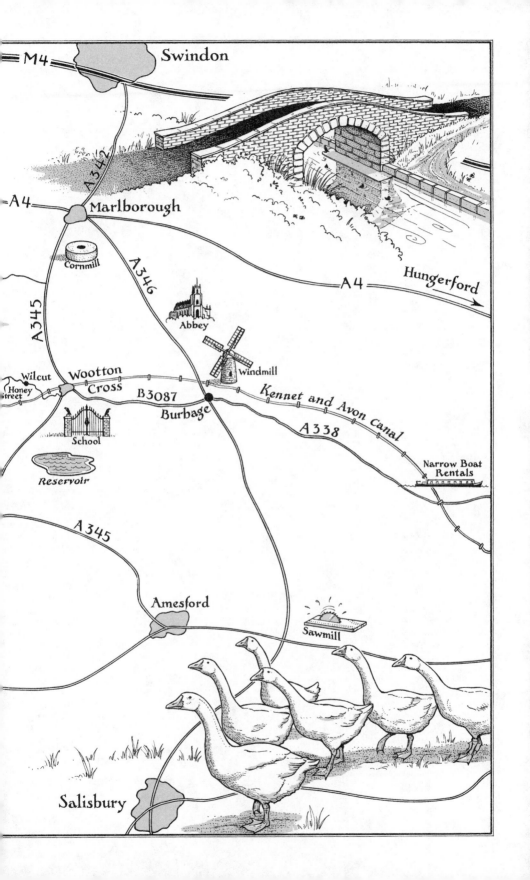

part
two

13

I*T WAS FIVE FIFTY-FIVE* in the afternoon when Detective Constable Robin Payne received the call he'd been waiting for, three weeks after the conclusion of his training course, two weeks after his official appointment as a detective constable, and less than twenty-four hours after he'd decided that the only way to relieve his anxiety—stage fright, he called it—was to phone his new detective sergeant at home and request to be included in the first case that came up.

"Eager to be someone's blue-eyed boy, are we?" Sergeant Stanley had asked him shrewdly. "Looking to be CC before you're thirty years old?"

"I just want to use my skills, Sarge."

"Your skills, is it?" The sergeant had sniggered. "Believe me, sonny, there'll be plenty of chances to use your skills—whatever they might be—before we're through with you. You'll be ruing the day you ever put your name up for CID."

Robin doubted that, but he reached into his past for an explanation that the sergeant might understand and accept. "My mum brought me up to prove myself."

"You've years to do that."

"I know. But will you anyway, sir?"

"Will I what, sprat?"

"Let me be part of the first case that comes up."

"Hmph. P'rhaps. We'll see what we'll see" had been the DS's response. And when he'd called to grant the request, he'd finished by saying, "So let's see you engage in some proving, Detective."

As he left the narrow high street of Wootton Cross behind him, Robin admitted to himself that his earnest request to be assigned to the first case that came up might not have been the best of ideas. His stomach was clenched fiercely round six dried-up tea sandwiches which he'd been in the process of ingesting at his mother's engagement party—DS Stanley's telephone call having blessedly rescued him from the unappetising sight of his mother and her corpulent and shiny-pated intended slavering over each other—and at the moment it seemed intent upon heaving those sandwiches upward and ejecting them outward. What in God's name would DS Stanley conclude about his rookie DC if Robin was sick when he looked at the corpse?

And it *was* a corpse that he was driving out to view, according to Stanley, a child's corpse that had been found along the bank of the Kennet and Avon Canal.

"Right beyond Allington," Stanley had informed him. "There's a lane that runs by Manor Farm. Cuts through the fields then heads southwest to a bridge. Body's out there."

"I know the spot." Robin hadn't lived in the county for all of his twenty-nine years without doing his share of country walking. For ages country walking had been the single best way to escape his mother and her asthma. All he ever needed to hear was a place name from the countryside—Kitchen Barrow Hill, Witch Plantation, Stone Pit, Furze Knoll—and a mental image of that location clicked into place in his brain. Geographical perfect pitch, one of his teachers had called it when he was in school. You've a natural future in topography, cartography, geography, geology, so what'll it be? But none of that had interested him. He wanted to be a policeman. He wanted to right wrongs. He was, in fact, quite passionate to right wrongs. "I can be there in twenty minutes," he had told his sergeant. He'd gone on to ask anxiously, "But nothing'll happen before I get there, will it? You won't draw any conclusions or anything like that?"

DS Stanley had snorted. "If I have the case solved by the time you arrive, I'll keep it to myself. Twenty minutes, you say?"

"I can do it in less."

"Don't kill yourself, sprat. It's a body, not a fire."

Nonetheless, Robin made the drive in quarter of an hour, heading north towards Marlborough first, then veering northwest just beyond the village post office, where he clipped along the country road that bisected the lush farmland, the downs, and the myriad tumuli, barrows, and other prehistoric sites which together constituted the Vale of Wootton. He'd always found the vale a peaceful place, his first choice for tramping away the tribulations that were sometimes inherent to living with an invalid mother. It was no more so than on this late afternoon in May when the breeze was ruffling the fields of hay and when his invalid mother was about to be taken off his hands. Sam Corey wasn't right for her—twenty years too old, all pats on the arse and nuzzles at the neck and sly winks and dim remarks about bouncing on the box springs "when I get you alone, sweet pear"—and Robin couldn't see what she wanted with him. But he'd smiled when he was required to smile, and he'd lifted his glass to toast the happy couple with warm champagne. And at the sound of the telephone he'd made his escape and tried to put from his mind the antics those two would get up to once he'd shut the front door. One didn't like to think of one's mum rolling round with a lover, especially this lover. It just wasn't nice.

The hamlet of Allington lay in a curve of the road, like the knob of an elbow. It consisted of two farms whose houses, barns, and assorted outbuildings were the most significant structures in the area. A paddock served as the hamlet's boundary, and in it a herd of cows were lowing, their udders swollen with milk. Robin skirted this paddock and cut through Manor Farm, where a harried-looking woman was shooing three children along the verge in the direction of a thatched, half-timbered house.

The lane DS Stanley had described to Robin was really just a track. It fronted two houses with red-tiled roofs and made a neat incision between the fields. Exactly the width of a tractor, it bore ruts from tyres and along its centre ran a vein of grass. Barbed-wire fencing on either side of the track served to enclose the fields, all of them cultivated and all of them verdant with approximately twelve inches' growth of wheat.

Robin's car lurched along the track, in and out of the ruts. It was more than a mile to the bridge. He babied the Escort along and hoped its suspension wasn't suffering any permanent damage from yet another exposure to a country thoroughfare.

Up ahead, he saw the track make the slight rise that indicated it was passing over the hump of the Allington Bridge. On either side of this bridge, vehicles were drawn over to the strip of white dead nettle that served as the verge. Three of them were panda cars. One was a van. The other was a blue Ariel Square-Four motorcycle, DS Stanley's preferred mode of transportation.

Robin pulled up behind one of the panda cars. To the west of the bridge, uniformed constables—of which group he'd so recently been a part—were pacing along either side of the canal, one set with eyes cast down upon the footpath edging the south bank of the canal, the other set meticulously making their way through the thick vegetation on the opposite side, five metres away. A photographer was just completing his work beyond a thick growth of reeds while the forensic pathologist waited patiently nearby, white gloves on his hands and black leather case at his feet. Aside from the clucking of mallards and teals who paddled on the canal, no one was making a sound. Robin wondered if this was a reverence for death or merely the concentration of professionals on the job. He pressed his palms against his trousers to rid his hands of the sweat of anticipation. He swallowed, ordered his stomach to settle, and got out of the car to confront his first murder. Although no one had called it a murder yet, he reminded himself. All DS Stanley had said was "We've got a child's body," and whether it would be classified as a murder or not remained in the hands of the medical examiners.

DS Stanley, Robin saw, was at work on the bridge. He was talking to a young couple who huddled together, arms round each other's waist as if they needed to keep warm. As well they might do, since neither one of them was wearing much more than a stitch of clothing. The woman had on three palm-sized black triangles posing as a swimsuit. The man was wearing a pair of white shorts. The couple had obviously come from a narrow-boat that was moored in the canal east of the reeds. The words *Just Married* rendered in shaving cream on the windows of that boat indicated what they'd been doing in the area. Sailing the canal was a popular spring and summer activity. As were hiking the towpath, visiting the locks, and sleeping rough from Reading all the way to Bath.

DS Stanley looked up as Robin approached. He flipped his notebook closed, said to the couple, "Stay right here, won't you?" and shoved the notebook into the back pocket of his jeans. He fished in his leather motorcycle jacket and brought out a packet of Embassys, which he offered to Robin. They both lit up.

"Over here," DS Stanley said. He directed Robin to the slope leading down to the towpath. He used his thumb and index finger to hold his cigarette and he spoke as he always did, out of the side of his mouth, as if his every disclosure were a secret between his listener and himself. "Honeymooners." He gave a snort and used his cigarette to indicate their narrow-boat. "Hired that, they did. And considering it's a bit too early to be docking for the evening, *and* considering there i'n't a hell of a lot of scenery in the immediate environs for them to have a gaze at, I can guess what was on their minds when they decided to stop, can't you?" He kept his eyes on the narrow-boat and said, "Just have a look at her, sprat. The girl, I mean. Not the boat. The girl."

Robin did what he was told. The girl's bikini, he saw, had no back at all to its bottom, just an indecent inch-wide strip of material that disappeared between her firm golden buttocks. On one of these two buttocks the young man's left hand rested with a proprietary air. Robin heard DS Stanley take in breath between his teeth.

"Time for exercising one's marital prerogatives, I should guess. And I wouldn't mind having a nice little bite of that crumpet myself. Jaysus have mercy. The arse on that woman. You, sprat?"

"Me?"

"If you could do her."

Robin knew he was going tomatoes to the roots of his hair, and he lowered his head to hide this fact. He poked the tip of his shoe into the ground and flicked away cigarette ash in place of a reply.

"Here's what happened," DS Stanley was continuing, still out of the corner of his mouth. "They pull over to have some squeeze. Fifth time today but, what the hell, they're newlyweds. He gets out to moor the boat—his hands all a-quiver and his dick like a periscope that's looking for the enemy. He finds a place to drive in the stake for a mooring—you can see it at the end of the line, there, can't you?—but while he's about it, he finds the kid's body. He and Bronze Arse run like the dickens over to Manor Farm and put in the call to triple nines from there. Now they're eager to be out of here, and we both know why, don't we?"

"You don't think they had anything to do—"

"With this?" The sergeant shook his head. "But they want plenty to do with each other. Even finding a body doesn't douse some people's fires, if you get my drift." He flipped his cigarette in the direction of the mallards. It sizzled against the water. One of the ducks scooped it up. Stanley grinned, muttered "Scavengers," and said, "C'mon, then. Have a gander at your first. You're looking peakish, sprat. Y'aren't going to feed the kippers on me, are you?"

No, Robin assured him. He wasn't going to be sick. He was nervous, that was all. Setting a foot wrong in the presence of his superior officer was the very last thing he wanted to do, and fear of setting a foot wrong had put his nerves in a jangle. He wanted to explain this to Stanley, he wanted also to express his gratitude that the detective sergeant had granted his request to be assigned to a case, but he stopped himself from doing either. There was no need to cast doubt upon himself at the moment, and expressing gratitude under the circumstances did not seem the appropriate behaviour of a detective constable.

Stanley called out to the couple who had discovered the body, "You two. Don't wander off. I'm not through with you," and led Robin down to the towpath. "Right. So let's see what kind of marbles you've got in the attic," he said. He indicated the constables on either side of the canal. "That's a probable exercise in futility. Why?"

Robin observed the constables. They were orderly, they were silent, they kept pace with each other. They were focused on their work and suffered no distractions. "Futility?" he repeated. To gain thinking time, he took a moment to stub out his cigarette on the sole of his shoe. He put the stub in his pocket. "Well, they're not going to find any footprints, are they, if that's what they're looking for. Too much grass on the towpath, too many wildflowers and weeds on the bank. But—" He hesitated, wondering if he should seem to be correcting what appeared to be his sergeant's hasty conclusion. He decided to take the risk. "But there are other things besides footprints that they might find. If this is a murder. Is it, sir?"

Stanley ignored the question, his eyes narrowed and another cigarette at his mouth, ready for lighting. "Such as?" he asked.

"If it's a murder? Such as anything. Fibres, cigarette ends, a weapon, a label, a clump of hair, the wad from a shotgun shell. Anything."

Stanley ignited his cigarette with a plastic lighter. It was shaped like a woman bent over, grasping her ankles. The flame shot out of her arse. "Nice," Stanley said. Robin couldn't decide if the sergeant was referring to his answer or the lighter.

Stanley tramped along the towpath. Robin followed. They headed in the direction of the reeds. There, the pathologist was in the process of climbing up the canal bank through a thickly knotted yellow skein of golden saxifrage and cowslip, with mud and algae clinging to the sides of his Wellingtons. Above him, two forensic biologists waited, their collection cases open. Next to them, a body bag was spread out on the towpath, ready for use.

"So?" Stanley said to the pathologist. He'd apparently come to the scene directly from a tennis game because he was wearing tennis whites and a sweatband round his forehead, an incongruous accompaniment to his knee-high black boots.

"We've some fairly decent wrinkling on both of the hands and on the sole of one foot," he said. "Body's been in the water for eighteen hours. At the most, twenty-four."

Stanley nodded. He rolled his cigarette between his fingers. He said to Robin, "Have a look, then, sprat," and to the pathologist with a smile, "Our Robbie here's still a virgin, Bill. Want to go five pounds on him making us a technicolour rainbow?"

A look of distaste passed across the pathologist's face. He joined them on the towpath and quietly said to Robin, "I doubt you'll be sick. The eyes are open, which always gives one a start, but there's no sign of decomposition yet."

Robin nodded. He took a breath and settled his shoulders. They were watching him—both the sergeant and the pathologist, not to mention the constables, the photographer, and the biologists—but he was determined to show them nothing other than professional disinterest.

He descended the canal bank through the matting of wildflowers. The silence round him seemed to intensify, making him hypersensitive to his own body's noise: the jet-engine sound of his breathing, the jackhammering of his heart, the timberfall of his feet as they crushed the flowers and the weeds. Mud plopped and sucked against the soles of his shoes as he came to the reeds. He skirted these.

The body lay just beyond them. Robin saw one foot first, lying out of the water and tucked into the reeds as if the child had been anchored there for some reason, then the other foot, which was in the water and wrinkled upon the sole, as the pathologist had said. His eyes travelled up the legs to the buttocks and from there to the head. This was turned on its side, the eyes open partway and heavily congested. Short brown hair floated outward from the head, undulating gently on the surface of the water, and as Robin stared at the corpse, racking his brain for the right question to ask—knowing that he knew it, knowing that it was planted firmly somewhere inside his brain, second nature to him, practically planned in advance, a question that would indicate he was on automatic pilot—he saw a quick flit of silver at the child's partially opened mouth as a fish darted up for a taste of dead flesh.

He felt light-headed. His hands were clammy. Miraculously, however, his mind clicked into gear. He took his eyes off the body, found the right question, and asked it in a voice that didn't quaver. "Boy or girl?"

In answer, the pathologist said, "Bring the bag," and joined Robin at the edge of the canal. One of the constables lowered the bag's zipper. Two others, in Wellingtons, waded into the water. With a nod from the pathologist, they flipped the body over. "Preliminarily, girl," the pathologist said in answer as her immature hairless pubes were exposed. The constables moved the body from the canal to the bag, but before they raised its zipper, the pathologist dropped to one knee next to the child. He pressed down on her chest. A delicate froth of white bubbles—not far different from soapsuds—seeped out of one nostril. "Drowned," he said.

Robin said to DS Stanley, "Not a murder, then?"

Stanley said with a shrug, "You tell me, sprat. What are the possibilities?"

As the body was removed and the forensic biologists descended the bank with their bottles and their bags, Robin considered the question and what answers would be reasonable. He caught sight of the honey-mooners' narrow-boat and said, "She was someone on holiday? She fell from a boat?"

Stanley nodded as if thoughtfully considering the hypothesis. "No child reported missing though."

"Pushed from a boat, then? A quick shove wouldn't leave marks on the body."

"Nice possibility," Stanley acknowledged. "That makes it murder. What else?"

"One of the children from the area? Maybe Allington? Or perhaps All Cannings? One can hike across the fields and get here from All Cannings."

"Same problem as before."

"No report of someone missing?"

"Right. What else?" Stanley waited. He didn't appear the least impatient.

Robin put the final hypothesis into words, a contradiction of his preliminary conclusion. "Victim of a crime, then? Has she—" He shuffled from foot to foot and sought a euphemism. "Has she been . . . well, interfered with, sir?"

Stanley cocked an interested eyebrow. Robin hurried on.

"I suppose she might have been, mightn't she? Except there didn't seem to be . . . on the body . . . superficially . . ." He told himself to get a grip. He cleared his throat. He said, "It could be a rape, except there was no superficial evidence of any violence on the body."

"Cut on the knee," the pathologist said from the towpath. "Some bruising round the mouth and the neck. A couple of healing burns on the cheeks and the chin. First degree, those."

"Still," Robin began.

"There's more than one way to rape," Stanley pointed out.

"So I suppose . . ." He thought about what direction to head in and settled on saying, "We don't seem to have much to go on, do we?"

"And when we don't have much to go on?"

The answer was so obvious. "We wait for the postmortem."

Stanley tipped him a salute, finger to eyebrow. He said to the pathologist, "When?"

"I'll have preliminaries tomorrow. Mid-morning. Providing I get no more calls before then." He nodded at Robin and DS Stanley both, said to the constables, "Let's load her," and followed the body up to the van.

Robin followed their progress with his gaze. On the bridge the young couple still waited. As the small corpse was carried past them, the girl turned her head into her husband's chest. He drew her closer, one hand in her hair, one on her buttock. Robin looked away.

"What's next?" Stanley asked him.

Robin considered the question. "We need to know who she was."

"Before that."

"Before? We take formal statements from the couple and get their signatures on them. And then we look at the PNC. If no one's gone missing locally, perhaps she's been reported missing from somewhere else and already listed on the computer."

Stanley zipped his leather jacket and patted the pockets of his jeans. He brought out a key ring and jiggled it in his hand. "And before that?" he said.

Robin puzzled over this. He looked back at the canal for inspiration. He supposed he could suggest that they drag it, but for what?

Stanley took mercy on him. "Before the statement and before the PNC, we deal with that lot." He jerked his thumb upward in the direction of the bridge.

A dusty car had just pulled up. Out of it were climbing a woman with a notebook and a man with a camera. Robin saw them hurry to the honeymooners. They exchanged a few words that the woman jotted down. The photographer began clicking pictures.

Robin said, "Newspapers? How the hell could they have found out so fast?"

"At least it's not television," Stanley replied. "Yet." And he walked off to deal with them.

—⁂—

Dennis Luxford touched his fingers to Leo's flushed cheek. It was damp with tears. He adjusted the blankets round his son's shoulders and felt a twinge that was one part guilt and one part impatience. Why did the boy always have to make everything so bloody difficult? he wondered.

Luxford murmured his name. He smoothed Leo's bright hair and sat on the edge of his bed. Leo didn't stir. He was either deeply asleep or more adept at faking it than Luxford would have guessed. In either case, he was unavailable for further discussion with his father. Which was probably just as well, considering where every discussion between them kept ending up.

Luxford sighed. He thought of the word *son* and everything that single syllable implied about responsibility, guidance, blind love, and guarded hope. He wondered why he had ever supposed he might make a success of fatherhood. He wondered why he had ever thought of fatherhood in terms of its rewards. More often than not, being a father seemed like an endless obligation. It was a lifelong duty that expected him to possess a reservoir of perspicacity as it did interminable battle with his personal desires and tried his meagre reserves of forbearance. It was just too much for one man to bear. How, Luxford asked himself, did other men do it?

He knew at least one part of the answer. Other men did not have sons like Leo. One glance round Leo's bedroom—in combination with a dip into the past to recall what his own room and that of his brother had been like at Leo's age—told Luxford that much. Black-and-white movie stills on the walls: everyone from Fred and Ginger in formal attire to Gene, Debbie, and Donald tapping away in the rain. A stack of art books on a plain pine desk, next to them a drawing pad with a sketch of a kneeling angel, its perfect head-encompassing halo and demure folded wings marking it as an example of fourteenth-century fresco. A cage of finches: fresh water, fresh seed, fresh paper on its floor. A bookcase with hardcovers arranged by author, from Dahl to Dickens. And in one corner a wooden trunk with black iron hinges in which, Luxford knew, went completely disregarded a cricket bat, a tennis racket, a football, Rollerblades, a chemistry set, a collection of toy soldiers, and a miniature pair of those pyjama-things worn by karate experts.

"Leo," he said quietly, "what's to be done about you?"

Nothing, Fiona would have told him in firm reply. Nothing at all. He's fine. He's perfect. The problem is yours.

Luxford put Fiona's assessment out of his mind. He bent, brushed his lips against his son's cheek, and turned off the light on his bedside table. He sat on the bed until the sudden total darkness in the room melded in his vision with what outside light filtered through the closed curtains. When he could see the shapes of the furniture and the crisp lines of black frames from the pictures on the wall, he left the room.

Downstairs, he found his wife in the kitchen. She was standing at the work top, putting espresso beans into a coffee grinder. The moment his foot hit the tiles of the kitchen floor, she briskly clicked the grinder into a howl.

He waited. She poured water into a cappuccino machine. She plugged its flex into the socket. She packed the newly ground coffee into the filter, tamped it down like tobacco, and pressed the machine's on switch. An amber light began to glow. The machine began to purr.

She stood in front of it, ostensibly waiting for the espresso, her back to him.

He knew the signs. He understood the volume of unspoken messages a woman communicated by the simple expedient of showing a man the back of her head instead of her face. But he went to her anyway. He rested his hands on her shoulders. He swept her hair to one side. He kissed her neck. Perhaps, he thought, they could simply pretend. "That's going to keep you awake," he murmured.

"Which is quite fine with me. I've no intention of sleeping tonight."

She didn't add *with you*, but Luxford didn't need those words to know her exact frame of mind. He could feel it in the resistance of her muscles beneath his fingers. He dropped his hands.

Released, she fetched a cup and set it beneath one of the machine's two spouts. A rivulet of espresso began to purl from the filter.

"Fiona." He waited for her to look his way. She didn't. Her concentration was all on the coffee. "I'm sorry. I didn't mean to upset him. I didn't mean things to be carried so far."

"Then what did you mean?"

"I meant us to talk. I tried to talk to him at lunch on Friday, but we didn't get anywhere. I thought if I tried, with all three of us together, we might resolve matters without Leo causing a scene."

"And you can't bear that, can you?" She went to the refrigerator, where she brought out a carton of milk. She poured a meticulous measure of it into a small stainless steel jug. She went back to the cappuccino machine and set the jug onto the work top. "God forbid if an eight-year-old boy causes a scene, isn't that right, Dennis?" She made an adjustment on the side of the machine and began to steam the milk. She swirled the jug furiously. The hot air hissed. The milk began to froth.

"That's not a fair assessment. It's no mean feat attempting to counsel a child who sees every attempt at discussion as an invitation to hysteria."

"He was *not* hysterical." She slapped the milk jug onto the work top.

"Fiona."

"He was *not*."

Luxford wondered what else his wife wanted to call it: five minutes of his carefully prepared remarks upon the glories and the benefits of Baverstock School for Boys greeted by Leo's dissolving into tears as if he were a cube of sugar and his father the hot water. Tears acting as harbinger to sobs. Sobs giving way quickly to howls. Howls the precursors of feet beating on the floor and fists flailing into the pillows on the sofa. What *was* hysteria if not that maddening response to adversity that was so characteristically Leo?

Baverstock would breed it out of him, which was principally why Luxford was determined to wrest Leo out of this cocoon-like environment of Fiona's and thrust him into a more hard-edged world. He was going to have to cope with that world eventually. What did it profit the boy to allow him to continue avoiding what he needed so badly to come to terms with?

Luxford had chosen the perfect time to discuss it: All three of them were together, the happy family in the dining room gathered to partake of the evening meal. It was Leo's favourite, chicken tikka, which the boy had tucked into energetically as he chatted about a BBC documentary on dormice upon which, apparently, he'd taken extensive notes. He'd been saying, "D'you think we can make a habitat for them in the garden, Mummy? They generally prefer old buildings, you know, attics and the spaces between walls. But they're ever so nice, and I expect that if we created a proper habitat, then in a year or two—" when Luxford decided it was time to clarify once and for all exactly where Leo would be residing in that year or two he was talking about.

He said expansively, "I'd no idea you were interested in natural science, Leo. Have you given veterinary medicine any thought?"

Leo's mouth formed the word *veterinary*. Fiona glanced Luxford's way. Luxford decided to ignore the minatory quality of her expression. He gambolled on.

"Veterinary medicine is a fine career. But it requires some preliminary experience with animals. And you're going to have that experience in spades—why, you'll be head and shoulders above the other applicants—by the time you're ready for university. What you're going to especially like about Baverstock is something they call the model farm. Have I mentioned it?" He didn't give Leo a chance to reply. "Let me tell you about it." And he began his monologue, a paean to the glories of animal husbandry. He actually knew little about the school's model farm, but what he didn't know, he embellished upon unashamedly: afternoons in the sunlight in the hills in the wind, the joys of lambing, the challenge of cows, breeding stock, gelding stallions. Animals galore. Not dormice, of course, at least no legitimate dormice. But in the outbuildings, the barns, perhaps even in the garrets of the dormitories themselves, the occasional dormouse might be encountered.

He finished his discourse by saying, "The model farm is one of the societies, not one of the formal classes. But through it you'll have the sort of exposure to animals that can eventually lead you towards a lifelong career."

As he'd been speaking, Leo's gaze had moved from his father's face to the rim of his glass of milk. He fixed it there and the rest of his body became ominously still, except for one foot which Luxford could hear kicking rhythmically against his chair leg. *Kerklunk, kerklunk.* Loud then louder. Like Fiona's presentation of her posterior, Leo's fixed gaze, kicks, and silences were warning signs. But they were also a source of aggravation to his father. God damn it, he thought. Other boys went off to school every year. They packed their trunks, they put scoff in their tuck boxes, they selected a favourite memento of home, and off they went. Perhaps with butterflies in their stomachs, but with a show of outward courage on their faces. With an understanding that their parents knew best and most of all without a display of histrionics. Which, Luxford knew, this chairkicking was leading to, as inevitably as sunset heralds the night.

He tried the power of positive thinking. He said, "Imagine the new friends you'll make, Leo."

"Got friends," Leo said to his milk glass. He said it in that irritating Estuary English that was becoming so fashionable, a glottal stop in place of the *t* in *got.* Thank God public school would soon breed that out of him as well.

"Think of the loyalties you'll develop, then. They'll last through your life. Have I told you how many old Bavernians I still see in a single year? Have I told you how influential they've been in seeing to each other's career advancement?"

"Mummy didn't go to public school. Mummy stayed at home and went to school. Mummy had a career."

"Of course. A fine one. But—" God, the boy wasn't now considering becoming a fashion model like his mother, was he? Professional dancing had seemed bad enough, but fashion? *Fashion?* Striding down a runway with one's pelvis thrust forward, an elbow jutting out, a shirt unbuttoned, hips on the swing, one's entire body an implicit invitation to sample one's wares. The idea was unthinkable. Leo was no more ready to take on that kind of life than he was ready to fly to the moon. But if he persisted . . . Luxford wrested back control of his raging imagination. He said kindly, "It's rather different for women, Leo. Their focus in life is different, so their education is different. You need a man's education, not a girl's. Because you're going to live in a man's world, not a girl's world. Right?" No response. "Right, Leo?"

Luxford saw Fiona's eyes on him. This was dangerous ground—a veritable bog—and if he ventured upon it, he risked becoming mired in more than merely Leo's histrionics.

He took the risk anyway. This question was going to be settled and it was going to be settled tonight. "A man's world requires traits of character that are developed best in the public school, Leo. Backbone, deep inner resources, quick thinking, leadership skills, the ability to make decisions, self-knowledge, a sense of history. That's what I want for you, and, believe me, when you've completed your time at Baverstock, you'll thank me for my sense of vision. You'll say, 'Dad, I can't believe there was a time when I was reluctant to be at Baverstock. Thank you for insisting it was for the best when I didn't know—' "

"I won't," Leo said.

Luxford chose to ignore the open defiance. Open defiance was unlike Leo, and chances were he hadn't intended to sound rebellious. He said, "We'll go down there in advance of Michaelmas term and give the place a thorough look-over. That way you'll have a leg up on the other new boys when they arrive. You'll be able to show them around yourself. Won't that feel good?"

"I won't. I won't."

The second *won't* was higher, more insistent than the first. It was the flare that preceded the actual bombardment, an antecedent shot into the air to light the way for the bombs to follow.

Luxford tried to maintain calm. He said, "You will, Leo. This is, I'm afraid, a decision that's been made and is, therefore, not open to further discussion. It's natural to feel reluctant—even frightened. As I've said before, most people greet change with some degree of trepidation. But once you've had a chance to adjust—"

"No," Leo said. "No, no, no!"

"Leo."

"I won't!" He shoved his chair away from the table, and stood, preparatory to leaving in a temper.

"Put your chair back."

"I'm finished."

"Well I am not. And until you're excused—"

"Mummy!"

The appeal to Fiona—and all that appeal implied about the nature of their relationship—made a flash of red lightning pass across Luxford's vision. He reached out, grabbed his son's wrist, and yanked him back to the table. He said, "You will sit until you are told you're finished. Is that clear?"

Leo cried out. Fiona said, "Dennis."

"And you," to Fiona, "keep out of this."

"Mummy!"

"Dennis! Let him go. You're hurting him." Fiona's words acted as invitation. Leo began to cry. Then wail. Then sob. And what had been a dinner conversation quickly escalated into a brawl in which a screaming, kicking, fist-beating Leo had finally been carried to his room and dumped inside where—in consideration of his precious belongings—he would be highly unlikely to do anything more than to beat his head against the pillows of his bed. Which is apparently what he did, unto exhaustion.

Luxford and his wife had finished their dinner in silence. They'd cleaned the kitchen. Luxford had read the rest of the *Sunday Times* while Fiona had used the fading light to work in the vicinity of the pond in the garden. She hadn't returned to the house until half past nine, at which time he'd heard her shower running, at which time he'd gone to check on Leo and had found his son asleep. At which time he wondered for the hundred-thousandth time how he was going to resolve the discord in his home without pulling rank and acting like the sort of paterfamilias he completely despised.

Fiona was pouring steamed milk into her cup. She always complained about the exorbitant cost one was asked to pay for a third of a cup of espresso and two-thirds of a cup of froth the consistency of dandelion down, so she was making herself a caffe latte instead of a cappuccino. She used three tablespoons of froth for the top and shook cinnamon onto it. Then she meticulously took the filter from the machine and set it just as meticulously into the sink.

Everything about her said, I don't wish to discuss it.

A fool would have rushed forward. A wiser man would have taken the hint. Luxford chose to play Feste.

He said, "Leo needs the change, Fiona. He needs an environment that will require more of him. He needs an atmosphere that will give him some backbone. He needs an exposure to boys from good families and decent backgrounds. He can only benefit from Baverstock. You must see that."

She raised her caffe latte and drank. She pressed a small square napkin against the foam on her upper lip. She leaned against the work top, making no move to go to a more comfortable location in the house, which is what he would have done to conduct this conversation and she knew that damn well.

She held her cup at the level of her breasts. She studied its cinnamon-topped foam. Then she said, "What a hypocrite you are," speaking down to the foam. "You've always touted equality, haven't you? You even went so far as to demonstrate your belief in equality by marrying into a squalid little family—"

"Stop that."

"—from south London. Heavens. The other side of the river. The daughter of a plumber and a hotel maid. Where people say *toilet* instead of *the loo* and no one listening has a seizure or even knows why they ought to be having one. How did you ever manage such a descent? How was it possible, believing, as you obviously did, that what you really needed was an exposure to good families with decent backgrounds? Or did you do it just for the challenge?"

"Fiona, my decision about Leo has nothing to do with class."

"Your nasty little schools have everything to do with class. They have everything to do with meeting the right people and making the right connections and learning the right accent and making sure one's clothing, posture, outside activities, choice of career, and attitude towards everyone else can be labelled U. Because God help the person who tries to get along in life simply on talent and the credentials of his worth as a man."

She'd wielded her weapons well. It was the fact that she used them so seldom that made them wound so effectively. Trench fighters were all like that, Luxford knew. They bided their time, dodged incoming shells, and lulled the opposition into thinking their arms were insignificant.

Luxford said with some stiffness, "I want the best for Leo. He needs guidance. He'll get it at Baverstock. I'm sorry you fail to see it that way."

She looked up from her coffee. She looked directly at him. "What you want for Leo is change. You're worried about him because he seems . . . I suppose you'd choose the word *eccentric*, wouldn't you, Dennis? Rather than the word you really mean."

"I want him to have a sense of direction. He's not getting that here."

"He has plenty of direction. You merely don't approve of it. I wonder why." She sipped her coffee.

He felt the fingers of warning tapping against his spine. To acknowledge them, however, was to hand power to the coward. He said, "Don't play amateur psychologist with me. Read that rubbish if you must. I don't object and you seem to enjoy it. But I'd appreciate it if you wouldn't inflict your diagnoses upon our relationship."

"You're terrified, aren't you?" she said despite his words. "He likes dancing, he likes birds, he likes little animals, he likes singing in the school choir, he likes medieval art. How can you possibly interpret such horrors in your son? Is the fruit of your loins going to turn out a poof? And if that's the case, isn't sending him to a boys' school just about the worst environment you can put him in? Or is it just the opposite because the first time an older boy shows Leo what's what when men get naked together, he's going to recoil and miraculously have any aberrant tendencies driven right from his head by fear?''

He watched her. She watched him. He wondered what she could read from his face and whether she could tell how his body had tightened and that he could feel his blood racing to his extremities. From her face, he could see only the process she was going through to evaluate him.

He said, "I'd assume you'd know from your reading that some things can't be quashed."

"Sexual preference? Of course not. Or if it's quashed, it's quashed only indefinitely. But the other? It can be quashed forever."

"What other?"

"The artist. The soul of the artist. You're doing your best to destroy it in Leo. I'm beginning to wonder when it was you lost yours."

She left the kitchen. He heard the sound of her leather sandals slapping quietly against the wooden floor. She went in the direction of her sitting room. From the kitchen window he could see the light snap on in that wing of the house. As he watched, Fiona came to the window and closed the curtains.

He turned away. But in turning away, he came face-to-face with his disregarded dreams. A life in literature was what he'd intended, making his mark in the world of letters. He would become a twentieth-century Pepys. He'd had the words. The ideas had been second nature. He'd fallen asleep to their marriage nightly. Finest writer I've ever known, David St. James had introduced him last week. And what had it come to?

It had come to being realistic. It had come to putting food on the table. It had come to building a roof over his head.

It had also come to the exquisite pleasure of wielding power, but that was secondary. Primary was that it had come to growing up. As everyone did, as everyone must do, Leo included.

Luxford decided that they weren't through with their conversation, he and Fiona. If she was insistent upon playing the game of psychological analysis, surely she wouldn't be averse to an examination of her own motives with regard to their son. Her behaviour towards Leo could do with a decent scrutiny. Her placement of herself between the wishes of Leo and the wisdom of his father could also do with a period of study.

He went to find her, readying himself for another round of verbal fisticuffs. He could hear the sound of the television. He could see the shifting dark and light images blinking against the wall. His footsteps slowed. His determination to have it out with his wife lessened. She must be more upset than he had originally thought, he realised. Fiona never turned on the television unless she wanted her agitated brain to be lulled.

He went to the doorway. He saw that she was curled into a corner of the sofa, a pillow at her stomach, holding it for comfort. The desire for combat faded more completely at the sight of her. It dissolved altogether when she spoke, saying without turning her head to him, "I don't want him to go. Don't do this to him, darling. It isn't right."

Beyond her on the screen, Luxford saw that the nightly news was playing. The newsreader's face faded to an aerial view of the country-side somewhere. The screen showed the snaking of a river bisected by bridges, a patchwork of fields, cars bumping along a narrow lane.

Luxford said to his wife, "Boys are resilient." He went to the sofa and stood behind it. He touched her shoulder. "It's natural to want to hold on to him, Fi. What's not natural is giving in to the impulse when it's best to let him have a new experience."

"He's too young for new experiences."

"He'll do fine."

"And if he doesn't?"

"Why don't we just take things as they come?"

"I'm afraid for him."

"That's why you're his mother." Luxford changed his position, going to sit next to her, removing the pillow, drawing her into his arms. He kissed the cinnamon taste of her mouth. "Can't we present a united front in this? At least until we see how it works out?"

"Sometimes I think you're intent upon destroying everything in him that's special."

"If it's special and it's real, it can't be destroyed."

She twisted her head to look up at him. "Do you believe that?"

"Everything I always was is alive in me," he said, indifferent to whether he spoke the truth or a lie, merely wanting an end to their enmity. "Everything that's special will stay alive in Leo. If it's strong and real."

"Eight-year-old boys shouldn't have to endure an ordeal by fire."

"Their mettle can be tested. Whatever's strong will endure."

"And that's why you want him to have this experience?" she asked. "To test his determination to be who he is?"

He looked her squarely in the eye and lied without a twinge of conscience. "That's why."

He settled her against him and gave his attention to the television screen. The picture was of a reporter this time, speaking into a microphone, a tranquil expanse of water behind her that had appeared from the air to be a river but instead was, she said, ". . . the Kennet and Avon Canal, where late this afternoon the body of an unidentified girl—perhaps six to ten years old—was discovered by Mr. and Mrs. Esteban Marquedas, two honeymooners sailing a narrow-boat from Reading to Bath. Although the death is being investigated as a suspicious circumstance, no decision has been made yet as to whether it should be classified a murder, a suicide, or an accident. Police sources tell us that the local CID have been at the scene and at the moment the Police National Computer is being used to attempt to establish the child's identity. Anyone with information that might assist the police is being asked to telephone the constabulary in Amesford." She went on to give the telephone number which was printed across the bottom of the screen. She concluded by giving her name, her station's call letters, after which she turned and gazed at the canal water with an expression of solemnity which she no doubt felt appropriate to the occasion.

Fiona was saying something to him, but Luxford didn't register her words. Instead, he was hearing a man's voice saying *I'll kill her Luxford if you don't run that story* overlapping Eve's voice saying *I'll die before I cave in to you* which itself was overlapping his own interior voice repeating the facts he'd just heard on the news.

He got abruptly to his feet. Fiona said his name. He shook his head and tried to manufacture an explanation. All he could come up with was "Damn. I've forgotten to give Rodney the word about tomorrow's news meeting."

He went in search of a telephone as far from Fiona's sitting room as possible.

14

I*T WAS FIVE O'CLOCK* on the following afternoon when Detective Inspector Thomas Lynley received word of the canal death. He had just returned to New Scotland Yard, having completed yet another interview with the Crown prosecutors. He never much cared for having to investigate high-profile murders, and the case that the prosecutors were preparing for trial—which involved the asphyxiation of a member of the England cricket team—had placed him into the spotlight more than he liked. But the media's interest was waning as the case began to wend its way into the judicial system. That interest was unlikely to be stirred up again until the trial itself. So he was feeling as if he'd shed a millstone he'd been forced to carry round for weeks.

He'd gone to his office to put it into some kind of order. During the last investigation, its chaos had assumed gargantuan proportions. In addition to the reports, the notes, the transcripts of interviews, the crime scene documentation, and the collection of newspapers that had become part of the manner in which he'd handled the case, the incidents room had been disassembled shortly after the perpetrator's arrest, and its collection of charts, graphs, timetables, computer printouts, telephone records, files, and other data had been delivered to him for sorting, for filing, and for sending onward. He'd been working through the material for the better part of the morning when he'd left to keep his appointment with the prosecutors. He was determined to wade through it to the end before he left for the day.

Upon reaching his office, however, he found that someone had decided to assist in his Augean endeavours. His detective sergeant, Barbara Havers, was sitting cross-legged in the midst of a stack of folders, a cigarette dangling from her lips as she squinted through the smoke at a stapled report that lay open on her lap. Without looking up, she said, "How were you going about this, sir? I've been working for an hour, and whatever your method is, it doesn't make any sense to me. This is my first fag, by the way. I had to do something to settle my nerves. So clue me in. What's your method? Are there piles to be kept and piles to be sent on and piles to be tossed out? What?"

"Just piles so far," Lynley said. He removed his jacket and hung it on the back of a chair. "I thought you were going home. Isn't this one of your Greenford evenings?"

"Yes, but I'll get there when I get there. There's not exactly a hurry. You know."

He did. The sergeant's mother was ensconced in Greenford, a paying resident in a private home whose owner cared for the aged, the infirm, and—in the case of Havers' mother—the mentally disintegrating. Havers made the pilgrimage to see her as often as her irregular work schedule would allow, but from what Lynley had been able to gather from six months of the sergeant's laconic remarks about her visits, it was always a toss-up as to whether her mother would recognise her.

She took a deep drag from her cigarette before, in deference to his unspoken wishes, she crushed it out against the side of the metal wastepaper basket and sent it to join the rubbish. She crawled across a scattering of folders and reached for her shapeless canvas shoulder bag. She dug round in it and brought out a wad of belongings from which she extracted a smashed packet of Juicy Fruit. She unwrapped two sticks and crammed them into her mouth.

"How'd you let it get this bad?" She made an expansive gesture to take in the office and leaned against the wall. She balanced her left heel upon the toes of her right foot, admiring her shoes. She was wearing high-top red trainers. They made quite a fashion statement with her navy trousers.

" 'Mere anarchy is loosed upon the world,' " Lynley said in answer to her question.

"More like loosed upon this office," she replied.

"I suppose things got out of hand," he continued, and added with a smile, "but at least they didn't fall apart altogether. Which means, I should guess, that the centre will hold."

Her face drew in on itself—eyebrows meeting, mouth pursing, chin lifting towards nose—as she rooted through his words for a meaning. She said, "Who what where, sir?"

He said, "Poetry." He went to his desk and gloomily surveyed the mound of manila folders, books, maps, and documents that heaped across it. He said, " 'Things fall apart; the centre cannot hold;/Mere anarchy is loosed upon the world.' It's part of a poem."

"Oh. A poem. Lovely. Have I ever mentioned how much I appreciate your efforts to elevate my cultural consciousness? Shakespeare, was it?"

"Yeats."

"Even better. I like my literary allusions obscure. Back to the subject at hand. What're we going to do with all this?"

"Pray for a fire," he said.

The genteel clearing of a throat drew their attention to the door of Lynley's office. A vision of hot pink double-breasted suit stood there, with a cream silk jabot frothing copiously from her throat. At the jabot's centre an antique cameo nested. All their superintendent's secretary needed to complete the ensemble was a broad-brimmed hat, and she'd be one of the royals, decked out for Ascot.

"This is a sad state of affairs, Detective Inspector Lynley." Dorothea Harriman gave a melancholy shake of her head at the condition of his office. "You must be angling for a promotion. Only Superintendent Webberly could make a bigger mess. Although he could manage it with far less material."

"Care to lend a hand, Dee?" Havers said from the floor.

Harriman held hers up, the nails perfectly manicured. She said, "Sorry. Other duties call, Detective Sergeant. For you as well. Sir David wants to see you. Both of you, in fact."

Havers thudded her head against the wall. "Shoot us now," she groaned.

"You've had worse ideas," Lynley said. Sir David Hillier had just been promoted to Assistant Commissioner. Lynley's last two run-ins with Hillier had walked a tightrope between insubordination and all-out warfare. Whatever Hillier wished to see them about now, it probably wouldn't be pleasant.

"Superintendent Webberly's with him," Harriman offered helpfully, perhaps in encouragement. "And I have it on the very best authority that they've spent the last hour behind closed doors with the VIP-est of VIPs: Sir Richard Hepton. He came on foot and he left on foot. What d'you think of that?"

"Since the Home Office is a five-minute walk from here, I don't think anything," Lynley said. "Should I?"

"The Home Secretary? Coming to New Scotland Yard? Locking himself up with Sir David for an hour?"

"He must be a masochist," was Havers' assessment.

"About halfway through, they sent for Superintendent Webberly and nattered with him for another thirty minutes. Then Sir Richard left. Then Sir David and Superintendent Webberly sent for you two. They're waiting now. Above."

Above meant in Assistant Commissioner Sir David Hillier's new office, which he had moved into with lightning speed once his promotion had become official. It had an uninteresting view of Victoria Street, and its walls were as yet undecorated with Hillier's plethora of career-enhancing photographs, although these were already laid upon the floor as if someone had been deciding upon the most flattering arrangement. Central to them was an enlargement of Sir David receiving his knighthood. He knelt with hands clasped before him and head bowed. He hadn't looked so humble in years.

The man himself was in grey this afternoon, a bespoke suit that exactly matched his great wealth of hair. He was sitting behind his football field of a desk, his hands folded upon a leather-bound blotter in such a way that his signet ring winked in the overhead lights. Lying at a precise right angle to the blotter's edge was a yellow pad covered with Hillier's flowing, self-confident cursive.

Superintendent Webberly—Lynley's immediate supervisor—was perched uncomfortably at the edge of a sling-back chair of the ultra-modern design that Hillier favoured. He was holding a wrapped cigar and rolling it thoughtfully back and forth along his thumb. He looked bearlike in his cuff-frayed tweeds.

Hillier said to Lynley without preamble, "A child's body was found in Wiltshire last night. Ten years old. She's the daughter of the Home Office Undersecretary. The Prime Minister wants the Yard to handle the investigation. The Home Secretary wants the same. I suggested you."

Lynley's suspicions were immediately aroused. Hillier never suggested him for a case unless he had something unsavoury up his sleeve. Havers, he saw, was experiencing misgivings as well, because she glanced towards him quickly as if gauging his reaction. Hillier apparently recognised their doubts because he went on curtly. "I know there's been bad blood between us for eighteen months, Inspector. But we've both been at fault."

Lynley looked up, ready to question Hillier's use of the word *both*. Hillier seemed to realise this, because he went on to say, "My fault may be the larger. We all follow orders when we must. I'm no different to you when it comes to that. I'd like to let bygones be bygones. Can you do the same?"

"If you're assigning me to a case, I'll cooperate," Lynley said and added, "Sir."

"You're going to have to do more than cooperate, Inspector. You're going to have to meet with me when requested so that I can have ready reports for the Prime Minister and the Home Secretary. Which means you won't be able to play at holding back information as you've done in the past."

"David," Webberly said carefully. Off on the wrong foot, his tone implied.

"I think I've been forthright with the facts as I've known them," Lynley said evenly to Hillier.

"You've been forthright enough when I squeezed you," Hillier said. "But I don't want to have to squeeze you this time round. The investigation's going to be under everyone's microscope, from the Prime Minister's down to Tory backbenchers'. We can't afford to fail to work as a team. Someone's head is going to roll if we do."

"I can see what's at stake, sir," Lynley said. What was at stake was virtually everything, since the Home Office was responsible for the workings of New Scotland Yard in the first place.

"Good. I'm glad of it. Know this, then. Not an hour ago the Home Secretary ordered me to throw the best I've got onto the case. I chose you." It was the closest Hillier had ever come to offering a compliment, and he added, "Do I make myself clear?" in case Lynley didn't understand the oblique homage that the Assistant Commissioner was paying to his underling's talents.

"Quite," Lynley said.

Hillier nodded and began to recite the details: The daughter of Eve Bowen, Junior Minister at the Home Office, had been abducted the previous Wednesday, allegedly snatched en route between her music lesson and her home in Marylebone. Within hours, kidnapping notes had been delivered. Demands had been made. An audiotape of the child had been recorded.

"Ransom?" Lynley asked in reference to the demands.

Hillier shook his head. The kidnapper, he told them, wanted the child's natural father to identify himself in the press. The child's father wouldn't do it because the mother didn't want him to. Four days after the initial demand, the child was found drowned.

"Murdered?"

"No direct evidence of that yet," Webberly said. "But it's probable."

Hillier slid open one of the drawers of his desk and brought out a file, which he handed over. It contained, along with the police report, the official police photographs of the body. Lynley examined them slowly, noting the name of the child, Charlotte Bowen, and a case number printed on the back of each. There was, he saw, no significant mark of violence on the body. Superficially, its appearance was consistent with accidental drowning. Except for one thing. "No froth from the nostrils," he said.

"According to the local CID, the pathologist got it from the lungs. But only under pressure on the chest," Webberly said.

"That's an interesting twist."

"It is, isn't it?"

"Here's what we want." Hillier intervened impatiently. It was no particular secret to the others that his interest had never lain in crime scene evidence, in the statements of witnesses, in the corroboration of alibis, in the gathering and piecing together of facts. His main fascination was in the politics of policing, and this particular case promised an exposure to those politics in unheralded degree. "Here's what we want," he repeated. "Someone from the Yard at every level of the investigation, in every location, and at every juncture."

"That's a hot potato," Havers noted.

"The Home Secretary doesn't care whose tender feelings get trampled in what police district, Sergeant. He wants us involved in every area of the investigation, so that's what we're going to be. We'll have someone in Wiltshire heading up that end of the case, someone heading up the London end, and someone liaising with the Home Office and Downing Street. If an officer along the line has a problem with the set-up, he can be replaced with someone who hasn't."

Lynley handed the photographs to his sergeant, asking Hillier, "What have the Marylebone police given us so far?"

"Nothing."

Lynley looked from Hillier to Webberly and made note of the fact that Webberly had suddenly fixed his eyes to the floor. He said, "Nothing? But who's our liaison at the local station?"

"There isn't one. The local police haven't been involved."

"But you said the girl went missing last Wednesday."

"I did. The family didn't phone the police."

Lynley tried to digest this. Five days had passed since the girl's disappearance. According to Hillier and Webberly, phone calls had been received by one parent. A tape had been recorded. Letters had been penned. Demands had been made. The child in question was only ten years old. And now she was dead. He said, "Are they mad? What sort of people are we dealing with? Their child goes missing and they do nothing to—"

"That's not quite it, Tommy." Webberly raised his head. "They did try to get help. They brought someone in immediately. Last Wednesday night. It just wasn't the police."

The expression on Webberly's face made Lynley tense. He had the distinct impression that, Hillier's acknowledgement of his expertise aside, he was about to discover why he of all people had been assigned to this case. "Who was it?" he asked.

Webberly heaved a sigh and shoved his cigar into the breast pocket of his jacket. "I'm afraid this is where things get dicey," he said.

———

Lynley powered the Bentley in the direction of the Thames. He gripped the steering wheel hard. He didn't know what to think about what he'd just learned, and he was trying like the devil to keep from reacting. Just get there, he told himself reasonably. Get there in one piece and ask your questions so you can understand.

Havers had followed him as he strode across the underground car park. She'd said, "Sir, listen to me," and had finally hooked on to his arm when he'd continued on his way without reply, deep in thought. She hadn't been able to stop him, however, so she had resorted to planting her chunky body in his path. She'd said, "Listen. You'd better not go over there now. Cool off first. Talk to Eve Bowen. Get the story from her."

He'd gazed at the sergeant, nonplussed by her behaviour. He'd said, "I'm perfectly cool, Havers. Head out to Wiltshire. Do your part. Let me do mine."

She said, "Perfectly cool? What bullshit. You're about to go off at half-cock, and you know it. If Bowen hired him to look for her daughter—and Webberly *said* not fifteen minutes ago that she did—then Simon's activities from that moment on were professional activities."

"Agreed. So, I'd like to gather the facts from him. It seems a logical place to begin."

"Stop lying to yourself. You're not after facts. You're after vengeance. It's written all over you."

Clearly, Lynley realised, the woman was mad. He said, "Don't be absurd. Vengeance for what?"

"You know what. You ought to have seen your face when Webberly said what everyone's been up to since Wednesday. You went white to the lips and you haven't recovered."

"Nonsense."

"Is it? Look. I know Simon. So do you. What do you think he was doing? Do you imagine he sat on his thumbs just waiting for this girl to be found dead in the countryside? Is that what you think happened?"

"What happened," he said reasonably, "is the death of a child. And I think you'll agree that death might have been prevented had Simon, not to mention Helen, had the foresight to involve the police from the first."

Havers settled her hips. Her expression said *Gotcha*. Her words were, "And that's it, isn't it? That's at the root of what's bothering you."

"Bothering me?"

"It's Helen. Not Simon. Not even this death. Helen was into things up to her eighteen-carat-gold earrings and you didn't know. Right? Well? Am I right, Inspector? And *that's* why you're heading to Simon's house."

"Havers," Lynley said, "I've got things to do. Please get out of my way. Because if you don't remove yourself from my path immediately, you're going to find yourself assigned to another case."

"Fine," she said. "Lie to yourself. And while you're at it, pull rank and have done with it."

"I believe I just have done. And since this is your first opportunity to be at the head of at least one arm of an investigation, I suggest you consider your options wisely before you force my hand."

Her upper lip curled. She shook her head. "Holy hell," she said. "You can be a real prick." She turned on the heel of her high-top trainer and set off for her own car, slinging the strap of her canvas bag to her shoulder.

Lynley got into the Bentley. He fired it up with a gratifying but unnecessary roar. Within a minute, he was out of the underground car park and speeding in the direction of Victoria Street. His mind was trying to deal with the process of setting up an investigation. But it was doing battle with his heart which, as Havers had shrewdly assessed—blast her intuition—was fixed on Helen. Because Helen had deliberately lied to him last Wednesday night. All her insouciant chatter about nerves, about marriage, about their future together, was merely a blind, constructed to conceal her activities with Simon. And the result of that lie and of those activities was a little girl's death.

He stepped hard onto the accelerator. He was in the middle of eight tour coaches all simultaneously trying to escape the immediate environs of Westminster Abbey before he realised that, given the time of day, he should have taken a different route to the river. As it was, he had plenty of time to question his friends' incomprehensible behaviour and plenty of time to consider where that behaviour had led them when he finally negotiated the rush hour congestion round Parliament Square and headed south towards Chelsea.

Traffic was heavy. He vied for position with taxis and buses. At the rising cables and slender towers of Albert Bridge, he made the turn into the narrow crescent of Cheyne Walk, from there to Cheyne Row. He squeezed the Bentley into a space towards the top of the cramped little street, and he took up the case file on Charlotte Bowen's death. He strode back in the direction of the river, to the tall, umber-hued brick house at the corner of Cheyne Row and Lordship Place. It was utterly quiet in the neighbourhood, and he found that the silence was a momentary balm to him. In it, he took a steadying breath. All right, he thought, maintain control. You're here to get facts and that's all. This is the most logical place to begin and nothing you're doing could possibly be described as flying off at half-cock. His sergeant's recommendation that he see Eve Bowen first was merely a reflection of her inexperience. There was no point to seeing Eve Bowen first when here in this house was the information he needed to set his investigation in motion. That was the truth of it. Any claims that he was seeking vengeance and lying to himself were completely off the mark. Right? Right.

He used the door knocker. After a moment, he also used the bell. He heard the dog barking, then the telephone ringing. Deborah's voice said, "Good grief. Everything at once," and called to someone, "I'm getting the door. Can you catch the phone?"

A bolt was released. Deborah stood there, barefooted and barelegged in jeans cut off at the thigh, with flour on her hands and more of it liberally dusting her black T-shirt. Her face brightened when she saw him. She said, "Tommy! Good heavens. We were talking about you not five minutes ago."

He said, "I need to see Helen and Simon."

Her smile faltered. She knew him well enough. She could hear from his tone—despite his effort at dispassion—that something wasn't right. "In the kitchen. In the lab. I mean, Helen's in the kitchen and Simon's in the lab. Dad and I were just showing her . . . Tommy, has something . . . ? Is anything wrong?"

"Will you fetch Simon?"

He left her climbing hurriedly towards the top floor of the house. He himself went to the back. Here stairs led down to the basement kitchen. Rising from there, he could hear Helen's laughter and Joseph Cotter's voice. Cotter was saying, "Now, egg whites's the secret. That's what makes them brown proper and get nice 'n' glossy on top. But you separate the eggs first, see. Make a nice firm crack 'long the shell like this. Use the shell 'affs thisways to scoop the yolk back and forth till you got the whites separate."

"Is that honestly all there is to it?" Helen was saying in reply. "Lord, it's perfectly simple. Even an idiot could do it. Even *I* could do it."

"Simple it is," he said. "You give it a try."

Lynley descended the stairs. Cotter and Helen were on either side of the worktable at the centre of the kitchen, Helen wrapped in an enormous white apron, Cotter in shirtsleeves rolled to his elbows. Spread out between them were mixing bowls, baking pans, boxes of currants, bags of flour, and assorted other ingredients. Into one of the smaller bowls, Helen was in the process of separating her egg. The baking pans held the fruits of their labour: circular mounds of currant-spotted dough the circumference of teacups.

The St. Jameses' small dachshund spotted Lynley first. She had been busily licking the flour dust from the floor round Helen, but perhaps sensing his presence, she raised her head, saw him, and gave a sharp bark.

Helen looked up, each hand holding the half of an eggshell. Like Deborah's earlier, her face brightened with her smile. She said, "Tommy! Hello. Imagine the impossible. I've actually made scones."

"We need to talk."

"I can't at the moment. I'm about to be shown how to put the final touch on my masterwork, just as soon as I finish separating this egg. Which I *do* believe I'm rather excelling at, as Cotter will no doubt agree."

Cotter, however, had apparently read Lynley more accurately. He said, "I c'n finish up here. Quick as a wink. Nothing much to it. You go with Lord Asherton."

"Nonsense," she said.

"Helen," Lynley said.

"I can't leave my creation at the climactic moment. I've come this far with it and I want to see it through to the end. Tommy will wait for me. Won't you, darling?"

The endearment grated against his nerves. He said, "Charlotte Bowen is dead."

Helen's hands were suspended, still holding the eggshells. She lowered them. She said, "Oh God."

Cotter, making an obvious gauge of the atmosphere between

them, scooped up the little dachshund and took her lead from a hook that hung near the back door. He was gone without a word. In a moment, the gate on Lordship Place creaked open, then closed.

"What did you think you were doing?" Lynley asked her. "Tell me, Helen. Please."

"What's happened?"

"I just told you what's happened. The girl's dead."

"How? When?"

"It doesn't matter how or when. What matters is that she might have been saved. This might never have happened. She might have been back with her family right now had you possessed enough sense to inform the police what was going on."

She recoiled slightly. Her next words were faint. "That isn't fair. We were asked to help. They didn't want the police."

"Helen, I don't care what you were asked. I don't care who did the asking. A child's life was at risk and that life is gone. Over. Dead. She's not coming back. She drowned at the Kennet and Avon Canal and her body was left to rot in the reeds. So was it—"

"Tommy." St. James spoke sharply from the stairs above him. Deborah stood behind him. "We've got the point."

"Have you any idea what's happened?" Lynley asked.

"Barbara Havers just phoned me." He made his awkward way down the stairs to the kitchen. Deborah followed. Her face was the colour of the flour on her T-shirt. She and St. James took up positions with Helen, on the other side of the worktable from Lynley. "I'm sorry," St. James said quietly. "I wouldn't have had it end this way. I think you know that."

"Then why didn't you do something to prevent it?"

"I tried."

"Tried what?"

"To talk to them both, the mother and the father. To make them see reason. To get them to phone the police."

"But not to walk away. Not to force their hand. You didn't try that."

"Initially, no. I didn't. I admit to that. We none of us walked away at first."

"None of . . . ?" Lynley's eyes went to Deborah. She was twisting her hands in the bottom of her T-shirt. She looked perfectly wretched. He realised what St. James's words had just told him, compounding their sin a hundred thousand times. He said, "Deborah? Deborah took part in this mess? Jesus Christ, have you all completely lost your minds? If I force myself, I can understand Helen's involvement because at least she has a modicum of experience working with you. But Deborah? *Deborah*? She has as much business embroiling herself in a kidnapping investigation as the family dog has."

"Tommy," Helen said.

"Who else?" Lynley asked. "Who else took part? What about Cotter? Did he get involved? Or was it just you three cretins killing off Charlotte Bowen?"

"Tommy, you've said enough," St. James said.

"No. I haven't. And I doubt I ever will. You're responsible, the three of you, and I'd like you to see exactly what you're responsible for." He opened the case folder he'd brought from the car.

St. James said, "Not here."

"No? Rather not see how things turned out?" Lynley flipped a photograph onto the table. It landed squarely in front of Deborah. "Have a look," he said. "You might want to memorise it just in case you decide to kill any more children."

Deborah's fist went to her mouth, but it wasn't sufficient to cut off her cry. Roughly, St. James pulled her away from the table. He said to Lynley, "Clear out of here, Tommy."

"It won't be that easy."

"Tommy!" Helen extended a hand towards him.

"I want to know what you know," he said to St. James. "I want every piece of information you have. I want every detail, and God help you, Simon, if you forget to include a single fact."

St. James had taken his wife into his arms. He said slowly, "Not now. I mean it. Leave."

"Not until I've got what I came for."

"I believe you've just got that," St. James said.

"Tell him," Deborah said against her husband's shoulder. "Please, Simon. Just tell him. Please."

Lynley watched St. James carefully weigh the alternatives. He finally said to Helen, "Take Deborah upstairs."

"Leave her here," Lynley said.

"Helen," St. James said.

An instant passed before Helen chose. She said, "Come with me, Deborah," and to Lynley, "Or would you like to stop us? You're big enough to do so, and frankly I'm wondering if you draw the line at striking women these days. Since you apparently draw no other lines."

She swept past him, her arm across Deborah's shoulders. They climbed the stairs and shut the door behind them.

St. James was looking at the photograph. Lynley could see a muscle working furiously in his jaw. Outside at a distance, he could hear the dog barking. He could hear Cotter's shout. Then, finally, St. James looked up.

"That was particularly unforgivable," he said.

Although Lynley knew what St. James was referring to, he deliberately chose to misunderstand. "Agreed," he said evenly. "It was unforgivable. Now tell me what you know."

They observed each other across the worktable. A long moment passed during which Lynley wondered if his friend was going to cooperate with information or to retaliate with silence. Nearly thirty seconds went by before he had his answer, and St. James began to speak.

He told his story tersely without looking up. He took Lynley through each day that had passed since Charlotte Bowen had disappeared. He delineated his facts. He listed his evidence. He explained the steps he had taken and why. And when he was through, with his attention still fixed firmly to the photograph, he said, "There's nothing more. Leave us, Tommy."

Lynley knew it was time to relent. He said, "Simon—"

But St. James cut him off. "Go," he said.

Lynley obliged.

—⁂—

The study door was closed. It had been open when Deborah had admitted him into the house, so Lynley knew that's where Helen had taken her. He turned the knob without knocking.

Deborah was sitting on the ottoman, arms clasped round her stomach and shoulders hunched. Helen sat opposite her, on the sofa. She held a glass in her hand. She was saying, "Have a bit more, Deborah," to which Deborah was replying, "I don't think I can."

Lynley said Helen's name. In response, Deborah's body pivoted away from the door. Helen set the glass on the sofa's side table, touched Deborah's knee lightly, and came to Lynley. She stepped into the corridor and shut the door behind her.

Lynley said, "I was out of line. I'm sorry."

She offered a brittle smile. "No, you're not sorry. But I trust you're satisfied. I hope you've managed to leave no stone of spleen-venting unturned."

"Damn it, Helen. Listen to me."

"Tell me this. Is there anything else for which you'd like to excoriate us before you leave? Because I'd hate to see you be on your way without having fulfilled your desire to castigate, humiliate, and pontificate."

"You have no right to any outrage, Helen."

"Just as you had no right to adjudication."

"Someone's dead."

"It isn't our fault. And I refuse, Tommy. I refuse to bow my head, bend my knees, and beg for your sanctimonious pardon. I've done nothing wrong in this situation. Neither has Simon. Neither has Deborah."

"Aside from your lies."

"*Lies?*"

"You could have told me the truth last Wednesday night. I asked. You lied."

Her hand climbed to her throat. In the dim light of the corridor, her dark eyes seemed to grow even darker. "My God," she said. "You rotten little pharisee. I can't even *believe* . . ." Her fingers tightened to a fist. "This isn't about Charlotte Bowen, is it? This has nothing to do with Charlotte Bowen at all. You've come here and spewed like a broken sewer pipe because of me. Because I chose to keep something private in my life. Because I didn't tell you something that you had no right to know in the first place."

"Are you out of your mind? A child is dead—dead, Helen, and I think I can safely assume you know what that means—so what are you doing talking to me about rights? No one but the person in danger has any rights at all when a life is at risk."

"Except you," she said. "Except Thomas Lynley. Except silver-spoon-in-his-mouth Lord Asherton. That's what you're getting at: *your* God almighty rights, and in this particular case, the right to know. But not to know about Charlotte because she's just the symptom. She's not the disease."

"Don't twist this into a reflection on us."

"I don't need to twist it. I can see it straight on."

"Can you?" he asked. "Then see the rest. Had you put me in the picture, she might be alive. She might be at home. She might have walked away from her abduction and not ended up floating dead in a canal."

"Simply because I told you the truth?"

"That would have been a fairly good start."

"It wasn't an option."

"It was the single option that might have saved her life."

"Was it?" She backed away, regarding him with a look that he could only interpret as pitying. She said, "This is going to come as a surprise to you, Tommy, and I almost hate to be the one to inform you, considering what a blow it's going to be: You are not omnipotent and despite your tendency towards acting the part, you are also not God.

Now, if you'll excuse me, I'd like to see if Deborah's all right." Her hand reached for the knob of the study door.

"We're not finished," he said.

"Perhaps you aren't," she pointed out. "But I am. Entirely."

She left him facing the door's dark panels. He stared at them. He worked to control the overpowering urge to kick in the wood. He found that at some point during their conversation his hands had clenched with the need to strike. And he felt that need now, a longing to drive his fist through the wall or a window, to feel pain as much as to cause it.

He forced himself to move away from the study. He forced himself to make his way to the front door. Outside, he forced himself to breathe.

He could almost hear Sergeant Havers' assessment of his interview with his friends: Nice job, Inspector. I even took notes. Accusing, insulting, and alienating everyone. A brilliant way to ensure their cooperation.

But what else had he been supposed to do? Should he have congratulated them for their inept meddling? Should he have politely informed them of the child's demise? Should he have even used that fatuous, innocuous word—*demise*—to spare them lest they feel what they bloody damn well ought to feel at the moment: responsible?

They did the best they knew, Havers would have said. You heard Simon's report. They followed every lead. They tracked her movements on Wednesday. They showed her picture round Marylebone. They talked to the people who saw her last. What more would *you* have done, Inspector?

Done background checks. Tapped telephone lines. Put a dozen detective constables into Marylebone. Given the girl's photograph to the television news and asked for the public to report sightings of her. Entered her name and her description into the PNC. All that just for a start.

And if the parents didn't want you to make that start? Havers would have demanded. What then, Inspector? What would you have done had they tied your hands as they tied Simon's?

But they wouldn't have been able to tie Lynley's hands. One didn't phone the police, report a crime, and then determine the manner in which the police would investigate it. Surely St. James—if not Helen and Deborah—knew that much. It had been within their power from the very first to effect a completely different sort of investigation to the one they had engaged in. And all of them knew it.

But they'd given their word . . .

Lynley could hear Havers' argument, but it was growing faint. And her last point was the easiest to dismiss. Their word counted for nothing when it was weighed against the life of a child.

Lynley descended the steps to the pavement. He felt the release that came from knowing he was in the right. He walked back to the Bentley and was in the process of unlocking it when he heard his name called.

St. James was approaching him. His expression, Lynley saw, was unreadable and when he reached the car, he merely extended a manila envelope, saying, "You'll want these, I think."

"What is it?"

"A school photograph of Charlotte. The kidnapping notes. The fingerprints from the tape recorder. The prints I took from Luxford and Stone."

Lynley nodded. He accepted the material. In doing so, he found that, despite his belief in the inherent justice of his censure of his friends and of the woman he loved, he felt a discomfort when faced with St. James's deliberate courtesy and all which that courtesy implied. This discomfort was an irritant to him, reminding him as it did that there were obligations in his life that were often messy, ones that went beyond the mere confines of his job.

He looked away, towards the top of the street where Cheyne Row made a jog at whose elbow sat an ancient brick house in sad need of renovation. It could have been worth a fortune had someone cared enough to see to its repair. As it was, it was nearly uninhabitable.

He said with a sigh, "Damn it, Simon. What would you have had me do?"

"Have some faith, I suppose."

Lynley turned back to him. But before he could comment upon the remark, St. James went on, returning once again to a tone that conveyed nothing other than an adherence to the protocol called for by Lynley's earlier demand for information. "I'd forgotten one thing. Webberly's incorrect. The police in Marylebone have been involved, however tangentially. A PC ran off a vagrant from Cross Keys Close the same day that Charlotte Bowen was taken."

"A vagrant?"

"He may have been staying in some squats on George Street. I think you'll need to check him out."

"I see. Is that it?"

"No. Helen and I think he may not have been a vagrant at all."

"If not a vagrant, then what?"

"Someone who might have been recognised. Someone in disguise."

15

---

*R*ODNEY ARONSON SLIPPED the wrapper from his Kit Kat bar. He broke off a piece and popped it into his mouth. Blissfully, he guided his tongue through an exploration of the delicious little nodes and crevices created by the ingenious conjunction of cacao seeds and wafer. This afternoon's Kit Kat, whose consumption Rodney had postponed till his body's fiendish need for chocolate could no longer be ignored, was almost enough to make him put Dennis Luxford out of his mind. But not quite.

At the conference table in his office, Luxford was in the midst of examining two alternative dummies of tomorrow's front page, which Rodney had just delivered to him, per Luxford's request. As he studied them, *The Source* editor rubbed his right thumb along the crooked scar on his chin, while his left thumb followed the shape of his bicep beneath his white shirt. He was the perfect picture of contemplation, but the information Rodney Aronson had managed to assemble in the past few days prompted him to wonder how much of Luxford's performance was being manufactured spontaneously for his deputy editor's benefit.

Of course, the truth was that *The Source* editor didn't know that Rodney had been playing the hound to Luxford's fox, so his contemplation of the two dummy front pages might be genuine enough. Still, the fact of the two front pages' very existence brought Luxford's motivations into question. He could no longer argue that the Larnsey–rent boy story was hot enough to take up front page space. Not with the news of the Bowen child's death reverberating through the canyons of Fleet

Street ever since the official statement had been handed down from the Home Office this afternoon.

Rodney still could see the raised eyebrows and dropped jaws among his colleagues during the news meeting when Luxford had said what he wanted despite the fast-breaking news of the Bowen death: a dummy front page running a year-old picture of Daffy Dukane in *tête-à-tête* with MP Larnsey, which one of the photo historians had managed to unearth after a prolonged archaeological dig through the newspaper's photo files. Perhaps in direct response to his colleagues' roar of incredulous protest, Luxford had gone on to order another dummy front page, this one running a photograph of the Home Office Undersecretary, a photograph that was spontaneous, catching Bowen en route from one location to another. He didn't, Luxford said, want a studio photograph or a publicity photograph, and he wasn't about to run either one on the front page of his paper in conjunction with Charlotte Bowen's death. He wanted a recent picture, a picture from today. And if they couldn't produce that for him by the time the newspaper went to press, they would go with Sinclair Larnsey and Daffy Dukane for tomorrow's paper and sink the Bowen story somewhere inside.

"But this is our lead," Sarah Happleshort had protested. "Larnsey's dead meat. What difference does it make where the Bowen pictures come from? We're going to have to use a school picture of the kid, and that won't be recent. So who the hell cares if her mother's is?"

"I care," Luxford said. "Our readers care. The chairman cares. So if you want to run the story, get the picture to go with it."

Luxford was attempting to stymie them, Rodney suspected. He was betting on the fact that no one would be able to come up with a current picture by deadline.

But he had bet wrong, because at precisely half past five that afternoon, Eve Bowen had ducked out a side entrance at the Home Office, and *The Source*, who had staff photographers as well as free-lancers at every possible location where the Junior Minister might show her face —from Downing Street to her health club—had managed to catch her with the Home Secretary's solicitous hand on her elbow, guiding her towards a waiting car.

It was a clean, clear shot. True, she didn't look much like the grieving mother—no lace-edged handkerchief clutched to her eyes, no dark glasses to hide the bloodshot whites—but no one could argue that it wasn't the woman of the hour. Although from the expression on Dennis Luxford's face, it looked as if he intended to try.

"Do you have hard copy on the rest of this?" Luxford asked, having read the four brief paragraphs crammed into the space that remained once the headline was in place. This read *High Ranking MP's Daughter Found Dead!* in a combination of colours guaranteed to move papers from vendor to customer as quickly as thirty-five pence could change hands. In comparison to the *Larnsey & Daffy in Happier Times* on the other dummy, there was simply no contest.

Rodney fished the rest of the story's copy from a sheaf of papers he'd brought along. It was a draft that he'd had Happleshort print out in anticipation of just such a request from the editor. Luxford read it.

Rodney said, "It's solid. We started with the official statement. We built from there. Confirmations on everything. More information to come."

Luxford raised his head. "What sort of information?"

Rodney saw that Luxford's eyes were bloodshot. The flesh beneath them was the colour of plum skin. He readied himself to read the editor for the slightest nuance and said with a careless shrug, "Whatever information the cops and Bowen are holding back."

Luxford set the copy next to the front page dummy. Rodney tried to interpret the precision of his movements. Was he stalling for time? Devising a strategy? Reaching a decision? What? He waited for Luxford to ask the next logical question: What makes you think they're withholding information? But the question didn't come.

Rodney said, "Look at the facts, Den. The kid lives in London but was found dead in Wiltshire, and that's the limit to what we were told in the official statement from the Home Office, along with 'mysterious circumstances' and 'awaiting autopsy results.' Now, I don't know how you interpret that rubbish, but personally I think it reeks like dead cod."

"What do you propose to do?"

"Put Corsico on it. Which," Rodney hastened to add, "I've already taken the liberty of doing. He's just outside. Arrived back in the newsroom as I was bringing in the dummies for you. Shall I . . . ?" And Rodney used his arm to indicate his willingness to have Mitch Corsico join them. "He's done all there can be done on Larnsey," Rodney pointed out. "It seemed a waste not to use his talents on what's clearly going to be a bigger story. Agree?" He made the word so affable, so filled with eagerness to pursue the news. What could Luxford do but concur?

"Bring him in," Luxford said. He sank into his chair and rubbed thumb and forefinger into his temple.

"Right." Rodney popped another piece of Kit Kat into his mouth. He slid it into the pouch of his cheek so the chocolate could melt there, slowly entering his system like an IV drug. He went to the office door and opened it, saying expansively, "Mitch-boy. Get in here. Tell papa the news."

In the waiting area, Mitch Corsico hitched up his jeans, which he perennially wore beltless, and lobbed the core of an apple into the wastepaper basket near Miss Wallace's desk. He scooped up his denim jacket, wrestled a grubby notebook from its pocket, and clomped across Miss Wallace's cubicle in his cowboy boots, saying, "I think we've got something nice and dodgy for tomorrow. And I can guarantee we're the only ones on to it so far. Can we hold up the presses?"

"For you, my son, anything," Rodney said. "It's on the Bowen situation?"

"None other," Corsico said.

Rodney closed the door behind the young reporter. Corsico joined Luxford at the table. He said with a flip of his index finger towards the dummy front pages and the draft of the Bowen story, "This stinks. They gave us one effing fact—a dead body in Wiltshire—and then entertained us with the have-you-no-decency routine when we wanted more information. We had to work our arses off to get every other detail, none of which it would have slain them to share. The kid's age, her school, the condition of the body, exactly where it was found. You name it, we had to grub for it. Did Sarah tell you that?"

"She just handed over the finished story. Which, I might add, is as lovely a piece as you've ever done." Rodney went to Luxford's desk and looped his thigh over the corner. It was odd how hidden knowledge invigorated one. He'd been working ten hours so far today, and the way he was feeling, he could work ten more. "Bring us up to date," he said, and added to Luxford, "Mitch tells me he's got something that we're going to want to run tomorrow along with this." He indicated the dummy Bowen front page, projecting a confidence in the editor's forthcoming decision about which of the two dummies would actually be used.

Luxford had no real choice in the matter, as Rodney well knew. He may have temporised at the news meeting earlier by demanding two dummies and a current photo of Bowen that he believed unobtainable, but he was boxed in now. He was the editor of the paper, but he reported to the chairman, and the chairman would expect *The Source* to run the Bowen story front and centre. There would be hell to pay if Sinclair Larnsey's mug and not Bowen's decorated page one in the morning, and Luxford would be the one to pay it.

It was intriguing to Rodney to speculate upon why Luxford had dragged his feet on the front page decision. It was especially intriguing to engage in speculation in light of Luxford's assignation at Harrods with one of the story's principal players. How much of a coincidence could it possibly be that he'd met with Eve Bowen secretly just three days before her daughter was found dead? And how did that meeting fit in with everything that had followed it: Den's holding up the presses on the flimsiest of pretexts, Den's visit from the red-haired photographer and the stranger who'd decked her, Den's rushing off not ten minutes after that decking had occurred, and now this death. . . . Rodney had spent much of the weekend mulling the question of what Luxford was up to, and when the Bowen story broke, he'd immediately assigned Corsico to it, knowing that if there was dirt involved somewhere, Mitch was just the person to roll in it.

Now he grinned at Corsico. "Shovel it out for us."

Corsico took a moment to remove his trademark Stetson. He looked at Luxford as if awaiting a more official directive. Luxford gave a weary nod.

"Okay. First. Mum's the word at the police press office in Wiltshire," Corsico began. "No comment at the moment aside from the basics: who found the body, what time, where, its condition, etc. Bowen and her husband made the positive ID round midnight in Amesford. And this is where things start to get interesting." He shifted his bum from one cheek to the other, as if settling in for a pleasant natter. Luxford glued his eyes steadily upon the reporter and didn't move them. Corsico continued.

"I asked the press office the regular preliminaries. The name of the investigating officer, the time of the autopsy, the identity of the pathologist, the initial decision on the time of death. No comment to all of it. They're controlling the information flow."

"That's hardly news to stop the presses for," Luxford commented.

"Right. I know. They like to play games with us. It's the normal struggle for dominance. But I've a reliable snout at the police station in Whitechapel, and she—"

"What's Whitechapel got to do with anything?" To emphasise his irritation, Luxford glanced at his watch.

"Nothing directly. But wait. I phoned her and asked her to have a look at the PNC, just to see what kind of vitals I could get on the kid herself. But—and here's where it starts getting dodgy—there was no report on the police computer."

"What sort of report?"

"No report of the body having been found."

"And this is what you consider earth-shattering? This is what I'm to hold up the presses for? Perhaps the police just haven't got caught up in their paperwork.''

"That's a possibility. But there was also no report of the girl's having gone missing in the first place. Despite—and Whitechapel had to call in some chits to get this for me—the body's having been in the water up to eighteen hours.''

Rodney said, ''That *is* a nice bit.'' And with an evaluative glance at Luxford, ''I wonder what it means. What d'you think, Den?''

Luxford ignored the question. He lifted his knuckles to his chin and rested it on them. Rodney tried to read him. His expression looked bored, but surely his eyes seemed wary. Rodney nodded at Corsico to continue.

Corsico warmed to his topic. ''At first I thought it was no big deal that no one had reported the kid missing. After all, it was the weekend. Maybe someone had got their wires crossed. Parents thinking the kid was with the grandparents. Grandparents thinking the kid was with an aunt or uncle. The kid supposedly at a sleep-over somewhere. That kind of thing. But I thought it was worth checking on anyway. And it turned out I was right.'' Corsico flipped open his notebook. Several pages fluttered out. He scooped them up from the floor and stuffed them into a pocket of his jeans. He said, ''There's an Irishwoman who works for Bowen. Fat lady in baggy leggings, name of Patty Maguire. She and I had a chat about quarter of an hour after the Home Office made the announcement about the kid.''

''At the MP's house?''

''I was first on the scene.''

''That's my boy,'' Rodney murmured.

Corsico modestly lowered his gaze to his notebook and made much of studying it. Then he went on. ''I was delivering flowers, actually.''

Rodney grinned. ''Ingenious.''

''And?'' Luxford said.

''She'd been praying up a storm on her knees in the sitting room, and once I told her I'd be more than pleased to share her devotions— which took a good forty-five minutes, let me tell you—we had a cuppa in the kitchen and she spilled the beans.'' He jockeyed his chair about so that he was no longer facing the table, but instead facing Luxford. ''The kid went missing last Wednesday, Mr. Luxford. Supposedly she was snatched off the street, most likely by some pervert. But the MP and her husband never reported it to the cops. What d'you think of that?''

Rodney blew a soft whistle of amazement. Even he hadn't been prepared for this. He went to the door and swung it open, ready to call in Sarah Happleshort to revamp the front page.

Luxford said, "What are you doing, Rodney?"

"Getting Sarah in here. We need to move with this."

"Close the door."

"But, Den—"

"I said close the door. Sit down."

Rodney felt his hackles rise. It was the tone that got to him, that bloody assurance of Luxford's that his every command would be obeyed. "We've got a damn solid story going," Rodney said. "Is there some reason you want to quash it?"

Luxford said to Corsico, "What sort of confirmation have you got on this?"

"*Confirmation?*" Rodney said. "This is the naffing housekeeper he's been talking to. Who'd know better that the kid was snatched and the police weren't called?"

Luxford repeated, "Have you got confirmation?"

Rodney said, "Den!" and knew that Luxford would kill the story unless Corsico had been sharp enough to cover every conceivable base.

But Corsico came through. He said, "I spoke to someone at three of the divisional police stations in the Marylebone area: Albany Street, Greenberry Street, Wigmore Street. There's no record in any of the collators' offices of anyone reporting this kid missing."

"Dynamite," Rodney breathed. He wanted to crow, but he contained himself. Corsico went on.

"That didn't make sense to me. What parents wouldn't phone the cops if their kid disappeared?" He tilted his chair back and answered his own question. "I thought, perhaps, it might be parents who wanted her gone."

Luxford remained expressionless. Rodney gave a low whistle.

"So I thought we might get ahead of the game if I did some more digging," Corsico said. "Which is what I did."

"And?" Rodney asked, seeing the story begin to take shape.

"And I found out that Bowen's husband—a bloke called Alexander Stone—isn't the father of this kid in the first place."

"That's hardly news," Luxford pointed out. "Anyone who follows politics could have told you that, Mitchell."

"Yeah? Well, it was news to me, and an interesting twist. And when a twist comes up, I like to follow where it's leading. So I went to St. Catherine's and looked up the birth certificate to see who the father was. Because I figured we'd want to interview him eventually, right?

The grieving parent? With the death and all?" He grabbed his denim jacket and drove his fist into one pocket, then the other. He brought out a folded piece of paper, which he unfolded, smoothed against the top of the table, and handed over to Luxford.

Rodney waited, breath held in anticipation. Luxford looked the paper over, raised his head, and said, "Well?"

"Well what?" Rodney demanded.

"She hasn't given the father's name," Corsico explained.

"I can see that much," Luxford said. "But since she's also never identified him publicly, this hardly comes as an overwhelming surprise."

"Maybe not a surprise. But a possible connection and, more important, a definite way to spin the story."

Luxford returned the copy of the certificate to Corsico. As he did so, he seemed to study the young reporter, the way one might examine a life form one can't quite identify. "Where exactly are you heading with this?"

"No name entered on the birth certificate? No report of the kid's disappearance made to the police? It's all about withholding information, Mr. Luxford. It's the prevailing theme, the theme of this poor kid's birth in the beginning, the theme of her death in the end. We can spin the story round that for a start. If we do—and an editorial about the insidious nature of family secrets would be nice as well—then believe me, even a twit would be able to dig up the nasties about MP Bowen for *The Source* afterwards. Because if Larnsey and the rent boy are any measure of what we can expect from the public, as soon as we spin this story round Bowen's tendency to withhold crucial information, every enemy she has will be ringing us up with a tip that will take us right where we want to go."

"Which is where?" Luxford asked.

"To the guilty party. Which, I'll wager, is the ultimate piece of information she's withholding." Corsico raked his hair back into place. It immediately unraked itself. "See, it only makes sense that she knows who snatched the kid. It's either that or she arranged to have the kid snatched herself. Those two are the only possible explanations for why she didn't phone the cops straightaway. The only reasonable explanations as well. Now, if we tack that information onto the fact that she's kept the identity of the kid's dad a secret all these years . . . well, I think you can see where I'm heading, can't you?"

"Actually, I can't."

Rodney's antennae immediately went up. He'd heard that tone of Luxford's before. Deadly even, utterly polite. Luxford was playing out the rope. If he had it his way, Corsico was going to pick it up, loop it round his neck, and hang himself directly. And the story with him.

He started to intervene, saying in what he hoped was a decisive tone, "A solid piece of investigative journalism so far. Of course, Mitch will be taking it one step at a time, with confirmations all the way. Correct?"

But Corsico didn't get the hint. He said, "Listen, I've got twenty-five pounds that says there's a connection between the kid's disappearance and the father. And if we start sifting through Bowen's background, I've another twenty-five that says we'll find it."

Rodney silently told Corsico to still his blabber. He tried to give him the cut-throat sign to shut up, but the reporter was intent upon making his points. After all, Luxford had always loved them before. What reason was there for Corsico to think he wouldn't love them now? This was just another Tory they were going after. Hadn't Luxford been regaled by Corsico's every effort to sink the Tories so far?

"How tough could it be to find the connection?" Corsico was saying. "We've got the kid's birth date. We count back nine months from it and start nosing round Eve Bowen's background to see what she was up to then. I've even made a start." He rustled through two pages of his notebook, read for a moment, said, "Yeah. Here. The *Daily Telegraph*. She was a political correspondent for the *Daily Telegraph* then. That's our starting point."

"And where do you go from there?"

"Don't know yet. But I'll give you my best guess."

"Please do."

"I say she was shagging a major player in the Conservative Party, to grease her way onto some constituency's candidacy list. We're talking Chancellor of the Exchequer, Home Secretary, Foreign Secretary. Someone like that. Her pay-off was a seat in Parliament. So all we have to do is find out who was shagging her. Once we've got that, the rest of the story's just a matter of camping out on his doorstep till he's ready to talk to us. And that, you'll see, will be the connection we're looking for between this"—he waved the birth certificate—"and the kid's death."

"Charlotte," Luxford said.

"Huh?"

"The child in question. Her name was Charlotte."

"Oh. Right. Yeah. Charlotte." Corsico scribbled into his notebook.

Luxford placed his fingers on the dummy front page, straightening it to line up with his desk. In the silence among them, the sound from the newsroom was suddenly amplified. Telephones ringing, laughter welling up, an individual yelling, "Shit! Someone save me! I'm dying for a fag!"

Dying was it, Rodney thought. He could see what was coming as surely as he could see the next Kit Kat bar he was planning to inhale the moment this meeting was over. The only thing he couldn't see was exactly how Luxford was going to pull it off. Then the editor enlightened him.

He spoke to Corsico. "I expected far better of you," Luxford said.

Corsico stopped writing, although he kept his pencil poised. He said, "What?"

"Better reporting."

"Why? What's the—"

"Better work than this bullshit fairy tale you've just spun for me, Mitchell."

"Now, wait a second, Den," Rodney intervened.

"No," Luxford said. "You wait. Both of you. We're not talking about a member of the public here: Lucy Law-and-order who follows every dictate and toes every line. We're talking about a Member of Parliament. And not just any Member of Parliament but a Government Minister. Do you actually expect me to believe for an instant that a Government Minister—an undersecretary of bleeding state, for the love of God—would *ever* phone her local police station and report her daughter missing when she can walk down the hall and have the Home Secretary handle the problem personally for her? When she can demand discretion? When she can have as much secrecy as she wants? In a bloody Government that makes secrecy its watchword? She could make this case the highest priority at Scotland Yard and no police station in the country would be wise to the fact, so why the hell do you think some station in Marylebone would happen to have it on report? Do you actually want me to believe we have a front page story upon which we're going to build a case against Bowen because she didn't phone her local bobby?" He shoved his chair back and surged to his feet. "What kind of journalism is this? Get out of here, Corsico, and don't come back until you have a story we can run with."

Corsico reached for the copy of the birth certificate. "But what about—"

"What about it?" Luxford demanded. "It's a birth certificate without a name. There are probably two hundred thousand just like it and none of them constitute news. When you have the Home Secretary or the Commissioner of Police going on record with the story that they knew nothing about this kid's disappearance prior to her death, then we'll have something to hold up the presses about. In the meantime, stop wasting my time."

Corsico started to speak. Rodney held up his hand to stop him. He couldn't believe Luxford would go so far as to use this as a reason to kill the entire story, no matter how much he apparently wanted to. But he had to make sure. He said, "Okay. Mitchell, we go back to square one. We double-check everything. Get three confirmations." And he quickly went on before Corsico could argue. "What's the front page going to be for tomorrow, Dennis?"

"We'll go with the Bowen piece as written. No changes. And nothing about the absence of fantasy police reports."

"Shit," Corsico breathed. "My story's solid. I know it is."

"Your story's manure," Luxford said.

"That's—"

"We'll work on it, Den." Rodney caught Corsico by the armpit and quickly manoeuvred him out of the room. He shut the door behind them.

"What the *hell?*" Corsico demanded. "My stuff is hot. You know it. I know it. All that bullshit about— Look, if we don't run it, someone else will. Come on, Rodney. Jesus. I should just take this story over to the *Globe* and sell it to them. This is news. This is hot. And no one has it but us. Damn it. God *damn* it. I ought to—"

"Keep working on it," Rodney said quietly, casting a speculative look at Luxford's office door.

"What? I'm supposed to try to get the Commissioner of Police to talk to me about a Member of Parliament? What a bloody laugh."

"No. Forget him. Follow the trail."

"The trail?"

"You think there's a connection, don't you? The kid, the birth certificate, all that?"

Corsico settled his shoulders and adjusted his spine. If he'd been wearing a tie, he'd probably have straightened its knot. He said, "Yeah. I wouldn't be going after it if it wasn't there."

"Then find the connection. Bring it to me."

"And then what? Luxford—"

"Bugger Luxford. Dog the story. I'll do the rest."

Corsico flicked a glance at the door of the editor's office. "It's a hell of a story," he said, but for the first time he sounded uneasy.

Rodney grabbed his shoulder and gave it a jerk. "It is," he said. "Go after it. Write it. Give it to me."

"And then?"

"I'll know what to do with it, Mitch."

—⁓—

Dennis Luxford pressed the button that would switch on the monitor of his computer terminal. He dropped into his chair. The figures on the monitor began to glow, but his eyes didn't focus on them. Switching on the monitor was merely an excuse for something to do. He could turn to it and display an avid perusal of its gibberish should anyone suddenly walk into his office and expect to see *The Source* editor watching over the pursuit of a story that no doubt at this moment had every reporter in London doing industrious spadework into Eve Bowen's life. Mitch Corsico was only one of them.

Luxford knew how unlikely it was that Mitch Corsico and Rodney Aronson had been convinced by his show of editorial outrage. In all the years that he had run *The Source* and the *Globe* before it, he had never moved to block a story that held as much scurrilous promise as did this tale of MP Bowen's failure to phone the local police about the abduction of her child. And it was a Tory tale to boot. He should have been glorying in the number of pleasing opportunities such a story presented. He should have been rabid in his eagerness to mould the revelation that Evelyn had failed to phone the police into a clever and sententious indictment of the entire Tory party. There they were, religiously touting their Recommitment to Basic British Values, one of which—one could only presume—was supposed to be the Basic British Family. And when the family was threatened in the most heinous of fashions, through the abduction of a child, a noted Tory minister did not, our sources tell us, so much as involve the proper authorities in a search for that child. Here was an opportunity to massage meagre facts into a story that would portray the Tories once again as the flimflammers they truly were. And he had not only not grasped that opportunity. He had done his best to eradicate it.

At the most, Luxford knew, he had only bought some time. That Corsico had got on to the birth certificate so quickly—that he had a sensible plan for excavating Evelyn's past—told Luxford how unreasonable it was to expect the secret of Charlotte's birth to remain a secret now she was dead. Mitchell Corsico had the kind of initiative which he—Luxford—would once have revelled in. The boy's instinct for ferreting out the path to the truth was astounding, and his ability to cajole people into telling that truth was in itself a work of art. Luxford could hobble his progress by placing restrictions upon him, by laying down specious surmises about the Home Secretary and New Scotland Yard and ordering the boy to check each one out. But he could not halt that progress save by giving him the sack. Which would serve only to prompt him to take his notebooks, his Filofax, and his nose for news to a competitor, the *Globe* most likely. And the *Globe* wouldn't have Luxford's reasons for thwarting a story that would expose the truth.

Charlotte. God, Luxford thought, he'd never even seen her. He'd seen the propaganda photographs when Evelyn was standing for Parliament, the candidate posing at home with her devoted, smiling family at her side. But that had been the extent of it. And even then he'd passed over the pictures with nothing more than the contemptuous glance he gave to all the candidates' posturing during a general election. He hadn't really looked at the child. He hadn't bothered to study her. She was his, and all he actually knew of her was her name. And—now—the fact that she was dead.

He'd phoned Marylebone from the bedroom on Sunday night. When he'd heard her voice, he'd said tersely, "The television news. Evelyn, a body's been found."

She'd said, "My God. You monster. You'll stoop to anything to bend my will, won't you?"

"No! Just listen to me. It's in Wiltshire. A child. A girl. Dead. They don't know who she is. They're asking for information. Evelyn. *Evelyn.*"

She'd hung up on him. He hadn't talked to her since.

Part of him said she deserved to be ruined. She deserved a very public objurgation. She deserved to see every detail of Charlotte's genesis, her life, her disappearance, and her death put on display for the judgement of her countrymen. And she deserved to be toppled from her position of power as a result. But another part of him couldn't be a party to her downfall. Because he wanted to believe that whatever her sins, she had paid for them fully with the death of this child.

He hadn't loved her those few days in Blackpool, any more than she had loved him. Their shared experience had been nothing more than bodies connecting, their concupiscence heightened by the fact that they were polar extremes. They had nothing in common but their ability to debate their opposing viewpoints and their desire to be seen as the victor in every polemic they embarked upon. She was swift-witted and confident. He, a verbal swordsman, hadn't intimidated her in the least. Their disputes generally ended in draws, but he was used to decimating his opponents thoroughly and failing to decimate her with words, he had sought other means. He'd been young enough and stupid enough that he still believed a woman's submission in bed was a declaration of male supremacy. When he'd finished with her and was flush with the swagger of what he'd brought her to and how, he'd expected radiant eyes, a somnolent smile, followed by a delicate and decidedly feminine fading into the closest woodwork from which she would henceforth allow him to reign among their colleagues supreme.

The fact that she hadn't faded into any woodwork at all after the seduction, the fact that she had acted as if nothing had happened between them, the fact that her wits were, if anything, sharper than ever, served only to infuriate him first and then to make him want her more. At least in bed, he'd thought, there would be neither symmetry nor equality between them. At least in bed, he'd thought, what conquest there was would always be his. Men dominate, he'd believed, and women submit.

But not Evelyn. Nothing he did and nothing he swore that she felt ever took away her self-possession. Intercourse was just another battleground for them, with pleasure instead of words the weapon.

The worst of it was that she knew all along what he was trying to do to her. And the final time she'd come, on that last hurried morning when both of them had trains to catch and deadlines to meet, she'd raised his face shiny with her fluids to hers and she'd said, "I am not diminished, Dennis. In any way. Not even by this."

He was shamed by the knowledge that an innocent life had grown from their loveless mating. So indifferent had he been to the consequences of skewering her in the only way he could, he hadn't bothered to take a single precaution and he hadn't cared in the least whether she was taking any. He hadn't even thought of what they were doing in terms of possibly creating a life. He'd seen it only as mastery, a necessary step in proving to her—and above all to himself—his supremacy.

He hadn't loved her. He hadn't loved the child. He had wanted neither. He'd assuaged what few twinges of conscience he'd had by "taking care of matters" in a way that meant he would never be touched personally by either of them. So by rights he should feel nothing now, other than bitterness and shock that Evelyn's single-minded recalcitrance had cost a human life.

But the truth was that what he felt went far beyond bitterness and shock. He felt knotted inside by guilt, anger, anguish, and regret. Because while he was responsible for the life of a child he had never tried to see, he knew very well that he was also responsible for the death of a child he would never know. Nothing could change that fact for him now. Nothing ever would.

Numbly, he drew the computer's keyboard towards him. He accessed the story that would have saved Charlotte's life. He read the first line: "When I was thirty-six years old, I made a woman pregnant." Into the silence of his office—a silence undercut by the exterior noises from the newspaper he'd been hired to rebuild from nearly nothing—he recited the conclusion to the sordid story: "When I was forty-seven, I killed the child."

16

WHEN LYNLEY REACHED Devonshire Place Mews, he saw that Hillier had already been at work meeting the Home Secretary's demands for an efficient operation. Sawhorses had been erected at the entrance to the mews. These were manned by a police constable, while another constable stood guard at the front door of Eve Bowen's home.

Behind the sawhorses and swelling out onto Marylebone High Street, the media were gathered in the dusk. They were represented by several television crews who were in the process of fixing up lights to film their correspondents' evening reports, print journalists who were barking questions at the constable nearest to them, and photographers who were restlessly waiting for the opportunity to take pictures of anyone related to the case.

When Lynley stopped the Bentley to show his identification to the sawhorse guard, the reporters surged round the car. A babble of questions rose. Was the death being labelled a homicide? If so, were there any suspects yet? Was there truth to the rumour that the Bowen child had a history of doing a bunk whenever she was unhappy? Would Scotland Yard be working with the local police? Was it true that important evidence was going to be removed from the MP's house this evening? Would DI Lynley comment upon any aspects of the case that related to child abuse, to the white slave trade, to devil worship, pornography, and ritual sacrifice? Did the police suspect IRA involvement? Had the child been molested before she died?

Lynley said, "No comment." And, "Constable, clear a path please." He guided the Bentley into Devonshire Place Mews.

As he got out of the car, he heard brisk footsteps coming in his direction, and he turned to see Detective Constable Winston Nkata approaching from the far end of the mews.

"Well?" Lynley said when Nkata joined him.

"No score at all." Nkata surveyed the street. "Folks are home in all but two of the houses. But no one saw anything. They all knew the girl—seems like she was a friendly little bird who liked to chunter with most anyone who'd listen—but no one saw her last Wednesday." Nkata slipped a small leather-bound notebook into the interior pocket of his jacket. He followed it with a mechanical pencil, carefully retracting its lead first. He said, "Had a long chat with an older bloke, pensioner in a hospital bed on the first floor of Number Twenty-one, see? He keeps a pretty good eye on the street most days. He said nothing out of the ordinary went down last week at all, far as he could tell. Just the normal comings and goings. Postman, milkman, residents, the like. And 'ccording to him, the comings and goings at the Bowen place work just like a clock, so he'd know it if something p'culiar was happening."

"Any suggestion of tramps in the neighbourhood?" Lynley told Nkata what he'd learned from St. James.

Nkata shook his head. "Not a whisper of it, man. And that old bloke I mentioned? He'd be likely to remember. He knows what's what in the neighbourhood, top to bottom. Even told me who likes having it off with fine young specimens of the opposite sex when her man's not round. Which, he assured me, goes on three–four days a week."

"You made careful note of that, I take it?"

Nkata grinned and raised a hand in denial. "I'm living clean as dish soap these days. Have been for the last six months. Nothing sticks to my mum's favourite boy that I don't want stuck there. Believe it."

"I'm glad to hear the news." Lynley nodded towards Eve Bowen's house. "Has anyone been in or out?"

"Home Secretary was there for an hour or so. A tall, skinny bloke with serious hair after that. He was there quarter of an hour, maybe more. He brought a stack of notebooks and folders with him, and he left with an older piece, heavy-set bird with a canvas tote bag. Hustled her into the car and out of here fast. Housekeeper, I'd say by the look of her. Crying into the sleeve of her sweater. Either that or hiding her face from the photogs."

"That's all?"

"That's it. Unless someone parachuted into their back garden. Which, truth to tell, I wouldn't put past that lot for a moment. How'd they get here so fast, anyway?" Nkata demanded about the reporters.

"Assisted by Mercury or beamed down from the *Enterprise*. Take your pick."

"I should get so lucky. I got caught in a jam in front of Buck House. Why'n't they move that damn place to some other part of town? It's sitting smack in the middle of a roundabout, doing nothing but obstructing traffic."

"Which," Lynley noted, "certain Members of Parliament would find an apt metaphor, Winston. But not Ms. Bowen, I dare say. Let's have a talk with her."

The constable at the door took a look at Lynley's identification before he admitted them. Inside, another constable was seated on a wicker chair at the foot of the stairs. She was doing *The Times* crossword puzzle, and she got to her feet—a thesaurus in her hand—as Lynley and Nkata entered. She led them into the sitting room off which a dining area opened. At a table there, a meal was spread out: lamb chops congealing in their juices, mint jelly, peas, and potatoes. Two places were laid. A bottle of wine stood open. But nothing had been either eaten or drunk.

Beyond the dining table, french doors opened into the back garden. This had been designed as a courtyard, with terra-cotta paving stones on the ground, wide, well-kept flowerbeds edging them, and a small fountain trickling water at their centre. At a green iron table set off to the left of the french doors, Eve Bowen was sitting in the growing shadows with a three-ring notebook opened in front of her and a glass to one side, half filled with ruby-coloured wine. Five more notebooks were stacked on another chair next to her.

The constable said, "Minister Bowen, New Scotland Yard," and that was the extent of her introductions. When Eve Bowen looked up, the constable backed off and returned to the house.

"I've spoken to Mr. St. James," Lynley said after identifying himself and DC Nkata. "We're going to need to talk to you frankly. It may be painful, but there's no other way."

"So he's told you everything." Eve Bowen didn't look either at Lynley or at Nkata, who slipped his leather notebook from his pocket and made a preparatory adjustment to the length of lead in his pencil. Rather, she looked at the papers in front of her, loosened from the notebook. The light was fading too quickly for her to be able to read any longer, and she made no pretense of doing so. She merely fingered the edge of one of the papers as she waited for Lynley's response.

"He has," Lynley said.

"And how much have you shared with the press so far?"

"It's not generally my habit to speak to the media, if that's your concern."

"Not even when the media guarantee anonymity?"

"Ms. Bowen, I'm not interested in revealing your secrets to the press. Under any circumstances. In fact, I'm not interested in your secrets at all."

"Not even for money, Inspector?"

"That's correct."

"Not even when they offer you more than you make as a policeman in the first place? Wouldn't a nice size bribe—three or four months' salary, for instance—be a tempting circumstance under which you might find yourself suddenly possessed of an insatiable interest in every one of my secrets?"

Lynley felt rather than saw Nkata look his way. He knew what the DC was waiting for: DI Lynley's verbal umbrage at the insult to his integrity, not to mention Lord Asherton's umbrage at the more serious insult to his bank account. He said, "I'm interested in what happened to your daughter. If your past relates to that, it's going to become public knowledge eventually. You may as well prepare yourself for that. I dare say it isn't going to be as painful as what's happened already. May we talk about it?"

She favoured him with an evaluative gaze in which he read nothing from her, no ripple on the surface and no emotion in the eyes behind her spectacles. But apparently she'd reached a decision of some sort, because she dipped her chin fractionally in what went for a nod and said, "I phoned the Wiltshire police. We went out directly to identify her last night."

"We?"

"My husband and I."

"Where is Mr. Stone?"

Her eyelids lowered. She reached for her wineglass but she didn't drink from it. She said, "Alex is upstairs. Sedated. Seeing Charlotte last night . . . Frankly, I think all the way out to Wiltshire he was hoping it wouldn't be her. I think he'd even managed to convince himself of that. So when he finally saw her body, he reacted badly." She drew her wineglass closer, not picking it up but sliding it across the glass that served as top to the table. "As a culture, we expect too much of men, I think, and not enough of women."

"None of us know how we'll react to a death," Lynley said. "Until it happens."

"I suppose that's true." She gave the glass a quarter turn and examined how the movement affected its contents. She said, "They knew she had drowned, the police in Wiltshire. But they wouldn't tell us anything else. Not where, not when, not how. Especially that last, which I find rather curious."

"They have to wait for the results of the autopsy," Lynley told her.

"Dennis phoned here first. He claimed to have seen the story on the news."

"Luxford?"

"Dennis Luxford."

"Mr. St. James told me that you suspected him of being involved."

"Suspect," she corrected him. She removed her hand from the wineglass and began to straighten the papers on the table, evening out the corners and the sides in a movement much like a sleepwalker's. Lynley wondered if she had been sedated as well, her exercise of straightening them was so slow. She said, "As I understand it, Inspector, there's currently no evidence that Charlotte was murdered. Is that correct?"

Lynley was reluctant to put his suspicions into words despite his viewing of the photographs. He said, "Only the autopsy can tell us exactly what happened."

"Yes. Of course. The official police line. I understand. But I saw the body. I—" The tips of her fingers whitened where she pressed them against the tabletop. It was a moment before she went on, and during that moment they could all clearly hear the muffled babble of voices from the reporters not far away on Marylebone High Street. "I saw the entire body, not just the face. There was no mark on it. Anywhere. No significant mark. She hadn't been tied. She hadn't been weighted down in some way. She hadn't struggled against someone holding her underneath water. What does that suggest to you, Inspector? It suggests an accident to me."

Lynley didn't openly disagree with her. He was more curious to see where she was heading with her thinking than he was eager to correct her misconceptions about accidental drownings.

She said, "I think his plan went awry. He intended to have her held until I surrendered to his demands for public notice. And then he would have released her unharmed."

"Mr. Luxford?"

"He wouldn't have killed her or ordered her killed. He needed her alive to assure my cooperation. But somehow it all went wrong. And she died. She didn't know what was going on. She may have been frightened. So perhaps she escaped. It would have been like Charlotte to do that, to escape. Perhaps she was running. It was dark. She was in the country. She wouldn't have been familiar with the land. She wouldn't even have known the canal was there because she'd never been to Wiltshire before."

"Was she a swimmer?"

"Yes. But if she was running . . . If she ran, fell, hit her head . . . You see what could have happened to her, I expect."

"We aren't ruling out anything, Ms. Bowen."

"So you're considering Dennis?"

"Along with everyone else."

She moved her gaze to her papers and to the ordering of them. "There isn't anyone else."

"We can't draw that conclusion," Lynley said, "without a full examination of the facts." He pulled out one of the three other chairs that sat round the table. He nodded at Nkata to do the same. He said, "I see you've brought work home."

"Is that the first fact to be examined, then? Why is the Junior Minister calmly sitting in her garden with her work spread round her while her husband—who's not even the father of her child—is upstairs completely prostrate with grief?"

"I expect your responsibilities are enormous."

"No. You expect I'm heartless. That's the most logical conclusion for you to reach, isn't it? You have to observe my behaviour. It's part of your job. You have to ask yourself what sort of mother I am. You're looking for whoever abducted my daughter and for all you know, I may have arranged it myself. Why else would I be capable of sitting here looking through papers as if nothing had happened? I don't seem to be the sort who'd be desperate for something to stare at, something to play at working upon, to keep myself from tearing my hair out with grief. Do I?"

Lynley leaned towards her, placing his hand near where she'd placed hers, on top of one of the stacks of papers. He said, "Understand me. Not every remark I make to you is going to be a judgement, Ms. Bowen."

He could hear her swallow. "In my world, it is."

"It's your world we need to talk about."

On the papers, her fingers began to curl, the way they would had she decided to crumple the documents. It seemed to take an effort for her to relax them again. She said, "I haven't cried. She was my daughter. I haven't cried. He looks at me. He waits for the tears because he'll be able to comfort me if I give him tears and until I do, he's completely lost. There's no centre for him. There's not even a handhold. Because I can't cry."

"You're still in shock."

"I'm not. That's the worst of it. Not to be in shock when everyone expects it. Doctors, family, colleagues. All of them waiting for me to show them an acceptable and appropriately overt indication of maternal torment so that they'll know what to do next."

Lynley knew there was little point in delineating for the MP any one of the endless responses to sudden death he'd seen over the years. It was true that her reaction to her daughter's death wasn't what he would have expected from a mother whose ten-year-old has been abducted, held, and then found dead, but he knew that her lack of emotion didn't make her response any less genuine. He also knew that Nkata was noting it for the record, since the DC had begun writing almost as soon as Eve Bowen had started to speak.

"We'll have someone checking into Mr. Luxford," he told her. "But I don't want to investigate him to the exclusion of other possible suspects. If your daughter's abduction was the first step to remove you from political power—"

"Then we need to consider who other than Dennis would be interested in that end," she finished for him. "Is that right?"

"Yes. We've got to consider that. As well as the passions that would motivate someone to remove you from power. Jealousy, greed, political ambition, revenge. Have you thwarted someone in the Opposition?"

Her lips moved in a brief, ironic smile. "One's enemies in Parliament don't sit opposite the object of their antipathy, Inspector. They sit behind her with the rest of her party."

"The better to backstab," Nkata remarked.

"Quite. Yes."

"Your rise to power has been relatively swift, hasn't it?" Lynley asked the MP.

"Six years," she said.

"Since your first election?" When she nodded, he continued. "That's a brief apprenticeship. Others have been sitting on the back benches for years, haven't they? Others who might have been attempting to work themselves into the Government ahead of you?"

"I'm not the first case of a younger MP leaping past those with more seniority. It's a matter of talent as well as ambition."

"Accepted," Lynley said. "But someone equally ambitious who sees himself as equally talented may have developed a bad taste in his mouth when you leap-frogged over him to get your post in the Government. That bad taste may have grown into a strong desire to see you brought down. Through Charlotte's paternity. If that's the case, we're looking for someone who would also have been in Blackpool at that Tory conference where your daughter was conceived."

Eve Bowen cocked her head, examined him closely, and said with some surprise, "He did tell you everything, didn't he? Mr. St. James?"

"I did say I'd spoken to him."

"Somehow I thought he might have spared you the seamier details."

"I can't have hoped to proceed without knowing you and Mr. Luxford were lovers in Blackpool."

She raised a finger. "Sexual partners, Inspector. Whatever else we may have been, Dennis Luxford and I were never lovers."

"Whatever you'd like to call it, someone knows what went on between you. Someone's done his maths—"

"Or hers," Nkata pointed out.

"Or hers," Lynley agreed. "Someone knows that Charlotte was the result. Whoever that person is, he's someone who was in Blackpool all those years ago, someone with a probable axe to grind with you, someone who very likely wants to take your place."

She seemed to withdraw into herself as she reflected on his description of the potential kidnapper. She said, "Joel would be first to want to take my place. He runs most of my affairs as it is. But it's unlikely he—"

"Joel?" Nkata said, pencil to paper. "Surname, Ms. Bowen?"

"Woodward, but he would have been too young. He's only twenty-nine now. He wouldn't have been at the Blackpool conference. Unless, of course, his father was there. He may have gone with his father."

"Who's that?"

"Julian. Colonel Woodward. He's chairman of my constituency association. He's been a party worker for decades. I don't know if he was there in Blackpool, but he may have been. So may have Joel." She lifted her wineglass but didn't drink, holding it instead in both her hands and speaking to it. "Joel's my assistant. He has political ambitions. We clash at times. Still . . ." She shook her head in apparent dismissal of the consideration. "I don't think it's Joel. He knows my schedule better than anyone. He knows Alex's and Charlotte's as well. He has to. It's part of his job. But to do this . . . How could he have done? He's been in London. At work. All through this."

"The weekend long?" Lynley asked.

"What do you mean?"

"The body was found in Wiltshire, but that doesn't mean Charlotte was held in Wiltshire from Wednesday on. She could have been anywhere, even here in London. She could have been transported to Wiltshire sometime during the weekend."

"You mean after she was dead," Eve Bowen said.

"Not necessarily. If she was being held in the city and the site got too hot for some reason, she may have been moved."

"Then whoever moved her would have to know Wiltshire. If she was hidden there before . . . before what happened."

"Yes. Add that to the equation as well. Someone from the Blackpool time. Someone who envies you your position. Someone with an axe to grind. Someone who knows Wiltshire. Does Joel? Does his father?"

She was looking at her papers, then suddenly looking through them. She said to herself, "Joel mentioned to me . . . Thursday evening . . . he said . . ."

"This Woodward bloke has a connection to Wiltshire?" Nkata clarified before adding to his notes.

"No. It's not Joel." She sifted through the papers. She rejected them and shoved them into their notebook. She pulled another from the stack on the chair next to her. She said, "It's a prison. He doesn't want it. He's asked repeatedly to meet with me about it, but I've put him off because . . . *Blackpool*. Of course he was in Blackpool."

"Who?" Lynley asked.

"Alistair Harvie. In Blackpool all those years ago. I interviewed him for the *Telegraph*. I asked for the interview—he was newly elected to Parliament then, outspoken and brash. Very articulate. Clever. Handsome. The party's blue-eyed boy. There was speculation he'd be quickly assigned as PPS to the Foreign Secretary and even more speculation that he'd be Prime Minister within fifteen years. So I wanted a profile. He agreed and we set up a meeting. In his room. I thought nothing of it, until he made his first move. You've just got to know me, he said, and turnabout's fair play, isn't it, so I want to know you, to really know you. I think I laughed at him. I doubt I bothered to pretend misunderstanding in order to let him save face. That sort of come-on from a man has always made my flesh crawl."

She found what she'd been looking for in the second notebook she pulled from the stack. She said, "It's a prison. It's been in the works for two years now. It's going to be expensive, state of the art. It'll house three thousand men. And, unless he can stop it, it's going to be built in Alistair Harvie's constituency."

"Which is?" Lynley asked.

"In Wiltshire," she replied.

Nkata folded his lanky frame into the Bentley's passenger seat, one of his legs still out on the pavement. He balanced his notebook on his knee and continued to write.

"Put that into something readable for Hillier," Lynley told him. "Get it to him in the morning. Avoid him if you can. He's going to dog us every step of the way, but let's try to keep him at a distance."

"Right." Nkata raised his head to observe the front of Eve Bowen's house. "What do you think?"

"Wiltshire's first."

"This bloke Harvie?"

"It's a starting place. I'll get Havers on it at her end."

"At this end?"

"We dig." Lynley reflected on everything St. James had told him. "Start checking for double connections, Winston. We need to know who has a connection to Bowen as well as a connection to Wiltshire. We've got Harvie already, but that seems too neat to be true, doesn't it? So look at Luxford, the Woodwards. Look at Charlotte's music teacher Chambers, since he was last to see her. Look at Maguire, the housekeeper. Look at the stepfather, Alexander Stone."

"Think he wasn't as cut up as Ms. Bowen wanted us to believe?" Nkata asked.

"I think anything's possible."

"Including Bowen's involvement?"

"Check her out as well. If the Home Office was looking for a site in Wiltshire for their new prison, they'd have sent a committee to study locations. If she was part of that committee, she'd have developed some knowledge of the land. She may well have known where to order someone to hold her daughter if she herself is behind the abduction."

"There's a big why attached to that one, man. If she set up the snatch, what'd she stand to gain?"

"She's a creature of politics," Lynley said. "Any answer to that question would have to come from politics as well. We can see what she'd lose easily enough."

"If Luxford ran the story, she'd be dogmeat."

"That's what we're meant to think, aren't we? The focus has all been on what she stood to lose, and according to St. James, every principal involved—with the exception of the music teacher—has stressed that from the first. So we'll keep it in mind. But there's usually some profit in taking a route that's not being signposted so avidly for us. So let's also dig around for what MP Bowen stood to gain."

Nkata finished his notetaking with a precisely placed full stop. He used the book's thin marking ribbon to hold his place. He returned notebook and pencil to his pocket. He got out of the car. Once again he examined the front of the Junior Minister's house where the lone constable stood with arms folded across his chest.

He bent and made his final remark through the open window of the car. "This could get real nasty, couldn't it, 'spector?"

"It's already nasty," Lynley replied.

—⁊⁊—

A detour west from her digs in Chalk Farm to Hawthorne Lodge in Greenford put Barbara Havers onto the M4 long after rush hour. Not that her timing made all that much difference, as she soon discovered. A crash just before Reading, between a Range Rover and a lorry transporting tomatoes, had reduced the motorway to a respectful procession through crimson sludge. When she saw the endless unspooling of brake lights illuminating into the horizon, Barbara changed down gears, punched the Mini's radio buttons until she found a station that could tell her what the hell was going on ahead of her, and settled in for a wait. She'd looked at a map before leaving her house, so she knew that she could forsake the motorway and try her luck with the A4 if necessary. But that meant coming upon an exit, always a scarce commodity when one wished to cash in one's vehicular chips.

"Sod," she said. It would be an age before she managed to extricate herself from this mess. And her stomach was demanding immediate attention.

She knew she should have thrown together a meal and jammed it down her gullet before taking to the road. At the time, however, consuming a hasty dinner hadn't seemed as important as stuffing a few changes of clothes and a toothbrush into her holdall and dashing out to Greenford prior to the journey to Wiltshire in order to give her mother the Big News. I'm heading up one arm of an investigation, Mum. How's that for professional progress at last? Being placed in charge of anything more significant than fetching sandwiches from the fourth floor for Lynley was a major development in Barbara's life. And she had been eager to share it with someone.

She'd tried her neighbours, first. On her way to her own dwarf-sized lodgings at the bottom of the garden in Eton Villas, she'd stopped at the ground floor flat of the Edwardian building to share her news. But neither Khalidah Hadiyyah—who, at eight years old, was Barbara's most frequent social companion in barbecues on the lawn, trips to the zoo, and boat rides to Greenwich—nor her father Taymullah Azhar was there to react with appropriate rapture to her change in professional circumstances. So she'd packed up her trousers, pullovers, underwear, and toothbrush, and she'd headed for Greenford to tell her mother.

She'd found Mrs. Havers, along with her Hawthorne Lodge companions, in the alcove that served as the dining room. They were gathered round the table with Florence Magentry—their keeper, their nursemaid, their confidante, their director of activities, and gentle gaoler—who was assisting them in assembling a three-dimensional puzzle. From its boxtop, Barbara could see that it was meant to be a Victorian mansion when completed. At the moment, it looked like a relic of the Blitz.

"It's a fine challenge for us," Mrs. Flo explained, smoothing her already neat grey hair back into place in its perfect wedge. "We move our fingers round the pieces and our mind makes connections between the shapes that we see, the shapes that we feel, and the shapes that we need to build the puzzle. And when it's done, we have a lovely building to look at, don't we, my dears?"

There were murmurs of assent from the three other women round the table, even from Mrs. Pendlebury, who was completely blind and whose contribution to the activity appeared to be swaying in her chair and singing along with Tammy Wynette's demand that she stand by her man, which was emanating from Mrs. Magentry's old stereo. She held a piece of the puzzle in her palm, but instead of feeling its shape with her fingers, she pressed it to her cheek and crooned, "Sometimes it's hard to be a woman . . ."

Wasn't that the truth, Barbara thought. She took the chair Mrs. Flo had vacated, next to her mother.

Mrs. Havers was throwing herself into the activity with enthusiasm. She was busily attempting to assemble one of the mansion's walls, and as she did so, she confided in Mrs. Salkild and Mrs. Pendlebury that the mansion they were in the process of building was just exactly like the one she'd stayed in as a guest during her trip to San Francisco last autumn. "Such a beautiful city," she said rhapsodically. "Hills up and hills down, precious cable cars climbing, sea gulls sweeping in from the bay. And the Golden Gate Bridge. With the fog swirling round it like white candy floss . . . It's a sight to behold."

She'd never been there, not in the flesh. But in her mind she'd been everywhere and she had a half dozen albums crammed with travel brochures from which she'd religiously clipped pictures to prove it.

Barbara said to her, "Mum? I wanted to stop by. I'm on my way to Wiltshire. I'm on a case."

"Salisbury's in Wiltshire," Mrs. Havers announced. "It has a cathedral. I was married there to my Jimmy, don't you know. Have I mentioned that? Of course, the cathedral isn't Victorian like this lovely house. . . ." She reached for another puzzle piece in a hasty movement, shrinking away from Barbara.

"Mum," Barbara said. "I wanted to tell you because this is the first time I've been on my own. On a case. Inspector Lynley's handling part of it here, but I've been given the other part. Me. I'll be in charge."

"Salisbury's cathedral has a graceful spire," Mrs. Havers went on in a more insistent tone. "It's four hundred and four feet tall. Imagine that, the tallest in England. The cathedral itself is quite unique because it was planned as a single unit and built in forty years. But the building's true glory—"

Barbara took her mother's hand. Mrs. Havers stopped talking, flustered and confused by the unexpected gesture. "Mum," Barbara said. "Did you hear what I said? I'm on a case. I've got to leave tonight and I'll be gone a few days."

"The cathedral's greatest treasure," Mrs. Havers plunged on, "is one of the three original copies of the Magna Carta. Fancy that. When Jimmy and I were last there—we celebrated our thirty-sixth anniversary this year—we walked round and round the cathedral close and had tea in a sweet little shop in Exeter Street. The shop wasn't Victorian, not like this lovely puzzle we're making. This puzzle's of a San Francisco mansion. It's just like the one I stayed in last autumn. San Francisco's so lovely. Hills up and hills down. Precious cable cars. And the Golden Gate Bridge when the fog comes in . . ." She wrested her hand from Barbara's and plunked a puzzle piece into place.

Barbara watched her and knew her mother was studying her from the corner of her eye. She was trying to sort through the muddle of her mind in order to come up with a name or a label she could place upon the somewhat stout and generally untidy woman who'd come to join her at the table. Sometimes she identified Barbara as Doris, her sister long dead during World War II. Sometimes she recognised her as her own daughter. Other times, like this, she seemed to believe that if she kept talking, she could somehow avoid the inevitable admission that she hadn't the slightest idea who Barbara was.

"I don't come often enough, do I?" Barbara said to Mrs. Flo. "She used to know me. When we lived together, she always knew me."

Mrs. Flo clucked sympathetically. "The mind is a mystery, Barbie. You're not to blame yourself for something that's clearly beyond your control."

"But if I came more often . . . She always knows you, doesn't she? And Mrs. Salkild. And Mrs. Pendlebury. Because she sees you every day."

"It's not possible for you to see her every day," Mrs. Flo said. "And that's not your fault. That's nobody's fault. It's just the way life is. Why, when you set off to be a detective, you didn't know your mum would come to this, did you? You didn't do it to avoid her, did you? You just followed your path."

But she was glad to have the burden of her mother lifted from her shoulders, Barbara admitted, if only to herself. And that gladness was her second largest source of guilt. The first was the necessary lapse of time between each visit she could make to Greenford.

"You're doing your best," Mrs. Flo said.

The truth was that Barbara knew she wasn't.

Now, wedged between a snail-shaped caravan and a diesel lorry on the motorway, she thought about her mother and her own expectations gone unfulfilled. What had she honestly expected her mother to do upon hearing her announcement? I'll be heading up one part of an investigation, Mum. Wonderful, darling. Break out the champagne.

What a lump-headed thought. Barbara fumbled in her bag for her cigarettes, one wary eye fixed on the traffic ahead. She lit up, took a lungful of tobacco smoke, and celebrated in solitude the gratifying thought of being relatively on her own in an investigation. She'd be working with the local CID, naturally, but she wouldn't be answerable to anyone but Lynley. And since he would be safely tucked away in London duelling with Hillier, the meatiest part of the case was hers: the crime scene, the evaluation of evidence, the results of the autopsy, the search for where the child had been held, the scouring of the country-side for potential evidence. And the kidnapper's identity. She was de-termined to suss that out, ahead of Lynley. She was in the better position to do so, and doing so would be the coup of her career. Pro-mo-tion time, Nkata would have called it. Well and good, she thought. She was overdue.

She was finally able to depart the M4 at exit twelve, just west of Reading. This put her squarely upon the A4 and on a direct line to-wards the town of Marlborough, south of which lay Wootton Cross, at whose police station she was scheduled to rendezvous with the Ames-ford CID officers who had been assigned to the case. She was way behind schedule at this point, and when she finally pulled into the mousehole of a car park behind the squat square of bricks that went for the Wootton Cross police station, she wondered if they'd given her up altogether. The station was dark and looked unoccupied—not an un-usual circumstance for a village once the sun went down—and the only car besides her own was an ageing Escort in just about as bad condition as the Mini.

She parked next to the Escort and shouldered open her door. She took a moment to stretch her cramped muscles, admitting to herself that there were inherent advantages to working side by side with Inspector Lynley, not the least of which was his sumptuous car. When the worst of the kinks were loosened from her body, she approached the police station and squinted through the dusty glass of its locked back door.

This door gave onto a corridor that led to the front of the building. Doors stood open on either side of this corridor, but no squares of light fell from them onto the floor.

Surely they would have left a note, Barbara thought. And she scouted round the rectangle of concrete that served as the back step to make certain nothing had blown away. Finding only a crushed Pepsi can and three used condoms—safe sex was great, but she couldn't understand why its proponents never quite made the leap from coital protection to post-coital clean-up—she took herself to the front of the building. This stood at the junction of three separate roads, which ran into Wootton Cross and met one another in the village square at whose centre stood a statue of some obscure king looking mightily unhappy about being memorialised in an even more obscure country location. He faced the police station dolefully, sword in one hand, shield in the other, with his crown and his shoulders liberally freckled with pigeon poop. Behind him and across the street, the King Alfred Arms identified him for those capable of putting two and two together. This pub was doing a good night's business, if the music blaring from its open windows and the shifting bodies behind the glass were anything to go by. Barbara noted it as the next logical place to seek her police companions if the front of the station yielded her nothing.

Which was very nearly the case. A neatly printed sign on the door informed those seeking police assistance after hours that they were to telephone the constabulary in Amesford. Barbara gave a half-hearted knock on the door anyway, just in case the CID team purportedly awaiting her had decided to take a snooze. When no lights blinked on in response, she knew there was nothing for it but to brave the crowd and the music—which sounded remotely like "In the Mood" being played enthusiastically if not quite accurately by a band of septuagenarians with diminishing lung capacity—of the King Alfred Arms.

She hated skulking into pubs alone. She was always unnerved by that moment when all eyes shifted to the newcomer for a quick evaluation. But she was going to have to get used to evaluations, wasn't she, if she was to take charge of the Wiltshire end of this investigation. So the King Alfred Arms was as good a place as any to start.

She began to head across the street, automatically reaching back for her shoulder bag and her cigarettes to bolster herself with some nicotine courage. She reached in vain. She stopped herself cold. Her bag . . . ?

It was in the car, she realised, and upon mentally retracing her steps thus far as Supreme Poobah Head of the Wiltshire Team, she congratulated herself on being so hot to establish her credentials and throw her weight around that, as she recalled, she'd left her car door open, her shoulder bag inside, and her keys—helpfully—still in the ignition.

"Bloody hell," she muttered.

She did a quick about-turn and strode hastily back the way she'd come. She rounded the side of the police station, hurried up the drive, dodged a rubbish dumpster, and entered the tiny car park. Which is when she blessed her silent little trainer-shod feet.

Because a darkly garbed man was bent into the Mini and from what she could see he was in the process of industriously pawing through her bag.

17

BARBARA HURLED HERSELF at him. He was big, but she had the
advantage of surprise and fury. She gave a howl worthy of the
highest-ranking expert in the martial arts as she grabbed the bag-
snatcher round the waist, wrenched him from her car, and flung him
against it.

She snarled, "Police, yobbo! And don't you move a bloody eyelash."

He was off balance, so he did more than move an eyelash. He fell
face first to the ground. He writhed for an instant as if he'd landed on a
stone, and he appeared to be reaching for his right trouser pocket.
Barbara stomped on his hand.

"I said don't move!"

He said, voice muffled by his position, "My ID . . . pocket."

"Oh right," she said caustically. "What sort of ID? Pickpocket?
Bag-snatcher? Car thief? What?"

"Police," he said.

"Police?"

"Right. Can I get up? Or at least turn over?"

She thought, Great shit. What a way to begin. And then said suspiciously, "What were you doing going through my things?"

"Trying to see who the car belonged to. Can I get up?"

"Stay where you are. Turn over, but stay on the ground."

"Right." He didn't move.

"Did you hear what I said?"

"You're still on my hand."

She hastily removed her high-top from his palm. She said, "No
sudden movements."

He replied, "Got it." With a grunt, he worked his way onto his side, then onto his back. From the ground, he observed her.

"I'm DC Robin Payne," he said. "Something tells me you must be Scotland Yard."

—⚏—

He looked like a young Errol Flynn with a bigger commitment to the moustache. And he wasn't in black as Barbara had first thought. Rather, he wore charcoal trousers and a navy sweater, a V-neck with a white shirt beneath it. The collar of this was currently smudged with grime—as were the sweater and the trousers—courtesy of his fall to the ground. And his left cheek was oozing blood, a possible explanation for his writhing once she put him there.

"It's nothing," he said when Barbara grimaced at the sight of him. "I would have done the same."

They were in the police station, just. Constable Payne had unlocked the back door and gone to what seemed to be an old laundry room, where he turned the taps on and let water run into a stained concrete tub. A dirt-encrusted green bar of soap lay in a rusty metal holder near the taps, and before he used it, Payne took a pocket knife from his trousers and pared off the soap's deep incisions of grime. While the water was heating up, he pulled his sweater off and handed it to Barbara with a "Hold on to this for a second, won't you?" Then he washed his face.

Barbara looked about for a towel. A limp piece of terry cloth hanging from a hook behind the door seemed the only thing suitable. But it was filthy and it smelled of mildew. She couldn't imagine handing it to anyone with the expectation of its actually being used.

She thought, Bloody hell. She wasn't the sort of woman who carried scented linen handkerchiefs for tender moments such as these, and she didn't think the ball of crumpled tissues wadded into the pocket of her jacket would be the thing to offer him to complete his ablutions. She was considering a half-open ream of typing paper for its absorbancy potential—it was currently being used as a doorstop—when he lifted his head from the sink, ran his wet hands through his hair, and solved the problem for her. He pulled his shirt out of his trousers and used the tails of it for a towel.

"Sorry," Barbara said as he dried his face. She got a glimpse of his chest. Nice, she noted, just hirsute enough to be attractive without encouraging one to think of possible simian forebears. "I saw you in my car and I reacted without a thought."

"That's decent training," he said, dropping his shirttails and tucking them in all round. "It shows your experience." He gave a rueful grin. "And my lack of it. Which explains why you're Scotland Yard and I'm not. How old are you, anyway? I was expecting someone round fifty, my sergeant's age."

"Thirty-three."

"Whoa. You must be hot."

Considering her chequered career with New Scotland Yard, *hot* wasn't the word Barbara would have used to describe herself. It was only during the past thirty months of working with Lynley that she'd begun to regard herself as even lukewarm.

Payne took his sweater from her and gave it a brisk few shakes to rid it of the car park dirt. He pulled it over his head, ran his hands through his hair another time, and said, "Right. Now for the first aid kit, which must be somewhere . . ." He rooted on a cluttered shelf beneath the room's only window. A bristle-split toothbrush fell to the floor. Payne said, "Ah. Here," and brought forth a dust-covered blue tin from which he took a plaster that he applied to the cut on his face. He flashed Barbara a smile.

"How long've you been there?" he asked.

"Where?"

"New Scotland Yard."

"Six years."

He gave a silent whistle. "Impressive. You said you're thirty-three?"

"Right."

"When did you become a DC?"

"When I was twenty-four."

His eyebrows rose. He slapped his hands against the dust on his trousers. "I just made it three weeks ago myself. That's when I finished the course. But I suppose you can tell, can't you? That I'm green, I mean. Because of out there and what happened with your car." He straightened his sweater against his shoulders. They too, Barbara noted, were nice. He said, "Twenty-four," to himself with some admiration and then to her, "I'm twenty-nine. D'you think that's too late?"

"For what exactly?"

"To be heading where you are. Scotland Yard. That's what I'm shooting for, eventually." He toed a piece of loose lino boyishly. "I mean, when I'm good enough, which I obviously am not at the moment."

Barbara didn't know quite what to tell him about the lack of glory that generally went with her work. So she said, "You said you've been a

DC three weeks? Is this your first case?'' and had her answer when his toe dug more deeply into the loose lino.

He said, "Sergeant Stanley's a bit put out that someone from London's been assigned to head things up. He waited here with me till half past eight, then he cleared off. Said to tell you that you could find him at home if you decide you need him for something tonight.''

"I got caught in traffic," Barbara said.

"I waited till quarter past nine, then figured you might have been heading for Amesford, to our CID office. So I was going to set off there myself. Which is when you arrived. I saw you creeping round the building and thought you were someone trying to break in.''

"Where were you? Inside?''

He rubbed the back of his neck and laughed, lowering his head with embarrassment. "Truth to tell, I was taking a pee," he said. "Out behind that shed beyond the car park. I'd got outside all ready to leave for Amesford and decided it was easier to have a pee in the weeds than to unlock and relock the place all over again. I didn't even hear your car. What a twit, huh? Come on. It's this way.''

He went towards the front of the building, into an office that was sparsely furnished with a desk, filing cabinets, and ordnance survey maps hanging on the walls. A dusty-leafed philodendron stood in one corner, its pot sprouting a hand-lettered sign that read *No coffee- or cigarette-dumping. I'm real.*

Doubtless, Barbara thought sardonically. The plant looked sadly like most of her own attempts at indoor gardening.

She said, "Why've we met here and not in Amesford?''

"Sergeant Stanley," Robin explained. "He thought you might want to see the crime scene first. In the morning, I mean. To orient yourself. It's just a fifteen-minute drive from here. Amesford's another eighteen miles to the south.''

Barbara knew what another eighteen miles on a country road meant: a good thirty minutes more of driving. She would have saluted Sergeant Stanley's perspicacity had she not wondered about his intentions. She said with more determination than she felt, considering how little she actually looked forward to the event, "I'm going to want to stand in on the autopsy as well. When's that scheduled?''

"Tomorrow morning." Payne took from under his arm a small stack of manila folders that he'd brought in from his car. "So we'll have to be up with the birds to do the crime scene first. We've some preliminary stuff, by the way." He handed her the folders.

Barbara looked through the material. It comprised a second set of photographs of the crime scene, another copy of the police report taken from the couple who had discovered the body, detailed photographs shot in the morgue, a meticulous description of the corpse—height, weight, natural marks upon the body, scars, etc.—and a set of X-rays. The report also indicated that blood had been drawn for the toxicologist.

"Our man would have gone on with the autopsy," Payne said, "but the Home Office told him to hold off till you were in place."

"No clothing with the body?" Barbara asked. "I assume CID made a thorough check of the area."

"Not a stitch," he said. "On Sunday night the mother gave us a decent description of what the girl was wearing the last time anyone saw her. We've put the word out, but nothing's turned up yet. The mother said—" Here, he came to her side and flipped through several pages of the report, resting his bum on the edge of the desk. "The mother said that when she was snatched she'd have had specs on and schoolbooks with her, with a school emblem—St. Bernadette's—printed inside. She'd have had a flute with her as well. That information's gone out, along with the rest, to the other forces. And we've come up with this." He flipped a few more pages to find what he wanted. "We know the body was in the water twelve hours. And we know that prior to her death she was somewhere near heavy machinery."

"How's that?"

Payne explained. The first conclusion had been arrived at by the presence of a lifeless flea caught up in the child's hair: Combed out and placed under a watch-glass, the flea had taken an hour and a quarter to recover from its immersion in the water of the Kennet and Avon Canal, which was very close to the exact time required for the insect to revive after twelve hours' exposure to a hostile and liquid environment. The second conclusion had been reached by the presence of a foreign substance underneath the child's fingernails.

"What was it?" Barbara asked.

It was a compound based on petroleum: a naphthenic distillate containing stearic acid and lithium hydroxide, among other multi-syllabic ingredients. "It's the goop that's used to lubricate heavy machinery," he told her.

"Under Charlotte Bowen's fingernails?"

"Right," he said. It was used on tractors, combine harvesters, that sort of thing, he explained. He indicated the patched-up ordnance survey maps on the wall, continuing with, "We've hundreds of farms in the county—dozens in the immediate area—but we've gridded everything off and with some help from the forces in Salisbury, Marlborough, and Swindon, we'll be canvassing all of them, looking for some evidence that the kid was there. Sergeant Stanley's set that up. The teams began yesterday, and if they have any luck . . . Well, who knows what they could turn up? Although it's probably going to take forever."

Barbara thought she caught in his voice some doubt about his sergeant's approach, so she said, "You disagree with that plan?"

"It's plodwork, isn't it, but it has to be done. Still . . ." He walked to the map.

"Still what?"

"I don't know. Just thoughts."

"Care to share them?"

He glanced at her, clearly hesitant. She could tell what he was thinking: He'd made a fool of himself once that evening; he wasn't certain he wished to risk it again.

She said, "Forget the car park, Constable. We both were rattled. What's on your mind?"

"Okay," he said. "But it's only a thought." He pointed out locations on the map as he spoke. "We've the sewage works at Coate. We've twenty-nine locks that carry the canal up Caen Hill. That's near Devizes. We've reservoir pumps—wind pumps, these are—here near Oare, here and here near Wootton Rivers."

"I can see them on the map. What's your point?" Havers asked.

He held up his hand and directed her attention back to the map. "We've caravan parks. We've corn mills—these are wind, like the pumps—at Provender, Wilton, Blackland, Wootten. We've a sawmill at Honeystreet. And we've all the wharves where the narrow-boats get hired when people want to take one on the canal." He turned back to her.

"Are you saying that any one of these locations could be a source of the grease under the girl's fingernails? Places where she was held? Besides at a farm?"

He looked regretful. "I think so, sir." He caught himself on the last word and grimaced, saying, "Sorry, ma'am . . . ah sergeant . . . guv."

It was an odd feeling, Barbara realised, being seen as someone's superior officer. The deference was a pleasant change, but the distance it created was disconcerting. She said, "Barbara will do," and gave her attention to the map rather than to the constable's youthful embarrassment.

"We're talking about heavy machinery, which is what you'll find in all those places," Payne said.

"But Sergeant Stanley hasn't instructed his men to evaluate those locations?"

"Sergeant Stanley . . ." Again Payne hesitated. He tapped his front teeth together as if nervous about speaking frankly.

"What about him?"

"Well, it's the wood and the trees, isn't it. He heard axle grease, which meant axles, which meant wheels, which meant vehicles, which meant farms." Payne smoothed out a wrinkled corner of the map and used a drawing pin to tack it back into place. He seemed too intent upon the operation, which told Barbara much about his level of discomfort with the conversation. He said, "Oh hell, he's probably right. He's got decades of experience and I'm worse than green when it comes to this. As you've already noted. Still, I thought . . ." He made a neat segue from smoothing the map to studying his feet.

"It was well worth mentioning, Robin. All the other locations will need to be checked out. And better the idea coming from me to the sergeant than from you to the sergeant. You'll still have to work with him when this is all over."

He raised his head. He looked grateful and relieved all at once. Barbara couldn't remember what it felt like to be so new at a job and so eager to succeed. She found that she liked the constable, felt a certain sororial warmth towards him. He seemed quick-witted and affable. If he could ever get his embarrassment under control, he might actually make a good detective.

"Anything else?" she asked. "Because if not, I'll need to get on to my digs. I've got to phone London and see what's on at that end of things."

"Yes, your digs," he said. "Well. Yes."

She waited for him to tell her where Amesford CID had arranged for her to stay, but he was clearly reluctant to part with the information. He shifted his weight from one foot to the other, then pulled his car keys out of his pocket and jiggled them in his hand. "This is awkward," he said.

"There's no place to stay?"

"There is. There is. It's just that . . . We thought you were older, you see."

"So? Where've you put me? The pensioners' home?"

"No," he said. "Mine."

"Yours?"

He went on in a rush to explain that his mother was in residence, that the house was a bonafide B and B, that they were listed in the AA guide, that Barbara'd have her own bathroom—well, it was a shower actually, if she didn't mind a shower—that there was no real hotel in Wootton Cross, that there were four rooms above the King Alfred Arms if she'd rather . . . Because she was only thirty-three and he was twenty-nine and if she thought it didn't look right that she and he . . . in the same house . . .

The music was still issuing at cyclonic volume from the King Alfred Arms, "Yellow Submarine" with an interesting echo-chamber effect that was produced by the narrowness of the village streets. The band gave no auditory indication that their gig would be ending anytime soon.

"Where's your house?" Barbara asked Robin Payne. "From the pub, that is."

"Other end of town."

"Sold," she said.

Eve Bowen didn't turn on the lights as she entered Charlotte's bedroom. This was force of habit. Upon returning from the Commons, usually well past midnight, she always looked in on her daughter. This was force of duty. Mothers looked in on their children when mothers returned long after their children went to bed. Eve qualified as a mother, Charlotte qualified as children. Ergo, Eve looked in on Charlotte. She usually slid the bedroom door open. She readjusted the covers if they needed readjusting. She picked the stuffed Mrs. Tiggy-Winkle off the floor and placed her among Charlotte's other collected hedgehogs. She made certain Charlotte's alarm clock was set to the proper time. Then she went on her way.

What she didn't do was stare down at her daughter and think of her infancy, her babyhood, her growing childhood, her coming adolescence, and her prospective womanhood. She didn't marvel at the changes that time had wrought in her child. She didn't meditate upon their past life together. She didn't construct fantasies about their future. About her own future, yes. She did more than fantasise about her own future. She worked, she schemed, she planned, she produced, she manipulated, she confronted, she championed, she condemned. But as to Charlotte's future . . . She told herself that Charlotte's future was in Charlotte's hands.

Eve crossed the room in the darkness. At the head of the empty single bed, Mrs. Tiggy-Winkle nestled among a mound of gingham pillows, and Eve picked up the stuffed animal absently and ran her fingers over the thick, rough fur. She sat on the bed. Then she lay among the pillows, with Mrs. Tiggy-Winkle tucked into her arm. She thought.

She shouldn't have had the baby. She'd known that the moment the doctor had said "Oh a lovely lovely precious little girl" and laid the blood-covered, warm, and writhing thing on her stomach, with a choked whisper of "I know exactly what this moment feels like, Eve. I have three of my own." Everyone in the room—and it had seemed like dozens—had murmured appropriately about the beauty of the moment, about the miracle of birth, about the blessing of being safely delivered of a perfectly healthy, beautifully formed, and lustily crying baby. Wonderful, miraculous, awesome, amazing, incredible, astounding, extraordinary. Never in a single five minutes had Eve heard so many adjectives describing an event that had wrenched her body for twenty-eight agonising hours and left her wanting nothing so much as peace, silence, and, more than anything, solitude.

She had wanted to say, Take her away, get her off me. She could feel the bubbling loss of control that would provoke those words. It was working its way from the tips of her fingers in the direction of her lips. But she was a woman who, even *in extremis*, would always recall the importance of image. So she had touched her fingers to the unwashed head and then to the shoulders of the squalling infant, and she had produced a radiant smile for those in attendance. So that when the time came and the tabloids were eagerly sniffing round her past for a nasty titbit they could use to impede her rise to power, they wouldn't be able to get a crumb from anyone present at Charlotte's birth.

When she'd found herself pregnant, she'd considered abortion. Standing in the crush of passengers on the Bakerloo Line, she'd read the oblong advertisement posted above one of the windows—LAMBETH WOMEN'S HEALTH CENTRE: YOU HAVE A CHOICE—and wondered about the possibility of a quick trip to South London and an end to the interminable difficulties that a pregnancy was going to bring into her life. She'd thought about making an appointment, using a false name. She'd pondered effecting an alteration in her appearance and creating an accent for the occasion. But she rejected all of this as the hysterical fancy of a woman whose hormones were currently in a roil. Do not, she'd told herself, take any hasty decisions. Mull over each possibility and map out where each path might lead.

When she thought each course through, she knew that the only safe one was to have the child and keep it. Aborting could only too easily be used against her later on, when she presented herself as a lifelong champion of the family. Putting it out for adoption was a distinct possibility, but not if she was going to portray herself as A Working Mother, Like So Many of You, in the parliamentary campaigns that she was determined would be part of her future. She could hope to miscarry, but she was as healthy as a pack mule, with all of her parts in fine working order. And anyway, a miscarriage in her past could always evoke unnecessary whisperings of doubt in her future: Had she—an unmarried mother—done something to generate a miscarriage? Had she abused her body in some obscure way? Was there a history of drug or alcohol abuse that ought to be examined? And doubt was pernicious in politics.

Her original intention had been to keep the identity of the father a secret from everyone, including the father himself. But seeing Dennis Luxford unexpectedly five months after Blackpool had put an end to that plan. He was no fool. When from across the Central Lobby at Parliament, she saw his gaze run down her body and then fix itself upon her face, she knew the conclusion he'd reached. She'd excused herself from the MP whose opinion she'd been soliciting for the *Telegraph*. She'd gone into the Members' Lobby, where she was writing out a message for another MP and preparing to slip it into his slot, when Luxford appeared at her side. He'd said, "We need to have a coffee," to which she'd replied, "I don't think so." He'd taken her elbow. She'd said calmly, "Why don't you just print up announcements, Dennis?" Without a glance at the dozens of people teeming round them—from tourists to tacticians—he'd dropped his hand. "Sorry," he'd said. "I've no doubt of it," she replied.

She'd made it clear to him that his participation in their child's life would never be welcome. Aside from a single phone call one month after the birth in which he'd unsuccessfully attempted to discuss with her a "financial arrangement" he wished to make for Charlotte, he had not ventured to intrude upon them. She thought he might several times. First, when she stood for Parliament. Then when she married, a short time thereafter. When he hadn't done and the years rolled by, she'd thought she was free.

But we're never free of our pasts, Eve admitted in Charlotte's dark room. And once again she silently made a confession to the truth: She should never have had this child.

She turned on her side. She tucked Mrs. Tiggy-Winkle under her chin. She drew up her legs and drew in a breath. The stuffed animal smelled vaguely of peanut butter. Which Eve had told Charlotte a hundred thousand times she was *not* to eat in her bedroom. Had Charlotte actually disobeyed her again? Had she dirtied the toy—an expensive Selfridge's purchase—in direct defiance of her mother's wishes? Eve lowered her head to the hedgehog, buried her face in the stiffened fur, and sniffed rapidly, suspiciously, and repeatedly. It certainly smelled like—

"Eve!" His footsteps came rapidly across the room. Eve felt his hand on her shoulder. He said, "Don't. Not like this. Not alone." And then her husband attempted to turn her on the bed. When she tensed, he said, "Let me help you, Eve."

She was grateful for the darkness and for the hedgehog in whose fur she could keep her face hidden. She said, "I thought you were asleep."

She felt the bed give as he sat on its side. He reclined next to her and formed his body into a shape that cupped hers. His arm came round her.

"I'm sorry." His voice was low and she could feel his breath on the back of her neck.

"For?"

"Falling apart." She heard the tightness beneath his words. She sought and failed to find a way to tell him he didn't need to offer her comfort, especially when the comfort came at such a cost to himself. He went on. "I wasn't prepared. I didn't think it would end like this. With Charlie." His hand grasped hers where hers grasped the hedgehog. "Jesus, Eve. I can't even say her name without feeling like I'm falling into a bottomless pit."

"You loved her," Eve said, her voice a whisper.

"I can't even think what to do to help you."

She made him a gift of the only truth there was. "There's nothing anyone can do to help me, Alex."

His lips pressed against the back of her head. His hand squeezed hers so hard that her knuckles bruised each other and she bit into the hedgehog to keep from crying out. "You must stop this," he said. "You're blaming yourself. Don't. You did what you thought was best. You didn't know what would happen. You couldn't have known. And I went along. I agreed. No police. So we're both to blame if anyone is. I won't let you carry this burden alone. God *damn* it." His voice trembled on the word *damn*.

Hearing the tremble, she wondered how he would be able to handle the days ahead. She could see it was crucial that he not be faced with a confrontation with the media. They were bound to discover that she hadn't phoned the police when Charlotte went missing, and once they had that bone of information to chew on, they would gnaw upon it to get at the marrow of her reason for keeping the police in the dark. It was one thing if they questioned her. She was used to duelling with them, and even had she lacked the skill to prevaricate believably, she was the mother of the victim and thus if she didn't wish to answer questions shouted at her from the street by journalists, no one would conclude she was attempting to avoid them. Alex, on the other hand, was a different matter entirely.

She could picture him caught up in a verbal brawl with a dozen reporters hurling questions at him, each one more incendiary than the last. She could picture his temper flaring, his self-control snapping, and the story they wanted pouring out as a result. "I'll tell you why we didn't phone the fucking police," he would snarl. And then, instead of employing subterfuge, he would resort to the truth. He wouldn't intend to. He would start out with something like, "We didn't phone the police because of bastards like you, all right?" Which would lead them to ask what he meant. "Your slobbering need for a bleeding story. God spare us all when you want your damn story." Were you trying to spare Ms. Bowen from a story, then? Why? What story? Has she got something to hide? "No! No!" And on they would go from there, each question a noose getting tighter, encircling and closing in on the facts. He wouldn't give them everything. But he would give them enough. So it was essential—it was critical—that he never talk to the press.

He needed another sedative, Eve decided. Two more, probably, so that he could sleep through the night. Sleep was as essential as silence. Without it, one ran the risk of losing control. She made a move to get up, raising herself on one elbow. She took his hand, pressed it briefly against her cheek, and laid it on the bed.

"Where—"

"I'm going to get those pills the doctor gave us."

"Not yet," he said.

"Exhaustion doesn't help us."

"But the pills just postpone. You must know that."

She was immediately wary. She tried to read his face for a meaning, but the darkness that had protected her did the same for him.

He sat up. He spent a moment staring at his long legs, a time he seemed to use to gather his thoughts. Finally, he urged her up next to him. He put his arm round her and spoke against her head.

"Eve, listen to me. You're safe here. All right? You're completely and utterly safe with me."

Safe, she thought.

"Here, in this room, you can let go. I don't feel what you feel—I can't, I'm not her mother, I wouldn't presume to understand what a mother feels at a time like this—but I loved her, Eve. I—" He stopped. She could hear him swallow as he tried to maintain mastery over his sorrow. "If you keep taking the pills, you'll just be postponing having to go through the grieving. That's what you've been doing, isn't it? And you've been doing it because I fell apart. Because of what I said the other night about your not really living here, and not really knowing Charlie at all. God, I'm sorry for that. I just lost it for a moment. But I want you to know that I'm here now, for you. This is a place where you can let go."

And then he waited. She knew what she was supposed to do: turn to him, beg to be comforted, and produce a believable manifestation of grief. In short, she was to cease pulling her hat upon her brow and to give sorrow actions, at least, if she could not give it words.

"Feel what you need to feel," he murmured. "I'll be here for you."

Her brain worked feverishly to come up with a solution. When she had it, she lowered her chin and forced the tension from her body. "I can't—" She took an audible breath. "There's too much inside of me, Alex."

"That's no surprise. You can let it out a little at a time. We've all night."

"Will you hold me?"

"What sort of question is that?"

She was in his arms. She slipped her own arms round him. She said into his shoulder, "I've been thinking that I should have been the one. Not Charlotte. Me."

"That's normal. You're her mother."

He rocked her. She turned her head towards his. She said, "I feel dead inside. What difference would it make if the rest of me died?"

"I know how it feels. I understand."

He smoothed her hair. He rested his hand on the back of her neck. She lifted her head. "Alex, hold me. Keep me from falling apart."

"I will."

"Stay here."

"Always. You know that."

"Please."

"Yes."

"Be with me."

"I will."

When their mouths met, it seemed the logical conclusion to the conversation they'd been having. And the rest was easy.

—m—

"So they've divided the county into quadrants," Havers was saying on her end of the phone. "The DS down here—a bloke called Stanley—has had DCs checking out every farm. But Payne thinks—"

"Payne?" Lynley asked.

"DC Payne. He met me at the Wootton Cross station. He's with Amesford CID."

"Ah. Payne."

"He thinks farm machinery's too narrow a scope. He says the grease under her nails could have come from other sources. The locks along the canal, a sawmill, a corn mill, a caravan, a wharf. Which makes sense to me."

Lynley thoughtfully picked up the tape recorder that lay on the top of his desk amidst three additional photographs of Charlotte Bowen handed over by her mother, the contents of the envelope St. James had given him earlier in Chelsea, the photographs and reports that had been collected by Hillier, and his own scrawled compendium of everything St. James had related in his basement kitchen. It was ten forty-seven and he'd been finishing off a cup of tepid coffee when Havers phoned from her lodgings in Wiltshire with the terse announcement, "I'm dossing at a local B and B. Lark's Haven, sir," and an equally terse recitation of its phone number before she went into the facts she'd gathered. He'd taken notes from her report. He'd jotted down the axle grease, the flea, and the approximate time the body had been in the water, and he'd been listing place names from Wootton Cross to Devizes when her caveat regarding the restricted nature of Sergeant Stanley's investigation nudged against something he'd already heard that evening.

He said, "Hang on a minute, Sergeant," and he pressed the play button on the tape recorder to listen once again to Charlotte Bowen's voice.

"Cito," the child said. "This man here says you c'n get me out. He says you're s'posed to tell everyone a story. He says—"

"That's the girl?" Havers said from her end of the line.

"Wait," Lynley said. He pushed fast forward. The voice turned to a chipmunk chittering for a moment. He slowed the speed. The voice went on. ". . . I haven't got a loo. But there's bricks. A maypole."

Lynley pressed stop. "Did you hear it?" he asked. "She seems to be talking about where she's being held."

"She said bricks and a maypole? Yeah. Got it. Whatever it means." A man spoke in the background. Lynley heard Havers muffle the phone. Then she came back on the line and said in an altered voice, "Sir? Robin thinks the bricks and maypole give us a direction to go in."

"Robin?"

"Robin Payne. The DC here in Wiltshire. It's his mum's B and B I'm staying in. Lark's Haven. Like I said. His mum runs it."

"Ah."

"There's no hotel in the village, and with Amesford eighteen miles away and the body site here, I thought—"

"Sergeant, your logic is impeccable."

She said, "Okay. Yes. Right," and went on to delineate her plan for the next day. Body site first, autopsy second, a meeting with Sergeant Stanley third.

"Do some scouting round Salisbury as well," Lynley said. He told her about Alistair Harvie, his antagonism towards Eve Bowen, his presence in Blackpool eleven years past, and his opposition to the prison site in his constituency. "Harvie's our first direct link between the Tory conference and Wiltshire," Lynley concluded. "He may be too convenient a link, but he needs to be checked out."

"Got it," Havers said. She muttered, "Harvie . . . Salisbury," and Lynley could picture her scribbling into her notebook. Unlike Nkata's, it would be cardboard-covered, its edges sprouting dog-eared blooms. Sometimes, he thought, the woman seemed to be living in another century.

"You do have your mobile phone with you, Sergeant?" he verified pleasantly.

"Sod them," she said with equal affability. "I hate the bloody things. How did it go with Simon?"

Lynley deflected the question with a recitation of all the facts from his compendium, ending with, "He found a fingerprint on the tape recorder. In the battery compartment, which makes him think it's genuine and not a plant. SO4's running it, but if they come up with a name and we find we've got a member of the Old Lags Brigade behind the kidnapping, I've no doubt someone hired him to do the job."

"Which may lead us back to Harvie."

"Or to any number of people. The music teacher. The Woodwards. Stone. Luxford. Bowen. Nkata's checking everyone out."

"As to Simon?" Havers asked. "Things okay there, Inspector?"

"They're fine," Lynley said. "Perfectly fine."

He rang off on the lie. He downed the rest of the coffee—room temperature now—and tossed the empty cup into the rubbish. He spent ten minutes avoiding the thought of his encounter with St. James, Helen, and Deborah, and during this time he read through the police report from Wiltshire once again. After that he added a few lines to his notes. Then he organised the case material into separate and neat folders. Then he admitted he could no longer avoid the thought of what had passed between himself and his friends in Chelsea.

So he left the office. He told himself he was done for the day. He was tired. He needed to clear his mind. He wanted a whisky. He had a new Deutsche-Grammophon CD that he hadn't yet heard and a stack of business mail from his family home in Cornwall that he hadn't yet opened. He needed to get home.

But the closer he got to Eaton Terrace, the more he knew he should be driving to Onslow Square. He resisted the inclination by telling himself all over again that he had been in the right from the first. But it was as if the car had a will of its own because despite his determination to go home, throw a whisky down his throat, and soothe his savage breast with a few bars of Moussorgsky, he found himself in South Kensington instead of Belgravia, sliding into a vacant parking space a few doors to the south of Helen's flat.

She was in the bedroom. But she wasn't in bed, in spite of the hour. Instead, she had the wardrobe doors open and the drawers of the chest pulled out onto the floor, and she appeared to be in the middle of either a spate of late-spring housecleaning or a sartorial purge. A large cardboard box was sitting between the chest of drawers and the wardrobe. Into this box she was placing a carefully folded trapezoid of plum-coloured silk that he recognised as one of her nightgowns. In the box already were other garments, also precisely folded.

He said her name. She didn't look up. Beyond her, on the bed, he saw that she'd left a newspaper spread open, and when she spoke, it was in apparent reference to this.

"Rwanda," she said. "The Sudan, Ethiopia. I trifle away my life in London—in circumstances helpfully financed by my father—while all those people starve to death or die from dysentery or cholera." She glanced his way. Her eyes were very bright, but not with happiness. "Fate's ugly, isn't it? I'm here, with all this. They're there, with nothing. I can't justify it, so how do I find a balance?"

She went to the wardrobe and pulled out the plum dressing gown that matched the nightgown. She laid it carefully on the bed, tied its belt in a bow, and began to fold it.

He said, "What are you doing, Helen? You can't possibly be thinking of—" When she looked up, her bleak expression stopped his words.

"Going to Africa?" she said. "Offering someone my help? Me? Helen Clyde? How completely absurd."

"I didn't mean—"

"Good Lord, if I did that, I might ruin my manicure." She placed the dressing gown with the other clothes, returned to the wardrobe, flicked past five hangers, and pulled out a coral sundress. She said, "And anyway, it would be wildly out of character, wouldn't it? Making myself useful at the expense of my nails?"

She folded the sundress next. The care she took each time she gathered up another piece of the linen told him how much needed to be said between them. He started to speak.

She cut him off, saying, "So I thought at least I could send them some clothes. I could at least do that. And please don't tell me how ridiculous I'm being."

"I hadn't thought that."

"Because I know what it looks like: Marie Antoinette offering cake to the peasants. What on earth is some poor African woman going to do with a silk dressing gown when what she needs is food, medicine, and shelter, not to mention hope?"

She finished the sundress. She put it in the box. She returned to the wardrobe and whisked through more of the hangers. She chose a wool suit next. She took it to the bed. She used a lint brush against it, checked all of the buttons, found one loose, and went to the chest where she rummaged through one of its drawers on the floor and produced a small straw basket. She took a needle and a reel of cotton from it. She tried twice and failed to thread the needle.

Lynley went to her. He took the needle from her. He said, "Don't do this to yourself because of me. You were in the right. I was set off by the fact that you'd lied to me, not by the girl's death. I'm sorry for everything."

She lowered her head. The light from a lamp on the chest of drawers caught itself in her hair. When she moved, a colour like brandy shimmered through the strands.

He said, "I want to believe that what you saw this evening is the worst that I am. When it comes to you, something feral takes over. It subverts whatever sense of breeding I have. What you saw is the result. And it's nothing I'm proud of. Forgive me for it. Please."

She made no reply. Lynley found that he wanted to take her into his arms. But he didn't make a move to touch her because he was suddenly afraid, for the very first time, what it would mean if she repulsed him now. So he waited, his heart rather than his hat in his hand, for her to respond.

When she did, her voice was low. Her head was bent and her gaze was fixed on the box of clothing. She said, "Righteous indignation carried me through the first hour. How dare he, I thought. What sort of godhead does he think he is?"

"You were right," Lynley said. "Helen, you were right."

"But Deborah did me in." She closed her eyes as if to remove an image from them. She cleared her throat as if to shake off an emotion. "Simon didn't want to have anything to do with it from the first. But Deborah persuaded him to look into things. And now she feels she's responsible for Charlotte's death. She wouldn't even let Simon throw that picture away. She was taking it with her upstairs when I left."

Lynley couldn't have imagined feeling worse about what had happened among them, but now he did. He said, "I'll put things right somehow. With them. With us."

"You've dealt Deborah some sort of death blow, Tommy. I don't know what it is, but Simon knows."

"I'll talk to him. I'll talk to them both. Together. Separately. I'll do what needs to be done."

"You're going to have to. But I don't expect Simon will want to see you for a while."

"I'll give it a few days, then."

He waited for her to give him a sign even though he knew it was cowardly of him to do so. When she didn't, he realised that the next move, however difficult, would have to be his. He raised his hand to the small, defenseless curve of her shoulder.

She said quietly, "I'd like to be alone tonight, Tommy."

He said, "All right," although it wasn't and would never be so. He went out into the night.

18

WHEN HER ALARM WENT OFF at half past four the next morning, Barbara Havers awoke in her usual manner: She gave a startled cry and flung herself upright as if the pane of glass that was her dream had been shattered by a hammer and not by a noise. She fumbled for the alarm and silenced it, blinking into the darkness. A thin film of dim light the width of a finger seeped through a break in the curtains. She observed this and frowned, knowing she wasn't awakening in Chalk Farm and for a moment wondering where the hell she was. She sorted her thoughts. They constituted yesterday, London, Hillier, Scotland Yard, and the motorway. Then she recalled a jungle of chintz, lace pillows, overstuffed furniture, sentimental aphorisms rendered in needlepoint, and floral wallpaper. Yards of floral wallpaper. Miles of it, in fact. Lark's Haven B and B, Barbara concluded. She was in Wiltshire.

She swung herself to the edge of the bed and reached for the light. She squinted in its brightness and she fumbled her way to the foot of the bed for the plastic black mackintosh that did duty as her dressing gown whenever she travelled. She shrugged into it and crackled across the room to the basin where she turned on the water and, when her courage would allow, raised her head to the mirror.

She couldn't decide what was worse: the sight of her sleep-puffed face still bearing the imprint of the pillow along one of her cheeks or the reflection of more of the Lark's Haven wallpaper. In this case, it was yellow chrysanthemums, mauve roses, blue ribbons, and—blithely defying all reason and botany—blue and green leaves. This charming motif was repeated in both the bedspread and the curtains with an abandon that suggested Laura Ashley gone mental. Barbara could just hear all those foreign visitors, eager to experience life among the natives, exclaiming at the perfect Englishness of the B and B. Oh, Frank, isn't this *just* what we always expected an English cottage would look like? How delicious. How charming. How utterly sweet.

How bloody nauseating, Barbara thought. And it wasn't a cottage at all, anyway. It was a solid brick house just outside the village on the Burbage Road. But there was no accounting for taste, was there, and Robin Payne's mother seemed to like the place just fine.

"Mum did the redecorating last year," Robin had explained when he'd led the way to her room. A small ceramic plate on the mercifully unpapered door had announced her accommodation as Cricket's Hideaway. He added, "With Sam's tender guidance, of course," and rolled his eyes.

Barbara had met them both below in the sitting room: Corrine Payne and her "recently intended," as she called Sam Corey. They were billers and cooers of the first order, which seemed somehow in keeping with the overall atmosphere of the B and B, and when Robin had guided Barbara from her car to the kitchen and from there to the sitting room, the pair had made short work of communicating to her their mutual devotion. Corrine was Sam's "sweet pear." Sam was Corrine's "little chappie." And until Corrine saw the plaster covering the cut on her son's face, they only had eyes for each other.

The plaster was a momentary diversion from the hand patting, arm squeezing, thigh pinching, and cheek kissing. When she spied it, Corrine vaulted from the sofa and said, "Robbie! What've you done to your lovely face?" She called for her "little chappie" to fetch the iodine, the alcohol, and the cotton wool so that Mum could see to her precious boy, but before Sam Corey could do her bidding, Corrine's rising anxiety gave way to what was apparently an attack of asthma, and with a shout of "I'll see to it, sweet pear," her recently intended went in search of her inhaler instead. With Corrine drawing from it gratefully, Robin took the opportunity to hustle Barbara from the room.

"Sorry," he'd said in a low voice at the top of the stairs. "They're not always that bad. They've just got engaged. So they're a bit over the top about each other at the moment."

Barbara thought *a bit* was an understatement.

Robin went on somewhat miserably when she didn't reply. "We should have put you up at the King Alfred, shouldn't we? Or at a hotel in Amesford. Or at another B and B. This place is too much. They're too much as well. But he isn't always here, and I thought—"

"Robin, it's great. Everything's fine," Barbara interrupted supportively. "And they're . . ." *Bloody smarmy* was what she wanted to say.

But what she said was "They're in love." And "You know what it's like when you fall in love," as if she herself did.

Robin paused before opening the door for her. He seemed to register her as female for the very first time, which she found disconcerting without knowing why. He said, "You're quite nice, aren't you?" And then seemed to realise how his question might be taken. He hurried on with, "Look. Your bathroom's next door. I hope . . . Yes. Well, anyway, sleep well." Then he opened the door and left her in a hurry, suddenly having become all elbows, kneecaps, and shins in his haste to "let her settle in."

Well, Barbara thought, she was as settled in as she could hope to be in a room called Cricket's Hideaway. Her knickers and socks were unpacked. Her sweatshirt swung from a hook on the back of the door. Her shirts and trousers hung in the cupboard. Her toothbrush stood in a glass by the basin.

She was using this with her customary morning vigour when a knock on the door was followed by a breathy voice calling, "Ready for morning tea, Barbara?"

Mouth still lathered, Barbara opened the door to find Corrine Payne standing with a tray in her hands. Despite the ungodly hour, she was completely dressed, fully made-up, and expertly coiffed. Had she not been wearing different clothes from the previous night and had her nut-brown hair not been curled into a different style, Barbara would have assumed she'd never gone to bed.

She was wheezing slightly, but she flashed a smile as she entered, and she used her hip to shut the door behind her. She set the tray on top of the chest of drawers and said, "Whew. Got to catch myself here," and leaned against the chest, taking a few gulps of air. She said, "Spring and summer. They're the worst of the worst. All the pollen in the air." She waved towards the tray. "Tea. Go ahead. Be fine in a dash."

Barbara kept one eye leerily upon the other woman as she rinsed away her toothpaste. Corrine's breathing sounded like air being released from the stretched mouth of a balloon. It would certainly be a wonderful thing if she collapsed while Barbara was happily swilling down the Formosa Oolong.

But after a moment, during which Barbara heard footsteps padding down the corridor outside her door, Corrine said, "Better. Much much better," and indeed her breathing seemed to ease. She went on with, "Robbie's already up and about, and as a rule he'd be the one to bring up the tea." She poured Barbara a cup. It was strong, the colour of baked cinnamon. "But I always draw the line at letting him deliver morning tea to young ladies. Nothing's worse than a man seeing a woman in the morning before she's made herself presentable. Am I right?"

The single experience she'd had with a man some ten years in the past hadn't included the morning, so Barbara merely said, "Morning. Night. It's all the same to me," and sloshed some milk into the cup.

"That's because you're young and your skin's just as peachy as it ever was. And . . . How old are you? Do you mind my asking that, Barbara?"

Barbara briefly considered lopping off a few years for the hell of it, but since she'd already revealed her age to Robin, there was no real point in lying to his mother.

Corrine said, "Lovely. I remember what thirty-three was like."

Which, Barbara decided, wouldn't have been a difficult proposition. Corrine herself was well under fifty, something which had initially surprised Barbara when she'd seen the woman on the previous night. Her own mother was sixty-four years old. Since Robin Payne was so close to her in age, Barbara hadn't been prepared to find in his mother a woman who'd obviously given birth to him as a teenager. She wondered, with an uncharacteristic moment of bitterness, what it would actually be like to have a mother who was in the middle of life instead of nearing the end of it, to have a mother who was in possession of her faculties instead of losing a battle against dementia.

Corrine said, "Sam's a great deal my senior. You noticed, didn't you? Funny how things work out. I used to think I could never fall in love with a balding man. Robbie's father had a great deal of hair. Mounds of it. Everywhere." She smoothed out the lace runner that covered the top of the chest of drawers. "But he's been so good to me, has Sam. He has such enormous patience with this." She used three fingers to pat the hollow of her throat. "When he finally asked me, what could I say but yes? And it's all for the best since it frees up Robbie. He'll be able to marry his Celia now. She's a lovely girl, Celia. Perfectly lovely. So sweet. She's Robbie's intended, you know."

The gentleness in her voice was not deceiving. Barbara met her eyes and read the steely meaning there. She wanted to say, "Mrs. Payne, don't worry. I'm not after your son, and even if I were, he wouldn't be likely to succumb to my dubious charms." Instead, she said after another gulp of tea, "I'll just throw on some rags and be down in a couple of minutes."

Corrine smiled. "Fine. Robbie's doing your breakfast. You like bacon, I hope." And without waiting for a reply, she was gone.

Downstairs, Robin emerged from the kitchen just as Barbara reached the dining room. He had a pan in one hand from which he slid two fried eggs onto her plate. He said with a glance out of the window where, to Barbara's eye, the sky was still black with the night, "Dawn's not far. We'll have to be about it if you still want to see the canal by five."

As they'd walked from their cars to the house last night, she'd announced her intention of viewing the body site at the same time of day as the body had entered the water. Robin had winced—"That means we're out of here by quarter to five," he'd pointed out—but when she'd responded with "Fine. Set your alarm," he hadn't made any further protest. And now he seemed as awake as if he rose every day while it was still night, although he stifled a yawn as he wished her *bon appétit* and returned to the kitchen.

Barbara tucked into the eggs. She shovelled them down, and since no one was present to comment on her manners, she sopped up the yolk with toast. She crammed the bacon into her mouth, washed it down with orange juice, and was done. She gave a curious glance to her watch. Three minutes of gastronomy. Definitely a new record.

Robin was subdued on the way out to the crime scene. To her immediate gratitude, Barbara discovered that he was a smoker, so they lit up and happily filled his Escort with carcinogens. After a few minutes of silent nicotine intake, he guided the car off the Marlborough Road and onto a narrower lane that led behind the village post office and out into the country.

"I used to work there," he said suddenly with a nod at the post office. "I used to think I'd be trapped there forever. It's why I got such a late start at this CID business." He glanced her way, and seeming anxious to clarify what he'd just said and whatever worries his words might have aroused in her, he went on quickly. "But I've taken some extra courses to get a leg up."

Barbara said, "The first investigation is always the roughest. I know mine was. I expect you'll do just fine."

"I had five O levels," he went on earnestly. "I'd thought I'd try for university."

"Why didn't you?"

He tapped ash from his cigarette through a speck of an opening he'd created by slightly lowering his window. "Mum," he said. "The asthma comes and goes. She's had some bad spells over the years, and I didn't feel like I could leave her alone." He tossed another look her way. "I expect that sounds like I'm tied to her apron."

Hardly, Barbara thought. She considered her own mother—both of her parents in fact—and the years upon years of her adulthood that she had spent living in the family home in Acton before and after her father's death, a prisoner to one parent's ill health and the other's mental erosion. No one was more likely to understand what it meant to keep one's life on hold than Barbara. But she settled upon saying, "She has Sam now, so your freedom's on the horizon, isn't it?"

"You mean our 'little chappie'?" he asked sardonically. "Oh yes. Right. If the marriage comes off, I'll be cut loose. *If* the marriage comes off."

He had the sound of a man who'd been this close to liberty more than once before, only to have his hopes and plans quashed. Celia, Barbara thought, whoever she was, must have the aspiratory constitution of a congenital optimist.

The lane humped over a bridge that spanned the Kennet and Avon Canal. "Wilcot," Robin said, identifying the hamlet of thatched cottages strung along the canal's banks like misshapen beads on a necklace. He went on to tell her that the site wasn't too much farther, and Barbara examined her watch in the dashboard lights to see how close they would be to five A.M. when they arrived. It was four fifty-two. Right on schedule, she thought.

They spun deeper into the countryside and the road veered west. To the south lay farmland where the corn—glaucous with the coming daylight—swayed in the breeze from the car. To the north rose the downs, across which one of Wiltshire's white chalk horses stretched out its neck in a motionless gallop, an eerie presence that pierced the gloom.

When they pulled into the hamlet of Allington, the sky was shifting from black to the colour of Trafalgar Square pigeons. Robin said, "We're coming on it," but rather than drive her directly there, he made a complete circuit of the hamlet first, showing her the two means of access to it from the main road. One access was farther north and cut past Park Farm and half a dozen rough stucco houses with red-tiled roofs. The other was closer to Wilcot and the way they'd come, and it bisected much of Manor Farm, whose houses, barns, and outbuildings sat behind brick walls overgrown with greenery.

Both means of access conjoined at a knobby track, and it was into this track that they jounced, with Robin telling her—with apologies for his car's suspension—that it was a mile and a half farther along to the site.

Barbara nodded vaguely, but she was busy taking note of the area. Even at five in the morning, lights had been on in three of the houses.

No one had been outside, but surely if a vehicle had passed this way at this same hour earlier in the week, someone might have heard it, might have seen it, and might only be waiting for the right question to jog a memory.

She said, "CID's spoken at each of the houses?"

"First thing." Robin changed down gears to first, and the car lurched uneasily.

Barbara gripped the dashboard. "We may want to talk to them all again."

"Could do."

"They may have forgotten. Someone had to have been up. People are up right now. If a car passed by—"

Robin whistled through his teeth. It was the sound of a doubt, unwilling to be given voice.

"What?" she asked him.

"You're forgetting," he said. "It was on Sunday morning the body was dumped."

"So?"

He slowed for a crater-sized pothole. "You *are* from the city, aren't you? Sunday's rest day in the country, Barbara. Farm people are up before dawn six days a week. On the seventh they do like God suggested and have themselves a lie-in. They're probably up by six-thirty. But at five? Not on a Sunday."

"Damn," she muttered.

"It doesn't make things any easier," he agreed.

Where the track rose to meet a bridge, he pulled as far to the left as he could and switched off the engine, which sputtered three times and then settled into stillness. They got out into the morning air. Robin said, "Down this way," and led her to the other side of the bridge, where a declivity thickly grown with grass dropped to the towpath that ran along the canal.

Here reeds grew in abundance as did a wealth of wildflowers that speckled the dark green banks like pink, white, and yellow stars. Among the reeds, waterfowl nested and their sudden cries as they took to the air seemed to be the only sound for miles. West and east of the bridge, two narrow-boats were moored along the canal banks, and when Barbara turned to question Robin about them, he told her in explanation that they were trippers only, not permanent residents. They hadn't been here the day the body was discovered. They wouldn't be here tomorrow.

"Cruising up to Bradford-on-Avon," he said. "To Bath, to Bristol.

They're up and down the canal from May to September, the narrow-boats. They just dock for the night where they can create a mooring. City people, most of them." He smiled. "Like you."

"Where do they get the boats?"

He took out his cigarettes and offered her one. He used a match to light hers first, sheltering the flame from the breeze by cupping his hand round hers. His skin, she found, was smooth and cool.

"Hire them," he said in answer to her question. "Just about any spot where the canal's near a town, someone's hiring out narrow-boats."

"Such as?"

He rolled his cigarette between thumb and forefinger as he considered the question. "Hungerford for one. Kintbury. Newbury. Devizes. Bradford-on-Avon. Even Wootton Cross. There's a hiring spot there."

"Wootton Cross?"

"There's a wharf farther up the Marlborough Road. That's where the canal passes through the village. Boats are hired from there."

Barbara saw the spider-webbing of the case's complexities. She squinted through her cigarette's smoke, back to the track they'd driven on. She said, "Where does that lead if you keep heading down it?"

He followed the direction of her gaze and indicated the southeast with the hand that held his cigarette. "It keeps running through the fields," he said. "Ends in a copse of sycamores about three-quarters of a mile along."

"Anything there?"

"Just the trees. Fences where the fields meet. Nothing else. We went over it Sunday afternoon with a comb. We can have another look if you like, when we've a bit more light."

As it was, the light was continuing to grow from the eastern sky where a fan of pale grey was streaking into the pigeon-feather darkness like uncurling fingers. Barbara considered the offer. She knew how serious was their disadvantage in this investigation. Five days had passed since Charlotte Bowen's disappearance, six if one wanted to include this as one of them. Forty-eight hours had passed since the discovery of her body, and God only knew how many since her actual death. With every additional handful of sand that trickled through the hour-glass, the trail got colder, people's memories grew dimmer, and the possibility of successfully concluding the case grew more remote. Barbara knew this. At the same time, she knew she was feeling mightily compelled to go over ground that had once been gone over. Why? she wondered. But she knew the answer. This was her chance to make her mark—every bit as much as it was DC Payne's chance—and she meant to make the most of it.

That compulsion didn't serve the interests of Charlotte Bowen's family or justice, however. She said, "If your lot found nothing there—"

"Not even a jingle of a nothing," he said.

"Then let's stick with what we have." They'd paced some yards along the canal to the exact location where the body had lain near the reeds. Now Barbara led the way back to the bridge, an arched affair of bricks beneath which a patch of concrete formed a narrow shelf over the water. She flicked her cigarette into the canal, and when she caught Robin wincing, she said, "Sorry, but there's still not quite enough light and I need to see . . ." The water flowed to the west. "Two possibilities," she said. She slapped her hand against the arch of the bridge that rose in a curve above their heads. "He parks above, comes down the path, dashes under the bridge with the body. He's out of sight in what, ten seconds? He drops the body in the water here. The body floats. The current carries it over to the reeds."

She walked back to the towpath. Robin followed. Unlike her, he put out his cigarette on the heel of his shoe. He put its dog end into his pocket.

Faced with such scrupulous environmentalism, Barbara felt guilty enough to dive into the water after her own cigarette. But instead, she said, "Or he brought her here in a narrow-boat. He eased her out the back end of it—what is it, the prow? the bow? the stern?"

"Stern."

"Right. Okay. He eased her out the stern and just kept on cruising, another holiday maker out on the canal."

"So we've all the boat hiring spots to look into as well."

"It appears that way. Does Sergeant Stanley have a team on that?"

He tapped his front teeth together, just as he had done on the previous night when Sergeant Stanley's manner of handling the case had come up.

"Is that a no?"

"Is what—?" He looked confused.

"What you're doing with your teeth."

He touched his tongue to them, then gave a short laugh. "You don't miss anything. I'll have to watch my p's and q's."

"I dare say. And as to the sergeant . . . ? Come on, Robin. This isn't a test of loyalty. I need to know where things stand."

His oblique answer gave her the information she wanted. "If it's all right with you, I'd like to scout round a bit today. You've the autopsy to see to, right? And Sergeant Stanley will want to meet with you after that. You've things the Yard wants you to dig into. You've phone calls to make and people to talk to. You've reports to write. I see it like this: I could drive you round—and I'm happy to do it, make no mistake of that—and be your right-hand man, or I could be another set of eyes and ears. Out there." He lifted his chin as a means of pointing in the direction of the track, the car, and the rest of Wiltshire.

She had to admire his diplomacy. Once she was back in London, he'd still be working with Sergeant Stanley. Both of them knew that the delicate balance of that relationship had to be his primary concern if he wanted to advance in CID.

She said, "Right. That works for me." She headed up the acclivity towards the track. She heard his heavier footsteps behind her. At the top she paused and glanced back his way. She said, "Robin," and when he looked up, "I think you're going to do fine as a Jack."

His teeth flashed in a smile and he quickly ducked his head. The light was still bad, but had it been better, Barbara was sure she would have seen him blushing.

—⁂—

"I swear to *God* I didn't," Mitchell Corsico said hotly. "D'you think I'm crazy? D'you think I *want* to slit my own throat?" He hitched up his jeans in some agitation and paced what little space was available in Rodney Aronson's office while Rodney himself watched the investigative reporter from behind his desk and listened to the creak of his cowboy boots. He unwrapped an Aero bar with his usual attention to the delicacy of the operation, exposing a single bite-sized portion of the chocolate.

"I can't help reliving your threats of yesterday, Mitch," Rodney said, chocolate deposited into the pouch of his cheek. "Doubtless, you see our concerns."

The word *our* wasn't lost on Corsico. He said, "You didn't actually tell Luxford what I . . . Fuck it, Rodney, Luxford doesn't think I turned traitor, does he? You know I was just blowing off steam."

"Hmmm," Rodney said. "But the fact remains . . ." He let that morning's copy of *The Source*'s foremost rival complete the sentence for him. The *Globe* lay atop Rodney's desk. On its front page, next to a telephoto shot of MP Eve Bowen emerging from her car at her home in Marylebone, a one-hundred-forty-four-point headline blared:

MP Daughter Snatched, No Call Made to Police! The tabloid had had a veritable field day with the same story that Mitchell Corsico had presented—and Luxford had soundly rejected—on the previous afternoon.

"Anyone else could have got that information," Corsico said. "Maybe I was first on the scene—"

"Maybe?"

"All right. Fuck it. I was. But that doesn't mean I'm the only person that the housekeeper might have given the story to. She was cut up, like the kid was her own. She would've talked to anyone who acted sympathetic."

"Hmmm," Rodney said again. He'd learned long ago that to look contemplative was just about as good as actually being contemplative. So having emitted the appropriate noise of deep thinking, he made a diamond of his fingers and thumbs and placed them beneath his chin. "What to do," he murmured.

"What d'you mean?" Corsico demanded. "Has Luxford seen this?"

Rodney lifted one shoulder in reply.

"I'll talk to him. He knew I was apeshit, but he also knows I wouldn't give my own story to another paper."

"There's no by-line on the story, Mitch. You must see how that looks."

Corsico snatched the tabloid from Rodney's desk. He ran his gaze over the front page. Where one would expect to see *Exclusive: By Joe Reporter* boxed off beneath the headline, there was nothing at all. He threw the paper down. "So what're you saying? I gave the story to the *Globe*, told them to run it without my name, and advised them I'd be coming on board just as soon as I gave my notice to Luxford? Come on, Rodney. Have some sense. If I wanted to do that, I would've quit last night and you'd be sitting here now, looking at my name on page one of that rag."

He paced again. He prowled the width of the office. Outside in the newsroom, it was business as usual, but more than one glance in the direction of the deputy editor's glass-walled office told Rodney that others on the floor, besides himself, knew of the *Globe*'s coup. Heads ducked when he looked their way. They all felt the same, sick in the gut. Being scooped was as bad as being inaccurate. Worse, in fact. Inaccuracy still sold papers.

Rodney peeled away another portion of the Aero bar's wrapper. He used his tongue to manoeuvre a new piece of chocolate into place. His dentist had told him that if he didn't stop stowing chocolate between his molars and his cheek, he wouldn't have teeth left by the time he was sixty. But what the hell, he thought. There were worse things in life than owning a set of porcelain chompers.

"It looks bad," Rodney said. "Your stock round here is something of an iffy thing at the moment."

"Great," Corsico muttered.

"So you'll just have to get a story in for us, fast. For tomorrow's paper."

"Yeah? What about Luxford? He didn't want this sort of stuff yesterday"—He jabbed his index finger at the copy of the *Globe*—"without confirmation from Scotland Yard that Bowen hadn't gone straight to Victoria Street and just bypassed the local cops. So what makes you think anything's changed today? And don't tell me someone from Scotland Yard actually confirmed the *Globe*'s story. That's a real stretch, and I won't buy it."

"It *is* possible," Rodney said. He went on meaningfully with, "Snouts're everywhere, Mitch. As—and may I be sure of this?—you well know."

The fact that Corsico had received Rodney's message was implicit in his answer. He said, "Okay. Okay. So I was burning when I left here yesterday. So I went out and got pissed."

"Instead of working to confirm your story. As, I believe, you were directed to do." Rodney tut-tutted. "We don't want that sort of thing to happen again. I don't. Mr. Luxford doesn't. The chairman doesn't. Am I being clear?"

Corsico shovelled his left hand into the back pocket of his jeans. He brought forth his notebook. "All right, but it's not as bad as it seems. We're already getting tips, just like I said we would."

Rodney recognised the moment to relent. He said pleasantly, "That's excellent. I can—and will—pass that news upward. It'll be sure to please. What've you got?"

"Part obvious observation, part crackpot bullshit, part possibility." Corsico licked his lips and then his fingers. He used them to riffle through the pages of his notes. "The obvious first: Do we know the child was illegitimate, do we know that Bowen never named the father, do we know the kid went to a convent school. The bullshit next: This is a religious plot and the next kid will be kidnapped within twenty-four hours; a satanic cult that sacrifices children is on the prowl; white slavery is involved; child pornography is at the root of everything. Plus the usual loonies phoning in with sightings of the kidnapper, declarations of guilt, and revelations of paternity."

"Aren't people despicable," Rodney murmured.

"Too right." Corsico's eyes were on his notes. He used the nail of his index finger to flick one of the pages of his notebook back and forth. It was a nervous gesture that Rodney didn't miss.

He said, "And the part that's a possibility, Mitch? We still need our story."

"It's nascent. Not ready for print."

"Understood. Go on."

"Right. I was in early this morning, which is why I didn't see that." He acknowledged the *Globe* with a dip of his head. "I had the kid's birth certificate—the copy from St. Catherine's—you remember?"

"I'd hardly be likely to forget. Have you learned something, then?"

Corsico took a pencil from his shirt pocket. He made a mark in his notebook, then drove the pencil beneath his Stetson and raised its brim. "I did the maths."

"Maths?"

"On Bowen's pregnancy. If the birth wasn't premature, then nine months before it was the thirteenth of October. For a lark, I had a look through the microfilms to see what was going on then. I did two weeks on either side of the thirteenth." He read from his notebook. "A blizzard in Lancashire. A pub bombing in St. Albans. A serial killer. Genetic fingerprinting under scrutiny. Test tube babies in—"

"Mitchell, I've taken off the gloves, if you hadn't noticed," Rodney said. "So there's no need to regale me with the minutiae of your research. Is there a point you're reaching?"

Corsico raised his head from his notes. "The Tory conference."

"What about it?"

"The October Tory conference in Blackpool. That's what was going on nine months to the day of the Bowen kid's birth. We already know that Bowen was the political correspondent for the *Telegraph* then. She would have been covering the conference. She did cover it, in fact. I got that from the *Telegraph*'s morgue fifteen minutes ago." Corsico flipped his notebook closed. "So I wasn't far off yesterday, was I? Every bigwig in the party probably made an appearance in Blackpool during that conference. And she was bonking one of them."

Rodney had to admire the young man's tenacity. He was in full possession of the strength, determination, and resiliency of youth. He filed the information about the conference into his brain for future reference and said, "But where do you go with this, Mitch? It's one thing to speculate on the father's identity. It's another to find it. How many Tories in Blackpool are we talking about? Two thousand party members and two hundred MPs? Where do you propose to start looking?"

"I want to have a look at what kind of stories Bowen was filing from the conference. I'll check to see if she was following the work of any particular parliamentary committee. She may have interviewed someone and got hooked up that way. I'll talk to the lobby correspondents and see if they have anything as well."

"That's a start," Rodney acknowledged. "But as to having a story for tomorrow's paper . . ."

"Right. Right. We can't go with this stuff. Not yet, at least. But I'll phone my snouts right now. I'll see what they can give me."

Rodney nodded. He raised a benedictory hand. It communicated to Corsico that their interview was at a conclusion.

At the door to the office, Corsico turned back. He said, "Rod, you don't actually believe I gave that story to the *Globe*. Do you?"

Rodney directed his facial muscles to arrange themselves into an expression of earnest rectitude. "Mitchell," he said, "believe me now if never again. I know you didn't give that story to the *Globe*."

He waited until the door had closed on the reporter. He removed the rest of the wrapper from his Aero bar. He wrote *Blackpool* and *13 October* on the back of it, folded it into a square, and put it into his pocket. He popped the last piece of chocolate into his mouth. He chuckled and reached for his Filofax and his phone.

The pictures hadn't been difficult to find. Evelyn was, after all, in an exposed position. As a public servant in the process of establishing a brilliant career, she had been the focus of more than one newspaper article in the past six years. And long knowing the importance of a politician's image, she had generally posed for photographs with her family.

Dennis Luxford had three of them spread on his desk. While the staff of *The Source* went about the business of the day just outside his office, he examined the photographs of his daughter.

In one of them, she sat on a plump hassock in front of Evelyn and her husband, who were themselves seated on a sofa. In another, she gripped the mane of a horse while Eve, in jodhpurs, led her round a ring. In the third, she sat at a table ostensibly doing schoolwork, a stub of a pencil clutched in her hand, her mother bending over her and pointing to something on the paper on which the child was writing.

Luxford slid open one of the drawers of his desk and shifted items until he found the magnifying glass he used to read fine print. He used the glass against the pictures. He studied Charlotte's face.

Now that he actually saw her for the very first time—instead of looking at and dismissing her photograph along with her mother's as so much political fodder for the masses—he could see that his family was etched in her. She had her mother's hair and her mother's eyes, but the rest of her marked her immutably as a Luxford. The same chin as his sister's, the same wide brow as his own, the same nose and mouth as Leo's. She was stamped as his daughter every bit as indelibly as if she'd been branded with his name, instead of denied it.

And he knew nothing about her. Her favourite colour, the size of her shoes, the stories she had liked to read before bed. He had no idea what her aspirations had been, what stages she'd gone through, what dreams she'd dreamed. Such knowledge was the hostage of responsibility. When he'd dismissed one, he'd forfeited the other. Oh, he'd tipped his hat to paternity with a monthly visit to Barclay's, wearing the ceremonial chains of fatherhood for quarter of an hour as he made out deposit slips in the cause of self-absolution. But that was the extent of his involvement with his daughter, a non-involvement whose superficial purpose was to see to Charlotte's future beyond his own death but whose real purpose was to act as continual balm to his conscience during his life.

It had seemed so much the right thing to do. Evelyn had made her wishes clear. Since, with what he liked to believe was an atypical display of masculine egocentricity, he had designated her the injured party, he told himself that he could only see that her wishes were fulfilled. And they were so easy to comply with. She'd stated them in five simple words, "Stay away from us, Dennis." He'd been happy to do so.

Luxford laid the pictures side by side on his desk. He examined each under the magnifying glass a second, third, then a fourth time. And he found himself wondering if the child he was studying through the lens liked music, if she hated broccoli, refused to eat mushrooms, walked pigeon-toed, read the Narnia books, rode a bicycle, had ever broken a bone. Her features marked her as his, but his ignorance about her forced him to acknowledge that she had never been his. That fact was as clear today as it had been four months before her birth.

Stay away from us, Dennis.

Very well, he'd thought.

So his daughter was dead. Precisely because he'd stayed away, as instructed. Had he refused to play along, Charlotte would never have been kidnapped in the first place. There would have been no demands to acknowledge her paternity because that information would have been available to everyone, including Charlotte.

Luxford touched her head in the photograph and wondered what her hair had felt like. He couldn't imagine. He couldn't honestly imagine a single thing about her.

The immensity of his ignorance burned in him. As did the testimony that the ignorance made to his true worth as a man.

Luxford set the magnifying glass on top of one of the pictures. He pressed his thumb and index finger to the bridge of his nose and closed his eyes behind them. All of his life he'd played the game of power. At this moment he sought only prayer. Somewhere, there had to exist the words that could assuage the—

"I'd like a word, Dennis."

He jerked his head up. In a reflex movement, he dropped his arm to his desk and obscured the pictures. Standing in the doorway to his office was the only person who would have dared to open the door without knocking or without asking Miss Wallace to ring through and advise the editor of his arrival: *The Source* chairman, Peter Ogilvie. He said, "May I . . . ?" and flicked his soulless grey eyes in the direction of the conference table. It was a pro forma request. Ogilvie clearly intended to enter the office whether he was invited to do so or not.

Luxford rose from his desk. Ogilvie advanced. He led, as always, with his signature eyebrows, so long gone untrimmed that they resembled feather boas snaking across his forehead. The two men met in the centre of the room. Luxford offered his hand. The chairman slapped a folded tabloid into it.

"Two hundred and twenty thousand copies," Ogilvie said. "That is, of course, two hundred and twenty thousand above their daily circulation, Dennis. But that's only part of my concern."

Ogilvie had always been a hands-off chairman of the newspaper. He had more important concerns than the daily running of *The Source*, and he generally addressed himself to them from his massive office in his Hertfordshire home. He was a bottom-line man whose interest was fixed almost solely upon profit and loss.

Aside from receiving reports of a drastic alteration in the newspaper's profits, only one other event would bring Ogilvie into the London offices of *The Source*. Being scooped was a fact of life in the newspaper business, and Ogilvie—who'd been in the business, it sometimes seemed, since the time of Charles Dickens—would have been first to admit this. But being scooped on a story that had the potential of tarring the Tories was completely unacceptable to him.

So Luxford knew what Ogilvie had delivered into his hand. It was this morning's edition of his erstwhile paper, the *Globe*, with its headline about MP Bowen's failure to contact the police in the wake of her daughter's abduction.

"Last week we were ahead of every paper in the nation on Larnsey and the rent boy," Ogilvie said. "Are we slipping this week?"

"No. We had the story. I killed it."

Ogilvie's only reaction was in his eyes. For an instant they narrowed fractionally. The movement looked like a muscle twitching.

"Is this a loyalty issue, Dennis? Are you still tied to the *Globe* for some reason?"

"Would you like a coffee?"

"A believable explanation will do."

Luxford went to the conference table and sat. He nodded for Ogilvie to do the same. He hadn't come to work for Ogilvie without learning that to show any sign of weakness in the chairman's presence was to trigger his predilection for bug squashing.

Ogilvie eyebrowed his way to the table and pulled out a chair. "Tell me."

Luxford did so. When he was finished taking the chairman through his interview with Corsico and his reasons for killing the story, Ogilvie homed in on the most cogent point with typical journalistic acumen.

"You've run stories before now without multiple confirmations. What stopped you this time?"

"Bowen's position at the Home Office. It seemed reasonable to conclude that she would have by-passed her local police and gone directly to Scotland Yard. I didn't want to run a story indicting her for inaction only to end up with egg on my face when some high rider at the Yard jumped to her defence, waving his appointment diary, and claiming she'd been there within ten minutes of learning the girl had been snatched."

"Something which hasn't happened," Ogilvie pointed out, "in the wake of the *Globe*'s story."

"I can only assume the *Globe* got confirmation from someone at the Yard. I told my man to do the same. If he'd had it for me before ten last night, I'd have run the story. He hadn't. I didn't. There's nothing more to tell."

"There's one thing more," Ogilvie said in disagreement.

Luxford grew wary, but he used his chair to demonstrate his composure to the chairman, leaning back in it and lacing his fingers across his stomach. He didn't ask Ogilvie to elucidate upon his "one thing more." He merely waited for the other man to continue.

"We did a good job on Larnsey," Ogilvie said. "And we did it without multiple confirmations. Am I correct?"

There was no point to lying, since a conversation with Sarah Happleshort or Rodney Aronson would be sufficient to uncover the truth. "You are."

"Then tell me this. Set my mind at ease. Tell me that the next time we have these Tory louts by the balls, you're going to know how to squeeze. You're not going to let the *Mirror*, the *Globe*, the *Sun*, or the *Mail* apply the pressure for you. And you're not going to back off by requesting confirmation from three, thirteen, or three dozen bloody sources."

Ogilvie's voice rose emphatically with the last four words. Luxford said, "Peter, you know as well as I that Larnsey's situation was different to Bowen's. Multiple confirmations weren't necessary in his case. There was nothing open to doubt. He was caught in a car with his trousers unzipped and his dick in the mouth of a sixteen-year-old boy. In Bowen's case, what we have is a single statement from the Home Office and everything else floating somewhere between innuendo, gossip, and downright fabrication. When I have some facts that I can be assured are facts, rely upon them being printed on our front page. Until then . . ." He lowered his chair to its original position and faced the chairman squarely. "If you've a problem with how I'm running the paper, then you need to think about getting yourself another editor."

"Den? Oh. Excuse me. I didn't realise . . . Mr. Ogilvie. Hello."

Rodney Aronson had chosen his moment superbly. The deputy editor stood with one hand on the knob of Luxford's door—which Ogilvie had left partially open, the better that his raised voice might drift out into the newsroom and shake up the troops—and his disembodied head poking into the aperture.

"What is it, Rodney?" Luxford demanded.

"Sorry. I didn't mean to interrupt. The door was open and I didn't know . . . Miss Wallace isn't at her desk."

"How intriguing. Thanks for informing us."

Rodney's mouth curved in a thin smile that was belied by the sudden angry stretching of his nostrils. Luxford saw that he wasn't going to accept being embarrassed in front of the chairman without doing something to return the favour. He said affably, "Right. Sorry. Not thinking," and then displayed his weapon of choice with, "I just thought you'd like to know what we've got brewing on the Bowen situation."

He made the assumption that his remark gave him entrée to Luxford's office. He took a chair directly opposite the chairman.

"You were right," he said to Luxford. "The Home Secretary did make a call to Scotland Yard on behalf of Bowen. A personal call, in the flesh. A snout's confirmed it." He paused as if in homage to Luxford's wisdom in holding back on the story that the *Globe* was running. But Luxford knew that the last move Rodney would make was to risk attenuating the value of his own stock with Ogilvie by promoting Luxford's. So he prepared himself for what was to come and began to line up his mental soldiers for a skirmish. "But here's what's interesting. The Home Secretary didn't make this visit to the Yard until yesterday afternoon. Before that, the Yard hadn't heard word one about the kid's disappearance. So Mitch's story was gold."

"Rodney, we're not in the business of wasting time in confirming other newspapers' stories," Ogilvie pointed out. He said to Luxford, "Although if you've managed to get confirmation today, I'd like to know why you couldn't manage it yesterday."

Rodney intervened. "Mitch was beating the bushes like hell, from yesterday afternoon till midnight. His sources were dry."

"Then he needs new sources."

"I couldn't agree more. And when he saw the *Globe*'s front page this morning, he set about getting them. After I gave him some encouragement in my office."

"May I conclude from your smile that you've come up with something more?" Ogilvie asked.

Luxford noted that Rodney did not deny himself a look of triumph cast in his direction. He veiled it, however, with a show of caution that did service as a stiletto inserted neatly between Luxford's ribs. He said, "Please understand, Mr. Ogilvie. Den may not want to run with this new stuff, and I wouldn't disagree with his decision, if that's what it is. We've only just got it from our snout at the Yard, and he may be the only one willing to talk."

"What is it?"

Rodney's tongue flicked across his lips. "Apparently, there were kidnapping notes. Two of them. They were received the same day the kid went missing. So Bowen knew beyond a doubt that the kid had been snatched and still she did nothing to involve the police."

Luxford heard Ogilvie draw in a breath. He spoke before the chairman could do so, saying evenly, "Perhaps she phoned someone else, Rod. Have you or Mitchell considered that angle?"

But Ogilvie prevented Rodney from answering by holding up a large and bony hand. The chairman reflected on the information in silence. His glance rose—not heavenward to seek the Almighty's counsel—but wallward, where the chrome-framed display of *The Source*'s circulation-winning front pages were hung.

"If Ms. Bowen phoned someone else," he said thoughtfully, "then

I suggest we let her tell us that herself. And if she has no comment to make on our story, then that fact can be displayed—along with the others—for the public's consumption." His gaze dropped to Rodney. "And the contents?" he said genially.

Rodney looked blank. He massaged his beard in a movement that bought time and served to cover his confusion.

"Mr. Ogilvie is asking about the contents of the kidnapping notes," Luxford said in translation with cool courtesy.

The temperature of the statement wasn't lost on Rodney. "We don't know," Rodney answered. "Only that there were two."

"I see." Ogilvie spent a moment considering his options. He finally announced his decision with, "That's enough to build a story round. Is your man on it?"

"As we speak," Rodney said.

"Lovely." Ogilvie rose. He turned to Luxford and offered his hand. "Things are picking up, then. I can be assured, I trust, that I won't have to come into town again?"

"As long as every story is solidly founded," Luxford replied, "it'll run in the paper."

Ogilvie nodded. He said, "Nice work, Rodney," in a thoughtful fashion that was intended to communicate his evaluation of the two men's relative positions at the newspaper. He left the room.

Luxford went back to his desk. He slid the photographs of Charlotte into a manila folder and returned the magnifying glass to his drawer. He punched the button to light his computer's screen and dropped into his chair.

Rodney approached. "Den," he said in a casual, introductory tone.

Luxford checked his appointment diary and made an unnecessary notation in it. Rodney, he decided not for the first time, needed a lesson to teach him his place. But he couldn't think what the lesson would be while his mind was occupied trying to come up with options Evelyn might pursue to avoid becoming a target of the press. At the same time he wondered why he was concerned for her in the first place. After all, she'd dug her own grave in this matter and— The thought of graves chilled him, brought everything back to him in a sickening rush. It wasn't Evelyn's grave that had been dug. And she wasn't the only one who'd assisted in the digging.

". . . and generally because of that, as I'm sure you'll understand, I wasn't altogether up front with Ogilvie just now," Rodney was saying.

Luxford raised his head. "What?"

Rodney rested a sizable portion of his beefy thigh on the front of

Luxford's desk. "We don't have all the facts yet. But Mitch is on their trail, so I'd lay money on our having the truth within a day. You know, Den, sometimes I love that kid like he was my own."

"What are you talking about, Rodney?"

Rodney cocked his head. Not listening, Den? his expression said. Something on your mind? "The Tory conference in Blackpool," Rodney said gently. "Where someone put Bowen in the club. As I said a moment ago, she was there, covering the conference for the *Telegraph*. And the conference began nine months to the day before her kid was born. Mitch's on the trail right now."

"Of what?" Luxford asked.

"What?" Rodney repeated in gentle mockery. "Of Dad, of course." With admiration he looked at the framed front pages. "Think of what it'll do if we get an exclusive on this one, Den: Bowen's unidentified paramour speaks to *The Source*. I didn't want to mention the possibility of a story on the dad to Ogilvie. No sense in having him riding our backs every day when we may not be able to come up with a thing. But still and all . . ." He released his breath in a sigh that acknowledged *The Source*'s commitment to snuffling through the pasts of the country's most prominent personalities in order to find a succulent truffle of personal history that would send the newspaper's circulation into the double-digit millions. "It's going to be like an A-bomb going off when we run it," he said. "And we will run it, won't we, Den?"

Luxford didn't avoid Rodney's gaze. "You heard what I told Ogilvie. We'll run anything that's solid."

"Good," Rodney breathed. "Because this . . . Den, I don't know what it is, but I have a gut feeling that we're on to something as good as diamonds."

"Fine," Luxford said.

"Yes. It truly is." Rodney removed his thigh from the desk. He headed in the direction of the door. But there he paused. He pulled at his beard. "Den," he said. "Hell. I've just realised something. I don't know why I didn't think of it before. You're the man we're looking for, aren't you?"

Luxford felt the chill from his ankles to his throat. He didn't say a word.

"You can help us out, help Mitch out, that is."

"I? How?"

"On the Tory conference," Rodney said. "I forgot to mention. I drew in a chit over at the *Globe* and had a wander through their microfilms after I talked to Mitch."

"Yes? What about them?"

"Come on, Den. Don't hide your light on this one. The Tory conference? In Blackpool? Doesn't it ring any bells?"

"Should it?"

"I should certainly hope." His teeth flashed like a shark's. "Don't you remember? You were there yourself, writing editorials for the *Globe*."

"Was I," Luxford said. Not a question, a statement.

"Yes indeed. Mitch'll want to talk to you. So why don't you have a nice long think about who it was who might have bonked Bowen." He gave a slow wink and left the office.

19

B ARBARA USED the hem of her jersey to blot the cold sweat from her forehead. She got up from her knees. More disgusted with herself than she'd been in recent memory, she flushed the toilet and watched the unsightly contents of her stomach whirlpool into oblivion. She gave her body a vigorous mental shake and ordered herself to act like the head of a murder investigation instead of like a whinging teenager going weak in the knees.

Postmortem, she told herself roughly. What is it? Merely the examination of a corpse, undertaken to determine the cause of death. It's a necessary step in a murder enquiry. It's an operation performed by professionals on a hunt for any suspicious processes that could have contributed to the untimely cessation of physical functions. In short, it's a critical step in finding a killer. Yes, all right, it's the disembowelment of a human being, but it's also a search for the truth.

Barbara knew those facts well. So why, she wondered, had she been unable to go the distance with Charlotte Bowen's postmortem?

The autopsy had been performed in St. Mark's Hospital in Amesford, a relic of the Edwardian era built in the style of a French chateau. The pathologist had worked quickly and efficiently, but despite the professional atmosphere in the room, the initial thoracic-abdominal incision into the body had caused Barbara's hands to sweat in an ominous manner. She knew immediately that she was in trouble.

Stretched out on the stainless steel table, the body of Charlotte Bowen was virtually unmarked, save for some bruising round the mouth, some reddish burn marks on the cheeks and chin, and a scab-covered cut on one knee. Indeed, the little girl actually looked more asleep than dead. So it seemed like such a defilement of her innocence to cut into the pearl flesh of her chest. But cut the pathologist did, tonelessly reciting his findings into a microphone that dangled above his head. He snapped away her ribs like so many thin branches from a sapling and removed her organs for examination. By the time he had taken out the urinary bladder and sent its contents off for analysis, Barbara knew she wasn't going to be able to make it through what was to follow: the incision through the child's scalp, the peeling back of her flesh to expose her small skull, and the high-pitched whizzing of the saw as it cut through bone to get to her brain.

Is all this necessary? she wanted to protest. Bloody hell on a wafer, we *know* how she died.

But they didn't, really. They could offer speculations based upon the condition of her body and where it had been found, but the exact answers they needed could only come from this essential act of scientific mutilation.

Barbara knew that DS Reg Stanley was watching her. From his position by the scales on which each organ was separately weighed, the man was glued to every expression that crossed her face. He was waiting for her to run from the room, hand clamped over mouth. If she did so, he would be able to snort, "Just like a woman," in dismissal. Barbara didn't want to give him an opportunity to deride her to the men with whom she was supposed to be working in Wiltshire, but she knew it was going to come down to a choice: She could humiliate herself by being sick on the floor or she could exit and hope she found a lavatory before she was sick in the corridor outside.

Upon reflection, however—with her stomach ever tightening, her throat closing in, and the room beginning to swim in her vision—she realised that there was another alternative.

She gave a marked glance to her watch, feigned realising that she'd forgotten to do something, emphasised this by rustling through her notebook, and communicated her intentions to Stanley by miming a telephone call with one hand to her ear and her lips saying, "Must phone London." The DS nodded, but the caustic quality of his smile told her he wasn't convinced. Sod you, she thought.

Now in the ladies' lavatory, she rinsed out her mouth. Her throat burned. She cupped her hands for water and drank greedily. She splashed her face, dried off on the limp blue towelling that spooled forth unantiseptically from a dispenser, and leaned against the grey wall upon which the dispenser hung.

She didn't feel much better. Her stomach was emptied of its contents, but her heart was still full. Her mind was saying, Concentrate on the facts. Her spirit was countering with, She was only a kid.

Barbara slid down the wall to the floor and rested her head against her knees. She waited for her stomach to settle and for the chills to leave her.

The child had been so small. Forty-nine inches tall, less than six stone in weight. With wrists that looked as if an adult's single finger could encompass them. With limbs whose definition came from bird-like bones, not muscles. With thin, sloping shoulders and the clam-shell bareness of completely undeveloped pudendum.

So easy to kill.

But how? Her body showed no sign of struggle, no indication of trauma. It emanated no telltale odour of almonds, garlic, or winter-green. It bore no flush of carbon monoxide in the blood, no cyanosis of the face, the lips, or the ears.

Barbara slid her arm beneath her knee and looked at the time. They'd be done by now. They'd have some kind of answer. Faint or not, she needed to be there when the pathologist made his preliminary report. The derision she'd seen in Sergeant Stanley's eyes across the autopsy table was enough to tell her that she wouldn't be able to rely upon him for an accurate account of the information.

She forced herself to her feet. She went to the mirror over the basin. She had nothing to use as a means of improving her colour, so she would have to depend upon her limited Thespian powers to bluff her way through what would undoubtedly be Sergeant Stanley's suspicion that she'd recently sicked up in the loo. Well, it couldn't be helped.

She found him in the corridor not five steps away from the ladies' lavatory. Stanley was making a pretence of forcing a fuller stream of water from an antique porcelain drinking fountain. As Barbara came his way, he straightened from his endeavours, said, "Bloody useless thing," and pretended to catch sight of her. "Phone calls made, are they?" he asked, glancing towards the lavatory door in a way that communicated his intimate knowledge of where British Telecom had installed every phone box in Wiltshire. No box in there, Missy, his expression said.

"Quite," Barbara said and walked past him to return to the post-mortem room. "Let's get on with things, shall we?" She steeled herself to whatever grisly sight was beyond the door. She was relieved to see that her assessment of the time that had passed since she'd first left the room was correct. The autopsy was completed, the corpse had been removed, and all that remained as evidence of the procedure was the stainless steel table on which it had been performed. A technician was in the process of hosing this down. Ensanguined water sluiced across the steel and drained away through holes and channels on the sides.

Another body, however, awaited the ministrations of the pathologist. It lay on a trolley, partially covered by a green sheet, its hands still bagged and an identification tag tied to its right big toe.

"Bill," one of the technicians called in the direction of a cubicle at the far end of the room. "I've popped new tapes into the recorder, so we're ready when you are."

Barbara didn't relish the thought of standing through another autopsy in order to get information from the last one, so she headed towards the cubicle. Inside, the pathologist was drinking from a mug, his attention given to a miniature television on whose screen two sweating men were battling each other in a tennis match. The sound was muted.

He murmured, "Come on, you numbskull. His net game is murder and you know it. So get aggressive, put him on the defensive. Yes!" He saluted the tennis player with his mug. He saw Barbara and Sergeant Stanley and smiled. "I've fifty quid riding on this match, Reg."

"You need to go to Gamblers Anonymous."

"No. I just need a decent bit of luck."

"That's what they all claim."

"Because it's true." Bill switched off the television and nodded at Barbara.

Barbara could tell from his expression that he was about to ask her if she was feeling better and she didn't think she needed to give Sergeant Stanley any fodder for his suspicions. So she took her notebook from her shoulder bag and said with a tilt of her head in the direction of the other corpse in the outer room, "London's waiting for word from me, but I'll try not to keep you from your other work long. What can you tell me?"

Bill looked to Stanley as if for an indication of who was in command. Behind her, Barbara could sense the sergeant giving some sort of limited papal dispensation because the pathologist began to make his report. "The superficial indications are all consistent, although none of them are very pronounced." And then he cooperatively translated this introductory remark by adding, "The conditions apparent to the naked eye—while not as well-defined as is usual—all support one cause of death. The heart was relaxed. On the right side, the auricle and ventricle were engorged with blood. The air vesicles were emphysematous, the lungs were pale. The trachea, bronchi, and bronchioles were all lined with froth. Their mucosa was red in colour and congested. There were no petechial haemorrhages under the pleura."

"What does that all mean?"

"She drowned." Bill took a sip from his mug. He used a remote control pad to turn off the television.

"When exactly?"

"There's never an *exactly* with drownings. But I'd say she died roughly twenty-four to thirty-six hours before the body was found."

Rapidly, Barbara did her maths. She said, "But that puts her in the canal on Saturday morning, not on Sunday." Which meant, she realised, that someone in Allington may well have seen the passage of a car carrying the girl to her death. Because on Saturday the farmers rose at five as usual, according to Robin. It was only on Sunday that they stayed in bed. She swung to Stanley and said, "We'll need to have men go back to Allington and question everyone at the houses. With Saturday, not Sunday, in mind this time. Because—"

"I didn't say that, Sergeant," Bill said blandly.

Barbara returned her focus to him. "Didn't say what?"

"I didn't say she was in the canal for twenty-four to thirty-six hours before she was found. I said she was dead for that length of time before she was found. My speculation as to the time she was in the canal hasn't changed from twelve hours."

Barbara sifted through his words. "But you said she drowned."

"She drowned, all right."

"Then are you suggesting that someone found her body in the water, removed it from the canal, and returned it later?"

"No. I'm telling you that she didn't drown in the canal at all." He drank down the rest of his coffee and set his mug on top of the television. He went to a cupboard and dug in a cardboard box for a clean pair of gloves. He said, slapping the gloves against his palm, "Here's what happens in a typical drowning. A single strong inspiration on the part of the victim while under water carries foreign particles into the body. Under the microscope, the fluid taken from the victim's lungs shows the presence of those foreign particles: algae, silt, and diatoms. In this case, those algae, silt, and diatoms should match the algae, silt, and diatoms from a sample of water taken from the canal."

"They didn't match?"

"That's right. Because they weren't there in the first place."

"Couldn't that mean that she didn't take that—what did you call it—'single inspiration' under water?"

He shook his head. "It's an automatic respiratory function, Sergeant, part of terminal asphyxia. And at any rate, there was water in the lungs, so we know she inhaled after submersion. But under analysis, the water in her lungs didn't match the canal water."

"I assume you're saying she drowned somewhere else."

"I am."

"Can we tell from the water in her body where she died?"

"Could do, in some circumstances. In these circumstances, no."

"Why not?"

"Because the fluid in her lungs was consistent with tap water. So she could have died anywhere. She could have been held down in a bathtub, dunked into a toilet, or dangled by her feet with her head in a basin. She could even have drowned in a swimming pool. Chlorine dissipates quickly and we'd have found no trace of it in the body."

"But if that happened," Barbara said, "if she was held down, wouldn't there have been an indication of that? Bruising on her neck and shoulders? Ligature marks on the wrists or ankles?"

The pathologist shoved his right hand into a latex glove and snapped it snugly against his skin. "Holding her down wasn't necessary."

"Why not?"

"Because she was unconscious when she was put into the water. Which is why all the typical signs of drowning were less marked than normal, as I first said."

"Unconscious? But you've mentioned no blow to the head or—"

"She wasn't struck to render her unconscious, Sergeant. She wasn't, in fact, molested in any way, before or after death. But the toxicology report shows that her body was riddled with a benzodiazepine. A toxic dose, as a matter of fact, considering her weight."

"Toxic, but not lethal," Barbara clarified.

"That's right."

"And what did you call it? A benzo—what?"

"A benzodiazepine. It's a tranquilliser. This particular one is diazepam, although you might know it from its more common name."

"Which is?"

"Valium. From the amount in her blood—in combination with the limited signs of drowning on the body—we know she was unconscious when she was submerged."

"And dead when she got to the canal?"

"Oh yes. She was quite dead when she got to the canal. And had been, I'd say, close to twenty-four hours."

Bill put on the second glove. He rooted in the cupboard for a gauze mask. He said, bobbing his head towards the outer room, "This next one is going to be rather malodorous, I'm afraid."

"We were just leaving," Barbara said.

—⁂—

As she followed Sergeant Stanley on the route back to the car park, she reflected on the import of the pathologist's findings. She'd thought they were making slow progress, but now it seemed they were back to square one. Tap water in Charlotte Bowen's lungs meant that she could have been held anywhere prior to her death, that her drowning could have been accomplished in London just as easily as in Wiltshire. And if that were the case, if the girl had been murdered in London, then she could have been held captive in London as well, with more than enough time to kill her in town and then to drive her body to the Kennet and Avon Canal. Valium suggested London as well, a tranquilliser prescribed to assist one in dealing with life in the metropolis. All that was necessary for a Londoner to have kidnapped and done away with Charlotte was that he or she possess some knowledge of Wiltshire.

So chances were good that it was all for nought that Sergeant Stanley had gridded off the land, and chances were equally good that it was equally for nought that Sergeant Stanley had deployed more than a score of policemen in a search for where Charlotte Bowen had been held captive. And chances were, it seemed, outstandingly excellent that she herself had agreed to the deployment of Robin Payne on the wildest of goose chases in which he would waste an entire day scouting round boat-hiring locales, not to mention sniffing up sawmills, canal locks, windmills, and reservoirs.

What a bloody waste of manpower, she thought. They were looking for a needle that probably didn't exist. In a haystack the size of the Isle of Wight.

We need something to go on, she told herself. A witness to the abduction stepping forward, an article of Charlotte's clothing found, one of the girl's schoolbooks recovered. Something more than a body with grease under her nails. Something that could tie that body to a place.

What would it be? she wondered. And in this vast landscape—if indeed it was here and not in London—how on earth were they going to find it?

Up ahead of her, Sergeant Stanley had paused on the steps. His head was bent into the lighting of a cigarette. He offered her the packet, which she saw as an unspoken truce between them. Until she also saw his lighter. It was a naked woman, bent at the waist, and the flame shot out of her arse.

Bloody hell, Barbara thought. Her stomach was unsettled, her head felt fuzzy, and her mind was trying to sort through the facts. And here she was, forced into keeping company with Mr. Misogyny disguised as Sergeant Plod. He was waiting for her to go hot in the face and make some sort of ultrafeminist remark that he could take back to his CID cronies for a chuckle.

All right, she thought. So naffing happy to oblige, you twit. She took the lighter from his hand. She turned it round. She doused its flame, lit it, doused it again. She said, "Utterly remarkable. Incredible, actually. I wonder if you've noticed."

He went for the bait. "Noticed what?" he asked.

And she reeled him in. "That if you drop your trousers and stick your arse in the air, this lighter is a dead ringer for you, Sergeant Stanley." She smacked it back into his palm. "Thanks for the fag." She walked to her car.

—⁂—

The squats on George Street were aswarm with members of the scene-of-crime team. With their kits, their envelopes, their bottles, and their bags, they scurried through the building that St. James and Helen had earlier explored. On the top floor, they were rolling up the carpet for analysis in the lab and giving particular attention to the collecting of fingerprints.

As they puffed the black dust onto woodwork and doorknob, windowsill, water tap, glass pane, and mirror, the prints emerged. There were hundreds of them, and they looked like the torn and severed wings of ebony insects. The print officers were lifting and recording all of them, not just those that fitted into the same classification as the one St. James had lifted from the battery compartment of the tape recorder. There was a very good chance that more than one person was involved in Charlotte Bowen's disappearance. An identifiable print could take them to that person and be the break they were looking for, if the squat proved to be significant in the case.

Lynley directed them to pay particular attention to two locations: the bathroom mirror and the water taps beneath it, and the window overlooking George Street where a pane had been cleaned, ostensibly to give someone a view through a gap in the buildings to St. Bernadette's on Blandford Street. Lynley himself was in the matchbox-sized kitchen where he was going through cupboards and drawers in a search for anything that St. James might have missed during his own inspection of the site.

There was little enough, and he noted that St. James had accurately listed all of it for him with his typical scrupulous attention to detail during their conversation on the previous afternoon. In one cupboard stood the red tin cup; in a drawer lay the single tine-bent fork and five rusty nails; on the work top stood two grimy jars. There was nothing else.

As water *plinked* softly into the sink, Lynley bent to the dusty work top and gave it a closer scrutiny. He examined it at eye level, looking for anything that might have gone unnoticed against the motley Formica. He directed his eyes from the wall to the outer edge of the work top, from the outer edge to the strip of metal that held the sink in position. Then he saw it. A fragment of blue—not much larger than a chip from a tooth—was wedged into a slight bubble of space between the metal stripping round the sink and the work top itself.

Using a thin blade from one of the scene-of-crime kits, he gently prised the blue fragment from its lodging. It had a vaguely medicinal scent, and when he scratched his fingernail against it in the palm of his hand, he saw it was friable. Part of a drug? he wondered. Some sort of detergent? He bottled it, marked it, and put it into the hands of one of the crime scene officers, telling her to arrange for its identification as soon as possible.

He went out of the flat, into the airless corridor. Because it was boarded up, there was little ventilation in the building. The scent of rodents, decomposing food, and excrement was heavy in the air, a scent heightened and cooked by the late spring's warm weather. This particular attribute was the one Detective Constable Winston Nkata commented upon when he came up the stairs as Lynley descended to the flat on the second floor. With a perfectly ironed white handkerchief pressed to his mouth and nose, the constable muttered, "This place is a cesspool."

"Watch where you're stepping," Lynley advised him. "God knows what's under that rubbish on the floor."

Nkata picked his way to the door of the flat as Lynley entered it. He joined him. "I hope these blokes're getting combat pay."

"It's all part of the glory of policework. What've you come up with?"

Nkata dodged the more significant piles of rubbish that the crime scene officers were sifting through. He went to the window and unlatched it, letting in an insubstantial stream of air. This was apparently enough to satisfy him because he lowered his handkerchief although he still winced at the smell.

"I been checking with the cops in Marylebone," he said. "The station in Wigmore Street's the one with constables who do the walk through Cross Keys Close. It's one of them would've seen the bum that Mr. St. James was telling you about."

"And?" Lynley said.

"Bust," Nkata said. "None of their regular blokes or birds remember rousting a dosser from the area. They been busy—tourist season and all that—and they don't keep score of who they hustle off what street when. So no one's willing to say there wasn't any rousting going on. But no one's willing to have a sit with our sketch man to get a picture of the bloke."

"Blast," Lynley said. There went their hopes of a decent description of the vagrant.

"Which is what I thought exactly." Nkata smiled and pulled on his ear. "So I took a little liberty here and there."

Nkata and his liberties had uncovered more than one piece of vital information. Lynley's interest heightened. "And?"

The DC reached into his jacket pocket. He'd taken one of their sketch artists out to lunch, he explained with a duck of his head that told Lynley the artist was one of the feminine persuasion. They'd dropped by Cross Keys Close on the way and paid a visit to the writer who'd given Helen Clyde the description of the tramp who'd been run out of the maze of mews the very day that Charlotte Bowen had disappeared. With the artist working and the writer providing her with the details, a likeness of the man had been composed. And, taking a little more liberty and an admirable amount of initiative, Nkata had had the foresight to ask the artist to draw a second sketch, this one *sans* the scraggly hair, the whiskers, and the knitted cap that all could be part of a disguise.

"Here's what we came up with." He handed over the two sketches.

Lynley studied them as Nkata continued. He'd made copies of both, he said. He'd distributed them among the constables who were currently out on the street attempting to pinpoint the place from which Charlotte had disappeared. He'd given others to the constables who were checking the local doss-houses to see if they could get a name for this bloke.

"Send someone to show the drawings to Eve Bowen," Lynley said. "Her husband and housekeeper as well. And that gentleman you were telling me about last night: the one who watches the street from his window. One of them may be able to give us something."

"Got it," Nkata said.

In the corridor, two members of the crime scene team were labouring with the rolled carpet from the floor above. It lay heavy on their shoulders like an obligation unmet, and one of them cried out, "Steady on, Maxie. I got only so much space to manoeuvre," as they staggered towards the stairs. Lynley went to assist. Nkata, more reluctantly, joined them, saying, "Smells like dog piss, this."

"Probably saturated with it," Maxie said. "It'll smell quite smart on your jacket, Winnie."

The others chuckled. With much stumbling, groaning, and fumbling about in the ill-lit corridors, they made their way to the ground floor of the building. Here, at least, there was more light and better air since the metal and boards had been removed from the front door to give them access to the interior. They carried the roll of carpeting through this door and shoved it into a waiting van on the street. Nkata made much of brushing himself off afterwards.

Back on the pavement, Lynley thought about what the detective constable had told him. While it was true that with the number of tourists wandering about the area looking for Regent's Park, the wax museum, or the planetarium, the local police might not keep in mind the occasional dosser they ordered to move along, it did seem reasonable to conclude that someone might be able to identify him with the assistance of what they now had: the sketch. He said, "You'll need to talk to the local force again, Winston. Show that picture round the canteen. See if it jogs a memory."

"There's another thing," Nkata noted. "And you're not going to like it much. They got twenty specials on the force as well."

Lynley cursed quietly. Twenty special constables—volunteers from the community who wore a uniform and walked a beat like any other policeman—meant twenty more individuals who might have seen the vagrant. The complexities of the case seemed to be increasing exponentially with every passing hour.

"You'll have to run the sketch by them as well," Lynley said.

"Not to worry. Will do." Nkata removed his jacket and inspected its shoulder where he'd balanced the roll of carpet. Satisfied with what he saw, he shrugged back into it and took a moment to adjust the cuffs of his shirt. He gave an evaluative glance to the building they'd just come out of, then said to Lynley, "You think this's the place where the kid was stowed?"

"I don't know," Lynley answered. "It's a possibility, but then so is the rest of London at the moment. Not to mention Wiltshire." He reached without thinking for the inside pocket of his jacket where, before he'd abjured them sixteen months ago, he'd always kept his cigarettes. It was odd how hard a habit died. The ceremony of igniting a thin tube of tobacco was somehow connected to the process of his thinking. He needed to do one in order to stimulate the other. At least that's how it felt at moments like this.

Nkata must have understood, because he fished in his trousers and brought forth an Opal Fruit. He passed it to Lynley without speaking and found another for himself. They unwrapped the sweets in silence, while behind them in the squat the work of the crime scene team went on.

"Three potential motives," Lynley said. "But only one of them really makes sense. We can argue that this entire affair was a bungled attempt to increase *The Source*'s circulation—"

"Hardly bungled," Nkata pointed out.

"Bungled in that it couldn't have been Dennis Luxford's intention that the child would die. But if that's our motive, we still have to dig up the *why* behind it. Was Luxford's job in jeopardy? Had another tabloid taken a chunk of *The Source*'s advertising? What was going on in his life that might have prompted the kidnapping?"

"Maybe both was going on," Nkata said. "Job troubles. And less advert revenue."

"Or were both the crimes—the kidnapping and the murder—designed by Eve Bowen to bring herself into the limelight with an outpouring of public sympathy?"

"That's cold," Nkata said.

"Cold, yes. But she's a politician, Winston. She wants to be Prime Minister. She's on the fast track already, but perhaps she became impatient with the process of getting to the top. She thought about a shortcut and her daughter was the answer."

"A woman'd be a monster to think like that. It's unnatural."

"Did she seem natural to you?"

Nkata sucked reflectively on his Opal Fruit. "Here's the deal," he finally said. "White women, I don't have truck with them. A black woman's honest about what she wants and when. And how, yes, she even tells a man how. But white woman? No. White woman's a mystery. White women always seem cold to me."

"But did Eve Bowen seem colder than the others?"

"She did. But then, that coldness? It's just a matter of degree. All white women seem icy about their children. You ask me, she was just who she was."

That might, Lynley thought, be a far more open-eyed assessment of the Junior Minister than was his own. He said, "I'll accept that. Which leaves us with motive number three: Someone is intent upon toppling Ms. Bowen from power. Just as she's claimed to have thought from the first."

"Someone who was there in Blackpool when she had her do with Luxford," Nkata said.

"Someone who stands to benefit if she takes a fall," Lynley said. "Have you done background on the Woodwards yet?"

"Next on my list," Nkata told him.

"Get on it, then." Lynley fished out his car keys.

"What about yourself?"

"I'm going to pay a call on Alistair Harvie," Lynley said. "He's from Wiltshire, he's no friend of Bowen's, and he was in Blackpool for the Tory conference."

"You think he's our man?"

"He's a politician, Winston," Lynley said.

"Doesn' that give him a motive?"

"Quite," Lynley said. "For just about everything."

—⁓—

Lynley found Alistair Harvie at the Centaur Club, which was conveniently located less than quarter of an hour's walk from Parliament Square. Housed in the former residence of one of the mistresses of Edward VII, the building was a showplace of Wyatt cornices, Adam fanlights, and Kauffmann ceilings. Its elegant architecture was a tribute to the country's Georgian and Regency past—with decorative details rendered in everything from plaster to wrought iron—but its interior design made a statement about the present and the future. Where once the great drawing room on the club's first floor might have contained an array of Hepplewhite furniture and fashionably dressed inhabitants enjoying a languid afternoon tea, now it contained a veritable traffic jam of athletic equipment and sweat-drenched men in shorts and T-shirts who grunted and groaned through leg squats, bench presses, and vertical butterflies.

Alistair Harvie was among them. In running shorts, trainers, and a terrycloth headband catching the perspiration that trickled from his extremely well-sculpted greying hair, the MP ran bare-chested on a treadmill that faced a mirrored wall, in which the exercisers could watch and meditate upon their physical perfections or lack thereof.

That is what Harvie appeared to be doing as Lynley approached him. He ran with arms bent, elbows held to his sides, and eyes anchored upon his own reflection. His lips were drawn back in what could have been either a smile or a grimace and as his feet thudded upon the rapidly moving track, he breathed evenly and deeply like a man who enjoyed testing his body's endurance.

When Lynley produced his warrant card and held it at Harvie's eye level, the MP did not stop running. Nor did he look concerned by this visitation from the police. He merely said, "Did they let you in below? What the hell's happened to privacy round here?" He spoke in the unmistakable plummy voice of the old Wickhamist. "I'm not finished with this. You're going to have to wait seven minutes. By the way, who told you where to find me?"

Harvie had the look of a man who'd take all too much pleasure in sacking the mousy little secretary who'd given Lynley the information in a burst of nerves upon seeing his police identification. So Lynley said, "Your schedule isn't much of a secret, Mr. Harvie. I'd like a word please."

Harvie didn't react to a policeman's producing an equally cultivated public school voice. He merely commented, "As I said. When I'm finished." He pressed his sweat-banded right wrist to his upper lip.

"I'm afraid I haven't the time to wait. Shall I question you here?"

"Have I forgotten to pay a parking fine?"

"Perhaps. But that's not the province of CID."

"CID, is it?" Harvie kept up his speed on the treadmill. He spoke between carefully regulated breaths. "Criminal investigation of what?"

"The kidnapping and death of Eve Bowen's daughter, Charlotte. Shall we talk about it here, or would you prefer the conversation take place somewhere else?"

Harvie's eyes finally left his own reflection and settled on Lynley's. They watched him speculatively for a moment as a bandy-legged exerciser with an excessively protuberant stomach clambered onto the treadmill next to them and began fumbling with its dials. It rumbled into action. Its user yelped and began to run.

Lynley said in a manner designed to carry if not to the rest of the room then at least to the treadmill runner next to them, "You've no doubt heard that the child was found dead Sunday evening, Mr. Harvie. In Wiltshire. Not all that great a distance from your home in Salisbury, I believe." He pressed his hands against the pockets of his jacket, as if looking for a notebook in which to record Alistair Harvie's statement. He said in the same manner, "So what Scotland Yard would like to know is—"

"All right," Harvie snapped. He adjusted a dial on the treadmill. His pace began to slow. When the running track stopped, he stepped off and said, "You have all the subtlety of a Victorian costermonger, Mr. Lynley." He grabbed a white towel that draped over the treadmill's railing. As he rubbed it up and down his bare arms, he said, "I'm going to shower and change. You can join me if you want to scrub my back, or you can wait in the library. The choice is yours."

The library was a euphemism for the bar, Lynley found, although it made obeisance to its name by offering a fan of newspapers and magazines on a mahogany table in the room's centre and by containing two walls of bookshelves whose leatherbound volumes didn't look as if they'd been opened during the current century. Some eight minutes later, Harvie took his time getting to Lynley's table. He stopped to exchange a few words with an octogenarian who was playing patience with a fiercely proud rapidity. Then he paused by a table at which two pinstripe-suited youths were poring over the *Financial Times* and making entries into a laptop computer. After imparting his wisdom upon them, Harvie said to the barman, "Pellegrino and lime, George. No ice please," and finally joined Lynley.

He'd changed from his workout clothes into his Member of Parliament ensemble. In best public school fashion, he wore a navy blue suit just tatty enough to suggest that a family retainer had broken it in for him first. His shirt, Lynley noted, was a perfect match for his percipient blue eyes. He pulled out a chair at the table and, once seated, unbuttoned his jacket and touched his fingers to the knot—then to the length—of his tie.

"Perhaps," Harvie said, "you can tell me what your interest is in interviewing me about this business." A bowl of mixed nuts sat in the centre of the table. He picked out five cashews and rested them in the palm of his hand. "Once I know why you're here, I'll be more than happy to answer your questions."

You'll answer my questions one way or another, Lynley thought. But he said, "Feel free to phone your solicitor if you think it's necessary."

Harvie popped one of the cashews into his mouth. He bounced the rest of them in his hand. He said, "That would take some time, of which, I believe, you recently mentioned you have very little to waste. Don't let's play games with each other, Inspector Lynley. You're a busy man, and so am I. In fact, I have a committee meeting in twenty-five minutes. So I can give you ten. And I suggest you use them wisely."

The barman brought his Pellegrino water to the table and poured it into a goblet. Harvie nodded his thanks, ran a wedge of lime round the glass's rim, then plopped the piece of fruit into the water. He popped another cashew into his mouth and chewed it slowly, watching Lynley as if he were gauging him for a response.

There didn't seem a point to verbal duelling, especially in a situation in which his adversary was primed by his vocation to win at any cost. So Lynley said, "You've been an outspoken opponent of a new prison in Wiltshire."

"I have. It may provide a few hundred jobs for my constituency, but at the cost of destroying several more hundred acres of Salisbury Plain, not to mention bringing a highly undesirable specimen of human being into the county. My constituents oppose it with very good reason. I am their voice."

"This puts you at loggerheads with the Home Office, I understand. And with Eve Bowen in particular."

Harvie rolled his remaining cashews in his palm. "You can't be suggesting I engineered the kidnapping of her daughter because of that, can you? That would hardly be an efficacious approach to moving the prison site to another location."

"I'm interested in exploring your entire relationship with Ms. Bowen."

"I have no relationship with her."

"I understand that you first met her in Blackpool some eleven years ago."

"I did?" Harvie looked perplexed, although Lynley was more than willing to discredit this perplexity as a demonstration of the politician's ability to dissemble.

"It was a Tory conference. She worked as a political correspondent for the *Telegraph*. She did an interview with you."

"I don't recall it. I've done hundreds of interviews in the last decade. I'd hardly be likely to remember any one of them in detail."

"Perhaps the outcome of it might jog your memory. You wanted sex with her."

"Did I?" Harvie took up his Pellegrino and tasted it. He seemed more intrigued than offended by Lynley's revelation. He leaned towards the table and picked through the nuts to fish out more cashews. He said, "That doesn't surprise me. She wouldn't have been the first reporter I wanted to take to bed at the conclusion of an interview. Did we do it, by the way?"

"Not according to Ms. Bowen. She rejected you."

"Did she? Well, I can't think I would have put very much effort into seducing her. She isn't my type. It was probably more a case of my testing the waters to gauge her reaction to the idea of a bonk than actually wanting to screw her."

"And if she'd been willing?"

"I've never been an advocate of celibacy, Inspector." He looked across the room, towards an embrasure that enclosed a window seat of tattered red velvet. Through the windows, a garden was in full bloom and the heliotrope flowers of a wisteria drooped grapelike against the glass. "Tell me," Harvie went on, turning from the sight of the flowers.

"Am I supposed to have kidnapped her daughter as retaliation for that rejection in Blackpool? A rejection, mind you, that I don't recall but one that I'm willing to admit might have occurred?"

"As I've said, in Blackpool she was a reporter for the *Telegraph*. Her circumstances have changed rather markedly since then. Yours, in contrast, haven't changed at all."

"Inspector, she's a woman. Her stock has been rising politically more because of that than because she possesses any particular talents over and above my own. I am—like you, I might add, and like all our brothers—a victim of the feminist outcry for more women in positions of responsibility."

"So if she weren't in her position of responsibility, a man would be."

"In the best of all worlds."

"And possibly that man would be yourself."

Harvie finished his cashews and wiped his fingers on a cocktail napkin. He said, "What am I to conclude from that comment?"

"If Ms. Bowen were to resign her post at the Home Office, who stands to gain?"

"Ah. You see me as waiting in the wings, the understudy who's desperately hoping that 'break a leg' comes to mean more than a wish of good luck for the leading actress. Is that correct? Don't bother to answer. I'm not a fool. But the question reveals how little you know about politics."

"Nonetheless, if you'll answer it," Lynley said.

"I'm not opposed to feminism *per se*, but I'll admit to a belief that the movement is getting out of hand, especially in Parliament. We have better things to occupy our time than engaging in dialogues over whether tampons and stockings should be sold in the Palace of Westminster or a crèche provided for the female MPs with small children. This is the centre of our government, Inspector. It is not the Department of Social Services."

Getting a straight answer from the politican, Lynley decided, was like trying to stab a greased snake with a toothpick. "Mr. Harvie," he said, "I don't want to make you late for your committee meeting. Please answer the question. Who stands to gain?"

"You'd like me to incriminate myself, wouldn't you, but I stand to gain nothing if Eve Bowen resigns her post. She's a woman, Inspector. If you want to know who gains the most if she stands down as Junior Minister, then you need to be looking at the other women in the Commons, not at the men. The Prime Minister isn't about to replace a female appointee with a man, no matter his qualifications. That's not going to happen in the present climate, not with his current rating in the polls."

"And if she stands down as a Member of Parliament altogether? Who gains then?"

"She wields more power from her position in the Home Office than she could ever hope to wield as a simple MP. If you're looking at who gains what if she stands down, then study the people whose lives are most affected by her presence in the Home Office. I'm not one of them."

"Who is?"

He went for the nuts again, picking two almonds from the bowl as he considered the question. "Gaolbirds," he said. "Immigrants, coroners, passport holders." He started to put an almond in his mouth, but stopped abruptly and lowered his hand.

"Someone else?" Lynley said.

Carefully, Harvie placed the nuts by his goblet. He said more to himself than to Lynley, "This sort of thing . . . What's happened to Eve's daughter isn't their normal way of making a point. Besides, in the present environment of cooperation . . . But if she were to stand down, they *would* have one less enemy . . ."

"Who?"

He looked up. "With the cease-fire being called and the negotiating going on, I can't really think they'd want to cock things up. But still . . ."

"Cease-fire? Negotiating? Are you talking about—"

"I am," Harvie said gravely. "The IRA."

Eve Bowen, he explained, had long maintained one of the hardest lines in Parliament on dealing with the Irish Republican Army. Developments towards peace in Northern Ireland had done nothing to allay her suspicions about what the Provos' real intentions were. In public, of course, she gave lip service to supporting the Prime Minister's attempts at resolving the Irish question. In private she voiced her belief that the INLA—always more extreme than the Provisional IRA—were a good bet to revamp themselves and emerge as an active and violent force against the peace process.

"She thinks the Government ought to be doing more to prepare itself for the moment the talks break down or the INLA takes action," Harvie said. Her belief was that the Government needed to be ready to deal with potential problems at their source and not run the risk of facing another decade of bombs going off in Hyde Park and Oxford Circus.

"How does she propose the Government do that?" Lynley asked.

"By examining ways both to broaden the powers of the RUC and to escalate the number of troops deployed to Ulster—all this on the sly, mind you—while still claiming a stalwart belief in the negotiating process."

"That's a risky business," Lynley said.

"Isn't it just." Harvie went on to explain that Eve Bowen was also a proponent of heightening the police undercover presence in Kilburn. Their purpose would be to identify and monitor London supporters of any maverick elements within the IRA who were intent upon smuggling weapons, explosives, and guerrillas into England in anticipation of not getting what they wanted from the peace talks.

Lynley said, "It sounds as if she has no belief that a resolution can be found."

"That's a fair assessment. Her formal position is twofold. First, as I've already said, that the Government needs to be prepared for the moment talks with Sinn Fein break down. And second, that those six counties voted to be part of the British Empire and by God they deserve the British Empire's protection to the bitter end. It's a popular sentiment among those who like to believe there actually *is* a British Empire any longer."

"You disagree with her views."

"I'm a realist, Inspector. In two decades, the IRA have demonstrated rather well that they're not going away because we clamp them in gaol without benefit of counsel whenever we get the chance. They're Irish, after all. They breed continually. Put one in gaol and ten more of them are out there procreating beneath a picture of the Pope. No, the only sensible way to end this conflict is to negotiate a settlement."

"Something Eve Bowen would be reluctant to do."

"Death before dishonour. Despite what she says in public, Eve believes at heart that if we negotiate with terrorists now, where will we be in ten years' time?" He looked at his watch and downed the rest of his water. He got to his feet. "This isn't typical of them, kidnapping and killing a politician's child. And I couldn't say that either event—as horrible as they must be for Eve—would result in her standing down from her position. Unless there's something connected to those events that I don't know . . . ?"

Lynley made no reply.

Harvie rebuttoned his jacket and adjusted his cuffs. "At any rate," he said, "if you're looking for someone who'll benefit mightily should she stand down, then you need to consider the IRA and its splinter groups. They could be anywhere, you know. No one knows better how to meld inconspicuously into a hostile environment than an Irishman with a cause."

20

ALEXANDER STONE saw Mrs. Maguire out of the corner of his eye. He was staring into the clothes cupboard in Charlotte's bedroom when the housekeeper came to the door. She had a plastic bucket in one hand while the other hand clutched a limp bouquet of rags. She'd been washing windows for the past two hours, her lips moving soundlessly and ceaselessly in prayer, her eyes dribbling tears as she scrubbed away dirt and polished the glass.

"If I'm not disturbing you, Mr. Alex." Her chin dimpled when she looked round the room where Charlotte's belongings were just as she'd left them nearly a week ago.

Alex said past the dull ache in his throat, "No. Go ahead. It's all right." He reached into the cupboard and fingered a dress, red velvet with an ivory lace collar and matching cuffs. Charlie's Christmas dress.

Mrs. Maguire shambled into the room. The water in the bucket sloshed about like the insides of a boozer's stomach. Like his own stomach, in fact, although it wasn't drink this time that was acting upon him.

He reached for a child-sized tartan. As he did so, he heard behind him the sound of the curtains being drawn back, followed by the sound of Charlie's stuffed animals being moved from the window seat to the bed. He squeezed his eyes shut at the thought of the bed, where last night in this very room he had fucked his wife, riding her frantically to Destination Orgasm as if nothing had happened to change their lives forever. What had he been thinking of?

"Mr. Alex?" Mrs. Maguire had dipped one of her rags into the bucket. She had squeezed it out and now she held it in her reddened hands, twisted into a shape like a rope. "I'm not wishing to cause you further grief. But I know the police phoned an hour ago. And as I didn't have the heart to intrude on Miss Eve's sorrow, I'm wondering if you might find a way to tell me that won't cause your dear soul more torment. . . ." Her eyes became liquid.

"What is it?" He sounded abrupt although he didn't intend that. It was only that the last thing he wanted was to be the object of anyone's compassion.

"Can you tell me, then, how it was with Charlie? I've read only the newspapers and, like I said, I haven't wanted to ask Miss Eve. I'm not intending to be ghoulish, Mr. Alex. It's just that I can pray more from the heart for her repose if I know how it was with her."

How it was with Charlie, Alex thought. Having her take that rapid skip at his side so that she could keep up with him when they walked together; teaching her to cook chicken with lime sauce, the first dish he himself had learned; tracking down the hedgehog hospital with her and watching her wander delighted—small fists clutched to her bony little chest—among the cages. That's how it was with Charlie, he thought. But he knew what information the housekeeper wanted. And it wasn't about how Charlie had lived.

"She drowned."

"In that place they showed on the telly?"

"They don't know where. Wiltshire CID say she was drugged with tranquillisers first. Then drowned."

"Sweet blood of Jesus." Numbly, Mrs. Maguire turned to the windows. She rubbed her wet rag against one of the panes, saying, "Holy Mother of God," and Alex heard the catch in her breath. She picked up a dry rag and applied it to the wet pane. She gave careful attention to the corners where grime collected and was most easily overlooked. But he heard her snuffling and he knew she'd begun to weep again.

"Mrs. Maguire," he said, "you've no need to keep coming here every day."

She turned. She looked stricken as she said, "You're not telling me you want me out of here?"

"God no. I only meant that if you want some time off—"

"No," she said firmly. "I'll want no time off." She went back to the windows, wetting her rag for the second pane. She washed it as thoroughly as she had done the first, before she said hesitantly and in an even lower voice, "She wasn't . . . Mr. Alex, forgive me, but Charlie wasn't interfered with, was she? She wasn't . . . Before she died, he didn't use her ill, did he?"

"No," Alex told her. "There's no evidence of that."

"God's mercy," Mrs. Maguire responded.

Alex wanted to ask her how it was merciful on the part of her God to allow the child's life to be taken in the first place. What was the point of kindly sparing her the preliminary terror and torture of rape, sodomy, or some other form of molestation, when she was going to end up discarded like someone's disappointed hopes, floating dead in the Kennet and Avon Canal? But instead, he woodenly went back to the clothing and tried to complete the mission Eve had sent him on.

"They're releasing the body," she had said to him. "We need to give the mortuary something for her to wear in the coffin. Will you see to that for me, Alex? I don't think I could bear to go through her things just yet. Will you do it? Please?"

She'd been colouring her hair in the bathroom. She was standing at the basin, a towel round her shoulders. She was sectioning off her hair in perfectly straight rows with the tail end of a comb and squeezing dye from a bottle onto her scalp. She even had what looked like a small paintbrush, which she employed with precision to cover all the hairs at their roots.

He'd watched her in the mirror. He hadn't slept the previous night once they'd finished with each other. She'd urged the sedatives on him and gone to bed herself, but he'd wanted nothing more to do with drugs and he'd told her so. So he'd wandered the house—from their bedroom to Charlie's room, from Charlie's room to the sitting room, from the sitting room to the dining room where he'd sat and looked out at the garden where, until dawn, he could see nothing but shapes and shadows—and then he'd ended up watching her calmly colouring her hair, with fatigue dragging at his limbs and a growing despair pulling at his heart. "What do you want her to wear?" he'd asked.

"Thank you, darling." She applied the dye in a streak from forehead to crown. She daubed the paintbrush through it. "We'll have a viewing, so it should be something that works for that."

"A viewing?" He hadn't thought—

"I want a viewing, Alex. If we don't have one, it's going to appear that we have something to hide from the public. We don't. So we need to have a viewing and she needs to be dressed in something appropriate for it."

"Something appropriate." He felt like her echo, unwilling to think because he was afraid of where thinking might take him. He forced himself to add, "What do you suggest?"

"Her velvet dress. The one from last Christmas. She wouldn't have outgrown it yet." Eve slid the tail end of the comb into her hair and picked up another section to be dyed. "You'll need to find her black shoes as well. And there are socks in the drawer. A pair with lace round the ankles would be good, but make sure you don't choose one with a hole in the heel. We can probably do without any underthings. And a ribbon for her hair would be nice if you can find one somewhere that matches the dress. Ask Mrs. Maguire to choose one for you."

He'd watched her hands, moving so proficiently. They wielded the bottle, the comb, the paintbrush without a shake or a quiver.

"What is it?" she'd finally said to his reflection when he hadn't moved to see to the task she'd given him. "Why are you watching me like that, Alex?"

"They have no leads?" He knew the answer already but he needed to ask her something because asking a question and listening to the answer seemed the only way he would be able to reach a point of understanding who and what she actually was. "There's nothing? Just the grease under her fingernails?"

"I've withheld nothing. You know exactly what I know." She watched him watching her and for a moment she ceased the work on her hair. He thought about how she always claimed to envy the fact that despite his forty-nine years, his hair had not yet begun to grey while hers had started the metamorphosis when she was thirty-one. He thought about how many times he had responded to that envy, saying, "Why dye it at all? Who cares about your hair colour? I sure as hell don't," and how she had replied, "Thank you, darling, but I don't like the grey, so while I can still do something that looks remotely natural to get rid of it, I intend to." All those times, he'd thought with a mental shrug that it was a woman's inherent vanity that prompted Eve to seek out the dye bottle, not very much different to her act of growing an overlong fringe to cover the scar cutting through her eyebrow. But he saw now that the key words he could have used to understand her had always been the same: *something that looks remotely natural.* And failing to hear them for what they were, he had also failed to understand her. Until this moment, it seemed. And even now he wasn't certain that he knew her.

"Alex, why are you staring at me?" she'd asked him.

He'd brought himself round, saying, "Was I? Sorry. I was just thinking."

"About what?"

"Dyeing hair."

He saw the flicker of her eyelids. In her competent fashion, she was making a quick assessment of the direction in which any response of hers would lead their conversation. He'd seen her do it countless times before when talking to constituents, to journalists, to adversaries.

She placed the bottle, the paintbrush, and the comb on the top of the cistern. Then she turned to face him. "Alex." Her face was composed, her voice was gentle. "You know as well as I that we must find a way to go on."

"Is that what last night was about?"

"I'm sorry you weren't able to sleep. I only got through last night myself because I took a sedative. You could have done as well. I asked you to take one. It doesn't seem fair of you to decide that simply because I was able to sleep and you weren't—"

"I'm not talking about the fact that you were able to sleep, Eve."

"Then what are you talking about?"

"What happened before that. In Charlie's room."

A movement of her head gave the impression that she was withdrawing from his words, but she stated simply, "We made love in Charlotte's room."

"On her bed. Yes. Was that part of going on with our lives? Or was it part of something else?"

"What are you getting at, Alex?"

"I was just wondering why you wanted me to fuck you last night."

She let the words hang in the air between them while her mouth formed the word *fuck* as if she would echo it much the way he'd been echoing her. A muscle quivered beneath her right eye. "I didn't want you to fuck me," she said quietly. "I wanted you to make love to me. It seemed—" She turned from him. She picked up the comb and the bottle of dye, but she didn't lift them to her head. She didn't raise her head, in fact, so all he could see of her was the reflection in the mirror of the neat cornrows of dye lining her scalp. "I needed you. It was a way—even for only thirty minutes—it was a way to forget. I didn't think about our being in Charlotte's room. You were there, and you were holding me. That's what mattered at the moment. I'd been dodging the press, I'd been meeting with the police, I'd been trying—God, I'd been *trying*—to forget what Charlotte looked like when we identified her body. So when you lay next to me and put your arms round me and told me it was all right to do what I'd been avoiding—to feel, Alex —I thought . . ." She raised her head then. He saw how her mouth pulled down spasmodically at the sides. "I'm sorry if it was wrong to want sex then, in her room. But I needed you."

They looked at each other in the mirror. He realised how much and how badly he wanted to believe that she was telling the truth. "For what?" he asked.

"To let me be how I needed to be. To hold me. To help me forget for a moment. Which is what I'm doing now, with this." She indicated the dye, the comb, the paintbrush. "Because, it's the only way . . ."

She swallowed. The muscles strained in her neck. Her voice broke on "Alex, it's the only way I seem to be able to hold on to—"

"Oh Jesus, Eve." He turned her to him and pressed her against him, mindless of the dye that transferred from her hair to his hands and his clothes. "I'm sorry. I'm exhausted and not thinking and . . . I can't help myself. She's everywhere I look."

"You need to get some rest," she said against his chest. "Promise me that you'll use those pills tonight. You can't collapse on me. I need you to be strong because I don't know how much longer I can be strong myself. So promise me. Tell me you'll take those pills."

It was little enough to promise. And he needed sleep. So he agreed and went on his way to Charlie's room. But his hands were stained with the dye of Eve's hair, and when he lifted them to the hangers in the clothes cupboard and saw the brown streaks that hid the colour of his flesh, he knew that there was very little chance that one sedative or five would be able to allay the unresolved misgivings that kept him from sleep.

Mrs. Maguire was speaking to him from the windows of Charlie's room. He caught the last words ". . . little mule when it came to her clothes, wasn't she?"

He roused himself, blinking against the pain behind his eyes. "I was thinking. Sorry."

"Your mind's as full as your heart, Mr. Alex," the housekeeper murmured. "You have no need to apologise to me. I was just yammering anyway. God forgive me, but the truth of the matter is that sometimes it feels better to talk to another human being than to talk to Our Lord."

She abandoned her bucket, her rags, and her windows, and came to stand next to him. She took a small white blouse from Charlie's cupboard. It had long sleeves and tiny white buttons down the front, and its rounded collar was frayed at the neck.

"Charlie hated these school blouses," she said. "The good Sisters mean well, but God knows what gets into their heads at times. They told the girls they had to keep these blouses buttoned right up to the top for reasons of purity. If they didn't, a black mark was put against them in the deportment book. Our Charlie didn't want black marks, but she couldn't abide the blouses being closed so tight round her neck. So she worried the top of every one of them. You see how loose she's made this top button? And how the threads are unravelling? She did that to all of them, squirming her fingers between the blouse and her neck. She hated these blouses like they were sent from the devil, our Charlie."

Alex took the blouse from her. He couldn't tell if it was the work of his exhausted imagination or if the scent was still on the material. But it smelled like Charlie. It seemed saturated with her little-girl odours of licorice, school rubbers, and pencil shavings.

"They didn't fit her right," Mrs. Maguire was saying. "Most days when she got home, she'd be flinging her uniform on the floor and the blouse on top of it. Sometimes, she'd tramp them down with her shoes. And those shoes, God love her, she didn't like them either."

"What did she like?" He should have known. He must have known. But he couldn't remember.

"From her clothes, d'you mean?" Mrs. Maguire asked. She reached with quick assurance past the dresses and skirts, the proper coats and jerseys, and said, "This."

Alex looked down at the faded Oshkosh overalls. Mrs. Maguire rustled through the clothing and brought out a striped T-shirt. "And this," she said. "Charlie wore them together. With her trainers. She loved her trainers as well. She wore them without laces, with the tongues hanging out. I told her, did I not, that ladies don't dress like scamps, Miss Charlotte. But when, I ask you, did Charlie care a fig for what ladies dressed like?"

"The overalls," he said. "Of course." He'd seen her in them a hundred times or more. He'd heard Eve say, "You are *not* going out with us dressed like that, Charlotte Bowen," every time Charlie had bounced down the stairs and out to the car with her overalls on. "I am, I am!" Charlie would crow. But Eve always prevailed and the result saw Charlie grumbling and squirming in a picture-perfect lacy dress—in her Christmas dress, by God—and black patent leather shoes. "This stuff is *scritchy*," Charlie moaned, and with a scowl she tugged at the collar. Just as she must have tugged at her white school blouses, worn buttoned to the top for reasons of purity so that no black marks went down against her in the book.

"Let me have these." Alex took the overalls from the hanger. He folded them along with the T-shirt. He saw the laceless trainers in the corner of the cupboard and scooped them up as well. For once, he thought, in front of God and everyone, Charlie Bowen would wear what she liked.

—⁂—

In Salisbury, Barbara Havers found MP Alistair Harvie's constituency association office without much trouble. But when she showed her identification and requested some routine background information on the MP, she came up against the strong will of his association chairman. Mrs. Agatha Howe wore a haircut at least fifty years out of date and a shoulder-padded suit straight out of a Joan Crawford film. The moment she heard the words *New Scotland Yard* in conjunction with the name of their esteemed Member of Parliament, she shared only the fact that Mr. Harvie had been in Salisbury from Thursday night until Sunday evening—"as always, he's our MP, isn't he?"—but her lips tightened over the additional information that Barbara sought. She made it clear that neither crowbar nor Semtex nor unveiled threats regarding the consequences of failing to assist the police would pry those lips open, at least not until Mrs. Howe had "a word with our Mr. Harvie." She was the sort of woman Barbara always itched to squash beneath her heel, the sort who assumed that her jolly hockey sticks education gave her some right of supremacy over the rest of mankind.

As Mrs. Howe consulted her diary to see where she might locate their MP at this time of day in London, Barbara said, "Right. Do what you want. But you might want to know that this is a rather high-profile investigation, with journalists dusting out everybody's cupboards. So you can talk to me now and I can be on my way or you can take a few hours to track down Harvie and run the risk of the press finding out that he's just become part of our enquiry. That should make a nice headline in tomorrow's papers: *Harvie Under the Gun.* How big's his majority, by the way?"

Mrs. Howe's eyes slitted to fingernail width. She said, "Are you actually threatening me? Why, you little—"

"I think you mean to say *Sergeant,*" Barbara cut in. " 'Why, you little Sergeant.' Right? Yes. Well, I certainly understand your sentiments. Rough stuff having my sort come in here and offend your sensibilities. But time's rather an issue for us, and I'd like to get on with things if I can."

"You'll have to wait until I speak to Mr. Harvie," Mrs. Howe insisted.

"I can't do that. My guv at the Yard is requiring daily reports and mine is due to him"—here Barbara studied the wall clock for effect— "just about now. I'd hate to have to tell him that Mr. Harvie's constituency chair refused to cooperate. Because that'll turn the light on Mr. Harvie himself. And everyone'll wonder what he's got to hide. And since my guv gives reports to the press every night, Mr. Harvie's name is bound to come up. Unless there's no reason for it to do so."

Mrs. Howe saw the dawn of reason, but she wasn't chairman of the local Conservative association for nothing. She was a dealmaker and she made her requirements clear: tit for tit, tat for tat, and question for question. She wanted to know what was going on. She put the desire obliquely, stating, "The constituency's interests are foremost in my mind. They must be served. If for some reason Mr. Harvie has come across some impediment to serving our interests . . ."

Blah de blah blah, Barbara thought. She got the point. She made the deal. What Mrs. Howe learned from her was that the investigation in question was the one heading up the nightly news and the same one headlining the morning and evening papers—the kidnapping and drowning of the ten-year-old daughter of the Home Office Undersecretary. Barbara didn't tell Mrs. Howe anything that she couldn't have learned for herself by doing something more than spending her time checking up on Mr. Harvie's movements in London and bullying the local constituency office's ageing secretary. But she imparted it all confidentially, with an air of *seulement entre nous, darling,* that was apparently convincing enough for the constituency chairman to part with some pearls of information in exchange.

Mrs. Howe didn't much like Mr. Harvie, as Barbara soon discovered. He was too much the cat with the cream round the ladies. But he had a way with the voters and he'd managed to fend off two serious challenges by the Liberal Democrats, so he was owed some loyalty for that.

He'd been born in Warminster. He'd gone to school at Winchester, and then on to university at Exeter. He'd read economics, successfully managed investment portfolios at Barclay's Bank right here in Salisbury, worked hard for the party, and ultimately presented himself as a potential candidate for Parliament when he was twenty-nine years old. He'd held his seat for thirteen years.

He'd been married to the same woman for eighteen years. They had the politically required two children, a boy and a girl, and when not away at school—which, of course, they were at the moment—they lived with their mother just outside Salisbury in the hamlet of Ford. The family farm—

"Farm?" Barbara interrupted. "Harvie's a farmer? I thought you said he'd been a banker?"

The farm was his wife's inheritance from her parents. The Harvies lived in the house, but the land was worked by a tenant. Why? Mrs. Howe wanted to know. Her nose quivered. Was the farm important?

Barbara didn't have a conclusive answer to that question even when she saw the farm some forty-five minutes later. It sat at the very edge of Ford and when Barbara lurched to a stop in the farm's trapezoidal-shaped courtyard, the only creatures who came out to greet her Mini were six extremely well-fed white geese. Their clamorous honking raised enough ruckus to alert anyone who might have been in the immediate vicinity. When no one came out of the steel-walled barn with pitchfork at the ready or out of the imposing brick and tile house with rolling pin rampant, Barbara concluded that she had the farmyard, if not its surrounding fields and pastures, to herself.

From her car, with the geese still furiously honking at a menacing Doberman volume, Barbara made her bow to scoping out the scene. The farmyard comprised the house, the barn, an old stone linhay, and an even older dovecote constructed of bricks. This last caught her attention. It was cylindrical in shape, topped with a slate roof and a glassless lantern cupola that gave birds access to the interior of the building. One side of it was overgrown with ivy. Gaps in the roof marked spots where tiles had either been removed or broken off. Its deeply recessed door was splintered and grey with age, crusty with lichen and looking as if no one had opened it within the last twenty years.

But something about it dragged at her memory. She catalogued the details in an attempt to decide what that something was: the slate roof, the lantern cupola, the heavy growth of ivy, the battered door . . . Something Sergeant Stanley had said, the pathologist had said, Robin Payne had said, Lynley had said . . .

It was no good. She couldn't remember. But Barbara was troubled enough by the sight of the dovecote to ease the Mini's door open into the beaks of the angry geese.

Their honking rose to a frenzied pitch. They were better than watchdogs. Barbara opened her glove box and rooted through its contents to see if she had something edible that might occupy them while she had a look round. She came up with a half bag of salt and vinegar crisps which she herself briefly regretted not having found the previous night when she'd been caught in traffic without a restaurant in sight. She sampled them. Slightly stale, but what the hell. She thrust her arm out of the open window and scattered the crisps on the ground, as a libation to the avian gods. The geese tucked in at once. The problem was solved, at least temporarily.

Barbara tipped her hat to formality by ringing the doorbell at the house. She did the same by calling a cheerful "Hullo?" into the barn. She walked the length of the yard, sauntering at last to the dovecote as if a perusal of it were the natural outcome of her wanderings.

The doorknob rattled loosely in the wood of the door. It was gritty with rust. It didn't turn, but when Barbara pushed upon the wood with her shoulder, the door creaked open some seven inches before its movement was thwarted by its own rain-swollen condition and an uneven patch in the old stone floor. A sudden flutter of wings told Barbara that the dovecote was at least partially in use. She squeezed herself inside as the last of the birds escaped through the lantern cupola.

Light, thick with rising dust motes, filtered down from that cupola and from the gaps in the roof. It illuminated tier upon tier of nesting boxes for the birds, a stone floor lumpy with pungent guano, and in this floor's centre a ladder with three fractured rungs which had once been used to collect eggs in the days when pigeons and doves were themselves raised as poultry.

Barbara did her best to dodge all bird droppings that were still shimmering with their youth. She approached the ladder. She saw that although it was fixed at its top to an upright pole by means of an extended rung, it wasn't intended to be stationary. Rather, it had been designed to move round the dovecote, giving the potential egg-gatherer easy access to all of the nesting boxes that lined the circumference of the building from a height of about two feet from the floor to the roofline some ten feet above.

The ladder, Barbara found, was still mobile despite its age and condition. When she pushed upon it, it creaked, hesitated, then began to move. It followed the curve of the brick walls of the dovecote in a movement achieved by means of the upright pole. Fitted to a primitive gear-and-sprocket device in the lantern cupola, the pole revolved and thus rotated the ladder.

Barbara looked from the ladder to the pole. Then from the pole to the nesting boxes. Where some of them had collapsed over time and had gone unreplaced, she could see the unfinished brick walls of the dovecote behind them. They were rough-looking, those walls, and where they didn't wear the speckling of bird droppings, in the subdued light, they looked redder than they had looked outside with the sun upon them. Odd, that red. Almost as if they weren't bricks at all. Almost as if—

She remembered with a rush. It was bricks, Barbara thought. Bricks and a pole. She could hear Charlotte's tape-recorded voice as Lynley had played it for her over the phone. *There's bricks and a maypole*, the child had said.

Barbara felt the hair stir on the back of her neck as she looked from the bricks to the pole in the centre of the room. Holy hell, she thought, Jesus Christ, this is it. She made a move to go to the door, which is when she realised that the geese outside had gone completely silent. She strained to hear the slightest noise from them. Even a mild satiated honk would do. But there was nothing. They couldn't still be eating those crisps, could they? she wondered. Because there hadn't been enough to last this long.

This realisation suggested that someone had thrown them a hand-ful of additional food once Barbara had gone into the dovecote. This in turn suggested that she wasn't alone in the farmyard any longer. This in its own turn suggested that if she wasn't alone and if whoever was out there was as intent upon silence as she, then whoever was out there was probably at this very moment creeping from barn to house to linhay. He held a pitchfork raised or perhaps a carving knife, his eyes a little wild, Anthony Perkins come to slice Janet Leigh to ribbons. Except that Janet Leigh had been in a shower, not in a dovecote. And she'd thought she was safe, whereas Barbara knew quite well that she wasn't. Particu-larly not here, where the location, the structure, the bricks, and the pole all made a claim upon her powers of deduction at the very same time as they seemed to close in on her so that any moment with her bowels gone loose and her palms gone sweaty—

Bloody hell, Barbara thought. Get a grip, all right? Get a bleeding, flaming, sodding little *grip*.

She needed a crime scene team to go over this building in a search for anything that would place Charlotte here. The axle grease, a hair from her head, a fibre from her clothes, her fingerprints, a drop of her blood from the cut on her knee. That's what was called for, and making the arrangements was going to take some decided finesse, both with Sergeant Stanley, who wasn't likely to greet her directive with the joy of the newly converted, and with Mrs. Alistair Harvie, who was more than likely going to pick up the phone and place a call to her husband and put him on the alert.

She'd tackle Stanley first. No reason to hunt down Mrs. Harvie and get her knickers in a twist before concerted knicker-twisting was actu-ally called for.

Outside, she discovered that the silence of the geese was due to the position of the car. She'd parked it in such a way that the sun reflecting off its rusting wings had created a patch of warmth on the earth, and upon this warmth the birds were basking contentedly among the re-mains of Barbara's offering of salt and vinegar crisps.

She tiptoed to the Mini, alternating her eyes from the birds to the barn, from the barn to the fields beyond it, from the fields to the house. Still, not a soul was in sight. A cow lowed in the distance and a plane flew overhead, but otherwise nothing and no one stirred.

She slipped into the car as noiselessly as possible. She said, "Sorry, old chaps," to the geese and started the engine. The birds leapt to life, honking, hissing, and flapping their wings like a visitation from the Furies. They pursued Barbara's car from the farmyard onto the lane. There, she thudded her foot onto the accelerator, shot through the hamlet of Ford, and headed in the direction of Amesford and Sergeant Stanley's waiting embrace.

The sergeant was enthroned in the incidents room, receiving homage in the form of reports from two teams of constables who had been at work probing the countryside for the past thirty-two hours in their respective sections of Sergeant Stanley's grid. The men from Section Number 13, the Devizes-to-Melksham patch, had nothing to report save an unexpected run-in with a caravan owner who apparently operated a thriving business in everything from ganja to bombers to blow. "Dealing from the car park in Melksham," one of the constables said incredulously. "Right behind the high street, if you can believe. He's in the nick now." The team from Section Number 5, the Chippenham-to-Calne patch, had little more. But they were giving a detailed explanation of their every movement to Sergeant Stanley anyway. Barbara was about to wrest them from their chairs and drop kick them back out into the street to get on with things so that she could arrange for the crime scene team to be sent to the Harvie farm, when one of the constables from Section Number 14 burst through the swinging doors of the incidents room, announcing, "We've got it."

His declaration mobilised everyone, including Barbara. She'd been practising patience by attempting to return a phone call from Robin Payne—which had apparently been placed from the call box inside a tea room in Marlborough, from what she was able to gather from the somewhat mentally deficient waitress who answered Barbara's return call upon the twenty-fifth ring—and by directing a young female constable to do some digging through Alistair Harvie's schooldays at Winchester. But now Sergeant Stanley's gridwork looked as if it was about to pay off.

Stanley waved the remaining talkers in the room to silence. He'd been seated at a round table, arranging a collection of wooden toothpicks into the crisscrossing walls of a log cabin as he listened to the reports, but now he stood. He said, "Give, Frank."

Frank said, "Right." He didn't bother with preliminaries. He just said with some excitement, "We've got him, Sarge. He's in interview room number three."

Barbara had a horrified vision of Alistair Harvie in leg irons without benefit of either caution or counsel. She said, "Got who?"

"The bugger that snatched the kid," Frank replied with a dismissive look in her direction. "He's a mechanic from Coate, works on tractors out of a garage near Spaniel's Bridge. One mile exactly from the canal."

The room erupted. Barbara was among those who stormed the

ordnance survey map. Frank pointed to the location with an index finger whose nail had an arch of mustard imbedded beneath it.

"Right here." The constable indicated a dogleg in the lane that led from the hamlet of Coate north towards the village of Bishop's Canning. Along the canal, it was three and a half miles from Spaniel's Bridge to the spot where Charlotte's body had been dumped, one and a half miles to that same spot if one used lanes, tracks, and footpaths to reach it instead of relying upon the meandering motorway. "The sod's claiming he doesn't know a thing, but we've got the goods on him and he's ready to be grilled."

"Right." Sergeant Stanley rubbed his hands together as if ready to do the honours. "Interview which did you say?"

"Three." Frank added scornfully, "Bugger's doing a real fine job of leaf-shaking, Sarge. You give him a good taste of muscle, and he's going to crack. I swear."

Sergeant Stanley settled his shoulders, preparing to take on the task. Barbara said, "What goods?" Her question went ignored. Stanley set off towards the door. Barbara felt her insides heat up. This wasn't the way they were going to play it. She said sharply, "Hang on, Reg," to Stanley, and when the sergeant did a deliberately slow pirouette in her direction, "Frank, you said you have the goods on this bloke . . . what's his name anyway?"

"Short. Howard."

"Fine. So what are the goods you've got on Howard Short?"

Frank looked to Sergeant Stanley for direction. Stanley gave a fractional lift of his chin as a response. The fact that Frank would need to get permission from Stanley infuriated Barbara, but she chose to ignore it and waited for his answer.

"School uniform," the constable said. "This bloke Short, he had it in his garage. Planning to use it for a rag, he claimed. But the Bowen kid's nametag is sewn into it, big as can be."

—⁂—

Sergeant Stanley dispatched the crime scene team to Howard Short's garage outside of Coate. He set off towards interview room number 3 with Barbara hard upon his heels. She caught him up and said, "I want another team in Ford. There's a dovecote with—"

"A dovecote?" Stanley stopped in his tracks. "A bleeding *dovecote*, did you say?"

"We have an audiotape of the girl," she told him, "made a day or two before she died. She's talking about where she's being held. The dovecote fits her description. I want a team of evidence officers out there. Now.''

Stanley leaned towards her. She realised for the first time that he was a truly unattractive man. At this proximity she could see the in-grown whiskers on his neck and the pockmarks round his mouth. He said, ''You clear that with our guv. I'm not sending evidence officers round the countryside because you get an itch that you want scratched.''

''You'll do what I tell you,'' Barbara said. ''And if you don't—''

''What? You going to sick up on my shoes?''

She grasped his tie. ''Your shoes'll be fine,'' she told him. ''But I can't promise much about the state of your balls. Now, are we clear on who's going to do what?''

He blew a puff of stale tobacco breath in her face. ''Cool down,'' he said softly.

''Bugger you and enjoy it,'' she replied. She released his tie with a shove against his chest. ''Take some advice, Reg. This is a battle you can't hope to win. Have some sense and know it before I have you pulled from the case.''

He lit a cigarette with his lady's arse lighter. ''I've an interview to conduct.'' He spoke with the assurance of a man who'd had tenure on the force for too many years. ''You want to sit in on it?'' He walked down the corridor, saying, ''Get us some coffee, room three,'' to a clerk who was hurrying by with a clipboard in her hand.

Barbara told her anger to recede. She wanted to jump on Stanley's pitted face, but there was no point to going eyeball to eyeball with him. It was clear that he was determined not to blink so long as his adversary was a woman. She'd have to use other means to neutralise the little bastard.

She followed him along the corridor and turned right to the inter-view room. There, Howard Short was seated on the edge of a plastic chair. A twentyish boy with the eyes of a frog, he was wearing the grease-splotched overalls of his profession and a baseball cap that had the word *Braves* scrolled across the front. He was clutching his stom-ach.

He spoke before either Stanley or Barbara had a chance to make a comment. He said, ''This's about that little girl, isn't it? I know it is. I could tell when that bloke went through my rag bag and found it.''

''What?'' Stanley asked. He straddled a chair and offered his packet of cigarettes to Short.

Howard shook his head. He clutched his stomach more tightly. ''Ulcer.''

"What?"

"My stomach."

"Bury it. What'd they find in the rag bag, Howard?"

The boy looked to Barbara as if seeking reassurance that someone was going to be on his side. She said, "What was in the bag, Mr. Short?"

"That," he said. "What they found. The uniform." He rocked on his chair and moaned. "I don't know nothing about this little kid. I just buy—"

"Why'd you snatch her?" Stanley said.

"I didn't."

"Where'd you keep her? In the garage?"

"I didn't keep no one . . . no little girl . . . I saw it on the telly like everyone else. But I swear I never seen her. I never seen her once."

"You liked stripping her though. You have a nice pop when you got her naked?"

"I never! I never did it!"

"You a virgin, then, Howard? Or a poufter? What is it? Don't like the girls?"

"I like girls fine. I'm only saying—"

"Little ones? You like them little as well?"

"I didn't snatch this kid."

"But you know she was snatched? How's that?"

"The news. The papers. Everybody knows. But I didn't have nothing to do with it. I only got her uniform—"

"So you knew it was hers," Stanley interrupted. "Right from the start. Is that it?"

"No!"

"Come out with it. It'll go easier if you tell us the truth."

"I'm trying. I'm telling you that the rag—"

"You mean the uniform. A little girl's school uniform. A dead little girl's uniform, Howard. You're just a mile away from the canal, aren't you?"

"I never did it," Howard said. He rolled forward on his arms, increasing the pressure against his stomach. "Hurts bloody awful," he grunted.

"Don't play games with us," Stanley said.

"Please, c'n I have some water for my pills?" Howard inched his arm away from his stomach, reached in his overalls, and pulled out a plastic pill box that was shaped like a spanner.

"Talk first, pills later," Stanley said.

Barbara jerked open the door of the interview room to call for some water. The clerk from whom Stanley had ordered the coffee stood there with two plastic cups of it. Barbara smiled, said, "Thanks awfully," with much sincerity, and handed her cup over to the mechanic.

She said, "Here. Use this for your pills, Mr. Short," and she pulled a chair out from the table and placed it next to the quaking young man. She said firmly, "Can you tell us where you got the uniform?"

Howard popped two pills into his mouth and drank them down. The position of Barbara's chair forced the boy to turn in his own, offering only his profile to Stanley. Barbara gave herself a mental pat on the back for shifting the power so adroitly. Howard said, "From the jumble stall."

"What jumble stall?"

"At the church fête. We have a church fête every spring and this year's was Sunday. I took my gran because she had to work in the tea booth for an hour. It wasn't worth taking her to the fête, going home, and coming back, so I hung about. That's when I got the rags. They were selling them in the jumble stall. Plastic bags of rags. One pound fifty each. I bought three because I use them at work. It was for a good cause." He added this earnestly. "They're raising money to restore one of the windows in the chancel."

"Where?" Barbara asked. "Which church, Mr. Short?"

"In Stanton St. Bernard. That's where my gran lives." He looked from Barbara to Sergeant Stanley. He said, "I'm telling the truth. I didn't know nothing about that uniform. I didn't even know it was in the bag till the cops dumped it out on the floor. I hadn't even opened the bag yet. I swear it."

"Who was working the stall?" Stanley interjected.

Howard licked his lips, looked Stanley's way, then back to Barbara. "Some girl. A blonde."

"Girlfriend of yours?"

"I didn't know her."

"Didn't chat her up? Didn't catch her name?"

"I only bought the rags off her."

"Didn't make a play? Didn't think about what it would be like to roger her?"

"No."

"Why? Too old for you? D'you like them young?"

"I didn't know her, okay? I just bought those rags like I said, at the jumble stall. I don't know how they got there. I don't know the name of the bird 'at sold them to me. Even if I did, she pro'ly doesn't know how they got there either. She was just working the stall, collecting money and handing over the bags. If you need to know more, you should pro'ly ask—"

"Defending her?" Stanley said. "Why's that, Howard?"

"I'm trying to help you lot!" Short shouted.

"I bet you are. Just like I bet you took that little girl's uniform and stowed it with the rags once you bought them at the fête."

"I never!"

"Just like I bet you snatched her, drugged her, and drowned her."

"No!"

"Just like—"

Barbara stood. She touched Short's shoulder. "Thanks for your help," she said firmly. "We'll look into everything you've said, Mr. Short. Sergeant Stanley?" She canted her head towards the door and left the interview room.

Stanley followed her into the corridor. She heard him say, "Balls. If that little sod thinks—"

She swung round to face him. "That little sod nothing. *You* start thinking. Bully a witness like that and we end up with sod all, which is what we nearly got from that kid."

"You believe that rubbish about tea booths and blondes?" Stanley snorted. "He's dirty as used-up engine oil."

"If he's dirty, we'll nail him. But we'll do it legitimately or not at all. Got it?" She didn't wait for an answer. "So send that school uniform to forensics, Reg. Check every inch of it. I want hairs, I want skin, I want blood, I want dirt, I want grease, I want semen. I want dogshit, cowshit, birdshit, horseshit, and anything else that might be on it. Okay?"

The sergeant's upper lip gave a roll of distaste. "Don't waste my manpower, Scotland Yard. We know it's the kid's. If we need to verify, we'll show it to her mother."

Barbara planted herself six inches from his face. "Right. We do. We know it's hers. But we don't know her killer, do we, Reg? So we're going to take that uniform, and we're going to comb it, tape it, fibre-optic it, laser it, and do just about anything else we can do to it to get something from it that will lead us to her killer. Whether it's Howard Short or the Prince of Wales. Am I making myself clear, or do you need it spelled out in writing from your CC?"

Stanley sucked slowly in on one side of his cheek. "Right," he said. And added under his breath, "Fuck you, guv'nor."

"You should be so lucky," Barbara said. She turned and went back to the incidents room. Where in the hell, she wondered, was Stanton St. Bernard?

21

DESPITE THE FACT that a maintenance man was in the process of hanging Assistant Commissioner Sir David Hillier's photographs for him, the AC had not wished to postpone his daily update. Nor had he wished to move it to a location from which he might not be able to supervise the appropriate placement of his pictorial history. So Lynley had been forced to deliver his report in hushed tones at the window, suffering through Hillier's interruptions. These interruptions weren't directed towards him. Rather, they were directed towards the maintenance man who was attempting to hang the photographs in such a way as to prevent their glass from reflecting the afternoon sunlight. Sunlight not only faded the pictures, it also obscured their subject from the admiration of anyone who might walk into the office. That was not acceptable.

Lynley concluded his report and waited for the AC's comment. Hillier admired his mundane view of Victoria Street and pulled on his chin as he thought about what he'd heard. When he finally spoke, his lips barely moved, in deference to the need for confidentiality. "I have a press conference in a half hour," he said. "I'll need to give them something to chew on for tomorrow." He made it sound as if he were considering what kind of bait to throw to the sharks. "What about this mechanic Havers has in Wiltshire? What was his name again?"

"Sergeant Havers doesn't think he's involved. She's running tests on the Bowen girl's uniform, which might give us something. But she isn't suggesting that what the uniform tells us will tie Charlotte Bowen to the mechanic."

"Still . . ." Hillier said. "It's nice to be able to say that someone is out there assisting the police in their enquiries. She's checking into his background?''

"We're checking into everyone's background."

"And?"

Lynley was reluctant to part with what he knew. Hillier had a propensity to showboat for the press, all in the name of the Yard's proficiency. But the papers already knew too much, and their interest wasn't in seeing that justice was done. Rather, it lay in seeing that a story was broken more quickly than their competitors got to it.

"We're looking for a link. Blackpool-Bowen-Luxford-Wiltshire."

"Looking for links isn't going to make us shine with the press and the public, Inspector."

"We've got SO4 dealing with the prints from Marylebone and we've got a sketch of a possible suspect. Tell them we're analysing evidence. Then release the sketch. That should satisfy."

Hillier examined his face speculatively. "But you've more, haven't you?"

"Nothing firm," Lynley said.

"I thought I was clear when I handed you this case. I don't want you holding back on reports."

"There's no point to my muddying the waters with conjecture," he said, and he added, "Sir," to pour oil where the waters weren't so much muddied as potentially troubled.

"Hmph." Hillier knew that to be called *sir* wasn't exactly to be *tutoyer*ed by Lynley. He seemed about to respond with a directive that would put them at loggerheads. But a knock on his office door announced the intrusion of his personal secretary, who said from behind the wood, "Sir David? You wanted thirty minutes' notice before the press conference. I've the make-up man here."

Lynley stopped his mouth from quirking at the thought of Hillier in pancake and mascara facing the news media's cameras. He said, "I'll get out of your way, then," and took the opportunity to escape.

In his own office, he found Nkata sitting at his desk, telephone pressed to his ear. He was saying, "DC Winston Nkata . . . Nkata, woman . . . *Nkata*. N-k-a-t-a. You tell him we need to talk. Fine?" He hung up the phone. He saw Lynley in the doorway and began to rise.

Lynley waved him back to the seat and took another, Havers' usual chair in front of his desk. He said, "Well?"

"Some Bowen-Blackpool connections," Nkata replied. "Bowen's constituency chairman was there at the Tory conference. A bloke called Colonel Julian Woodward. Know him? Him and me, we had ourselves a pleasant little chat in Marylebone right after I left you at the squat."

Colonel Woodward, Nkata told Lynley, was a retired Army man some seventy years old. A former instructor in military history, he'd retired at sixty-five and moved to London to be nearer to his son.

"Apple of his eye, that Joel," Nkata said in reference to the Colonel's son. "I got the 'pression that the Colonel'd do just about anything for him. He got the bloke his job with Eve Bowen, you know. And he took him along to Blackpool for that Tory conference."

"Joel Woodward was there? How old was he then?"

"Nineteen just. He'd 'triculated at UCL at the time, getting set to read politics. He's still there. Been working part-time on a doctorate since he's twenty-two. That's where he is at this moment, according to Bowen's office. He was next on my list to have a natter with, but I couldn't track him down. Been trying since noon."

"Any connection to Wiltshire? Any reason either of the Woodwards would want to bring down Eve Bowen?"

"I'm still working on Wiltshire. But I got to say the Colonel has plans for Joel. Political plans and he doesn't care who knows."

"Parliament?"

"You got it. And he's no admirer of Ms. Bowen, either."

Colonel Woodward, Nkata went on, was a firm believer in a woman's place. And it wasn't in politics. The Colonel himself had been married and widowed three times and not one of his wives had felt the necessity to prove herself in any arena other than in the home. While he acknowledged that Eve Bowen had "more balls than our esteemed premier," he also confessed to not liking her much. But he was cynical enough to know that to keep the Conservative Party in power, the constituency needed the best possible candidate to stand for election, and the best possible candidate might not always be someone with whom he felt in tune.

"He's looking to replace her?" Lynley asked.

"Love to replace her with his boy," Nkata said. "But no way is that going to happen unless someone or something pushes her out of power."

Intriguing, Lynley thought. And supportive of what Eve Bowen herself had said in slightly different words: In politics, one's fiercest enemies wore the guise of friends.

"What about Alistair Harvie?" Nkata asked.

"Snake oil."

"Politician, man."

"He didn't seem to know anything about Bowen and Luxford in Blackpool, claimed not to know that Bowen had been there."

"You believe him?"

"I did, frankly. But then Havers phoned in."

Lynley told Nkata what Sergeant Havers had reported. He concluded with, "And she was able to dig up some background on Harvie's years at Winchester as well. He has just about everything one would expect to see on his résumé of activities at the school. But one activity stood out among the rest. He was involved in ecology and cross-country trekking for his last two years there. And most of the trekking was done in Wiltshire, on Salisbury Plain."

"So he knows the countryside."

Lynley reached across the desk for a paper-clipped fan of telephone messages that had been placed near his phone. He put on his spectacles and flipped through the messages, asking, "Anything more on the tramp?"

"Not a squeak so far. But it's early on that one. We're still tracking down all of the Wigmore Street specials to give them a look at the sketch. And none of the blokes checking the local doss-houses've reported in yet."

Lynley tossed the messages back onto the desk, removed his spectacles, and rubbed his eyes. "It feels as if we're making snail's progress."

"Hillier?" Nkata asked wisely.

"The usual. He'd like it wrapped up within twenty-four hours, all for the glory of the Yard. But he knows the odds and he's not going to argue that we're not facing a tremendous disadvantage." Lynley thought of the reporters he'd seen at Eve Bowen's house on the previous night, thought of the newsagents' stands he'd seen that morning with *Police Hunt Underway* and *MP Said No Cops* scrawled across the notice boards that advertised the contents of the day's lead story. "Blast them," he muttered.

"Who's that?" Nkata asked.

"Bowen and Luxford. Tomorrow marks a week from the kidnapping. If they'd brought us in the first hour she went missing, we'd have been through with this mess by now. As it is, we're trying to heat up a cold trail, asking potential witnesses—with no interest in the matter and nothing at stake—to remember something that they might have seen six days after the fact. It's madness. We're relying on luck, and I don't much like that."

"But luck'll do it, more often'n not." Nkata leaned back in Lynley's chair. He looked remarkably like someone who belonged behind the desk. He stretched his arms and locked his hands behind his neck. He smiled.

It was the smile that told Lynley. "You've got something more."

"I do. Oh, I do."

"And?"

"It's Wiltshire."

"Wiltshire connected to whom?"

"Well, that's where things get real intriguing."

—⁓—

Traffic slowed them down both in Whitehall and the Strand, but between crawling along and stopping altogether, it gave Lynley the opportunity to read the article in the *Sunday Times* magazine that Nkata had unearthed in his day of digging through the pasts of the suspects. The article was six weeks old. Entitled "Turning Round a Tabloid," its featured subject was Dennis Luxford.

"Seven whole pages," Nkata remarked as Lynley looked through it and scanned the paragraphs. "The happy family at home, at work, at play. With everyone's background there in black and white. Lovely, huh?"

"This," Lynley said, "could be the break we're looking for."

"That's what I thought," Nkata agreed.

At *The Source*, Lynley's police identification made little impression upon the receptionist who gave him a look that said, I've seen blokes like you before. She phoned upstairs and said only, "Cops. Scotland Yard," into the miniature mouthpiece of her headset. She added, "You got that right, luv," with a guffaw, managing to drop every *t* in the sentence. She made out visitors' badges in a rounded, childish script and slipped them into plastic holders. She said, "Eleventh floor. Use the lift. And don't go snooping where you don't belong, hear?"

When the lift doors opened on the floor in question, a grey-haired woman met them. She was slightly stoop-shouldered, as if with too many years of bending over filing cabinets, typewriters, and word processors, and she introduced herself as Miss Wallace, confidential, private, and personal secretary to *The Source* editor, Mr. Dennis Luxford.

She said, "If I might check your identification personally?" and her withered cheeks shook as if with the effrontery of the question. "We can't be too careful when it comes to visitors. Newspaper rivalry. Perhaps you know what I mean?"

Again, Lynley showed his identification. Nkata did the same. Miss Wallace scrutinised both warrant cards diligently before murmuring, "Very well," and leading them towards the editor's office. It was obviously a dog-eat-dog business, getting the nation's scandal sheets onto the streets. The wisest tabloids put their trust in the fact that everyone was suspect when it came to ownership of a story, even people claiming to be the police.

Luxford was at a conference table in his office, seated with two other men who appeared to be the head of circulation and the head of advertising if the graphs, charts, tables, and dummy pages of the tabloid were anything to go by. When Miss Wallace first interrupted them, swinging open the door and saying, "I do beg your pardon, Mr. Luxford," the editor's response to her was a sharp, "God damn it, Wallace, I thought I made myself clear on the topic of interruptions." His voice sounded frazzled. From behind the secretary, Lynley could see that he didn't look much better.

"They're from Scotland Yard, Mr. Luxford," Miss Wallace said.

Advertising and Circulation looked at each other, becoming interest incarnate at this turn of events. Luxford said to them, "We'll go over the rest of this later," and didn't get up from his position at the head of the conference table until they and Miss Wallace were out of the room. Even when he did rise, he remained in place with the graphs, charts, tables, and dummy tabloid pages spread out in front of him. He said sharply, "This'll be all over the newsroom in forty-five seconds. You couldn't have phoned first?"

"Circulation meeting?" Lynley asked. "How are the numbers these days?"

"You haven't come to discuss our numbers, I dare say."

"I'm interested, nonetheless."

"Why?"

"Circulation is everything to a newspaper, isn't it?"

"I expect you know that. Advertising revenues depend on circulation."

"And circulation depends upon the quality of the stories? Their veracity, their contents, their depth?" Lynley produced his identification yet another time, and while Luxford examined it, he himself examined Luxford. The man was dapperly dressed but jaundiced in colouring. The whites of his eyes didn't look much better than the condition of his skin. "I would assume that one of the primary considerations any editor has is his paper's circulation," Lynley said. "You've been intent upon building yours, according to what I've just read in the *Sunday Times* magazine. No doubt you'd like to keep building it."

Luxford handed back the identification. Lynley returned it to his pocket. Nkata had strolled to the wall next to the conference table. On it hung framed front pages. Lynley read the headlines: One dealt with a Tory MP with four mistresses, a second with speculation over the love life of the Princess of Wales, a third with television stars from a salutary, family-oriented, postwar drama who had been discovered living in a *ménage à trois*. Wholesome reading to accompany one's equally wholesome breakfast cereal, Lynley thought.

"What's this line of talk all about, Inspector?" Luxford asked. "You can see that I'm busy. Can we get to the point?"

"Charlotte Bowen is the point."

Luxford flicked his eyes from Lynley to Nkata. No fool, he wasn't about to give them one scrap of information until he knew what they had.

"We know you're the girl's father," Lynley said. "Ms. Bowen confirmed that last night."

"How is she?" Luxford picked up one of the graphs, but he didn't look at it. Instead, he looked at Lynley. "I've phoned her. She won't return my calls. I haven't spoken to her since Sunday night."

"I expect she's dealing with the shock," Lynley said. "She didn't think things would turn out as they have."

"I've the story written," Luxford told them. "I would have run it had she given me the go-ahead."

"Doubtless," Lynley said.

At the dryness of his tone, Luxford looked at him shrewdly. "Why have you come?"

"To talk about Baverstock."

"Baverstock? What in God's name . . . ?" Luxford looked to Nkata as if expecting the constable to answer. Nkata merely pulled out a chair and sat. He reached in his pocket and produced notebook and pencil. He made both of them ready to record Luxford's words.

"You entered Baverstock School for Boys as an eleven-year-old," Lynley said. "You were there until you were seventeen. You boarded."

"What of it? What's that got to do with Charlotte? You told me you'd come to talk about Charlotte."

"During those years you belonged to a group called the Beaker Explorers, an amateur archaeological society. Is that correct?"

"I liked to grub round in the dirt. Most boys do. I don't see what importance this has in your investigation."

"This society—the Beaker Explorers—ranged far and wide, didn't they? Studying barrows, earthworks, stone circles, and the like? Becoming familiar with the lay of the land?"

"What if we did? I fail to see what this has to do with anything."

"And you were the society's president during your last two years at Baverstock, weren't you?"

"I was also editor of the *Bavernian Biannual* and the *Oracle*. And to complete your budding picture of my schooldays, Inspector, I failed utterly at every attempt to make the cricket first eleven. Now, tell me if you will. Have I left anything out?"

"Only one detail," Lynley said. "The school's location."

Luxford's eyebrows drew together for a moment. His look was speculative.

"Wiltshire," Lynley said. "Baverstock School is in Wiltshire, Mr. Luxford."

"There are a great many things in Wiltshire," Luxford said. "And most of them are far more notable than Baverstock."

"I wouldn't disagree. But they don't have the advantage of Baverstock, do they?"

"What advantage is that?"

"The advantage of being less than seven miles from the site where Charlotte Bowen's body was found."

Slowly, Luxford replaced the graph he'd been holding, laying it among the others on the table. He greeted Lynley's disclosure in absolute silence. Outside the building, eleven floors below them, an ambulance howled its two-note warning to clear traffic in the street.

"Quite a coincidence, wouldn't you say?" Lynley asked him.

"That's all it is and you know it, Inspector."

"I'm reluctant to take your word for that."

"You can't possibly believe I had anything to do with what happened to Charlotte. The idea's mad."

"Which end of the idea? Your being involved in Charlotte's kidnapping or your being involved in her death?"

"In either. What do you think I am?"

"A man with concerns about his newspaper's circulation. And consequently a man looking for a story that no one else has."

Despite his protests and despite whatever he might have been trying to hide from Lynley, Luxford's attention fell briefly upon the graphs and charts on the table, the lifeblood of his newspaper and his job. That single dropping of his glance contained more information than anything he might have said.

"At some point," Lynley continued, "Charlotte would have had to be transported out of London in a vehicle."

"I had nothing to do with it."

"Nonetheless, I'd like to have a look at your car. Is it parked nearby?"

"I want a solicitor."

"Certainly."

Luxford crossed the room to his desk. He shuffled through some papers and unearthed a leatherbound telephone directory, which he opened with one hand as he grabbed the phone with the other. He had punched in two numbers before Lynley spoke again.

"Constable Nkata and I will have to wait for him, of course. Which might take some time. So if you've concerns about how the newsroom is interpreting our visit, you might want to consider how they'll construe our cooling our heels outside your office door while we wait for the arrival of your solicitor."

The editor punched in four more numbers. His hand hovered over the phone before he reached the seventh. Lynley waited for him to make the decision. He saw a vein throbbing in the other man's temple.

Luxford crashed the telephone receiver into its cradle. "All right," he said. "I'll take you to the car."

The car was a Porsche. It sat in a parking garage redolent of urine and petrol, not five minutes away from *The Source* building. They walked there in silence, Luxford several steps ahead of them. He'd stopped only to put on his jacket and to tell Miss Wallace that he'd be out for quarter of an hour. He'd looked neither right nor left as he led them to the lift, and when a bearded man in a safari jacket had called out, "Den, could I have a word please?" from the door of an office at the far side of the newsroom, Luxford had ignored him. He'd ignored everyone else as well.

The car was on the fifth level of the garage, dwarfed between a dirty Range Rover and a white van with GOURMET ON THE GO written on its side. As they approached it, Luxford removed a small remote control unit from his pocket. This he used to deactivate the Porsche's alarm system. The beep echoed in the concrete structure like a hiccupping bird.

Constable Nkata didn't wait for an invitation. He put on a pair of gloves, opened the car's passenger door, and slid inside. He explored the contents of the glove box and the contents of the console between the seats. He lifted the floor mats of both passenger's side and driver's side. He dug his hands into the recessed compartments in the doors. He got out of the car and moved the seats forward to give himself access to the space in the back.

Luxford watched all of this wordlessly. Brisk footsteps sounded somewhere nearby, but he didn't look to see if Nkata's search was being observed. His face was impassive. It was impossible to tell what was going on beneath the surface of his stolid exterior.

Nkata's feet scrambled against the concrete as he worked his lanky frame farther inside the car. He gave a grunt, to which Luxford responded.

"You can't possibly hope to find anything remotely related to your investigation in my car. If I were going to transport a ten-year-old child out of town, I'd hardly use my own vehicle, would I? I'm not a fool. And the idea of secreting Charlotte in a Porsche is absurd. A Porsche, for the love of God. There's not even enough room inside of it to—"

" 'Spector," Nkata interrupted. "Got something here. 'Neath the seat."

He backed out of the car. He was grasping an object in his closed fist.

"It can't be anything to do with Charlotte," Luxford said.

But he was wrong. Nkata straightened up and showed Lynley what he'd found. It was a pair of spectacles. Round in shape and framed in tortoiseshell, they were nearly identical to the spectacles that Eve Bowen wore. The only difference was that this pair had been made for a child.

"What in God's name . . . ?" Luxford sounded astonished. "Whose are those? How did they get in my car?"

Nkata rested the spectacles in a handkerchief that Lynley extended to him, spread across his palm. "I dare say we'll discover these belonged to Charlotte Bowen," Lynley said. He nodded at Nkata and added, "Constable. If you will."

Nkata recited the caution. Unlike Havers, who always enjoyed the drama created by ceremoniously reading it from the back of her note-book, Nkata merely repeated it from memory and without inflection. Still, Luxford's face transformed. His jaw loosened. His eyes widened. He swallowed, and when Nkata had finished, he began to speak.

"Are you completely mad?" he demanded. "You know I had nothing to do with this."

"You might want to phone your solicitor now," Lynley said. "He can meet us at the Yard."

"Someone put those glasses in the car," Luxford insisted. "You know that's what happened. Someone who wants it to look as if I—"

"Make arrangements to have the car impounded," Lynley told Nkata. "Phone the lab and tell them to be ready to go over it."

"Right," Nkata said. He headed off to take care of it, the leather soles of his shoes sounding tympanically as they came down smartly against the concrete, the noise rebounding off the ceiling and the walls.

Luxford said to Lynley, "You're falling into his hands, whoever he is. He put those glasses in the car. He's been waiting for the moment when you'd stumble on them. He knew you'd get to me eventually, and you have. Don't you see? You're playing the game his way."

"The car was locked," Lynley pointed out. "It was armed as well. You deactivated the alarm yourself."

"It isn't locked all the time, for God's sake."

Lynley moved to the passenger door and shut it.

"The car isn't locked all the time," Luxford repeated in some agitation. "It isn't armed either. Those glasses could have been put inside anytime."

"When specifically?"

The editor was momentarily taken aback. Clearly, he had not expected his argument to carry water with such speed.

"When isn't the car locked and armed?" Lynley said. "That shouldn't be too difficult a question to answer. It's an expensive vehicle. It's not a heap you might leave unlocked on the street. Or in a parking garage. Or a car park somewhere. So when isn't it locked and armed, Mr. Luxford?"

Luxford's mouth moved round the words, but he didn't say them. He had seen the trap an instant before it was sprung upon him, but he obviously knew it was too late to retreat from its jaws.

"Where?" Lynley asked.

"At my home," Luxford finally said.

"Are you certain of that?"

Luxford nodded numbly.

"I see. Then I believe we need to have a talk with your wife."

—⁂—

The drive to Highgate was endless. It was a straight shot northwest through Holburn and Bloomsbury, but the route took them through the worst traffic in the city, compounded this night by a car fire just north of Russell Square. Lynley navigated through the congestion, all the time wondering how Sergeant Havers could stand to make the commute every day to Westminster from her digs in Chalk Farm, which was one of the neighbourhoods they passed through some forty minutes into their journey.

Luxford said little. He asked to phone his wife and make her aware of his arrival in the company of a DI from Scotland Yard, but Lynley refused him. When the newspaperman said, "I need to prepare her. She doesn't know about any of this. About Eve. About Charlotte. I need to prepare her," Lynley replied by telling him that his wife might well know far more than he thought, which is why they were going to see her in the first place.

"That's ridiculous," Luxford asserted. "If you mean to suggest that Fiona is any way involved in what's happened to Charlotte, you're mad."

"Tell me," Lynley said in return. "Were you married to Fiona at the time of the Blackpool Tory conference?"

"I was not."

"Were you involved with her?"

Luxford was silent for a moment. When he did reply, he said only, "Fiona and I weren't married then," as if that fact alone had given him licence to pursue Eve Bowen.

"But Fiona knew that you were in Blackpool?" Lynley asked. Luxford said nothing. Lynley glanced his way, saw the whiteness round his mouth. "Mr. Luxford, did your wife—"

"Yes. All right. She knew I was in Blackpool. But that's all she knew, all she ever knew. She doesn't follow politics. She's never followed politics." He raked his hand through his hair in agitation.

"As far as you know, she's never followed politics."

"She was a model, for God's sake. Her life and her world were her body, her face. She'd never even bothered to vote before I knew her." Luxford rested his head wearily against the seat. He said, "Brilliant. Now I've made her sound like a twit," and he rolled his head to the left and gazed dully through the window. They were passing Camden Lock Market, where a juggler stood at the edge of the pavement, plying his trade with antique pewter platters. They winked fitfully in the day's late light.

Luxford said nothing more until they reached Highgate. His home was on Millfield Lane, a villa that stood directly opposite two of the ponds that formed the east boundary of Hampstead Heath. When Lynley made the turn between the two brick pillars that marked the driveway to *The Source* editor's home, Luxford said, "At least let me go inside first and have a word with Fiona."

"I'm afraid that's not possible."

"Can't you have some bloody decency?" Luxford demanded. "My son's at home. He's eight years old. He's completely innocent. You can't expect me to include him in this exhibition you're planning."

"I'll watch what I say while he's present. You can take him to his room."

"I hardly think—"

"That's the extent of the compromise, Mr. Luxford."

Lynley parked behind a late-model Mercedes-Benz that was itself parked beneath a portico. The portico overlooked the villa's front garden, which appeared to be more a wildlife refuge than a traditional display of carefully manicured lawn and burgeoning herbaceous borders. When Luxford got out of the Bentley, he went to the edge of this garden, where a flagstone path disappeared into the shrubs. He said,

"They're usually watching the birds feed at this time of day." He called his wife's name. Then he called to his son.

When no answering cry came from beneath the trees, he turned back to the house. The front door was closed, but not locked. It opened into a marble-floored foyer at the centre of which a flight of stairs rose to the first floor of the house.

"Fiona?" Luxford called. His voice was distorted by the stone floor and plaster walls of the foyer. Again no one responded.

Lynley shut the door behind them. Luxford went through an archway to their left. Here a drawing room was banked by bay windows that gave an unobstructed view of the ponds on the heath. He continued to call his wife's name.

The house was utterly hushed. Luxford went from one room to another throughout the sprawling villa, but as he did, it became evident to Lynley that this trip to Highgate had been in vain. Fortuitously or not, it was clear that Fiona Luxford was not there to answer his questions. When her husband came down the stairs, Lynley said to him, "You'll want to phone your solicitor, Mr. Luxford. He can meet us at the Yard."

"They should be here." Brow furrowed, Luxford looked from the drawing room where Lynley had waited for him to the entry and the heavy front door. "Fiona wouldn't go out without locking the front door. They should be here, Inspector."

"Perhaps she thought she'd locked it."

"She wouldn't think. She'd know. It locks with a key." Luxford went back to the door and pulled it open. He called his wife's name, more a shout this time. He called his son's name. He strode back down the slope of the driveway towards the lane where, just inside the walls of his property, a low white building stood. It comprised three garages, and as Lynley watched, Luxford entered the building through a green wooden door, an unlocked green wooden door, Lynley noted. So perhaps there was mild support for Luxford's claim as to how Charlotte's glasses came to be in his car.

Lynley stood in the portico. He let his gaze sweep over the garden. He was thinking about insisting that Luxford lock up the house and climb back into the Bentley for the drive to Scotland Yard, when his eyes fell upon the Mercedes in front of him. He decided to test the newspaperman's assertions about where and when his own car was locked. He tried the driver's door. It opened. He slid inside.

His knee nudged a pendent object near the steering column. A muted metallic jangling sounded. The car's keys, he saw, hung from the ignition on a large brass ring.

On the floor of the passenger's side of the car a woman's shoulder bag lay. Lynley reached for this. He opened it, rustled past a compact, several lipstick tubes, a brush, a pair of sunglasses, and a chequebook, and pulled out a leather purse. It contained fifty-five pounds, a Visa card, and a driving licence with *Fiona Howard Luxford* printed on it.

A sense of disquiet rose in him, like insects buzzing too close to his ears. He was getting out of the car, the shoulder bag looped over his hand, when Luxford hastened back up the driveway.

"They sometimes take their bikes onto the heath in the afternoon," he said. "Fiona likes the ride to Kenwood House and Leo loves to look at the paintings. I thought they might have gone there, but their bikes are—" He caught sight of the shoulder bag.

"This was in the car," Lynley told him. "Have a look. Are these her keys?"

Luxford's expression gave Lynley the answer. Once the man saw the keys, he rested both hands against the bonnet of the car, looked out over the garden, and said, "Something's happened."

Lynley walked round the Mercedes to the other side. The front tyre was flat. He squatted to have a closer look. He ran his fingers along the treads and followed his fingers' progress with his eyes. He found the first nail a quarter of the way up the tyre. Then a second and a third nail together, some six inches above the first.

He said, "Is your wife generally home at this time of day?"

Luxford said, "Always. She likes to spend time with Leo after school."

"What time does his school day end?"

Luxford raised his head. His look was stricken. "Half past three."

Lynley looked at his pocket watch. It was after six. His disquiet heightened, but he said the reasonable thing. "They may have both gone out."

"She wouldn't leave her bag. She wouldn't leave the keys in the car. And the front door unlocked. She wouldn't do that. Something's happened to them."

"There's no doubt a simple explanation," Lynley said. Which was usually the case. Someone seemed to be missing who was all the while engaged in the most logical of activities, activities that the panicked spouse would have recalled had the panicked spouse not panicked in the first place. Lynley considered what Fiona Luxford's activities might be, looking for cool reason in the face of Luxford's growing apprehension. "The front tyre's gone flat," he told Luxford. "She's picked up three nails."

"*Three?*"

"So she may have taken the boy somewhere on foot."

"Someone's flattened it," Luxford said. "Someone's flattened the tyre. Listen to me, won't you? Someone's flattened that tyre."

"Not necessarily. If she was heading out to pick him up from school and found the tyre flat, she—"

"She wouldn't." Luxford pressed his fingers to his eyelids. "She *wouldn't*, all right? I won't allow her to fetch him."

"What?"

"I make him walk. I make him walk to school. It's good for him. I've told her it's good for him. It'll toughen him up. Oh God. Where are they?"

"Mr. Luxford, let's go inside and see if she's left a note somewhere."

They went back to the house. Maintaining his calm, Lynley instructed Luxford to check every possible spot where his wife might have left him a message. He followed him from the basement gym to a desk in a second floor aerie. There was nothing. Anywhere.

"Your son had no appointments today?" Lynley asked. They were descending the stairs. Luxford's face wore a fine sheen of perspiration. "Your wife had no appointments? Doctor's? Dentist's? A place they may have gone together by taxi or underground? By bus?"

"Without her bag? Without her money? Leaving her keys in the car? For God's sake, have some sense."

"Let's rule out all the possibilities, Mr. Luxford."

"And while we're ruling out all the bloody possibilities, she's out there somewhere . . . Leo's out there somewhere . . . God damn!" Luxford hit his fist on the stair rail.

"Do her parents live nearby? Do yours?"

"There's no one nearby. There's nothing. Nothing."

"Any friends she might have taken the boy to see? Any colleagues? If she's discovered the truth about you and Eve Bowen, she may well have decided that she and your son—"

"She hasn't discovered the truth! There is no possible way that she could have discovered the truth. She should be here in the house or out in the garden or riding her bicycle and Leo should be with her."

"Has she a diary that we might—"

The front door swung open. Both of them spun towards it as someone outside pushed at it forcefully. It flew to the wall and slammed against it. A woman stumbled into the house. Tall, with tumbling hair the shade of honey and dirt streaking her wine-coloured leggings, she was breathing raggedly and she clutched her chest as if her heart were in seizure.

Luxford cried, "Fiona!" and pounded down the rest of the stairs. "What in the name of heaven . . . ?"

Her head flew up. Lynley saw she was ashen. She cried out her husband's name, and he caught her in his arms.

"Leo," she said. Her voice was wild. "Dennis, it's Leo. It's Leo. Leo!"

And she raised her clenched hands to the level of his face. She opened them. A small boy's school cap fell to the floor.

—·—

Her story came out in tatters, torn from her uneven breathing. She'd expected Leo no later than four. When he hadn't arrived by five, she was irritated enough with his thoughtlessness to set out after him and give him a thorough talking-to when she found him. He knew, after all, that he was always to come directly home after school. But when she tried to take the Mercedes down the driveway, she'd found a tyre was flat, so she set off on foot.

"I walked every route he might have taken," she said, and she listed them for her husband as if to prove her point. She sat on the very edge of a sofa in the drawing room, her hands trembling badly as they curved round a tumbler of whisky that Luxford had poured for her. He squatted in front of her, steadying her grip and occasionally reaching forward to push the hair from her face. "And after I'd walked them all—every route—I came home along the cemetery. And the cap . . . Leo's cap . . ." She raised the whisky glass to her mouth. It clattered unsteadily against her teeth.

Luxford seemed to know what she was unwilling to put into words. "In the cemetery?" he asked. "You found Leo's cap? In the cemetery?"

Tears spilled from her eyes.

"But Leo knows not to go into Highgate Cemetery alone." Luxford sounded puzzled. "I've told him, Fiona. I've told him time and again."

"Of course he knows, but he's a boy. A little boy. He's curious. And the cemetery . . . You know how it is. Overgrown, wild. A place for adventure. He passes right by it every day. And he'd have thought—"

"My God, has he talked to you about going in there?"

"Talked to . . . ? Dennis, he's grown up with that cemetery practically in his back garden. He's seen it. He's been interested in the tombs and catacombs. He's read about the statues and—"

Luxford rose to his feet. He drove his hands into his pockets and turned away from her.

"What?" she asked. Her voice arced with more panic. "What? *What?*"

He swung round on her. "Did you encourage him?"

"To what?"

"To visit the tombs. The catacombs. To have adventures in that bloody cemetery. Did you encourage him, Fiona? Is that why he went?"

"No! I answered him. I answered his questions."

"Which piqued his curiosity. Which stimulated his imagination."

"What was I supposed to do when my son asked questions?"

"Which led him to jump the wall."

"Are you making me responsible? You, who insisted he walk to school, who downright *demanded* that I never baby him by—"

"Which no doubt led him straight to some pervert who decided he needed an afternoon's switch from Brompton Cemetery to Highgate."

"Dennis!"

Lynley intervened quickly. "You're ahead of yourself, Mr. Luxford. There may be a simple explanation."

"Bugger your simple explanations."

"We need to phone the boy's friends," Lynley went on. "We need to talk to Leo's headmaster as well as his teacher. It's just two hours past the time he was due home, and chances are you're falling into panic for nothing."

As if in support of Lynley's words, the telephone rang. Luxford sprang across the room and snatched up the receiver. He barked a hello. Someone on the other end spoke. His left hand grabbed the mouthpiece and cupped it.

"Leo!" he said. His wife surged to her feet. "Where the hell are you? Do you have any idea of the state you've put us into?"

"Where is he? Dennis, let me speak to him."

Luxford held his hand up to stop his wife. He listened in silence for less than ten seconds. Then he said, "Who? Leo, who? God damn it. Tell me *where* . . . Leo! Leo!"

Fiona grabbed the phone. She cried her son's name into the mouthpiece. She listened, but obviously listened in vain. The phone clattered from her hand to the floor.

"Where is he?" she said to her husband. "Dennis, what's happened? Where's Leo?"

Luxford turned his face to Lynley. It looked carved from chalk.

"He's been taken," he said. "Someone's kidnapped my son."

part three

22

"*THE MESSAGE WAS VIRTUALLY IDENTICAL* to the one Luxford received about Charlotte," Lynley said to St. James. "The difference was that this time the child delivered it personally."

" 'Acknowledge your firstborn child on page one?' " St. James asked.

"A slight variation of that. According to Luxford, Leo said, 'You're to run the story on page one, Daddy. Then he'll let me go.' And that's all."

"According to Luxford," St. James repeated. He saw that Lynley followed his thinking.

"When Luxford's wife grabbed the phone, the line had gone dead. So the answer is yes: He was the only one of us to speak to the boy." Lynley reached for the balloon glass that St. James had placed for him on the coffee table in his Cheyne Row study. He meditated upon its contents as if he would find the answer he was looking for floating on the surface. He looked fairly done in, St. James noted. Permanent exhaustion went hand-in-glove with his line of work.

"It's not a pretty thought, Tommy."

"Even less pretty when one considers that the story our putative kidnapper wants to see on page one will actually run in Luxford's paper tomorrow. There was quite enough time to alter the front page and go to press with it once we'd heard from Leo. That's rather convenient, wouldn't you agree?"

"What have you done?"

He'd done what was called for by the situation, Lynley explained, despite his unease and his growing suspicions about Dennis Luxford. Thus, constables were assigned to Highgate Cemetery, where they were looking for clues to the boy's disappearance. Other constables were walking the routes Leo might have taken once he left his junior school on Chester Road. The media had been given photographs of the boy to broadcast with the nightly news for potential sightings of him. Wiretaps were in the works, to trace all incoming calls to Luxford.

"We've taken the nails from the tyres as well," Lynley finished. "And dusted the Mercedes for prints, for what little good that activity's probably going to do us."

"What about the Porsche?"

"The glasses were Charlotte's. Eve Bowen confirmed."

"Does she know where you found them?"

"I didn't tell her."

"She may have been right all along. About Luxford. His involvement. His motivations."

"She may have been. But if she is, we're dealing with an ability to dissemble that's roughly on a par with people like Blunt." Lynley swirled the brandy in his glass before he shot the liquor back. He set the glass on the coffee table and leaned forward, elbows resting on his knees. He said, "SO4's given us a match on the fingerprints. Whoever put his thumb on the inside of that tape recorder also left his print in the squat on George Street. Once on the edge of the bathroom mirror, a second time on the windowsill. That was good work, Simon. I don't know when—or even if—we would have got to the squat if you hadn't brought it to our attention."

"Thank Helen and Deborah. They ran across it last week. Both of them insisted that I give it a look."

At this, Lynley studied his hands. Behind him, night's darkness pressed against the windows, splintered by a streetlamp a few doors away from St. James's house. Inside the house, the silence between the two men was broken by the sound of music, floating down from the top floor where Deborah was working in her darkroom. St. James recognised the song with a slight stirring of discomfort: Eric Clapton's ode to the son he had lost. He immediately regretted having mentioned Deborah at all.

Lynley raised his head. "What have I done? Helen told me I dealt her a death blow."

St. James felt the unintended irony of the words like a subtle bruise on his psyche. But he knew he couldn't betray his wife's trust. He said, "She's sensitive when it comes to children. She still wants them. And the adoption process moves forward roughly like flies crossing flypaper."

"She connected what I said about killing children to the difficulty she's had with her pregnancies, then."

Lynley's astute remark was an indication of how well he actually knew Deborah. It was also too close to the truth for St. James's liking. He spoke past a raw soreness from which he thought he'd recovered at least twelve months in the past. "It's not as simple as that."

"I didn't intend to hurt her. She must know that. I flew off without thinking. But it was because of Helen, not Deborah. May I apologise to her?"

"I'll tell her what you've said."

Lynley looked as if he would argue the point. But there were lines in their friendship that he wouldn't cross. This was one of them; both of them knew it. He rose, saying, "My temper got the better of me last evening, Simon. Havers warned me off coming, but I wouldn't listen. I regret the whole scene."

"I haven't been gone from the Met so long that I've forgotten what the pressure's like," St. James said. He walked with Lynley to the front door and followed him out into the cool night. The air felt damp against his skin, as if a mist were rising from the Thames a short distance away.

"Hillier's handling the media," Lynley said. "At least that's not on my back."

"But who's handling Hillier?"

They chuckled companionably. Lynley took his car keys from his pocket. "He wanted to go to the media with a suspect this afternoon, a mechanic Havers dug up in Wiltshire who had Charlotte Bowen's school uniform in his garage. He had nothing else, though, as far as we know." Contemplatively, he examined the keys in his hand. "It's too spread out, Simon. From London to Wiltshire and God knows how many points in between. I'd like to settle on Luxford, on Harvie, on someone, but I'm beginning to think more than one person's behind what's happened."

"That was Eve Bowen's thought."

"She might well be right, although not the way she assumed." He told St. James what MP Alistair Harvie had claimed about Bowen, the IRA, and its potential splinter groups. He ended with, "It's never been the IRA's way of working: kidnapping children and taking their lives. I want to reject the idea out of hand. But I can't, I'm afraid. So we're checking into backgrounds to see what's there."

"The housekeeper's Irish," St. James offered. "Damien Chambers as well. The music teacher."

"The last one to see Charlotte," Lynley noted.

"He has a Belfast accent, for what it's worth. He has more potential than the housekeeper, I think."

"Why?"

"He had someone with him the night Helen and I went to see him,
someone upstairs. He claimed it was a woman and attributed his nerves
to first-night trauma: The scene is set for seduction and strangers arrive
to question him about the disappearance of one of his music pupils."

"Not an unreasonable reaction."

"Quite. But there's another connection between Chambers and
what happened to Charlotte Bowen. I hadn't really thought about it till
you mentioned the IRA."

"What's that?"

"The name. In the note Bowen received, Charlotte is referred to as
Lottie. But out of all the people I spoke to about the girl, only Damien
Chambers and her schoolmates called her Lottie. So I'd check into
Chambers if I were you."

"One more possibility," Lynley agreed.

He said goodnight and walked to his car. St. James watched him
drive off before he turned and went back into the house.

He found Deborah still in the darkroom on the top floor, her music
now switched off. She'd completed her developing and the door was
open, but he saw that she wasn't finished working despite the hour. She
was bent over the work top, studying something with a magnifying
glass. One of her old proof sheets, he suspected. It was her habit to
gauge her creative growth by constantly comparing where she was at
the moment with where she had come from.

Caught up in her study, she didn't hear him say her name. He
entered the darkroom, where he saw over her shoulder why she was so
absorbed, and he instantly knew that he couldn't tell her a second child
had been abducted. She wasn't looking at one of her proof sheets.
Rather, she was using the magnifying glass to scrutinise the photograph
of Charlotte Bowen's body that Lynley had dropped in front of her in
anger on the previous afternoon.

St. James reached for the magnifying glass. She started with a cry
and dropped the glass on top of the picture.

"You frightened me!"

"Tommy's come and gone."

Her eyelids lowered. She restlessly fingered the edges of the picture.

"He's apologised for what he said to you, Deborah. It was the heat
of the moment. He didn't mean it. He would have come up here to talk

to you himself, but I thought it was best that I bring you the message. Would you have preferred to see him?"

"What Tommy meant isn't important. What he said was the truth. I kill children, Simon. You and I know it. What Tommy doesn't know is that Charlotte Bowen just wasn't the first."

St. James felt the cold weight of his spirit sinking. His mind cried out, Not now, not again. He wanted to disappear from the room and to wait for Deborah to come out of her funk, but because he loved her, he forced himself to call upon patience and reason. "It's been a long time. How many years will it take for you to forgive yourself?"

"I can't adhere to a timeline you've established for me," she replied. "Feelings aren't like scientific formulae. You don't add remorse to understanding and come out with peace of mind. At least I don't. What goes on inside people—or at least inside me—isn't like mixing molecules, Simon."

"I'm not suggesting that it is."

"You are. You look at me, you think, Well, it's been a good number of years since she had the abortion, which according to my calculations should be more than enough time to put it behind her. And you conveniently forget what I've been through since then. How many times you and I have tried . . . have tried and have failed because of me."

"We've had this discussion before, Deborah. It never gets us anywhere. I don't blame you. I never have done. So why do you insist upon blaming yourself?"

"Because it's *my* body. Because it's *my* failure. I own it. It's mine."

"And if it were mine?"

"What?" She sounded suddenly wary.

"Would you want me to torture myself with recriminations? Would you want me to see every error I made—every decision gone wrong—as yet another result of my body's inability to reproduce? Is that even rational thinking?"

He could feel her distance herself from the discussion. Her features grew remote as she shut herself down. She said politely, "There you have the source of our conflict. You want me to think rationally."

"That's hardly unreasonable."

"You don't want me to feel."

"What I want," he said, "is for you to think about what you're feeling. And you're avoiding what I asked. So answer the question."

"Which one?"

"Would you want me to torture myself? Because of something that my body can't do? Something I myself may have caused but also something that now is completely beyond my control? Would you have me torture myself over that?''

She was silent. Her head lowered and she sighed unevenly. ''Of course not. How can I argue with that? Oh, of course not, of course not, Simon. Forgive me.''

''Can we put this at rest, then?''

''We can try. I can try. But this—'' She touched the curve of Charlotte's head in the picture. She drew a deep breath. ''Here's what it is: I asked you to become involved. You wouldn't have. You didn't want to. But I asked you and you did it for me.''

He reached past her and took the photograph. He put his arm round her shoulders and drew her out of the darkroom and into the laboratory beyond it. He laid the picture of Charlotte Bowen facedown on the nearest worktable, and when he spoke, it was against Deborah's hair. ''Listen to me, my love. You have complete power over my heart. I'll never argue with you about that. But I have control over my mind and my will. You may have asked me to look into Charlotte Bowen's disappearance, but asking alone doesn't make you responsible. Not when the final decision was mine. Are we clear on that now?''

She turned so that she was easily in his arms. ''It's because of who and what you are,'' she whispered in answer to the question he hadn't asked. ''I want so badly to make a child with you because of who and what you are. If you were a lesser man, I don't think it would even bother me to fail.''

He tightened his hold on her. He let his heart open and damned all the consequences, which was the way of love. ''Deborah, believe me,'' he said in reply. ''Making a child is the easiest part of it.''

—⁂—

Dennis Luxford found his wife in the bathroom. The female police constable in the kitchen had said only that Fiona had asked to be left alone before she'd gone upstairs, so the first place Luxford looked for her when he returned from *The Source* office was Leo's bedroom. But the room was empty. He turned woodenly from the sight of the art book open on Leo's desk, from the sight of an unfinished sketch of Giotto's Virgin cradling the body of her Son. His chest felt as if blood clots were constricting it, and he found he needed to stop in the doorway until he was able to breathe without difficulty again.

He checked all the other rooms as he came upon them. He called his wife's name softly because softness seemed to be required, and even if it hadn't been, that's all he could manage. He went through the study and the sewing room, through the spare rooms and their bedroom. When he found her, she was sitting in the dark on the bathroom floor, forehead on her knees and arms covering her head. Moonlight, laced by the tree leaves outside the bathroom window, created a penumbra on the marble. In this lay the crushed cellophane from a large packet of jam mallows and, on its side, an empty carton for milk. Luxford could smell the rank odour of vomit that was released into the air each time his wife exhaled.

He picked up the empty jam mallows packet and placed it in the rubbish basket along with the milk carton. He saw the still unopened fig rolls at Fiona's side, and he eased them up from the floor and placed them in the rubbish, where he covered them with the cellophane from the other biscuits in the hope that she wouldn't find them later.

He squatted in front of his wife. When she lifted her head, even in the subdued lighting, he could see the sweat on her face.

"Don't start doing this to yourself again," Luxford said to her. "He'll be home tomorrow. I promise you that."

Her eyes looked dull. She reached lethargically for the fig rolls and found them missing. She said, "I want to know. And I want to know now."

He'd left without telling her anything. To her agonised cries of What's happening, where is he, what are you doing, where are you going, he'd shouted only that she needed to control herself, that she needed to calm down, that she needed to let him get back to the newspaper where he could run the story that would bring their son home. She'd cried, What story? What's happening? Where's Leo? What's Leo got to do with a story? And she'd grabbed on to him to keep him from leaving her. But he'd wrested himself away and left her anyway, tearing back to Holborn by taxi and cursing the police who'd robbed him of his Porsche which would have made shorter work of the journey than did the lumbering Austin and its cigarette-smoking driver.

He lowered himself to the floor. He searched for a way to tell her about everything that had happened in the past six days as well as about the events of nearly eleven years ago that served as these past six days' history. He realised that he should just have brought *The Source* story home for her to read. It would have been simpler than uselessly looking for a way to begin that would soften the impact of what he had to tell her about the lie he'd been living for more than a decade.

He said, "Fiona, I made a woman pregnant at a political conference eleven years ago. That child—a girl called Charlotte Bowen—was kidnapped last Wednesday. The kidnapper wanted me to admit to having fathered her and to admit it on the front page of the newspaper. I didn't. She was found dead on Sunday night. That same man—whoever took Charlotte—has Leo now. He wants the story in the paper. So I'm running it tomorrow."

Fiona parted her lips to speak but said nothing. Then slowly her eyes closed and she turned her head away.

He said, "Fi, it's something that just happened between me and the woman. We weren't in love, it didn't really mean anything, but there was a spark between us and we didn't turn away from it."

"Please," she said.

"You and I weren't married," he said, anxious to make everything clear to her. "We knew each other, but we weren't involved. You'd said you weren't ready for that. Do you remember?"

She brought her hand up and balled it between her breasts.

"It was sex, Fiona. That's all it was between us. It was simply sex. Mindless. Without affection. Something that happened and then was forgotten by both of us." He was saying too much, but he couldn't seem to stop. He needed to find the right words so that when hearing them, she would be compelled to answer and to give him a sign that she understood or at least forgave. He said, "We were nothing to each other. We were bodies in a bed. We were . . . I don't know. We just *were*."

She brought her face back to his in a torpid movement. She searched his features as if reading them for the truth. She said in a toneless voice, "Did you know about the child? Did this woman tell you? Have you known all along?"

He thought about lying. He couldn't bring himself to do so. "She told me."

"When?"

"I've known about Charlotte from the first."

"From the first." She whispered the phrase as if mulling it over. She said it once more. Then she reached above her head, where a thick green towel hung from a rail. She pulled the towel down and stuffed it into a ball in her arms. She began to weep.

Wretchedly, Luxford reached out to hold her. She shrank away. He said, "I'm sorry."

"This has all been a lie."

"What has?"

"Our life. Who we are to each other."

"That's not true."

"I've held nothing back from you. But that hasn't meant anything because all the time you . . . Who you really were . . . I want my son," she cried. "Now. I want Leo. I want my son."

"I'll have him here tomorrow. I swear it to you, Fi. On my life, I *swear* it."

"You can't," she wept. "You haven't the power. He's going to do what he did to the other."

"He isn't. Leo will be all right. I'm doing what he's asked. I didn't do that for Charlotte, but I'm doing it now."

"But she's dead. She's *dead*. He's a murderer now as well as a kidnapper. So how can you think that with murder hanging over his head, he'll actually let Leo—"

He grabbed her arms. "Listen to me. Whoever's got Leo has no reason to harm him because he has no quarrel with me. What's happened has happened because someone wanted to destroy Charlotte's mother and discovered a way to do it. She's in the Government. She's a Junior Minister. Someone's looked into her background and found out about me. The scandal—who I am, who she is, what occurred between us, how she's misrepresented it all these years—the scandal will finish her. And that's what this has been all about: finishing off Eve Bowen. She was willing to risk maintaining her silence when Charlotte went missing. She convinced me to do the same. But I'm not willing to do it now that someone's got Leo. So the situation's different. And Leo will not be harmed."

She had the towel at her mouth. She watched him over it. Huge eyes, frightened. She looked like a trapped animal, facing its death.

He said, "Fiona, trust me. I'll die before anyone hurts my own child."

He heard what he'd said before the silence even had a chance to sweep in after his words. He could see from her face that she'd heard it as well. He dropped his grip on her arms. He felt his own statement—and its implicit damnation of his behaviour—crush him.

He said what he knew his wife was thinking. Better for him to put it into words than to have to hear it from her. "She was my child as well. I did nothing. And she was my child."

Sudden anguish welled up in him. It was the same anguish he'd held in check since seeing the news and fearing the worst on Sunday night. But it was amplified now by the guilt of having abdicated his responsibility towards a life he'd been a party to creating, and it was deepened by the knowledge that his inaction over the past six days had now provoked the abduction of his son. He turned away from his wife, unable to face her expression any longer. "God forgive me," he said. "What have I done?"

They sat in the darkness together. They were inches from each other but they did not touch, one of them not daring, the other not willing. Luxford knew what his wife was thinking: Flesh of his flesh, Charlotte had been his child as much as Leo was, and he had not rushed—mindless of the consequences—to save her. What he didn't know was the conclusion she'd reached about what his inaction said of him as a man to whom she was tied by ten years of marriage. He wanted to weep, but he'd long ago lost the ability to depurate himself through the means of emotion. One couldn't walk the path he'd chosen so many years ago upon coming to London and still remain a sentient creature. If he hadn't known that before, he knew now that it was an impossibility. He'd never been so lost.

"I can't say it's not your fault," Fiona whispered. "I want to, Dennis, but I can't."

"I don't expect it. I could have done something. I let myself be led. It was easier because if everything worked out, you and Leo would have never learned the truth. Which is what I wanted."

"Leo." Fiona said his name haltingly. "Leo would have liked to have a big sister. Very much, I think. And I . . . I could have forgiven you anything."

"Except the lie."

"Perhaps. I don't know. I can't think about it now. I can think only of Leo. What he's going through, how frightened he must be, how alone and worried. I can think only of that. And of the fact that it may already be too late."

"I'm going to get Leo back," Luxford said. "He isn't going to harm him. He won't get what he wants if he does. And he's getting what he wants tomorrow morning."

Fiona went on as if her husband hadn't spoken. "What I've been wondering is how it could have happened at all. The school's not far, not even a mile from here. All the way, the streets are safe. There's nowhere to hide. If someone grabbed him off the pavement, someone else had to see it. Even if someone lured him into the cemetery, someone else would have noticed. And if we can find that person—"

"The police are looking."

"—then we'll also find Leo. But if no one saw . . ." She stumbled on the word.

"Don't do this," Luxford said.

She went on regardless. "If no one saw anything out of the ordinary, then don't you see what it has to mean?"

"What?"

"It means that whoever took Leo was someone Leo knows. He wouldn't willingly walk off with a stranger, Dennis."

—𝕞—

Rodney Aronson gave an indifferent wave to Mitch Corsico as he came into the winebar in Holborn Street. The reporter nodded in acknowledgement, paused to have a word with two competitors from the *Globe*, and strode through the haze of cigarette smoke with the confidence of a man who knows he's onto the story of his life. His cowboy boots fairly sang against the roughhewn floor. His face glowed. He looked, in fact, as if he could levitate altogether. Fool that he was.

"Thanks for meeting me, Rod." Corsico removed his hat and swung a chair back from the table. He lifted one leg across the seat cowboy fashion.

Rodney nodded. He speared another hoop of calamari and he washed it down with a swill of Chianti. He was hoping to get a decent buzz from the plonk, but so far it had settled sloshily into his stomach without doing a thing to tingle his head.

Corsico perused the menu and flipped it aside. He tossed a trendy "double cap, no cinnamon, chocolate biscotti" to a passing waiter and dug out his notebook. He gave a cautionary glance towards the *Globe* reporters he'd spoken to on the way in, and he followed it with another glance round at the closer tables to scope out potential eavesdroppers. Three overweight women with the sort of unattractive haircuts Rodney always associated with radical feminists and aggressive bull dykes were at the table closest to theirs, and from what they were saying about "the fooking movement" and "those cock-sucking pigs," Rodney felt total confidence in the fact that they wouldn't be the least interested in whatever information Corsico had insisted upon laying out for him at a safe but neutral location. But he allowed the young reporter his moment of intrigue and said nothing as Corsico hunched forward over both notebook and table, protecting his information by curving his shoulders round it.

"Shit, Rod," he said. Rodney noticed that he spoke from the side of his mouth: Alec Guinness in surreptitious public conversation with a valuable spook. "I've got it, and it's hot. You aren't going to believe it."

Rodney forked up another calamari hoop. He added some red pepper flakes to heat up the already spicy sauce. The wine wasn't getting to his head as he wished, so perhaps the pepper would at least get to his sinuses. "What is it?"

"I started out with that Tory conference, the one in Blackpool. Okay?"

"I follow."

"I dug into the *Telegraph* stories about it. The ones she filed before, the ones during, the ones after. Okay?"

"Haven't we trodden this ground before, Mitch?" After what he'd discovered in the past two hours, the thought that Corsico would be insisting upon a clandestine meeting for nothing more important than a rehash of what he already knew was more than discomposing to Rodney. It was head-bashing. He chewed with vigour.

"Wait," Corsico said. "I compared those stories to the conference itself. And then to what was happening in the lives of the story subjects before, during, and after the conference."

"And?"

Corsico snatched his notes from the table as the waiter appeared with his double cappuccino and his chocolate biscotti. The drink was served in a cup the approximate size of a wash basin. The waiter said, "Cheers," and Corsico sank what looked like a tongue depressor covered in knobs of plastic into the liquid. "Sugar," he explained to Rodney's querying look. He dunked the stick up and down like a toilet plunger. "It melts off in the espresso."

"Super," Rodney said.

Corsico used both hands to raise the cappuccino to his mouth. He gave himself a froth moustache, which he wiped off on the sleeve of his plaid shirt. He was a noisy drinker, Rodney noted with a shudder. There was nothing more unappetising than listening to someone slurp while one was attempting to eat.

"She filed stories from that conference like she was covering the scoop of the century," Corsico continued. "It was like she was afraid that someone was going to pull her off her expense account if she couldn't justify the whoop-de-do she was having in Blackpool. She did one to three pieces each day. Shit. Can you believe that? And some real boring stuff it was. It took me an age to read them then to compare them to anything that looked interesting in the lives of the major players. But I managed it." He flipped open his notebook and then inserted the chocolate biscotti cigar-like between his molars. He chomped. Crumbs spewed forth.

Rodney brushed one from the side of his bowl. He said, "And?"

"The Prime Minister," Corsico said. "Of course he wasn't PM then, but that makes the situation even seamier, doesn't it? It gives him something rather significant to hide in the here-and-now."

"How did you put this together?" Rodney asked curiously, always intrigued by the intricate workings of the human imagination.

"With some heavy legwork, let me tell you." Corsico slurped more cappuccino and referred to his notes. "Two weeks after that conference in Blackpool, the PM and his wife separated."

"They did?"

Corsico grinned. A piece of chocolate was wedged between two of his teeth. "Didn't know that, I expect, did you? That separation lasted nine months and, as we know, didn't end in divorce. But I thought the nine months was an interesting time frame—all things considered—wouldn't you agree?"

"Nine months rings all sorts of bells for me," Rodney said. He finished off his calamari and poured himself a final glass of wine. "Perhaps you'd like to tell me what the bell-ringing heralds."

"Just wait till you hear." Corsico settled his buttocks happily into his chair. "I spoke to five different maids who worked at the hotel where the conference was held. Three of them still work there. Two of those three confirmed that the PM had a woman with him—just for the evenings, mind you, it was nothing official—and the woman wasn't his wife. Now, what I propose to do tomorrow is to take some pictures of Bowen up to Blackpool and see if I can get confirmation from one of the maids that she was the PM's dollybird. If either of them will confirm—"

"What did you offer them?"

Corsico looked blank for a moment and chewed noisily as he thought about the question.

"Are we paying them for the story or just giving them their fifteen minutes somewhere inside *The Source?*"

"Hey, Rod," Corsico protested. "If they're going to go on record, they're going to want to be recompensed for the stress. That's how we've always played it. Right?"

Rodney sighed. "Wrong." He blotted his mouth with his napkin and crumpled it on the table. As Corsico watched in confusion—clearly incapable of comprehending this sudden change in the publishing philosophy of his own newspaper—Rodney reached into one of the capacious pockets of his khaki jacket and produced tomorrow's paper with its redesigned front page, which had come to his attention due to a phone call from one of the news editors, a man whose loyalty Rodney had managed to cull through years of keeping silent about his wee-hours life in one of the seedier fleshpits of Soho. He tossed it in front of the reporter and said, "You might want to have a look at that. It's hot, as they say, off the bloody presses."

Rodney watched Corsico read what he himself had virtually memorised while waiting in the winebar. The three-hundred-and-thirty-point headline and its accompanying photograph said just about everything: *Father of Bowen Love-Child Steps Forward* explained what Dennis Luxford's mug was doing decorating the front page. When Corsico saw it, he reached blindly for his cappuccino. He read and slurped with equal fury. He stopped once to look up and say, "Holy *shit*," but he returned rabidly to the paper without requiring a reply. Which, Rodney knew, was what everyone else was going to be doing once this paper hit the streets in the morning. It would outsell the *Globe*, the *Mirror*, and the *Sun* as well, by at least one million copies. It would require successive stories as follow-up. And the papers they appeared in would outsell the *Globe*, the *Mirror*, and the *Sun* in their part.

Rodney watched glumly as Corsico—fulfilling every journalist's dream—avidly made the jump with the story, turning to the inside page where it continued. When he was finished, he threw himself back in his chair and stared at Rodney. "Geez," he said. "Rodney. *Shit*."

"Exactly," Rodney said.

"Why's he done it? I mean, what's he turning into these days, a man of conscience or something?"

Or something, Rodney thought. Or definitely something. He refolded the newspaper and returned it to his pocket.

"Damn," Corsico said. "Shit. Hell. I could have sworn that my story on the PM was as solid as . . ." His glance flew to Rodney. "Hey. Wait a flash here. You don't think that Luxford's covering for Downing Street, do you? Geez, Rod. Could he be a closet Tory?"

"Not a closet one," Rodney said, but the irony was lost on the younger man.

"Of course, our numbers are going to go through the roof now, aren't they?" Corsico said. "And the chairman's going to kiss his arse. But our numbers've been steadily building since Luxford came on board, so why's he done it? What the hell does it mean?"

"It means," Rodney said, pushing his chair away from the table and signalling to the waiter to bring him his bill, "that the shoot-out is officially over. For now."

Corsico looked at him blankly.

Rodney explained. "The black hats and white hats? Dodge City? Tombstone? The O.K. Corral? Place it where you will, Mitchell. It all turns out the same."

"What?" Corsico demanded.

Rodney looked at the bill and reached for his money. He threw down twenty pounds as he threw in the towel. "The guys in the black hats have won," he said.

23

KNACKERED *DIDN'T DESCRIBE* how Barbara Havers felt as she switched off the Mini's ignition at the top of the Lark's Haven driveway. She was done in, blown out, beat, and burned down. She listened listlessly to the car's engine gargle for a good fifteen seconds before it finally succumbed to petrol deprivation. When this miracle of modern mechanics ultimately supervened, she flicked the headlamps off and shoved her car door open. But she didn't get out.

The day had been largely a bust. Now it was becoming a quagmire. She'd spoken to Lynley and learned the news of Leo Luxford's disappearance in a conversation that had consisted of Lynley's concise recitation of the facts and her own "What? Bloody hell! *What?*" offered with rising intensity after each piece of information he imparted. They had not a single clue as to the whereabouts of the eight-year-old boy, he told her in conclusion, and only his father's word for the fact that the child had been on the telephone in the first place.

"So what do you think?" Barbara asked him. "How's our Luxford smelling these days?"

Lynley's response was laconic. They couldn't risk treating this as anything other than a kidnapping, he told her. Which was what he would be doing in London, in conjunction with working on the Bowen case. She was to soldier on with the murder investigation in Wiltshire. There was little doubt that the two cases were connected. What did she have? he wanted to know.

She was forced to admit to the worst. After her last confrontation with Sergeant Stanley over the deployment of the scene-of-crime team, she'd thrown her weight round Amesford CID. She'd got up DS Stanley's nose and had a moderate row with the sergeant's CC about Stanley's lack of cooperation. She didn't mention to Lynley the sergeant's cigarette lighter or his attitude towards her. Lynley would have little sympathy with her over that. He would opine that if she wished to make her way in what was largely a man's world, she was going to have to learn to kick arses and not expect her superior officer at Scotland Yard to do the kicking for her.

"Ah," he said. "Business as usual, is it?"

She went on to give him the rest of the information that comprised her day's dismal report. She'd managed to get the scene-of-crime team out to Ford to go over the dovecote that had looked so promising at Alistair Harvie's farm. Harvie's wife had given her most cooperative permission for the team to examine the building, but this hadn't caused Barbara to deduce the MP's complete innocence in the matter of the dead girl's disappearance. Rather, Barbara concluded that Harvie's wife was either a fine actress or that she knew nothing about her husband's nefarious goings-on behind her back. And while it was hard to believe that a ten-year-old girl could have been held in the dovecote a mere thirty yards from the farmhouse without Mrs. Harvie's knowledge, desperate circumstances called for equally desperate conclusions: While there was a chance that Charlotte had been in the dovecote, Barbara was going to have the dovecote examined.

She gleaned nothing from the exercise other than the crime scene team's taking a decided scunner to her. Which was nothing compared to how the doves themselves felt.

The only light at the end of the day's tunnel of disappointments was the information from forensic that the components of the grease found under Charlotte Bowen's fingernails exactly matched the components of the grease found in Howard Short's garage in Coate. But both samples of grease were a common brand of axle grease, and Barbara had to admit that finding axle grease under someone's fingernails or anywhere else in a farming community was about as earth-shattering as finding fish scales on the shoe soles of someone who worked at Billingsgate Market.

Her only hope for a solid break at this point was Constable Payne. She'd had four separate telephone messages from him during the day, each one marking his progress across the county. The first had been the one she'd received from Marlborough. The next were from Swindon, Chippenham, and Warminster. They'd finally managed to make voice contact on this last call, quite late in the day upon Barbara's less-than-victorious return to the Amesford station from the Harvie dovecote.

"You sound clapped out," Robin commented.

Barbara gave him a compendium of the day's events, beginning with the autopsy and ending with the waste of time and manpower at the dovecote. To all this he listened in silence from his phone box—with the roar of lorries passing nearby—and when she was finished, he said astutely, "And Sergeant Stanley's being a nasty clot as well, isn't he?" He didn't give her a chance to respond. He went on with "It's his way, Barbara. It's nothing to do with you. He tries that game on with everyone."

"Right. Well." Barbara shook a cigarette from her packet and lit it. "We're not completely out of leads at this end." And she told him about Charlotte Bowen's uniform, where it had been found, and where the mechanic Howard Short had claimed he got it.

"I've got my own leads," Robin had said. "The local police stations have been answering some questions that Sergeant Stanley never thought to ask."

He wouldn't say more than that. But his voice was keyed up with an excitement that he seemed eager to control, as if it weren't the appropriate emotion for a detective constable to be experiencing. He said only, "I've a bit more checking to do round here. If it's solid, you'll be the first to know."

Barbara was grateful for the constable's consideration. She'd burned more than half a bridge with Stanley and the sergeant's chief constable during the day. It would be nice to have something—a decent clue, a piece of evidence, an eyewitness to anything—that might undo the damage she'd done to her credibility with the investigators' useless traipse out to the dovecote that afternoon.

She'd spent the rest of the day and on into the evening fielding reports from the constables who were still tirelessly working Sergeant Stanley's grid system. Aside from the mechanic in possession of Charlotte's school uniform, they'd come up with nothing. Once she'd talked to Lynley and learned of Leo Luxford's abduction, she'd called the teams back to the office, brought them up-to-date on the second kidnapping, and distributed the boy's photograph and vital statistics.

Now she hoisted herself from the Mini and plodded through the darkness towards the house, steeling herself for yet another immersion into the Laura Ashley nightmare of Lark's Haven. Corrine Payne had given her a key to the front door, so Barbara headed there rather than go through the kitchen as she had done on the previous night with Robin. The lights were on in the sitting room, however, and when she turned the key in the lock and swung the door open, Corrine's breathy, asthmatic voice called out, "Robbie? Come and see a surprise, darling boy."

The injunction made Barbara pause. A shudder passed over her.

Too many times she'd heard a call so exactly similar—Barbie? Barbie? Is that you, Barbie? Come and see, come and see—and too many times she'd responded to find her mother wandering somewhere in the vast playing field of her growing dementia: perhaps planning a holiday to a destination she would never see, perhaps caressing and folding the clothes of a brother dead nearly two decades, perhaps sitting splay-legged on the kitchen floor making biscuits from flour and sugar and jam directly on the dirty yellow lino.

"Robbie?" Corrine sounded chesty, as if a few minutes with the inhaler were in order. "Is that you, darling? My Sammy's just left, but we've a visitor here still and I absolutely insisted that she not stir an inch till you got home. You'll want to see her straightaway, I dare say."

"It's me, Mrs. Payne," Barbara called. "Robin's still working."

Corrine's *oh* spoke volumes. It's only the slug, her tone implied. She was seated at a card table that had been set up in the centre of the sitting room. A game of Scrabble was in progress on it, with Corrine's opponent an attractive, young freckle-faced woman with a head of fashionably styled hair the colour of champagne. Beyond them on the fitted shelves, Sky television was showing an old Elizabeth Taylor film with the sound turned off. Barbara studied the picture. Taylor swathed in chiffon, Peter Finch in dinner clothes, a howlingly artificial jungle atmosphere, and a scowling native butler. *Elephant Walk*, she concluded. She always loved the climactic scene when the pachyderms finally smashed Peter Finch's villa to bits.

A third chair was drawn up to the card table, and the little pew for holding the Scrabble letters was still set up, marking Sam Corey's former place. Corrine saw Barbara's eyes take in this third place, and she casually removed the extra letter holder lest Barbara plunk herself down for a few attempts at double and triple words scores. She was, after all, pure hell with an *x*, and Corrine must have instinctively known it.

"This is Celia," Corrine said in introduction of her companion. "I may have already mentioned that she's my Robbie's—"

"Oh, please, Mrs. Payne. Don't." Celia spoke with an embarrassed laugh and a flush of pink blooming against her round cheeks. She was plump but not fat, the sort of woman one saw comfortably nude and reclining on sumptuous sofas in paintings identified as *Odalisque*. So this was the future daughter-in-law, Barbara thought. It was nice, for some reason, to realise that Robin Payne wasn't the sort of man who needed a woman with a body like a broom straw.

Barbara extended her hand across the table and said, "Barbara Havers. Scotland Yard CID." Then she wondered why she'd added that last, as if she had no other identity.

"You're here about that little girl, aren't you?" Celia asked. "It's a terrible thing."

"Murder generally is."

"Well, our Robbie shall get to the bottom of it," Corrine said stoutly. "Make no mistake of that." She plunked two letters onto the board: *c* and *a* before a *t*. She meticulously counted up her score.

"Are you working with Rob?" Celia enquired. She reached for a digestive biscuit that sat in a wreath of other biscuits on a floral plate at the edge of the table. She took a feminine bite from it. Barbara would have shoved the whole thing into her mouth, chomped it up heartily, and washed it down with whatever fluid was immediately available. In this case it was tea, contained in a pot that was covered by a quilted cozy. The cozy—like everything else in the house—was an Ashley creation. Barbara noted that Corrine didn't rush to remove it so as to offer her a cuppa.

It was time, she knew, to exit stage left. If Corrine's *oh* hadn't told her that much, her current lapse in hospitality had.

"Robbie's working for the sergeant," Corrine clarified. "And she's happy to have him, aren't you, Barbara?"

"He's a good policeman," Barbara said.

"He is indeed. First in his class from that detective school. Not two days after he finished the course and there he was in the middle of a case. Isn't that right, Barbara?" She watched Barbara shrewdly, clearly looking to measure a reaction, perhaps one that Barbara might give to her assessment of Robin's abilities.

Celia's round cheeks grew rounder and her blue eyes shone, perhaps at the thought of her beloved's certain rise to prominence in his chosen field. "I knew he'd make a success of CID. I told him that before he went on the course."

"And not just any case, mind you," Corrine said as if Celia hadn't spoken. "But this particular case. This Scotland Yard case. And this case, my dear"—with a pat on Celia's hand—"will be the making of our Robbie."

Celia smiled appealingly, her teeth pulling against her lower lip as if to contain her pleasure. In the meantime on the telly, the elephants were getting restless. One particularly huge bull was lumbering towards the estate's outer wall, following the age-old path to water that Peter Finch's father had so arrogantly blocked with his impressive villa. Approximately twenty-two minutes until elephant tramp-down, Barbara thought. She'd seen the film at least ten times.

She said, "I'll just say goodnight. If Robin comes in within the next half hour, will you have him come by my room? We've some facts to sort out."

"I'll certainly tell him, but I imagine our Robbie'll be a bit taken up with things right here," Corrine said with a meaningful nod at Celia who was studying her tiles. "He's waiting until he's settled completely into the new job. Once he knows his way about, then he'll be making some big changes in his life. Some permanent changes. Won't he, dear?" Another pat on Celia's hand. Celia smiled.

Barbara said, "Yes. Well. Congratulations. All the best," and felt like a fool.

Celia said, "Thank you," and gently laid five tiles onto the Scrabble board. Barbara glanced at the word. Celia had added to Corrine's *cat*, making it *catamite*. Corrine frowned at it in some confusion and reached for a dictionary, saying, "Are you certain, dear?" Barbara saw her eyes widen when she read the definition. She caught the merriment on Celia's face, which was quickly quelled when Corrine closed the dictionary and looked her way. "It's something to do with rock formations, isn't it?" Celia asked with spurious innocence.

Corrine said, "My goodness," with her hand at her chest. "My goodness . . . I need . . . Oh goodness . . . just a breath . . ."

Celia's expression altered. She got to her feet. Corrine gasped, "All of a sudden, dear . . . Where've I put . . . Where's my magic air? Has Sammy . . . Has he moved it?"

Celia quickly managed to find the inhaler next to the television. She hurried it to Corrine and put a steadying hand on her shoulder as the older woman pumped it vigorously into her mouth. Celia looked repentant for *catamite*, the obvious cause of Corrine's distress.

Interesting, Barbara thought. This is how their relationship would probably be played out over the next thirty or so years. She wondered if Celia had twigged to that fact.

Barbara heard the kitchen door open and then slam shut as Celia returned to her seat at the table. Rapid footsteps came on and Robin's voice called urgently, "Mum? Are you here? Is Barbara about?"

It wasn't the right question from what Barbara could tell from Corrine's expression. But it was also a question that didn't need answering, since Robin came through to the sitting room and stopped in the doorway. He was grubby from face to feet; there were cobwebs in his hair. But he grinned at Barbara and said, "There you are. Wait till you hear. Stanley's going to brick it when he finds out."

"Robbie, darling?" Corrine's voice—winded and weary—diverted her son's attention from Barbara to the card table. Celia rose.

She said, "Hullo, Rob."

He said, "Celia." He looked from his intended to Barbara in some confusion.

Barbara said, "I was just heading upstairs. If you'll excuse—"

"You can't!" Robin gave her a supplicatory glance. Then he said to Celia, "I'm in the middle of something. Sorry, but I can't just drop it." And his expression telegraphed the unspoken message that he hoped someone would rescue him from the awkwardness of the situation.

Clearly, Corrine didn't intend to and Celia didn't want to. And while Barbara might have complied with his desire for deliverance out of sheer friendship, she didn't know how to accomplish it. That sort of conversational legerdemain was the bailiwick of women like Helen Clyde.

Corrine said, "Celia's been waiting for you since half past eight, Robbie. We've had ourselves the loveliest visit. I told her that it's been far too long since we last had her at Lark's Haven and I know you mean to rectify that now you're working with CID. Any day now, I said to her, Robbie's going to slip something special onto your finger. Just you wait and see."

Robin looked agonised. Celia looked mortified. Barbara felt the back of her neck begin to sweat. She said, "Yes. Right," in a hearty fashion, and made a determined turn towards the stairs. "I'll just say goodnight, then. Robin, you and I can—"

"No!" He followed her.

Corrine called out, "Robbie!"

Celia cried, "Rob!"

But Robin was hot on Barbara's heels. She heard him behind her, saying her name urgently. He caught her up at the door to her room and grabbed her arm, which he quickly released when she turned to face him.

"Look," she said. "This is becoming something of a mess, Robin. I can stay in Amesford just as easily as here, and after tonight, I think that's best."

"After tonight?" He looked towards the stairs. "Why? That? You mean Celia? Mum? All that? Forget about it. It isn't important."

"I don't think you'd get Celia or your mum to agree with you."

"Bugger them both. They're not important. Not now. Not to-night." He wiped his arm across his forehead. In its wake, he left a deposit of grime. "I've found it, Barbara. I've been out there all day. I've been crawling through every odd hole I could think of. And I've bloody well found it."

"What?" she asked.

His dirty face looked triumphant. "The place where Charlotte Bowen was held."

—៷៷—

Alexander Stone watched as his wife placed the telephone receiver into the cradle. Her expression was impossible to decipher.

He'd heard only her end of the conversation. This had consisted of, "Do *not* phone me. Don't you *ever* phone me. What do you want?" And then her words sounded as if they were caught somewhere in her throat. "He's *what*? . . . When? . . . You rotten little . . . Don't you *dare* try to make me believe . . . You bastard. You filthy bastard." The last word rose towards a shriek. She clenched her fist at her mouth to contain it. He could hear a man's voice continuing to talk earnestly as Eve put down the phone. She was rigid but quivering, as if electricity were hurtling through her body and holding her in place.

"What is it?" Alex asked her.

They'd gone to bed. Eve had insisted upon it. She'd said he looked exhausted and she herself was worn down and both of them needed to get some rest if they were to make it through the coming days of funeral obligations. But their ascent to their bedroom hadn't been so much for sleep, he'd realised, as it had been a means by which they could circumvent conversation. In darkness, one of them or both of them could lie motionless, breathe deeply, feign sleep, and avoid. But they hadn't yet turned off the light when the phone rang.

Eve rose from the bed. She slipped into her dressing gown and belted it. But the belting was a savage yanking on the rope of satin, and that savage yanking gave her away.

"What's happened?" Alex repeated.

She walked to the bank of clothes cupboards against the wall. She opened the doors. She tossed a black coatdress onto the bed, turned back to the cupboard, and dropped a pair of shoes onto the floor.

Alex got out of bed himself. He took her by the shoulder. She jerked away.

"God damn it, Eve. I asked—"

"He's running the story."

"What?"

"You heard me. That shabby little cockroach is running the story. Front page. Tomorrow. He thought"—and here her features puckered with bitterness—"he thought I'd like to know in advance. To prepare myself for the other journalists."

Alex looked at the phone. "That was Luxford, then?"

"And who else?" She went to the chest and pulled on a drawer. It stuck and she wrenched it, giving a grunt. She rooted up underclothes, a slip, stockings. She threw them onto the bed alongside the coatdress. "He's played me for a fool from the very beginning. And tonight he thinks he's finished me off. But I'm not dead yet. Not by a long shot. As he shall see."

Alex tried to fit the pieces together, but one of them was clearly missing. "The story?" he repeated. "About the two of you? Blackpool?"

"For God's sake, what other story is there, Alex?" She began tugging underclothes onto her body.

"But Charlie's—"

"This isn't about Charlotte. This was never about Charlotte. Why can't you see that? Now he claims his miserable son's been kidnapped and the kidnapper's making the same demand. Isn't *that* convenient." She stalked to the bed. She shoved her arms into the coatdress, jerked its padded shoulders into position, and fumbled with its gold buttons.

Alex watched her, dazed. "Luxford's son? Kidnapped? When? Where?"

"What does it matter? Luxford's squirrelled him off somewhere and now he's using him exactly the way he planned to use Charlotte."

"What are you doing, then?"

"What does it look like I'm doing? I'm heading him off."

"How?"

She shoved her feet into her shoes and faced him squarely. "I didn't cave in when he snatched Charlotte. He intends to make the most of that now. He's going to use the whole story to make me look barbaric: Charlotte's disappearance, the demand for the story, my refusal to cooperate in the face of Luxford's desperate and heartfelt pleas that I do so. And in contrast to my barbarism, we have Luxford's sanctity: To save his son, he's going to do what I wouldn't do to save my daughter. Do you see it now, or do I have to spell it out more clearly? He's going to look like St. Christopher with the Christ Child on his shoulders and I'm going to look like Medea. *If* I don't do something to stop him. Now."

"We must phone Scotland Yard." Alex made a move to do so. "We must see if his story checks out. If the boy's really been kidnapped—"

"He hasn't been kidnapped! And it won't gain us anything to phone the police, because you can be sure Luxford's thought of every detail this time. He's hidden the little monster somewhere remote. He's phoned the police and played out the drama. And even as you and I waste time having a little chat about what he's up to and why, he's written the story and it's flying off the presses and within seven hours it'll be on the streets. Unless I do something. Which is what I fully intend to do. All right? Do you get it?''

Alex got it. He saw it in the hard line of her jaw, the rigid carriage of her body in the shoulders and backbone, the stony look of her eyes. He got it completely. What he didn't understand—about himself, about her—was what had kept him from getting it before.

He felt cast adrift. The vastness of space seemed to envelop him. From a great distance he heard himself say, ''Where are you going, Eve? What are you doing?''

''I'm pulling in chits.'' She went into the bathroom, where he could see her rapidly applying a patina of make-up to her face. She didn't use her typical precision for the activity. She merely flogged her cheeks with blusher, swatted her eyelashes with mascara, and whipped a lipstick across her lips. That done, she ran a brush through her hair and took up her spectacles from the shelf above the basin where she always laid them at night.

She returned to the bedroom. ''He's made one mistake, aside from what happened to Charlotte,'' she said. ''He's assumed I'm powerless. He's assumed I won't know where to turn and when. He's wrong about that, as he'll see within hours. If it goes my way—and believe me, it will—I'll have an injunction so tight that he won't be able to print a word of that story—or any other story—for the next fifty years. And that will finish him as he deserves to be finished.''

''I see,'' Alex said, and although the question felt pointless, an obdurate need to hear her speak at least a form of the truth compelled him to ask it. ''And what about Charlie?''

''What *about* Charlotte? She's dead. She's a victim of this mess. And the only way to give her death meaning is to make certain it wasn't in vain. Which is what it will be if I don't stop her father and stop him now.''

''For yourself,'' Alex said. ''For your career. For your future. But not really for Charlie.''

''Yes. All right. Of course. For my future. Or did you expect that I'd crawl into a hole—doing what Luxford wants me to do—because she's been killed? Is that what you wanted?''

''No,'' he said. ''I didn't want that. Just, I thought, a period of mourning.''

She took a threatening step towards him. ''Don't start on me. Don't tell me what I feel and what I don't. Don't tell me who I am.''

He raised his own hands in a gesture of surrender. ''I wouldn't do that. Not now.''

She went to the bedside table where she took up her shoulder bag. She said, "We'll talk later." She left the room.

Alex heard her footsteps on the stairs. He heard the bolts to the front door being drawn. A moment later he heard her car start. The journalists had decamped for the night, so she would have no trouble getting out of the mews. Wherever she was going, there was no one to follow her.

He lowered himself to the edge of the bed. Head in his hands, he stared at the carpet, at the sight of his feet—so white and so useless—resting on that carpet. His heart was as empty of his wife's presence as was the room and the house itself. He felt the immensity of the vacuum within him and wondered how he could have deluded himself for so long.

He'd made excuses for every warning sign she'd given him. In a few years, he'd thought, she would trust enough to open her heart. She was merely wary and this wariness was the logical outcome of the career she'd chosen, but in time she'd slough off her fears and hesitations and allow her spirit to rise to meet his. When that happened, they'd build upon the meeting of their spirits. And the building would be a family, a future, and love. He only needed patience, he'd told himself. He only needed to prove to her how deeply rooted and unswerving was his devotion. When he was able to do that, their lives would take on a newer and richer order, one that was defined by children—brothers and sisters to Charlie—for whom he and Eve would be a steady presence, enriching their lives.

It was all a lie. It was the fairytale that he told himself when he didn't want to see the reality being played out in front of him. People didn't really change. They merely dropped their personae when they considered it safe to do so, or when trying circumstances forced their exterior shells to shatter like childhood's most cherished beliefs. The Eve he loved was, in reality, no different to Father Christmas, the Tooth Fairy, the Bogey Man, or the Grim Reaper. Alex was a fantast. And, playing the role he'd designed for her, she'd been as fantastic as he'd wanted her to be. So the lie was his. As was its consequence.

Heavily, he pushed himself to his feet. Like his wife, he went to the clothes cupboard and began to dress.

—⁂—

Robin Payne drove. He headed west on the Burbage Road at a furious clip. He talked quickly, recounting his movements in the county that day. It was the bricks and the maypole, he told Barbara. Hearing about them had given him an idea, but there were so many possibilities that he wanted to check out each one of them before positing any as a site where Charlotte Bowen may have been held. This was farmland, after all, he said in dubious clarification of the point he was attempting to make. Wheat was its primary crop.

"What has wheat to do with Charlotte Bowen?" Barbara asked. "Nothing in the autopsy—"

Wait, Robin told her. Clearly, this was his moment of glory. He wanted to savour it in his own way.

He'd been everywhere, he explained. As far west as Freshford, as far south as Shaftsbury, but since he had a decent idea of what they were looking for because of those bricks and that maypole referred to by the girl—not to mention because of the wheat—the search covered an enormous expanse of territory but not an equally enormous number of individual locations. Still and all, he'd had dozens to crawl through, which is why he looked like such a grub.

"Where're we going?" Barbara asked. They hurtled through the darkness, the road unlit, trees growing thickly right up to the verge.

"Not far," was all he would reply.

As they passed through a village of brick and thatch, she told him what had occurred in London, giving him all the details that Lynley had earlier given to her. When she was finished covering everything from the fingerprint match to the search for the vagrant, she concluded with the disappearance of Leo Luxford.

Robin Payne clutched the steering wheel tightly. "Another?" he demanded. "A little boy this time? What the hell's going on?"

"He may be in Wiltshire, like Charlotte."

"What time'd he go missing?"

"After four this afternoon." She saw him frown as he worked a thought over. "What?" she asked.

"I was only thinking . . ." Robin changed down gears as they made a left turn, heading north this time on a narrower road that was posted Great Bedwyn. "The timing's not right, but if he—what's his name again?"

"Leo."

"If Leo was snatched round four, I was thinking he could be stashed out here as well. Where Charlotte was stashed. Except the snatcher would have already moved him to the county, wouldn't he, long before I even got to the spot? And I would have found him my-self—out there—" He gestured through the windscreen into the dark-ness. "Only I didn't find him." He blew out a breath. "Damn. So maybe this isn't the right place after all and I've brought you out on a midnight wild-goose chase."

"It wouldn't be the first wild-goose chase of my day," Barbara said. "But at least the company's decent this time round, so let's play it to the end."

The road began to narrow into a lane. The headlamps illuminated just the roadway, the ivy-draped trees that lined it, and the edge of the farmland that began beyond the trees. The fields were fully planted here, just as they were planted near Allington. But unlike Allington, here the hay was replaced by wheat.

As they approached another village, the lane narrowed further. The verges became inclines on which scattered houses were built at the very edge of the road. The houses multiplied into another brick and thatch village where mallards slumbered on the banks of a pond and a pub called The Swan was closing for the night. The last of its lights were extinguished as Robin and Barbara spun past, still heading north.

Robin slowed his Escort perhaps a half mile beyond this village. When he made a right turn, it was into a lane so narrow and overgrown that Barbara knew she would not have been able to distinguish it from the rest of the night-shrouded landscape had she been alone. This lane began to rise quickly towards the east, bound on one side by the glitter of wire fencing, bound on the other by a line of silver birches. The roadway was potted by craters. And the field beyond the fencing was knotted by weeds.

They came to a break in the birches, and Robin turned into it, onto a track that jostled them over boulders and through ruts. The trees were thick here but shaped by generations of wind; they loomed over the track like sailors bending into a storm.

The track ended at a fence of wire and posts. To their right, an old rail gate hung at an angle like a listing boat, and it was to this gate that Robin led Barbara, after rooting through the Escort's boot and bringing out a torch, which he handed over to her. He himself took out a camping lantern, slinging it over his arm and saying, "It's just this way."

This way led through the old gate, which Robin shoved forward roughly into a hillock of dried mud. The gate closed off a paddock in the middle of which a huge conical shape rose into the sky, looking in the darkness like a spaceship come to land. This structure was on the highest point of ground in the surrounding area, and field after field fell away from it into the black on three of its sides while on the fourth— perhaps fifty yards in the distance—the shadowy form of a crumbling building near the road they'd driven in on gave testimony to a former dwelling.

The night was perfectly silent. A chill was in the air. The heavy smell of damp earth and sheep dung hung over them like a cloud about to burst. Barbara grimaced and wished she'd at least thought to bring a jacket to ward off the cold. The smell of the place she would have to endure.

They tramped across a heavy webbing of grass to get to the structure. As they did, Barbara raised her torch to shine against its exterior. She saw the bricks. They soared up into the darkness and were capped with an ice cream mound of white metal roof. Angling upwards and downwards from the circular eave of that roof were the splintery remains of four long wooden arms the length of which had once been covered by what looked like shutters. Now there were ragged gaps in the arms where storms had torn the shutters from their housings through the years, but enough of the original shape remained to make it instantly clear what she was looking at when Barbara shot her torchlight against it.

"Windmill," she said.

"For the wheat." Robin swung his unlit lantern out in a gesture that encompassed not only the sloping fields to the south, east, and west of where they stood, but also the unlit dwelling that hulked to the north of them, back near the road. He said, "Time was, there were flour mills along the River Bedwyn, before water was diverted to make the canal. When that happened, places like this sprang up and took over. They went great guns till there was factory roller milling. Now they're falling to ruin, if someone doesn't take an interest in saving them. This one's been vacant for a good ten years. The cottage as well. That's it back by the road."

"You know this place?"

"Oh, I do." He chuckled. "And every other place within twenty miles of home where a randy little bloke of seventeen used to take his favourite bird on a summer's night. It's part of growing up in the country, Barbara. Everyone knows where to go if they want a bit of trouble. I'd expect the city is much the same, isn't it?"

She would hardly know. Neither spooning in the mooning nor snogging in the fogging had ever been among her regular pursuits. But she said, "Quite. Right."

Robin grinned that sort of grin that says mutual background information has just been exchanged and another notch has been carved in the staff of friendship. If he knew the truth about her dismal love life, Barbara thought, he'd be categorising her as the anomaly of the century, not looking at her as if they had a common history of grope-and-clutch that was differentiated only by the trysting locations. She hadn't groped and clutched with anyone as a teenager and what she'd done as an adult was so far removed from her memory that she couldn't even recall with whom the rapturous moment had been enacted. Someone called Michael? Martin? Mick? She couldn't recollect. She could remember only a great deal of cheap wine, enough cigarette smoke to pollute a small town, deafening music that sounded like Jimi Hendrix on speed—which was probably normal Jimi Hendrix now she thought of it—and floor space shared by six other couples all engaged in rapturous moments of their own. Ah, to return to the joys of one's twenties.

She followed Robin beneath a rickety gallery that ran round the exterior of the mill at first floor height. They passed two worn millstones that lay on the ground growing lichen and stopped at an arched wooden door. Robin started to open it—hand raised to press against the wood—but Barbara stopped him. She shone her torchlight against the door, examined its old panels from top to bottom, and then directed her light to a deadbolt at shoulder height. It was brass, new, and not at all worn by the weather. She felt her stomach tighten at the sight of this and what it possibly meant in contrast to the disrepaired mill itself and the cottage that had once housed its owners.

"That's what I thought," Robin said into her quiet speculation. "When I saw it, after tramping through water mills, sawmills, and every other windmill in the county, I had to take a fast pee or I thought I'd wet myself on the spot. There's more inside."

Barbara dug her hand into her shoulder bag and brought out a pair of gloves. She said, "Have you—?"

"These," he replied, and pulled some crumpled work gloves from the pocket of his jacket. When their hands were protected, Barbara nodded towards the door and Robin shoved it open, the deadbolt currently not in use. They stepped inside.

The room was brick-floored and brick-walled. It was windowless. It was tomb-cold and damp, and it smelled of must, mouse droppings, old fruit.

Barbara shuddered in the frigid air. Robin said, "Want my jacket?"

She said no as he squatted on the floor and lit the lantern he'd brought. He cranked a knob on it until it was at its fullest illumination. With its glow breaking up the darkness, there was no need of the torch. Barbara switched this off and stood it on a stack of wooden crates at the far side of the little circular room. These crates were the source of the old fruit scent. Barbara prised up one of the slats. Dozens of someone's long-forgotten apples lay wizened within.

Another, more subtle smell tinctured the air as well, and Barbara tried to identify and locate its source as Robin retreated to a narrow stairway that led to a trapdoor in the ceiling. He lowered himself to one of the steps and watched her for a moment before he said, "It's waste."

"What?"

"The other smell. It's waste."

"Where's it coming from?"

He nodded towards the other side of the crates. "It looked to me like someone was meant to . . ." He shrugged and cleared his throat, perhaps displeased with his moment of failing objectivity. "There isn't a toilet here, Barbara. There's only that."

That was a yellow plastic bucket. Barbara saw the sad little mound of faeces inside. It lay in a pool of liquid from which rose the acrid scent of urine.

Barbara blew out a breath on the words, "Right. All right." And then she began to look round the floor.

She found the blood in the centre, on a brick that was slightly out of line with its brothers, and when she raised her head from the drops and looked at Robin, she saw that he'd found the blood on his earlier visit as well. She said, "What else?"

He said, "The crates. Have a look. The right side. Third from the bottom. You might want more light."

She used the torch. She saw what he'd seen. A wisp of three fibres had become caught in a splinter at the edge of one of the crates. She bent to these, held the light closer to them. She couldn't be sure because of the shadows beyond the crates, so she took a tissue from her shoulder bag and held it behind them for contrast. They were green, the same muddy green of Charlotte's school uniform.

She felt her pulse increase, but she told herself not to count any chickens. After the dovecote in Ford and the garage in Coate, she wasn't up for taking any hasty decisions. She looked back at Robin.

"On the tape," she said. "She mentioned a maypole."

"Follow me. Bring the torch."

He climbed the stairway and pushed against the trapdoor in the ceiling. When Barbara followed him, he extended his hand and pulled her up behind him into the first floor chamber of the mill.

Barbara looked about, quelling a sneeze. Her eyes watered in reaction to the amount of dust in the chamber, and she rubbed them against the arm of her pullover. When Robin said, "I may have bollixed up some of the evidence round here," she shot the torchbeam along the line of his arm and saw the footprints: small and large, child and adult. They overlapped each other and smeared each other. As a result, it was impossible to tell if one child or ten—or one adult or ten—had been in the room. He said, "I got myself in a lather when I saw the fibres and blood down below, and I charged up here straightaway. I didn't think about the floor until it was too late. Sorry."

Barbara noted that the floorboards were so warped that none of them had really taken a decent print. They displayed the shape of shoe soles, but not their markings. She said, "Don't worry about it. They don't look very useful."

She directed her beam from the floor to the circular wall. To the left of the trapdoor, there was a single window that had been boarded up; beneath it lay a pile of old tools the likes of which Barbara had never seen before. Some were fashioned from metal and some from wood. These were the old dressing tools, Robin said. They were used on the millstones, which were a floor above them. That's where the grinding had been done.

Dusty cogs lay near the tools, as did two wooden pulleys and a coil of rope. Above them, the brick wall was speckled white with lichen, and damp seemed to cling to the air. At the height of the ceiling not far above their heads, an enormous notched wheel was suspended on its side. Part of the mechanism for running the mill, this was the great spur wheel and it was centred between two matching gears. Running through a hole in this wheel, from the floor they stood upon up through the ceiling and presumably to the very top of the windmill, was a fat iron pillar that was knobby with rust.

"Charlotte's maypole," Barbara said as she shone her beam along its length.

"That's what I thought," Robin said. "It's called the main shaft. Here. Look up."

He took her arm and led her to stand directly beneath the great spur wheel. He closed his hand over hers and steadied the torchlight onto one of the wheel's cogs. Barbara could see that the cog bore a coating of a gelatinous-looking substance that had the appearance of cold honey.

"Grease," Robin said. After making sure she had seen it, he lowered her arm and directed the light onto the spot where the main shaft was attached to the floor. The same substance lacquered this joining point. As Robin squatted by it and indicated a section, Barbara saw what had made him come racing home to find her, what had made him ignore his mother's meaningful dialogue about his future bride. This was more important than a future bride. There were fingerprints in the old axle grease at the main shaft's base. And they belonged to a child.

"Bloody hell," Barbara murmured.

Robin got to his feet. His eyes were anxiously fastened on her face.

She said, "I think you may have done it, Robin." And she felt herself smiling for the first time all day. She said, "Sod it all. I think you've gone and bloody *done* it, you twit."

Robin smiled but looked abashed by the compliment. Still, he said eagerly, "Have I? You think?"

"I definitely think." She squeezed his arm and allowed herself a quick hoot of excitement. "Okay, London," she exulted. "This is it." Robin laughed at her exhilaration and she joined him in laughing and shot a fist into the air. Then she sobered and guided herself back to her role as head of the team. She said, "We'll need the crime scene boys out here. Tonight."

"Three times in one day? They're not going to be happy with that, Barbara."

"Bugger them. I'm happy as hell. What about you?"

"Bugger them," Robin agreed.

They descended the stairs. Beneath them, Barbara saw a crumpled blue blanket. She inspected this. She drew it out from beneath the stairs, and as she pulled upon it, something rattled from it onto the floor. She said, "Hang on," and bent to inspect the small object that lay in a trough of mortar between two bricks. It was a figurine, a tiny hedgehog, ridged on the back, with a pointed snout. It was one-sixth the size of her palm, perfect to be clutched in a child's small hand.

Barbara picked it up and showed it to Robin. "We'll need to see if the mother can ID this."

She went back to the blanket. The coarse material was damp, she noted, damper than the room's moisture might have produced. And the idea of damp, of moisture, of water, quelled her spirits and reminded her of the manner in which Charlotte Bowen had died. There was a piece to the puzzle that remained elusive.

She turned back to Robin. "Water."

"What about it?"

"She was drowned. Is there water nearby?"

"The canal's not far and the river's—"

"She drowned in tap water, Robin. A bathtub. A basin. A toilet. We're looking for tap water." Barbara thought of what they'd seen so far. "What about the cottage? The one near the road. How ruined is it? Is there water there?"

"I expect it's long been turned off."

"But it had running water when someone lived there, didn't it?"

"That was years ago." He removed his work gloves and stowed them in the pocket of his jacket.

"So it could have been turned on—even for a short time—if someone found the main valve on the property."

"Could have been. But it's probably well water, this far from the village. Wouldn't that show up different to water from the tap?"

It would, of course it would. And the fact of that flaming tap water in Charlotte Bowen's body just complicated matters another degree. "There's no tap in here, then?"

"In the mill?" He shook his head.

"Sod," Barbara muttered. What had the kidnapper actually done? she wondered. If this was the site where Charlotte Bowen had been held, then surely she'd been held here alive. The faeces, the urine, the blood, and the fingerprints all gave mute testimony to that. And even if that putative evidence of her presence could be explained away through another means, even if the child had been dead when she was brought to this site, what would have been the point of risking being seen in the act of carrying her body into the mill to stow it for a few days? No, no. She was alive when she was here. Perhaps for days, perhaps only for hours. But she was alive. And if that was the case, then somewhere close by was a source of tap water that had been used to drown the girl.

Barbara said, "Go back to the village, Robin. There was a call box outside the pub, wasn't there? Phone for the scene-of-crime team. Tell them to bring lights, torches, the works. I'll wait here."

He looked to the door, to the darkness beyond it. He said, "I'm not keen on that plan. I don't like your being here by yourself. If there's a killer round—"

"I can cope," she said. "Go on. Make the call."

"Come with me."

"I need to secure the scene. That door was open. Anyone can come along and—"

"My point exactly. It's not safe. And you've not come out here armed, have you?"

He knew she wasn't armed. No detective was armed. He wasn't armed himself. She said, "I'll be fine. Whoever took Charlotte has Leo Luxford right now. And since Leo isn't here, I think it's safe to assume that Charlotte's killer isn't here either. So go make that phone call and come right back."

He mulled this over. She was about to give him a helpful shove towards the door, when he said, "Right, then. Keep the lantern lit. Give me the torch. If you hear anyone—"

"I'll get one of the dressing tools and pound him a good one. And I'll keep him pounded till you get back."

He grinned. He headed for the door. He paused for a moment

before turning back to her. He said, "This sounds a bit out of line, I suppose, but—"

"What?" She was immediately wary. Having Sergeant Stanley out of line was enough. She didn't need Robin Payne to join him. But the constable's words—and the way he said them—surprised her.

"It's just that . . . You're not exactly like other women, are you?"

She'd known for some time that she wasn't like other women. She'd also known that what she *was* like wasn't particularly attractive to men. So she looked him over, wondering what he was getting at and not completely certain she wanted the point clarified.

"What I mean is, you're rather special, aren't you?"

Not as special as Celia popped into Barbara's mind. But what dropped off her tongue was "Yeah. So are you."

He watched her across the width of the windmill. She swallowed against a sudden lump of dread. She didn't want to think of what she suddenly feared. She didn't want to think of why she feared it. She said, "Go make that call. It's getting late and we've hours of work ahead of us here."

Robin said, "Right." Still, he hesitated a long moment in the doorway before he turned away and headed back towards his car.

The cold swept in. With Robin's departure it seemed to seep outward from the walls. Barbara wrapped her arms round herself and slapped her hands against her shoulders. She found that her breathing had become erratic and she stepped outside the door to take in the night air.

Forget it, she told herself. Maintain a grip. Get to the bottom of this case, tie up loose ends, and head back to London as soon as possible. But don't—do *not*—engage in idle fantasy.

The point was water. Ordinary water. Tap water. In Charlotte Bowen's lungs. That's what she ought to be considering at the moment and that's what she was determined to do.

Where had the girl been drowned? Bathtub, wash basin, kitchen sink, toilet. But which sink? What toilet? Which bathtub? Where? If every clue they'd uncovered was tied to London, then the tap water was somehow tied to London as well, if not geographically then personally. Whoever had used tap water to drown Charlotte was someone who was also associated with London where she had been taken. The principals were her mother—with her prison site in Wiltshire—and Alistair Harvie—with his constituency here. But Harvie was a blind road; he had to be. As for her mother . . . What kind of monster would arrange the kidnapping and the murder of her only child? Besides, according to Lynley, Eve Bowen was poised on the brink of losing everything now that Luxford was going to run the story. And Luxford—

Barbara drew in a quick breath at the sudden recollection of a single fact from among the many which Lynley had given her over the phone a few hours before. She strode away from the windmill, into the paddock. She moved out of the carpet of light that poured forth from the windmill's door. Of course, she thought. Dennis Luxford.

In the darkness she could just make out the downward slope of fields to the south of the windmill and beyond them the distant rise of land again, above which hung a speckled-bright mantle of stars. To the west the scattered lights of the nearby village sequinned the darkness. To the north lay the weed-knotted fields they'd driven along to arrive at this place. And somewhere nearby—she knew it, she believed it, and she would prove it to herself as soon as Robin returned—sat Baverstock School for Boys.

This was the connection she was looking for. This was the tie that bound London to Wiltshire. And this was the unbreakable bond between Dennis Luxford and the death of his child.

24

LYNLEY HADN'T REALIZED how much Helen had become part of the fabric of his life until he had breakfast alone the next morning. He'd skipped breakfast entirely on the previous day, thereby avoiding a prolonged and solitary engagement over eggs and toast. But since he'd skipped dinner as well, he was feeling light-headed by midnight. He could have done with a snack at that point, but he wasn't up to rustling round the kitchen. He decided instead just to pass out in bed and take care of his need for sustenance in the morning. So he left a note in the kitchen—"Breakfast. For one."—and Denton had complied with his usual dedication to Lynley's nutrition.

Half a dozen serving dishes were lined up on the sideboard in the dining room. Two kinds of juice stood ready in jugs. Cornflakes, Weetabix, and muesli were arranged next to a bowl and another jug of milk. Denton's strong suit was that he always followed directions. His weakness was not knowing when to stop. Lynley could never decide if the younger man was a frustrated actor or an even more frustrated set designer.

After a bowl of cereal—he chose the Weetabix—he dipped into the serving dishes and helped himself to eggs, grilled tomatoes, mushrooms, and bangers. It was not until he sat down with this second course that he became aware of how uncomfortably silent the entire house was. He ignored the illusion of claustrophobia that the silence produced. He gave his attention to *The Times*. He was wending his way through the editorial page—two columns and seven letters on the hypocrisy of the Tory Party's Recommitment to Basic British Values as reflected in the recent actions of the East Norfolk MP and his Paddington rent boy—when he realised he'd read the same castigatory paragraph three times without the slightest idea of its contents.

He pushed the newspaper away. There'd be plenty more to read when he got his hands on this morning's edition of *The Source*. He raised his head and looked at what he'd been avoiding since he'd entered the dining room: Helen's empty chair.

He hadn't phoned her last night. He could have done. He might have used as an excuse the fact that he'd seen St. James and made his apologies for the row he'd provoked among them on Monday afternoon. But there had been a strong emotion underlying the activity Helen had been engaged in on Monday night—that winnowing of utterly useless clothing for the poor of Africa—and if he spoke to her, he was fairly certain that he'd learn exactly what the emotion was. Since her current frame of mind and heart had obviously arisen from his lashing out at her and at his friends, Lynley knew that to approach her now was to run the risk of hearing something he didn't wish to hear.

Avoiding her was sheer emotional cowardice, and he knew it. He was attempting to pretend all was right with his world in the hope that pretending would make it so. Skipping breakfast yesterday had been part of the pretence. Better to rush off with his mind fully occupied by details of the investigation than to find his heart clouded by the fear that through his bullheaded stupidity, he may have lost or at least irreparably damaged what he prized most. Giving His human creations the ability to love had to be the Divinity's most ingenious act of self-amusement, Lynley thought. Let them fall for each other and then drive each other mad, He must have schemed. What a bloody good laugh it will be to watch the chaos that ensues when I get the man-woman chemistry just right.

Chaos had certainly ensued in his life, Lynley admitted. From the moment eighteen months ago when he'd realised he'd come to love Helen, he'd felt like Crane's man in pursuit of the horizon. The more he tried to reach his destination, the endlessly farther it seemed to recede.

He pushed away from the dining table and crumpled up the linen napkin as Denton came into the room. "Were you expecting the Micawbers for breakfast?" Lynley enquired pleasantly.

Typically the allusion was lost on the younger man. If it hadn't been created by Andrew Lloyd Webber for consumption in the West End, it simply didn't exist. "Pardon?" Denton said.

"Nothing," Lynley said.

"Dinner tonight, then?"

Lynley nodded towards the sideboard. "Reheat that."

Denton saw the dawn. "Did I cook too much? It was just that I didn't know for certain if *one* really meant *one*." He directed a wary look at Helen's chair. "I mean, I did get your note, but I thought Lady Helen might actually . . ." He somehow managed to look earnest, regretful, and concerned simultaneously. "You know. Women."

"Clearly not as well as you know them," Lynley said. He left Denton to clear away the remains. He took himself off to New Scotland Yard.

Havers phoned him as he was negotiating his way through the commuters, the suitcase laden travellers, and the double-decker tour coaches that clogged every artery near Victoria Station. They'd found the probable location where Charlotte Bowen had been held, she reported in a voice that attempted to sound casual but didn't quite manage to carry it off without giving a hint of the pride she felt in her achievement. It was a windmill not far from Great Bedwyn and, more important, less than a mile from the Kennet and Avon Canal. Not the same spot along the canal where the body had been dropped, mind you, but with a narrow-boat hired expressly for the purpose, the killer could have stowed her body below deck, putted happily along to Allington, dumped her in the reeds, and gone on his way. Or, conversely, he could have driven her there because it wasn't that far and Robin had pointed out . . .

"Robin?" Lynley asked. He braked to avoid hitting a mohawk-haired boy with a ring through his left nipple and a push-chair curiously draped with black netting.

"Robin Payne. Remember? The DC I'm working with? I'm staying at his—"

"Oh yes. Right. That Robin." He hadn't remembered. He'd been too consumed with his own affairs to remember. But he remembered now. And from the lilt of Havers' voice, he found himself wondering what, other than the identity of a killer, was in the process of being detected in Wiltshire.

She went on to tell him that she'd left the crime scene team to go over the windmill. She'd be returning there as soon as she ate. She hadn't eaten yet because she'd got in so late and she hadn't slept much on the previous night and she thought she deserved a bit of a lie-in, so . . .

"Havers," Lynley told her, "carry on. You're doing fine."

He wished he could have said the same for himself.

At New Scotland Yard, Dorothea Harriman generously imparted the news in passing that AC Hillier was on the prowl, so Detective

Inspector Lynley might want to keep his head low until something other than the Bowen case came up to occupy the Assistant Commissioner's attention. Lynley said to her curiously, "You know what I'm working on, Dee? I thought all this was top secret." To which she replied serenely, "Nothing's secret in the ladies' loo."

Brilliant, he thought.

The top of his desk was a landslide of accumulating information. Centred among the folders, reports, faxes, and telephone messages was a copy of this morning's *Source*. Appended to it was a note in Winston Nkata's microscopic script. Lynley put on his spectacles and read it: *Ready for the shit to hit?* He detached the note and looked at the tabloid's front page. From what he could see, Dennis Luxford had followed the kidnapper's instructions to the letter, writing the article without sparing either himself or Eve Bowen. He'd accompanied it with relevant dates and time frames. And he'd associated it with the kidnapping and murder of Bowen's daughter. He wrote about taking responsibility for Charlotte's death by being reluctant to reveal the truth before this moment, but he made no mention of what had prompted him to write the story: the abduction of his son. He was doing everything possible to ensure the boy's safety. Or so it seemed.

This would certainly escalate the media frenzy that was feeding upon Eve Bowen. It brought Luxford into the spotlight, true, but the tabloids' interest in him would be small potatoes compared to their desire to have at her. That consideration—what Eve Bowen was going to face and how accurately she had predicted having to face it—stirred disquiet in Lynley. He set *The Source* aside and began to go through the other material on his desk.

He scanned the autopsy report that Havers had faxed him from Wiltshire. He read what he already knew: The drowning had not been accidental. The child had been rendered unconscious first, so that she would die without a struggle. The substance that had been used to drug her was a benzodiazepine derivative called diazepam. Its common name was Valium. A prescription drug, it was sometimes used as a sedative, sometimes used as a tranquilliser. In either case, enough of it in the bloodstream produced the same effect: unconsciousness.

Lynley highlighted the drug's identification in the report and set the fax aside. Valium, he thought, and he riffled through the other paperwork before him, looking for the forensic report he'd ordered the previous day at the Marylebone squat. He found it attached to a message requesting that he phone someone named Figaro at SO7, the forensic science lab across the river. As he punched in the number, he read the attached report from the lab's chemistry division. They'd completed their analysis of the small blue chip that Lynley had found in the kitchen of the squat on George Street. As he had suspected, it was indeed a drug. And it was diazepam, they concluded, a benzodiazepine derivative with the common name Valium. Bingo, Lynley thought.

A woman's voice came on the line, saying brusquely, "Figaro." And when Lynley identified himself, she went on. "Exactly what kind of strings are you pulling over there, Inspector Lynley? We've a six-week backload of work sitting here and when the goodies from that Porsche came through the lab yesterday, we were told to move them to the head of the class. I had people working here all night."

"The Home Secretary's interested," Lynley said.

"Hepton?" She gave a sardonic laugh. "He'd do better to be interested in the rise in crime, wouldn't he? Those National Front yobbos were raising hell outside my mum's house last night. In Spitalfields, this is."

"If I see him, I'll mention it," Lynley said. He added, hoping to move her along, "I'm returning your call, Miss—"

"Doctor," she said.

"Sorry. Doctor Figaro."

"Right. Let's see." He heard the slapping sound of slick-covered journals falling on each other, then the crinkling noise of papers being turned. "Porsche," she muttered. "Where did I . . . Here . . . Let me just . . ."

Lynley sighed, removed his spectacles, and rubbed his eyes. They felt tired already and his day was just beginning. God knew what they'd feel like fifteen hours from now.

As Dr. Figaro continued to rustle on her end of the line, Winston Nkata appeared in the doorway. He gave a thumbs-up sign—apparently in reference to whatever was contained in the leatherbound notebook he held open in his palm—and Lynley motioned him over to a chair.

Figaro said into his ear, "Right. We've a match on the hairs."

"Hairs?" Lynley asked.

"From the Porsche, Inspector. You wanted it swept, didn't you? Well, it was swept, and we picked up some hair in the back. We've got blond and brown. And the brown is a match for the hair from the Bowen house."

"What hair from the Bowen house?"

Nkata held up his hand. He mouthed, "The kid's. I fetched it."

"*What* hair . . . ?" Figaro sounded indignant. "Who's running the show over there these days? We were pounding our skulls for you blokes till two in the morning and now you're telling me—"

Lynley interrupted with what he hoped was an adequate explanation of how the hair had momentarily slipped his mind. Figaro sounded partially placated, which was enough for him. He rang off and said to Nkata, "Good initiative, Winston. Again."

"We do aim to please," the constable said. "Was it a match for the kid's, then? In Luxford's car?"

"It was."

"Makes things interesting, that. You think they're a plant? Along with the specs?"

It was a definite possibility. But Lynley disliked thinking in the direction that Dennis Luxford had yesterday insisted he think. "Let's keep our options open." He nodded at the notebook. "What do you have?"

"Best news there is."

"Which is what?"

"A phone call from Bayswater. It just came in."

"Bayswater?" Nothing seemed less likely than a phone call from Bayswater to provide the best news of his day. "What's this about?"

Nkata smiled. "How'd you like to have a natter with that tramp?"

—⁕—

Contrary to St. James's speculations about the vagrant, there'd been no disguise. The man, as he'd been described and sketched, was absolutely real. His name was Jack Beard, and when Lynley and Nkata got to him, he wasn't happy about being detained at the nearest police station to the Bayswater soup kitchen where he'd gone to take his morning meal. He'd been tracked there from a doss-house in Paddington, where a single viewing of the sketch in the hands of a detective constable had prompted a quick identification from a reception clerk eager to rid the building of the noxious police presence. He'd said, "Why, that's old Jack Beard, that is," and described what he knew of Jack's daily routine. This apparently consisted of prowling through dustbins for the salable odd bit and dropping in on charitable organisations for meals.

In the police station's interview room, the first thing Jack Beard declared to Lynley was, "I ain' done nothing to no one. Wha's this about, then? Who are you, Mr. Fancy Suit? I need me a fag."

Nkata nicked three cigarettes from the duty sergeant and handed one over to the tramp. Jack puffed at it hungrily, holding it to his mouth, pinched between a scabby index finger and a black-nailed thumb as if someone might take it away from him. He looked suspiciously from Lynley to Nkata, from beneath a fringe of greasy grey hair.

"I fought for Queen and country," he said. "Likes of you can't say as much, I d'say. What'd you want with me?"

"We've been told you go through dustbins," Lynley said.

"Anything in a dustbin's a toss-out. I c'n keep wha' I find. Ain't no law says I can't. I been going through bins since twelve years back. I never caused no trouble. I never took nothing but were in the bin."

"There's no question of that. You're not in trouble, Jack."

Jack's eyes shifted between the police officers again. "So wha's this, then? I got stuff to do. I got my regular route to be walking."

"Does your regular route take you into Marylebone?"

Nkata opened his notebook. Jack looked wary. He puffed locomotively at his cigarette. "Wha' if it does? Ain' no law says I can't look in dustbins wherever they be. You show me the law says I can't look where I wants."

"In Cross Keys Close?" Lynley asked. "Do you check the dustbins there as well?"

"Cross Keys wha'? I dunno the place."

Nkata unfolded a copy of the sketch that had been made of Jack Beard. He placed it on the table in front of the man. He said, "There's a writer-bloke living in Cross Keys Close who says you been there, Jack. Wednesday last, he says, you were going through the dustbins. He saw you good enough to describe to our sketch artist. This look like you, man? What d'you think?"

"I dunno the place. I'm telling you honest. I dunno no Cross Keys. I didn' do nothing. You got to let me out."

Lynley read the confusion on the old tramp's face. The pungent smell of fear was on him. He said again, "Jack, you're not in trouble. This isn't about you. A young girl was kidnapped from the area round Cross Keys Close on Wednesday last, not so long after you were there. We'd—"

"I didn't take no girl!" Jack crushed his cigarette against the table top. He tore the filter from a second cigarette and lit it. He swallowed and his eyes—yellow where they should have been white—watered suddenly. He said, "I did my time. Five years I did. I been clean since."

"You've been to prison?"

"Break'n'enter. Five years in the Scrubs. But I learnt my lesson. I never been back. But my head's no good and I forget easy so I never worked much. I do the dustbins now. Tha's all I do."

Lynley sifted through what he'd said and found the cogent point. He said to Nkata, "Constable, tell Jack about Cross Keys Close, please."

Nkata, apparently, had also seen the problem. He took back the sketch, and as he returned it to his jacket pocket, he said, "It's a squir-relly group of mews, this place. Maybe ten yards from Marylebone High Street, off Marylebone Lane near a fish and chips shop called the Golden Hind. There's a street nearby—a cul de sac—where the backs of offices look down on a pub. This's on the corner where the mews begin, place called the Prince Albert. Got some picnic tables out on the pave-ment. And the dustbins—"

"Prince Albert, you say?" Jack Beard asked. "You say Prince Al-bert? I know the place."

"So you were there?" Lynley asked. "On last Wednesday?"

"May've been."

Lynley thought through their facts for something to jog the tramp's memory. He said, "The man who gave us your description said that you were rousted from the area by a constable, probably a special constable. Does that help?"

It did. Jack's face showed umbrage. "I never been rousted before," he declared. "Not there. Not nowhere. Never once."

"You go there regularly?"

" 'Course I do. It's part o' me regular route, that spot. I don't make no noise. I keep the rubbish neat. I never bother no one. I take my bags and when I find something I c'n flog somewheres—"

Lynley cut in. The tramp's daily economic machinations were not of interest to him. The events of that particular Wednesday were. He produced Charlotte's photograph, saying, "This is the girl who was abducted. Did you see her on Wednesday last, Jack?"

Jack squinted at the picture. He took it from Lynley and held it at arm's length. He studied it for a good thirty seconds, all the time puff-ing at his defiltered cigarette. "Don't recall 'er," he said. And now that he realised he was off the hook of the police's interest, he became more expansive. "Don't ever get much out of the bins in that spot. Just the odd bit now and again. Bent fork. Broke spoon. Old vase with a crack'n it. Little statue or something. Sort o' rubbish gen'rally needs fixing before I c'n flog it. But I always go coz I like to keep my rounds reg'lar, just like the postman and I never bother no one and don't never look like I mean anyone harm. I never had no trouble there before."

"Just this one Wednesday?"

"Tha's it. Tha's right. It was like . . ." Jack fingered his nose as he sought the appropriate metaphor. He removed a flake of tobacco from his tongue, examined it on the end of his fingernail, and shoved it up onto his gums. He said, "It was like someone wanted me out o' there, mister. Like someone called the cops to roust me just to make sure I was dead gone before something pecul'ar went down."

—m—

Lynley and Nkata watched the constable shut the door on the panda car and whisk Jack Beard away, back to his interrupted morning meal in Bayswater where, the vagrant told them, he was expected to "help with the washing up as a payback for the chuff, see."

Nkata said, "He's not our man, then. You didn't want his dabs, just to make sure?"

"We don't need his fingerprints," Lynley replied. "He's done time. They're on file. If he was a match for the prints we've lifted, we'd have already been told."

Lynley thought about what the old man had told them. If someone had phoned the police to have him removed from Cross Keys Close prior to Charlotte Bowen's abduction, then it had to be someone who'd been watching the area, who'd been loitering in the area, or who lived in the area. He realised which possibility was most likely, and he recalled what St. James had told him on the previous night about Charlotte's nickname and who had used it. He said, "Winston, what do we hear from Belfast? Have the RUC reported back yet?"

"Not yet. Think I should shake their tree?"

"I do," Lynley said. "But shake it from in the car. We need to pay a visit to Marylebone."

—m—

The location of Baverstock School for Boys didn't turn out to be the linchpin of the investigation, as Barbara had hoped it might. It was in the vicinity, true. But its land didn't border on the windmill's land, contrary to her speculations. Instead, it stood just outside Wootton Cross, on a vast acreage that had once been the estate of a wheat baron.

Robin had informed her as much on their way back to Wootton Cross late the previous night. They were going to pass right by the Baverstock gates, he'd told her, and he pointed them out—immense wrought iron structures that hung open between two falcon-topped brick pillars—as they spun by. He'd said, "Where does Baverstock fit into the picture?"

"I don't know." She sighed and lit a cigarette. "I had a thought. . . . One of our London suspects is an old boy from Baverstock. Luxford. The newsman."

"He's a real toff, then," Robin had said. "You don't get into Baverstock unless you've got a scholarship or your blood type's right."

He sounded the way she usually felt about such places. She said, "Your blood wasn't, I take it?"

"I went to primary school in the village. Then to the comprehensive in Marlborough."

"No old Baverstock boys on your family tree?"

He glanced her way. He said simply, "There's no one at all on my tree, Barbara. If you know what I mean."

She did indeed. She couldn't have lived in England all her life without knowing what he meant. Her own relations were about as socially consequential as dust motes, although not quite so numerous. She said, "My family go back to the Magna Carta and beyond, but not in any way you'd want to shout about. No one could pull himself up by his bootstraps because no one had boots till the turn of the century."

Robin chuckled and gave her another glance. It was hard to ignore that this one was admiring. "You sound like being no one is nothing to you."

"To my way of looking at it, you're no one only if you think you're no one."

They'd gone their separate ways at Lark's Haven, Robin into the sitting room, where his mother was waiting up for him despite the hour, Barbara up the stairs to collapse into bed. But not before she heard Corrine saying, "Robbie, Celia was only here tonight because—" and Robin interrupting with, "There'll be no discussion about Celia. Keep your mind on Sam Corey and off of me." Corrine countered with a trembly, "But little chappie," to which Robin curtly responded, "That's Sam, Mum, isn't it?"

Barbara fell asleep wondering how much Robin must bless the deliverance that Sam Corey's engagement to his mother promised him. She was still thinking this the next morning when she concluded her call to Lynley and found the three of them—Sam Corey, Corrine, and Robin—in the dining room.

Corrine and Sam had their heads together over a tabloid. Corrine was saying, "Just imagine it, Sammy. My goodness. My *goodness*," in her wheezy voice. Sam was holding one of her hands and rubbing her back as if to assist with her breathing, and all the time he shook his head somberly at what the tabloid was revealing. It was *The Source*, Barbara saw. Sam and Corrine were reading the story that Dennis Luxford had written to save his son.

Robin was stacking breakfast dishes onto a tray. When he carried the tray into the kitchen, Barbara followed. Better to eat at the sink, if necessary, than to swallow down breakfast in the presence of lovebirds who'd probably prefer to be left on their own.

Robin stood at the cooker where he was heating a pan, presumably for her eggs. His face, Barbara noted, was shuttered and withdrawn, not at all the face he'd worn when they'd exchanged their confidences on the previous night. His words seemed to explain the change in him. "He's run the story, then. That bloke Luxford in London. D'you think that'll be enough to free the boy?"

"Don't know," Barbara admitted.

He knifed up a wedge of butter and flopped it into the pan. Barbara had intended to have only a bowl of cereal—she was nearly two hours behind schedule because of her lie-in—but it was rather pleasant to watch Robin making breakfast for her, so she changed her plans and vowed to make up for the time loss by chewing *allegro*.

Robin increased the heat and watched the butter melting. "Do we keep looking for the boy?" he asked. "Or do we hold off and see what happens next?"

"I want to have a look round that windmill in daylight."

"D'you want company? I mean, you know where the mill is now, but I could always . . ." He gestured with the egg turner to complete his sentence. Barbara wondered what that sentence might have been. I could always show you round? I could always hang about? I could always be there if you need me? She didn't need him though. She had done a fairly nice job of not needing anyone for years. And she told herself that she very much wanted to keep things that way. He seemed to read this on her face, because he graciously gave her an opening to continue avoiding indefinitely, saying, "Or I could start checking on the narrow-boat rentals. If he took the girl from the windmill to Allington via the canal, he's going to have needed a boat."

"It's something that should be dealt with," Barbara said.

"I'll see to it, then." He broke two eggs into the pan and wielded salt and pepper over them. He turned down the heat and popped two pieces of bread into the toaster. He seemed, Barbara thought, unaffected by her unspoken desire to see to her day's work alone, and she found herself feeling a small but insidious spider of disappointment attempting to spin a web against her skin. She brushed it off. There was work to be done. One child was dead and another was missing. Her fancies were secondary to that.

She left him doing the washing up. He'd asked her if she needed a refresher on the route to the windmill, but she was certain she could find it without written directions. She took a minor curiosity-inspired detour on the way, however, and turned in through the gates at Baverstock School for Boys. Baverstock, she realised as she drove under the great canopy of beeches that framed the drive, was probably the main source of employment for the village of Wootton Cross. The school was enormous, and it would require an equally enormous staff to run it. Not only teachers, but groundsmen, caretakers, cooks, launderers, matrons, and the lot. As Barbara took in the pleasing arrangement of buildings, playing fields, shrubbery, and gardens, she felt once again the stubborn nudging of an instinct that told her that this school was somehow involved in what had happened to Charlotte Bowen and to Leo Luxford. It was too coincidental that Baverstock—Dennis Luxford's own school—should be so beguilingly close to the site where his daughter had been held.

She decided a modified prowl was in order. She parked near a lofty-roofed structure of random rubble that she took for the chapel. Across a swept gravel walk from this, a small neatly painted wooden sign pointed the way to the headmaster's office. That'll do, Barbara thought.

Classes were obviously in progress, since there were no boys to be seen other than one lone black-robed young man who came out the door to the headmaster's office as Barbara went in it. He clutched schoolbooks under his arm, said, "Pardon," politely, and hurried towards a low doorway across the quad out of which Barbara could hear a group of less-than-enthusiastic voices chanting the multiples of nine.

The headmaster couldn't see the detective sergeant from London, Barbara was told by his secretary. The headmaster, in fact, wasn't on the school grounds. He wouldn't be in for most of the day, so if the detective sergeant from London wished to make an appointment for later in the week . . . The secretary poised a pencil over the headmaster's engagement diary and waited for Barbara to respond.

Barbara wasn't exactly sure *how* to respond since she wasn't exactly sure what had brought her to Baverstock in the first place other than the vague and unsettling feeling that the school was somehow involved. For the first time since coming to Wiltshire, she fleetingly wished that Inspector Lynley were with her. He never seemed to have any vague or unsettling feelings about anything—other than Helen Clyde, that is, and about her he appeared to have nothing *but* vague and unsettling feelings—and faced with the headmaster's secretary, Barbara realised that she could have done with a good Inspector-Sergeant confab before sauntering into this office without an idea in the world as to what she'd do once she got here.

She chose as her opening gambit, "I'm investigating the murder of Charlotte Bowen, the girl who was found in the canal on Sunday," and she was pleased to see that she had the secretary's full regard at once: The pencil lowered to the engagement diary and the secretary—whose name plate identified her merely as Portly, an inaccuracy if there ever was one since she was skeletally thin, not to mention at least seventy years old—became all attention.

"This girl was the daughter of one of your old boys," Barbara went on. "A bloke called Dennis Luxford."

"Dennis?" Portly put heavy emphasis on the first syllable. Barbara took this as indication that the name had rung a bell.

"He must have been here some thirty years ago," Barbara prompted.

"Thirty years ago, nonsense," Portly said. "He was here last month."

—m—

When he heard footsteps coming up the stairs, St. James raised his head from a set of crime scene photographs, which he was examining to refresh his memory prior to an appearance at the Old Bailey. He heard Helen's voice. She was saying to Cotter, "I *could* do with a coffee. And bless you a thousand times for asking. I slept right through breakfast, so anything that'll see me at least partway to lunch . . ." Cotter's voice from below said that coffee would be on its way to her forthwith.

Helen came into the lab. Curiously, St. James glanced at the wall clock. She said, "I know. You were expecting me ages ago. I'm sorry."

"Rough night?"

"No night. I couldn't sleep, so I didn't set the alarm. I thought I hardly needed it since I wasn't doing much more than staring at the ceiling." She dropped her shoulder bag onto the worktable and immediately took off her shoes. She padded over to join him. "Except that's not quite true, is it? I did set the alarm, originally. But when I still wasn't sleeping by three in the morning, I simply unset it. For psychological reasons. What are we working on?"

"The Pancord case."

"That terrible creature who killed his grandmother?"

"Allegedly, Helen. We're on the defence's side."

"That poor socially deprived and fatherless child who is wrongly accused of tapping a hammer against an eighty-year-old woman's skull?"

"The Pancord case, yes." St. James went back to the pictures, using his magnifying glass. He said, "What psychological reasons?"

"Hmmm?" Helen had begun going through a stack of reports and correspondence, preparatory to organising the former and answering the latter. "For unsetting the alarm, you mean? It was supposed to set my mind free of the anxiety of knowing I *had* to fall asleep within a certain period of time in order to get enough rest before the alarm went off. Since anxiety keeps one awake in the first place, I thought that if I relieved myself of at least one source of anxiety, I could fall asleep. I did, of course. Only I didn't wake up."

"So the method has dubious merits."

"Darling Simon, it has no merits at all. I still didn't fall asleep before five. And then, of course, it was asking altogether too much of my body to waken itself by half past seven."

St. James set the magnifying glass next to a copy of the DNA study done on semen from the scene of the crime. Things did not look good for Mr. Pancord. He said, "What other sources have you?"

"What?" Helen looked up from the correspondence. Her smooth hair swung back from her shoulders with the movement, and St. James could see how the skin beneath her eyes looked puffy.

He said, "Turning off the alarm was supposed to relieve one source of anxiety. But you've others?"

"Oh, just the usual psychic neuritis and neuralgia." She made the comment airily enough, but he hadn't known her more than fifteen years for nothing.

He said, "Tommy was here last night, Helen."

"Was he." She said it as a statement. She attended to a letter written on vellum. She read through it before looking up and saying with reference to its contents, "A symposium in Prague, Simon. Will you accept? It's not till December, but the timeline's short if you want to prepare a paper to deliver."

"Tommy made his apologies," St. James said steadily, as if she hadn't been trying to divert him. "To me, that is. He would have spoken to Deborah as well, but I thought it best to deliver the message."

"Where is Deborah, by the way?"

"St. Botolph's Church. She's doing more pictures." He watched as Helen walked to the computer, switched it on, and accessed a file. He said, "The Luxford boy's been taken, Helen. With the same message received from the kidnapper. So that's been thrown onto Tommy's plate as well. He's walking an awfully fine line at the moment. While I realise that doesn't go far to explain—"

"How can you always—*always*—forgive him so easily?" Helen demanded. "Has Tommy never done anything that's made you believe it's time to draw the line on your friendship?" Hands in her lap, she spoke the words to the computer screen rather than to him.

St. James thought about her questions. They were certainly reasonable enough, given his spotted history with Lynley. One disastrous automobile accident and one previous relationship with St. James's own wife were on the account books of their friendship. But he'd long ago accepted his own part in both of those situations. And while he was happy about neither of them, he also knew that a continual pawing through his mental and emotional state with regard to the past was largely counterproductive. What had happened, had happened. And that was the end of it.

He said, "He has a rotten job, Helen. It tries the soul more than anything we can imagine. If you spend enough time examining the underbelly of life, you go in one of two directions: Either you become callous—just another nasty murder to look into—or you become angry. Callous works best because it keeps you functioning. Anger you can't let get in the way. So you push it aside for as long as you can. But eventually, something comes up and you blow. You say things you don't mean. You do things you wouldn't otherwise do."

She lowered her head. Her thumb smoothed the skin that capped the knuckles of her folded hand. She said, "That's it. The anger. His anger. It's always there, just beneath the surface. It's in everything he does. It has been for years."

"The anger comes from his work. It's nothing to do with you."

"I know that. What I don't know is whether I can bear to live with it. There it will always be—Tommy's anger—like an unexpected dinner guest when one hasn't any food."

"Do you love him, Helen?"

She gave a short, miserable, unhappy laugh. "Loving him and being able to spend my life with him are two entirely different things. I'm sure about one, but not the other. And every time I think I've put my doubts to rest, something happens and they all begin rumbling again."

"Marriage isn't a place for people who want peace of mind," St. James said.

"Isn't it?" she asked. "Hasn't it been? For you?"

"For me? Not at all. It's been a prolonged exposure to a field of battle."

"How can you endure it?"

"I hate being bored."

Helen laughed wearily. Cotter's heavy footsteps sounded against the stairs. In a moment, he appeared in the doorway, a tray in his hands. "Coffee all round," he said. "I've brought you some biscuits as well, Lady Helen. You look like you could do with a decent bite o' chocolate digestive."

"I could do," Helen said. She left the computer and met Cotter at the worktable nearest the door. He slid the tray onto its surface, dislodging a photograph that fluttered to the floor.

Helen bent for it. She turned it right side up in her hands as Cotter poured their coffee. She sighed and said, "Oh God. There's no escaping." She sounded defeated.

St. James saw what she was holding. It was the photograph of Charlotte Bowen's drowned body that he'd taken from Deborah the night before, the same photograph that Lynley had thrown down like a gauntlet in the kitchen two days earlier. He should have tossed it away last night, St. James realised. That blasted picture had done quite enough damage.

He said, "Let me have that, Helen."

She held it, still. "Perhaps he was right," she said. "Perhaps we *are* responsible. Oh, not in the way he meant. But in a larger way. Because we thought we could make a difference when the truth is that no one makes a difference, anywhere."

"You don't believe that any more than I do," St. James told her. "Give me the picture."

Cotter took up one of the coffee cups. He disengaged the photograph from Helen's fingers and handed it over to St. James. St. James placed it face down among the pictures he'd been studying earlier. He accepted his own coffee from Cotter and said nothing more until the other man had left them.

Then he said, "Helen, I think you need to decide about Tommy once and for all. But I also think you can't use Charlotte Bowen as an excuse to avoid what you fear."

"I'm not afraid."

"We're all afraid. But trying to elude the fear that we might make a mistake . . ." His words died as his thoughts dried up. He'd been in the act of setting his coffee cup on the worktable as he spoke and his eyes had fallen on the photograph he'd just placed there.

Helen said, "What is it? Simon, what's wrong?" as he felt blindly for his magnifying glass.

By God, he realised, he'd had the knowledge all along. He'd had this photograph in his house for more than twenty-four hours, and thus for more than twenty-four hours the truth had been available to him. He saw this quickly and with dawning horror. But he also saw that he'd failed to recognise the truth because he'd been aware only of Tommy's offences against them. Had he been less concerned with keeping his reactions under icy control, he might have exploded himself, exhausted his own anger and, anger spent, returned to normal. And then he would have known. He would have seen. He had to believe that because he had to believe that under normal circumstances he would have noticed what was before his eyes right now.

He used the magnifying glass. He studied the shapes. He studied the forms. He told himself again that under different circumstances he would have recognised—he swore it, he believed it, he knew it absolutely—what he should have seen on the picture from the first.

25

*W*HEN ALL WAS SAID AND DONE and she was driving back to the Burbage Road, Barbara Havers decided that giving the inspiration of the moment full sway had been . . . definitely inspired. Over a cup of tea, which she had produced from a samovar that would have done justice to Irina Prozorov's twentieth birthday, Portly had thoroughly indulged herself in a soul-cleansing gossip that, guided by Barbara's incisive questions, ultimately touched upon the subject at hand: Dennis Luxford.

Since Portly had held her position at Baverstock School from the dawn of man onwards—or so it seemed by the number of pupils she recalled—Barbara was regaled with countless of the secretary's favourite tales. Some of the tales were general: everything from a prank involving dried mustard and toilet tissue that was played upon the Board of Governors on Speech Day forty years ago, to the ceremonious dunking of the headmaster into the newly dedicated swimming pool this last Michaelmas term. Some of the tales were specific: from Dickie Wintersby—now fifty years old and a prominent London banker—who had been gated for making indecent advances towards a terrified third-former, to Charlie O'Donnell—aged forty-two, now a QC *and* a member of the Board of Governors—who'd been caught on the school farm by his housemaster, making even more indecent advances towards a sheep. It didn't take long for Barbara to discover that Portly's specific memories tended to home in on the lubricious. She could report on which boy had been called on the carpet for solo masturbation, mutual masturbation, buggery, bestiality, fellatio, and coitus (interruptus or otherwise), and she did so with gusto. Where she got a bit vague was in instances when the boy in question had apparently kept his almond in the shell.

Such was the case with Dennis Luxford, although Portly held forth for a good five minutes on sixteen other boys from Dennis Luxford's same year who were gated for a full term after being revealed as making regular nookie with a village girl charging two pounds a pop. No snogging this, Portly declared, but the real thing, out in the old icehouse, with the girl coming up preggers as a result, and if the sergeant would like to see *where* the historic bonking occurred . . .

Barbara guided her back to the chosen subject, saying, "As to Mr. Luxford . . . ? And actually, I'm more interested in his recent visit, although this other material is really quite interesting and if I only had more time . . . You know how it is. Duty and everything."

Portly looked disappointed that her tales of randy teenagers running rampant had failed to please. But she said that *duty* was her watchword—when it wasn't *salacity*—and she pursed her lips as her mind contended with Dennis Luxford's recent visit to Baverstock.

It was about his son, she finally reported. He'd come to see the headmaster about getting his son enrolled for Michaelmas term. The boy was an only child—a rather wilful only child, if Portly wasn't mistaken—and Mr. Luxford had thought he would benefit enormously from an exposure to the rigours and the joys of Baverstock life. So he'd met with the headmaster, and after their meeting the two men had done a tour of the school so that Mr. Luxford could see how it had changed in the years since he had been a pupil.

"A tour?" Barbara felt her fingertips tingle with the implications. A good prowl round the grounds, ostensibly in the cause of inspecting the school prior to committing his son to it, might well have been how Luxford had refamiliarised himself with the local environment. "What sort of tour?"

He'd seen the classrooms, the dormitories, the dining hall, the gymnasium. . . . He'd seen everything as far as Portly could recall.

Had he seen the grounds? Barbara wanted to know. The playing fields, the school farm, and beyond?

It seemed to Portly that he had. But she wasn't certain, and to assist her memory, she took Barbara into the headmaster's office where an artistically rendered map of Baverstock School for Boys hung on the wall. It was surrounded by dozens of photographs of Bavernians through the decades, and as Portly studied the map as a visual aid to her memory, Barbara studied the pictures. They featured Bavernians in every conceivable situation: in classrooms, in the chapel, serving meals in the dining hall, marching in black academic gowns, giving speeches, swimming, canoeing, biking, rock climbing, sailing, playing sports. Barbara was skimming over them and wondering how much lolly a family had to lay out to get their little nob into a place like Baverstock when her attention fell on a photo of a small group of hikers, haversacks on their backs and walking sticks in hand. The hikers didn't interest Barbara as much as where they were posing for their picture. They stood assembled in front of a windmill. And Barbara was willing to lay money on the fact that it was the same windmill in which Charlotte Bowen had been held captive only last week.

She said, "Is this windmill on Baverstock land?" and indicated the picture.

Goodness no, Portly said. That was the old mill near Great Bedwyn. The archaeological society hiked there every year.

Hearing the words *archaeological society*, Barbara flipped through the pages of her notebook, looking for the scribblings she'd made during her telephone conversation with Inspector Lynley. She found them, read through them, and located the information she needed at the bottom of the page: Dennis Luxford's schooldays as faithfully and meticulously reported by Winston Nkata. As she had suspected, *The Source* editor had been a member of the archaeological society. It was called the Beaker Explorers.

Barbara made her farewells as quickly as possible and shot out to her car. Things were looking up.

She remembered the route to the windmill, and she followed it without further detours. Crime scene tape marked off the track leading into the mill, and she parked just beyond this tape on a verge thickly grown with drooping wildflowers of purple and white. She ducked under the yellow tape and walked towards the mill. She noted the fact that because of the birches that grew along the road as well as those growing along the path she now walked, the mill was at least partially hidden. And even if that hadn't been the case, there wasn't a soul nearby. It was the perfect spot for a kidnapper with a child in tow or for a killer removing that same child's body.

The mill had been sealed up the previous night, but Barbara did not need to enter it. She'd remained while the evidence was being collected, marked, and bagged, and the crime scene team's thoroughness had left her with no doubts about their competence. But darkness had prevented her from observing the windmill as part of a larger landscape, and it was to see this landscape now that Barbara had returned.

She shoved open the old gate and strode out from beneath the birches. Inside the paddock, she realised why the mill had been built on this particular spot. Last night had been calm, but today the breeze was a brisk one. In it, the arms of the old mill creaked. Had the structure still been operational, its sails would have been spinning and its stones grinding wheat.

Daylight exposed the surrounding fields. They fell away from the mill, planted with hay, with maize, and with corn. Aside from the ruined miller's cottage, the closest habitation was some half mile away. And the closest living creatures were sheep who grazed just to the east of the mill behind a wire fence. In the distance, a farmer rumbled his tractor along the edge of a field and a crop duster banked to skim along the green tops of whatever was growing beneath him. But if there had been any witness who could offer testimony to what had happened where Barbara stood—at the windmill—that witness bleated among the sheep.

Barbara walked to their paddock. They munched, indifferent to her presence. She said to them, "Come on, you lot. Cough it up, now. You saw him, right?" But they continued to munch.

One of the sheep disengaged from the others and came in Barbara's direction. For a moment she thought absurdly that the animal had actually paid heed to her words and was approaching with communication in mind, until she saw that its destination wasn't her but rather a low trough near the fence, at which it lapped up water.

Water? She went to investigate. Within a small three-sided shelter of bricks at the far end of the trough, a tap rose out of the ground. It was pitted from the weather, but when Barbara put on a glove and tried to turn it, there was no resistance from rust or corrosion. The water flowed out, clear and sweet.

She remembered Robin's words though. This far from the nearest village, it would likely be well-water. She needed to be sure.

She drove back to the village. The Swan was open for its lunchtime customers and Barbara pulled her Mini to a stop between a mud-encrusted tractor and an enormous antique Humber. When she entered, she was greeted by the usual momentary silence that a stranger encounters when coming into a country pub. But when she nodded at the locals and stopped to pat a Shetland sheepdog on the head, conversation resumed. She approached the bar.

She ordered a lemonade, a packet of salt and vinegar crisps, and a slice of the day's special: leek and broccoli pie. And when the publican presented her with her meal, she offered her police identification along with the £3.75.

Was he familiar, she asked the publican, with the recent discovery of a child's body in the Kennet and Avon Canal?

But local gossip had apparently made prefatory remarks unnecessary. The publican replied, "So that's what all the ruckus was about up on the hill last night."

He hadn't actually seen the ruckus himself, he confessed, but old George Tomley—the bloke who owned the farm south of the windmill—had been up with his sciatica tormenting him till long past midnight. George'd seen all the lights and—sciatica be damned—he'd gone to investigate. He could tell it was police business of some kind, but he'd assumed it was kids again, up to no good.

Hearing this, Barbara knew that there was obviously no need to obfuscate, circumvent, or prevaricate. She told the publican that the mill was the site where the girl had been held before she'd been drowned. And she'd been drowned in tap water. There was a tap on the property. So what Barbara wanted to know was if the water from that tap came from a well.

The publican declared that he hadn't the first clue about where the mill water came from, but old George Tomley—the same old George Tomley—knew nearly everything about property hereabouts and if the sergeant wanted to talk to him, old George was sitting right by the dart board.

Barbara took her pie, crisps, and lemonade over to George straightaway. He was massaging his bad hip with the knuckles of his right hand while with his left he thumbed through a copy of *Playboy*. In front of him lay the remains of his lunch. He too had ordered the day's special.

Water? he wanted to know. Whose water?

Barbara explained. George listened. His fingers massaged and his glance drifted down to the magazine and back up to Barbara as if they were making an unfavourable comparison.

But he was forthcoming with the information. Wasn't no well on any property hereabouts, the old man told her when she'd concluded her explanation. It was all main water, pumped up from the village and stored in a tank that was buried in the field next to the windmill. Highest point of land, that field, he told her, so that water flows out by force of gravity.

"But it's tap water?" Barbara pressed him.

As ever was, he told her.

Brilliant, Barbara thought. Pieces were clicking into place. She had Luxford in the vicinity recently. She had Luxford at the windmill in his youth. Now she needed to put Charlotte's school uniform into his hands. And she had a fairly good idea how to do that.

To Lynley, Cross Keys Close looked like a haunt of Bill Sikes. Twisting into a canyon of buildings off Marylebone Lane, its narrow alleys were completely devoid of human life and virtually untouched by the day's sunlight. As Lynley and Nkata entered the area, having left the Bentley parked in Bulstrode Place, Lynley wondered what had ever possessed Eve Bowen to allow her daughter to wander round this vicinity alone. Had she never been here herself? he wondered.

"Place gives me the jumps." Nkata echoed Lynley's thoughts with his words. "Why's a little bird like Charlotte coming round this place?"

"That's the question of the hour," Lynley admitted.

"Hell, in winter she'd be walking through here in the dark." Nkata sounded disgusted. "And that's practic'ly an invitation to . . ." His footsteps faltered, then stopped altogether. He looked at Lynley, who paused three paces ahead of him. "An invitation to trouble," he concluded thoughtfully. And then went on with, "You think Bowen knew about Chambers, 'Spector? She could've done her own digging right there at the Home Office and come up with the same dirt we got on the bloke. She could've sent the bird to him for her lessons and planned everything out herself, knowing we'd twig to his background eventually. And when we did—which we've just done—we'd set our sights on him and forget about her."

"The scenario plays well," Lynley said, "but let's not run before our horse to market, Winston."

Shakespearean allusions, no matter how apt, were lost on Nkata. He said, "Do what to who?"

"Let's talk to Chambers. St. James thought he was hiding something on Wednesday night, and St. James's instincts are generally sound. So let's see what it was."

They hadn't given Damien Chambers the benefit of knowing they were coming. Nonetheless, he was at home. They could hear the music of an electric keyboard filtering out of his tiny house, and this music ceased abruptly midbar when Lynley rapped with the brass treble-clef door knocker.

A limp curtain at the window flicked as someone within the house checked out the visitors. A moment later, the door opened the wary width of a young man's pale face. This was thin and framed by wispy chest-length hair.

Lynley showed his identification, saying, "Mr. Chambers?"

Chambers seemed to make an effort not to look at Lynley's warrant card. "Yeah."

"Detective Inspector Thomas Lynley. Scotland Yard CID." Lynley introduced Nkata. "May we have a word, please?"

He didn't look happy to do it, but Chambers stepped away from the aperture and swung the door open. "I was working."

A tape recorder was playing and the mellifluous and undoubtedly RADA voice of an actor was intoning, "The storm continued unabated into the night. And as she lay in her bed and thought of what they'd once been to each other, she realised that she could no more forget him than could she—"

Chambers silenced the machine. He said in explanation, "Abridged talking books. I'm doing the music bits in between the scenes," and he rubbed his hands down the sides of his jeans as if with the intention of wiping sweat from them. He began removing sheet music from the chairs, and he pushed two music stands out of the way. He said, "You can sit if you like," and he went through a doorway into the kitchen and ran water there. He returned with a glassful. In it, a slice of lemon floated. He set this glass on the edge of his electric keyboard and seated himself behind it as if with the intention of continuing his work. He played a single chord but then dropped his hands to his lap.

"You're here about Lottie, aren't you?" he said. "I've rather expected it. I didn't think that bloke last week would be the only one to come round if she didn't turn up."

"Did you expect her to turn up?"

"I'd no reason not to. She always liked to make mischief. When they told me she was missing—"

"They?"

"That bloke who came here on Wednesday night. Last week. He had a woman with him."

"Mr. St. James?"

"I don't remember his name. They were working for Eve Bowen. They were looking for Lottie." He took a sip of his water. "When I saw the story in the paper—what happened to Lottie, I mean—I thought someone would come round sooner or later. That's why you're here, isn't it?" He asked the question casually. But his expression was moderately anxious, as if he sought reassurance rather than information from them.

Without answering directly, Lynley said, "What time did Charlotte Bowen leave here on Wednesday?"

"Time?" Chambers looked at his watch. It was fastened to his thin wrist with a strap made from twine. A braided leather bracelet accompanied it. "After five, I'd say. She stayed to chat—she usually did that—but I sent her on her way not too long past the end of her lesson."

"Was anyone in the alley when she left?"

"I didn't see anyone hanging about, if that's what you mean."

"So consequently, no one was out there to see her leave."

Slowly, the musician's feet drew up under his chair. He said, "What are you getting at?"

"You've just said that there was no one in the alley who might have seen Charlotte leaving here at quarter past five. Am I correct?"

"That's what I said."

"So it follows that there was also no one in the alley to confirm—or to refute, for that matter—your claim that she ever left your home in the first place."

His tongue went out and passed over his lips, and when he next spoke, the Belfast in him bled through his words, spoken in haste and with rising concern: "What are you on about, then?"

"Have you met Charlotte's mother?"

"Of course I've met her."

"So you know she's a Member of Parliament, don't you? And a Junior Minister at the Home Office as well?"

"I suppose. But I don't see what—"

"And with a little effort to discover her views—which wouldn't be much of an effort at all since you're one of her constituents—you might have come to understand where she stands on certain controversial issues."

"I'm not political," Chambers said in immediate response, but the very stillness of his body—every nerve held in check lest he somehow betray himself—acted to give the lie to his words.

Lynley recognised the fact that his presence alone in Chambers' house was every Catholic Irishman's nightmare. The spectres of the Birmingham Six and the Guildford Four crowded the small room, made already overfull by the ominous proximity of Lynley and Nkata, both English, both Protestant, both well over six feet tall, both in their prime, and one bearing the sort of facial scar that suggested violence had once been part of his life. And both policemen. Lynley could sense the Irishman's fear.

He said, "We've had a talk with the RUC, Mr. Chambers."

Chambers said nothing. One of his feet rubbed against the other and his hands crawled up to hide in his armpits, but otherwise he maintained his calm. "That must have been a dead boring conversation."

"They had you pegged as a lout. Not exactly an IRA chummy, but someone well worth watching. Where do you suppose they got that idea?"

"If you want to know if I've sympathised with Sinn Fein, I have,"

Chambers said. "But so has half the population of Kilburn, so why don't you drive round there and roust them out? There isn't a law against taking a side, is there? And besides, what can it matter now? Things're cooled off."

"Taking a side doesn't matter. But taking a stand is different. And the RUC have you taking a stand, Mr. Chambers. From right round your tenth birthday onwards. Are you preparing to take more stands, I wonder? Unhappy with the peace process? Think Sinn Fein have sold out, perhaps?"

Chambers rose. Nkata got to his feet as if to intercept him. The black man towered over the musician by at least ten inches. He outweighed him by a good seven stone. Confronted by him, Chambers said, "Hang on, all right? I only want a drink. Something stronger than water. The bottle's in the kitchen."

Nkata looked to Lynley for direction. Lynley indicated the kitchen with a nod. Nkata fetched a glass and a bottle of John Jameson.

Chambers poured himself a shot of the whisky. He drank it down and recapped the bottle. He stood for a moment with his fingers on the bottle's cap, in a position that suggested he was considering his options. Finally, he shoved his long hair back from his face and returned to his seat. Nkata did likewise. Chambers, apparently now fortified for disclosure, said, "If you've talked to the RUC, then you know what I did: what any Catholic kid in Belfast was doing. I threw rocks at British soldiers. I threw bottles. I banged dustbin lids. I set fire to tyres. Yes, the police slapped my hands for that, and they did no different to my mates, all right? But I outgrew causing the soldiers aggro, and I went to university. I studied music. I have no IRA connections."

"Why teach music here?"

"Why not teach it here?"

"It must seem at times a hostile environment."

"Yeah. Well, I don't get out much."

"When was the last time you were in Belfast?"

"Three years ago. No, four. My sister's wedding." He dug a cardboard-framed photograph from a pile of magazines and sheet music that stood on a large stereo speaker. He handed it over.

It was a picture of a large family all gathered round a bride and groom. Lynley counted eight siblings and saw Chambers at their edge, looking ill at ease and slightly apart from the group who, aside from him, were standing arm in arm.

"Four years," Lynley noted. "A fairly long time. None of your family are in London now?"

"No."

"And you've not seen them?"

"No."

"That's curious." Lynley returned the picture.

"Why? Because we're Irish, d'you expect us to live in each other's knickers?"

"Are you at odds with them?"

"I don't practise the Faith any longer."

"Why's that?"

Chambers shoved his hair back behind his ears again. He pressed several keys on the electric keyboard. A dissonant chord sounded. "Look, Inspector, you came here to talk about Lottie Bowen. I've told you what I know. She was here for her lesson. After it, we chatted. Then she left."

"And no one saw her."

"I can't help that. I'm not responsible for that. If I'd known she was going to get snatched, I would have walked her all the way home. But I had no reason to believe there was any danger round here. No one's house gets burgled. No one gets mugged. No drug deals go down. So I let her go off on her own and something happened and I feel like hell about it but I'm not involved."

"I'm afraid you'll need corroboration for that."

"Where am I supposed to get it?"

"I expect you can get it from whoever was upstairs when Mr. St. James was here on Wednesday. If someone—other than Charlotte Bowen, that is—was actually here in the house with you. May we have her name and address, please?"

Chambers' chin dimpled as he sucked nervously against the inside of his lower lip. His eyes looked distant, as if he were examining something no one else could see. It was the look of a man who had something worth hiding.

Lynley said, "Mr. Chambers, I don't need to tell you how serious a situation you're in. You've a background that touches marginally upon the IRA; we've the daughter of an MP—with a history of unconcealed hostility towards the IRA—first missing then murdered; you're associated with that daughter; you're the last person known to have seen her. If there's someone out there who can assure us you had nothing to do with Charlotte Bowen's disappearance, then I'd suggest you produce her straightaway."

Again Chambers touched the black keys on the electric keyboard. Sharps and flats issued forth in no particular order. He breathed out a word that Lynley didn't catch and then finally said in a low voice and without looking at either of the other men, "All right. I'll tell you. But it can't get out. If the tabloids catch hold of the story, it'll smash things to bits. I couldn't cope with that."

Lynley thought that unless the musician was having a clandestine affair with a member of the Royal Family or the Prime Minister's wife, he was hardly likely to be of interest to the tabloids. But what he said was, "I don't speak to journalists, tabloid or otherwise. That's generally handled by the police press bureau."

This was, apparently, enough reassurance, although Chambers required another shot of John Jameson before he spoke again.

It wasn't a woman he was with on Wednesday night, he told them, keeping his eyes averted. It was a man. His name was Russell Majewski, although the Inspector might better recognise him by his professional name: Russell Mane.

Nkata said to Lynley, "A telly bloke. He plays a cop."

He played, Chambers said, an oversexed police detective whose patch was the eponymous West Farley Street, a gritty drama about crime, detection, and punishment set in South London. It was currently a smash hit on ITV, and his part had launched Russell Mane—if not into the entertainment stratosphere—then at least into heightened public awareness. This is what every actor wanted: recognition for his talent. But with recognition came certain expectations that the actor in question actually *be* in real life at least somewhat like the character he played. Only in this instance Russell wasn't at all like his character. He'd never even *been* with a woman other than on screen. Which is why they—Russell and Damien—went to such pains to keep their relationship a secret.

"We've been together three years, nearly four." He looked everywhere but at either Nkata or Lynley. "We're careful because people are phobic, aren't they? And it's shortsighted to think they're anything else."

Russ lived here, Chambers concluded. He was filming at the moment and he wouldn't be back till nine or ten that night. But if the police needed to talk to him . . .

Lynley handed over his card. He said, "Tell Mr. Mane to phone."

Back in the alley with the door shut behind them and the music once more emanating from within, Nkata said, "Think he knows our Special Branch blokes have him under the daily microscope?"

"If he doesn't," Lynley said, "he'll be thinking of it now."

They walked in the direction of Marylebone Lane. Lynley sorted through what they knew so far. They were amassing an appreciable amount of information and evidence: from fingerprints to a prescription drug, from a school uniform recovered in Wiltshire to a pair of spectacles found in a car in London. There had to be a logical way in which everything they were amassing was connected. All they needed was the clarity of vision that would enable them to see a pattern. Ultimately, everything they had and everything they knew had to be tied to one person. And that was the person who possessed the knowledge about Charlotte Bowen's paternity, the ingenuity to carry off two successful abductions, and the audacity to operate in the full light of day.

So what sort of person was it? Lynley wondered. There seemed to be only one reasonable answer: Their perpetrator had to be someone who, if even seen with the children, knew being seen did not necessarily mean being caught.

Piranhas, Eve Bowen thought. She'd thought jackals earlier, but jackals were by their nature carrion eaters, while piranhas went after living—and preferably bleeding—flesh. The reporters had been gathering all day: outside her constituency office and the Home Office as well as in front of One Parliament Square. They were accompanied by their cohorts—the *paparazzi* and the press photographers—and together this group milled about on the pavement, where they drank coffee, smoked cigarettes, ate jam doughnuts and packets of crisps, and surged round anyone who might give them a titbit of information as to the fate, the state of mind, or the reaction of Eve Bowen to the disclosures made by Dennis Luxford in today's *Source*. As the reporters surged, they fired off questions and shot off pictures. And woe betide the victim of their attention who attempted to shield a face or parry an enquiry with a sharp retort.

Eve thought last night had been hell. But each time the front door to the constituency office opened to the babble of voices and the flashing of camera lights, she knew the hours between Dennis Luxford's phone call and her final realisation that she could do nothing to stop his story had only been Purgatory.

She'd done her best. She'd pulled in every debt and every chit, sitting with the phone pressed to her ear hour after hour as she contacted judges, QCs, and every political ally she'd ever established. Each phone call was to the same purpose: to quash *The Source* story that Luxford had claimed would save his son. Each phone call produced the same result: the conclusion that such quashing was not going to be possible.

Throughout the night she heard every variation on why a court injunction was out of her reach, despite her power in the Government:

Did the story in question—she would not reveal the exact details to any recipient of her phone calls—actually constitute libel? No? He's writing the truth? Then, my dear, I'm afraid that you haven't a case. Yes, I do realise that details from our pasts might sometimes prove embarrassing to our presents and our futures, but if those details comprise the truth . . . Well, one can only keep a stiff upper lip and hold one's head high and let one's current actions speak for who one is, can't one?

This isn't exactly a Tory newspaper, is it, Eve? I mean, one could ask the PM to phone and rattle a cage or two if the editor of the *Sunday Times* or the *Daily Mail* or even, perhaps, the *Telegraph* had been planning to run a story seriously detrimental to a Junior Minister. But *The Source* was a Labour sympathiser. And one couldn't reasonably expect a little bout of verbal thumb-squeezing to produce an agreement not to print an anti-Tory story in a Labour tabloid. As a matter of fact, should someone even attempt to thumb-squeeze a man like Dennis Luxford, there's little doubt that an editorial would expose that fact the very same day the story ran. And how would that look? How would that make the Prime Minister look?

That final question was a thinly veiled prod to action. What it really asked was how *The Source*'s story was ultimately going to reflect on the PM, who had personally raised Eve Bowen to her current position of political power. What it really suggested was a course of action should that same story be likely to put more egg on the already yolk-smeared face of the man who'd had to endure the humiliation of one of his party colleagues cavorting in a parked automobile with a rent boy just twelve days ago. The Prime Minister's Recommitment to Basic British Values had already taken some serious body blows, Eve was being told. If Ms. Bowen—not only an MP but also, unlike Sinclair Larnsey, a Government Minister—believed that there was the slightest possibility of *The Source*'s article causing the Premier any more embarrassment . . . well, certainly Ms. Bowen knew what course she ought to take.

Of course she knew. She was to fall upon her sword. But she didn't intend to plunge earthward without putting up a desperate fight.

She'd met with the Home Secretary that morning. She'd arrived in Westminster in darkness, long before *The Source* hit the street and hours before her normal arrival, so she eluded the press. Sir Richard Hepton met her in his office. He'd apparently dressed in what came immediately to hand upon receiving Eve's phone call at quarter to four. He wore a rumpled white shirt and the trousers to a suit. He had put on neither jacket nor tie, merely a cardigan. He had not shaved. Eve knew that it was his way of telling her that their meeting would perforce be a brief one. Obviously, he would have to return home in good time to shower, to change, and to prepare himself for the day.

It was fairly clear that he thought her call was the result of two days spent grieving her daughter's death. He thought she was there to demand stronger action on the part of the police, and he had come to mollify her in whatever way he could. He had no idea what lay behind Charlotte's disappearance. Despite experience in the Government which might have taught him contrary, he assumed that things, at least with his Junior Ministers, were what they seemed.

He said, "Nancy and I received the message about the funeral, Eve. Of course we'll be there. How are you coping?" His expression was watchful as he asked the question, adding, "These next few days aren't going to be easy. Are you getting enough rest?"

Like most politicians, Sir Richard Hepton asked questions that were really references to another topic entirely. What he wanted to know was why she had phoned him in the middle of the night, why she had insisted they meet at once, and above all why she was displaying a disturbing potential to act like an hysterical woman, which was the least desirable characteristic in a member of the Government. He wished to give her leeway because she'd suffered a monstrous loss, but he didn't want the immensity of that loss to undermine her ability to cope.

She said, "*The Source* is going to run a story tomorrow—this morning, rather—that I want to advise you about in advance."

"*The Source?*" Hepton observed her without a change in expression. He played political poker better than anyone Eve knew. "What sort of story, Eve?"

"A story about me, about my daughter. A story, I should guess, about what led to her death."

"I see." He shifted his elbow to the arm of his chair. The leather creaked, which emphasised the stillness of the entire Home Office as well as the silence of the streets outside. "Were there—" He paused thoughtfully, and his face looked pensive. He seemed to be making a selection from among several conclusions. "Eve, were there problems between you and your daughter?"

"Problems?"

"You said the story would be about what led to her death."

"This isn't a child abuse story, if that's what you mean," Eve clarified. "Charlotte wasn't abused. And what led to her death had nothing to do with me. At least, not in that way."

"Then perhaps you'd better tell me in what way you're involved."

She began by saying, "I wanted you to know because so often in the past when the tabloids launch into someone in politics, the Government's taken completely by surprise. I didn't want that to happen in this case. I'm making a clean breast of it, so we can think what to do next."

"Advance knowledge is a useful weapon," Hepton acknowledged. "Acquiring it has always allowed me to see with a much clearer vision."

Eve didn't miss how he'd changed the pronoun to singular. She also didn't miss the absence of any word or even guttural sound that she could take for reassurance. Sir Richard Hepton knew that something nasty was in the wind. And when an odour pervaded his well-kept house, he was a man who knew how to open windows.

She began to talk. There was no real way to colour the story in an appealing hue. Hepton listened with his hands clasped on top of his desk and his face the same noncommittal mask that she'd seen him wear at so many meetings in the past. When she'd covered every relevant detail of her week-long Blackpool fling with Dennis Luxford—as well as every detail relating to Charlotte's disappearance and subsequent murder—she realised how rigid her body had become. She could feel the nervous tension in the spasmodic tightening of muscles from her neck to the base of her spine. She tried to make her body relax, but she could not trick it into believing that her political fate wasn't hanging in the balance of this one man's interpretation of her behaviour eleven years ago.

When she was finished speaking, Hepton rolled his leather chair away from the desk and slowly swung it to one side. He raised his head and seemed to be scrutinising the portraits of three monarchs and two prime ministers on the opposite wall. He rubbed his thumb along his jaw; his silence was so profound that Eve could hear the sandpaper sound of his whiskers as his thumb rubbed against their grain.

She said, "I dare say Luxford's operating with two motivations: newspaper circulation and political damage. He means to outsell the *Globe*. He means to wound the Government. With this story, he does both with one stroke."

"Perhaps. Perhaps not." He sounded thoughtful. Eve could tell from his tone that the Home Secretary was assessing the possible responses they might make to this story. Damage containment was paramount.

She said, "Certainly this can be turned against Luxford, Richard. If I'm painted as a hypocrite, what exactly is he? And when the police uncover him as the mastermind behind Charlotte's abduction—"

Hepton lifted an index finger to stop her. He continued to think. The fact that he was tossing round options without making her a party to what those options were was not lost on Eve. She knew that her best interests lay in saying nothing more, but she couldn't keep herself from attempting a final act of salvage.

"Let me talk to the Prime Minister. Surely if he's fully apprised of what led up to Dennis Luxford's writing this story—"

"Without question," Hepton said slowly. "The PM must be made aware of what's happening with no delay."

Greatly relieved, she said, "I can go over to Downing Street straightaway. He'll see me at once if he knows what's at stake. And better that I go now—while it's dark and before the newspapers arrive on the streets—than to wait until the story's out and the reporters start gathering."

"He faces a Q and A at the Commons tomorrow," Hepton went on, his voice contemplative.

"Which is all the more reason why he needs to know about Luxford now."

"The Opposition—not to mention the press—will eat him alive if we're not careful. So he can't confront that Q and A without having this matter completely settled."

"Settled," Eve repeated. There was only one way to settle the matter within the time frame Hepton had established. She continued, feeling desperate, "Let me talk to him. Let me attempt to explain. If I fail to persuade him to—"

Hepton interrupted, still in that contemplative tone of voice. Eve realised that it gave him distance from her. It was the same tone of voice a monarch would have used in reluctantly pronouncing a death sentence upon a loved one. "After the Larnsey debacle, the PM must be made to appear decisive, Eve. Conciliation is absolutely out of the question." Then he finally looked at her, "You see that, don't you? You do see that?"

She felt a loosening within her as her future—as if it had been contained in her muscles, her organs, and her blood—began to drain away. Years of careful planning, years of effort, years of political machinations, were wiped out in an instant. Whatever she was to create out of the time to come, she knew that the creation would not be a person of substance in the Palace of Westminster.

Sir Richard Hepton seemed to read this on her face. He said, "I know resignation is a blow, but it doesn't mean you have nothing ahead of you. You can be rehabilitated. Look at John Profumo. Who would have thought one man so disgraced would be able to turn himself so much around?"

"I don't intend to be a puling social worker."

Hepton cocked his head and looked paternal. "I didn't intend to suggest that, Eve. Besides, you're not finished in government. You'll still have your seat in the Commons. Standing down as Junior Minister doesn't mean you lose everything."

No. Just most of everything, Eve thought.

So she'd written the letter that the Home Secretary required of her. She wanted to think the PM would refuse to accept her resignation, but she knew otherwise. People put their trust in their elected leaders, he would intone religiously from the steps of Number Ten. When that trust is eroded, the elected leaders must go.

She'd gone from the Home Office the short distance to Parliament Square. She was there when her assistant arrived. In that quick aversion of his eyes from hers, Eve saw that Joel Woodward had heard about the headlines. Naturally. It would have been on the morning news and Joel always watched the news while he thrust his cereal down his throat.

It quickly became clear that everyone else in the Parliament Square building was aware of the Luxford story as well. No one addressed her, people quickly nodded and just as quickly looked away, and in her office voices spoke in the hushed tones of those who have experienced a firsthand encounter with death.

Reporters began phoning as soon as the telephone lines were open for the day. "No comment" didn't satisfy them. They wanted to know if the MP from Marylebone was going to refute *The Source*'s claim. "There can't be 'no comment,' " Joel carefully reported one of them as saying. "It's either the truth or a lie, and if she doesn't plan to file a suit for libel, I expect we know which way the wind's blowing."

Joel wanted her to deny the paper's allegations. He couldn't believe that the object of his Tory wet dreams had a side to her that didn't quite mesh with the Party's stated beliefs.

She did not hear from Joel's father until mid-morning. And then she heard from him only through Nuala, who phoned her from the Constituency Association's office and told her that Colonel Woodward was assembling a meeting of the Association Executive. Nuala recited the summons to appear and the time of the meeting. Then she lowered her voice and said kindly, "Are you all right, Ms. Bowen? It's dead wild over here. When you come, try to get in the back way. Reporters are five deep on the pavement."

They'd been ten deep by the time she'd arrived. Now in the constituency office, Eve readied herself for the worst. The Association Executive had not required that she attend their preliminary discussion. Colonel Woodward had merely stuck his head in her office and demanded to know the name of her daughter's father. He didn't ask the question in an amicable fashion, nor did he attempt to couch it in a euphemism. He barked it out like a military order and, in doing so, let her know unconditionally what the lay of the political landscape was.

She attempted to go about the day's business, but there was little enough of it. She wasn't normally in the constituency office until Friday so aside from dealing with the post, there was nothing else to do. No one was waiting to speak to the local MP except the reporters, and one word of encouragement to them would be madness. So she read letters and answered them, and when she wasn't doing that, she paced.

Two hours into the Executive's meeting, Colonel Woodward came for her. He said, "You're wanted now," and turned on his heel, heading in the direction of the Executive's conference room. As he walked, he brushed at the shoulders of his herringbone jacket to rid it of dandruff, of which he had an ample supply.

The Association Executive sat round a rectangular mahogany table. Jugs of coffee, used cups, yellow pads, and pencils littered its surface. The room was greatly overheated—both by their bodies and by the intensity of the two hours of discussion—and Eve thought about asking that someone open a window. But the proximity of the reporters outside forced her to reject the idea. She took the empty place at the foot of the table and waited for Colonel Woodward to return to its head.

"Luxford," he said. He may as well have said *dog shit*. And he locked his beetle-browed gaze upon her so that she could read the force of his—and hence the Executive's—full displeasure. "We don't know what to make of this, Eve. An affair with an anti-monarchist. A scandal monger. A Labour supporter. For all we know, a Communist or Trotskyite or whatever else these people call themselves. You couldn't have chosen much more abominably."

"It was a long time ago."

"Are you suggesting he wasn't then as I've described him?"

"On the contrary, I'm suggesting I wasn't then who I am now."

"Praise God for small favours," Colonel Woodward said. There was a restless stirring round the table. Eve took a moment to look each member of the Executive full in the face. In their willingness or their reluctance to return her gaze, she could see how they stood with regard to her future. The majority, it seemed, were on Colonel Woodward's side.

She said to them all, "I made a mistake in my past. I've paid for it in coin larger than anyone in public life has ever paid for an act of indiscretion: I've lost my child."

There was a general murmur of acknowledgement and expressions of sympathy from three of the women. Colonel Woodward moved quickly to quell any tide of condolence that might build to a wave of support by saying, "You've made more than one mistake in your past. You've also lied to this body, Miss Bowen."

"I don't believe I've—"

"Lies of omission, Miss. Lies growing out of subterfuge and hypocrisy."

"I've acted in the interests of my constituency, Colonel Woodward. I've given the constituency my devotion, my full attention, and my effort. If you can find an area in which I've been deficient when it comes to the citizens of Marylebone, you might be willing to point it out to me."

"Your political efficacy is not the issue," Colonel Woodward said. "We held this seat in your first election by an eight-hundred-vote majority only."

"Which I increased to twelve hundred votes last time round," Eve replied. "I told you from the first that it takes years to build the sort of majority you have in mind. If you give me the leeway to—"

"The leeway to what?" Colonel Woodward demanded. "Surely you don't mean the leeway to maintain your seat?"

"That's exactly what I mean. If I stand down right now, you'll have a by-election on your hands. In the current climate, what do you expect the outcome of that election to be?"

"And if you don't stand down, if we let you stand for Parliament again after this Luxford business, we'll lose to Labour anyway. Because despite what you may think about your ability to attain absolution from the electorate, no voter, Miss Bowen, is likely to forget the gulf between how you've portrayed yourself and who you actually are. And even if the voters were that forgetful, the Opposition will be only too happy to dredge up every insalubrious detail from your past as a reminder if you're our candidate at the next election."

The words *insalubrious detail* seemed to echo round the room. Eve saw the members of the Executive look to their yellow notepads, their pencils, and their coffee cups. Discomfort wafted off them in nearly visible waves. None of them wanted this meeting to turn into a dogfight. But if they expected her to bend to their collective will, then they were going to have to make that will perfectly clear. She would make no offer to stand down at once and thereby hand her seat over to the Opposition.

She said calmly, "Colonel Woodward, we all have the Party's interests at heart. At least, I assume so. What is it you'd like me to do?"

He peered at her suspiciously. It was her second sentence that set him on edge. He said, "I disapprove of you, Miss. I disapprove of who you are, of what you did, and of how you attempted to hide it. But the Party is more important than my dislike of you."

He needed to castigate her, Eve realised. He needed to do it in as public a forum as the situation and their mutual interest in damage control would allow. She could feel the angry blood pounding through her veins, but she remained motionless in her chair, saying, "I completely agree to the importance of the Party, Colonel Woodward." And again added, "What is it that you'd like me to do?"

"We have only one option. You're to remain in your seat until the Prime Minister next calls a General Election."

"And then?"

"Then we're through with you. You're through with Parliament. You'll stand down in favour of whomever we select to run."

She looked round the table. She could see that this plan was a compromise, the unhappy marriage of demanding her immediate resignation and allowing her to continue at her post indefinitely. It bought her as much time as the Prime Minister could string out before the winds of political change that had been building for months forced him into calling a General Election. When that election rolled round, her career was finished. It was finished as of this moment, actually. She'd keep her seat in the House of Commons for a time, but everyone sitting in the meeting room knew who among them would be wielding the real power.

"You've always disliked me, haven't you?" she said to Colonel Woodward.

"Not without good reason," the colonel replied.

26

*B*ARBARA HAVERS SENSED that she was getting closer to the truth the moment she located Stanton St. Bernard. The village was a collection of farms, barns, and cottages strung along five intersecting tracks and country lanes. It hosted a spring, a well, a shoe box of a post office, and the modest church which had sponsored the fête whose jumble stall had contained the bag of rags in which Charlotte Bowen's school uniform had been found. But it wasn't the presence of this church that stimulated Barbara's interest. It was the location of the village itself. A mere half mile to its south, the Kennet and Avon Canal flowed between fields planted with hay and with maize, and it rolled tranquilly towards Allington, a little more than two miles to the west. Barbara made a brief circuit of the village to ascertain these details before heading to the church. By the time she had parked her Mini and climbed out to breathe the manure-hung air, she felt confident that she was tracing the path walked by a killer.

She found the vicar and his wife in the garden of a narrow-windowed house identified by a sign as The Rectory. They were both on their knees in front of an abundantly planted flower bed, and for a moment Barbara thought that they were praying. She waited at the gate, which seemed a respectful enough distance, but then their voices carried over to where she was standing.

The vicar said, "We should have a fine show from the ranunculi, my dear, if the weather cooperates," to which his wife replied, "But we've seen the best of the ornithogalum, haven't we? You must pull it out. With the women's league tea coming fast upon us, I must have the garden in order, pet."

Hearing this clearly non-theological exchange, Barbara called out a hullo and pushed the gate open. The vicar and his wife sat back on their heels. They were kneeling on a tartan car rug. As she got closer, Barbara saw that the vicar had a hole in the ankle of one of his black socks.

They were apparently preparing to do some work. They'd laid out an array of pristine gardening tools at their knees. These tools were arranged on a large square of wrapping paper. On the paper was drawn what appeared to be an overall plan for the garden. It was heavily smudged and marked with countless notations. The vicar and his wife, it seemed, took to the soil with the passion of zealots.

Barbara introduced herself and produced her identification. The vicar brushed his hands together and got to his feet. He helped his wife up, and as she tidied everything from her denim skirt to her greying hair, he introduced himself as the Reverend Mr. Matheson and identified his wife as "my bride Rose."

His wife laughed shyly at this appellation and took her husband's arm. She slid her hand down it till their fingers met and twined. The vicar said to Barbara, "How may we help you, my dear?"

Barbara told them she'd come to talk about the recent church fête, and Rose suggested they do their talking while she and the vicar attended to the garden. "It's difficult enough to carve an hour from Mr. Matheson's day to see to our plants," she confided, "especially when he'd do just about anything to avoid a grub round the flower beds. So now I've got him here, I must strike while the iron is hot."

Mr. Matheson looked abashed. "I've a black thumb, Rose. God didn't see fit to make botany one of my talents, as you know."

"I do," Rose said fervently.

Barbara said, "I'd be happy to help as we talk."

Rose appeared delighted with this suggestion. "*Would* you?" She dropped back to her knees on the car rug. Barbara thought she was about to offer a prayer of thanksgiving upon the occasion of the Lord's sending her a helper. Instead, she plucked a hand rake from among the tools and handed it over, saying, "We'll work the soil first. Loosen initially, fertilise secondarily. That's how one makes things grow."

"Right," Barbara said. She didn't have the heart to reveal the fact that her own thumb was more coal-coloured than green. The heavenly gates were doubtless decorated with the hundreds of plants she'd sent to their just rewards over the years.

Mr. Matheson joined them on the rug. He began tearing out the ornithogalum and tossing its remains onto the lawn. While they worked on either side of Barbara, the couple chatted amiably about the fête. It was a yearly event—*the* yearly event if their enthusiasm was anything to go by—and they used it as a means of raising money to replace the windows in the church. "We mean to go back to stained glass," Mr. Matheson explained. "Now, some of the wardens accuse me of being too High Church because of those windows—"

"They accuse you of popery," Rose said with a gentle laugh.

Mr. Matheson waved off the accusation by flipping a trailing stem of ornithogalum over his shoulder. "But when I have those windows in place, they'll think differently, just wait and see. It's all in what one is used to. And when our present doubting Thomases become used to the way the light changes, the way both contemplation and devotion are absolutely and irrevocably *altered* in the more subdued light . . . a light like nothing they've ever seen . . . unless, of course, they've been to Chartres or Notre Dame—"

"Yes, pet," Rose said firmly.

Her words brought the vicar round. He blinked, then chuckled. "I do go on, don't I?"

"It's nice to have a love of something," Barbara said.

Rose was industriously weeding among the ranunculi. "Indeed," she said, and yanked at a particularly well-rooted dandelion. "But one does sometimes wish Mr. Matheson's loves were more generally Anglican in nature. He was rhapsodising about the west facade of Reims Cathedral in the presence of the Archdeacon two weeks ago, and I thought the poor man would have a stroke." She deepened her voice. " 'B-b-but my good Matheson, it's a *Papist* structure.' " She clucked. "Such a scene Mr. Matheson caused."

Barbara made the appropriate tsk-tsking noises, then brought them to the subject of the fête again. She was interested in the jumble stall, she explained. An article of clothing, a school uniform that was tied to a murder investigation, had been found in a rag bag that had come from that stall.

Mr. Matheson rose from his efforts with the ornithogalum. He said disbelievingly, *"Murder* investigation?" as his wife said, "School *uniform?"* with an equal amount of disbelief.

"The little girl who was found in the canal Sunday evening. In Allington. You've heard?"

Of course they had heard. Who hadn't heard? Allington wasn't a stone's throw away, and the hamlet was part of Mr. Matheson's parish.

"Right," Barbara said. "Well, it was her school uniform that was found in the rags."

Rose thoughtfully plucked at a weed that, under Barbara's observation, didn't look much different to the plants growing next to it. She frowned and shook her head. "Are you sure it was her uniform?"

"It had her name sewn into it."

"All in one piece?"

Barbara looked at her blankly, assuming she was referring to Charlotte's name. She said, "Pardon?"

Was the uniform in one piece, Mrs. Matheson wanted to know. Because, she explained, the rags themselves would not have been. Rags were by their definition . . . well, rags. Any clothing that was found unacceptable for sale *as* clothing was cut into squares and placed into bags and offered as rags for sale at the jumble stall during the fête. But there would have been no uncut garment among her rags, Mrs. Matheson said. Prior to the fête, she and her daughter—whom she referred to in an Austenian fashion as "the young Miss Matheson"—had gone through the jumble one piece at a time and they did all the cutting themselves. "So as not to offend any of the parishioners," Rose confided. "If they knew that one of their neighbours might be making a judgement about the suitability of their offering . . . Well, they probably would stop giving altogether, wouldn't they? So we do it ourselves. We always have done." Therefore, she concluded, attacking a patch of clover with vigour, a school uniform in good condition would not have passed through her hands and ended up among the rags. And if it had been in bad condition, it would have been cut into squares like the rest of the unsuitable garments.

This was an interesting turn of events, Barbara thought. She dug round a plant with her hand rake and mulled over the information. She said, "When was the fête, exactly?"

"Saturday last," Rose said.

"Where was it?"

Right in the church grounds, they told her. And everything for the jumble stall had been collected in cardboard boxes in the church vestibule over a period of four weeks. Mrs. Matheson and her daughter—the aforementioned young Miss Matheson—had dealt with it every Sunday night right there in the church crypt.

"That's when we did the cutting," Mrs. Matheson said. "It's easier to take it one week at a time than to wait till the end and do it all at once."

"Organisation is the key to a successful fête," Mr. Matheson confided. "We made three hundred and fifty-eight pounds and sixty-four pence on Saturday, didn't we, Rose?"

"Indeed we did. But there was, perhaps, a tiny bit too much grease on the coin toss plates. Not enough prizes were won at that booth and people got a wee bit miffed."

"Nonsense," her husband scoffed. "It's all in a proper cause. With those windows in place, the congregation shall see—"

"We know, pet," Mrs. Matheson said.

Assuming that the uniform was not among the jumble as originally seen by Mrs. Matheson, Barbara asked who had access to the discarded clothing once it was already sorted, cut, and bagged.

Mrs. Matheson crawled into the flower bed on the trail of a creeping weed that was speckled with tiny yellow flowers. She said, "Access to the jumble? Anyone, I suppose. We kept it in the crypt, and the crypt's not locked."

"Church isn't locked either," Mr. Matheson added. "I won't hear of it. A place of worship should be available to the penitent, the mendicant, the wretched, and the sorrowful at any hour of the day or night. Totally absurd to expect one's congregation to feel prayerful on the vicar's schedule, wouldn't you say?"

Barbara told them she would say. And before the vicar could expound further on his religious philosophy—which she could see he was warming to do since he abandoned the ornithogalum and rubbed his hands together—she asked if they'd seen any strangers in the area in the days prior to the fête. Or even, she added, on the morning of the fête.

The Mathesons looked at each other. They shook their heads. Of course, Mr. Matheson added, at the *actual* fête there were always people one didn't know since the event was advertised in every nearby hamlet and village, not to mention in Marlborough, Wootton Cross, and Devizes. For that was one point of a fête, wasn't it? Besides raising money, one always hoped to return another soul to the Lord's safekeeping. And what better way to do it than to encourage lost souls to mingle among the already saved.

This complicated matters, Barbara realised. Worse, it left the field wide open. "So," she said, "anyone could have got to those rag bags, opened one of them, and stowed the uniform inside. Either in the crypt before the fête or sometime during the fête itself."

During the fête was unlikely, Mrs. Matheson said. Because the stall was manned, and if a stranger had opened one of the bags, surely she would have *seen* him doing so.

Did she run the stall herself, then? Barbara asked.

She did, Mrs. Matheson replied. And when she wasn't there, the young Miss Matheson was. Did the sergeant wish to speak to the young Miss Matheson?

Barbara did, so long as she didn't have to twist her tongue round "the young Miss Matheson" more than once. But she wanted to have a picture of Dennis Luxford in her hand during the conversation. If Luxford had made a more recent sojourn to Wiltshire than his month-ago visit to Baverstock School indicated—if he'd been prowling round

Stanton St. Bernard within the past week—someone somewhere was likely to have seen him. And what better place to start looking for that someone than right here?

She told the vicar and his wife that she would return with a photograph for them to inspect. She told them she'd want to have their daughter take a look at it as well. What time did the young Miss Matheson finish school for the day?

The Mathesons tittered. They explained their tittering with the information that the young Miss M wasn't in school, at least not any longer, but thank you for thinking we're still youthful enough to have a school-aged child. One shouldn't be prideful about one's appearance, but the sergeant wasn't the first person to remark upon the astounding youthfulness of this couple who had given their lives to God. The truth was that when one devoted a life to serving the Lord *and* got a decent amount of fresh air as they were doing now—

"Right," Barbara said. "Where can I find her?"

At Barclay's in Wootton Cross, Rose said. If the sergeant wanted the young Miss Matheson to look at a photo before the end of her workday, she could take it by the bank. "Just ask for Miss Matheson in New Accounts," Mrs. Matheson said proudly. "It's quite a proper job."

To which the vicar added earnestly, "She even has her own desk."

—⁓—

Winston Nkata took the call from Sergeant Havers, so Lynley heard only one side of it, most of which consisted of "Right . . . Brilliant, that move, Sarge . . . He was at Baverstock *when?* . . . Ooooh, nice, that . . . And what's the word on the narrow-boats?" When the conversation ended, the DC told Lynley, "She needs a picture of Luxford faxed to Amesford CID. She says she's got a noose round his neck and it's tightening fast."

Lynley turned the car left at the first opportunity and began to weave northward towards Highgate and the Luxford home. While he drove, Nkata brought him up-to-date on the sergeant's activities in Wiltshire. He concluded with, "Interesting that Luxford never mentioned it to us, him being in Wiltshire last month, don't you think?"

"It's a remarkable omission," Lynley agreed.

"If we can tag him hiring a narrow-boat—which is what the sarge's honey is up to at the moment, then—"

" 'The sarge's honey'?" Lynley clarified.

"That bloke she's working with. Don't you hear her voice get fuzz all over it when she says his name?"

Lynley wondered what a voice with fuzz on it sounded like. He said, "I haven't been aware of voice fuzz."

"Then you're wearing earmuffs. Those two are sweet on each other, man. You just mark my words."

"A conclusion you've drawn from the sound of the sergeant's voice?"

"Right. And it's natural. You know what it's like when you work close with someone."

"I'm not certain I do," Lynley said. "You and I have been together for several days now, but I'm feeling no particular longing for you."

The other man laughed. "All in good time."

In Highgate, Millfield Lane had become an encampment of journalists. They clung round the front of the Luxford home like a host of unshakeable bad memories, and accompanying them were news vans, cameramen, banks of television lights, and three neighbourhood dogs who were snarling over possession of the journalists' discarded mealtime rubbish. Across the street, pedestrians, neighbours, and assorted gawkers had assembled to the east of the Highgate ponds. And as Lynley's Bentley parted the crowd in front of the Luxford driveway, three bicyclists and two Rollerbladers lurched to a stop and joined in the confusion.

A police presence at the bottom of the driveway had so far managed to keep the press at bay. But as the constable in charge moved the sawhorse to one side, a reporter dodged past him with two photographers on his heels. They raced for the villa at the top of the slope.

Fingers on the door handle, Nkata asked, "Want me to put the collar to that lot?"

Lynley watched them dash in the direction of the portico. One of the photographers began shooting pictures of the garden. "They won't get anything useful," he said. "You can bet that Luxford isn't answering his door."

"Getting a dose of his own though, with this lot sharking through the waters like they are."

"It's a nice little irony," Lynley acknowledged, "if you like that sort of thing."

He pulled to a stop behind the Mercedes. At his knock, a constable opened the door. The reporter shouted past Lynley, "Mr. Luxford! Answer a few questions from the *Sun*? What's your wife's reaction to this morning's—"

Lynley grabbed the man by the back of his shirt collar. He thrust him at Nkata, who seemed only too pleased to shove the reporter back in the direction of the street. Upon cries of "Bleeding police bru*tality*," they entered the house.

The constable said tersely, "You got our message?"

Lynley said, "What message? We were in the car. Winston was on the phone."

The constable said in a low voice, "Things are breaking. There's been another call."

"From the kidnapper? When?"

"Not five minutes ago." He led the way into the drawing room.

The curtains were closed to keep the Luxfords at peace from tele-photo lenses. The windows were shut to keep them safe from prying ears. But the result was a close and tenebrous atmosphere that even broken by illuminated table lamps felt tomblike and unnaturally still. Evidence of meals largely uneaten lay on coffee tables, ottomans, and the seats of chairs. Cups of film-topped tea and ashtrays coughing up cigarette ends and burnt tobacco crowded the surface of a grand piano, where an unfolded copy of that day's *Source* shed its pages onto the floor.

Dennis Luxford sat, head in his hands, in an armchair next to the telephone. As the police crossed towards him, he raised his head. Simultaneously, DI John Stewart—one of Lynley's divisional colleagues at the Yard and the very best man for any job requiring meticulous attention to detail—came into the drawing room from the other direction. He was wearing a set of headphones round his carrot-thin neck and speaking into a cordless phone. He nodded at Lynley, said into the phone, "Yes . . . Yes . . . Blast. We'll try for more next time . . . Right," and snapped the mouthpiece closed. He said to Luxford, "Nothing, Mr. Luxford. You did your best but there wasn't enough time," and to Lynley, "You've heard?"

"Just now. What was it?"

"We've got it on tape." He led Lynley to the kitchen. On a centre island that stood between a work top and a stainless steel cooker, a taping system had been set up. It consisted of a recorder, a half dozen spools of tape, earphones, flex, and wiring that seemed to run everywhere.

DI Stewart rewound the tape and then played it back. Two voices spoke, both ostensibly male, one of them Luxford's. The other sounded as if the caller were speaking from the throat and through completely clenched teeth. It was an effective way to distort and disguise the voice.

The message was brief, too brief to be able to trace the call itself: *"Luxford?"*

"*Where's my son? Where's Leo? Let me talk to him.*"

"*You got it wrong, fucker.*"

"*Got what wrong? What are you talking about? For God's sake—*"

"*Shut up. And hear me good. I want the truth. The story. The kid dies without the truth.*"

"*I wrote it! Haven't you seen the paper? It's on the front page! I did what you asked, exactly as you asked. Now, give me my son or—*"

"*You wrote it wrong, fucker. Don't think I don't know. Do it right by tomorrow, or Leo dies. Like Lottie. You got that? Tomorrow or he dies.*"

"*But* what—"

The tape ended as the phone went dead.

"That's it," Stewart said. "Not enough time for a trace."

"What now, Inspector?"

Lynley turned towards the voice. Luxford had come to the kitchen door. He was unshaven, he looked unwashed, and his clothes were the same that he'd worn the previous day. The cuffs and the open collar of his white shirt were grimy with his body's perspiration.

" 'You got it wrong,' " Lynley said. "What does he mean?"

"I don't know," Luxford said. "As God is my witness, I do *not* know. I did what he told me to do, to the letter. I don't know what more I could have done. Here." He was carrying a copy of the morning's *Source*, and he extended it to Lynley. He blinked rapidly, eyes red-lidded and bloodshot.

Lynley looked at the paper more closely than he had done upon seeing it earlier that day. The headline and the accompanying photograph were all the kidnapper could have hoped for. They barely required the reader to consume the story that they illustrated. And anyone with the reading skills of a seven-year-old would have been able to comprehend the prose that Luxford had used in assembling his article, at least on the front page. Lynley skimmed it, seeing that the first paragraph alone contained the pertinent answers to who, where, when, why, and how. He did not read on when he came to the end of what the front page held.

"That's what happened as best I remember it," Luxford said. "I may have got some detail wrong. I may have left something out—God knows I don't remember the room number in the hotel—but everything I *could* remember is in that story."

"Yet you got it wrong. What could he mean?"

"I don't know, I tell you."

"Did you recognise the voice?"

"Who the hell could have recognised the bloody voice? It sounded like he was talking with a gag in his mouth."

Lynley glanced beyond him, back towards the drawing room. "Where's your wife, Mr. Luxford?"

"Upstairs. Lying down."

"Got agitated about an hour ago," Stewart added. "She took a pill and had a lie-down."

Lynley nodded at Nkata, who said, "She's upstairs, Mr. Luxford?"

Luxford seemed to realise the intent behind the question, because he exclaimed, "Can't you leave her alone? Does she have to know this now? If she's finally sleeping—"

"She may not be sleeping," Lynley said. "What sort of pill has she taken?"

"Tranquilliser."

"What kind?"

"I don't know. Why? What's this all about? Look. Good Christ. Don't wake her and tell her what's happened."

"She may already know."

"Already? How?" Then Luxford appeared to put it all together, because he said quickly, "You can't still think Fiona has *anything* to do with this. You saw her yesterday. You saw her state. She isn't an actress."

"Check her," Lynley said. Nkata left to do so. "I need a picture of you, Mr. Luxford. I'd like a picture of your wife as well."

"What for?"

"My colleague in Wiltshire. You didn't mention you'd been in Wiltshire recently."

"When the hell was I in Wiltshire?"

"Does Baverstock jog your memory?"

"Baverstock? You mean when I went to the school? Why should I have mentioned a visit to Baverstock? It had nothing to do with anything that's happened. It had to do with enrolling Leo." Luxford seemed to be trying to read Lynley for his assessment of guilt or innocence. He also seemed to glean that assessment because he went on with, "Jesus. What's happening? How can you stand there watching me as if you expect my flesh to start bubbling? He's going to kill my son. You heard it, didn't you? He's going to kill him tomorrow if I don't do what he wants. So what the hell are you doing wasting time interviewing my wife when you could be out there doing something—*anything*— to save my son's life? I swear to God, if something happens to Leo after this . . ." He appeared to notice that he was breathing roughly. He said blankly, "God. I don't know what to do."

DI Stewart did. He opened a cupboard, found a bottle of cooking sherry, and poured half a tumblerful. He said to Luxford, "Drink this."

As Luxford was doing so, Nkata returned with the newspaperman's wife.

If Lynley had thought Fiona Luxford was involved in the death of Charlotte Bowen and the subsequent kidnapping of her son, if he'd thought she had made the recent phone call herself from a cellular phone somewhere within this house, those thoughts were laid to rest instantly by the woman's appearance. Her hair was flattened, her face was swollen, her lips were chapped. She was wearing a crumpled oversized shirt and leggings, the shirt stained in the front as if she'd been sick on it. The smell of sickness was heavy on her, in fact, and she clutched a blanket round her shoulders as if for protection rather than for warmth. When she saw Lynley, her steps faltered. Then she saw her husband and seemed to read disaster on his face. Her own face crumpled.

She said, "No. He isn't. He *isn't*," on an ever-rising scale of fear.

Luxford took her into his arms. Stewart poured more sherry. Lynley led them all back to the drawing room.

Luxford gently eased his wife onto the sofa. She was trembling violently, so he adjusted the blanket round her and circled her shoulders with his arm.

He said, "Leo isn't dead. He isn't dead. All right?"

Weakly, she leaned into his chest. She plucked at his shirt. She said, "He'll be so frightened. He's only eight . . ." And she squeezed her eyes shut.

Luxford pressed her head against him. He said, "We'll find him. We'll get him back." The look he directed towards Lynley asked the unspoken question: How can you believe that this is a woman who engineered the kidnapping of her own son?

Lynley had to admit that her culpability was unlikely. From what he'd seen of Fiona Luxford since her arrival home yesterday afternoon with her son's school cap clutched in her hand, she had not struck a single false note. It would take more than a fine actress to carry off the performance of overwrought anxiety that he'd seen from this woman. It would take a sociopath. And his intuition told him that Leo Luxford's mother was not a sociopath. She was simply Leo's mother.

This conclusion, however, did not yet exonerate Dennis Luxford. There was still the fact that a search of his Porsche had produced Charlotte's spectacles and hairs from her head. And while these might have been plants, Lynley could not dismiss the newspaperman as a suspect. He watched him closely as he said, "We need to examine the newspaper story, Mr. Luxford. If you've got it wrong, then we need to know why." Luxford looked as if he was about to protest, about to argue that their time and their energy could be better spent combing the streets for his son than combing his printed words for an error that could be corrected and thus somehow placate a homicide. Lynley said in answer to that unspoken protest, "The investigation is gaining ground in Wiltshire. We've made progress here in London as well."

"What sort of progress?"

"Among other things, a positive ID on those glasses we found. Hairs from the girl as well. In the same location." He didn't add the rest: Mr. Luxford was standing on shaky ground, so he might want to cooperate as fully as possible.

Luxford got the message. He wasn't a fool. But he said, "I don't know what else I could have written. And I don't see where this direction will take us."

His doubt wasn't unreasonable. Lynley said, "Something may have happened during that week you and Eve Bowen spent together in Blackpool, something that you've forgotten. That incident—a chance remark, a botched encounter of some sort, an appointment or assignation that you cancelled or failed to keep—could be the key to our rooting out whoever is behind what happened to Charlotte and to your son. If we uncover what it is that you left out of the story, we may see a connection to someone, a connection that at the moment is beyond our reach."

"We need Eve for this," Luxford said. When his wife raised her head, he went on with, "There's no other way, Fi. I've written all that I can remember at this point. If there's something left out, she's the only one who can tell me. I have to see her."

Fiona turned her head. Her gaze was dull. "Yes," she said. But the word was dead.

Luxford said to Lynley, "Not here though. With the vultures outside. Not here. Please."

Lynley handed his keys to Nkata, saying, "Fetch Ms. Bowen. Take her to the Yard. We'll meet you there."

Nkata left. Lynley studied Fiona Luxford. He said, "You must be strong for the next several hours, Mrs. Luxford. DI Stewart will be here. The constables will be here as well. If the kidnapper phones, you must try to prolong the conversation to give us a chance at a trace. He may be a killer, but if your son's the last card he's holding, he's not going to harm him while there's still a possibility that he can get what he wants. Do you understand?"

She nodded but didn't move. Luxford touched her hair and said her name. She drew herself up, blanket clutched to her chest. She nodded again. Her eyes became filmed by a transparency of tears, but she didn't shed them.

Lynley said to the other DI, "I'll need your car, John."

Stewart tossed him the keys, saying, "Run over a few of those swine at the end of the drive while you're at it."

Luxford said to his wife, "Will you be all right? Shall I phone someone to stay with you before I go?"

"Go," she said, and it was clear her mind was completely in order on at least one subject. "Leo's the only thing that matters."

27

*L*YNLEY HAD DECIDED in advance that there was little profit in having his meeting with Dennis Luxford and Eve Bowen in an interview room. They might have been disconcerted by the presence of a tape recorder, the absence of windows, and a system of lighting engineered to sallow the complexion and rattle the nerves. But effecting a loss in their self-possession wasn't as important at this point as was garnering their cooperation. So he took Luxford directly to his office, and there they waited for Nkata's return with the Marylebone MP.

Dorothea Harriman thrust a stack of messages in Lynley's direction as they passed her desk. She said in apparent reference to these, "SO7 reporting in on the George Street squat. SO4 on Jack Beard's fingerprints. Wigmore Street on the Special Constables. Two reporters—one from *The Source* and the other from the *Mirror*—"

"How did they get my name?"

"Someone's always willing to blab, Detective Inspector Lynley. Just look at the royals."

"They blab on themselves," Lynley pointed out.

"How times have changed." She referred back to the messages. "Sir David twice. Your brother once—he says not to phone back. It was just about having solved the problem at the Trefalwyn's dairy. Does that make sense?" She didn't wait for an answer. "Your tailor once. Mr. St. James three times. He says you're to phone him as soon as you can, by the way. And Sir David says he wants his report pronto."

"Sir David always wants his report pronto." Lynley took the messages and stuffed them into his jacket pocket. He said to Luxford, "This way," and sat the newsman in his office. He phoned SO4 and SO7 to hear what they had to say about Jack Beard and about the squat. The information was complete but not altogether useful. Jack Beard's criminal record was confirmed by the Fingerprint Office, but his prints were no match for any that they'd found. The carpet from the squat had been examined, and it was going to take at least another week to sort through everything they'd found in it and on it: hairs, semen, blood, urine, and enough food droppings to keep a flock of pigeons happy for hours.

When Nkata arrived with Eve Bowen, Lynley handed the rest of the messages to the DC, along with the photograph of Dennis Luxford that *The Source* editor had provided him. As Nkata hurried off to send the picture to Havers in Wiltshire, to deal with the messages, and to compile a report that would keep the Assistant Commissioner content for another day, Lynley shut the door behind him and turned to Eve Bowen and the man who had fathered her child.

The MP said, "Was this entirely necessary, Inspector Lynley? Do you have any idea how many photographers were waiting to capture the timeless moment when your constable came for me?"

"We could have come to your office," Lynley replied. "But I doubt you would have appreciated that. The same photographers who caught you leaving with DC Nkata would have had a field day recording Mr. Luxford's appearance at your door."

She hadn't acknowledged Dennis Luxford's presence. She didn't do so now. She merely crossed to one of the two chairs in front of Lynley's desk and sat on the edge of it, her back like a shaft. She was wearing a black coatlike dress, double-breasted with six gold buttons. It was politician's clothing without a doubt, but it looked uncharacteristically rumpled, and a ladder in her black stockings, down by the ankle, threatened to snake whitely up the rest of her leg.

She said in a composed voice but without looking in his direction, "I've stepped down at the Home Office, Dennis. And I'm finished in Marylebone. Are you happy now? Fulfilled? Complete?"

"Evelyn, this was *never*—"

"I've lost just about everything," she interrupted. "But there's still hope, according to the Home Secretary. In twenty years, if I keep my nose clean, I could turn myself into John Profumo. Admired, if neither respected nor feared. Isn't that something worth looking forward to?" She gave a false little laugh.

"I wasn't involved," Luxford said. "After everything that's happened, how can you even think I was behind this horror?"

"Because the pieces fit into place so nicely: one, two, three, four.

Charlotte was taken, the threat was made, I failed to capitulate, Charlotte died. That focused attention on me where you wanted it and prepared the way for piece number five."

"Which is what?" Luxford asked.

"Your son's disappearance and the subsequent necessity to ruin me." She finally looked at him. "Tell me, Dennis. How are the newspaper's circulation numbers? Did you finally manage to outdistance the *Sun?*"

Luxford turned away from her, saying, "Good God."

Lynley went to his desk. He sat behind it and faced the two of them. Luxford slumped in his chair, unshaven, his hair unwashed and largely uncombed, his skin the colour of putty. Bowen maintained her unyielding posture, her face like a mask that was painted on her flesh. Lynley wondered what it would take to gain her assistance.

He said, "Ms. Bowen, one child is already dead. Another may die if we don't move quickly." He took the copy of *The Source* that had been at Luxford's house and laid it upside down on his desk so that its lead story was facing the other two people. Eve Bowen glanced at it distastefully, then averted her eyes. "This is what we need to talk about," Lynley said to her. "There's something in here that's incorrect or something that's missing. We need to know what it is. And we need your help to know it."

"Why? Is Mr. Luxford looking for tomorrow's lead? Can't he develop it on his own? He's managed to do that so far."

"Have you read this story?"

"I don't wallow in muck."

"Then I'll ask you to read it now."

"If I refuse?"

"I can't think your conscience will bear the weight of an eight-year-old's death. Not fast upon the heels of Charlotte's murder. And not if you can do something to stop it. But that death will occur—make no mistake about it—if we don't act now to head it off. Please read the story."

"Don't play me for a fool. Mr. Luxford's got what he wants. He's run his little front page article. He's destroyed me. He can carry on for days picking through my remains for additional stories, and I've no doubt he'll do it. But what he won't do at this point is murder his own son."

Luxford lunged forward and grabbed the paper. "Read it!" he snarled. "Read the God damn story. Believe what you want, think what you will, but read this fucking story or so help me God, I'll—"

"What?" she asked. "Move from character assassination to the real thing? Are you capable of that? Could you plunge the knife? Could you pull the trigger? Or would you just rely on one of your henchmen to do the job again?"

Luxford threw the paper into her lap. "You manufacture reality as you go along. I'm through trying to make you see the truth. Read the story, Evelyn. You didn't want to act to save our daughter, and I have no power to change that fact. But if—"

"How dare you refer to her as *our* daughter. How dare you even suggest that I—"

"But *if*"—Luxford's voice grew louder—"if you think I'm going to sit on my hands and wait for my son to be the second victim of a psychopath, you have completely misread me. Now, read the bloody story. Read it now, read it carefully, and tell me what I've got wrong so I can save Leo's life. Because if Leo dies . . ." Luxford's voice splintered. He got to his feet and went to the window. To the glass he said, "You have reason enough to hate me. But don't take your vengeance out on my son."

Eve Bowen watched him the way a scientist watches a specimen from which she hopes to glean some empirical information. A career of distrusting everyone, maintaining her own counsel, and keeping an eye open for backbench backstabbers had not prepared her to accept anyone's credibility. Inherent suspicion—the simultaneous bane and necessity of political life—had brought her to her present state, taking as its hostage not only her position but also, most horribly, the life of her child. Lynley saw clearly that that same suspicion, in conjunction with her animosity for the man who had made her pregnant, prevented her from making the leap of faith that would allow her to help them.

He couldn't accept this. He said, "Ms. Bowen, we've heard from the kidnapper today. He's said he's going to kill the boy if Mr. Luxford doesn't correct whatever facts are incorrect in this story. Now, it isn't necessary for you to believe Mr. Luxford's word. But I'm going to ask you to believe mine. I heard the tape of the phone call. It was made by one of my CID colleagues who was in the house when the call came through."

"That doesn't mean anything," Eve Bowen said. But her remark was less certain than her earlier statements had been.

"Indeed. It doesn't. There are dozens of clever ways to fake a telephone call. But assuming for the moment that the call was genuine, do you want a second death on your soul?"

"I don't have the first one on my soul. I did what I had to do. I did what was right. I'm not responsible. He—" She lifted her hand to gesture at Luxford. For the first time, the hand was trembling slightly.

She seemed to see this and dropped the hand to her lap where the tabloid lay. "He . . . Not I . . ." She swallowed, stared at nothing, and finally said again, "Not I."

Lynley waited. Luxford turned from the window. He started to say something, but Lynley shot him a look and shook his head. Outside Lynley's office, telephones were ringing and he could hear Dorothea Harriman's voice. Inside the office, he held his breath, thinking, *Come on, come on. Damn you, woman. Come on.*

She crumpled the edges of the tabloid. She pushed her spectacles more firmly into place. She began to read.

The telephone rang. Lynley snatched it up. Sir David Hillier's secretary was on the line. When could the AC expect an update on the investigation from his subordinate officer? When it's written, Lynley told her, and dropped the phone.

Eve Bowen turned to the inside page where the story continued. Luxford remained where he was. When she had completed her reading, she sat for a moment with her hand covering the newsprint and her head raised just enough so that her gaze rested on the edge of Lynley's desk.

"He said I've got it wrong," Luxford told her quietly. "He said I have to write it correctly for tomorrow or he'll kill Leo. But I don't know what to change."

"You haven't." Still she wouldn't look at him and her voice was muted. "You haven't got it wrong."

"Has he left out something?" Lynley asked.

She smoothed the paper. "Room 710," she said. "Yellow wallpaper. A watercolour of Mykonos on the wall above the bed. A minibar with very bad champagne, so we drank some of the whisky and all of the gin." She cleared her throat. Still, she looked at the edge of the desk. "Two nights we met for a late dinner out. One night was at a place called Le Château. The other night was an Italian restaurant. San Filippo. There was a violinist who wouldn't stop playing at our table until you gave him five pounds."

Luxford didn't seem able to look away from her. His expression was painful to see.

She continued. "We always separated long before breakfast because that was wise. But the last morning we didn't. It was over, but we wanted to prolong the moment before we parted. So we ordered room service. It came late. It was cold. You took the rose from the vase and . . ." She took off her glasses and folded them in her hand.

"Evelyn, I'm sorry," Luxford said.

She raised her head. "Sorry for what?"

"You said you wanted nothing from me. You wouldn't have me. So all I could do was put money in the bank for her—and I *did* that much, once a month, every month, in her own account—so that if I died, so that if she ever needed anything . . ." He seemed to realise how inconsequential and pathetic his act of taking responsibility had been, cast against the immensity and sheer enormity of what had passed within the last week. He said, "I didn't know. I never thought that—"

"What?" she asked sharply. "You never thought what?"

"That the week might have meant more to you than I realised at the time."

"It meant nothing to me. You meant nothing to me. You mean nothing to me."

"Of course," he said. "I know that. Of course."

"Is there anything else?" Lynley asked.

She returned her glasses to her nose. "What I ate, what he ate. How many sexual positions we tried. What difference does it make?" She handed the tabloid back to Lynley. "There's nothing more from that week in Blackpool that could be of interest to anyone, Inspector. The interesting item has already been printed: For nearly a week, Eve Bowen fucked the left-wing editor of this scurrilous piece of filth. And she spent the next eleven years pretending otherwise."

Lynley directed his attention to Luxford. He considered the words he'd heard on the taped conversation. There did indeed seem nothing else to print to ruin the MP any more thoroughly than she'd already been ruined. This left only one possibility, as unlikely as that possibility seemed: The MP had never been the kidnapper's target.

He began sifting through the files and reports on his desk. Towards the bottom of the mass of material, he found the photocopies of the two initial kidnapping notes. The originals were still with SO7 where the lab was running the lengthy procedure of lifting fingerprints from the paper.

He read the note that had been sent to Luxford, first to himself and then aloud. " 'Acknowledge your firstborn child on page one, and Lottie will be freed.' "

"I acknowledged her," Luxford said. "I claimed her. I admitted it. What more can I do?"

"If you did all that and you still got it wrong, there's only one feasible explanation," Lynley said. "Charlotte Bowen wasn't your first-born child."

"What are you saying?" Luxford demanded.

"I think it's fairly obvious. You have another child, Mr. Luxford. And someone out there knows who that child is."

—m—

Barbara Havers returned to Wootton Cross near teatime with the photograph of Dennis Luxford, which Nkata had faxed to Amesford CID. It was grainy—and its graininess wasn't exactly improved by making several photocopies of it—but it would have to do.

In Amesford, she'd done her best to avoid another run-in with DS Reg Stanley. The detective sergeant had been barricaded in the incidents room behind a fortress of telephone directories. And since he'd had a telephone pressed to his ear and was barking into it as he lit a cigarette with his obnoxious lady's-arse lighter, Barbara had been able to give him a businesslike but otherwise meaningless nod after which she'd gone in search of her fax from London. Once she'd found it and made her copies, she'd hunted down Robin who'd completed his circuit of the narrow-boat hiring locations. He'd come up with three possibilities and he seemed ready to discuss them with her, but she said, "Brilliant. Well done, Robin. Now go back to the possibles and have a go at them with this." She handed over the photocopied picture of Dennis Luxford.

Robin had looked at it and said, "Luxford?"

"Luxford," Barbara replied. "Our strongest candidate for Public Enemy Number One."

Robin had studied the picture for a moment before he said, "Right then. I'll see if anyone recognises him round the boats. What about you?"

She told him she was still on the trail of Charlotte Bowen's school uniform. "If Dennis Luxford slipped that uniform in among the jumble in Stanton St. Bernard, someone had to have seen him. And that's what I'm after."

She'd left Robin fortifying himself with a cup of tea. She'd clambered back into the Mini and headed north. Now she swung round the statue of King Alfred that stood at the crossroads in Wootton Cross, and she drove past the diminutive police station where she'd first met Robin—thinking, as she drove, Was it only two nights ago? She found Barclay's Bank in the high street, between Bull in a China Shop (firsts and seconds) and Mr. Parsloe's Exceedingly Good Cakes (baked fresh daily).

Barclay's was experiencing a quiet afternoon. The place was noiseless, more like a church than a bank. At the far end, a railing marked the area reserved for the operational bigwigs. In this section, cubicles were set up in front of a row of offices. When Barbara asked for "Miss Matheson in New Accounts," a red-headed man with unfortunate teeth directed her towards the cubicle nearest to an office marked Manager. Perhaps, Barbara thought, it was her proximity to this greatness from which the parents of "the young Miss Matheson" derived such pride in their offspring's employment.

Miss Matheson was seated at her desk, her back to Barbara and her face to a computer. She was rapidly inputting data from a sheaf of papers, using one hand to flip from sheet to sheet and the other to fly competently among the keys. She had, Barbara noted, an ergodynamically appropriate chair and her posture was a credit to her erstwhile typing instructor. This wasn't a woman who was going to suffer from carpal tunnel, wry neck, or curvature of the spine. Looking at her, Barbara straightened her own slouch to a rodlike position that she felt fairly confident of being able to hold for at least thirty seconds.

She said, "Miss Matheson? Scotland Yard CID. Could I have a word?"

As she was speaking, the other woman swivelled round in her chair. Barbara's "Could I have a word?" faded to a mumble, and her admirable posture crumbled like a breeze-hit house of cards. She and "the young Miss Matheson" stared at each other. The latter said, "Barbara?" while Barbara said, "Celia?" and wondered what it meant that following the trail of Charlotte Bowen's uniform had taken her in the direction of Robin Payne's intended bride.

Once they recovered from the confusion of seeing each other in an unexpected place, Celia took Barbara upstairs to the employees' lounge, saying, "It's time for my break anyway. I don't expect you've come to open an account, have you?"

The lounge was at the top of a flight of stairs carpeted in a soil-hiding brown. It shared space with a storage room and a unisex lavatory, and it contained two tables and the sort of ergodynamically inappropriate plastic chairs that, in quarter of an hour's break, probably could undo whatever good might be accomplished by sitting in their antitheses the rest of the day. An electric kettle stood on an orange Formica work top, surrounded by cups and boxes of tea. Celia plugged in the kettle and said over her shoulder, "Typhoo?"

Barbara saw the box of tea before she made a fool of herself and said *Gesundheit*. "Fine," she replied.

When the tea was ready, Celia brought two mugs to the table. She used a packet of artificial sweetener; Barbara went straight for the real poison. They were stirring and sipping in the fashion of two wary wrestlers come to the mat when Barbara divulged the reason for her visit.

She brought Celia up to snuff on the discovery of Charlotte

Bowen's school uniform—where it had been found, by whom, and among what—and she noted that the young woman's expression went from guarded to surprised. She removed the picture of Dennis Luxford from her shoulder bag as she concluded, saying, "So what we're wondering is whether this bloke looks familiar to you. Do you recognise him as someone you saw at the fête? Or near the church sometime prior to the fête?"

She handed the photo over. Celia set her tea mug on the table and smoothed the picture flat, holding her hands on either side of it. She looked at it closely and shook her head, saying, "Is that a scar on his chin, then?"

Barbara herself hadn't noticed, but now she looked again. Celia was right. "I'd say so."

"I would have remembered the scar," Celia said. "I'm fairly good with faces. It helps with the customers round here if one can call them by name. I generally use a mnemonic device to help me along, and I would have used that scar."

Barbara didn't want to know what Celia had used in her own case. But she thought it was best to run her through a memory test. She pulled out a picture of Howard Short that she'd snagged while in the CID office. She asked Celia if she recognised him.

This time the response was positive and immediate. "He came to the jumble stall," she said, and she added in an appealing show of honesty that no doubt would have pleased her parents, "but I would have known him anyway. It's Howard Short. His gran comes to our church." She took a sip of her tea. Barbara noted that she was a silent sipper despite the tea's heat. Good breeding will out.

"He's an awfully sweet boy," Celia noted, and passed the picture back to Barbara. "I hope he hasn't got himself into trouble."

Barbara thought that Celia couldn't be much older than Howard Short, so designating him "an awfully sweet boy" seemed a little condescending. Nonetheless, she said, "He seems clean at the moment although he's the one who had the Bowen girl's uniform."

"Howard?" Celia sounded incredulous. "Oh, he can't have anything to do with her death."

"That's what he claims. He says the uniform was just mixed up with the rags in a bag he bought from your stall."

Celia confirmed Howard's story about having bought the rags from her, but she also confirmed her mother's story about how the rags came to be rags in the first place. She went on to describe the jumble stall itself: One portion held racks of hanger-hung clothing, another held tables of folded goods, another held a display of shoes—"We never do sell many of those," she admitted—and the plastic rag bags were in a large box in the stall's far corner. They didn't need to be under anyone's watchful eye because they were, after all, just bags of rags. There was no great monetary loss to the church if one was pinched, although it was distressing to think that someone had used a well-meaning event like the yearly Stanton St. Bernard fête to dispose of something linked to a murder.

"So someone could have placed the uniform in a bag without being noticed by someone else at the till?" Barbara asked.

Celia had to admit that it was possible. Unlikely but possible. The jumble stall was, after all, a popular feature of the yearly fête. Mrs. Ashley Havercombe of Wyman Hall near Bradford-on-Avon generally donated heavily of her personal garments, and there was always a frenzy to get to those in the earliest hours of the day, so during that time . . . Yes, it was possible.

"But you didn't see this man? You're certain?"

Celia was certain. But she hadn't manned the jumble stall all day, so Barbara would do well to show her mother that picture. "She's not as good with faces as I am," Celia said, "but she likes to chat with people, so if he was there, she may have had a few words with him."

Barbara doubted that Luxford would have been so simple-minded as to cache his daughter's uniform among the rags and then underscore his presence by having a chat with the vicar's wife. Nonetheless, she said, "I'm heading back to Stanton St. Bernard from here."

"Not going to Lark's Haven, then?" Celia offered the question in a casual manner as she used her well-shaped thumbnail to trace a decoration on her mug. Barbara looked at the mug and observed the decoration: a fat pink heart with *Happy Valentine's Day* written above it. Idly, she wondered if it had been a gift.

She said, "At the moment? No. Too much work left to do," and she pushed her chair back from the table and made a movement to return the pictures to her bag.

Celia said, "I wondered about everything at first—none of this is really like him, actually—but I worked it all out last night."

Barbara said, "Pardon?" and sat there dumbly with one hand suspended and the pictures dangling from them like an offering gone rejected.

Celia made an unnecessarily scrupulous study of the centre of the table where a dog-eared stack of newsletters bore the title *Barclay's Beat* in fuchsia lettering. She took a deep breath and said with a faint smile, "When he came back from the course this last week, I couldn't understand what had happened to change things between us. Six weeks ago we were everything to each other. Then all of a sudden we were nothing."

Barbara tried to make the cognitive leap into comprehension. *He* would be Robin. *Things* would be their relationship. *The course* would be Robin's time in a CID Detectives Course. She got that much, but Celia's prefatory statement about working it all out left her in the dark. So she said, "Hey, listen. CID's a tough go. This is Robin's first case, so he's bound to be a little preoccupied because he wants to make a success of the investigation. You shouldn't take it to heart if he seems a little distant. That goes with the job."

But Celia maintained her own line of thought. "At first I thought it was because of Corrine's engagement to Sam. I thought, He's uneasy because he's worried that his mother hasn't known Sam as long as she ought to know a man before agreeing to marry him. Robbie's conservative that way. And he's awfully attached to his mother. They've always lived together. But even that didn't seem enough of a reason to make him unwilling to . . . well, to *be* with me. If you know what I mean." She gave Barbara her attention then. She watched her steadily. She seemed to be waiting for some sort of answer to an unspoken question.

Barbara felt entirely unequipped to make a response. The toll paid for their choice of careers by her CID colleagues at the Yard was a heavy one, and she didn't think it would much soothe the other woman to learn of the trail of broken marriages and aborted relationships that her fellow officers left behind them. So she said, "He has to get comfortable in the job. He has to find his sea legs, if you know what I mean."

"Sea legs aren't what he's found. I saw that when I saw you together last night at Lark's Haven. He didn't expect to find me waiting for him. And when he saw me, I didn't even register on his brain. That just about says it, wouldn't you agree?"

"Says what?"

"He met you at that course, Barbara. The detective course. And that's where things started."

"Things? Started?" Barbara felt incredulity spreading through her. It pricked at her brain as she finally understood what Celia was suggesting. "You've been thinking that Robin and *I* . . ." The idea was so ludicrous that she couldn't even complete the sentence. She stumbled on with, "The two of us? Him? With me? Is that what you think?"

"It's what I know."

Barbara fumbled in her bag for her cigarettes. She felt a little dazed. It was hard to believe that this young woman with her fashionable haircut and her fashionable clothes and her slightly plump but undeniably *pretty* face could look upon her as competition. Her, Barbara Havers, with her unplucked eyebrows, her rat's nest of hair, her baggy brown trousers and overlarge pullover both worn to camouflage a body so dumpy that the last man who'd looked on her with desire had done so in another decade and under the influence of so much alcohol that— Bloody hell, Barbara thought. Sodding wonders will never cease.

She said, "Celia, put your mind at rest. There's nothing going on between me and Robin. I just met him two nights ago. As a matter of fact, I tossed him to the ground and stamped on his hand in the bargain." She grinned. "You know, what you see as desire is probably only Robin considering how best to take revenge when he gets the chance."

Celia didn't join her in the jollity. She stood and took her cup to the work top where she ran water into it and placed it carefully among the others stacked helter-skelter into a dish drainer. She said, "That doesn't change anything."

"What doesn't change anything?"

"When you met him. Or how. Or even why. I know Robin, you see. I can read his face. Things are over between us, and you're the reason." She wiped her fingers on a kitchen towel, then brushed her hands together as if to rid them of dust, of Barbara, and most particularly of this encounter. She offered Barbara a formal smile. "Is there anything else you need to speak with me about?" she asked in a voice that she doubtless used with banking customers whom she completely loathed.

Barbara stood as well. "I don't think so," she said. And she added as Celia moved towards the door, "You aren't right, you know. Really. There's nothing going on."

"Not yet, perhaps," Celia said and descended the stairs.

—⁂—

The black officer with the hybrid accent wasn't available to drive her home, so Lynley arranged for an unmarked police car to fetch Eve Bowen from the underground car park and whip her up the ramp onto Broadway. Eve had thought that the change in vehicles—from the ostentatious silver Bentley to this unassuming and less-than-spotless beige Golf—would put the newshounds off her scent. But she was wrong. Her driver made some evasive manoeuvres round Tothill, Dartmouth, and Old Queen Streets, but he was dealing with experts in the field of pursuit. While he shook off two cars whose drivers made the mistake of assuming his destination was the Home Office, a third car picked them up flying north along St. James's Park. This driver was speaking into a car phone, which did much to guarantee there would be others on Eve Bowen's tail before she got anywhere near Marylebone.

The Prime Minister had given his from-the-steps-of-Number-Ten acceptance of her resignation shortly after noon, looking solemn and mouthing all the appropriate sentiments of a man obliged to toe-dance between the opprobrium expected from one who had hung his hat on the peg of A Recommitment to Basic British Values and the acknowledgement required from a fellow Tory to an esteemed Junior Minister who had served him tirelessly and with distinction. The PM managed to strike the right note of regret while simultaneously distancing himself from her. He had, after all, fairly decent speech writers. Four hours later, Colonel Woodward had spoken from the front door of the Constituency Association office. His words had been terse but eminently suitable for the nightly news sound bite: "We elected her; we're keeping her. For now." And ever since those two oracles had decreed her fate, the reporters had been hungry to record her reaction, in words or in pictures. Either would do.

She didn't ask the constable at the wheel of the Golf if the reporters knew that Dennis Luxford had been inside Scotland Yard to meet with her. At this point it didn't make much difference. Her connection to Luxford had become old news the moment Luxford's tabloid had printed it for public consumption. The only matter that now counted with the reporters was the acquisition of a fresh angle on her story. Luxford had scooped every paper in London, and there wasn't an editor from Kensington to the Isle of Dogs who wasn't sledgehammering his staff into remembering that fact. So from this moment until the next news sensation seized the public's fancy, reporters would hound her for some new twist they could use to sell their papers. She could try to outwit them, but she couldn't hope that they would show her any mercy.

They had plenty for tomorrow, courtesy of both the Prime Minister and her Constituency Association Chairman. They had enough to make their current pursuit of her very nearly superfluous. But there was always the chance of something more delectable falling their way. And by God they weren't going to miss an opportunity to shovel another mound of dirt onto her grave.

The constable continued his attempts to elude pursuit. His mastery of the streets of Westminster was so absolute that Eve wondered if he'd done previous duty as a London cabbie. But he was still no match for the fourth estate. When it became apparent that, however circuitously, he was heading for Marylebone, the newshounds merely phoned their colleagues who'd been loitering round Devonshire Place Mews. When

Eve and the Golf finally made the right turn off Marylebone High Street, they were awaited by a phalanx of camera-toting, notebook-wielding, and otherwise shouting individuals.

Eve had always given the appropriate amount of lip-service to the Royal Family. She was a Tory, so it was expected of her. But despite her inner and unspoken certainty that they were nothing more than a brain-less drain on the economy, she found herself wishing that one of them—any of them, it didn't even matter who—had done something this day to merit the rabid attention of the press. Anything to get them off her own back.

The mews was still blocked off, manned by a constable who was ensuring that her home was still off limits. Despite her resignation and no matter what came of that resignation in the next few days, the mews would stay blocked off until the furor died down. She had Sir Richard Hepton's promise of that much. "I don't throw my own to the wolves," he'd said.

No. He just threw them in the general vicinity of the wolves, Eve concluded. But that was politics.

Her driver asked if she wanted him to come inside the house with her. *To secure the premises* was the expression he used. She told him such security wasn't required. Her husband was waiting for her. No doubt he'd already heard the worst. She wanted only privacy.

She heard the cameras shooting off their rapid-fire pictures as she ducked from the car to her doorway. The reporters were shouting from behind the barrier, but their questions were yammered against a back-drop of traffic from the high street and the noise from the outdoor boozers swilling their beers at the Devonshire Arms. She ignored it all. And once she closed the front door behind her, she couldn't really hear it either.

She shot the bolts home. She called out, "Alex?" and went to the kitchen. Her watch gave the time as 5:28, post-tea, pre-dinner. But there was no sign of either meal having been consumed or prepared. It didn't matter terribly much to her. She wasn't hungry.

She climbed the stairs to the first floor. By her count, she'd been wearing the same clothes for eighteen hours now, since leaving the house the previous night for her barren attempt to fend off disaster. She could feel the clammy touch of her dress cradling her armpits, and her underpants clung damply to her crotch like an inebriate's palm. She wanted a bath, a long, hot soak in a tub with scented oil and a beauty mask to scrape the filth from her skin. After that she wanted a glass of wine. She wanted it white and chilled with a musky aftertaste that would remind her of bread-and-cheese picnics in France.

Perhaps that's where they'd go, until things died down and she was no longer the Fleet Street scandalmongers' flavour-of-the-month. They would fly to Paris and hire a car. She would lean back in her seat and close her eyes and let Alex drive her wherever he wished. It would be good to get away.

In their bedroom, she stepped out of her shoes. She called, "Alex?" again, but only silence answered. Beginning to unbutton her dress, she went back to the corridor and called his name again. Then she remembered the time and realised he'd be at one of his restaurants, where he usually was in the afternoon. She herself was never home at this hour. Doubtless the house, which seemed so preternaturally quiet, was really quite in order. Still, the air seemed hushed, the rooms seemed so breathlessly waiting for her to discover . . . what? she wondered. And why did she feel such a certainty that something was wrong?

It was nerves, she thought. She'd been through hell. She needed that bath. She needed that drink.

She stepped out of her dress, left it in a lump on the floor, and went to the cupboard for her dressing gown. She pulled open the doors. And there it was. She saw what the silence had been trying to tell her.

His clothes were gone: every shirt, every suit, every pair of trousers and shoes. They were so thoroughly gone that not a single wisp of slut's wool had been left behind to give evidence that someone had once used this length of now-empty rod, this line of shelves, and this wooden tree to store garments and shoes.

The chest of drawers was the same. As were the bedside table and, in the bathroom, the vanity and the medicine cabinet. She couldn't imagine how long it had taken him to remove every vestige of himself from the house. But that's exactly what her husband had done.

She made certain of this by checking the study, the sitting room, and the kitchen. But everything that had marked his presence in the house—as well as in her life—was gone.

She thought, Bastard, *bastard*. He'd chosen his moment so well. What better means of driving the sword through her flesh than to wait until he could make her public humiliation complete. There was no doubt that those carrion eaters waiting on Marylebone High Street had seen him leaving, Volvo packed to the bursting point. And now they were waiting to record her reaction to this final moment of her life's obliteration.

Bastard, she thought again. The filthy bastard. He'd taken the easy course, slinking out of here like a puling adolescent when she wasn't around to ask any questions or demand replies. It had been simple for him: Just pack up, go, and leave her to face the chorus of questions. She could hear them now: Is this a formal separation? Is your husband's leaving related in any way to this morning's revelations by Dennis Luxford? Was he aware of your affair with Mr. Luxford prior to the story in today's *Source*? Has your stand on the sanctity of marriage altered in the past twelve hours? Is divorce in the offing? Have you any statement at all that you'd like to make in regards to—

Oh yes, Eve thought. She had plenty of statements. She just wouldn't be making them to the press.

She went back to the bedroom and hurriedly dressed. She applied fresh lipstick. She combed her hair and smoothed her fingers over her eyebrows. She went to the kitchen where the calendar hung. She read the word *Sceptre* on Wednesday's square in Alex's neat hand. How propitious, she thought. The restaurant was in Mayfair, less than ten minutes by car.

She saw the reporters snap to attention behind the police barrier when she pulled her car out of the garage. There was a general scramble among them as those with vehicles in the vicinity made a race for them to follow her. At the barrier, the constable leaned into her car and said, "Not a good plan to set out alone, Ms. Bowen. I can have someone here in—"

"Move the sawhorse," she told him.

"This lot's going to be on your tail like mad hornets."

"Move the sawhorse," she repeated. "Move it now."

His look said *bloody stupid bitch*, but his mouth said, "Right." And he swung aside the wooden barrier to give her access to Marylebone High Street. She gunned her car through a fast left turn and sped in the direction of Berkeley Square. Sceptre was tucked away at the corner of a cobblestone mews just southwest of the square. It was a handsome building of brick and vines with a profusion of lush tropical plants in the entry.

Eve arrived well in advance of the reporters, who'd had the disadvantage of consuming time in scuttling for their cars and adhering to the rules of the road, which she herself had ignored. The restaurant wasn't open for business yet, but she knew that the kitchen staff had probably been there since two and before. Alex would be among them. She went to the side door and rapped on it sharply with her brass key ring. She was inside the dry storage room, face-to-face with the pastry chef, before the trailing reporters were even out of their vehicles.

"Where is he?" she asked.

The pastry chef said, "Working on a new aioli. We've a swordfish special tonight, and he—"

"Spare me the details," Eve said. She brushed past him and went to the kitchen, past the enormous refrigerators and the open-fronted cabinets where the pots and pans shimmered in the bright overhead lights.

Alex and his head chef were at a work top, conversing over a mound of minced garlic, a bottle of olive oil, a heap of chopped olives, a bouquet of cilantro, and a currently untouched collection of tomatoes, onions, and red chilis. Round them, the preparations for the evening's dinner were in full swing as assistants made soup, prepared the night's starters, and washed everything from arugula to radicchio. The mixture of scents would have been intoxicating had she been hungry. But food was the last thing on her mind.

She said, "Alex."

He looked up.

She said, "I want a word." She was aware of an instant's hush after she spoke, but it was followed by the kitchen noise rising again with pot-banging determination. She waited for him to play the puling adolescent a second time in twenty-four hours: "Can't you see I'm busy? This will have to wait." But he didn't do that. He merely said to his chef, "We need to get our hands on some nopalitos before tomorrow," and then to Eve, "The office."

A bookkeeper was seated in the office's only chair. At a desk she was dealing with a mound of bills. She appeared to be in the midst of arranging them into some sort of order, and she looked up when Alex opened the door. She said, "I swear we've been overcharged again from that stall in Smithfield, Alex. We need to change suppliers or do something to—" She suddenly seemed to register the fact that Eve was standing behind her husband. She lowered the account she'd been referring to and looked round the room as if seeking a place to which she could retreat.

Alex said, "Five minutes, Jill. If you wouldn't mind."

She said, "I've been longing for a cup of tea." She got to her feet and hurried past them. Eve noted that the other woman didn't look her in the eye.

Alex shut the door. Eve had expected him to appear mortified, embarrassed, regretful, or even belligerent. She didn't expect to find on his face a bleak desolation that lined it deeply.

She said, "Explain yourself."

"What would you like me to say?"

"I wouldn't *like* you to say anything in particular. I want to know what's going on. I want to know why. I think you owe me that much."

"You've been home, then."

"Of course I've been home. What did you think? Or did you expect the reporters to be the ones to inform me my husband has left me? I take it you managed the move right in their view?"

"I did most last night. The rest this morning. The reporters weren't there yet."

"Where are you staying?"

"That isn't important."

"Isn't it? Why?" She looked towards the door. She recalled the expression that had crossed the bookkeeper's face when she'd seen her standing behind Alex in the corridor. What had it been? Alarm? Dismay? Cat with the canary? What? She said, "Who is she?"

Wearily, Alex closed his eyes. It seemed a struggle for him to open them again. "That's what you think this is all about? Another woman?"

"I'm here to understand what this is about."

"I can see that. But I don't know if I can explain it to you. No, that's not true. I can explain. I can explain and explain right into tomorrow, if that's what you want me to do."

"It's a start."

"But the end of my explaining will be the beginning of it. You won't understand. So it's better for both of us to walk away from each other, to cut our losses and spare each other the worst."

"You want a divorce. That's it, isn't it? No. Wait. Don't answer yet. I want to make certain I understand." She walked to the desk, placed her bag upon it, and turned to face him. He stayed where he was by the door. "I've just passed through the worst week of my life, with more to come. I've been asked to stand down from the Government. I've been told to vacate my parliamentary seat at the next election. My personal history is in the process of being smeared all over the national tabloids. And you want a divorce."

His lips parted as he took a breath. He looked at her but not with anything that resembled recognition. It was as if he'd retreated to another world in which the inhabitants were altogether different from the woman who shared the office with him at this moment. "Listen to yourself," he said in an exhausted murmur. "Fuck it, Eve. Just listen for once."

"To what?"

"To who you are."

His tone wasn't cold and it wasn't defeated. But it was resigned in a way she'd never heard before. He was speaking like a man who'd drawn a conclusion, but whether she comprehended that conclusion appeared to be a matter of indifference to him. She crossed her arms and cradled her elbows. She pressed her fingernails into her skin. She said, "I know damn well who I am. I'm the current fodder for every paper in this country. I'm the object of universal derision. I'm yet another victim of a journalistic frenzy to mould public opinion and effect a change in the Government. But I'm also your wife, and as your wife I want some straight answers. After six years of marriage, you owe me something more than psychospeak, Alex. 'Just listen to who you are' isn't exactly sufficient grounds for anything other than an escalating row. Which is what this is going to turn into if you don't explain yourself. Am I being clear?''

"You've always been clear," her husband replied. "I was the one in a fugue. I didn't see what was in front of my face because I didn't want to see it."

"You're talking absolute nonsense."

"To you, yes. I can see that it would be. Before this last week, I would have thought it nonsense myself. Rubbish. Rot. Complete bullshit. Whatever you will. But then Charlie disappeared, and I had to look at our life straight on. And the more I looked at it, the more offensive our life became."

Eve stiffened. The distance between them seemed comprised not only of space but of ice. She said, "And what exactly did you expect our life to be like with Charlotte kidnapped? With Charlotte murdered? With her birth and her death made a source of titillation across the country?"

"I expected you to be different. I expected too much."

"Oh, did you? And what is it that you expected of me, Alex? A hairshirt? Ashes smeared on my face? My clothing ripped? My hair hacked off? Some sort of ritual expression of grief that you could approve of? Is that what you wanted?"

He shook his head. "I wanted you to be a mother," he said. "But I saw that all you ever really were was someone who'd mistakenly given birth to a child."

She felt anger grasp her in its hot, violent fist. She said, "How *dare* you suggest—"

"What happened to Charlie—" He stopped. The rims of his eyes became red. He cleared his throat roughly. "What happened to Charlie was really all about you from the first. Even now, with her dead, it's all about you. Luxford's running that story in the paper was all about you as well. And this—me, my decision, what I've done—that's nothing more than something about you, another dent in your political aspirations, something to explain away to the press. You live in a world where how things look has always taken precedence over how things are. I was simply too stupid to realise that until Charlie was murdered." He reached for the doorknob.

She said, "Alex, if you walk out on me now . . ." But she didn't know how to complete the threat.

He turned back to her. "I'm sure there's a euphemism—perhaps even a metaphor—that you can give the press to explain what's happened between us. Call it what you will. It makes no difference to me. Just so long as you call it over."

He swung the door open. The sounds from the restaurant's kitchen rose round him. He began to leave the office, then hesitated, looking back at her. She thought he was going to say something about their history, their life together, their now abortive future as husband and wife. But instead he said, "I think the worst was wanting you to be capable of love, and through that wanting, believing you were."

"Are you going to talk to the press?" she asked him.

His answering smile was wintry. "My God, Eve," he said. "Jesus. My God."

28

*L*UXFORD FOUND HER in Leo's bedroom. She was sorting through his drawings and placing them into neat piles by topic. Here were his meticulous copies of Giotto's angels, Madonnas, and saints. There were quick line sketches of frail ballerinas and top-hatted dancers. Next to them sat a small stack of animals, mostly squirrels and dormice. And all by itself in the centre of the desk lay a drawing of a small boy sitting dejectedly on a three-legged stool, behind the bars of a prison cell. This last looked like an illustration from a children's book. Luxford wondered if his son had copied it from Dickens.

Fiona appeared to be studying this last picture. She was holding the top of a pair of Leo's plaid pyjamas to her cheek. She rocked gently in the chair, a barely perceptible movement with her face pressed against the worn flannel.

Luxford couldn't conceive how she would be able to endure the newest blow he'd come to deal her. He'd wrestled with his past and with his conscience all the way from Westminster to Highgate. But he'd managed to find no easy way to tell her what the kidnapper was requiring of him now. Because the full horror was that he didn't have the information that was being demanded of him. And he hadn't been able to create a single way to tell his wife that their son's life sat in the pan of a balance into whose other pan Luxford could place nothing.

"There were calls," Fiona said quietly. She didn't look away from the drawing.

Luxford felt a surge in his guts. "Did he—"

"Not from the kidnapper." She sounded empty, as if every emotion had been wrung out of her. "Peter Ogilvie first. He wanted to know why you held back the story on Leo."

"Good God," Luxford whispered. "Who's he been talking to?"

"He said you're to phone him at once. He said you're forgetting your obligations to the paper. He said you're the key to the biggest story of the year, and if you're holding back on your own newspaper, he wants to know why."

"Oh God, Fi. I'm sorry."

"Rodney phoned as well. He wants to know what you want on tomorrow's front page. And Miss Wallace wants to know if she should allow Rodney to continue using your office for the news meetings. I didn't know what to tell any of them. I said you'd phone when you could."

"Sod them."

She rocked gently, as if she'd managed to divorce herself from what was going on. Luxford bent to her. He touched his mouth to the honey-coloured hair at her crown. She said, "I'm so afraid for him. I imagine him alone. Cold. Hungry. Trying to be brave and all the time wondering what's happened and why. I remember reading once about a kidnapping where the victim was put in a coffin and buried alive, with an air supply. And there was only so much time to find her before she suffocated. And I'm so frightened that Leo's been . . . that someone may have hurt him."

"Don't," Luxford said.

"He won't understand what's happened. And I want to do something to help him understand. I feel so useless. Sitting here, waiting. Not being able to do a thing while all the time someone out there holds my whole world hostage. I can't bear thinking of his terror. And I can't think of anything else."

Luxford knelt by her chair. He couldn't bring himself to say what he'd been saying to her for more than twenty-four hours: We're going to get him back, Fiona. Because for the very first time, he wasn't sure: of Leo's safety or of anything else. He felt he was walking on ice so brittle that one precipitate step would destroy them all.

Fiona stirred, turned in her chair to face him. She touched the side of his head and dropped her hand to his shoulder. "I know you're suffering as well. I've known that from the first, but I didn't want to see it because I was looking for someone to blame. And you were there."

"I deserve the blame. If it hadn't been for me, none of this would have happened."

"You did something unwise eleven years ago, Dennis. But you aren't to blame for what's happened now. You're a victim as much as Leo is. As much as Charlotte and her mother were victims. I know that."

The generosity of her forgiveness felt like a claw tightening round his heart. Guts roiling, he said, "I must tell you something."

Fiona's grave eyes watched him. "What was missing from the story in this morning's paper," she concluded. "Eve Bowen knew. Tell me. It's all right."

It wasn't all right. It could never be all right. She'd spoken about looking for someone to blame and until this afternoon he'd been doing the same thing. Only in his case he'd been blaming Evelyn, using her paranoia, her odium, and her gross stupidity as reasons why Charlotte was dead and Leo was hostage. But now he knew where true responsibility lay. And sharing that knowledge with his wife was going to shatter her.

She said, "Dennis, tell me."

He did. He began with what little Eve Bowen had been able to contribute to the story in the newspaper, he continued with Inspector Lynley's interpretation of the phrase *your firstborn child*, and he concluded with a verbalisation of what he'd been contemplating ever since leaving New Scotland Yard. "Fiona, I don't know this third child. I never knew of its existence before now. As God is my witness, I don't know who it is."

She looked dazed. "But how can you possibly not know . . . ?" As she realised what his ignorance implied, she turned away from him. "Were there so many of them, Dennis?"

Luxford sought a way to explain who he had been in the years before they'd met, what had driven him, what demons had trailed him. He said, "Before I knew you, Fiona, sex was something I just did."

"Like brushing your teeth?"

"It was something I needed, something I used to prove to myself . . ." He gestured aimlessly. "I don't really know what."

"You don't? You don't really know? Or you don't want to say?"

"All right," he said. "Manhood. An attraction to women. Because I was always afraid if I didn't keep proving to myself how deadly attractive I was to women . . ." He looked back, as she did, to Leo's desk, to the drawings, their delicacy, their sensitivity, their heart. They represented the fear he'd lived his life in avoidance of facing. Finally, it was his wife who gave it voice.

"You'd have to deal with having been so deadly attractive to men."

"Yes," he said. "That. I thought there must be something wrong with me. I thought I was somehow giving off something: an aura, a scent, an unspoken invitation. . . ."

"Like Leo."

"Like Leo."

She reached forward then for the picture of the little boy that their son had drawn. She held it up so that the light caught it directly. She said, "This is how Leo feels."

"We'll get him back. I'll write the story. I'll confess. I'll say anything. I'll name every woman I've known and beg each one to step forward if—"

"Not how he feels right now, Dennis. I mean this is how Leo feels all the time."

Luxford took the picture. Holding it closer, he could see the boy was meant to be Leo. The white hair identified him, as did the too-long legs and the fragile ankles, exposed because the trousers were outgrown and the socks were rucked. And he'd seen that defeated posture before, only last week in the restaurant in Pond Square. A closer inspection of the sketch showed him that another figure had been in it initially. Erased now, the faint outline remained, enough to see the paisley braces, the crisp shirt, and the etching of a scar across the chin. This figure was overly large—inhumanly large—and it loomed over the child like a manifestation of his future doom.

Luxford crumpled the picture. He felt beaten down. "God forgive me. Have I been that hard on him?"

"As hard as you've been on yourself."

He thought of his son: how watchful he was in his father's presence, how careful not to make a mistake. He recalled the times the boy tried to accommodate his father by toughening his walk, roughing up his voice, avoiding the words that might brand him a sissy. But the real Leo always bled through the persona he worked so hard to produce: sensitive, easily given to tears, open-hearted, eager to create and to love.

For the first time since, as a schoolboy, he'd accepted the importance of masking emotion and soldiering on, Luxford felt anguish ballooning dangerously in his chest. But he shed no tears. "I wanted him to be a man," he said.

"I know that, Dennis," Fiona replied. "But how could he be? He can't be a man until he's allowed to be a little boy."

Barbara Havers felt deflated when she saw that Robin's car wasn't in the drive of Lark's Haven upon her return from Stanton St. Bernard. She hadn't consciously thought about seeing him since her odd conversation with Celia—Celia's conclusion about the nature of their relationship being too stupid to dignify by considering it—but when she saw the vacant spot where he usually left his Escort, she breathed out, "Oh hell," and realised that she'd been counting on talking the case through with a colleague, much in the way she talked through cases with Inspector Lynley.

She'd been back to the rectory in Stanton St. Bernard where she'd shown the photograph of Dennis Luxford to Mr. Matheson and his wife. They'd stood with it under the light in their kitchen—each holding a side of it—and one saying to the other, "What do you think, pet? Is he someone familiar?" and the other answering, "Oh my dear, my memory's a useless old thing," and both of them tentatively concluding that this was a face they hadn't seen. Mrs. Matheson said she would have probably remembered the hair, noting with a sheepish little smile that she always "did like a young man with a lovely head of hair." Mr. Matheson, whose hair was rather sparse, said that unless he'd engaged in some sort of liturgical, personal, or religious dialogue with an individual, he never did much remember faces. But still, if this one had been at the church, in the graveyard, or at the fête, his face would have looked at least somewhat familiar. As it was . . . They were sorry but they couldn't remember him.

Barbara acquired no different answer from anyone else in the village. Nearly everyone she met wanted to help, but no one was able to. So, knackered and hungry, she returned to Lark's Haven. It was long past time to phone London anyway. Lynley would be waiting to assemble something suitable to keep AC Hillier out of their hair.

She trudged to the door. There'd been no word on Leo Luxford. DS Stanley was employing his grid once again, with a heavier concentration on the area round the windmill. But they'd had no indication that the kid was even in Wiltshire, and showing his picture in every hamlet, village, and town had produced nothing but a montage of shaking heads.

Barbara wondered how two children could disappear so thoroughly. Having grown up in a sprawling metropolitan area, she herself had been drilled endlessly in her childhood with the only injunction that was secondary to "look both ways before crossing the street." This was "and never talk to strangers." So what had happened with these two children? Barbara wondered. No one had seen them dragged screaming off the street, which meant that each of them had gone willingly. So had they never been told to be wary of strangers? Barbara found this impossible to believe. So if they *had* been drilled with that timeless injunction as she had been, then the only conclusion was that whoever had taken them wasn't a stranger to them at all. So who was common to both these children?

Barbara was too hungry to look for a link. She needed to eat—she'd stopped and bought a Corned Beef Crispbake ("just pop it in the oven") for that express purpose at Elvis Patel's Grocery—and after she ate, perhaps she'd have the blood sugar and the brainpower necessary to make sense of the data she had and to look for a connection between Charlotte and Leo.

She glanced at her watch as she went in the front door, Crispbake in hand. It was nearly eight o'clock, the perfect hour for elegant dining. She hoped Corrine Payne wouldn't mind if she commandeered the oven for a while.

"Robbie?" Corrine's wispy voice came from the direction of the dining room. "That you, darling?"

"It's me," Barbara said.

"Oh. Barbara."

Since the dining room was on Barbara's route to the kitchen, she couldn't avoid a meeting with the woman. She found her standing over the dining table on which was spread out a length of sprigged cotton. Corrine had pinned a pattern to this and was in the process of cutting it.

Barbara said, "Hullo. Mind if I use the oven?" and she lifted the Crispbake for Corrine's inspection.

"Robbie isn't with you?" Corrine slid the scissors beneath the material. She snipped along the pattern.

"Still on the job, I expect." Barbara winced, realising after she'd said it that she'd chosen a rather unfortunate expression.

Corrine smiled down at her work and murmured, "Yourself as well, I suppose?"

Barbara felt her neck itch. She tried to speak airily. "Masses of stuff to be done. I'll just heat this up and get out of your way." She headed towards the kitchen.

"You almost had Celia convinced," Corrine said.

Barbara stopped. "What? Convinced?"

"About you and Robbie." She continued to cut along the line of the pattern. Was it imagination, Barbara wondered, or had Corrine's scissors picked up the pace? "She phoned here not two hours ago. You didn't expect that, did you, Barbara? I could tell by her voice, of course—I'm very good at that—and while she didn't want to tell me, I had the story out of her. I think she needed to talk. One does, you know. Would you like to talk to me?" She looked up and met Barbara's gaze quite pleasantly. But the way she raised her scissors sent hackles running like mice up and down Barbara's spine.

Barbara wasn't one for subterfuge. She'd missed that coursework entirely during her days at school. She often thought her inability to master feminine wiles was the main reason she spent every New Year's

Eve listening to the radio and eating most of a St. Michael's Toffee Pecan Dream Pie. So she thrashed round in her head for an appropriate response that would direct Corrine Payne onto another topic, but she ended up saying, "Celia's got the wrong idea about me and Robin, Mrs. Payne. I don't know where she got it, but it's altogether wrong."

"Corrine," Corrine said. "You're to call me Corrine." She lowered the scissors and began to cut again.

"Right. Corrine. So I'll just pop this in the oven and—"

"Women don't get 'wrong ideas,' Barbara. We're far too intuitive for that. I've seen the change in Robbie myself. I simply didn't know what name to put upon it until your arrival. I understand why you might lie to Celia." On the word *lie*, the scissors snapped with excessive energy. "She is, after all, Robbie's intended. But you're not to lie to me. That won't do at all." Corrine gave a gentle cough as she concluded. Barbara noticed for the first time that her breathing was congested. She watched as the older woman patted her chest smartly, smiled, and said, "Nasty old asthma. Too much pollen in the air."

"Rough in the springtime," Barbara said.

"You can't imagine how rough." Corrine had moved round the table as she'd continued her cutting. She now stood between Barbara and the kitchen door. She cocked her head and produced an affectionate smile. She said, "So tell me, Barbara. No lies to Corrine."

"Mrs. Pay—Corrine. Celia's upset because Robin's preoccupied. But that's always the way it is in a murder investigation. One gets caught up. One forgets about everything else for a while. But when the case is over, life gets back to normal, and if she'll just be patient, she'll see I'm telling the truth."

Corrine tapped the tip of the scissors against her lip. She examined Barbara appraisingly and when she returned to her cutting, she returned to her theme of choice as well. "Please don't take me for a fool, dear. That's unworthy of you. I've heard you together. Robbie's tried to be discreet. He's always been terribly thoughtful that way. But I've heard him going in to you in the night, so I'd prefer we be honest with each other about everything. Lies are so unpleasant, aren't they?"

The implication rendered Barbara speechless for a moment. She stammered, "Going in? Mrs. Payne, are you thinking that we've been—"

"As I said, Barbara, you may feel the need to lie to Celia. She is, of course, his intended bride. But you mustn't lie to me. You're a guest in my home, and that isn't very nice."

Paying guest, Barbara wanted to clarify as Corrine's scissors began to pick up speed. Soon to be ex-guest if she could pack her belongings fast enough. She said, "You've got everything wrong, both you and Celia. But let me clear out. It'll be better for everyone."

"And give you greater access to Robbie? Through a place where you can meet and do your business with perfect freedom?" Corrine shook her head. "That wouldn't be proper. And it wouldn't be fair to Celia, would it? No. I think it's best that you stay right here. We'll get this sorted out as soon as Robbie gets home."

"There's nothing to sort. I'm sorry if Robin and Celia are having troubles, but it's nothing to do with me. And you'll only embarrass the hell out of him if you try to make a case that he and I . . . that we . . . that he's been . . . I mean while I've been here . . ." Barbara had never felt so flustered.

"Do you think I'm making this up?" Corrine asked. "Are you accusing me of producing a falsehood?"

"Not at all. I'm only saying you're mistaken if you think—"

"*Mistaken's* no different from lying, dear. *Mistaken's* the word we use in place of *lying.*"

"Maybe you do, but I—"

"Don't argue with me." Corrine's breath caught raspily in her chest. "And don't deny. I know what I've heard and I know what it means. And if you think that you can open your legs and take my Robbie from the girl he's meant to marry—"

"Mrs. Payne. Corrine."

"—then you had better think again. Because I'm not going to stand for it. Celia's not going to stand for it. And Robbie . . . Robbie . . ." She gasped for a breath.

"You're getting yourself worked up over nothing," Barbara said. "You're going red in the face. Please. Sit down. I'll talk if you want to. I'll try to explain. Just settle down or you'll make yourself ill."

"And wouldn't you like that?" Corrine waved the scissors in a way that set Barbara's nerves on edge. "Isn't that *just* what you've had planned from the first? With his mum out of the way, no one else would be here to make him realise he's about to throw his entire life away for a piece of rubbish when he could have . . ." The scissors clattered to the table. She reached for her chest.

"Hell," Barbara said. She made a move towards Corrine. Gasping stertorously, Corrine motioned her off. Barbara said, "Mrs. Payne, be rational. I met Robin just two nights ago. We've spent a grand total of about six hours in each other's company because we've not been working the same part of the case. So think about it, won't you? Do I look like a *femme fatale* to you? Do I look like someone Robin would want to sneak in to in the middle of the night? And after an acquaintance of only six hours? Does that make sense?"

"I've been watching the two of you." Corrine struggled for breath. "I've seen. And I know. I know because I phoned to—" Her fingers grasped her chest.

Barbara said, "It's nothing. Please. Try to stay calm. If you don't, you're going to—"

"Sam and I . . . We set the date and I thought he'd want to be . . . first one . . ." She wheezed. "To know . . ." She coughed. She wouldn't give in. "But he wasn't there, was he, and we both know why and aren't you ashamed—ashamed, *ashamed*—to be stealing another woman's man." The sentence drained her. She crumpled over the table. Her breathing sounded as if she were sucking in air through the eye of a needle. She grabbed on to the length of material she'd been cutting. She dragged it with her as she sank to the floor.

"Flaming hell!" Barbara leapt forward. She shouted, "Mrs. Payne! Hell! Mrs. Payne!" She grabbed the other woman and turned her onto her back.

Corrine's face had altered from red to white. Blue edged her lips. "Air," she panted. "Breathe . . ."

Barbara dropped her back to the floor without ceremony. She surged to her feet and began to search. "The inhaler. Mrs. Payne, where is it?"

Corrine's fingers weakly moved in the direction of the stairway.

"Upstairs? In your room? In the bathroom? Where?"

"Air . . . please . . . stairs . . ."

Barbara tore up the stairs. She chose the bathroom. She flung open the medicine cabinet. She swept a half dozen medications into the basin beneath it. She flung out toothpaste, mouthwash, plasters, dental floss, shaving cream. There was no inhaler.

She tried Corrine's room next. She pulled drawers from the chest and dumped out their contents. She did the same with the bedside table. She looked on the bookshelves. She went to the clothes cupboard. Nothing.

She raced into the corridor. She could hear the woman's agonised breathing. It seemed to be slowing. She shouted, "Shit! *Shit!*" and hurled herself at a cupboard, where she drove in her arms and began throwing everything onto the floor. Sheets, towels, candles, board games, blankets, photo albums. She'd emptied the cupboard in less than twenty seconds with no more success than she'd had anywhere else.

But she'd said *stairs*. Hadn't she said *stairs*? Hadn't she meant . . . ?

Barbara raced back down the stairs. At the foot of them stood a half-moon table. And there among the day's post, a lush potted plant, and two pieces of decorative crockery sat the inhaler. Barbara snatched it up and dashed back to the dining room. She placed it into the woman's mouth and pumped frantically. She said, "Come on. Oh God. Come on," and she waited for the medical magic to work.

Ten seconds passed. Twenty. Corrine's respiration finally eased. She kept breathing with the assistance of the inhaler. Barbara kept holding her lest she slip away somehow.

And that's how Robin came upon them, less than five minutes later.

—⁓—

Lynley ate his dinner at his desk, courtesy of the fourth floor. He'd phoned Havers three times—twice at Amesford CID and once at Lark's Haven, where he'd left a message with a woman who'd said, "Rest assured, Inspector, I'll make certain she gets it," in the sort of deadly polite tone that suggested what Barbara was going to get might include far more than his request that she phone London with her day's summary of her part of the investigation.

He'd phoned St. James as well. There, he'd spoken only to Deborah who said her husband hadn't been home when she herself had returned from a day's shooting in St. Botolph's Church just a half hour before. She said, "Seeing the homeless there . . . It puts everything in perspective, doesn't it, Tommy?" Which gave him an opportunity to say, "Deb, about Monday afternoon. I have no excuse other than to say I was acting like a boor. No, I *was* a boor. That whole bit about killing children was inexcusable. I'm terribly sorry." To which, after a thoughtful and entirely Deborah-like pause, she replied, "I'm sorry as well. I'm rather vulnerable when it comes to that sort of thing. Children. You know." To which he said, "I know. I know. Forgive me?" To which she replied, "Ages ago, dear Tommy," although it had only been forty-eight hours since the harsh words had passed between them.

After speaking to Deborah, he'd phoned Hillier's secretary to give an approximate time when the AC might expect his report. Then he'd phoned Helen. She'd told him what he already knew—that St. James wanted to speak to him and had been wanting to speak to him since noon that day. She'd said, "I don't know what it's all about. But it has something to do with that picture of Charlotte Bowen. The one you left at Simon's. On Monday.''

Lynley said, "I've spoken to Deborah about that. I've apologised. I can't unsay what I said, but she seems willing to forgive me.''

"That's quite like her.''

"It is. Are you? Willing, that is.''

There was a pause. He picked up a pencil and used it to doodle on top of a manila folder. He sketched out her name like a schoolboy. He imagined her gathering resources for a reply. He heard the sound of crockery at the other end of the line and realised that he'd interrupted her dinner, which was the first reminder he'd had that he hadn't thought much about eating since breakfast.

He said, "Helen?''

She said, "Simon tells me I must decide. Into the fire or off the stove altogether. He's an into-the-fire man himself. He says he likes the excitement of an uncertain marriage.''

She'd gone right to the heart of the matter between them, which was unlike her. Lynley couldn't decide if this was good or bad. Helen tended to use indirection to find her direction out. But he knew there was truth to what St. James had told her. They couldn't go on like this indefinitely, one of them hesitant to make a complete commitment, the other willing to accept that hesitation rather than having to face rejection. It was ridiculous. They weren't in the frying pan. For the last six months they hadn't even got close to the burner.

He said, "Helen, are you free at the weekend?''

"I'd planned a lunch with Mother. Why? Won't you be working, darling?''

"Possibly. Probably. Definitely, if this case isn't closed.''

"Then what—?''

"I thought we might get married. We have the licence. I think it's time that we used it.''

"Just like that?''

"Directly into the fire.''

"But what about your family? What about my family? What about guests, the church, a reception . . . ?''

"What about getting married?'' he persisted. His voice was light enough, but his heart was full of trepidation. "Come along, darling. Forget about the frippery. We can do that part of it later if you like. It's time to make the leap.''

He could almost feel her weighing her options, attempting to explore in advance every possible outcome of permanently and publicly tying her life to his. When it came to making decisions, Helen Clyde was the least impetuous woman he knew. Her ambivalence maddened him, but he'd long ago learned that it was part of who she was. She could spend quarter of an hour trying to decide what stockings to don in the morning and an additional twenty minutes poring over her earrings for the perfect pair. Was it any wonder that she'd spent the last eighteen months trying to decide first if, then when, she would marry him?

He said, "Helen, this is it. I realise the decision is difficult and frightening. God knows I have doubts myself. But that's only natural, and there comes a time when a man and a woman have to—"

"Darling, I know all that," she said reasonably. "There's no real need to give me a pep talk."

"There isn't? Then, for God's sake, why won't you say—?"

"What?"

"Say yes. Say that you will. Say something. Say anything to give me a sign."

"I'm sorry. I didn't think you needed a sign. I was only considering."

"What, for God's sake?"

"The most important detail."

"Which is?"

"Heavens. I expect you know that as well as you know me: What on earth shall I wear?"

He told her he didn't care what she wore. He didn't care what she wore for the rest of their lives. Sackcloth and ashes, if she chose. Blue jeans, leotards, satin and lace. She laughed and said she would hold him true to his words. "I have just the accessories to go with sackcloth."

Afterwards, he realised just how hungry he was, and he went to the fourth floor, where the special sandwich of the day was avocado and prawn. He bought one, along with an apple, and he took both back to his office with the apple balanced on a cup of coffee. He'd downed half of this makeshift meal when Winston Nkata came to the door, a piece of notebook paper in his hand. He looked perplexed.

"What is it?" Lynley asked.

Nkata ran his finger along the scar on his cheek. He said, "I don't know what to make of it." He lowered his lanky frame into one of the chairs and referred back to his paper. "I just got off the phone with the Wigmore Street station. They been working on the specials since yesterday. Remember?"

"The special constables?" When Nkata nodded, Lynley said, "What about them?"

"You remember that none of the Wigmore Street regulars rousted that bloke from Cross Keys Close last week?"

"Jack Beard? Yes. So we assumed it was one of the volunteers at the station. Have you located him?"

"Can't be done."

"Why not? Aren't their records accurate? Has there been a change in personnel? What's happened?"

"No to both and nothing to the last," Nkata said. "Their records are fine. And the same person coordinates the specials as always has done. In the last week, there's no one quit. And no one added onto the roster."

"So what are you telling me?"

"That Jack Beard wasn't rousted by a special constable. Or by a regular Wigmore Street constable either." He leaned forward in his chair, crumpled up the paper, tossed it into the rubbish. "I got the feeling that Jack Beard wasn't rousted by anyone at all."

Lynley thought about this. It didn't make sense. They had two independent corroborative statements—aside from the tramp's own—that Beard had indeed been shooed off from those Marylebone mews the very same day Charlotte Bowen had disappeared. While both of the statements had initially been gathered by Helen, officers on the case had taken formal statements from the very same people who had witnessed the exchange between the vagrant and the constable who'd run him out of the close. So unless there was a conspiracy among Jack Beard and the inhabitants of Cross Keys Close, there had to be another explanation. Such as, Lynley supposed, someone posing as a constable. Police uniforms weren't impossible to come by. They could be hired in a costume shop.

The implications behind this line of thought made Lynley uneasy. He said more to himself than to Nkata, "We've an open field."

"It looks to me like we got a field with nothing on it."

"I don't think so."

Lynley looked at his watch. It was too late to start phoning costume shops now, but how many could there be in London? Ten? Twelve? Less than twenty, surely, and first thing tomorrow morning—

The telephone rang. It was reception. A Mr. St. James was waiting below. Would the inspector see him? Lynley said he would. Indeed he would. He sent Nkata to fetch him.

St. James didn't bother with the social niceties when he entered Lynley's office with Winston Nkata five minutes later. He merely said, "Sorry. I couldn't wait any longer for you to return my calls."

Lynley said, "It's been madness round here."

"Right." St. James took a seat. He was carrying a large manila envelope, which he set on the floor, balanced against his chair leg. He said, "Where are you with it? The *Evening Standard* was concentrating on an unnamed suspect in Wiltshire. Is that the mechanic you were telling me about last night?"

"Courtesy of Hillier," Lynley said. "He wants the public to know how well their taxes are being spent in the area of law enforcement."

"What else do you have?"

"A great number of loose ends. We're looking for a way to tie them together."

He brought St. James up-to-date on the case, both the London end of it and the Wiltshire end of it. St. James listened intently. He interjected the occasional question: Was Sergeant Havers certain that the photograph she'd seen at Baverstock was of the same windmill where Charlotte Bowen had been held? Was there a connection between the church fête at Stanton St. Bernard and anyone associated with the case? Had any of Charlotte's other belongings been found—the rest of her uniform, her schoolbooks, her flute? Could Lynley identify the regional accent of whoever it was who had phoned Dennis Luxford's home that afternoon? Had Damien Chambers any relations in Wiltshire, specifically any relations involved in policework there?

"We haven't gone that route with Chambers," Lynley said. "His politics put him in the IRA camp, but his connection to the Provos is fairly remote." Lynley outlined the facts that they had gathered on Chambers. He ended with, "Why? Have you something on Chambers?"

"I can't forget the fact that he was the only person, aside from her schoolmates, who called her Lottie. And because of that, he's the only link that I can make between Charlotte and whoever killed her."

"But there's lots of folks who might've known what the bird was called without calling her that themselves," Nkata pointed out. "If her schoolmates called her Lottie, her teachers would've known it. Her mates' parents would've known it. Her own parents would've known it. And that's not even taking into account her dancing teacher, the leader of her choir, the minister where she went to church. As well as anyone who might've heard someone yelling her name when she was walking down the street."

"Winston has a point," Lynley said. "Why are you focused so firmly on the name, Simon?"

"Because I think that revealing his knowledge of Charlotte's nickname was one of the mistakes the killer made," St. James said. "Another was the thumbprint—"

"—inside the tape recorder," Lynley concluded. "Are there more mistakes?"

"One more, I think," St. James reached for the manila envelope. He opened it and slid its contents onto Lynley's desk.

Lynley saw that the contents comprised the photograph of Charlotte Bowen's dead body. It was the photograph he had tossed at Deborah and then left behind after their row.

St. James said, "Have you the kidnapping notes?"

"Copies only."

"Those'll do."

The notes came easily to Lynley's hand since he'd made use of them only a few hours earlier when Eve Bowen and Dennis Luxford had been in his office. He took them up and set them next to the photograph. He waited for his brain to make a connection between them. As he did so, St. James came round to his side of the desk. Nkata leaned forward.

"I had a long look at the notes last week," St. James said. "On Wednesday night, after seeing both Eve Bowen and Damien Chambers. I was restless, trying to fit pieces together. So I spent some time assessing the writing." As he spoke, he indicated each point he was making by placing the rubber end of a pencil against it. "Look at the way he forms his letters, Tommy, the *t* and the *f* especially. The crosspiece of each leads into the formation of the letter behind it. And look at the *w*'s, always alone, unconnected to the rest of the word. And notice the *e*'s. They're always connected to what follows them, but never connected to what precedes them."

"I can see the two notes are the work of the same hand," Lynley said.

"Yes," St. James said. "And now look at this." He turned over the photograph of Charlotte Bowen, exposing her name, which had been written on the back. "Look at the *t*'s," he said. "Look at the *e*'s. Look at the *w*."

"Christ," Lynley whispered.

Nkata got to his feet. He joined St. James, on the other side of Lynley's chair.

"That's the reason I asked about Damien Chambers' connection to Wiltshire," St. James said. "Because it seems to me that someone—like Chambers—passing along the information to an accomplice in Wiltshire is the only way that whoever wrote her name on the back of this picture could have known her nickname when he wrote these two notes as well."

Lynley considered all of the facts they had. They led, it seemed, to one reasonable, frightening, and ineluctable conclusion. Winston Nkata straightened from his examination of the notes and gave that conclusion voice.

He blew out a lungful of air, saying, "I think we got ourselves some serious trouble."

"My thought exactly," Lynley responded and reached for the phone.

29

A T THE SIGHT OF BARBARA and his mother on the floor, Robin went as white as mash at high tea. He cried out, "Mum!" and dropped to his knees. He reached for Corrine's hand tentatively, as if she might dissolve at too rough a touch.

Barbara said, "She's okay. She had a spell, but she's okay now. I tore the place up looking for her inhaler though. I've left a mess upstairs."

He didn't seem to hear her. He said, "Mum? What happened? Mum? Are you all right?"

Corrine made a feeble movement towards her son. She said, "Sweet chappie. Robbie," in a weak murmur, although her breathing had vastly improved. "Had a spell, darling. But Barbara . . . saw to me. Quite all right in a moment. Don't worry."

Robin insisted that she go to bed at once. "I'll phone Sam for you, Mum. Is that what you'd like? Shall I ask Sam to come round?"

Her eyelids fluttered as she shook her head wearily. "Just want my little boy," she murmured. "My Robbie. Just like old times. All right with you, darling?"

"Of course it's all right." Robin sounded indignant. "Why wouldn't it be all right? You're my mum, aren't you? What're you thinking?"

Barbara had a good idea what Corrine was thinking, but she said nothing. She was more than happy to hand the other woman over to Robin's care. She helped him get his mother to her feet and then assisted the two of them up the stairs. He went into the bedroom with her and shut the door. From behind it, Barbara could hear their voices,

Corrine's fragile and Robin's soothing, like a father speaking reassuringly to a child. He was saying, "Mum, you've got to take more care. How can I give you over to Sam if you won't start taking more care?"

In the corridor, Barbara knelt among the wreckage she'd made of the linen cupboard. She began sorting through the sheets and the towels. She'd got as far as the board games, the candles, and the vast miscellanea that she'd earlier flung to the floor, when Robin came out of his mother's bedroom. He pulled the door shut gently behind him.

He said hastily, "Hang on there, Barbara," when he saw what she was doing. "I'll see to that myself."

"I'm the one who created the havoc."

"You're the one who saved my mother's life." He came to her and extended his hand. "Up," he said. "And that's an order." He softened his words with a smile, adding, "If you don't mind being ordered round by a lowly DC."

"You're hardly lowly."

"I'm glad of that."

She took his hand and allowed herself to be raised to her feet. She hadn't made much progress with the mess. She said with a dip of her head towards the floor, "I did pretty much the same with her bedroom. But I expect you saw that."

"I'll put it right. I'll do the same here. Have you had your dinner?"

"I was going to heat up something from the grocery."

"That won't do."

"No. It's fine. Really. A Crispbake."

"Barbara . . ." He made her name sound like a prefatory remark. His tone was low and all of a sudden underscored with a feeling she couldn't define.

She said quickly, "I got the Crispbake at Elvis Patel's. Have you been in that shop? With a name like that, I had to stop in. Sometimes I think I should've been born in the fifties because I've always had a thing for blue suede shoes."

"Barbara . . ."

She plunged on with more determination. "I was taking it to the kitchen to heat it up. That's when your mum had her spell. I almost couldn't find the inhaler. The way I tossed the house, it looks like—" She hesitated. His expression had become rather intense, the sort of intense that probably would have conveyed an encyclopaedia of unspoken meaning to a woman with more experience, but to Barbara it conveyed nothing other than a wary feeling that she was wading in waters deeper than she had previously thought. He said her name a third time and she felt as if a hot rash was breaking out across her chest. What in hell did those intent eyes of his mean? More, what did it mean when he said *Barbara* the same tender way she usually said *more clotted cream*? She went on in a hurry. "Anyway, your mum had her spell not ten minutes after I got home. So I never had a chance to heat the Crispbake."

"So you could do with a meal," he said reasonably. "And I could do with a meal as well." He took her arm and she could tell that the gentle pressure he placed upon it was intended to guide her towards the stairs. He said, "I'm a good cook. And I've brought home some lamb chops that I'll grill for us. We've got fresh broccoli and some decent-looking carrots." He paused and looked at her directly. It was some sort of challenge and she wasn't entirely sure how to read it. "Will you let me cook for you, Barbara?"

She wondered if *cook for you* was some sort of new age double entendre. If so, she couldn't suss out its meaning. She had to admit she was hungry enough to bolt down a wild boar, so she decided that it could hardly hurt their working relationship if she let him whip up a quick dinner for her. "Okay," she said. Still, she felt that she would be accepting the meal under completely false pretences if she didn't make clear to Robin what had passed between her and his mother earlier. Obviously, he saw her as Corrine's saviour and was perhaps feeling a tender gratitude for the part she'd played in the evening's drama. And while it was true that she'd saved Corrine, what was also true was that she was the *agent provocateur* behind Corrine's asthma attack as well. He needed to know that. It was only fair. So she disengaged his hand from her arm and said, "Robin, we need to talk about something."

At once, he looked guarded. Barbara knew that feeling. *We need to talk about something* generally heralded the other shoe's dropping, and in this case it could only drop in one of two locations: on their professional relationship or their personal relationship . . . if they even had a personal relationship. She wanted to reassure him in some way, but she was too inexperienced in man-woman talk to do so without looking like an idiot. So she just blundered on.

"I spoke to Celia today."

"Celia?" If anything, he looked even more guarded. "Celia? Why? What's going on?"

Brilliant, Barbara thought. He was building defences and she'd only made her initial remark. "I had to see her about the case—"

"What's Celia got to do with the case?"

"Nothing as it turns out, but I—"

"Why talk to her, then?"

"Robin." Barbara touched his arm. "Let me say what I have to say, okay?"

He looked uncomfortable, but he nodded although he said insistently, "Can't we talk below? While I make our dinner?"

"No. I need to tell you this now. Because you might not want to cook dinner for me afterwards. You might feel the need to take some time tonight to straighten things out with Celia." He looked perplexed, but before he had a chance to question her, she hurried on. She explained what had happened, first at the bank with Celia, then at Lark's Haven with his mother. He listened to it all—going grim in the face at the start, saying, "Damn," in the middle, standing silent at the end. When he didn't make a remark within thirty seconds of her having concluded, she persisted. "So I think it's for the best that I clear out of here after our meal. If your mum and your girlfriend have the wrong idea—"

"She's not my—" He cut in quickly, but he stopped himself before finishing. He said, "Look, can we talk about this downstairs?"

"There's nothing more to talk about. Let's clean up this mess, and then I'll pack my things. I'll have dinner with you, but then I've got to get out of here. There's no other choice." She bent to the task a second time. She began to gather up a scattered Monopoly game whose money and property cards were mixed in with the markers from an ancient game of Snakes and Ladders.

He reached for her arm again and stopped her. This time his grip was quite firm. He said, "Barbara. Look at me," and his voice—like his grip—was utterly altered, as if *man* had suddenly taken the place of *boy*. She felt an odd lurch in her heartbeat. But she did as he asked. He guided her upwards again. He said, "You don't see yourself as others see you. I've recognised that from the first. I expect you don't see yourself as a woman at all, a woman who might be of interest to a man."

She thought, Holy shit. But what she said was, "I think I know who and what I am."

"I don't believe it. If you knew who and what you are, you wouldn't have told me what Mum thinks about us—what Celia thinks about us—in the way that you did."

"I just gave you the facts." Her voice was steady. She liked to think it was even light. But she was acutely aware of his proximity and everything that his proximity implied.

"You gave me more than the facts. You told me that you didn't believe."

"Believe what?"

"That what Celia and Mum have seen is true. That I feel something for you."

"And I do for you. We've been working together. And when you work with someone, there's a camaraderie that develops that might—"

"What I've been feeling goes beyond camaraderie. Don't tell me you haven't recognised that because I won't believe you. We click together, and you know it."

Barbara didn't know what to say. She couldn't deny that there had been a small spark between them from the beginning. But it had seemed so unlikely that anything could come of it that she'd first ignored the spark and later doused it as best she could. That was the logical way to proceed, she'd told herself. They were colleagues, and colleagues shouldn't become enmeshed. And even if they hadn't been colleagues, she wasn't so thick-headed that she'd for a moment forgotten the negative baggage she carried round with her: most notably her face, her figure, her manner of dress, her brusque demeanour, and her porcupine personality. Where was the man on earth who would ever see through all that rubbish to who she actually was?

He seemed to read her mind. He said, "It's the inside of people that's important, not the outside. You look at yourself and you see a woman who'd never appeal to a man. Right?"

She swallowed. He hadn't moved away from her yet. He was expecting some sort of response, and she was going to have to make one sooner or later. Either that, or she would have to run to her room and slam the door. So say something, she told herself. Answer him. Because if you don't . . . because he's moving closer . . . because he might very well think . . .

The words gushed out of her. "It's been a long time. I haven't actually been with a man in . . . I mean . . . I'm just no *good* at this . . . Don't you want to phone Celia?"

"No," he said. "I don't want to phone Celia." He closed the scant distance between them and kissed her.

Barbara thought, Bloody hell, flaming saints, holy shit. Then she felt his tongue in her mouth and his hands on her face, then her shoulders, then her arms, then seeking her breasts. And she ceased to think. He moved against her. He backed her to the wall. He stood so that she could feel all of him, so that there would be no mistaking his intentions. Her mind said, No, best run, best hide. Her body said, Finally and bloody well time.

The telephone rang. The noise broke them apart. They stood staring at each other, breathless, guilty, bodies hot, eyes wide. They spoke simultaneously, Barbara with, "You'd better—" Robin with, "I ought to—"

They laughed. Robin said with a smile, "Let me get that. Stay where you are. Don't move an inch. Promise?"

"Yes. All right," Barbara said.

He went into his bedroom. She could hear his voice: the soft *hullo*, the pause, and then, "Yes. She's here. Hold on." He came out of the room with a cordless phone. He handed it to Barbara, saying, "London. Your guv."

Sodding hell, she thought. She ought to have phoned Lynley by now. He'd have been waiting for her report since late afternoon. She put the phone to her ear as Robin opened the linen cupboard and bent to the task of stowing its contents away once more. She could still taste the flavour of him in her mouth. She could still feel the pressure of his hands on her breasts. Lynley couldn't have called at a less opportune moment.

She said, "Inspector? Sorry. We've had a bit of a crisis here. I was just about to phone you."

Robin looked up at her, grinned, and went back to the work at hand.

Lynley said quietly, "Is the constable with you?"

"Of course he is. You just spoke to him."

"I mean with you now. In the same room."

Barbara saw Robin look up at her again. He cocked his head quizzically. She shrugged her shoulders at him and said to Lynley, "Yeah," but she could hear her voice rise as she made the confirmation into a question. Robin went back to his work.

Lynley said to someone else in his office, "He's with her," and then he went on, his voice terse and unlike him, "Listen carefully, Barbara. Keep yourself still. There's a very good chance Robin Payne's our man."

Barbara felt glued to the spot. She couldn't have reacted had she even tried. She opened her mouth and somehow the words "Yes sir" came out, but that was the limit of what she could say.

He said, "Is he still there? In the room? With you?"

"Oh quite." Barbara moved her gaze jerkily from the opposite wall to Robin, where he squatted on the floor. He was stacking up photo albums.

Lynley said, "He wrote the kidnapping notes; he wrote Charlotte's name and the case number on the back of the crime scene pictures. St. James has gone over them all. The writing's a match. And we've confirmation from Amesford CID that Payne did the writing on the back of those pictures."

"I see," Barbara said. Robin was putting the Monopoly game back into order. Money here. Houses there. Hotels next to them. She stole a glance at one of the Chance cards. *Get out of gaol free.* She wanted to howl.

"We've traced his movements over the last few weeks," Lynley was continuing. "He was on holiday, Barbara, which gave him the time to be in London."

"That *is* news, isn't it?" Barbara said. Past Lynley's words, however, she heard what she should have heard before, what she would have heard had she not been blinded by the thought—or was it the hope, you twit?—of a man's potential interest in her. She could hear each of them speaking and the very contradiction of what they had said should have waved red flags of warning in her face:

"I made CID *just three weeks ago,*" Robin's voice, "*that's when I finished the course.*"

But Celia had said, "*When he came back from the course last week . . .*"

And Corrine had cried, "*When I phoned . . . he wasn't there.*" And that last was most telling of all. Barbara could hear it echoing round her skull. He wasn't there, he wasn't there, he wasn't there at the detective course. Because he was in London, setting his plan in motion: trailing Charlotte, tracking Leo, getting to know each child's movements and mapping the route he would use when it came time to snatch them.

Lynley was saying, "Barbara. Are you there? Can you hear me?"

She said, "Oh yes, sir. Quite. The connection's fine at this end." She cleared her throat because she knew she sounded odd. "I was just pondering all the whys and wherefores. You know what I mean."

"His motive? There's another child out there somewhere. Beyond Charlotte and Leo, Luxford has a third child. Payne knows its identity. Or the identity of its mother. That's what he wants Luxford to put in the paper. That's what he's wanted from the first."

Barbara watched him. He was reaching to gather up a collection of candles, which had spilled from the cupboard. Red, bronze, silver, pink, blue. How could it be? she wondered. He looked no different than he'd looked before when he'd been holding her, when he'd been kissing her, when he'd been acting as if he wanted her.

She said, carrying on the charade but still looking for the slightest chance, "So the facts are perfectly straight, then? I mean, Harvie looked so bloody *clean*, didn't he? I know we had the Wiltshire connection from the first, but as to the rest . . . Hell, sir, I hate to throw a wrench, but have you checked every angle?"

"Are we certain Payne's our man?" Lynley clarified.

"That's the question," Barbara said.

"We're within an inch of certainty. What's left is the print."

"Which one is that?"

"The one St. James found inside the recorder. We're bringing it to Wiltshire—"

"Now?"

"Now. We need a confirmation from Amesford CID. They'll have his prints on file there. When we make the match, we'll have him."

"And then?"

"Then we do nothing."

"Why?"

"He's got to lead us to the boy. If we take Payne before that, we run the risk of losing the child. When Luxford's paper comes out in the morning without the story Payne wants to see in it, he's going to head for the boy. That's when we'll grab him." Lynley continued, his words low and urgent. He told her she was to carry on as before. He told her that Leo Luxford's safety was paramount. He emphasised that they must wait and do nothing and let Payne lead them to where he had the boy hidden. He told her that once they had confirmation on the fingerprint, Amesford CID would put the house under surveillance. All she had to do until that time was to carry on as normal. "Winston and I are leaving for Wiltshire now," he told her. "Can you maintain things where you are? Can you carry on? Can you go back to whatever you were doing before I phoned?"

"I expect so," she said, and she wondered how the hell she was going to manage it.

"Fine," Lynley said. "As far as he knows, we're closing in on Alistair Harvie, then. You carry on exactly as before."

"Yes. Right." And then she paused and added for good measure, as if in response to something else Lynley said, "Tomorrow morning? Right. That's no problem. Once you've got Harvie in the nick, he'll tell you what he's done with the boy. You won't need me out here any longer, beating the bushes. What time do you want me at the Yard?"

"Well done, Barbara," Lynley said. "Hold fast as you are. We're on our way."

Barbara punched the button to disconnect the call. She watched Robin at work on the floor. She wanted to pounce on him and beat both truth and reality from him. And she wanted the result of that beating to be that Robin was as he'd first seemed. But she knew she was powerless to do anything at the moment. Leo Luxford's life was far more important than her coming to understand two minutes of clutch-and-grope amid the towels and the bedsheets of the linen cupboard. As she said, "Shall I put the phone . . . ?" Robin looked up at her, and she saw why he had been so intent upon cooking the dinner, upon straightening up the mess she had made, upon keeping her occupied with him and distracted from what she'd inadvertently uncovered in the linen cupboard. He'd picked up the candles. He was preparing to stow them back inside the cupboard. But among the tapers in his grasp was a silver candle that wasn't actually a candle at all. It was part of a flute. Charlotte Bowen's flute.

Robin got to his feet. He shoved what he held along one side of a stack of towels. Barbara saw, among the detritus on the floor, another section of the flute lying next to the case from which it had fallen. He scooped this up among a handful of pillowcases. He put it in the cupboard. Then he took the phone from her and said, "I'll stow it," and he grazed her cheek with his fingers as he passed her on the way to his room.

She expected his spurious ardour to have undergone a change once the flute was out of sight. But when he came back to her, he smiled as he approached. He ran a finger along her jaw and bent to her.

Barbara thought of the lengths to which she would go in the line of duty. This wasn't one of them. His tongue felt like a reptile in her mouth. She wanted to snap her jaws shut and grind her teeth until she could taste his blood. She wanted to knee him in the balls so that stars shot out of his miserable eye sockets. She wasn't about to roger a homicide for love, for money, for Monarch, for country, for duty, or for the sick thrill of it all. But that, she realised, was the very reason Robin Payne wanted to roger her. The sick thrill of it all. The great big belly laugh of having it off with the very cop who was trying to track him down. Because that's what he'd been doing all along, in one form or another. He'd been having it off metaphorically at her expense.

Barbara could feel the anger burning holes in her chest. She wanted to smash in his face. But she could hear Lynley telling her to carry on. So she considered how best to buy time. She didn't think it would be difficult. She had an excuse right here in the house. She pulled away from Robin's kiss and said in a whisper, "Bloody hell, Robin. Your mum. She's just in her room. We can't—"

"She's asleep. I gave her two pills. She'll be out till morning. There's nothing to worry about."

So much for plan one, Barbara thought. And then in a flash she registered what he'd said. Pills. *Pills*. What *sort* of pills? She needed to get back to the bathroom posthaste because she had little doubt of what she would find among the prescriptions she'd swept from the shelves of the medicine chest. But she wanted to be sure.

Robin enclosed her, one arm on the wall, the other hand on the back of her neck. She could feel the tensile strength in his fingers. How easy it must have been to hold Charlotte Bowen beneath the water until she died.

He kissed her again. His tongue probed. She stiffened. He withdrew. He looked at her intently. He was, she saw, nobody's fool. "What?" he asked her. "What's going on?"

He knew something was up. And he wasn't going to take the bait if she again tried to hook him with her concerns about his mother. So she told him the truth because something about him that she hadn't seen before—a predatory sexuality—told her there was a possibility that he would interpret the truth in a way that would serve her needs. "I'm afraid of you."

She saw the suspicion flicker in his eyes. She kept hers steadily, trustingly on his.

"I'm sorry," she went on. "I tried to tell you before. It's been ages since I've been with a man. I don't much know what to do any longer."

The flicker in his eyes went out. He himself moved in. "It'll all come back to you," he murmured. "I promise."

She suffered through another kiss. She made what she hoped was an appropriate sound. In answer to this, he took her hand. He guided it to him. He curved her fingers round him. He tightened them to squeeze him. He groaned.

Which gave her the excuse to break away. She was careful to sound breathless, confused, dismayed. "This is going too fast. Robin, hell. You're an attractive man. God knows you're sexy. But I'm just not ready for . . . I mean, I need a bit of time." She rubbed her knuckles fiercely into her hair. She gave a laugh that was meant to sound rueful. She said, "I feel completely inept. Can't we slow things down? Give me a chance to—"

"But you're leaving tomorrow," he pointed out.

"Leaving . . . ?" She caught herself at the edge of the precipice. "But that's only to London. And how long does it take to get to London? Eighty miles? No time at all if you want to be there bad enough." She offered him a smile and cursed herself for spending so little time in her life practising womanspeak. "So do you? Want to be in London? Bad enough, I mean?"

He ran his finger down the bridge of her nose. He used three fingers to smooth against her lips. She remained immobile and ignored the impulse to snap her way down to the third knuckle.

"I need some time," she said again. "And London's not far. Will you give me some time?"

She was out of her minuscule bag of dubious female tricks. She waited to see what would happen next. She wouldn't have said no to a *deus ex machina* at about this time. Someone zipping down from on high in a fiery chariot would have been just the ticket. But she was in Robin's hands as much as he was in hers. She was saying, Not now, not here, not yet. The next move was entirely up to him.

He touched his mouth to hers. He slid his hand down the front of her. He cupped her so quickly between the legs that she might not have felt the gesture at all except for the fact that he did it hard so that once his hand was gone, she could still feel its hot pressure. "London," he said. And he smiled. "Let's have dinner."

—m—

She stood at her bedroom window, straining her eyes out into the dark. There were no streetlamps on the Burbage Road, so she had to depend on the moonlight, the starlight, and the occasional lights from a passing vehicle to reveal a sign that Lynley's promised police surveillance was in place.

Somehow, she had gagged down her dinner. She couldn't remember now what else he'd cooked other than the lamb chops. There'd been serving dishes on the dining room table, and she'd picked from them in a semblance of eating. She'd chewed, she'd swallowed, she'd drunk a glass of wine after switching it with his—just as a precaution— when he'd gone into the kitchen to fetch the vegetables. But she'd tasted nothing. The only one of her five senses that had appeared to be functioning was her sense of hearing. And she'd listened to everything: to the sound of his footsteps, to the rhythm of her own breathing, to the scrape of their knives against china, and most of all to the muted noises from outside. Was that a car? Were those the soft thuds of men taking up position? Was that a doorbell ringing somewhere, allowing the police access to a house from which they could wait for Robin to make his move?

Conversation with him had been torture. She'd been acutely conscious of the risk of asking the wrong questions—in the guise of a growing intimacy between them—that would inadvertently betray her knowledge of his guilt. To avoid doing that, she had talked instead.

There was little enough to sustain conversation and less that she wished to share with him. But if he was to believe that she harboured a dream of seeing him upon her return to London, she knew she had to keep stars in her eyes and happy anticipation in her voice. She had to look at him directly. She had to make him think she wanted him conscious of her lips, her breasts, her thighs. She had to make him talk, and when he did, she had to hang on his words as if they were the manna for which she was starving.

It wasn't exactly an act she had perfected. By the end of the meal, she was utterly clapped out. By the time they'd cleared the dishes from the table, her nerves were strung taut.

She'd said she was ready to drop, the day had been a long one, she'd need to make an early start in the morning, she was due at the Yard at half past eight, and with traffic what it was . . . If he didn't mind, she'd take herself off to bed.

He hadn't minded. He'd said, "You've been through it today, Barbara. You deserve a decent kip." He'd walked with her to the foot of the stairs and caressed the back of her neck as a goodnight.

Once she was out of his line of vision, Barbara waited to hear the movements that would tell her he'd returned to the dining room or to the kitchen. When the sounds of crockery being washed floated up to her, she slipped into the bathroom where earlier she'd sought out Corrine's inhaler.

Breath held and moving as noiselessly as possible, she'd shifted through the prescription bottles that lay in the basin where she'd tumbled them. She read labels eagerly. She came across drugs for nausea, for infection, for discomfort, for diarrhoea, for muscle spasms, and for indigestion, all of them prescribed for the same patient: Corrine Payne. The bottle she was looking for wasn't there. But it *had* to be . . . if Robin was who Lynley thought he was.

Then she'd remembered. He'd given Corrine pills. If they'd been with the other prescriptions originally, he would have had to root through the basin—as she had just done—to find them. Finding them, he would have scooped up the bottle and shaken two pills into his hand and . . . What had he done with the bloody bottle? It wasn't replaced in the medicine cabinet. It wasn't on the basin's ledge. It wasn't in the wastebasket. So where . . . ? She saw it, sitting on the top of the cistern. She gave a mental crow of triumph and grasped it in her hand. *Valium*, she read on its label. And the directions to the patient: *Take one tablet at the onset of stress.* And the additional small warning label: *May cause drowsiness. Do not mix with alcohol. Take only as directed.*

She'd returned the bottle to the top of the cistern. Gotcha, she thought. She'd gone to her room.

She'd made quarter of an hour's bedtime noises. She thunked herself onto the bed and turned out the light. She waited five minutes and then slipped to the window. Which is where she now stood, watching and waiting for a sign.

If she knew they were there—and Lynley had said they would be—then she should see some sign of them, shouldn't she? An unmarked van? A dim light behind a curtain in that house across the road? A movement near those trees by the drive? But she saw nothing at all.

How long had it been since Lynley's call? she wondered. Two hours? More? He'd phoned from the Yard, but they were setting off at once, he'd said. They'd make good time on the motorway if there hadn't been a smash-up somewhere. The country roads to Amesford were a bit of a problem, but surely they would have arrived by now. Unless Hillier had stopped them. Unless Hillier had demanded a full accounting. Unless bloody sodding Hillier had thrown his usual wrench in the works . . .

She heard Robin's footsteps in the corridor outside her door. She flew to the bed and scrambled beneath its covers. She forced herself to breathe the breath of the living dead, and she laboured to hear her door's knob turn, her door swing open, and his stealthy tread come across the room.

Instead, she heard noise in the bathroom. He was peeing like a fire hose. It went on and on. Then the toilet *whooshed*, and when its noise receded, she heard a *ticky-click* that she recognised. Pills being rattled round in a bottle.

She could hear the pathologist's explanation so clearly, as if he were standing right here in the room. "She was drugged before she was drowned," he'd said, "which explains why there are no significant marks on the body. She wouldn't have been able to put up a struggle. She was unconscious when he held her under the water."

Barbara shot upright. She thought, The boy. He isn't going to wait for the paper tomorrow. He's going after the boy tonight and he's using the Valium to do it. She cast the covers to one side and silently darted to the door. She ventured a hair's crack opening.

Robin came out of the bathroom. He went across to his mother's room and opened her door. He watched for a moment, appeared satisfied, then turned in Barbara's direction. She shut her door. There was no bolt. Nor was there time to race to the bed before he reached her. She stood with her head pressed against the wood. She prayed, Walk on, walk on, walk on. She could hear him breathing on the other side of the wood. He tapped quietly. She did nothing. He whispered, "Barbara? Asleep? Can I come in?" And then he tapped again. She pressed her lips together and held her breath. A moment later she heard him on the stairs.

He lived in the house. So he knew there was no bolt on her door. So he hadn't wanted in, because if he had wanted in, he would have walked in. So he had only wanted to assure himself that she was asleep.

She eased her door open. She could hear him below. He'd gone into the kitchen. She crept down the stairs.

He'd closed the kitchen door behind him, but he hadn't latched it completely. She cracked it the width of a strand of yarn. She could hear more than she could see: a cupboard opening, an electric can opener whirring, the sound of metal clinking on tile.

Then he passed within her line of vision, a large red Thermos in his hand. He rummaged in a cupboard and brought out a small chopping block. Onto this he placed four blue tablets. He crushed them into powder with the back of a wooden spoon. He neatly swept this powder into the Thermos.

He moved to the cooker where something was heating. He stirred for a minute. She could hear him whistling under his breath. Then he carried a pan to the Thermos and funneled into it hot steaming liquid, tomato soup by the smell of it. After he capped the Thermos, he scrupulously cleaned away all evidence of his work. He gave a glance round the kitchen, patted his pockets, brought forth his car keys. He went out into the night, switching the kitchen lights off behind him.

Barbara raced for the stairs. She flew up them and dashed to her window. His Escort was rolling silently—and lightlessly—down the drive towards the road. But they would see him once he hit the street. Then they would follow.

She looked right, then left. She waited. She watched. Robin's car started once it slid into the road. He switched on his headlamps and headed west, in the direction of the village. But no one followed. Five seconds went by. Then ten. Then fifteen. No one.

"Shit!" Barbara whispered. "Bloody sodding . . . God *damn!*" She grabbed her keys. She pounded down the stairs. She dashed through the kitchen and into the night. She hurled herself into her Mini. She started it with a bellow, ground its gears to find reverse, and shot down the drive and into the Burbage Road. She drove without headlamps, tearing in the direction of the village. She prayed. And she alternated the prayers with curses.

In the centre of the village, she braked where the road forked on either side of the statue of King Alfred. If she took the left fork, she would be heading south towards Amesford. The right fork led north towards Marlborough and towards the country lane that passed through the Vale of Wootton, through Stanton St. Bernard, through Allington, and past that ghostly chalk horse that had been galloping across the downs for a thousand years. She chose the right fork. She floored the accelerator. She whizzed past the dark-enshrouded police station, past Elvis Patel's Grocery, past the post office. The Mini felt airborne as it took the bridge that arched over the Kennet and Avon Canal.

Once beyond the canal, she was out of the village and into the beginning of farmland. She scanned the horizon. She squinted hard at the road ahead of her. She cursed Hillier and everyone else she could think of who might have cocked up the surveillance plans. She heard Lynley's voice telling her that the boy's safety was paramount, that Payne would go after him once the tabloid story didn't appear. She saw Charlotte Bowen's body as it looked during her autopsy, and she pounded the steering wheel, shouting, "Damn you! Where've you gone?"

Then she saw it: Headlamps flashed against a windbreak of trees some quarter of a mile ahead of her. She shot towards that light. It was her only hope.

He wasn't speeding as she was. In his mind there would be no need. As far as he was concerned, his mother was asleep and Barbara was asleep. Why draw attention to himself by tearing along the road as if pursued by demons? So Barbara gained on him, and when he cruised past a brightly lit petrol station outside of Oare, she saw that indeed it was Robin Payne's Escort that she was following. Perhaps, she thought, there was a God after all.

But no one followed her. Which told her that she was completely on her own. Without a weapon, without a plan, and without a complete understanding of why Robin Payne had set out on a path to destroy the lives of so many people.

Lynley had said that there was a third child fathered by Dennis Luxford. Since the kidnapping note had ordered the newspaperman to acknowledge his *firstborn* child, and since acknowledging Charlotte Bowen hadn't served the interests of the kidnapper, the only possible conclusion was that there was an older child. And this was a child whom Robin Payne knew about. Knew about and was angry about. Angry enough to kill. So who . . . ?

He'd changed, Celia said. Directly he returned from what she had assumed to be his detective course, Robin had changed. When he'd left Wootton Cross, she'd assumed they would be marrying. When he'd returned, she felt the gulf between them. She'd concluded that gulf meant another woman in Robin's life. But what if Robin had discovered something about her? About Celia? About Celia's involvement with another man? About Celia's involvement with Dennis Luxford?

Up ahead, Robin turned left off the main road into a lane, his headlamps illuminating his twisting progress through the farmland. A left turn meant he was heading into the north section of the Vale of Wootton. When Barbara reached the lane, she risked flashing her own lights for an instant to see exactly where he was going. She read the sign for Fyfield, Lockeridge, and West Overton. And next to it, with an arrow indicating the direction, the universally understood image for a site worthy of historical note: the keep of a castle, rendered brown on white metal, with clear crenellation so that no one could mistake it for anything else. Bingo, Barbara thought. Windmill first. Castle next. Robin Payne, as he had said himself, had long known all the best places in Wiltshire to get into mischief.

Perhaps he'd even been there with Celia. Perhaps that was specifically why he'd chosen it. But if this was all about Celia Matheson and her illicit liaison with Dennis Luxford, when had it occurred and how? Charlotte Bowen had been ten years old at her death. If she wasn't Luxford's firstborn child, then whoever was, obviously, was older. And even if the child was older by only a few months, that would put Celia Matheson's involvement with Dennis Luxford into her teenage years. How old was Celia anyway? Twenty-four? At the most twenty-five? For her to have had a fling with Luxford, for her to have produced a child older than Charlotte Bowen as a result of that fling, she would have been boffing Luxford when she was only fourteen. That wasn't beyond the realm of possibility since children had babies all the time. But although Luxford seemed a thoroughly unsavoury character—if his newspaper was anything to go by—nothing Barbara had heard about him had made her conclude he was attracted to teenagers. And when one considered Portly's description of Luxford while he was a pupil at Baverstock, especially when one considered the contrast Portly had painted between Luxford and the other boys, one had to conclude—

Wait, Barbara thought. Bloody flaming *hell*. She increased her grip on the steering wheel. She could see Robin's car twisting along the road, tunneling beneath some trees, curving upward on a slight acclivity. She followed along, eyes alternately on his car and on the lane she was driving, and she summoned out of her memory the salient details from what Portly had said. A group of boys from Baverstock—upper-sixth boys, Dennis Luxford's own age—had regularly met one of the village girls for sex in the old ice house on the grounds of the school.

They'd paid her two pounds each for her favours. She'd come up pregnant. There'd been a ruckus afterwards, expulsions and all the trimmings. Right? So if that local girl had carried her pregnancy to full term, if she had delivered a healthy living baby who was living still, then the child of that ice-house coupling between the village girl and the rank of randy boys would be today—Barbara did her maths—twenty-nine years old.

Holy flipping shit, Barbara thought. Robin Payne didn't know about Luxford's child. Robin Payne thought he *was* Luxford's child. How he'd come to that conclusion Barbara couldn't have guessed. But she knew it for the truth just as she knew he was leading her to the child he believed was his half-brother. She could even hear what he'd said to her the night they drove past Baverstock School. *There's no one at all on my family tree.* She'd thought he meant no one of significance. Now she understood that he'd meant exactly what he'd said. No one at all, at least not legitimately.

Getting himself assigned to the case had been a masterstroke, really. No one would have a second thought when the eager young DC asked to take part. And when he offered his own home to the Scotland Yard sergeant—so close to the scene of the body dump, no decent hotel in the village, his own mummy in residence to keep everything on the up and up, the house a bonafide B and B—what better way to keep his fingers on the pulse of the case? He'd known how far they were getting every time he spoke to Barbara or heard her talk to Lynley. And when she fed him the line about the bricks and the maypole from Charlotte's tape recording, he'd been in heaven. She'd handed him the "clue" he needed in order to be the one to find the windmill. Where, no doubt, he had made certain to snag Charlotte's uniform on those crates before he folded it up and packed it into one of the vicar's rag bags on a visit to the Mathesons. Of course the Mathesons wouldn't have thought of Robin as a stranger come to creep round the church. He was their daughter's intended, their daughter's true love. That he was also a killer had escaped their notice.

Barbara's attention locked onto Robin's Escort. He was turning again, this time south. His car began to climb the rise of a hill. Barbara had the distinct feeling they were nearing their target.

She made the turn after him, slowing now. There was nothing out here—they'd passed the last farm at least three miles back—so she had little thought of losing him. She could see his headlamps bobbing in the distance. She crept along at an even stretch behind him.

The lane narrowed to a deeply rutted track. To its left a hill climbed, thickly grown with trees. To its right a vast field fell away into the darkness, fenced off from the lane with wire and posts. The track began to curve round the side of the hill, and Barbara slowed even more. Then some hundred yards ahead of her, Robin's car halted in front of a split-rail gate. This blocked off the road, and as Barbara watched, Robin got out of his car and shoved the gate open. He drove in, closed the gate behind him, and continued on his way. The moonlight illuminated his destination. Perhaps another hundred yards beyond the gate stood the ruins of a castle. She could see the crumbling wall that surrounded it and the frothlike scalloping of moonlit shrubs and trees just inside. And within the wall's confines rose what little remained of the castle itself. She could make out two round, crenellated towers at either end of a collapsing wall and some twenty yards from one of the towers the roof of a building: perhaps a kitchen, a bakehouse, a solar, or a hall.

Barbara manoeuvred her Mini to the edge of the track just outside the closed gate. She switched off the ignition and clambered out, keeping well to the left side of the track where the hillside rose, overgrown with trees and with shrubs. A sign on the gate identified the structure as Silbury Huish Castle. A secondary sign indicated that it was open to the public only on the first Saturday of every month. Robin had chosen his location well. The road was bad enough to deter most tourists from wandering in, and even if they ventured this far on an off-day, they'd be unlikely to risk trespass for the opportunity of gazing upon what appeared to be little more than a ruin. There were plenty of other ruins in the countryside, and those far easier to get to than this one.

Ahead, Robin's Escort stopped near the castle's outer wall. His headlamps made bright arcs against the stones for a moment. Then they were extinguished. As Barbara crept forward to the split-rail gate, she saw his shadowy form get out of his car. He went to the boot and rustled round in it. He removed one object that he set on the ground with a *clink* against stone. A second object he held, and from it a bright cone of light shot forth. A torch. He used it to light his way along the castle wall. It was only a moment before he was out of sight.

Barbara hurried to the boot of her own car. She couldn't risk a torch—one glance over his shoulder to see he was being followed and Robin Payne would make her dead meat. But she wasn't about to venture into and among those ruins without a weapon of some sort. So she threw onto the ground the contents of the Mini's boot, cursing herself for having used it for so long as a receptacle for anything she had a mind to stow. Buried beneath blankets, a pair of Wellingtons, assorted magazines, and a bathing suit at least ten years old, she found the tyre jack and its accompanying iron. She grabbed this latter. She tested its weight in her hand. She smacked the curved end of it sharply into her palm. It would have to do.

She set off after Robin. In his car he'd followed the track to the castle. On foot, following the track wasn't necessary. She cut across a stretch of open land. This was a vista that long ago would have given the castle's inhabitants visual warning of a coming attack, and Barbara kept this fact in mind as she dashed across it. She moved in a crouch, knowing that the moonlight that made her progress less difficult also made her visible—if as a shadow only—to anyone who happened to look her way.

She was making quick, easy, unimpeded progress when nature got in her way. She stumbled against a low shrub—it felt like a juniper—and unsettled a nest of birds. They shot up in front of her. Their *chack, chack, chack* bounced and echoed, it seemed, round every stone in the castle walls.

Barbara froze where she was. She waited, heart pounding. She made herself count to sixty, twice. When nothing stirred from the direction Robin had taken, Barbara set off again.

She reached his car without incident. She looked inside for the keys, praying to see them dangling from the ignition. They were gone. Well, it had been too much to hope for.

She followed the curve of the castle wall as he had done, picking up the pace now. She'd lost the time she'd intended to gain by avoiding the track. She needed to make up that time through any means. But stealth and silence were crucial. Aside from the tyre iron, the only other weapon she had was surprise.

Round the curve of the wall she came to the remains of the gatehouse. There was no longer a door attached to the old stones, merely an archway above which she could dimly see a worn coat of arms. She paused in an alcove created by the half-tumbled gatehouse wall, and she strained to listen. The birds had fallen silent. A night breeze susurrated the leaves on the trees that grew within the castle walls. But there was no sound of voice, footfall, or rustling clothes. And there was nothing to see except the two craggy towers raised towards the dark sky.

These contained the small oblong slits which would have shed sunlight on the spiral stone stairways within the towers. From these slits some defence of the castle could have been made as men-of-arms raced upward to the crenellated roof. From these slits also, dim light would have shone had Robin Payne chosen either of the towers in which to hold Leo Luxford hostage. But no light filtered from them. So Robin had to be somewhere in the building whose roof Barbara had noted some twenty yards from the farthest of the towers.

She could see this building as a shadowy form in the dim light. Between the gable-roofed structure and the archway where she stood in what felt like a teacup of darkness, there was little enough to hide her. Once she ventured out of the gatehouse and beyond the trees and shrubs at the wall, there would be only the random heaps of foundation stones that marked the sites where once the living quarters of the castle had stood. Barbara studied these heaps of stones. It appeared to be ten yards to the first group where a right angle of rubble would give her protection.

She listened for movement and sound. There was nothing beyond the wind. She dashed for the stones.

Ten yards closer to the castle's remaining structure allowed her to see what it was. She could make out the arch of the Gothic lancet windows and she could see a finial at the apex of the roof sketched against the dusky sky. This was a cross. The building was a chapel.

Barbara glued her gaze to the lancet windows. She waited for a flicker of light from within. He had a torch. He couldn't be operating in total darkness. Surely in a moment he'd give himself away. But she saw nothing.

Her hand felt slick where it held the tyre iron. She rubbed it against her trousers. She studied the next stretch of open ground and made a second dash to a second heap of foundation stones.

Here she saw that a wall lower than the castle's outer walls had been built round the chapel. A small roofed gatehouse whose shape mirrored the chapel itself acted as shelter for the dark oblong of a wooden door. This door was closed. Another fifteen yards gaped between her position and the chapel's gatehouse, fifteen yards in which the only shelter was a bench from which tourists could admire what little remained of the mediaeval fortification. Barbara hurtled herself towards this bench. And from the bench she dashed to the chapel's outer wall.

She slithered along this wall, tyre iron gripped fiercely, scarcely allowing herself to breathe. Hugged to the stones, she gained the chapel's gatehouse. She stood, her back pressed to the wall, and listened. First, the wind. Then the sound of a jet far above. Then another sound. And closer. The scrape of metal on stone. Barbara's body quivered in reply.

She eased her way to the gate. She pressed her palm against it. It gave an inch, then another. She peered inside.

Directly in front of her, the chapel door was closed. And the lancet windows above it were as black and as sightless as before. But a stone path led round the side of the church and as Barbara slid within the gate, she saw the first glimmer of light coming from this direction. And that sound again. Metal on stone.

An unattended herbaceous border grew profusely along the outer wall that bounded the chapel's environs, overspreading the stone path with tendrils, with branches, with leaves, and with flowers. Here and there this overgrown border had been trampled, and observing this, Barbara was willing to bet that the trampling hadn't been done by some first-Saturday-of-the-month visitor who had risked his car's suspension by venturing out to this remote location.

She glided across the path to the chapel itself. She sidled along the rough stones of its external wall till she gained the corner. There, she paused. She listened. First she heard the wind again, a swelling and receding that rustled through the trees on the hillside nearby. Then the metal on stone, more sharply now. Then the voice.

"You'll drink when I say to drink." It was Robin, but not a Robin she had heard before. This wasn't the uncertain and untried detective constable she'd been speaking to for the last few days. This was the voice of a thug and a killer. "Have we got that straight?"

And then the child's voice, reedy and frightened. "But it doesn't taste right. It tastes—"

"I don't care how it tastes. You'll drink it up like I tell you and be happy to have it or I'll force it down your throat. You understand? Did you like having it forced down your throat last time?"

The child said nothing. Barbara inched forward. She ventured a look round the corner of the chapel and saw that the path led to a set of stone steps. These steps curved downward through an arch in the chapel wall. They appeared to lead to a vault. Light fingered its way up these stairs. Too much light for a torch, Barbara realised. He must have taken his lantern as well. He'd had it with him when they'd gone to the windmill. That must have been what he'd removed from the boot of his car.

She flexed her fingers round the tyre iron. She pressed forward slowly along the chapel wall.

Robin was saying, "Drink, God damn it."

"I want to go home."

"I don't give a shit what you want. Now, take this—"

"That hurts! My arm!" The boy cried out.

A scuffling followed. A blow fell. Robin grunted. And then his voice snarled, "You little turd. When I tell you to drink . . ." And the sound of flesh hitting flesh, striking hard.

Leo shrieked. Another blow fell. Robin meant to kill him. Either he'd force the drug into him and wait the few minutes for him to drop off and drown him then as he'd done to Charlotte, or he'd kill him with violence. But either way, Leo was going to die.

Barbara raced the length of the path towards the light. She had surprise on her side, she told herself. She had the tyre iron. She had surprise.

She rushed down the steps with a howl and flung herself into the vault. She crashed the wooden door fully back against the stones. Robin had a tow-haired boy's head caught in the crook of his arm and his hand was forcing a plastic cup to his lips.

She saw in an instant how he meant to do it this time. The vault was an ancient burial chamber. Six lead coffins spanned a trench in the floor. In this trench lay a pool of algae-slimed water that gave off an odour of rot, human filth, and disease. That's the water that would be in Leo's body. Not tap water this time, but something infinitely more challenging for the pathologist to play about with.

"Let him go!" Barbara shouted. "I said bloody let him go!"

Robin did so. He shoved the boy to the floor. But he didn't back away and cower at having been caught out as a killer. Instead, he came at her.

Barbara swung the tyre iron. It connected with his shoulder. He blinked but came on. She swung it again. His hand shot up and grabbed it. He wrenched it from her grasp and flung it to one side. It slid across the stone floor. It clanked against a coffin and fell into the trench with a splash. Robin smiled at the sound. He advanced.

Barbara yelled, "Leo! Run!" but the child seemed mesmerised. He crouched near the coffin that the tyre iron had struck. He watched them from between his fingers. He cried, "No! Don't!"

Robin was fast. He had her against the wall before she knew what was happening. He drove his fists into her, one to the stomach to shove her into the stones and then, jerked forward, another to the kidneys. She felt heat sear through her, and she grabbed his hair in her fingers. She twisted hard and pulled his head backwards. She sought his eyes with her thumbs. He jerked back instinctively. She lost her grip. He powered his fist into her face.

She heard her nose break. She felt the pain of it spread across her face like a shovel on fire. She fell to one side, but she grabbed on to him. She took him down with her. They hit the stones.

She scrambled on top of him. Blood gushed from her nose and onto his face. She gripped his head between her hands. She lifted it. She pounded it onto the stone floor. She drove her fists into his Adam's apple, then against his ears, his cheeks, his eyes.

She shouted, "Leo! Get out of here!"

Robin's hands grabbed for her throat. He thrashed beneath her. Through a mist in her eyes she saw Leo move. But he was backing away. He wasn't running for the door. He was crawling between the coffins as if to hide.

She screamed, "Leo! Get out!"

With a grunt, Robin threw her off him. She kicked out savagely as she hit the ground. She felt her foot hit his shin and as he sank back, she jumped to her feet.

She drew her hand across her face. It came away crimson. She shouted for Leo. She saw the colour of his hair—bright light against the dull lead of the coffins—and then Robin surged to his feet as well.

"Fucking . . . God *damn* . . ." He charged, head lowered. He ploughed her against the wall. He grunted. He battered her face with sharp blows.

A weapon, Barbara thought. She needed a weapon. She had nothing. And if she had nothing, they were lost. She was. Leo was. Because he would kill them. He would kill them both because she had failed. Failed. Failed. The thought of it—

She shoved him away from her, her shoulder driving desperately into his chest. He pounded her back, but she caught him to her, arms at his waist. She dug in her feet for purchase and when his weight shifted, she drove her knee upward, seeking his groin. She missed and he grabbed the advantage. He threw her against the wall. He grabbed her by the neck. He plunged her to the floor.

He stood above her, looked to the left and the right. He was seeking a weapon. She saw it as he did. The lantern.

She grabbed his legs as he lunged to get it. He kicked her face, but she pulled him down. When he thudded to the floor, she crawled on top of him, but she knew her strength was nearly spent. She pressed against his throat. She locked her legs round his. If she could hold him here, if the boy could get away, if he had the sense to run into the trees . . .

"Leo!" she shouted. "Run! Hide!"

She thought she saw him moving at the edge of her vision. But something about him wasn't right. Hair not bright enough. Face gone ghoulish, limbs looking dead.

He was terrified. He was only a kid. He didn't understand what was going on. But if she couldn't make him see that he had to get out, get out fast, get out now, then . . .

"Go!" she cried. "Go!"

She felt Robin heave. Legs, arms, and chest. With a burst of power he flipped her off him again. But this time she couldn't get to her feet. He was on her just as she'd been on him. Arm at her throat, legs locked onto legs, breathing hotly into her face.

"He *will* . . ." Wildly, he gulped in air. "Pay. He *will*."

He increased the pressure. He ground himself onto her. Barbara saw a blur of white buzzing round her. And the last thing she saw was Robin's smile. It was the look of a man for whom justice was being done at last.

30

*L*YNLEY WATCHED CORRINE PAYNE lift the cup to her mouth. Her eyes were groggy and her movements sluggish. "More coffee," he said to Nkata grimly. "Make it black this time. And stronger. Double strength. Triple if you can."

Nkata responded warily. "Cold shower might do the same trick." He went on as if in rebuttal to the statement that Lynley didn't bother to make: They had no female DC with them. They could hardly undress the woman themselves. "Wouldn't have to take off her clothes, would we? We could just douse her good."

"See to the coffee, Winston."

Corrine murmured, "Little chappie?" and her head lolled forward.

Lynley shook her by the shoulder. He pulled back the chair and lifted her to her feet. He walked her the length of the dining room, but her legs had all the strength of cooked spaghetti. She was as useful to them as a kitchen utensil. He muttered, "Damn it, woman. Come out of it. *Now*," and as she stumbled against him, he realised how badly he wanted to rattle her into oblivion. Which told him how large his anxiety had grown in the thirty minutes since arriving at Lark's Haven.

The plan should have come off without a hitch. Departure from the Yard, a drive to Wiltshire, a comparison of DC Payne's police fingerprints with the prints from the tape recorder and the squat. And after that, a surveillance set up so that when Payne went after the Luxford boy in the morning—which he was sure to do when he saw *The Source* sans the story he wanted—it would be no trying matter to track him, to arrest him, and to restore the child to his parents in London. What had cocked things up was Amesford CID. They couldn't find a fingerprint officer for love or money, and once they had managed to locate such a creature, it had taken him more than an hour to get to the station. During that time, Lynley had done verbal combat with DS Reg Stanley, whose response to the idea that one of his detectives was behind two kidnappings and one murder was, "Effing nonsense, that. Who are you blokes anyway? Who sent you here?" and a derisive snort when he understood that they worked with the Scotland Yard sergeant who'd apparently become his *bête noire.* Cooperation didn't appear to be high on his list of personal attributes at the best of times. At this—the worst of times—it apparently had disappeared altogether.

Once they had the confirmation they were seeking—which absorbed the length of time it took for the fingerprint officer to put on his glasses, turn on a high intensity lamp, take out a magnifying glass to hold over the fingerprint cards, and say "Double loop whorls. Child's play. They're the same. Did you actually bring me from my poker game for this?"—the surveillance team was gathered quickly. There were murmurs among the constables when it became clear who the object of the surveillance was, but a van was dispatched, radio contact was set up, and positions were assigned in short order nonetheless. It was only when the first message came back that the suspect's car was gone, as was the car of the Scotland Yard DS, that Lynley and Nkata went out to Lark's Haven.

"She's followed him somewhere," Lynley told Nkata as they whipped northward through the night towards Wootton Cross. "He was in the room when I spoke to her. He must have read the truth on her face. Havers is no actress. He's making his move."

"Maybe he's gone off to see his woman," Nkata observed.

"I don't think so."

Lynley's feelings of trepidation heightened when they got to the house on the Burbage Road. It was completely dark—which suggested that everyone had gone to bed—but the back door was not only unlocked, it was open. And a deep tyre mark in the flower bed along the drive suggested that someone had left in haste.

Lynley's radio crackled as he and Nkata made for the open back door. "You want back-up, Inspector?" a voice asked from the van, which was parked a few yards down the road.

"Maintain your position," Lynley told the officer. "Things don't seem right. We're having a look inside."

The back door led into a kitchen. Lynley flipped on the lights. Everything appeared to be in order, as was the case in the dining room and the sitting room beyond.

Upstairs they found the bedroom Havers was using. Her old St. George-and-the-dragon sweatshirt hung limply by its label from a hook on the door. Her bed was tousled—but only the counterpane and the blanket, with the sheets still folded neatly in place. This suggested that she'd either taken a nap, which was highly unlikely, or that she'd feigned sleep, which was more in keeping with his instructions to her to carry on normally. Her misshapen shoulder bag was on the top of the chest of drawers, but her car keys were missing. So she must have heard Payne leaving the house, Lynley thought. She must have grabbed up her keys, and she must have given chase.

The thought of Havers by herself on the trail of a killer sent Lynley to the window of her bedroom. He flicked back the curtains and observed the night, as if the stars and the moon could tell him in which direction she and Robin Payne had gone. Damn and blast the infuriating woman, he thought. What the hell had she been thinking of, setting out after him alone? If she got herself killed—

" 'Spector Lynley?"

Lynley turned from the window. Nkata stood in the doorway. "What is it?"

"Woman in one of the other bedrooms. Out like a dead tuna. Seems like she's drugged."

Which is how they came to be pouring coffee down Corrine Payne's throat while she murmured alternately for her "little chappie" or for Sam. "Who's Sam when he's someone?" Nkata wanted to know.

Lynley didn't care. He only wanted the woman coherent. And when Nkata brought another pot of coffee into the dining room, he sat Corrine at the table and began sloshing it into her.

"We need to know where your son is," Lynley said. "Mrs. Payne, can you hear me? Robin's not here. Do you know where he's gone?"

Her eyes seemed to focus this time, the caffeine finally working on her brain. She darted them from Lynley to Nkata, upon whose visage they widened in absolute terror.

"We're police officers," Lynley said before she could set up a howl at the sight of an unknown—and therefore inherently threatening—black man in her pristine dining room. "We're looking for your son."

"Robbie's a policeman," she told them in answer. Then she seemed to read *We're looking for your son* for a fuller meaning. "Where's Robbie?" she demanded. "What's happened to Robbie?"

"We need to talk to him," Lynley told her. "Can you help us, Mrs. Payne? Can you give us an idea where he might be?"

"Talk to him?" Her voice rose slightly. "Talk to him why? It's night. He's in bed. He's a good boy. He's always been good to his mummy. He's—"

Lynley put a steadying hand on her shoulder. She was breathing unevenly.

She said, "Asthma. Sometimes my breath goes."

"Have you medicine?"

"An inhaler. The bedroom."

Nkata fetched it. She pumped it vigorously and it seemed to restore her. The combination of the coffee and the medicine brought her round to herself. She blinked several times as if fully awakened. "What do you want with my son?"

"He's taken two children from London. He's brought them to the country. One of them is dead. The other may very well still be alive. We need to find him, Mrs. Payne. We need to find that child."

She looked utterly dazed. Her hand closed over her inhaler and Lynley thought that she would use it again. But instead she stared at him. Her face was a study in absolute incomprehension.

"Children?" she said. "My Robbie? You're mad."

"I'm afraid not."

"Why, he wouldn't hurt children. He wouldn't consider it. He loves them. He means to have children of his own. He means to get married to Celia Matheson this very year and have children by the score." She drew the edges of her bathrobe closer as if suddenly chilled. She went on with, "Are you trying to tell me—are you actually trying to suggest to me—that my Robbie's a *per*vert?" in a hushed and disgusted voice. "My Robbie? My son? My very own son who won't touch his little peepee unless I put it into his hands myself?"

Her words hung there between them for an instant. Lynley saw Nkata raise his eyebrows in interest. The woman's question suggested waters that were cloudy if not deep, but there was no time to draw inferences. Lynley went on.

"The children he's taken have the same father. Your son appears to have a grievance with this man."

If anything, the woman looked more nonplussed than before. She said, "Who? What father?"

"A man called Dennis Luxford. Is there a connection between Robin and Dennis Luxford?"

"*Who?*"

"Dennis Luxford. He's editor of a tabloid called *The Source*. He went to school in this area, at Baverstock, some thirty years ago. The first child your son took was Luxford's illegitimate daughter. The second is Luxford's legitimate son. Apparently, Robin believes there's a third child, a child older than the other two. He wants Dennis Luxford to name that child in the newspaper. If Luxford doesn't, the second child he's taken will die."

The change came over her slowly as Lynley spoke. Each sentence seemed to shutter her face further. Finally, she dropped her hand to her lap. She said faintly, "Editor of a paper, you said? In London?"

"Yes. He's called Dennis Luxford."

"Dear God."

"What is it?"

She said, "I didn't think . . . He wasn't actually meant to believe . . ."

"What?"

"It was so long ago."

"What?"

The woman said nothing beyond, "Dear God."

Lynley's nerves strung out another degree. "If you can tell us something that will lead to your son, then I suggest you do it and do it now. One life is gone. Two more are at stake. We've no time to waste and less to reflect. Now—"

"I didn't really know who it was." She spoke to the tabletop, not to either of the men. "How could I have done? But I had to tell him something. Because he kept insisting . . . He kept asking and asking. He gave me no peace." She seemed to shrivel into herself.

Nkata remarked, "This is nowhere, man."

"Find his bedroom," Lynley said. "Something there may tell us where he's gone."

"But we got no—"

"To hell with a warrant, Winston. Havers is out there. She may be in trouble. And I don't intend to sit round here waiting for—"

"Right. I'm finding it." Nkata made for the stairs.

Lynley heard the constable moving briskly down the upstairs corridor. Doors opened and shut. Then the sound of drawers and cupboard doors being moved to and fro combined with Corrine Payne's continuing jabber.

"I never thought," she was saying. "It just seemed so simple when I saw it in the paper . . . When I read . . . When it said Baverstock . . . of all places, Baverstock . . . And he *could* have been one of them. Really, he could have been. Because I didn't know their names, you see. I never asked. They just came to the ice house. Mondays and Wednesdays . . . Lovely boys, really . . ."

Lynley wanted to shake her, to jar loose her teeth. She was talking aimlessly while time trickled away. He shouted, "Winston! Is there anything to go on?"

Nkata clattered back down the stairs. He was carrying cuttings from a newspaper. He looked grave. He handed the cuttings over to Lynley, saying, "This was in a drawer in his room."

Lynley looked at the cuttings. They were from the *Sunday Times* magazine. He spread them on the table, but he didn't need to read. It was the same article that Nkata had shown him earlier in the week. He read its title a second time: "Turning Round a Tabloid." Its contents constituted a minor biography of Dennis Christopher Luxford, and this biography was accompanied by glossy pictures of Luxford, his wife, and their son.

Corrine reached out and weakly traced the outline of Dennis Luxford's face. She said, "It said Baverstock. It said he went to Baverstock. And Robbie wanted to know . . . His dad . . . He'd been asking for years . . . He said he had the right . . ."

Lynley finally understood. "You told your son that Dennis Luxford is his father? Is that what you're saying?"

"He said I owed him the truth if I was going to marry. I owed him his real dad once and for all. But I didn't know, you see. Because there'd been so many. And I couldn't tell him that. I couldn't. How could I? So I told him there was one. Once. At night. I hadn't wanted to do it, I told him, but he was stronger than me, so I had to. I just had to or else I'd be hurt."

Nkata said, "Rape?"

"I never thought Robbie would . . . I said it was long ago. I said it didn't matter. I told him *he* was what mattered now. My son. My lovely love. He was what mattered."

"You told him Dennis Luxford raped you?" Lynley clarified. "You told your son Dennis Luxford raped you when you were both teenagers?"

"His name was in the paper," she murmured. "It said Baverstock as well. I didn't think . . . Mercy. I don't feel very well."

Lynley shoved himself away from the table. He'd been standing over her, but now he needed distance. He was incredulous. A little girl was dead and two other lives now hung in the balance because this woman—this utterly loathsome woman—hadn't wanted her son to know that his father's identity was a mystery to her. She'd taken a name out of a hat, out of nowhere, out of the sky. She'd seen the word *Baverstock* in the magazine article and she'd used that one word to condemn a ten-year-old to die. God. It was madness. He needed some air. He needed to be out on the road. He needed to find Havers before Payne got to her.

Lynley turned to the kitchen, to the door, to escape. As he did so, his radio spurted to life.

"Car coming, Inspector. Slow. From the west."

"Get the lights," Lynley ordered. Nkata moved quickly to extinguish them.

"Inspector?" the radio crackled.

"Stay where you are."

At the table, Corrine stirred, saying, "Robbie? Is it Robbie?"

Lynley said, "Get her upstairs."

She said, "I don't *want*—"

"Winston."

Nkata moved to her. He raised her up. "This way, Mrs. Payne."

She clutched onto the chair. "You won't hurt him," she said. "He's my little boy. You won't hurt him. Please."

"Get her out of here."

As Nkata guided Corrine to the stairs, the headlamps from a car swept light across the dining room. An engine rumbled, growing louder as the car approached the house. Then its noise ceased with a burble and a cough. Lynley slipped to the window and eased the curtain away from the glass.

The car had pulled beyond his line of vision, towards the back of the house where the kitchen door still stood open. Lynley moved quietly round the table in that direction. He deadened the sound on his radio. He listened for movement outside.

A car door opened. Seconds passed. Then heavy footsteps approached the house.

Lynley made his own move, quickly, to the door between the kitchen and dining room. He heard a deep, guttural cry—sounding as if it were being savagely stifled—from just outside the house. He waited in the darkness with his hand on the light switch. When he saw the shadowy figure on the steps, he flipped the switch on and shot the room full of light.

"Christ!" he cried. He shouted to Nkata as Sergeant Havers sagged against the door.

—⁂—

She held a child's body in her arms. Her eyes were swollen, and her face was welts, bruises, and blood. More blood soaked the front of her dingy pullover. It stained her trousers from her hips to her knees. She squinted at Lynley from her ruined face. "Bloody hell," she said through mushrooming lips. One of her teeth was broken. "You took your time."

Nkata charged into the room. He brought himself up short at the sight of Havers, whispering, "Holy Jesus."

Lynley said to him over his shoulder, "Get an ambulance," and to Havers, "The boy?"

"Asleep."

"He looks like hell. You both look like hell."

She smiled, then winced. "He went swimming in a trench to look for my tyre iron. He clobbered Payne a good one. Four good ones, in fact. Tough little bloke. Though he'll probably need a tetanus shot after jumping in that water. It was filthy. A breeding ground for every disease ever known to man. It was in a burial vault. There were coffins, see. It was a castle. I know I was supposed to wait, but when he took off and no one followed, I thought it best to—"

"Havers." Lynley stopped her. "Well done."

He went to her, took the child from her arms. Leo stirred but didn't wake. Havers was right. The boy was streaked with everything from grime to algae. His ears looked as if they were growing moss. The palms of his hands were black. His fair hair appeared green. But he was alive. Lynley handed him to Nkata.

"Phone his parents," he said. "Give them the word."

Nkata left the room.

Lynley turned back to Havers. She hadn't moved from the door. Gently, he drew her away from it, away from the light and into the dining room where it was still dark. He sat her down.

"He broke my nose," she whispered. "And I don't know what else. My chest hurts bad. I think it's some ribs."

"I'm sorry," Lynley said. "Christ, Barbara. I'm sorry."

"Leo got him," she said. "He bashed him proper."

Lynley squatted in front of her. He took out his handkerchief and used it tenderly against her face. He blotted away the blood. But more blood oozed out. Where the hell, he wondered, was the blasted ambulance?

" 'Course I knew he didn't really care for me," she said. "But I went along with it. It seemed the right thing to do."

"It was," Lynley said. "It was right. You were right."

"And I gave him a dose of his own in the end."

"How?" Lynley asked.

She chuckled and grimaced with pain. "I locked him in the crypt. I thought I'd see how he'd like the dark for once. The bastard."

"Yes," Lynley said. "That's what he is."

She wouldn't go off to hospital until she made certain they knew where to find him. She wouldn't even allow the paramedics to attend to her until she had drawn Lynley a map. She hunched over the table and bled onto the Laura Ashley cloth that covered it. And she drew her map with a pencil that she had to guide with both of her hands.

She coughed once and blood burbled from her mouth. Lynley took the pencil from her and said, "I see. I'll fetch him. You need a hospital now."

She said irrationally, "But I want to be there to see things through."

"You have done," he said.

"Then what now?"

"Now you take a holiday." He squeezed her shoulder. "You damn well deserve one."

She surprised him completely by looking stricken. "But what'll you—" she began but cut her own words off as if she was afraid she would cry should she say them.

He wondered what she meant. What would he what? Then he understood as he heard movement behind him and Winston Nkata returned to join them. "Got the parents," he told them. "They're on their way. How're you doing, Sarge?"

Havers' eyes were fixed on the tall DC. Lynley said to her, "Barbara, nothing's changed. You go to the hospital."

"But if a case comes up—"

"Someone else will handle it. Helen and I are getting married at the weekend. I'll be away from the Yard as well."

She smiled. "Married?"

"Finally. At last."

"Bloody hell," she said. "We ought to drink to that."

"We will," he said. "But not tonight."

Lynley found Robin Payne where Sergeant Havers had said she'd left him: in the macabre vault that lay below the chapel on the grounds of Silbury Huish Castle. He was crouched in a corner as far as possible from the grisly lead coffins, his hands covering his head. When Constable Nkata shone the beam of his torch upon the other policeman, Payne raised his face into the light and Lynley felt a brief and atavistic satisfaction at the sight of his injuries. Havers and Leo had given almost as good as they'd got. Payne's cheeks and forehead were deeply bruised, scratched, and scored. Blood matted his hair. One eye was swollen shut.

Lynley said to him, "Payne?"

The detective constable responded by rising with a wince, drawing the back of his fist across his mouth, and saying, "Get me out of here, will you? I've been locked in by some yobbos. They flagged me down on the road below and—"

"I'm Sergeant Havers' partner," Lynley cut in.

That silenced the young man. The putative yobbos—convenient to whatever story he'd been cooking up since Havers had abandoned him here—seemed to dissipate from his thoughts. He moved closer to the wall of the vault, and after a moment he said in a remarkably assured tone of voice considering his circumstances, "Where's my mum, then? I must talk to her."

Lynley told Nkata to read Payne the caution. He told one of the other DCs from Amesford CID to radio ahead for a doctor to meet them at the station. As Nkata obliged and the other officer went off to make arrangements for medical assistance, Lynley observed the detective constable who'd brought death, ruin, and despair into the lives of a group of people he'd never met.

Despite Payne's injuries, Lynley could still see the youthful—and spurious—innocence of his face. It was a superficial innocence that, in conjunction with a disguise that no thinking observer might have thought a disguise, would have served him well. Dressed in the uniform he'd worn as a constable prior to joining Amesford CID, he would have rousted Jack Beard from Cross Keys Close in Marylebone, and no one looking upon him and upon his rousting would have cause to think he was anything other than what he appeared to be: not a kidnapper clearing the scene before luring his victim to her abduction but instead a policeman on the beat. Dressed in that same uniform with that innocent face shining resplendently with his good intentions, he would have talked Charlotte Bowen—and later Leo Luxford—into accompanying him. He would have known that children are warned from their mothers' breasts not to talk to strangers. But he would have also known that children are told they can trust the police. And Robin Payne had a face that was designed for trust. Lynley could see that beneath its injuries.

It was an intelligent face as well, and a surfeit of intelligence had been necessary to plan and to carry out the crimes that Payne had committed. Intelligence would have told him to use the George Street squat while he was in London so that he could come and go with ease while tracking his victims—whether dressed as a uniformed constable or dressed as a civilian—without taking the chance that a hotel's receptionist might note him and later connect him, even remotely, to the abduction of two children and the murder of one of them. And that same intelligence in combination with his professional experience would have led him to plant evidence that would direct the police towards Dennis Luxford. Because one way or another, he'd meant to bring Dennis Luxford to some form of justice. Clearly, the man he believed to be his father was at the centre of everything Payne had done.

The horror lay buried in the fact that in striking out against Luxford, he'd been striking at a phantasm birthed from a lie. And it was this knowledge that scratched against the door of Lynley's intentions at this moment of confrontation with the killer.

Kidnapper. Homicide. On the drive to the castle, Lynley had planned out this first meeting between them: how he'd yank Robin Payne to his feet, how he'd bark out the order for the caution to be read, how he'd slap on the handcuffs and shove him out into the night. Murderers of children were less than pond scum. They richly deserved to be treated as such. And Robin Payne's tone when requesting to talk to his mother—so completely assured, so absent of remorse—seemed nothing more than an illustration of his real malevolence. But observing the younger man and casting that observation into the light of what he'd learned about his background, Lynley felt only a tremendous sense of defeat.

The chasm between the truth and what Robin Payne believed to be the truth was simply too wide for Lynley's anger and outrage to bridge, no matter the assurance of the detective constable's request. Lynley heard Corrine Payne's words echoing inside his skull as Nkata drew the other DC's hands behind him and locked his wrists together: "You won't hurt him. Please. He's my little boy." And hearing these words, Lynley realised that there was little enough point to hurting Robin Payne. His mother had already done damage enough.

Still, he needed one final bit of information that would allow him to close the case with at least a modicum of peace of mind. And he was going to have to jockey for position carefully in order to get that bit of information. Payne was clever enough to know that all he needed to do was to keep silent and Lynley would never secure the last piece to the puzzle of what had happened. But in his request to talk to his mother,

Lynley saw how he could mete out a meagre form of justice at the same time as he obtained from the constable the last fact he needed to connect him irrefutably both to Charlotte Bowen and to her father. The only way to get to the truth was going to be to speak the truth. But it wouldn't be for him to do the talking.

"Fetch Mrs. Payne," he told one of the Amesford DCs. "Bring her to the station."

The DC's expression of surprise told Lynley that he'd assumed Payne's request to talk to his mother was being granted. He said uneasily, "Bit irregular, that is, sir."

"Right," Lynley replied. "All of life is irregular. Fetch Mrs. Payne."

—⚏—

They made the drive to Amesford in silence, the nighttime landscape flying by in a darkness only occasionally split by the lights of a passing car. Before them and behind them rolled an escort of police vehicles, their radios doubtless crackling as the report went out that Payne had been apprehended and was being brought to the station. But inside the Bentley there was no sound. From the moment he'd asked to speak to his mother, the detective constable had not said another word.

It wasn't until they finally reached the Amesford police station that Payne spoke. He saw a single reporter with notebook in hand and a single photographer with camera at the ready, both of them waiting at the station door, and he said, "It's not about me, all this. The story'll come out. People will know. And I'm glad of it. I'm that bloody glad. Is Mum here yet?"

They had the answer to that question when they got inside. Corrine Payne approached them, her elbow in the hand of a plump, balding man who wore a pyjama top tucked into his grey and beltless herringbone trousers.

"Robbie? My Robbie?" Corrine reached out to her son, her lips quivering round his name. Her eyes filled. "What've these dreadful men *done* to you?" And then to Lynley, "I told you *not* to hurt him. Is he badly injured? What's happened to him? Oh, Sam. *Sam.*"

Her companion quickly slid his arm round her waist. He murmured, "Sweet pear. Be easy now."

"Put her in an interview room," Lynley said. "Alone. We'll be along directly."

A uniformed constable took Corrine Payne's arm. She said, "But what about Sam? *Sam!*"

He said, "I'll be right here, sweet pear."

"You won't go away?"

"I won't leave you, love." He kissed the tips of her fingers.

Robin Payne turned away. He said to Lynley, "Can we get on with things, then?"

Corrine was led off to the interview room. Lynley took her son to meet with the doctor, who was waiting for them with a medical bag opened, instruments displayed, and gauze and disinfectant neatly arranged. He made quick work of examining his patient, speaking in a low voice of the possibility of concussion and the need to keep watch over the injured man for the next few hours. He applied plasters where necessary and used sutures to bind together a nasty wound on Payne's head. "No aspirin," he said as he completed his work, "and don't let him sleep."

Lynley explained that sleep was not in Robin Payne's immediate future. He took him along the corridor—where he noted that Payne's colleagues averted their eyes as they passed—and brought him into his mother's presence.

Corrine was sitting away from the interview room's single table. Her feet were flat on the floor. She held her bag on her lap with both hands curved round its handle in the attitude of a woman about to depart.

Nkata was with her. He lounged against the far wall with a cup in his hand. He sipped from this. Steam rose round his face. The scent of chicken broth tinctured the air.

Corrine's hands tightened on her bag when she saw her son. But she didn't move from her chair. "These men have told me something dreadful, Robbie. Something about you. They've said you've done some terrible things, and I've told them they're wrong."

Lynley shut the door. He drew out a chair from the table and used his hand on Payne's shoulder to indicate that he was to sit. Payne cooperated, but said nothing.

Corrine went on, stirring in her chair but still not making a move to go to her son. "They've said you killed a little girl, Robbie, but I told them that was out of the question. I told them how much you've always loved children, and how you and Celia mean to have a packet of them just as soon as you marry. So we'll get all this silliness straightened out directly, won't we, dear? I expect it's all a terrible mistake. Someone's got himself into a muddle over something, but that someone's certainly not you, is it?" She tried a hopeful smile, but her lips couldn't manage it. And, despite her words, her eyes betrayed her fear. When Payne didn't answer her question at once, she said earnestly, "Robbie? Isn't that so? Haven't they been talking nonsense, these two policemen? Isn't this all a dreadful mistake? You know, I've been thinking that perhaps, it's due to that sergeant's staying with us. Perhaps she's told some silly tales about you. A woman scorned will do anything, Robbie, anything at all to get revenge."

"You didn't," he said.

Corrine pointed to herself in some confusion. "I didn't what, dear?"

"Get revenge," he said. "You didn't. You wouldn't ever. So I did."

Corrine offered him a faltering smile. She shook an admonishing finger at him. "If you mean the way you've behaved in these past few days towards Celia, you naughty boy, then she's the one who should be sitting in this chair, not I. Why, that girl has the patience of a saint when it comes to waiting for you to speak your mind, Robbie. But we'll clear up your misunderstandings with Celia just as soon as we deal with the misunderstandings here." She watched him brightly. It was clear that her son was supposed to follow her lead.

"They've got me, Mum," Payne said.

"Robbie—"

"No. Listen. It isn't important. What's important now is that the story gets out and that it gets out proper. That's the only way he's going to pay. I thought at first I could get him through his money—make him pay through the nose that way for what he'd done. But when I first saw her name, when I realised that he'd done to someone else just bloody exactly what he'd done to you . . . That's when I knew that taking money from him wouldn't be enough. He needed to be shown for what he is. That'll happen now. He's meant to suffer because he got away clean, Mum. I did it for you."

Corrine looked flustered. If she understood, she was giving no indication of that fact. "What exactly are you saying, dear Robbie?"

Lynley pulled a second chair out from the table. He sat where he could observe both mother and son. He said with deliberate brutality, "He's explaining that he kidnapped and killed Charlotte Bowen and that he kidnapped Leo Luxford for you, Mrs. Payne. He's explaining that he did it as a form of vengeance, to bring Dennis Luxford to justice."

"Justice?"

"For having raped you, for having made you pregnant, and for having abandoned you thirty years ago. He knows he's been caught out—holding Leo Luxford at Silbury Huish Castle is hardly a testimony to his innocence, I'm afraid—so he wants you to know why he set on this course of action in the first place. He did it for you. Knowing that, would you like to put him straight on past history?"

"For me?" Again the fingers pointed to her chest.

"I asked you and asked you," Payne told his mother. "But you would never say. You always thought I was asking for myself, didn't you? You thought I wanted to satisfy my curiosity. But it wasn't ever for me that I wanted to know, Mum. It was for you. He needed to be dealt with. He couldn't leave you like he did and never face the music. That's just not right. So I've made him face it. The story'll come out in all the papers now. And he'll be finished like he deserves."

"The papers?" Corrine looked aghast.

"No one but me could have done it, Mum. No one but me could even have planned it. And I don't have a single regret. Like I said, you weren't the only one he did the job on. Once I knew that, I knew he had to pay."

It was his second reference to another rape, and there was only one possible identity of that alleged rape's victim. Payne's having brought the subject up gave Lynley the opening he'd been looking for. "How did you know about Eve Bowen and her daughter, Constable?"

Payne still spoke to his mother. "See, he'd done the job on her as well, Mum. And she'd come up pregnant just like you. And he'd left her just like he did with you. So he had to pay. I thought I'd take him for money at first, a nice wedding present for you and Sam. But when I looked into it and saw her name on his account, I thought Cor, what's this? And I sussed her out."

Her name on his account. I thought I'd take him for money. Money. Lynley suddenly remembered what Dennis Luxford had told Eve Bowen during their meeting at his office. He'd opened a savings account for their daughter, money to be used should she ever be in need of it, his meagre way of accepting the burden of her birth. Looking for anything to destroy Luxford's life, Robin Payne must have come across this account, which then gave him access to the editor's most closely kept secret. But how had he done it? This was the final link that Lynley was seeking.

"After that it was easy," Payne went on. He leaned across the table in his mother's direction. Corrine backed fractionally into her chair. "I went to St. Catherine's. I saw there was no name for the dad on her birth certificate, just like on mine. That's how I knew that Luxford had done to someone else what he'd done to you. When I saw that, I didn't want his money. I only wanted him to tell the truth. So I tracked the little bird down through her mum. Then I trailed her. And when the time was right, I snatched her. She wasn't meant to die, but when Luxford wouldn't come clean, there was no other way. You see that, don't you? You understand? You look dead pale, but you're not to worry. Once the story comes out in the papers—"

Corrine waved her fingers in some agitation to stop his words. She opened her handbag and dug out her inhaler. She pumped it into her mouth.

"Mum, you're not to make yourself ill," Payne said.

Corrine breathed, eyes closed, hand on chest. "Robbie, dearest," she murmured. Then she opened her eyes and offered him an affectionate smile. "My dearest dearest *lovely* boy. I don't know how we've come to have this terrible misunderstanding."

Payne watched her blankly. He swallowed and said, "What?"

"Where on earth, my dearest, did you get the idea that this man is your father? Certainly, Robbie, you couldn't have got it from me."

Payne stared at her without comprehension. "You said . . ." His tongue slipped out and wetted his lips. "When you saw the *Sunday Times*, the story about him . . . You said . . ."

"I said nothing at all." Corrine replaced her inhaler in her handbag. She shut the bag with a snap. "Oh, I may have said this man *looks* familiar, but you're terribly mistaken if you think that I identified him in any way. I might even have said that he looks vaguely like the boy who used me so ill all those years ago. But I wouldn't have said more because it *was* all those years ago, Robbie my dear. And it was only one night. One dreadful horrible heartbreaking night that I'd like more than anything to simply forget. Only how can I ever forget it now that you've done this to me? Now there'll be newspapers and magazines and the telly, all of them bombarding me with terrible questions that'll dredge everything up, that'll make me remember, that'll cause Sam to think . . . perhaps even to leave . . . Is that what you wanted? Did you want Sam to leave me, Robbie? Is that why you've done this terrible thing? Because you're about to lose me to another man and you wanted to ruin it? Is that it, Robbie? Did you want to destroy Sam's love for me?"

"No! I did it because he made you suffer. And when a man makes a woman suffer, he's got to pay."

"But he didn't," she said. "It wasn't . . . Robbie, you misunderstood. It wasn't this man."

"It was. You said. I remember how you passed me the magazine article, how you pointed at Baverstock, how you said, 'This is the man, my Robbie. He took me to the ice house one night in May. He had a bottle of sherry with him. He made me drink some and he had some and then he pushed me onto the ground. He tried to choke me, so I submitted. And that's what happened. This is the man.' "

"No," she protested. "I never said that. I may have said he *reminds* me—"

Payne slapped his hand on the table. "You said 'This is the man'!" he shouted. "So I went to London. So I followed him. So I trailed him to Barclay's and then I came home and I went to Celia and I nuzzled her proper and I said, 'Show me how this computer-thing works. Can we look up accounts? Anyone's accounts? How about this bloke's? Cor, how amazing.' And there was her name. So I tracked her down. I saw he'd done to her mum what he'd done to you. And he had to pay. He . . . had . . . to . . . pay." Payne slumped in his chair. For the first time, he sounded defeated.

Lynley realised that the circle of information was finally complete. He recalled Corrine Payne's words: *He means to marry Celia Matheson.* He put them together with what the constable had just said. There was only one possible conclusion to be reached. Lynley said to Nkata, "Celia Matheson. Bring her in."

Nkata moved towards the door. Payne stopped him, saying wearily, "She doesn't know. She isn't involved. She won't be able to tell you anything."

"Then you tell me," Lynley said.

Payne observed his mother. Corrine opened her handbag. She drew out a handkerchief that she used to press against her nose and beneath her eyes. She said in a faint voice, "Do you need me for anything further, Inspector? I'm feeling rather unwell, I'm afraid. Perhaps if you'll be so good as to call Sam to fetch me . . . ?"

Lynley gave a nod to Nkata, who slid out of the room. As they waited for him to return with Sam, Corrine spoke one more time to her son. "Such a terrible misunderstanding, dear. I can't think how it came to happen. I simply can't think . . ."

Payne dropped his head. "Get her out of here," he said to Lynley.

"But Robbie—"

"Please."

Lynley ushered Corrine Payne from the room. They met Nkata with Sam in the corridor. She fell into the man's plump arms. She said, "Sammy, something dreadful has happened. Robbie's not himself. I tried to talk to him, but he won't be made to see reason any longer and I'm so afraid—"

"Hush," Sam said and patted her back. "Hush now, sweet pear. Let me take you home."

He headed back towards reception with her. Her voice floated back to them, saying, "You won't leave me, will you? Say you won't leave?"

Lynley went back into the interview room. Payne said to him, "Can I get a fag, please?"

Nkata said, "I'll see to it," and went for the cigarettes. When he'd returned with a packet of Dunhills and a book of matches, the other DC lit up and smoked for a moment in silence. He looked shell-shocked. Lynley wondered how he would take it when—and if—his mother ever resorted to speaking the truth about his birth. It was one thing to believe oneself the product of an act of violence. It was another to know oneself to be the product of anonymous and mindless sex, initiated by an exchange of cash, hurriedly and wordlessly completed with nothing more in one mind but a rush to orgasm and nothing more in the other mind but what the collected pounds and pence would be spent on when the act was done.

"Tell me about Celia," Lynley said.

He'd used her, Payne told him, because she worked at Barclay's in Wootton Cross. Oh, he'd known her before—he'd known her for ages, in fact—but he'd never really thought much about her till he saw how she could help him with Luxford.

"One evening when she was late at work, I got her to let me into the bank," he said. "She has a cubicle that she works in and she showed it to me. She showed me her computer as well and I got her to access Luxford's accounts because I wanted to see how much I could take him for. I got her to do other accounts as well. I made it a game and buried Luxford in the middle. And while she did it—while she accessed the accounts—I did her."

"You had sex with her," Lynley clarified.

"So she'd think I was hot for her," Payne finished, "and not just hot for her computer."

He flicked ash from his cigarette onto the tabletop. He tapped an index finger against it and watched the wedge of ash disintegrate.

"If you believed Charlotte Bowen was your half-sister," Lynley said, "and a victim just like you, why did you kill her? That's the only thing I don't understand."

"I never thought of her like that," Payne replied. "I only thought of Mum."

—⚹—

They tore westward on the motorway, hazard lights blinking to clear out the right lane. Luxford drove. Fiona sat next to him in a position she hadn't altered from the moment they'd got into the Mercedes in Highgate. She had her seat belt on, but she leaned forward against it as if her posture could make the car go faster. She did not speak.

They'd been in bed when the call had come through. They'd been lying in the darkness holding each other, neither of them speaking because it seemed there was nothing left to say. Dwelling on memories of their son subjected his disappearance to a permanence they couldn't bear to speak of. Talking of Leo's future ran the risk of an assumption that a vengeful god might seek to thwart. So they talked of nothing, lying beneath the covers and holding each other with no expectation of sleep or peace of mind.

The phone had rung before they'd gone to bed. Luxford had let it ring three times as he'd been instructed by the police detective who was still below in the kitchen, hoping for the call that would break the case. But when Luxford had picked up the receiver, Peter Ogilvie had been on the other end.

He'd said in his crisp I'll-brook-no-nonsense voice, "Rodney tells me a snout at the Yard places you there with Eve Bowen this afternoon. Were you planning to run that story, or just let the *Globe* have it? Or perhaps the *Sun?*"

"I've nothing to say."

"Rodney claims you're involved in this Bowen matter up to your eyeballs, although eyeballs wasn't the part of the anatomy he used. He suggests you have been from the first. Which tells me where your priorities lie. Not with *The Source.*"

"My son's been kidnapped. He may well be murdered. If you think I ought to be concentrating on the paper at a time like this—"

"Your son's disappearance is unfortunate, Dennis. But he hadn't disappeared when the Bowen story was breaking. You held back on us then. Don't deny it. Rodney followed you. He saw you meet with Bowen. He's been doing double his job since the Bowen girl's death and before."

"And he's made sure you knew it," Luxford said.

"I'm giving you the opportunity to explain yourself," Ogilvie pointed out. "I brought you on board to do for *The Source* what you did for the *Globe.* If you can assure me that tomorrow morning's lead story will fill in the gaps in the public's information—and I mean all the information, Dennis—then we'll call your job secure for at least another six months. If you can't give me that assurance, then I shall have to say it's time we parted company."

"My son's been kidnapped," Luxford repeated. "Did you even hear that?"

"All the more power for the front page story," Ogilvie said. "What's your answer?"

"My answer?" Luxford had looked at his wife, who sat at the end of the chaise longue in the bay window of their bedroom. She still held Leo's pyjama top. She was folding it carefully into a square on her lap. He wanted to go to her. He said to Ogilvie, "I'm out of it, Peter."

"What's that supposed to mean?"

"Rodney's been after my job since day one. Give it to him. He deserves it."

"You don't mean that."

"I've never meant anything more."

He'd replaced the phone and gone to Fiona. He'd undressed her gently and put her to bed. He got in next to her. They watched the pattern of moonlight work its slow way across the wall and onto the ceiling.

When the phone rang three hours later, Luxford's heavy heart told him to let it keep ringing. But he went through the routine that the police had prescribed for him, and on the fourth ring he picked it up.

"Mr. Luxford?" The man's voice was soft. His words carried the melodic accent of the West Indian grown to adulthood in South London. He identified himself as Constable Nkata and added Scotland Yard CID as if Luxford had forgotten him in the intervening hours since they had last met. "We have your son, Mr. Luxford. It's all right. He's fine."

Luxford had only been able to say: "Where?"

Nkata had said Amesford police station. He'd gone on to explain how he'd been found and by whom, why he'd been taken, where he'd been held. He'd ended by giving Luxford directions to the station and the directions were the only part of the brief speech that Luxford remembered or cared to remember as he and Fiona sped onwards in the night.

They left the motorway at Swindon and tore south towards Marlborough. The thirty miles to Amesford felt like sixty—one hundred and sixty—and during them Fiona finally began to speak.

"I made a bargain with God."

Luxford glanced at her. The headlamps from a passing lorry washed her face with light.

She said, "I told Him that if He gave Leo back to me, I would leave you, Dennis, if that's what it took to make you see reason."

"Reason?" he asked.

"I can't think what it would be like to leave you."

"Fi—"

"But I will leave you. Leo and I will go. If you don't see reason about Baverstock."

"I thought I'd already made it clear that Leo doesn't have to go. I thought you'd understood from my words. I know I didn't say it directly, but I assumed that you realised I've no intention of sending him away after this."

"And once the horror of 'this'—as you call it—wears away? Once Leo begins to irritate you again? Once he skips instead of stalks? Once he sings too beautifully? Once he asks to be taken to the ballet for his birthday instead of to a football game or a cricket match? What will you do when you again begin to think he needs some toughening up?"

"I pray I'll hold my tongue. Is that good enough, Fiona?"

"How could it be? I'll know what you're thinking."

"What I think isn't important," Luxford said. "I'll learn to accept him as he is." He looked towards her again. Her expression was implacable. He could tell there was no bluff behind her words. He said, "I love him. For all my faults, I do love him."

"As he is or as you want him to be?"

"Every father has dreams."

"A father's dreams shouldn't become his son's nightmares."

They passed through Upavon, manoeuvred a roundabout, continued south in the darkness. To the west an occasional glitter of lights marked sleepy villages that sat on the edge of Salisbury Plain. East Chisenbury, Littlecott, Longstreet, Coombe, Fittleton. As Luxford drove past their signposts, he thought about his wife's words and how closely one's dreams ally to one's fears. Dream to be strong when you're weak. Dream to be rich when you're poor. Dream to climb mountains when you're caught in the masses scrabbling about on the valley floor.

His dreams for his son were merely a reflection of his fears about his son. Only when he let go of his fears would he be able to relinquish his dreams.

"I need to understand him," Luxford said. "And I will understand him. Let me try. I will."

He followed the route Constable Nkata had given him as they reached the outskirts of Amesford. He pulled into the car park and stopped next to a panda car.

Inside the station, the bustle of activity suggested the middle of the day and not the middle of the night. Uniformed constables passed through the corridors. A three-piece suit carrying a briefcase announced himself as Gerald Sowforth, Esq., a solicitor demanding to see his client. A white-faced woman came through reception leaning heavily on the arm of a balding man, who patted her hand and said, "Let's just get you home, my pear." A team of paramedics were answering questions put to them by a plainclothes police officer. A lone reporter was making angry enquiries of a sergeant behind the reception counter.

Luxford said loudly over the head of the reporter, "Dennis Luxford. I'm—"

The woman who'd come into reception began to keen, shrinking into her companion's side. She said, "Don't leave me, Sammy. Say you won't leave!"

"Never," Sammy told her fervently. "Just you wait and see." He allowed her to hide her face against his chest as they passed Luxford and Fiona and went out into the night.

"I'm here for my son," Luxford said to the sergeant.

The sergeant nodded and picked up a phone. He punched in three numbers. He spoke briefly. He rang off.

Within a minute the door next to the reception counter opened. Someone said Luxford's name. Luxford took his wife's arm and together they passed into a corridor that ran the length of the building.

"This way," a female constable said. She led them to a door, which she opened.

Fiona said, "Where's Leo?"

The constable said, "Wait here, please." She left them alone.

Fiona paced. Luxford waited. They both listened to the sounds outside in the corridor. Three dozen footsteps passed without stopping during the next ten minutes. And then a man's quiet voice finally said, "In here?" The door opened.

When he saw them, Inspector Lynley said immediately, "Leo's all right. It's taking a bit of time because we've had a doctor examining him."

Fiona cried, "A doctor? Has he—"

Lynley took her arm. "It's just a precaution. He was filthy when my sergeant brought him in, so we're trying to clean him a bit as well. It won't be much longer."

"But he's all right? He *is* all right?"

The inspector smiled. "He's more than all right. He's largely the reason my sergeant's alive. He took on a murderer and gave him something on the skull to remember him by. If he hadn't done that, we wouldn't be here now. Or at least if we were, we'd be having an entirely different conversation."

"Leo?" Fiona asked. "Leo did that?"

"He jumped into a drainage trench to find the weapon first," Lynley explained. "And then he wielded a tyre iron like a young man who was born to crack open skulls." He smiled again. Luxford could tell he was trying to put Fiona at ease. He covered her hand and led her to a chair. "Leo's quite the young lout," he said. "But that's exactly what was called for in the circumstances. Ah. Here he is."

And there he was, carried in the arms of Constable Nkata, his fair hair damp, his clothes brushed but filthy, his head resting against the black constable's chest. He was asleep.

"Dead knackered," Nkata told them. "They kept him awake long enough for the doc to check him over, but he fell asleep while they were washing his hair. Had to use hand soap on that, 'm afraid. You'll want to give him a good scrubbing when you get him home."

Luxford went to the constable and took his son in his arms. Fiona said, "Leo. Leo," and touched his head.

Lynley said, "We'll leave you alone for a while. When you've said your hellos, we'll talk again."

As the door closed softly, Luxford carried his son to a chair. He sat, holding him, wondering at the meagre weight of him, feeling every bone in his body as if he were touching each for the very first time. He closed his eyes and breathed in the smell of him: from the detergent pungency of his badly washed hair to the sour muck of his clothing. He kissed his son's forehead, then both of his eyes.

These fluttered open, sky blue like his mother's. They blinked, then adjusted. He saw who held him.

"Daddy," he said, then automatically made the adjustment—with an altering of voice—that Luxford had long insisted upon. "Dad. Hullo. Is Mummy with you? I didn't cry. I was scared, but I didn't cry."

Luxford tightened his arms round the boy. He lowered his face to the crook of Leo's shoulder.

Fiona said, "Hello, darling," and knelt by the chair.

"I expect that was the right thing to do," Leo said to her stoutly. "I didn't cry once. He kept me locked up and I was awfully scared and I *wanted* to cry. But I didn't. Not once. That was good, wasn't it? I did right, I think." His face wrinkled round the eyes and on the forehead. He squirmed to have a better look at his father. "What's wrong with Dad?" he asked his mother, perplexed.

"Nothing at all," Fiona said. "Daddy's just doing your crying for you."

acknowledgements

Wootton Cross and the Vale of Wootton do not exist. But I thank those individuals who helped with its creation: Mr. A. E. Swaine of Great Bedwyn, Wiltshire, who shared the beauties of Wilton Windmill with me; Gordon Rogers of High Ham, Somerset, and the kind people of the National Trust who made High Ham Windmill available to me; the good police constables of Pewsey who fielded questions and who allowed their police station to stand in for Wootton Cross's.

I'm greatly indebted to Michael Fairbairn, political correspondent from the BBC, who spent time with me at the Houses of Parliament and who graciously answered innumerable questions during the course of this novel's creation; to David Banks, who allowed me access to the *Mirror* and Maggie Pringle, who answered my questions and made arrangements for me to visit the newspaper's offices in Holburn; to Ruth and Richard Boulton, who always respond graciously to every question, no matter how trivial; to Chief Inspector Pip Lane, who keeps me at least somewhat within the boundaries of reasonable policework; to my agent Vivienne Schuster and my editor Tony Mott, who support my efforts and make encouraging noises when necessary.

In the United States, I'm grateful to Gary Bale of the Orange County Sheriff's Department for his words of wisdom on everything from fingerprinting to toxicology; to Dr. Tom Ruben and Dr. H. M. Upton for supplying me with medical advice when necessary; to April Jackson of the *Los Angeles Times* for fielding miscellaneous questions on journalism; to Julie Mayer for reading yet another draft; to Ira Toibin for his kind and consistent support; to my editor Kate Miciak for listening

to endless variations on plot and theme; to my agent Deborah Schneider for her wisdom and her belief in the project.

It should be remembered that this is a work of fiction. It should also be remembered that any errors or missteps in the novel are mine alone.